Catherine

SUSAN HOPLEY

OR

THE ADVENTURES

OF

A MAID SERVANT

Elibron Classics
www.elibron.com

SUSAN HOPLEY:

OR,

THE ADVENTURES

OF

A MAID SERVANT.

BY

MRS. CROWE,

AUTHOR OF
"LILLY DAWSON," "NIGHT SIDE OF NATURE,"
ETC. ETC.

LONDON:
G. ROUTLEDGE & CO., FARRINGDON STREET.
1852.

SUSAN HOPLEY.

CHAPTER I.

WORTHY, excellent Susan! methinks I see her now, in her neat, plaited cap, snuff-coloured stuff gown, clean white apron, and spectacles on nose, plying her knitting needles, whose labours were to result in a comfortable pair of lamb's-wool stockings for my next winter's wear, or a warm waistcoat for poor old Jeremy; or in something, be it what it might, that was to contribute to the welfare and benefit of some human being; and I believe, if it had so happened that the whole human race had been miraculously provided to repletion with warm stockings and waistcoats, that Susan, rather than let her fingers be idle and not be doing something for somebody, would have knit jackets for the shorn lambs and blankets for the early calves.

Excellent Susan! she is dead now; and sadly, sadly I miss her; for when, by the death of my wife and the marriage of my children, I grew a lone old man, she became my companion as well as my housekeeper. During the day, whilst I looked after my farm, or wandered over the fields with my gun in my hand, or wrote or read in my library, she was engaged with her household affairs, and superintending the servants; but with the tea-urn, in the evening, came Susan, so neat, so clean, with her honest, benevolent face, which although it was not handsome, was the pleasantest face I ever looked upon; and whilst she made my tea —by the bye, the flavour of teas is sadly falling off, I observe; it's nothing like what it was in Susan's time—but whilst she poured me out the pleasant beverage, and sweetened it exactly to my taste—it's very odd; one would think a man ought to know his own taste, but I always put in too much sugar or too little; and in trying to repair the error, I regularly make things worse— but, as I was saying, whilst she presided at my tea-table, or plied her knitting needles, sometimes I read aloud, but more generally we used to talk over old times and past adventures—and pleasant chat it was! Some people, if they had listened to us, might have thought there was a sameness in our conversation—a repetition of old stories—but they never wearied us; I think I liked them better every night; and so did she.

A 2

At length, one evening, it occurred to us that what amused us so much, might perhaps amuse other people. "Suppose, we write our histories," said I, "Susan; I think we could make out three volumes of adventures before we settled down into this quiet life, which furnishes nothing to tell. In the evening, we can collect our materials and arrange our plan: and on wet days, when I can't get out, I'll put it all on paper: and we shall then be able to judge how it reads. I've a notion it wouldn't be a bad story. The world don't want extraordinary events, and improbable incidents, to amuse it now. They have found out that, ' the proper study of mankind is man;' and he who can paint real life and human nature, has the best chance of being read. It has often been said that few biographies would be uninteresting, if people would or could disclose the exact truth with all its details. Let us make the experiment, and relate simply, without addition or subtraction, the events of our early years. Nearly all are dead now who would be pained by the disclosures; and we have but to conceal the names of places and of people, and wait a few years, and perhaps when you and I are both gone, some kind friend may revise our manuscript, and give it to the world; and we may thus, by furnishing our quota to the amusement of mankind, pay back some part of the pleasure we have derived from the excellent tales that have cheered our evening fireside."

Susan liked the idea; and accordingly we lost no time in putting our plan into execution. Whether the result of our labours will ever see the light—whether it will be considered worth publishing "by the trade," or worth reading by the public, is more than I can foresee; but this I know, that the occupation it furnished, afforded Susan and myself many a pleasant hour: and that come what may of it, it will not be all *lost labour.*

HARRY LEESON.

<hr />

CHAPTER II.

WHICH GIVES AN ACCOUNT OF SUSAN'S BIRTH, EDUCATION, AND FIRST SERVICE.

SUSAN HOPLEY was a native of the village of Mapleton—at least so we choose to call it—in the south-eastern part of England; where her father was a day-labourer on the farm of a Mr. Whitehead. He was an industrious sober man, his wife a worthy woman, and their family consisted only of Susan, and a boy named Andrew, who was a few years younger. But the mother was weakly, and unable to undertake anything more than the care of her house and children; and the father's wages was only just sufficient to supply his family with the necessaries of life; leaving nothing to spare for education, which was then much more expensive and of much more difficult attainment than it is now. So Mrs. Hopley brought up her children in the fear of God, taught them to spell out words in the Bible, and to be honest and true, and love their neighbours; and trusted in Providence for the rest.

Thus they lived happily enough till Susan was thirteen, and Andrew ten: but then the always infirm health of the mother began to give way; and with the expense of doctors, and one thing or another, the family were beginning to fall into difficulties; when the cleanly appearance and orderly conduct of the children at church, happened, fortunately, to attract the notice of Mrs. Leeson. This lady was the daughter of a former curate of Mapleton, where she had been born and bred; and when very young, had fallen in love with an officer of the king's troops that were quartered in the village. As the regiment was ordered abroad, and the young lady could not part with him, they were married; and she followed him about the world for several years, and was near him in many battles. It was even said, that she had once saved his life, by seeking him out amongst a heap of bodies where he had been left for dead. He had been desperately wounded, and was lying there so far gone, that he could never have survived the night, had she not stretched herself beside him on the ground, and, by folding him in her arms, contrived to keep some warmth in his blood, till she could get assistance in the morning.

At length, Major Leeson, who was a good deal older than his wife, beginning to feel some effects from the hardships he had undergone, they resolved to leave the army, and set themselves down for life in the village where they had first met. They had not much money; he had his half-pay, and she had two hundred a-year allowed her by her mother's brother, Mr. Wentworth, of Oakfield; but as they had no children, and a great deal of love for one another, they had enough. However, after they had lived in this way for some time, Mrs. Leeson, to her own surprise and that of everybody else, found herself in the family way, and was brought to bed of as lovely a little boy as eyes ever looked upon. Great was the joy at his birth, and a happy family they were till the child came to be about six or seven years old; but then the expenses of his education, and the means of setting him afloat in the world began to be thought of; and after much deliberation, and many hard struggles, it was resolved that the major should apply to be placed on full-pay again, in order that, at the end of a few years, he might obtain leave to sell his commission, and thus secure something for little Harry against his parents died.

Sad, sad was the parting, for the husband and wife had never been separated before; and they still loved each other as they had done in their young days. But they trusted in God and their constant love; and the major sailed for the West Indies, where the regiment he was appointed to was stationed.

He had been gone some time, when the illness of the labourer's wife, and the consequent distress of the family, reached the ears of Mrs. Leeson; who thereupon went to the cottage to see how

she could be of use to them. Little as she had to spare, there was
nobody in the village so serviceable to the poor as she was, particularly after the major left her; and, indeed, alleviating their dis-
tresses, and superintending the education of her dear Harry,
seemed to be all that constituted her pleasure in life. "I do believe, poor lady," said Susan, whose own words we shall frequently
take the liberty of using, "I do believe that she sought to win the
prayers of the poor, and to make Heaven her friend, for the sake
of her dear husband that was far away."

Many were the comforts and alleviations she afforded Mrs.
Hopley, whose health continued daily to decline: but the greatest
of all was, that she undertook to have Andrew and Susan taught
to read and write; and to procure them such other instruction as
was likely to be useful in their situations, and enable them to earn
their bread respectably. "Heaven bless her for it!" Susan would
say, when she came to this part of our story: "many's the day I
have had reason to say so!"

Mrs. Leeson had a worthy, excellent servant called Dobbs, who
had been brought up in her father's family; and who, when the
young lady married, had followed her fortunes, and accompanied
her through all her dangers and difficulties; and who was still fast
by her side, watching over little Harry, and as fond of him as if
he'd been her own. "I often think, sir, when I remember Dobbs,"
Susan would say, "that there are few friends more valuable than
an attached and worthy servant. People that don't think it worth
their while to make a friend of a good servant, lose more in life
than they think of."

Now, Dobbs had had a very good education from Mrs. Leeson's
father; and as she did not forget that part of her catechism which
taught her to do to others as she would they should do to her, she
very willingly undertook, at the request of her mistress, to impart
to Susan and Andrew such instruction as was needful.

Whilst Mrs. Hopley lived, the children only spent certain hours
of the day at Mrs. Leeson's; devoting the rest to the care and
attendance of their sick parent; but when the poor mother died,
whose passage to the grave was smoothed by knowing that they
had found a friend, and were rescued from the peril she had most
apprehended—namely, that when she was gone, they would be
thrown amongst the idle and disorderly children of the village,
and forget all the good and virtuous principles she had taught
them—then, when she was laid at rest in the humble churchyard,
Mrs. Leeson took Susan altogether to be under Dobbs, and do
what little she was able in the house, till she had learned the duties
of a servant. Andrew lived with his father for a time, earning a
trifle when he could, by weeding or picking stones; but he still
punctually attended Mrs. Dobbs's instructions; and often, when
they were over, was allowed to play a game at marbles or trap-ball
with Master Harry, or take a walk with him in the fields; for
Andrew was a steady, well-behaved boy, and to be depended on.
As for Harry, his education was superintended by the clergyman

of the village; at whose house he spent a considerable part of every day, and under whose instructions he made great progress.

As soon as Andrew was old enough, Mrs. Leeson completed her kindness, by procuring him a situation in the establishment of her uncle, Mr. Wentworth, of Oakfield; and there, by his good conduct, he rose from being stable-boy to be footman; and a great favourite with his master he was, as well as with honest Mr. Jeremy, the butler.

Susan had been living about five years in Mrs. Leeson's service, when she learned from Dobbs that the major's regiment was ordered home. For several weeks before, both she and Dobbs had observed an alteration in Mrs. Leeson; her step was lighter and quicker, her face brighter, and sometimes as she went about the house, they heard her sweet voice carolling a few snatches of some old song; and Dobbs would say, "There she is, bless her! singing the major's favourite tune as blithe as she used to be in old times." She had her husband's picture over the mantelpiece in the drawing-room, and her first glance in the morning as she entered the room, and the last at night when she left it, was towards that face she loved so dearly. It was most times a melancholy look—a look of fond affection, and of deep regret for the precious hours of life so wasted; for, by her, all that were not spent with him, were scarcely counted. But now the expression changed; she met his eye with a joyous greeting; and there was a brightness in hers, and an involuntary smile upon her lip, that told of pleasant thoughts and glad anticipations.

"It's my opinion," said Dobbs to Susan, "that there's been some good news from the major in that last letter! for I saw her sitting before the glass to-day trying a new way of dressing her beautiful hair; and yesterday she went into the village and bought some pink and blue ribbons to trim her morning caps. I shouldn't be surprised if we see him soon."

"I declare the same thought struck me," said Susan, "for since she's given orders to have the carpets taken up, and the house cleaned, I remark, that whenever she's directing what's to be done, she keeps glancing up at the picture every moment, as if she was asking his opinion."

"And then do you see," said Dobbs, "how she flings her arms about little Harry every now and then; and laughs a gay laugh, as if there was a hidden fountain of joy in her heart that was running over. Mark my words, we shall hear news of the major before it's long."

Dobbs was right. "One day soon after this," (and here we shall let Susan tell her own story,) "we saw Mrs. Leeson come hurrying up the little garden that was in front of the house with flushed cheeks and an eager step; and presently afterwards her bed-room bell rang twice for Dobbs. We guessed directly that she had been out to meet the postman, and that there was news; and so it proved. The major was coming home directly; but as the colonel was absent, and he had the command of the regiment, he was not

sure whether he should be able to leave it immediately on landing
or not. If he could not get away, he promised to send her a line
the moment the vessel got into port, that she and Harry might
hasten to meet him. He added, too, that he had made a very
advantageous arrangement for parting with his commission to a
young nobleman, who didn't care for money, but who wanted to
get into a regiment that was not likely to be sent to a foreign
station for some years.

"Oh, Mr. Harry, there was joy! I shall never forget her sweet
face when first I saw it after she had got the news. Beautiful she
always was; but now, as Mr. Poppleton, the curate said, she was
radiant, and looked ten times younger and handsomer than ever.
She told Dobbs that the major had before hinted that there was an
early prospect of his coming home; but that she had not courage
to mention it till she was certain, fancying she could bear a disappointment better if she had never communicated her hope to anybody.

"As this letter had been written immediately before the fleet
was to sail, of course the major himself, or the summons to meet
him at Portsmouth, might be hourly expected; and there was such
preparations—such a joyous bustle!—and dear Harry, he was so
busy too! There was the house to be got ready, the clean curtains
to be put up, the carpets to be laid: whatever was much worn or
looked shabby to be replaced; and there was her own dress, and
Harry's dress to be thought of; and the garden to be trimmed,
and the trunks to be packed. Oh, heavens! the joy of much
loving! But, oh! the pain!

"Well, sir, all was ready, and we rejoiced that time had been
given us to complete everything; but now it was all listening and
watching; every sound of a wheel that was heard approaching,
every coach that passed through the village, even the latch of the
garden gate being lifted, brought us all to the window. Master
Harry's lessons were laid aside, for he had too much to ask, and
too much to hear about his dear papa, to give his mind to them;
whilst the mother, anticipating the pride and delight of the father
when he looked at his noble boy, had not the heart to chide him—
and every morning when the sun rose, it was to be to-day; and
every night when he set, it was to be to-morrow. With the
earliest dawn, we could hear Mrs. Leeson opening her window to
observe the weather; and Harry spent half the day waving his
handkerchief in the wind, to be sure it was still blowing from the
right quarter. And it did blow from the right quarter; and calm
beautiful summer weather it was, as ever shone out of the
heavens!

"Well, at last we saw the postman coming with a letter, and
we all felt certain it was the right letter, for there were not many
came to the house; and sure enough it bore the Portsmouth post
mark; and Harry, who got hold of it first, and who did not know
his papa's hand, cried out, 'He's come! he's come!' But the
letter was from Mr. Wentworth. Happening to be in London, he

had heard that the telegraph had announced the fleet was in sight, and he had gone down to Portsmouth to meet the major. But the letter said, that although the fleet was come in, the transport in which Major Leeson had embarked had parted company with the others, and was not yet arrived, but it was expected hourly.

"I was in the room when my mistress read the letter, for we were all too anxious to keep out of it; and I shall never forget her face. Oh! the change that came over it! The falling from the great hope to the heavy fear! She said nothing, but she turned very pale; and her lips trembled, and her hand shook; and Harry looked at her with an amazed and serious look, for the child felt damped too—'What, ma?' he said. 'Soon, love; soon!' she murmured, as she kissed his forehead, and the words came with a deep gasp and a great swelling of the heart. Then she rose and went to her bed-room; and Dobbs and I knew that she passed almost all that day upon her knees. Sometimes we could distinguish her foot pacing the room; but whenever there was silence, we knew that she was praying; and at night it was the same. I don't think she ever passed another night in her bed till she laid herself down in it to rise no more.

"Well, sir, the sun rose and set—but still no tidings came. For her, the blow had been struck the first day by Mr. Wentworth's letter; there was something prophetic in that deep love of hers—she saw it all from the beginning. Poor Harry couldn't believe it; and he hoped on, and we hoped on; but she hoped no more.

"She seldom spoke; sometimes she would throw her arms round Harry, and utter such a cry! Surely it was the cry of a broken heart. I never heard anything like it but from her lips. Few, I hope, ever suffered what she did. Then she would bid Andrew or me take Harry out into the fields and amuse him as well as we could. She didn't like to cloud his young days with sorrow, or inure him to the sight of wretchedness so early. Then the picture! oh that picture! One day I happened to be passing the drawing-room door when it was a little ajar, and hearing a deep sob, I turned my head that way. She was on her knees, and her arms were stretched out towards it, as if she was inviting him to come to her. Her hair was pushed back from the forehead, her lips were apart, and her eyes staring with such eagerness on the countenance, that she looked as if she expected the energy of her grief and love could animate the canvas, and impart life and being to the form she loved so dearly.

"Well, sir, she drooped and drooped from day to day; I am sure she prayed for death, and her truest friends could not wish her to live.

"It was not many months afterwards, that we knelt by her bedside and closed her sweet eyes—and we that loved her best, thanked God when we did so."

CHAPTER III.

As soon as Mrs. Leeson was dead, Mr. Wentworth, and Miss
Fanny his daughter, who had neglected nothing they could think
of to comfort her during her lifetime, took poor little Harry with
them to Oakfield, which they had promised his mother should
henceforth be his home; and when she was laid in her grave, and
the house at Mapleton was given up, Dobbs and Susan followed.
Dobbs was only to stay till Harry was somewhat reconciled to his
loss, which he felt bitterly, poor child; and till she had met with a
situation to suit her; but Miss Wentworth took Susan into the
family altogether, and appointed her to the situation of under-
housemaid.

Mr. Wentworth was a gentleman who had made a very large
fortune in the wine trade; and he had his house of business still
in the city, where affairs were conducted under the superinten-
dence of an old and much valued clerk, of the name of Simpson;
whilst he himself resided chiefly with his daughter at Oakfield.
She was his only child, and the pride and delight of his heart; and
well did she merit all the affection he bore her.

Most fortunate Susan thought herself, on all accounts, to obtain
so excellent a situation; and one which placed her near those she
most loved, her brother and little Harry. Andrew now wore a
livery; he was grown a nice young man, and had won the good-
will of all the family by his diligence and good temper. As soon
as Harry was considered sufficiently recovered, he was placed at a
boarding-school about ten miles from Mapleton; and then Dobbs
quitted Oakfield, and accepted a situation as cook and housekeeper
in a gentleman's family in London.

Harry had been at school between three and four months, and
Susan was looking forward to the approaching midsummer vacation, when she was desired to prepare a room for Mr. Gaveston,
who was expected on a visit: and she soon learned from the
servants, that the visit was to terminate in a marriage. This
gentleman was a distant relative of Mr. Wentworth's, who had
brought him up, and provided handsomely for him by giving him
a share in the wine business. He had hitherto resided a good deal
at Bordeaux, where Mr. Wentworth was connected with several
houses of eminence; always, however, spending some months of
every year in England; and during these visits, he had contrived
to make himself so completely master of the affections of poor
Fanny, that though (heiress as she was to all her father's wealth,
and endowed with many charms of mind and person into the
bargain) she had hosts of suitors, she would listen to none of them,

but persisted in giving her young heart, and engaging her fair hand, to Walter Gaveston.

It was pretty evident to everybody but herself, that Mr. Gaveston was not the husband her father would have selected for her; but he was too indulgent and too just to oppose her wishes on a subject so material to her happiness, unless he could have given her convincing reasons for his objection; and this he could not. He had originally been very fond of Walter, who was a clever, handsome, forward boy; but of late years he had felt a sort of growing dislike to him that he could hardly account for; and that he was himself half inclined to look upon as idle antipathy or weak prejudice. He had nothing exactly to allege against him; and sometimes after examining his own mind, and searching for the motive of his own alienation, he would end by saying, "D—n the fellow! I believe it's only that I don't like the expression of his face." Nobody did like the expression of his face, that looked at it with unprepossessed eyes; but poor Fanny's were witched—and if she ever remarked that the prospect of her marriage was disagreeable to her father, she attributed the dissatisfaction wholly to his dread of parting with her, and not at all to the nature of the alliance she was about to form.

In spite of the displeasing expression we have alluded to, there could be no doubt that Mr. Gaveston was a very fine looking man; and one likely to attract the eye and admiration of the fair sex in general. His features were regular and manly; he had a beautiful set of teeth, dark hair and eyes, a complexion bronzed into a very becoming hue by the sun of the South, and a figure that formed a perfect model of strength and agility. And, accordingly, there were few men who excelled so much in all manly exercises; whether he walked, rode, or danced, the performance was perfect; he was the best cricket-player about the country, the most fearless huntsman, and the best shot. He was equally remarkable for his proficiency in all games of skill—cards, billiards, nothing came amiss to him. Then he was an excellent judge of a horse, very fond of attending races, and understood all the intricacies of betting, edging, and jockeyship in general. Of classical learning or deep reading he had very little; but he had a great deal of general information; knew something of most people that were making any sensation in the world; and was seldom at a loss upon any subject of fashionable or popular discussion.

Such was the man that had won Fanny Wentworth's affections, and to whom she was to be united in the ensuing month of August. Many preliminaries, of course, were to be arranged. Dresses to be prepared, settlements drawn up, and entertainments given; and when Harry returned to Oakfield for the vacation, he found the house full of gaiety and commotion.

"I think it right to inform you," said Mr. Wentworth one day to Mr. Gaveston, when the subject of settlement was under discussion, "that since the death of Harry Leeson's parents, I have adopted him, and look upon him as my son. I was always fond

of the boy, who is as fine a little fellow as ever lived; and I loved
his father and mother, and would do it for their sakes if I did not
do it for his own. The arrangement I propose to make is this—
and I have given Olliphant directions to prepare the settlements
and my will at the same time. You are at present possessor of a
sixth share of the business—I will make that a fourth. Whatever
fortune I give my daughter now, or whatever I leave her, I shall
vest in trustees for her use, to descend from her to her children;
or if she have none, to be disposed of as she pleases, with the exception of ten thousand pounds, of which you will have the life-
rent, should you survive her. This, with a fourth share of the
business, will, I hope, be considered sufficient. Are you satisfied
with that arrangement?"

"Quite, sir, quite," replied Mr. Gaveston; and he endeavoured
to look very satisfied indeed.

"With respect to Harry Leeson," continued Mr. Wentworth,
"he will be entitled by my will to two shares of the wine business, and to ten thousand pounds, to be paid free of all deductions.
The fourth share I intend giving to old Simpson, on whom the
management of the whole must rest. I shall also appoint him
guardian and trustee for Harry. All this I do with Fanny's
entire approbation."

How far these arrangements were agreeable to Mr. Gaveston
may be doubted; but, at all events, he reiterated the assurances
of his entire satisfaction, and Mr. Wentworth did not trouble himself to investigate further.

Mr. Gaveston's pursuits—riding, cricketing, sporting, and so
forth—were naturally very attractive to Harry; and, as he was a
spirited boy, he was glad enough to be allowed to share in them
whenever he was permitted. Mr. Gaveston seemed willing enough
to encourage this disposition, and, amongst other things, he took
upon himself to teach Harry to ride; but, on the plea that a boy
should be afraid of nothing, he one day set him on a young horse
of his own, before the child had any seat, and allowed him to
follow the hounds; the consequence of which was, that the horse
ran away, and if Andrew (who, happening to see Harry start, had
felt uneasy, and gone after them to observe how he got on) had
not been at hand, and stopped the horse with one hand, whilst he
caught Harry with the other to break his fall, it would in all probability have proved the poor little fellow's first and last hunt.
Mr. Gaveston charged Harry not to tell his uncle, "for," said he,
"if you do, you'll have a log tied to you for the future, and there'll
be an end of your sport." Harry did not tell; but Andrew, who
thought the boy's life would be in jeopardy if this sort of thing
went on, did; and Mr. Wentworth set his veto against any future
lessons in equitation from Mr. Gaveston. "He hasn't caution
enough," he said, "to be trusted with a boy of that age. Harry
shall have proper instruction, and a safe pony to begin with."

It was not long after this that a second accident occurred to
Harry, no less likely to have proved fatal than the first.

There was in the grounds at some distance from the house, a large pond or lake on which lay an old boat, which was rarely used, except Harry sometimes got leave to take a row in it with one of the men-servants, but he was strictly enjoined never to enter it alone.*

"One day, as I was standing at Miss Wentworth's bedroom window," (for here we shall let Susan once more tell her own story,) "I saw somebody coming through the trees towards the house. He was a good way off when I first caught sight of him, but I observed that he was walking slowly, and that every now and then he stopped and seemed to be looking all round as if to see whether anybody was at hand. When he emerged from amongst the trees, and got upon the open lawn, he began to run; and I then perceived that it was Mr. Gaveston, with his coat off, and looking very pale. He approached the house rapidly, and I was just wondering what could have happened to him, when I heard a loud scream from Miss Fanny, and a great bustle below; and on running down to see what was the matter, I overtook her rushing out of the house, followed by Mr. Gaveston, and all the maid-servants, crying out that Harry Leeson was in the pond.

"Now, it happened that it was hay-making time, and as the weather was considered unsettled, every man about the estate was in the fields, at least a quarter of a mile from the pond, and quite in an opposite direction from the house; but there was a shorter cut across than going by the water; and Mr. Gaveston said he would run there as fast as he could and send assistance; and as he set off Miss Wentworth called after him, 'For God's sake, despatch somebody to the village for a surgeon!' So away we all ran—we to the pond, who could be of no use in the world when we were there; and Mr. Gaveston, who perhaps might, to the hay-field, in search of aid which never could have arrived in time. What chance little Harry had of being saved by either party may be imagined; but Providence sent him help.

"My brother Andrew, who, like me, doted on Harry, for his dear mother's sake as well as his own, was always glad when he could invent anything to amuse him; and, having something of a mechanical turn, he often employed his leisure hours in contriving toys and playthings for him: and it chanced that the day before this accident happened, he had been down with the child to the pond, to try the sailing of a little vessel that he had been at work on some time. On first launching it, it turned over: but, after hewing it away a little, he brought it to do, and much delighted Harry was with it.

"In order that no time might be lost with the hay, Mr. Wentworth, who had gone to town in the morning, had desired that the men should have a luncheon of bread and cheese and beer in the

---

* This incident has some resemblance to one in the Third Number of "Master Humphrey;" but it was written many months before Mr. D.'s work appeared.

fields, and not return till the day's work was over. This the
maids had carried out to them; but, finding the beer run short,
Mr. Jeremy, the butler, told Andrew to step to the house and
fetch another can.

"Now, when Andrew had sat down with the others to eat his
bread and cheese he had missed his knife; and as it was a very
nice one, that Harry had saved up his own pocket-money to buy,
and which he had given him as a birthday present, he would have
been very sorry to lose it. 'I dare say,' thought he, 'I left it at
the pond yesterday;' and as it would not make many minutes'
difference, he resolved to run round that way and look for it.

"Just as he came in sight of the pond, he fancied he heard a
cry that proceeded from that direction, and he hastened forward;
but when he reached it he saw no one, nor indeed anything unusual, except that the boat was reeling from side to side as if it
were on the waves of the sea. Now, there was no motion in the
water, for, as I said before, though it was deep, it was but a pond;
and the day was calm, cloudy, and still threatening rain, but not a
breath of wind was stirring.

"Andrew looked at the boat—thought of the cry—and jumped
into the water. He could not swim; but he didn't stop to remember that. Fortunately the boat was at hand, and he was
active and strong. He caught the child by the jacket, and when
the water threw him up, he struggled to get hold of it. Once he
failed, and they went down together; but the second time he succeeded; and when we reached the pond, we found him sitting in
the boat with Harry in his lap, rubbing the child's chest and
stomach, and doing the best he could to restore him.

"'Don't be frightened,' he cried to us, 'Master Harry's coming
to, but look for the oars amongst the grass, and push them towards
me.'

"We did so; and then he brought the boat ashore, and carried
the child up to the house in his arms, where he was soon in a warm
bed, and so far recovered that there was nothing to fear for his
health.

"It was nearly an hour after this, I dare say, that Miss Wentworth and I, who were sitting by Master Harry's bedside, heard
Mr. Gaveston's foot entering the hall below, and coming hastily
up stairs. He was now as red as he had before been pale, and
bursting open the door, he exclaimed, 'My dear Fanny, I am
sure you'll never forgive me; and if you do, I never can forgive
myself. If it hadn't been for Andrew's providential arrival, the
dear boy must inevitably have been drowned.' With the noise
he made, Harry, who had fallen asleep, opened his eyes; and
holding out his hand and smiling on him, he said, 'It was an
accident, nobody could help it; but wasn't it brave of Andrew to
jump into the water to save me when he couldn't swim?'

"'I thought you could swim, Walter,' said Miss Wentworth.

"'No,' replied he, 'I never could learn.'

"'But how in the world did it happen?' said Fanny. 'How came you in the water, Harry?'

"'I can't think,' said Harry. 'We had got into the boat to sail my little vessel, and I was leaning over the side, when all at once the boat dipped down, and I went over. What made it dip down so suddenly I can't tell. Perhaps you came too quickly to my side?' said he to Gaveston.

"'I'm afraid I did,' answered Gaveston. 'I thought you were leaning over too far, and without reflection I stepped across to take hold of you. However, you know, those that are born to be hanged will never be drowned. It's all very well as it has turned out; and the less that's said about it the better.'

"'I think we'd better not tell my uncle,' said Harry. 'He'll forbid my going to the pond any more, and then I can't sail my vessel.'

"'That he certainly will,' said Mr. Gaveston. 'You'll be tied up, depend upon it, if you tell him.'

"'He must be told,' said Fanny. 'He detests concealments; and if he finds it out afterwards, he'll be much the more displeased.'

"'How should he find it out?' said Mr. Gaveston.

"'Everything is found out sooner or later,' replied Fanny."

CHAPTER IV.

SUSAN HAS AN EXTRAORDINARY DREAM, WHICH IS THE FORERUNNER OF ILL NEWS.

THE period of the wedding was fast approaching, and a day was already appointed for signing the settlements, when Mr. Gaveston received a letter from a confidential friend at Bordeaux, intimating that the bankruptcy of one of the houses with which Mr. Wentworth was connected, was supposed to be impending; and that it was of the last importance that he, Mr. Gaveston, should lose no time in repairing to the spot.

The serious consequences that might arise from a neglect of this caution, induced Mr. Wentworth to consent to the immediate departure of his intended son-in-law, and the postponement of the wedding; though, at the same time, he declared that he did not believe there was any foundation for the report.

"Râoul and Bonstetten are much too steady men to fail," said he; "however, you may as well go; the marriage can as well take place in October as now." Perhaps Mr. Wentworth was not sorry for the respite. "I have an idea," continued he, "of going down to the sea for a couple of months; and you can join us there on your return. The doctor says, that that poor fellow Andrew will never recover perfectly till he has undergone a course of warm sea-bathing; and as he got his illness in doing me a great service, the least I can do is to contribute all I can to his recovery."

Andrew had never been well since the day he jumped into the water to save Harry. He was very warm at the moment from working in the hayfield and running on his errand; and having remained some time in his wet clothes, being too anxious about Harry to think of himself; the chill had brought on a rheumatic fever, from which he had not perfectly recovered. Nothing could exceed the attention shown him by the family during his illness; and as for Harry, he could scarcely be induced to quit his bedside to take needful rest and sleep. And signal as was their kindness appeared Andrew's gratitude; he "only hoped," he often told Susan, "that he might find means during his life of testifying his sense of their great goodness to him."

Mr. Gaveston departed; when the young man got better, Harry returned to school, and not long afterwards, Mr. and Miss Wentworth, accompanied by Andrew, set out on their excursion. There had been, at one time, an idea of taking Susan; Miss Wentworth happening just then to be without a maid: the one that was to attend her after her marriage not having arrived. However, this was finally given up, and they went alone.

"It was a lovely morning when they set out," said Susan; "just the last week in August; and we all assembled in the portico to see them off. I shall never forget it—Miss Fanny looking so fresh and so pretty, in her grey silk pelisse, and little straw bonnet lined with pink; and the dear old gentleman, with his broad-skirted brown coat, and his wide-brimmed hat, looking so smiling and so benevolent as he bade us good-by; and then handing his daughter into the carriage as proud as an emperor—he'd reason to be proud of her, for she was a sweet creature; and as good as she was pretty!

"'We shall bring back Andrew to you quite well, Susan,' said master, putting his head out of the window.

"'God bless you, sir,' said I, 'and my mistress too; and I wiped the tears from my eyes with the corner of my apron.

"'Good-by, sister,' said Andrew, giving me a last kiss, and jumping up behind. 'All's right!' cried he; the postilions cracked their whips, and away they went. Lord! Sir; how little we poor mortals know what is before us!

"Well, Sir, nothing particular occurred after this till we received a letter to say the family would be home on the evening of the sixteenth—we were then in the month of October. The letter was written by Andrew at his master's desire; and he concluded by saying that he had quite recovered his health, and was as well as ever he had been. Then there followed a passage which I did not well understand, and which I promised myself to ask him the meaning of when he came back. He said, 'Mr. Gaveston is arrived, and the marriage is to take place in November; but if I had courage to do *something*, I think I could prevent it; but I don't know how to act without assistance.'

" On the morning of the 16th, when we were all prepared, there came another letter from Andrew, to say that they should not be back till the 18th. Mr. Gaveston had a bet on a boat-race that he wanted to see the result of; they had therefore arranged to start on the 17th, sleep at Maningtree that night, and reach home the next day to dinner.

" On the same evening, that is, on the 16th, as we were sitting in the servants' hall after supper, there came a ring at the back-door. I remember we were all talking about Mabel, the dairy-maid, who had just got up and left the room, as she usually did, the moment meals were over. It was very well known that Andrew was in love with her; and as she was a beautiful creature, there was not a man in the house but was his rival; and they were not a little jealous because they fancied she showed him more favour than the rest. But, for my part, I always saw that Mabel had no thoughts of Andrew more than of the others; and that she was much too proud to listen to a poor boy who had nothing but his livery. However, more out of envy, I believe, than because they thought it, they insisted that she liked him, recalling several little kindnesses that she had shown him during his illness, and prophesying that now he had recovered it would soon be a match. But Mr. Jeremy, the butler, was of a different opinion. 'No, no,' said he, 'them little knows Mabel that looks to see her married to a footman. Mabel comes of a proud family—they were gentry once, as I've heard—howbeit, they never knew themselves nor their stations. Mabel was rocked in the cradle of pride, and she fed upon the bread of pride—and she'll have a fall, as all such pride has.'

" ' Well, she'll fall to Andrew,' said the coachman: 'that'll be a fall.'

" ' No, no,' said Mr. Jeremy, ' it'll be a worse fall than falling to an honest young fellow like Andrew. Mark my words. I was never deceived in no man, nor woman neither; and I ar'n't now.'

" Just as the butler had said those words, came the ring I spoke of; and as I happened to be going up stairs to look at my fires, I said I would see who it was.

" When I opened the door, I saw by the light of the candle I held in my hand, a stout man in a drab coat, with his hat slouched over his eyes, and a red handkerchief round his throat, that covered a good deal of the lower part of his face; so that between the hat and the handkerchief, I saw very little of his features except his nose; but that was very remarkable. It was a good deal raised in the bridge, and very much on one side; and it was easy to see that whatever it had been by nature, its present deformity had been occasioned by a blow or an accident. He did not look like a common man, nor yet exactly like a gentleman; but something between both; or rather like a gentleman that had got a blackguard look by keeping bad company. However, sight is quick, or I should never have had time to make out the little that I tell you; for whether he thought that I looked at him more

B

than he liked, or what, I don't know, but he dropped a stick he
had in his hand, and in stooping to pick it up, he contrived to
knock the candle out of mine, and there we were both in the
dark.

"As I did not quite like his appearance, and could not help
thinking he had done this on purpose, I got frightened, suspecting he wanted to make a rush and get into the house, so I
pushed the door and tried to slam it in his face; but he was
stronger than I was; and putting his hand against it, firmly, but
without violence, he said, in a quiet sort of a voice, that had certainly nothing in it to alarm me, 'When do you expect Mr.
Wentworth home?'

"Well, sir, the way he spoke, and his asking such a natural
harmless question, made me think myself a fool, and that his
putting out the candle had been an accident; so answering him as
civilly as I could, to make up for my rudeness, I said that they
would be home on the 18th to dinner, adding that we had expected
them sooner, but that they were to sleep upon the road.

"'Thank ye,' replied he, turning away. 'I don't know exactly
which way I should go, amongst all these buildings,' he added,
looking round—'I suppose that's the stables, with the light in the
window?'

"'No, sir, that's the dairy,' said I, 'the stables are on the other
side. But if you go straight across you'll find your way.' 'Good
night,' said he, and away he went, whilst I proceeded up stairs to
look after my fires. When I returned to the servants' hall, so
little did I think of the matter, that I only told them when they
asked who had rung, it was a person called to inquire when master
would be home.

"On the following day, which was the 17th, nothing particular
occurred; and on the 18th we were all prepared for the family,
with the cloth laid, and the fires blazing, and everybody on the
watch for the carriage. But the dinner hour came and passed,
and tea time came, and supper time came, and still no signs of
those we were looking for. The servants sat up till half-past
eleven, wondering and guessing all manner of reasons for the
delay: and then thinking all chance was over for that night, they
went to bed. But for my part, I somehow or other felt so uneasy,
that I was sure I shouldn't sleep, so I fetched a book, and sat
myself down in an arm-chair by master's bed-room fire, which, as
well as Miss Fanny's, I resolved to keep in, in case they might
have been impeded by accident, and yet arrive, cold and uncomfortable, in the course of the night.

"I scarcely know how it was, but my thoughts, in spite of
myself, took a melancholy turn. All the misery that had followed
the disappointment about Major Leeson's arrival recurred to my
mind, and I could not help anticipating that some ill news was to
follow upon this. I thought of the odd passage in Andrew's letter,
wondering what it could mean, and what it was he wanted to do.
I knew he disliked Mr. Gaveston very much, and that the dislike

was mutual. Andrew could not forgive him for having exposed Harry Leeson to so much danger; and, one day, when he was not aware that he was within hearing, he had called him a cowardly rascal for running away and leaving the child in the water. This, together with Andrew's having told Mr. Wentworth of the hunting accident, had made Mr. Gaveston his enemy; and I was often afraid of my brother's getting into some trouble through it; for much as he was a favourite with his master and mistress, of course he could not have stood against Mr. Gaveston's influence if it had been exerted against him.

"All these things now took possession of my mind, and I kept pondering upon them, till insensibly my waking thoughts became dreams, and I gradually sunk into a slumber, in which the same train of ideas seemed to be continued. At first, the images were all confused and mingled together—there was something about my master, and mistress, and Mr. Gaveston, and Andrew—there was trouble and strife—but nothing which I could reduce afterwards to any form; but what followed, was as distinct on my mind when I awoke—ay, and is so still, as any circumstance that ever occurred to me in my waking hours.

"I thought I was sitting in master's arm-chair by his bed-room fire, just as indeed I was, and that I had just dropped asleep when I heard a voice whisper in my ear, 'Look there! who's that?' Upon that I thought I lifted up my head and saw my brother Andrew sitting on the opposite side of the fire in his grave clothes, and with his two dead eyes staring at me with a shocking look of fear and horror—then I thought he raised his hand slowly, and pointing with his thumb over his shoulder, I saw two men standing close behind him; one had a crape over his face, and I could not see who he was; but the other was the man with the crooked nose, who had rung at the bell two nights before. Presently they moved forwards, and passing me, went into my master's dressing-closet, which was behind where I was sitting. Then I fancied that I tried to rouse myself, and shake off my sleep, that I might look after them, but I could not; and when I turned my eyes again on the chair where Andrew had been sitting, instead of him I saw my master there with a large gash in his throat, and his eyes steadfastly fixed on me, whilst he pointed to something at my back; he seemed to try to speak, but his jaw fell, and he could make no sound. Whilst I was staring at this dreadful sight, shivering with horror, I thought that, though I could not see them, I was yet conscious that the two men had come out of the closet, and were standing close behind him, one with an open clasp-knife in his hand, and the other with a lantern; then I thought my brother Andrew suddenly came between us, and whispered, 'No, no; let her sleep! let her sleep!' and with that the light was suddenly extinguished, and I could see no more.

"Well, sir, the moment the light seemed to go out, I awoke in reality; and as I did so, I fancied I heard a door gently closed, and the sound of feet moving softly away; but I was almost in darkness, and could distinguish nothing. The bit of candle I had taken up with me had burned to the socket and gone out; and the fire, though there were some red ashes yet in the grate, shed but a faint glimmer on the hearth.

"What between cold, and fear, and horror, I felt as if my blood was frozen in my veins; and although I'd have given the world to move, and call the other servants who slept over-head, I found it impossible at first to stir my limbs; and there I sat with my eyes staring on the imperfect outline of the chair where I had seen Andrew and my master sitting just before, expecting to see them there again; and my ears straining for a sound with that dreadful intensity that fear gives one, till I fancied I distinguished the approach of a horse's feet; presently, I became sure of it; I thought there were two horses; they drew near as if they came from the stables, passed under the window, turned the corner of the house, and then receding, I heard no more of them.

"Till the morning light began to peep in through the chinks of the shutters, I couldn't summon courage to move. Gradually, when it illuminated the objects around me sufficiently, I forced myself to survey the room, and with a great effort to turn my head and look behind me; but everything, as far as I could see, was just as it was when I went to sleep. By-and-by, as the light grew stronger, I arose and opened the door that led out upon the stairs; but nothing unusual was to be seen or heard. Then I went to the dressing-closet; there, too, I could perceive no change. I tried my master's drawers and boxes, which had been all locked when he went away—and locked they were still. Finally, I examined the other rooms, both on that floor and below; but all was right. Nothing could I find to induce the suspicion that my dream was anything but a dream.

"Well, sir, you know how differently one feels about things in the broad daylight that have frightened and puzzled us in the dark; and you may imagine that the lighter it grew, the more absurd my terror appeared to me; till at last, by the time the sun was up, I was ready to laugh at myself for my folly: and when the servants came down stairs and found me warming myself by the kitchen fire, and looking very pale, I merely said that I had fallen asleep in master's arm-chair, and had awakened shivered and uncomfortable. I did not mention my dream, for I knew it must appear ridiculous to others—and I had no pleasure in recalling the disagreeable images that the light had dispersed. However, I did remark to Mr. Jeremy, that I had heard horses passing under the window in the night; but he said it was probably nearer morning than I had imagined, and that it was the farm horses going to their work; and this I thought likely enough."

CHAPTER V.

ILL NEWS.

ON the morning succeeding the night Susan had passed so un-pleasantly in her master's bed-room, when the servants assembled at breakfast, it was remarked that Mabel had not made her appearance; and Mrs. Jeremy, the housekeeper, who was a pre-cise personage, sent Susan to tell her, that if she did not attend at the appointed hours, she must go without her meals. Mabel, however, was not to be found in her dairy, nor anywhere about the house; and it was concluded that after doing her morning's work, she had gone to visit her sister Grace, who lived in the village, a couple of miles off. Nothing more, therefore, was thought of her till the gardener came in some time afterward, and said, that being attracted by the lowing of the cows, who had all assembled close to the park paling, he had been to see what was the matter, and discovered that they had not been milked. Further inspection of them and of the dairy proved this to be the case. Mrs. Jeremy vowed vengeance against the delinquent, and desired Susan, who understood the business, to supply her place for the immediate occasion. But when several hours elapsed and Mabel did not appear, her absence began to excite surprise as well as displeasure; more especially, when one of the men who had been to Mapleton with a horse to be shod, returned saying, he had called at Grace Lightfoot's to inquire if she was there, but that Grace assured him she had not seen her sister since the morning before. Upon this, Mabel's room, which adjoined the dairy, was examined, and, from various indications, it was con-cluded that she had not slept there on the previous night. Her clothes were all found, except her bonnet and shawl, and such as she might be supposed to have worn; and there was nothing dis-covered that could throw the smallest light on the cause of her absence, except it was, that a man's glove was found on the floor; but whose glove it might be, remained an enigma that time only could solve. Mabel Lightfoot, beautiful and haughty as we have described her, had never been known to countenance the atten-tions of any man, either in her own station or a higher; nor was it suspected that any of the latter class were in pursuit of her. Andrew Hopley was the most favoured, or rather, the least dis-dained, of her admirers; and even to him she had never shown anything that amounted to encouragement.

Conjecture was therefore at a fault; and no one could suggest any probable solution of the mystery, as hour after hour passed, and the messengers that had been sent in search of her returned, and brought no tidings.

One circumstance recurred to Susan's mind, but it seemed almost too vague and unimportant to draw any conclusions from, and therefore she made no mention of it. It was, that on the night the man with the crooked nose had rung at the back door, she had heard Mabel in conversation with some one as she passed her room: it was as she was returning to the kitchen after she had been up to look at her fires, and consequently not many minutes after she had seen him. The voice was that of a man: she thought nothing of it at the time, concluding it was some member of the family; but it now recurred to her that the stranger's saying he could not find his way, (in which there was certainly no difficulty,) and inquiring what place that was with the light in the window, might be a *ruse* to discover the dairy-maid's quarters.

Susan, however, kept these reflections to herself; and, indeed, her thoughts were very much diverted from the mystery of Mabel's departure, by her anxiety for the arrival of the family and her brother, from whom the morning's post had brought no tidings; and when she had finished her household duties, she sat down with her needlework at one of the windows that looked towards the park gate, to watch for the first approach of a carriage.

It was nearly three o'clock in the afternoon, when the sound of wheels announced an arrival. Not doubting it was the family, Susan started from her seat, but before she ran down stairs to meet them, she waited a moment to catch a glimpse of her brother in the rumble; but great was her disappointment when the vehicle drew near, to perceive it was not the expected carriage, but a hack post-chaise, in which sat a single traveller—a man, and a stranger.

Concluding it was some one seeking Mr. Wentworth about business, as was not uncommon, she had reseated herself and resumed her work, when the door opened, and Mr. Jeremy the butler entered with a face announcing "as a book where men might read strange matters," that he had something extraordinary to communicate.

"Is there anything wrong, sir?" said Susan, whose apprehensions of some unknown disaster were so much excited as to require little prompting.

"I am afraid there is," replied Mr. Jeremy; "but what, I don't know. The man that's come in the post-chaise is a constable from Maningtree; and he says you, and I, and my wife, are to accompany him back immediately; and that you are to take with you all the letters you have received from Andrew since he went away."

"But what can be the meaning of that?" said Susan.

"I can't make it out," replied Jeremy. "However, we must go, that's certain; and as it's getting late, the sooner we set off the better. So tie up what you'll want in a handkerchief, and make haste down. Mrs. Jeremy's gone to get ready."

In a state of amazement and confusion indescribable, Susan

proceeded to obey Mr. Jeremy's commands; and in a very short time they were prepared to set off.

"I hope nothing has happened to my brother?" said she to the man when she met him in the hall below.

"Are you the footman's sister?" said he, eyeing her curiously.

"Yes, sir," replied Susan. "There's nothing wrong with him, I hope, is there?"

"Wait till you get to Maningtree," replied the man, shaking his head significantly; "you'll hear it all soon enough."

The unexpected summons, the mystery attending it, and these hints and inuendoes, whilst they perplexed Mr. and Mrs. Jeremy, threw poor Susan into an agony of alarm. That something had occurred in which Andrew was concerned was evident: and again the strange passage in his letter about the marriage, the visit of the man with the crooked nose, Mabel's disappearance, and her own dream, all presented themselves vividly to her mind; and although she could not tell how, nor see the links that united them, she could not help fancying that all these circumstances belonged to the same chain of events.

It was towards nine o'clock in the evening when the chaise drove up to the door of the King's Head Inn at Maningtree. Several persons were lounging about the street; and when the carriage stopped, and the constable, who was seated on the dicky, jumped off to open the door, there appeared a manifest desire on the part of the bystanders to obtain a glimpse of the travellers; and Susan heard a voice in the crowd say—"I believe one of them's the young man's sister;" whilst some cried, "Which is she?" and others ejaculated, "Poor thing!" Mr. Jeremy, with whom both Susan and Andrew were great favourites, heard all this too: and leaving his wife to the care of the constable, he kindly gave the poor girl his arm; who, trembling, and ready to sink into the earth with fear and agitation, could scarcely support herself, as, preceded by a waiter, they were conducted to a small parlour at the extremity of the passage.

After procuring her a glass of water and a vial of hartshorn, the butler desired to be conducted to his master; to which the waiter replied, that Mr. Vigors the constable had gone up to let the gentleman know they were arrived; and presently afterwards Mr. Vigors appeared at the door, beckoning Mr. Jeremy to follow him.

When Jeremy entered the room above, he saw seated round a table, on which were decanters, glasses, and the remains of a dessert, four gentlemen, one of whom was Mr. Gaveston, the other three were strangers. On missing Mr. Wentworth, his first words were, "I hope nothing has happened to my master, sir?"

"You have not heard?" said Mr. Gaveston, with an appearance of surprise.

"Nothing," answered Jeremy. "The constable wouldn't tell us why we were sent for."

"You desired me not, you know, sir," said Vigors, who still stood by the door, with his hat in his hand.

"Very true," answered Gaveston, "I had forgotten. I think you may go now, Mr. Vigors, we shall not want you for the present;" and Vigors withdrew. "Take a glass of wine, Jeremy," continued Gaveston, "you've bad news to hear."

"I should be glad to know what it is at once, sir," said Jeremy, who was a straightforward sort of man, and entertained the most entire distrust of Mr. Gaveston's sympathy or civilities.

"Nothing less than the death of your master, Jeremy," replied Gaveston, taking out his pocket-handkerchief and covering his face with it: "that rascal Andrew has robbed and murdered him."

"Andrew!" cried Mr. Jeremy. "Lord, sir, the thing's unpossible!" for, grieved as the honest man was to learn the death of his master, his astonishment and incredulity at an accusation that appeared to him so monstrous, for the moment overpowered his other feelings.

"I fear it's too true," observed one of the gentlemen, whose name was Sir Thomas Taylor, and who was a magistrate for the county.

"Where is Andrew, sir?" said Jeremy; "does he confess it?"

"Gone off! escaped with his booty!" answered Gaveston, removing the handkerchief from his face.

"When did it happen?" inquired the butler.

"The night before last," answered he; "and though pursuit has been made in every direction—I myself have scoured the country, and hav'n't been off my horse till this evening—yet we can gather no tidings of the rascal. Once I thought I was upon his track; the description answered him exactly, and there was an evident desire of concealment; but the young man had a woman with him, therefore that couldn't be Andrew, you know, Mr. Jeremy."

Mr. Jeremy was silent.

"Andrew was never supposed to be connected with any woman that ever I heard of, was he?" repeated Mr. Gaveston.

"Not that I know of," answered Jeremy. "Andrew Hopley I take to be as good a young man as ever lived; and I should as soon suspect myself of such an act as I'd suspect him."

"But the thing's certain," replied Mr. Gaveston, "why else should the fellow make off?"

"It can't be denied that appearances are strongly against him," said Sir Thomas Taylor; "at the same time we know that these are sometimes fallacious—and previous good character is not without its weight."

"I remember a remarkable case of circumstantial evidence," said the coroner, "where appearances were quite as condemnatory as in this instance, and yet the suspected person was innocent; and what was extraordinary, the real criminal ultimately proved to be——"

"But, I repeat, is there any other way of accounting for the fellow's evasion than by supposing him guilty?" said Gaveston.

"There's no telling," answered Sir Thomas. "I remember a

case in which the supposed criminal proved himself to have been one of the vic——"

"Oh, no doubt such mistakes do occur occasionally," interrupted Gaveston: "but they are rare, and cannot by any means be admitted as precedents; or the consequence would be to throw so much discredit and uncertainty on circumstantial evidence,—which, remember, gentlemen, is very often all the evidence we can get at,—that the march of justice would be altogether embarrassed and impeded. But to pursue what I was saying—Andrew was never suspected of an attachment to any woman: was he, Jeremy?"

"There's few young men as have reached Andrew's years without," answered Jeremy. "Andrew may have fancied a girl as well as another; but there's no harm in that."

"Oh, none—none in the world!" exclaimed Gaveston, with an air of extreme candour. "No, no; all I wanted to know for, was because, as I mentioned, a suspicious person was observed on the road in company with a woman."

Jeremy was silent. There was something in all this inexplicable to him. He was an uneducated, but a very clear-headed man, and one who, to use his own phrase, was rarely deceived in man or woman. Of Andrew he entertained the highest opinion, founded on observation and experience, having known the lad from his childhood; whilst to Mr. Gaveston he had an antipathy so decided, that he used to liken it to the horror some people have of cats; and declare that he always felt an uncomfortable sensation when he was near him. Then, as for Mabel's having gone off with Andrew, which appeared to be the conclusion that would be drawn when her absence was known, and which, in short, he could not help suspecting was the insinuation Mr. Gaveston was driving at, he was as sceptical about that as the young man's guilt. He not only believed her incapable of countenancing or taking a part in the crime, but he was satisfied that she cared very little for Andrew; and was altogether actuated by views of a very different nature. He was even aware that Mr. Gaveston himself had offered to pay her more attention than was quite consistent with his engagement to Miss Wentworth; and he had observed them more than once in private conversation.

"To what amount is the robbery, sir?" said he.

"Forty or fifty pounds," replied Gaveston. "At all events, whatever money Mr. Wentworth had in his portfolio is gone; as well as my pocket-book and watch. Is your wife below?" added he.

"She is, sir," answered Jeremy, "and Susan also."

"I should like to ask her a few questions—Mrs. Jeremy, I mean. I think we may as well have her up?"

"Just as you please," said the other gentlemen.

"I'll fetch her," said Jeremy, "if you wish to see her."

"No," said Gaveston; "stay where you are; I'll send the waiter for her."

"Mrs. Jeremy," said he, when the housekeeper made her appearance, "I suppose you have heard what has happened?"

"The waiter has just told me as I came up stairs," said Mrs. Jeremy, weeping—"Good Lord! that one should be so deceived in anybody! I'd have staked my life Andrew was as honest a lad as ever lived."

"And how do you know but what he is still?" said her husband.

"You'd a good opinion of him, too, then; had you, Mrs. Jeremy?" said Gaveston.

"An excellent one, sir," replied the housekeeper. "I never knew a better young man—at least, than he *seemed* to be."

"It's strange," said Gaveston, "and almost staggers one; only that his making off tells so decidedly against him. If we could only get upon his track, and find where he's gone—by the bye, Mrs. Jeremy, Andrew was not connected with any woman that you know of, was he?"

"No, sir," answered the housekeeper. "Andrew was a very virtuous youth, as far as ever I knew. I believe he was fond of a young woman—one of his fellow-servants, but there was nothing between them more than should be."

"You're sure they were not married?" said Mr. Gaveston.

"Oh, no, sir," replied Mrs. Jeremy. "Indeed, I don't think Mabel had any mind to him."

"Did he correspond with her during his absence?" inquired Mr. Gaveston.

"I believe he did write her a letter," answered the housekeeper.

"If I had known this before, we should have sent for her also," said Mr. Gaveston; "and I think it would be right to do so still. What do you say, gentlemen?"

"Perhaps it might be as well," said Sir Thomas; "and desire her to bring the letter with her."

"We'll despatch Vigors again," said Mr. Gaveston; "and we may get her here time enough for the inquest to-morrow."

"I'm sure I don't know whether he'll find her," said Mrs. Jeremy; "for we missed her this morning, and she wasn't come back when we left Oakfield."

"How!" said Mr. Gaveston, suddenly turning round on his chair with a look of astonishment, and glancing at the other gentlemen—"missed her? what do you mean?" Whereon Mrs. Jeremy narrated the particulars of Mabel's disappearance, and the ineffectual search that had been made for her.

"And you've reason to believe that she did not sleep in her own apartment last night?" said Mr. Gaveston.

"So we think," replied the housekeeper.

"Pray, what sort of a girl is this Mabel?" said he. "If I recollect, she's rather pretty."

"She's very handsome," replied Mrs. Jeremy. "She was thought the prettiest girl in the county, high or low."

"Just describe her person," said Mr. Gaveston. "What was the colour of her hair?"

"Her hair is black," replied Mrs. Jeremy, "and her——"

"Stop a moment," said Mr. Gaveston, whilst he appeared to be searching for something in his pockets, whence he presently drew a scrap of white paper. "This is a memorandum I made from the people's description of the two persons that had attracted observation: the man answers to Andrew exactly. Now let us hear about the woman. Perhaps you'll compare as she goes on, Sir Thomas," and he handed the paper to the magistrate.

"She has black hair and blue eyes," continued Mrs. Jeremy.

"And what's her complexion?" said Mr. Gaveston, "and her height?"

"Her complexion's a beautiful white and red; and she's neither tall nor short—much about my height," replied the housekeeper.

The description and the memorandum tallied exactly; and the consequent conclusion was, that Andrew and Mabel had gone off together; and that the persons Mr. Gaveston had heard of were the fugitives. Upon which he declared his determination to spare neither trouble, expense, nor personal exertion, to discover them; and announced his intention of mounting his horse the moment the inquest was over, and never to relax in the pursuit till he had traced them to their concealment. In the meantime, a messenger was despatched to Oakfield, to ascertain if Mabel had returned, or if any news of her had been obtained.

Poor Susan first learned her misfortune from the lips of Mr. Jeremy: and it would be needless to enlarge on her amazement, grief, and incredulity; and the only consolation she had was in finding that the butler, of whose discernment she had a high opinion, was as unwilling to believe in Andrew's guilt as she was. Still, the question of "Where the devil is he?" which the worthy man blurted out ever and anon, in the height of his perplexity, was a most confounding one, and "Where is Mabel?" not much less so.

Susan suggested that he too might have been murdered; but then his body would have been found as well as Mr. Wentworth's; or he might have been carried off for some purpose by the criminals; but Mr. Jeremy objected that carrying off people against their will in England was no easy matter in these days. Finally, she suggested that he might have become aware of the murder, and of the direction taken by those who had perpetrated it, and have gone in pursuit of them. This supposition appeared, at once, the most probable and the most consoling; and to it they ultimately inclined.

Still, through the sleepless hours of the ensuing night, strange thoughts would find their way into Susan's mind; and again and again her dream, and the visit of the man with the crooked nose, recurred to her, though how to connect them with the catastrophe she could not tell. However, the following morning was appointed for the inquest, when it was possible some light might be thrown on the mystery; and in tears, prayers, and interminable conjectures, she passed the intervening hours.

CHAPTER VI.

THE INQUEST.

THE particulars elicited on the inquest were briefly as follows:—
It appeared that on the evening of the 17th, about eight o'clock,
Mr. Gaveston had arrived at the King's Head Inn on horseback,
and inquired what beds there were for a family that was following.
He was informed that, being ball night, there were none in the
inn, but that the party could be well accommodated over the way,
in a house that, being unoccupied, the host had the use of during
the full season. He inspected the rooms, and approved of them;
but expressed a wish that, as the weather was bad, the young lady
might be provided with a bed in the inn if one became vacant.
He then went away, and no more was seen of him till towards
nine o'clock, when the family arrived, and he met the carriage at
the door. In the meantime, a person had called to say, that " the
bed engaged some days before for a Mr. Smith, who purposed to
attend the ball, would not be wanted:" and Mr. Gaveston immediately secured this apartment for Miss Wentworth.

It next appeared that Mr. Wentworth had inquired for his
servant several times in the course of the evening, but that Andrew
was not to be found; but on interrogating the waiter, he admitted
that the house was so full of servants belonging to the gentry
attending the ball, and he was himself so busy, that he had taken
little pains to seek him. At length, on Mr. Wentworth's becoming impatient, he had discovered him standing amongst others at
the ball-room door, where he declared he had been the whole
time.

About eleven o'clock the family had retired to bed, and nothing
more was heard of them till the following morning; when Mr.
Gaveston came over to the inn in a state of considerable agitation,
and said he had been robbed of his pocket-book and watch. On
hearing this, the chambermaid, waiter, and boots, had accompanied
him across the way, where they searched every part of his room
without discovering the missing articles. Mr. Gaveston then
inquired where that fellow Andrew was; and they had proceeded
to the servants' apartment, but he was not there; and, on investigation, no one appeared to have seen anything of him since the
night before.

Mr. Gaveston then proposed their visiting Mr. Wentworth, to
learn if he had been robbed too; and after knocking and receiving
no answer, they opened the door, and discovered the unfortunate
gentleman lying on the floor, with a stream of blood issuing from
a wound in his throat, and a severe contusion of the head, which,
it was the opinion of the surgeon, had been occasioned by a blow
that had rendered him insensible before the wound in the throat
was inflicted. From the appearance of his bed it was supposed he

had quitted it in haste on being alarmed. His watch was gone; and his portfolio, which lay on the dressing-table, was found open and rifled.

When Andrew's room came to be examined, there were also evident indications of his having left his bed precipitately. The clothes were dragged nearly off, and, as well as the pillow, were lying on the floor. A chair that stood by the bedside was overturned, and under it were found a leathern purse containing a few shillings, and a silver watch, which Susan recognised as belonging to her brother. No clothes were found in the room but one stocking, which lay near the window, and appeared to have been dropped. The window was open, and as the room was on the ground-floor, there was every reason to conclude he had escaped that way. At the door of his bed-room were found his boots, which the man, whose office it was to clean them, said he had taken away the night before, and placed there himself in the morning.

But the strongest circumstance against Andrew was a letter found on the table in his room, addressed to A. B., Post-office, Maningtree, and which ran as follows:—

"All's right—house full—no bed to be had but *Mr. Smith's*—sky as black as hell. I must cut till after dark. At eight o'clock I'll be hanging about the Checquers—word, How far to London?"

The letter was written in a good clerk-like hand, and well spelt.

This circumstance led to inquiries of the waiter as to who had engaged and given up Mr. Smith's bed; but he could give no information on the subject. He believed it to be the same person that had called on each occasion; and, as he wore a drab coat, he had supposed him a servant: but both visits were after dark. He had only left the notes at the door, and he could not say he should know him again.

However, he was able to produce the second note; and, on comparing it with the letter found in Andrew's room, the writing appeared to be the same.

The woman who kept the post-office was then interrogated, and admitted that she remembered on the evening in question that a man had knocked at the window and inquired if she had a letter for A. B. She knew it was a man by his voice, but had not seen him, because she had only opened a single panel in the window, and he had stood rather on one side. There was no post-mark on the letter, and it must have been dropped in on the spot. The man said, "How much?" she answered, "A penny," which he handed to her, and departed.

When all this evidence had been adduced, Mr. Gaveston and Mr. and Mrs. Jeremy were called to speak to Andrew's character. The two latter avowed the most favourable opinion of him; but Mr. Gaveston said he knew too little of the young man to have formed any; but he did not omit to mention Mabel's disappearance, and his conviction that she and Andrew were the persons he had traced on the road.

This circumstance, together with the letter found in the young

man's room, and the mysterious passage in the one he had written
to his sister, combined with his evasion, seemed to point him out
so decidedly as the criminal, that even Susan herself could not be
surprised at the verdict which was brought in of "Wilful murder
against Andrew Hopley;" more especially as the messenger that
had been sent to Oakfield returned without any tidings of the
dairymaid.

A considerable reward was then offered to any one that would
give such information as would lead to the detection of the delinquent, or of that of his accomplices, as, from the letter addressed
to A. B., it was concluded he had some; and hand-bills were
printed and distributed over the country with a description of his
person and that of Mabel. But little or nothing was elicited by
these proceedings. A coachman who drove one of the London
coaches, came forward to say that on the morning after the murder, a man wearing a drab coat, and mounted on a bright chestnut
horse, had passed him soon after dawn about twenty miles from
Maningtree. He was going at full speed, and the horse was
covered with foam; but the man having taken off his hat to wipe
his head, he perceived that he was quite bald behind. This,
therefore, could not be Andrew. And we may here observe, that
although every effort was used, and Mr. Gaveston devoted his
time for several weeks to the pursuit, no further information was
obtained; and it was finally concluded that Andrew, and his
paramour Mabel, had succeeded in making their escape from the
country.

"Well, sir," poor Susan would say, when we came to this part
of our story, "you may imagine what my situation was! A few
days—but a few hours before, I had been as happy as a person in
my circumstances could be. I was in a comfortable service, enjoying the favour of my master and mistress, and the good-will of
my fellow-servants; and I had a dear brother who was all the
world to me, and who had the good opinion of everybody that
knew him; and as we both meant to do our duty to our employers,
we had no fears for the future, nor any anxiety, except latterly
about Andrew's weak health. Now, how different was it! My
brother, my only connexion in the world (for our father had died
the year before), was declared a robber and a murderer—the worst
of murderers, for he had murdered his benefactor—he was a fugitive, hiding from justice, and a price was set upon his head—our
name was branded with infamy; and I not only knew that I must
leave the service I was in, but I doubted very much whether I
should be able to get another. Who would trust their life or
property to one of such a family? What signified my character
or my past conduct? They could not be better than Andrew's
had been; yet one night—one single night, had proved him the
most barbarous of villains. Why might not I prove the same?
How could I hope to earn my bread honestly when nobody would
trust me? Where could I look for a friend, having no natural

claim on any one, and knowing that my very name henceforth would be a terror to those that heard it? Would it not be better, I said to myself, to end my life at once, than drag on a miserable existence, exposed to insult, want, and every kind of wretchedness, till a lingering death terminates my sufferings, or till the cruelty of the world forces me to some act that might justify the ill opinion it entertains of us?"

"But then, again," I said, "if I could clear Andrew's character? If I could live to see the day when we might lift up our heads again, and cry to the world, 'You've wronged us!' For my heart still told me he was not guilty; and that if he were alive, he would surely come forward and vindicate himself; and if he were dead, his body would yet be found, and his wounds speak for him. Would it not be worth while to live through all the wretchedness the scorn of the world could inflict on me, to hail that day at last? But how was I to live if nobody would employ me? without money, without friends, without a roof where I could claim shelter, or a board where I could ask a bit of bread?"

Overwhelmed with these mournful reflections, Susan was sitting sadly in her room debating whether to live or die, when the housekeeper, who had been attending Miss Wentworth, came in, and, with tears in her eyes, bade her go to her young lady's room, who wished to speak to her. "I was so glad," said Susan, "to be permitted to see her, for it was what I had not expected, that I started up and followed Mrs. Jeremy immediately.

"Miss Wentworth was still in bed, for she had been seized with fainting fits when she heard of her father's lamentable end, and had never been able to rise since. I approached her bedside, weeping bitterly; but I met her eye without fear or shame; for I felt certain that neither I, nor mine, had ever injured her; and that much as she deserved pity, I deserved it still more. She held out her hand to me, and said, 'Poor girl! God help you!' and then her tears choked her voice. 'Amen! ma'am,' I sobbed out, 'for I have none else to help me now!'

"'Don't say that, Susan, don't say that!' said she. 'I'll help you; why should you suffer that are innocent?'

"'I believe in my soul that I am not more innocent than my brother, ma'am,' said I. 'If you can think that Andrew did this cruel wicked deed, think that I was privy to it—for one is as likely as the other.'

"'God in heaven only can know that!' said she.

"'And I on earth, ma'am!' I replied; 'and though I may never live to see it—though I may have starved on a dunghill or perished in the street before that time comes—it will come, ma'am. God will justify us; the day will come that Andrew will be cleared.'

"'I wish it may, Susan,' said she; 'for your sake, and for the sake of human nature. I had rather believe it was any one than Andrew, to whom my poor father had always been so kind.'

"A sad thought crossed me then—one that would intrude—
that I could not keep away—a dreadful thought—and as I looked
on her sweet, unsuspecting face, I wept *for her.*

"'However,' said she, 'we must leave it to heaven. If your
brother is innocent, I believe, with you, that the truth will some
day come to light and prove him so; but in the meantime, my
poor girl, what is to become of you? I cannot keep you in my
service; and, indeed, I should think you would not desire to
stay.'

"'I should desire it, and prefer it to all things,' I replied, 'if
it were possible; but I know it is not. I am aware that, not to
mention your own feelings, the world would blame you; and that
for many reasons it cannot be.'

"'I scarcely know what to recommend you to do,' said Miss
Wentworth, 'and I fear no one in the neighbourhood of Oakfield
would be willing to take you into their service. But I have been
thinking that if you were to engage a room at Mapleton, where
you are known, and where your father and mother lived respected,
that you might, perhaps, support yourself for the present by
needlework, till time and your own conduct have somewhat
abated the prejudice that I am afraid will be excited against you.
At all events, you can consider this plan: and in order to preserve
you from immediate distress, I have desired Jeremy to give you
ten pounds, besides your wages; and, as long as I hear you
deserve it, you shall always find me willing to befriend you.'

"All the tears I had shed before were nothing to what this
kindness drew from me. I could scarcely find voice enough to
bid God bless her; and to pray that the day might come when
she would be convinced that neither I nor my poor brother were
ever guilty of ingratitude to her or hers; or were capable of doing
anything to render us unworthy of her goodness."

It was arranged that Susan should go back to Oakfield on the
following morning, for the purpose of gathering together what
belonged to her, that she might be away before Miss Wentworth
returned. An elderly lady connected with the family had come
down to stay with her; and Susan saw too plainly that the
stranger did not regard her with such indulgent eyes as her kind
young mistress did. "Good heavens! Fanny," she heard her say,
as she closed the door, "how can you think of countenancing
that horrid woman?" whilst she shrunk away as the poor girl
passed her, as if she feared to be polluted by the contact of her
skirt.

The most earnest desire Susan had, after she had been dismissed from Miss Wentworth, was to go over to the house that
had been the scene of the catastrophe, and inspect every part of
it herself. But after Mr. Wentworth's body had been removed,
which was at the close of the first day's inquest, the house was
shut up, and the gate that led to it locked; and when she hinted
her wish to Mr. Jeremy, he advised her to say nothing about it,
as he was sure it would not be complied with.

Exhausted with fatigue and grief, poor Susan forgot her
troubles for some hours in a refreshing sleep; but early in the
morning she arose to prepare for her melancholy journey to
Oakfield.   When she was dressed, finding no one was yet stirring
in the house, she opened her window and sat down near it to
think over her projects for the future.   Immediately beneath the
window was a pump, to which, with the early dawn, came the
housewives of the village to fetch their daily allowance of water :
withered crones, and young maidens, and lads who, before they
went to their labour in the fields, carried their mother's pails to
fill, and little children, who tottered beneath the yoke they bore
on their shoulders.   Some, busy or diligent, did their errand
and hastened away; while others, less occupied or industrious,
lingered to talk over the gossip of the day.

The morning was tolerably bright and fine now; but it happened that the previous day's rain had affected the water, which,
looking thick and muddy, drew forth many complaints.   "Rain
or not rain, it never was over-good water to my mind," observed
a middle-aged woman.   "We'd much better at Totcombe, where
I come from, than any to be got here."

"Na, na," said an old crone, putting down her pails, and
setting her hands on her hips; "there's no better water at
Totcombe than there is at Maningtree, if we had the right use
on't, but they took it away from us; and this here pump, I grant
you, was never good for nothing.   When I was a girl, everybody
in the village fetched their water from the well, at the old house
there, over the way; but they were fine people as lived there in
those times—mighty fine people, with carriages and horses, and
ladies in their silks and their satins, and their hoops, and what
not; and one day they found out that our slopping about in the
grounds with our pails was a nuisance, and not to be tolerated no
how; so they took the privilege from us, and gave us this here
pump in exchange—but the water never was the same thing."

"And what came of it!" said another; "why, they never had
no luck arter.   The very next summer the little boy, that was the
only son they had, fell into the well and was drowned afore ever
they missed him; and then, when it was too late, they boarded it
up."

"Ay," said the crone, "they went to the dogs from that time,
and many said it was a judgment on 'em for taking away the
privilege of the poor, that we'd had time out o' mind.   First, the
boy was drowned, and the mother pined away after him of a
broken heart—then one went, then another.   At last, Squire
Remorden, as owned the place at that time, brought home a beautiful foreign lady—some said she was his wife, some that she
wasn't; howbeit, she sung like a robin-redbreast.   But one night
there came a carriage with four horses, galloping through the
street like mad, till it stopped at Remorden's gate, and out
stepped a dark man—they said he was her father.   Then shots
were heard, and presently the dark man came out, dragging the

c

lady by the arm, and after flinging her into the carriage, away
they went as fast as they came. Soon after this, Remorden went
away across the water, and we never saw him again: and then it
came out that he had spent more than he should, and was obliged to
live abroad till things came round. However, he soon died; and
then the estate fell to George Remorden, his nephew: a wild one
he was. At the end of two years he hadn't a rap to bless himself
with; and then the house was shut up, and has been going to ruin
ever since: and this here last business'll do for it entirely."

"And who does it belong to now?" inquired one of the
auditors.

"To that same Squire George, if he's alive," replied the
woman; "but it's years sin' we seen him here. He was a fine
young gentleman as you'd wish to see before he took to gaming
and bad company—and there wasn't a girl in the village but her
head was turned for him. There was Judith Lake—Lake the
carpenter's sister—she drowned herself for love of him. I remember the day, as if it was yesterday. We were going to
church—for it was a Sunday morning—and there was Mary
Middleton, and Bob Middleton, and Job Lake, and I; and Mary
was dressed out in a fine new bonnet, with sky-blue ribbons,
that Remorden had given her; and Bob was sulky about it,
and so was Job, for he had a mind to her himself; and when
we were going through the meadow by the mill-stream, Mary
called out, 'La! what's that in the water? I do think it's a
woman!' and sure enough, when they pulled her out, who should
it be but Judith Lake. But that didn't keep Mary from going
the same road. We soon missed her from the village, and Bob
saw her in London, where he went to seek her, dressed out like a
duchess, sitting in a play-house with Remorden. Bob waited for
him till he came out; and then what did he do but fetch him a
blow across the face that broke his nose, and laid him his length
on the pavement; but Mary wouldn't leave him for all Bob
could say to her, and we heard she died at last upon the streets.
But the Squire'll carry Bob's mark with him to the grave. Na,
na; the family never had no luck after they took the water from
us—serve 'em right, I say—devil help 'em!" and with this charitable conclusion the conclave broke up.

But now that the stage was clear, another dialogue became
audible, which was carried on by two girls that were leaning
against the house, immediately under the window.

"How much are you to have of it?" asked one.

"Mother says she'll give me ten shillings out of it," replied the
other; "and I don't know whether to buy a gown or a shawl with
the money."

"What luck!" said the first; "what sort of a gentleman was
he?"

"I didn't see him," said the other; "at least, I am not sure
whether I did or not; I wasn't at home when he came; but I
think, from mother's description, I did see him when I was

standing by the post-office talking to Lucy Walters. A stout gentleman in a drab coat came up and dropped a letter in the box. I dare say that was to the lady."

"I wonder whether it was one of the Miss Roebucks he comed after!" said the first.

"Like enough," said the second, "for they say one of 'em's got a sweetheart that the old gentleman don't like. And he told mother when he came, that he wanted to get speech of his sweetheart as she went to the ball without anybody's seeing him; and that was why he left his horse at our house and wouldn't ride into the town."

"I wonder if he did see her!" said the other.

"I don't know," said the second. "When he came back, it was the middle of the night, and I was in bed. Mother said he saddled his horse himself, and threw her the guinea, and away he went without saying a word. But, come along up to Thomson's; he'd got a beautiful gownpiece in the window yesterday, but I couldn't make up my mind whether to have that or a shawl for the ten shillings;" and away went the two girls to inspect Mr. Thomson's goods, and enjoy the luxury of indecision between two objects so desirable.

When Susan had had her breakfast, she sat down in a room that happened to be vacant, to wait till the coach came up; and as it was in the front, she had an opportunity of inspecting the fatal edifice over the way, more at her leisure than she had hitherto done.

It was a large square brick building, and it had a heavy, antiquated, formal look, that suited well with the name it bore, which was the *Old Manor House.* The place was encircled by a lowish wall, and there was a paved walk which led from the gate to the door; and Susan perceived that one of her objects in desiring to inspect the place would have been defeated. She had a notion that she might make some discovery by examining the ground under the window of Andrew's room; but the pavement extended to a considerable width all round the house; so that no footmarks could remain. Beyond this there appeared a largish wilderness of a garden and orchard, neglected and overgrown with weeds, shrubs, and fruit-trees past bearing.

"It's a dismal-looking place," said Susan to the chambermaid, who happened to come into the room; "but I should like to have gone over it, if they would have let me."

"You'd have seen nothing," replied Betty, "to throw any light on it. There wasn't a corner we didn't look into; but except the young man's watch, and purse, and stocking, there wasn't a thing left behind."

"And his boots," observed Susan.

"That's true," answered Betty; "and unless he'd a pair of shoes in his pocket, he must have gone away barefoot; for he didn't take a single article over with him when he went to bed, that I saw; and I lighted him to his room myself. The only

c 2

thing I found at all," continued the chambermaid, "was an old
shirt-button, such as gentlemen fasten their wristbands with; it
was on the pavement under the window of the footman's room:
but it may have been lying there weeks before, for anything I
know. Here it is," and she drew it from her pocket—"if you like
to have it, you're very welcome."

"I should," said Susan, as she examined it. It was a pair of
little studs united by a chain, with a bit of coloured glass in each;
on one was inscribed W. G., and on the other J. C. The first
were the initials of Mr. Gaveston; and though, even if the thing
were his, the discovery amounted to little or nothing, yet Susan
felt anxious to possess it, and accepted Betty's offer with thanks.

Whilst they were yet talking, they heard voices and the sound
of a horse's foot under the window; and on looking out, she saw
the ostler was bringing out Mr. Gaveston's mare, as he (Mr.
G.) was about to start, as he had announced, in quest of the
fugitives.

It was a beautiful animal of a bright bay colour, and had a coat
that, as the ostler remarked, you might see your face in; and he
led her admiringly up and down, patting her sleek sides and
stroking her taper legs, waiting till her master was ready to
mount.

"A nice bit of blood that," remarked the blacksmith, who had
been summoned to look at her shoes before she started, and was
now with other idlers lingering about the door to witness the
traveller's departure; "but them high-bred critturs arn't fit for
the road—it shakes the bones out of their bodies."

"It do," returned the ostler; "it knocks 'em to pieces. Two
years on the road tells sadly agen a oss. She's shook in the
shoulder, surely, sin' I seen her last. She was a nice crittur
then."

"What, she's an old acquaintance o' yours, Jem, is she?" said
the blacksmith, winking to the bystanders; for Jem was famous
for his recognition of the animals intrusted to his care.

"I never forgets a oss," replied Jem. "We Newmarket lads
never do, none on us. Bless you! they be a deal more memorable
like than Christ'ans, to them as is used to them. She was a nice
crittur two years agone. She won a sweepstakes of a hundred
guineas agen some of the best cattle on the course—I mean to say
them as wasn't quite thorough-bred, but she's good blood in her,
too."

"And did she belong to this here chap then?" asked the blacksmith, pointing with his thumb towards the house.

"I can't rightly say," answered Jem. "I remember there was
two or three rum coveys came down from Lunnun the night afore
the Darby, and bilked the knowing ones; and this here mare was
one on 'em. I worked at the Spread Eagle then, where they put
up. There war a chap among 'em as went by the name o' Nosey,
that I'd seen afore at Newmarket—my eyes! how he cleaned 'em
out!"

Mr. Gaveston now came from the house, accompanied by the landlord, and as they stood on the steps, the latter was heard to say—"No, no, sir, depend on it, nobody in this neighbourhood had any hand in it. I have lived here man and boy these forty years, and know everybody high and low about the place, from his honour Sir Thomas, down to black Cuddy, the born idiot. That letter may have been dropped into the office here, and as there was no postmark on it, I suppose it was. But you see, sir, on a ball night there's a concourse of people about, gentry and servants; and nobody knows who's who, nor thinks of asking any questions. Depend on it, sir, it's been some of them London chaps that have got hold of the lad, and planned the whole thing. But it'll come out, sooner or later. Some on 'em 'll peach—when a man's going to be tucked up, he likes to make a clean breast of it. He don't care much for his pals then."

"I believe you are not far wrong," said Mr. Gaveston, as he moved off the steps.

"A fine mare, sir," said the landlord, inspecting the girths, to ascertain that all was right—" and a nice 'un to go, I'll warrant her. Had her long, sir?"

"Almost since she could carry a saddle," replied Gaveston. "She's something the worse of hard work now—ar'n't you, Bess? Your ostler has done her justice, however," added he, drawing some silver from his pocket.

"I always take care to have a man in that situation that knows his business," answered the landlord—" this is a Newmarket lad, and I'll back him against any ostler in England."

"From Newmarket, are you?" said Gaveston, eyeing the man.

"Ees, sir," said Jem, " but I lived at the Spread Eagle at Epsom since that —and I think I've seen this here mare afore——"

"Very likely," said Mr. Gaveston, drily; and returning the silver to his pocket, he drew out a guinea, which having handed to the ostler, he mounted his horse and wishing the landlord " Good morning," rode away. " Humph!" said the blacksmith, winking at the ostler, "you be Newmarket, sure enough, Jem!"

" I war bred there," said Jem, with a knowing leer, and putting his tongue in his cheek.

Upon this the loungers dispersed; and the coach that was to convey Susan to Oakfield presently coming up, she took a friendly leave of Mr. Jeremy, who promised to call on her when he returned, and with a heavy heart, and a last look at the old Manor House, she mounted the roof and departed from Maningtree.

CHAPTER VII.

SUSAN RESOLVES TO SEEK HER FORTUNE IN LONDON.

Susan had a lover, as what young housemaid, or any other maid at twenty, has not? His name was William Dean, and he was the son of the miller of Mapleton—a man reputed well to do in the world. It would, therefore, have been a great match for the humble and parentless Susan, who had only her own two hands, and her good character, to make her way withal. But now, alas! the good character was gone, or at least under suspicion; and it was to be feared that the two hands, however industriously disposed, might not be able to earn her bread.

Before reaching Oakfield, the coach had to pass through Mapleton, and as Susan cast her eyes towards the mill, she could not help feeling some anxiety as to how William Dean would meet her. As her arrival was not expected, and as the coach did not stop in the village, few people recognised her; but she fancied that in the demeanour of those few she could already perceive a difference. They looked at her, she thought, with more curiosity than kindness; and there was something in the cool nod of the head, and the nudging the elbow of the next bystander, that made poor Susan's cheek burn, and inspired an earnest wish that there were some spot in the world where, unknowing and unknown, she might earn her subsistence, however hardly, and hide her drooping head till death relieved her from her sorrows, or justification from her shame.

When the coach reached the stile that led across the fields to Oakfield, Susan got down, and with her bundle in her hand, trudged onwards towards the park gates. No one could be on better terms with her fellow-servants than she was, and yet now she dreaded to meet them; and as she drew near the house, she slackened her pace, and the big drops chased each other down her cheeks at the thought of her altered fortunes.

"Susan!" cried a well-known voice, and she felt a friendly hand laid on her arm—"Susan, how are you? Let me carry your bundle; I have run all the way from the village to overtake you." It was William Dean, the faithful man.

"Oh, William!" said she, giving free vent to her tears—"I little thought you'd ever have seen me brought to this trouble."

"Keep a good heart, Susan," said the young man. "You're not to be blamed for others' faults."

"Sure, you don't think Andrew guilty, William?" said Susan, indignantly.

"I hope not," answered he. "But we heard here they'd proved it against him, and that he'd gone away with Mabel."

"I have no right to be angry at anybody's believing it," replied Susan. "But it's hard to bend one's mind to it. It's one of the greatest trials I have to go through—but I must bear that with the rest, till it please God to bring the truth to light. In the meantime, William, I am very much obliged to you for this kindness. I know it's what few would have done in your place; and I am very glad you have done it, because it gives me the opportunity of saying something that I had made up my mind to say the first time we met—that is, if I saw occasion—for I thought perhaps you would not wish to speak to me."

"That was a very unkind thought, Susan," said the young man.

"It would have been like the world, William," answered Susan; "but though you and I must keep company no longer, it will always be a pleasure to me to remember that you did not forsake me in my trouble."

"I have no intention of forsaking you, Susan," answered William; "I don't know whether Andrew's guilty or whether he is not—but as I said before, there is no reason why you should suffer for other peoples' faults."

"But I must suffer for them, William," answered Susan. "When one member of a poor family does a bad act, he takes the bread out of the mouths of the others."

"Then you'll have the more need of friends," replied William.

"Need enough," returned Susan; "but that's not the question now. What I wish to say is—and there's no time like the present to say it in—that we must keep company no longer. I'll bring no honest man to shame; and unless I live to see the day that I can hold up my head again, I'll live and die Susan Hopley."

Many were the arguments William used to shake this resolution, but Susan felt that she was right, and she remained unmoved. It was doubtless a severe trial to resign her lover, and to renounce the support and protection she so much needed; but the pain was much less severe than it would have been had he forsaken her; and she was sustained by the consciousness that she was giving him the best proof of her affection. "He may think himself strong enough to brave the world for me now," said she to herself, "but in after years he might meet many mortifications on my account, that would make him repent of his generosity, and blame me for taking advantage of it."

Susan remained at Oakfield but one night, and on the following day she removed to Mapleton, where she engaged a room, and gave out that she wished to take in needlework. A few charitable people sent her some; but she soon perceived that, from the smallness of the neighbourhood on the one hand, and the prejudice against her on the other, she would be obliged ere long to seek a livelihood somewhere else. In the meantime, she eked out her scanty gains by drawing on the little stock of money Miss Wentworth's liberality had supplied her with, and bore up against her troubles as well as she could.

One day, about a fortnight after she had been settled in her lodging, she heard a heavy foot ascending the narrow stairs, and presently Mr. Jeremy threw open her room door. It was his second visit, for he had called on her the day after he returned from Maningtree, and she saw by his manner and his portentous brow that he now came charged with ill news.

"What's the matter, sir?" said she, "for I'm sure by your face there's something wrong."

But Mr. Jeremy only threw himself into a chair, placed his hands on his knees, puffed out his cheeks, and after blowing like a whale, folded in his lips as if he were determined the secret should not escape him; so Susan, who knew his ways, looked at him in silence, and waited his own time. "No will!" said he, after a pause of some duration, and rather appearing to speak to himself than her—"No will! Whew! they may tell that to them as knows no better, but it wont go down with John Jeremy."

"What, sir," said Susan, "hasn't master left a will?"

"So they say," said he; "but I'll take my oath there was a will, and that I was by when it was signed; and not one only, but two —and what's more, to my certain knowledge, master took one with him when he went away, and left the other at Oakfield; for I was myself in his dressing-room the last morning when he took one of them out of the escritoir where they both lay, and put it into the portfolio just before I carried it down to the carriage."

"Then whoever took the money out of the portfolio, took that also?" said Susan.

"No doubt," answered Jeremy. "That's as plain as a pikestaff, though one can't see of what use it could be to them—but where's the other, Susan? That's the question. Master had his keys with him; and after Miss Wentworth came back, nobody ever opened the escritoir till Mr. Rice and Mr. Franklyn, who were appointed trustees and executors, went to search for the will."

Again Susan thought of her dream; but as she never mentioned it before, she felt that to do it now would be useless; and perhaps subject her to the suspicion of having invented it for the purpose of shifting odium from her own family to others.

"As they can't find either," continued Jeremy, "people say he must have taken both with him; but I know better."

"But after all, it wont signify much, will it?" said Susan. "The whole fortune will go to Miss Wentworth; and I'm sure she'll take care of Master Harry."

"Miss Wentworth wont be of age these two years," replied Jeremy, "and if she marries that Jackanapes before she's her own missus—whew!"

The marriage, however, was deferred for a twelvemonth; and all they had to hope was, that in that interval the lost document might be recovered.

The day before Christmas day, Susan's door was suddenly burst open, and in a moment she found Harry Leeson's arms about her neck. "Oh, Susan," he cried, bursting into tears, "do tell me the truth about Andrew. I wont believe it—I can't believe it— —Andrew that was always so good—and that went into the water to save my life—and that was so kind to poor Rover when he broke his leg—nobody shall make me believe it—but tell me Susan, where is he?"

"In heaven, my dear boy, I believe," answered Susan; "for I'm sure Andrew never did a thing in the world that he need hide his head for; and if he were alive, he'd have come forward before this to prove his innocence."

"But, perhaps," said Harry, "some wicked people have got him, and shut him up in a dungeon. I've read of such things."

"I thought of that too," replied Susan, "but they tell me that couldn't happen now, in this country at least."

"But if he's dead, what made him die?" said Harry. "Did anybody kill him? What should they kill poor Andrew for? He'd no money, had he?"

"No, dear child," said Susan; ".if they killed poor Andrew, it was not for money."

"Then what was it for?" asked Harry.

"It's hard to say," replied Susan. "Perhaps he had discovered their wicked intentions—or perhaps he was killed in trying to save his master."

"That's it!" cried Harry. "I'd bet anything that's it! But, Susan, where do you think they put him when they'd killed him?"

"Ah, there's the thing, Master Harry," said Susan. "They've made up their minds that he's a thief and a murderer, and they've offered a reward for his apprehension; but if, instead of that, they'd offered a reward for his body, perhaps the mystery might be cleared up. And there's the misfortune of being poor, Harry. If we were rich gentlefolks instead of poor servants, they wouldn't have been in such a hurry to condemn him; and if I had plenty of money, I might find out the truth yet."

"When I am a man," said Harry, his cheeks flushing and his eyes sparkling at the thought, "I'll find out the truth, I'm determined. Fanny says I shall be anything I like, and I mean to be a lawyer, or a doctor; and when I'm rich, I'll put in the paper that I'll give a hundred pounds to anybody that will tell me the truth about Andrew Hopley."

"Although I had little hope," Susan would say, "that the dear child would ever have it in his power to do what he promised, or that if he did the truth would be discovered by such means, yet it was a great comfort to me to hear him talk in this way; and I shed tears of joy to see the confidence his innocent mind had in Andrew's goodness; for I was sure if my poor brother was in heaven, and knew what was doing on earth, that the words of the child he had loved so much would rise up to him sweeter than the odour of the frankincense and myrrh that in the old time was offered to God upon the altars."

About a fortnight after this, Harry, who, since he came home for the vacation, had seldom passed two days without paying Susan a visit, entered her room with a countenance that plainly denoted something had happened to vex him. His cheeks were

crimson, the heavy drops still stood on his long dark lashes, and
his pretty lip was curled with indignation.

"Oh, Susan," he cried, throwing himself into a chair, "I wish
I was a man."

"What for, dear?" said Susan. "Don't be in a hurry to wish
away time. We know what is, but not what is to come."

"I do, though," he said, "that I might be revenged on Mr.
Gaveston!"

"Hush, Harry!" answered Susan. "We must leave vengeance
to God. But is Mr. Gaveston come to Oakfield?"

"Yes," said he; "he came the day before yesterday; and now I
shall be very glad when my holidays are over, and I go back to
school. I hate him!"

"But what has he done?" inquired Susan. "You didn't use to
hate him, did you?"

"No," replied Harry, "for he didn't use to give himself such
airs. When my uncle was alive, he wouldn't have dared to treat
me as he does, or to say anything against Andrew."

"And what does he say against Andrew, dear?" said Susan.

"Why, when I told him I was coming to see you, he said,
'Upon my word, young gentleman, you show a delicate taste in
the choice of your society, and remarkable gratitude towards your
benefactors! A promising youth, certainly!' And, oh, Susan, he
said it in such a spiteful, scornful manner, that it was worse than
the words; and I would have knocked him down for it if I had had
strength to do it."

"And what did you answer?" inquired Susan.

"I said," replied Harry, "that I loved my uncle and Fanny
too as well as ever he did, and better too, perhaps; but that I
wasn't going to forget that Andrew had saved my life at the risk
of his own, when other people had left me in the water to be
drowned; nor that you had helped Dobbs to nurse my poor
mamma through all her sickness; and that I should go to see you
as often as I liked."

"Well, and what then?"

"Then he said, in the same spiteful, disagreeable way, 'Pray
do, sir, by all means; I should be sorry to balk your inclinations.
But I shall take care that if you choose to keep up a connexion
with that rascally family, you shall pay your visits to them
elsewhere, and not in this neighbourhood. Pretty associates,
truly, you've selected, for a chap like you, that depends on charity
for his bread-and-butter. Now, I dare say,' said he, 'if you
choose, you could tell us where that scoundrel is hiding from the
gallows—of course you're in the secret.'—'Yes,' said I, 'I do believe
I know where Andrew is, and that's in heaven, where spiteful
people can't hurt him—but when I am a man, and have got money
of my own, Mr. Gaveston, I'll spend it all to find out the truth,
and get justice for Andrew and Susan; and I'll advertise in the
papers a great reward to anybody that'll tell me what's become of
him.'—Oh, Susan, if you had but seen his face when I said that!

He turned as white as that muslin you're hemming, with rage; and
I do believe, if he dare, he would have killed me. He did lift up
his hand to strike me; but though I am but a boy, I wouldn't
stand still to be beat by him, for I'd have given him blow for blow
as long as I could have stood up to him. But then he seemed to
recollect himself. I suppose he began to think how Fanny would
like his treating me so, if she heard of it; and he said, in a taunting,
jeering way, 'You're really a nice young gentleman! It's a pity
your mother had no more like you. Go your ways, sir—to the
devil, if you please! and the sooner the better;' and then he turned
away. But one thing, Susan, I'm so glad of—though I couldn't
keep from crying as soon as he was gone, I did keep in my tears
while he was speaking to me. I wouldn't have had him seen me
cry for a hundred pounds!"

This conversation alarmed Susan a good deal, for she saw in it
the confirmation of what she had always feared, that whenever
Gaveston had the power, he would show himself no friend to
Harry; so she told him, that though his visits were the only real
comfort she had known since her misfortune, she must forbid
his coming; "for," said she, "remember, dear, you have only
Miss Wentworth to look to for your education, and for everything; and although she might not herself object to your visits,
yet husbands and lovers have great power over women, and can
not only oblige them to do as they please, but very often can
make them see with their eyes, and hear with their ears; and if
you offend Mr. Gaveston, there is no telling what may happen.
He may do many things that you can't foresee, nor I neither. By
and by, Harry, when you're a man, and your own master, it will
be different; then, perhaps, we may meet again."

"And then," said he, brightening up with the glowing hopes of
a young heart that could not believe in disappointment—"and
then, Susan, when I have got a house of my own, you shall come
and live with me, and be my housekeeper. Wont that be nice?
I'll go back to school the very day the holidays are over, and
take more pains than ever to get on, that I may soon be able to
go into a profession, and keep a house;" and then he ran on with
all sorts of plans for their little establishment, amongst which he
proposed that Susan should be treasurer; "for," said he, "I am
very bad at keeping money; somehow or another, I always spend
it in nonsense, and things of no use, and afterwards I'm sorry—
and so, by the bye, I wish you'd do me the favour to accept this
half-crown that Mr. Gaveston gave me the other day. I don't
want it; and besides, if I did, I shouldn't like to keep any present
of his:" and as he said this, he laid the half-crown on the table.

"Keep it, my dear," said Susan, "you'll be glad of it at school,
and I assure you at present I am not distressed; if I were, I
wouldn't scruple to accept of it, for I know I should be welcome:"
but as she pushed the piece of money towards Harry, she perceived something on it which led her to examine it more closely.

Over the royal effigy was cut the following inscription: "6th

June, 1765." The characters appeared to have been made with a
knife, and Susan felt perfectly sure that she had seen that half-
crown before, and under circumstances that induced her at once
to alter her mind, and accept of Harry's gift.

It happened, the day before Mr. Wentworth left home on his
last fatal journey, that she was in his dressing-room when he was
arranging some papers in the portfolio he took with him. He had
emptied it of most of its contents, and laid them on the table
beside him, when in turning round he jerked the table, which was
but a small one, and they all fell to the ground. Susan assisted
him to pick them up—and when she had done so, he asked if that
was all.

"Yes, sir," replied she—"it's all I see; but I thought I heard
something roll away like money."

"No," answered Mr. Wentworth—"don't trouble yourself further—there was no money here."

"Yes, sir," said Susan, "there was; here it is under the drawers.
It's a half-crown."

"Keep it, then," said he, "for your pains," and he locked the
portfolio and left the room.

Whilst Susan was yet looking at it, however, he returned.

"Show me that half-crown," said he. "Is there anything on it?
Ah!" continued he, with a sigh, as he examined it, "I must not
part with this. Here's another, Susan, in its place;" and then he
folded the one she had found in a bit of white paper, and replaced
it in a corner of his portfolio.

Now Susan felt perfectly satisfied that this was the same half-
crown; but how it should have come into Mr. Gaveston's possession she could not imagine. That Mr. Wentworth had no design
of parting with it, was evident; and from the manner in which he
had put it away, there was no possibility of his doing so by mistake. It seemed almost certain that it must have been taken
from his portfolio at the time of the murder; but it was inexplicable, not only that Gaveston should have had it, and kept it so
long, but still more so that, if he knew whence it came, he should
have given it to Harry.

Susan, however, who was resolved to neglect nothing that could
throw the faintest light on the mystery she was so anxious to
penetrate, consented to keep the half-crown, and after making
Harry observe the inscription, she folded it in paper, and deposited it in the same little box with the shirt-studs.

Much did she debate whether or not to mention the circumstance, but the apprehension of not being believed, on the one
hand, and of injuring Harry still further with Gaveston, on the
other, decided her to remain silent for the present. Indeed,
although from foregone conclusions, she attached much importance to the accident herself, she could not expect it to have any
weight with other people. Gaveston would naturally deny any
acquaintance with the previous history of the half-crown; and his

having given it to the boy would be a strong confirmation of the truth of his assertions.

The displeasure she found she was likely to bring on Harry by remaining in the neighbourhood of Oakfield, quickened a determination she had been some time forming of trying her fortune in London, where, her unhappy story being less known, she hoped she might get employment. With this view she wrote to her friend Dobbs, explaining her motives, and requesting her advice; and Dobbs, whose kindly feelings towards her were in no way diminished by her misfortunes, recommended her to come up without delay, assuring her that "Lunnuners were not so nice as country people, and that she did not doubt being able to get her into a respectable situation."

With this encouragement, Susan, glad enough to leave a place where she was looked on coolly, and where she had no tie but little Harry, lost not a moment in preparing for her departure; and, having with many tears embraced her dear boy, and taken a kind leave of Mr. Jeremy, she mounted the coach that passed through Mapleton, and, bidding adieu to the place of her birth, and the scenes of her childhood, she started to try her fortune in London.

CHAPTER VIII.

SUSAN'S ARRIVAL IN LONDON—SHE FINDS A FRIEND IN NEED.

As Susan understood that the coach would not reach London till between ten and eleven at night, she made up her mind not to trouble her friend till the following day: and, with this view, she requested the coachman to set her down at some inn where she would be able to get a bed, as near as he could to Parliament-street, where Dobbs resided.

In compliance with this request, when they reached Charing-Cross, the driver suddenly pulled up; and calling out, "Now, young 'oman, here you are!—Quick, if you please! Help her down, Jack! Box in the boot—that's it!"—Susan in a moment found herself standing in the middle of the area, with her luggage beside her.

"Which is the inn, sir?" said she.

"Please to remember the coachman," said he.

In her confusion, Susan put her hand in her pocket; but, in truth, she knew she had nothing there; for she had only kept out the money she expected to want on the road—the rest she had packed for security in her box; and the expenses having exceeded her calculations, she had not a single sixpence left.

"If you'll show me the inn, and wait till I have unlocked my trunk"—she was beginning to say to the man—but without stay-

ing to hear the conclusion of her speech, he mounted his box,
ejaculating "D—n all such passengers!" and with a smack of the
whip, the coach was gone, and out of sight before Susan had
recovered her astonishment. "And there I stood," she used to
say, "in the middle of the place, close to the figure of the king on
horseback, with my luggage beside me, perfectly bewildered, and
not knowing in the world which way to turn, or what to do next."

Coaches and carriages whisked by her, but no one paused to ask
her what she was standing there for; and there were plenty of
foot-passengers going to and fro on the pavement, of whom she
might have inquired her way; but she had heard so much of the
dangers and dishonesty of London, that she trembled to turn her
eyes from her boxes, lest they should vanish from her sight for
ever. Just, however, as she had made up her mind to encounter
this peril, and venture as far as the pavement, rather than stand
where she was all night, a man who had been observing her from
a distance, crossed over and inquired if she was waiting for a
coach.

"No, sir," replied Susan; "I have just left the coach; but I am
a stranger in London, and I don't know which is the inn."

"Oh," said he, "if that's all, I'll show you the inn in no time.—
Is this your luggage?"

"Yes," replied Susan; "but I want somebody to carry it."

"I'll carry it," said he. "The inn isn't two minutes' walk—just
hoist up the trunk on my shoulder—that's your sort—now give
me the bandbox."

"I wont trouble you with that, sir," said Susan, grateful for
this unexpected aid—"I can carry it myself."

"No, no," said he—"give it to me; you do not know London.
Somebody'd snatch it out of your hand before you got the length
of a street;" and so saying, away he trudged with the two boxes,
and Susan after him, as hard as she could go. But with all her
efforts she found it impossible to keep up with him. Whilst he
held along the Strand, as the way was straight, and the lamps
pretty thickly set, she contrived to keep him in view; but when
he approached the neighbourhood of Drury-lane, and turned up a
street to the left, that was rather on the ascent and worse lighted,
he got the advantage of her, and she soon lost sight of him
altogether.

Poor Susan called out "Stop! stop!" and ran as fast as she could;
but little thought had he of stopping, and after being nearly
knocked down several times, and getting repeated blows from
people she ran against in her confusion, out of breath, frightened
and exhausted, she gave up the chase, and sitting down on the
step of a door, she burst into tears. They were bitter tears, for it
was a sad beginning—all her little stock of money gone, how was
she to live till she obtained a situation! And when she had found one,
how was she to go to it, when she had not an article of clothing in
the world but what she had on?

It is admitted that no loneliness can be worse than the loneliness of a great city; and Susan felt it so, as passenger after passenger passed, hurrying on their errands of pleasure or of business, or hastening to the shelter of their own roofs, heedless of the poor stranger, houseless and homeless, whose sobs met their ears. A few turned their head to look at her; but none stopped or spoke; for there, where vice and misery walk the streets by night, or keep unholy vigils in unblest abodes, the sight of woman's wretchedness is too common to excite either curiosity or compassion.

At length the cold and damp—for it had come on to rain hard—forced her to get upon her legs and move on; and considering her desperate condition, without a penny in the world even to procure a night's lodging, she thought, unwilling as she was to disturb the family, that she had better try and find her way to Dobbs, late as it was. But the difficulty was to find the way. Some to whom she ventured an inquiry abused her—some insulted her; one man flung his arm round her waist and said he'd go with her anywhere she liked; and she had much ado to get rid of him; and another told her if she did'nt leave him alone, he'd call the watch. As for the women she addressed, they were still worse;.and one, who being very gaily dressed, she took for a lady, swore a big oath, and bade her go to h—ll!

After running the gauntlet in this way for some time, without advancing in the least towards her object, Susan gave up the point; and resigning herself to what seemed inevitable, faint and weary as she was, she once more seated herself on a door-step, and folding her cloak about her, resolved to wait there till morning.

She had sat some time, and had nearly cried herself to sleep, when she was aroused by the opening of the door behind her, and looking round, she saw a lady stepping out, who, however, paused upon the threshold to speak to some one that, with a candle, appeared to be standing within the passage.

"Be sure you're ready in time," said the lady. "Remember the coach starts at six."

"Never fear that," replied a voice that struck upon Susan's ear as one not unfamiliar. "I am too glad to get away from this place, to risk staying an hour longer in it than I can help."

"Well, good by," said the lady. "I hope you'll have a pleasant journey, and meet with no disappointment."

"Good by!" answered the voice within. "I wish you were going with me." "I wish I were!" said the other. "Oh, I forgot to say, that you are to be sure and travel in the veil Mr. Godfrey sent you."

"Yes, he told me," replied the voice. There was another "Good by!" and a shake of the hand; and then the door closed and the lady stepped forward.

She was attired in a silk dress, red shawl, and straw bonnet; and by the light from the lamp which fell upon her face as she advanced, Susan discerned that she was young and pretty. Her voice, too, was gentle; and emboldened by that and the countenance, the poor wanderer determined on making a last attempt to

obtain the information she needed. Rising, therefore, to let her
pass, she dropped a curtsey, and said, " Would you have the goodness, ma'am, to tell me the way to Westminster? I am a poor
stranger from the country, and am quite lost."

At first she was about to pass on without heeding the question,
but at the last words she paused and looked back. " To Westminster!" said she; " you're a long way from Westminster. What
part of it do you want to go to?"

"To Parliament Street, ma'am," replied Susan.

"And don't you know your away about London at all?" said she.

"Not a bit, ma'am," answered Susan. "I never was in it till
about two hours ago, when I got off the coach that brought me
from the country; and since that," she added, giving way to her
tears, " a man that offered to carry my luggage has run away with
my boxes, which contained all I had in the world; and here I am,
without money, or a lodging for the night, and but one friend in
the whole place, and I can't find my way to where she lives."

"It's impossible you should, without some one to guide you, and
it's not my road," answered the lady. She hesitated a moment,
and then drawing nearer to Susan, she looked hard in her face
under her bonnet, as if to see whether she were speaking the
truth. The result of the investigation appeared to be satisfactory;
for she added, as if moved by a sudden impulse of compassion—
" Come with me! I'll give you shelter for a few hours; and in the
morning you can find your friend. There was a night in my life
when if some charitable soul had done as much for me, I mightn't
be the miserable wretch I am now. Come along!" And with that
she turned and walked rapidly up the street, Susan keeping close
by her side.

As she was young, pretty, well dressed, and according to Susan's
notions appeared to be a gentlewoman, the poor girl was so surprised at her last words, that she forgot everything else in wondering what they could mean; and as the lady herself seemed to be
in a reverie, they proceeded for some time in silence, which she
at length rather abruptly interrupted by saying, " What's your
name, and where did you come from?"

"My name's Susan Hopley, ma'am; and I come from Mapleton,"
answered our heroine—" And as I spoke the words," she used to
say, " I fell rather behind her; for I expected nothing else but that
she would have driven me away from her directly, and left me to
pass the night in the street. But, to my great relief, the name
didn't seem to strike her at all; and I felt much comforted to see
that the people in London were not so much occupied about
Andrew and me, and what had happened in the country, as I had
supposed."

"And what was your employment there?" said she.

"I was a servant," replied Susan. "But latterly, being out of a
situation, I took in needlework."

"And you are come to seek a situation here, I suppose?" said
the lady.

Susan answered that she was; and after this there was no more conversation till they reached the neighbourhood of Oxford-street, where she lived, and then slackening her pace a little, she said, "I'll put you into the room with my little girl; but as my husband might not be pleased at my taking a stranger into the house, you'll make no noise till I come to let you out in the morning. He'll be gone away before that."

She then, having stopped at a respectable-looking house, drew a key from her pocket, and let herself in; and beckoning Susan to follow her up stairs, she conducted her to the second floor, where there was a candle half burnt down standing in a basin.

"Take this," she whispered, giving her the light, and opening the door of a room which she motioned her to enter; and laying her finger on her lip, once more to enjoin silence, she closed the door and disappeared.

On looking round, Susan found herself in a comfortable, well-furnished apartment, with a four-post bed on one side, and a child's crib in the corner, in which lay sleeping as lovely an infant, of about four years old, as eyes ever looked upon. It was enjoying a sweet, calm sleep, with one little hand under its rosy cheek, and with a half smile playing round the pretty red lips, that showed its baby dreams were pleasant.

"What," thought Susan, as she hung over it admiringly, "can make the mother of such a cherub call herself a wretch? She cannot be very poor, or she couldn't afford to live in such a house as this. But we poor people are too apt to think there's no evil so great as poverty. Perhaps there are many as bad, and worse—and I ought to learn to bear my own trouble patiently, when I see that this pretty, kind young creature is not without hers. Heaven bless it, sweet soul!" she added, as she stooped down to kiss the infant's cheek; and as she lifted up her head again, she saw the lady standing beside her with a piece of bread and a glass of wine on a plate.

"My husband is not come home yet," said she, laying her hand kindly on Susan's arm, as if she were pleased at finding how she was engaged—"take this, it will do you good." She then kissed the child, and once more bidding the grateful Susan "Good night," left her to her repose. Without undressing, the weary traveller stretched herself upon the welcome bed, and was soon in a sound sleep.

This blessed oblivion, however, had not lasted long, when she was aroused by the sound of a man's voice, which, although proceeding from the next room, reached her distinctly through the thin partition. In the confusion of first awakening, she started up, imagining herself still on the top of the coach, and that the man was abusing her for not paying him; for the first words she distinguished were, "D—n it! no money! Don't tell me! What's become of the last ten pounds?"

"Gracious, George," said a voice which Susan recognised as that of her compassionate hostess, "how can you ask? Why, you know,

D

we owed every farthing of it, and more; and I was obliged to
divide it betweeen the tradespeople just to stop their mouths."

"Well, if you can't get any money from him, you must walk the
streets for it," replied the man; "for devil-a rap I have to give you.
I suppose he gave you the allowance for the child? If he stops
that, you can have him up before the magistrates, and he wont
like that just now, I can tell you."

"Yes," answered the lady, "he has promised me the allowance;
but that is not enough to pay the rent, and all the other things we
owe. Besides, how are we to get on when that's gone? I dare say
I shall get no more from him till you come back."

"I'll be d—d if I know what you're to do," answered the man,
"unless you choose to do what I tell you. I can't afford to pay
the piper any longer, and I wont, that's flat. And now I'll thank
you to let me have a little sleep, for I must be up at daylight to be
ready for the coach. I hope that girl will be ready. Did you tell
her to be punctual?"

"Oh, yes, she'll be ready," answered the lady. "But before you
go to sleep, do listen to a few words I have to say to you; for,
perhaps, it may be long before you return. I have been thinking
that if I could contrive to get money enough to set me up in some
sort of little shop that would provide me and my child with bread,
that I needn't be a burden to you or anybody else; and I want
you to help me to this."

"I can't help you to what I haven't got," answered the man, in
a drowsy tone.

"Yes, you could," answered she, "if you would persuade him
to do it. Tell him that I would on that condition renounce the
allowance for the child, and undertake to maintain her myself.
Will you, George?"

"Very well," said the man, in a tone that denoted he was half
asleep.

"I say, George, listen to me; will you ask him to do this?"
persisted she.

"D—n it, woman, hold your tongue, will you, or I'll make
you?" exclaimed the man, in a louder key.

"Only promise to do what I ask, and I'll not speak another
word," returned she. "I know very well, George, you're tired of
me now; but you did like me once, and then you promised that
I should always share whatever you had. I don't complain that
you have changed, and I have no right to reproach you. But do
me this one favour; it's all I'll ever ask of you!"

"Very well," replied the man, in rather a softer tone. "Perhaps, I'll try what I can do; but he's devilish hard to deal with.
He was a different sort of chap when he wanted me. And as to
my wishing to get rid of you, Julia, you know as long as the
game lasted, I've kept you like a lady, and you've wanted for
nothing; but now it's up, I tell you, and you must shift for
yourself."

"And so I will," replied she, "if you could only get him to put
me in an honest way of getting my living."

"Well, I'll see what I can do," said the man; "and now, d—n it, do let me get a little sleep."

Here the conversation terminated: and, much as Susan was impressed with it, her fatigue soon put an end to her reflections, and in a few minutes she was again buried in a profound sleep, from which she did not awake till she was roused by the joyous infantine laugh of the child in the morning. The mother was dressing.it, and between every article of clothes she put on, it was running away, and hiding itself behind the curtains of the bed. "It would have been a pretty sight to look on," Susan would say, "the fair young mother and the lovely child, if I had not had in my mind the conversation I had overheard in the night;—but that spoiled the picture, and I could have wept to think of the misery that was gathering round them. 'And that sweet face of thine,' thought I, as I looked at the infant, 'may be but a snare to thee, as thy poor mother's has doubtless been to her!' She was a pretty young creature, the mother, with delicate features, and soft, dove-like eyes, but already, although she was not more than twenty years of age, there were traces of melancholy and deep anxiety in her countenance. Perhaps, if I had not been so much in her secret, I might not have understood them so well; but as it was, I fancied I could read her story in her face."

When she had finished dressing the child, Susan arose and wished her good morning. She answered very kindly, hoping she had rested well, and had recovered her fatigue.

"Quite, ma'am, thanks to you," replied Susan; "and I am sure I shall never forget your goodness the longest day I have to live. It's what few would have done for a poor stranger."

"You are very welcome," replied Julia. "I wish I could do more to help you out of your difficulties. But I suppose when you have found your friend, you'll do pretty well; so after we have had some breakfast, I'll walk part of the way with you and put you on the road."

They then adjourned to the front room, where there was a fire; and Susan having assisted her to prepare the breakfast, they sat down together.

"And what made you leave the country, where I suppose you had friends, to come to London for the chance of doing better among strangers?" inquired Julia.

"I had plenty of friends in the country, ma'am," answered Susan, "and very good ones; and six months ago, I never expected to be as badly off as I am now, or to be obliged to look further for a home; but a circumstance happened that threw a suspicion on one of my family, and since that, I found people began to look coldly on me."

"Ah," said she, "that's the way of the world; at least, towards the poor;" and then she fell into thought and was silent.

As soon as breakfast was over, she put on her bonnet and shawl,

and they set off towards Parliament-street, leading the child between them, who, pretty soul, went skipping and prattling along,
as gay as the morning.

They had walked some distance, and had reached the neighbourhood of Soho, when, in passing through a narrow shabby
street, Julia requested Susan to take charge of the child a moment
whilst she called at a shop, and presently she turned into one
that, by the watches and trinkets in the window, Susan concluded
was a jeweller's; but a longer acquaintance with London life
would have taught her to recognise it as a pawnbroker's. She
had a small parcel in her hand when she went in, but she came
out without it; and, after walking a few steps, she said, "Here,
Susan, take this; it's not much, but it's better than nothing:"
and she had placed five shillings in her hand before she knew what
she was doing.

"My dear lady," answered Susan, who, after what she had
heard in the night could not bear to think of accepting her bounty,
"pray take it back again: I don't fear but I shall do very well
when I have found my friend. And, at all events, I am alone,
and able to bear up against a deal of hardship, but you have this
dear child to provide for, and I could never find it in my heart to
spend the money if I took it."

"She turned a sharp eye on me," Susan used to relate, "when
I said this, and I saw in a minute that I had betrayed myself;
for certainly there was nothing in her appearance or way of living
to justify me in supposing that she could not spare so small a
sum. The colour came into her cheeks, for she guessed how I
had gained my information; and I turned away my head, for I
felt my own getting red too. 'No,' she said, when she had recovered herself, though her voice was slightly altered—'no, keep
it; it wont make my situation better or worse, but it is awkward
for you not to have a shilling in your pocket in case of need.'

"I couldn't keep the tears that were already in my eyes from
running down my cheeks at these words, to think of her goodness, her youth, her troubles, and her sweet young child, and I
thought what a blessed thing it would be for anybody that was
rich to put her in the decent way she wanted to earn her bread,
and so perhaps save her from being driven by poverty and want to
more misery, and a worse way of life; but I could only bid God
bless her, and look down upon her with pity."

When they had reached the neighbourhood that Dobbs inhabited, and there was no further danger of Susan's losing her way,
Julia stopped, and said, "Now you are within a few doors of your
friend's house, and I may leave you."

"Dear lady," said Susan, "it's not likely that such a poor
creature as I am should ever have it in my power to make any
return for your goodness but my prayers, but if there ever should
be anything that a poor servant can do, be sure that I would go
as far to serve you or your dear little child here, as I would for
myself."

"I don't doubt it," replied Julia, "for I see you've a grateful heart, and I wish I was so situated that I could keep you with me. Such a friend would be a great comfort. Heaven knows I want one! But that's impossible; so good-by, and God bless you!"

"Amen, madam, and you!" said Susan—"and so shaking hands kindly, we parted, after a few hours' acquaintance, with our hearts as warm to each other, and as much trust and good-will, as if we had been friends all our lives."

CHAPTER IX.

LOVE AND MURDER.

IN an old château on the banks of the Garonne in the neighbourhood of Cadillac, and about fifteen miles from Bordeaux, dwelt an antique cavalier, called Don Querubin de la Rosa y Saveta. As his name implies, he was a Spaniard by birth, and was, in fact, a native of Upper Navarre; but a rather premature explosion of gallantry having brought him into perilous collision with a powerful and vindictive family of Arragon, his parents despatched him across the Pyrenees, to the care of Monsieur Râoul, a worthy exporter of claret, and an old acquaintance.

Although Don Querubin could show some quarters of nobility, he was the youngest son of a very indigent family; and after residing some months in the house of Monsieur Râoul, he began to discover that there was better fare to be met with at the table of an opulent Bordeaux merchant than cow-heel, onion-broth, tripe, or unsavoury stews, and that it was more agreeable to relish his fricandeaux and salmis with a good glass of Château Margaux than with the poor produce of the paternal vineyard. Overlooking the degradation, therefore, he consented to defile his pure blood by connecting himself with commerce, and in process of time became a partner in the house of Râoul, Bonstetten, and Company, of which firm he was still a member, although, being now advanced in years, an inactive one.

His Spanish pride, which, although subdued to his interest, was by no means eradicated, caused him to prefer inhabiting in solitary state the old castle we have mentioned, which he had christened the Château de la Rosa, to residing in the more gay and bustling city, although he sacrificed a great deal of comfort and society to his dignity. But in Bordeaux he was simply called Monsieur Rosa, whilst in the neighbourhood of his castle he was styled Monsieur le Marquis—a variation of nomenclature that made an incalculable difference in the old gentleman's happiness and self-complacency, and fully compensated for all the advantages he was content to forego to enjoy it. Besides, after the vengeance of his enemy was supposed to have relaxed, he frequently revisited the place of his nativity; and he found it more agreeable to his haughty relations to be invited to the Château de la Rosa, where his remnant of nobility still adhered to him, than to busy Bordeaux, where it was neither esteemed nor acknowledged.

Now, it happened that Monsieur le Marquis had the misfortune to be fitted by nature with some rather incongruous attributes; he was very ugly, very vain, and, withal, an inordinate admirer of beauty—of beauty of all shades and countries, but more especially of English beauty. He had been in love all his life, but he had been one of the most unsuccessful of lovers, particularly amongst the goddesses of his peculiar worship, the fair Englishwomen, not one of whom had he ever been able to persuade to listen to his vows. Nevertheless, he did not despair; he loved on as sanguine people live on, through a thousand disappointments, reviving again after each overthrow, ready to enter with fresh vigour on a new pursuit; and willing to attribute his failure to any cause in the world but his own want of merit; although with an extremely tall, spare figure, a sallow complexion, high aquiline nose, and long, yellow teeth, he certainly made but an ill representation of Cupid, especially as these charms were usually attired in a black velvet skull cap, called a calotte; a crimson damask dressing gown, and yellow slippers. But he found his consolation and his encouragement in his favourite song, which, with a cracked voice, he daily and hourly carolled out of tune:—

> That Love his triumphs dear should sell,
>   Is sure most just and fair,
> Since none but he rewards so well,
>   With joys beyond compare.
> Besides, 'tis clear the urchin's wise,
> For what is cheap we never prize.

"Here is a letter for Monsieur le Marquis," said his servant, entering his dressing-room, one morning, where he was shaving, and singing—

> That love his triumphs dear should sell.

"Let us see, Criquet," said the marquis; "where does it come from, eh?"

"It comes from England," said Criquet, holding it up to the light, and compressing the sides, that he might get a peep into it.

"Give it me," said Don Querubin, laying down his razor, though but half shaved.

"Stop," said Criquet, still endeavouring to penetrate the contents of the letter, "I see the words, 'beautiful girl.'"

"How? you see that?" said the marquis, turning briskly round on his chair.

"'Beautiful girl,'" repeated Criquet, slowly, "'her eyes are'—ah! I can't make out the colour of her eyes."

"Blue, Criquet!" cried Don Querubin, smacking his lips.

"Blue, by my marquisate! For doubtless she's an Englishwoman. But let us see; give me the letter, that we may ascertain what it's about."

"It's about a pretty girl," said Criquet; "that's clear."

"Nothing better, Criquet," said the marquis, with a knowing wink, whilst he broke the seal. "A-h!" continued he, drawing a long breath, as he threw himself back in his chair, and stretched out his legs, that he might the better relish a communication on so interesting a topic—"now, let us see;" and he commenced reading aloud as follows:—

"'Dear Sir,—In compliance with your request, I have, ever since my return to England, been looking out for something likely to suit you'—("How?" exclaimed the marquis, a little puzzled by this beginning); 'and I trust I have at length been so fortunate as to discover an object exactly to your taste.' ("What can it be, Criquet?" said the marquis. "Go on," said Criquet.) 'The young lady to whom I have ventured to promise your favour and protection is exceedingly desirous of travelling and visiting foreign parts.' ("That shows her sense," observed Criquet. "Softly," said Don Querubin; "where were we? Ah, I see—'travelling and visiting foreign parts.') 'She is a most beautiful girl'—"

"Didn't I say so?" said Criquet.

"'Her eyes—'" continued Don Querubin.

"Ah! now for the eyes!" said Criquet, rubbing his hands.

"'Her eyes are of a heavenly blue—' By the blood of my ancestors!" exclaimed the marquis, "I was sure of it. 'Her hair is perfectly black, and her complexion positively transparent.' Heavens! what incomparable charms!" cried the marquis, dropping the letter, as if paralyzed by the force of the description.

"Let us see the rest," said Criquet, picking it up, and proceeding to decipher its contents. "'Her teeth are like pearls,' (that's good;) 'her figure graceful, and her hands and feet models for a sculptor.' A thousand miracles!" "Why, she's an angel, Criquet," exclaimed the marquis. "I like the hands and feet," said Criquet. "But stay, there's more to come. 'This young person,'" continued he, "'is remarkably prudent, and entertains a peculiar preference for individuals of a certain age.'" "The very thing we want," said Criquet. "I admire her taste," said the marquis. "Go on, go on."

"'But,'" continued Criquet—("Ah, here comes a *but*, as usual), '*but* I will not conceal from you, that this lovely creature is ambitious.'"

"And why not?" said the marquis.

"'Ambitious,'" repeated Criquet, "'and desirous of raising herself to an elevated rank.'"

"She shall be a marchioness, Criquet," said Don Querubin. "I hope that will content her. De la Rosa y Saveta, eh?"

" 'Nevertheless,' " continued Criquet, reading, " 'being very young, for she is but seventeen—' "

"The tender lambkin!" exclaimed the marquis.

" ' Knowing little of the world, and being entirely ignorant of all foreign languages and customs—' "

"I'll teach her the language of love," said the marquis, sentimentally.

" 'Or customs,' " reiterated Criquet, " 'some slight ceremony, and a few unmeaning words read from a missal by our friend Criquet, who will make a capital priest'—(" The devil I shall !" said Criquet—' will be all that is necessary on the occasion.'

"The end spoils the beginning," said Criquet, nodding his head significantly.

"But that is villanous!" said the marquis, in an indignant tone.

"And pray who does the letter come from?"

"It's signed *Walter Gaveston*," answered Criquet. "Here's a postscript too."

"Read it," said Querubin.

" 'I have addressed the young lady, whose name is Mademoiselle Amabel Jones, to the house of Monsieur Râoul and Co., Bordeaux, where I expect she will arrive, escorted by a particular friend of mine, shortly after this reaches you.' "

"That's all," said Criquet, as he closed the letter, with a strong expression of contempt on his countenance.

"We shall marry her in reality," said the marquis.

"To be sure we shall," replied Criquet. "What do they take us for?—wretches without principle, without honour, to deceive a young creature that puts her trust in us! The very idea shocks me."

"You are an honest fellow, Criquet," said the marquis. "You are a man of honour."

"I hope so," said Criquet. "As for that rascal, Gaveston, he was never much to my taste. I'd never much opinion of him."

"Nor I," replied the marquis. "He's a hard man; he has no heart, no susceptibility. I doubt whether he was ever in love in his life."

"And it is said some awkward misunderstandings arose at the card-table when he was last here," said Criquet. "I know some gentlemen refused to play with him."

"A man that will deceive women, will deceive men when he hopes to do it with impunity," said the marquis.

"I have always remarked it," replied Criquet.

"True honour," continued the marquis, "is for every day's wear—for all times and for all places; it is not to be put off and on at pleasure."

"That's true," said Criquet. "He was not a man to employ on so delicate a mission."

"It was rather a jest than anything else," returned the marquis. "I have never thought of it since."

"But since she is coming," said Criquet, "we must make up our minds what we are to do."

"Marry her, of course," replied Querubin.

"With all my heart," responded Criquet, "provided always—"

"Provided what?" said the marquis.

"Why, there are certain points to be considered," said Criquet. "Suppose, for example, she was not exactly—hem!" and he shrugged his shoulders significantly.

"What do you mean, Criquet?" asked the marquis. "Isn't she as beautiful as an angel?"

"There's no denying that," replied Criquet; "at least, if she answers the description: but what's to become of us if she should not happen to be as virtuous as one?"

"But he particularly mentions her prudence," observed the marquis.

"That's true," replied Criquet; "but what is his word good for?"

"Fie, fie, Criquet," said Querubin. "We must not suspect the lovely creature."

"But, unfortunately, lovely creatures are not always as irreproachable as they should be," said Criquet.

"For my part," said the marquis, "I have always found their virtue impregnable."

"I fancy that depends on circumstances," said Criquet. "But, however, supposing that's all right, there's another question. What are we to do with Ma'm'selle Dorothée?"

"But if she does not love me?" replied Don Querubin. "Have I not persevered for three years without a shadow of success? I am satisfied she has some other attachment, or the thing would be impossible."

"That may be," answered Criquet. "I don't dispute it; but there are certain little emoluments that the young lady has touched occasionally, which she may, perhaps, be less willing to dispense with, than with the vows that accompanied them. Besides, if I mistake not, it was only yesterday that I found you at her feet."

"I can't deny it," replied Querubin. "And, moreover, I promised her a new shawl, which I was to give her this morning."

"And here she comes to claim it," said Criquet. "I hear the pattering of her feet in the corridor."

"Open the door, my friend, open the door, and we'll confess the whole affair to her with honour and candour," said the marquis.

"Come in, Ma'm'selle Dorothée," said Criquet, as he threw open the door, and admitted a pretty, arch-looking, black-eyed grisette, who walked into the room with all the consciousness of power in her step.

"Good morning, marquis," said Dorothée: "how are you to-day?"

"Quite well, my love—hem! that is, Ma'm'selle Dorothée, I mean."

"Ha! ha!" thought Dorothée. "He's angry because I wouldn't let him have a kiss yesterday. I must coax him a bit. Gracious! how blooming you are looking this morning! Stay, just let me set your cap a little on one side—there, so. Now, whip me, if you look more than thirty; you don't, indeed; and you know I never flatter you."

"Not often, certainly, Dorothée," replied the marquis. "But the good news I have just received has cheered me, I confess."

"From Spain, perhaps?"

"No, it's from England," replied the marquis. "It announces the approaching arrival of a young lady——"

"A young lady!" said Dorothée, raising her eyebrows.

"As beautiful, Dorothée, as yourself."

"And I hope a little more amiable," thought Criquet.

"It's to try me," thought Dorothée. "And pray what is she coming for?"

"For the sole purpose of honouring me with her hand and her affections," replied Don Querubin.

"Bah!" said Dorothée. "Before she has seen you?"

"It's true, however," replied the marquis. "This young lady is gifted with a remarkable degree of prudence; she has very proper notions about things, and entertains a decided preference for gentlemen of a certain age."

"That is, she says so, and you are flat enough to believe her," said Dorothée.

"Besides," said the marquis, "she is ambitious, and aspires to a distinguished alliance."

"For that part of the story, it's likely enough," said Dorothée. "And what do you mean to do with her when she arrives?"

"Marry her, assuredly." said the marquis, in as firm a voice as he could assume, for he felt rather awed by the thunder-cloud he saw gathering on Ma'm'selle Dorothée's fair brow; there was something very like truth in the marquis's manner, and she did not quite admire the aspect affairs were taking.

"You're telling me this to put me in a passion; I'm sure you are," said Dorothée, as the angry blood suffused her cheeks.

"By the blood of my ancestors, no!" answered Querubin. "Here is the letter, let Criquet read it to you. You will there learn her qualifications, and the favourable disposition she entertains towards me."

Not too much delighted at the office, however, Criquet undertook it; since the art of reading formed no part of Ma'm'selle Dorothée's accomplishments. She waited quietly till he reached the end of the epistle, (a certain passage of which, regarding the false marriage, he had the precaution to omit,) and then settling herself firmly on her feet, putting her two hands in the pockets of her apron, and fixing her bright black eyes on the marquis, she said, "Now, listen: if this woman comes here, I'll poison her!"

"Bah!" said the marquis. "You're joking."

"You think so?" said Dorothée. "You had better not put me to the proof. For three long years you have been courting me—it was but last night you entreated me to accept your hand—"

"And you refused it," said the marquis.

"No matter," answered she; "I mightn't always have refused it. Perhaps I came here this morning with certain intentions—I shall not say what, now—I might have owned that I loved you, for anything you know; but you shall never know now whether I do or not!" And passion here supplied the fountains that grief would have left dry.

"Nay, nay, Dorothée!" said Querubin, who was at a loss to find an argument against the tears. "Queen of my soul!"

"I am not the queen of your soul," sobbed she. "You never loved me; I see it plainly, now that it's too late."

"By heaven! but I did, and do," said Querubin, quite overcome.

"Then you wont marry her?" said Dorothée.

"But if she come to me all the way from England on purpose?" said the marquis. "What can I do, as a man of honour, but marry her?"

"Very well!" said Dorothée: "let her come, that's all. I ask no better. But mark me, for what I say, I'll do. If she comes here, I tell you again, I'll poison her!" and so saying, she quitted the room.

"By the great gods!" exclaimed Don Querubin, throwing himself back in his chair, and dropping his arms, "I pity her! She loves me to distraction!"

"It's to be regretted she never mentioned it before," said Criquet.

CHAPTER X.

THE DUKE AND THE DAIRYMAID.

On a certain evening, nearly about the period that the conversation detailed in our last chapter took place in the dressing-room of Don Querubin, in the Château de la Rosa, the unwieldy diligence from Harfleur, entering by the Barrière de Neuilly, rolled into the city of Paris, containing in the interior of its massive body its full complement of six goodly souls; and in the coupé, two, a lady and gentleman, bearing in air and aspect the most unequivocal symptoms of a recent importation across the channel. The lady was very young, exceedingly handsome, and neatly attired in the costume of her own country; and though without any appearance of fashion or of artificial polish, there was an air of simple and natural grace about her person and demeanour that left no room for regret that art had done little where nature had done so much. Her figure was light and agile, her eyes of a rich deep blue, her hair glossy black, and her complexion pure, delicate, and healthy.

The gentleman was many years older, perhaps about forty, with a countenance that yet showed some remains of beauty, and that appeared to have suffered more from dissipation and bad company, than from time. Its expression was so mixed as to be almost undefinable. There were some traces still surviving of good nature, and of a disposition to enjoy and be happy, that occasionally struggled through and illuminated the dark and complicated mask that puzzled the beholder; but then such a heavy cloud would suddenly fall and obscure these gleams of light, that the spectator felt as if a black crape veil had been unexpectedly interposed betwixt him and the object of his contemplation.

The prevailing expression, however, the one most frequently pervading both the countenance and manner, was that of extreme recklessness, mingled with a considerable degree of intrepidity. With respect to the costume, and general air and carriage of the person in question, it partook, in about equal degrees, of that of the horse-jockey, prize-fighter, and gentleman; and there was one feature in his face which inclined an attentive observer to believe that his society had not always been of the most peaceable description; namely, his nose, which had evidently been broken across the bridge, and had consequently acquired a very remarkable twist and elevation.

The evening was dark and excessively wet; and Paris, noisy, dirty, and ill-lighted, as it then was, did not present a very alluring aspect.

"Is this Bordeaux?" inquired the lady of her companion, as they drew up at the Barrière to deliver their passports.

"Not exactly," replied he; "we shall be there by and by. But I propose remaining here to-night, and perhaps for a few days to recruit, if you have no objection."

"Not any," answered she; "I shall be very glad of a little rest, for I am very tired, and my head aches dreadfully with jolting over those stony roads."

"Come, ladies and gentlemen!" cried the driver, when he had safely lodged the cumbrous vehicle in the court of the coach-office, in the Rue Nôtre Dame des Victoires. "Now! we are at the end of our journey. Have the goodness to get down. Give me leave to help you," added he, taking the fair traveller round her slender waist, and placing her on the ground.

"We want a lodging," said the gentleman, in indifferent French, and addressing himself to one of the clerks. "Is there anything to be got near here?"

"I have a splendid apartment at the gentleman's service," said a respectable looking man, advancing with his hat off, and bowing to the ground. "Allow me the honour of showing you the way; it's not five minutes' walk from this." And the luggage being intrusted to a commissionaire, the party immediately moved off, and were conducted by the stranger to a respectable looking house in the Rue des Petites Ecuries; where, after ascending a considerable number of dirty stone stairs, they found themselves in a very tolerable suite of apartments, decorated with faded yellow damask, and a due proportion of cracked mirrors, tarnished gilding, and marble slabs; and when the stove was heated, the girandoles lighted, and a good supper from the kitchen of a neighbouring traiteur was placed upon the table, accompanied by a bottle of Vin de Bordeaux, the travellers began to find themselves tolerably comfortable and disposed to conversation.

"You've heard of Paris, I dare say?" said the gentleman.

"Yes," replied the lady. "It's in France, isn't it?"

"Precisely," returned he. "The chief city, as London is of England; only much gayer and more agreeable."

"It may easily be that," replied she; "at least, for all I saw of London."

"That was not much, certainly," answered the gentleman, smiling. "But you'll see Paris under different circumstances."

"Is it on our road?" said she.

"Why, to say the truth," returned he, "it did not make much difference, and I thought it a pity to lose the opportunity; so here we are!"

"In Paris?" said she.

"In Paris," returned he; "where I think we may kill a little time pleasantly enough. You must not judge by what you've seen yet," added he, observing that the impression made by the dirty streets and dim lights was not altogether favourable. "You'll see things under a different aspect to-morrow. Besides, we are not in the fashionable quarter, exactly."

"I should like to live in the fashionable quarter," observed the the lady, "if we are to make any stay."

"By all means," replied the gentleman. "It's precisely what I intend. There is no place in the world where beauty sooner attracts notice than in Paris, especially foreign beauty. It has only to be seen in public places—the Thuilleries, for example."

"What sort of a place is that?" inquired the lady.

"It's the garden of the royal palace—the king's palace."

"Does he live there?" said she.

"He does usually," answered her companion.

"I should like to go there very much," responded the lady.

"I thought so," replied her companion. "Of course, it's the resort of the court, and myriads of gay cavaliers, young, handsome, and rich, are to be met with. I think it will be time enough to go to the Château de la Rosa when we have shown ourselves here a little. What say you?"

"I should like to go to the Thuilleries, by all means," returned the lady; "but I don't intend to give up being a marchioness."

"Certainly not, unless you gave it up for something better," replied the gentleman. "But there are more marquises in the world than Don Querubin who have an eye for beauty; young, handsome, and' rich ones into the bargain; not to mention counts, dukes, and princes, all as plenty as blackberries here. At all events, you can give it a trial. A little delay can do no harm; and we can go forward if we find things here don't answer our expectations. To-morrow, if you like, we'll move into a more fashionable quarter; and by the bye, we must think of how we'll call ourselves. We're in the passport as Mr. and Miss Jones— Colonel Jones would sound better, and be more likely to get us on."

"Why not Lord Jones?" said the lady.

"I'm afraid that wont do," returned he. "Lords are too well known. But there are fifty Colonel Jones's, and I may be one of them for anything the people here will know to the contrary."

"I don't like the name of Jones at all," replied the lady. "I like names of three syllables, at least: and I like two or three names, there were some people in our county that had two or three names, and they were always thought more of than others, on that account."

"But we'd better stick to Jones," returned the gentleman, "for fear of accidents, as it's in the passport."

"But we can add some more names to it," said the lady. "In our county there were the families of the Arlingtons, and the Darlingtons. I think Arlington Darlington Jones would sound very well."

"It's coming it rather strong," said the gentleman.

"I like it," said she.

"Then Arlington Darlington Jones let it be. We'll get some cards to-morrow, the first thing we do."

On the following morning after breakfast, Colonel and Miss Arlington Darlington Jones sallied forth in quest of fashionable lodgings, and at the Hotel Marbœuf, in the Rue St. Honoré, they found a suite of apartments likely to answer their purpose. On the first floor, large, lofty, and elegantly furnished, they appeared, to the fair Englishwoman, everything that was desirable.

"I think they'll answer extremely well," said the colonel to the showily-dressed lady who condescended to treat with him on the subject. "We'll order our luggage to be sent, and sleep here to-night."

"Excuse me!" said the lady, "but perhaps Monsieur would have the goodness to favour me with a reference; it's extremely unpleasant, but we are obliged to be cautious."

"Oh, by all means," replied the colonel, with the most unconcerned manner imaginable. "You are very right—very right indeed. Here is my card—Colonel Jones, Arlington Darlington Jones, you observe. You've only to send to the British Ambassador's, they'll recognise the name immediately. There are few better known in England, I flatter myself, than Jones."

"I am persuaded of it," responded Madame Coulin, with a deferential curtsey and a winning smile, dazzled by the splendour of the reference. "Persons of distinction are so easily recognised."

"As I am assured your inquiries will be answered satisfactorily," pursued the colonel, "I shall desire the luggage to be sent immediately. In the meantime, as we want to make a few purchases, you can perhaps favour us with the address of a milliner, a tailor, and so forth?"

"Certainly," replied Madame Coulin. "There is the excellent Monsieur Truchet just opposite; a man of the first respectability, and my own cousin, by the bye; an artist of the highest celebrity. And for a milliner, I shall take the liberty of recommending my sister, Madame Doricourt, Rue de Richelieu, No. 7. She has one of the first establishments in Paris, and I flatter myself the young lady will have every reason to be satisfied."

"I don't doubt it," responded the colonel; "and everything being arranged, I believe we may take our leave for the present. You'll have the goodness to receive our luggage; and we shall ourselves return in the course of the day. Good morning, madame!"

"Adieu, monsieur!" said the lady, as she curtsied them out of the saloon. "You will have the goodness to remember my sister's address; the worthy Monsieur Truchet you will find exactly opposite."

"Certainly," said Colonel Jones. "They may rely on our custom; the being connexions of yours is quite a sufficient recommendation; and we shall not fail to make use of your name."

"Gracious!" said she, as she looked over the gilt balustrade, and followed them with her eyes down the stairs, "those English folks! Never to ask the rent! But they're so rich, that's the reason. I'd made up my mind to take six hundred livres—but eight wont be a penny too much. Indeed, the apartments are cheap at eight; and eight it shall be. It will be just the same to him, I've no doubt"—a conclusion in which Colonel Jones, had he been appealed to on the subject, would have perfectly coincided.

The next visit of our travellers was to the gate of the British Ambassador's hôtel, where, having inquired if his lordship was at home, and being of course answered in the negative, the colonel threw down his card, begging it might be delivered to him without fail; so that, when presently afterwards, Madame Coulin arrived to make her perquisitions, the porter was prepared to say that he believed the gentleman was an acquaintance of his excellency, as he had just been there to make a visit.

The assistance of the worthy cousin, Monsieur Truchet, and of the sister, Madame Doricourt, were next put in requisition; and the colonel suggested to his fair companion the propriety of not exhibiting themselves in the more fashionable resorts till their appearance was improved by the result of these admirable artists' taste and science. They accordingly confined themselves to the obscurer parts of the city, taking their dinner at an inferior restaurateur's; after which the colonel conducted Miss Jones to the hôtel of Madame Coulin, who received them with the most flattering attention; and then proceeded to finish his own evening at a gaming-house in the Palais Royal.

On the second day, being duly equipped, they repaired at the accustomed hour of promenade to the Thuilleries, where the transcendant charms of Miss Jones soon attracted such a swarm of admirers, that their way was absolutely impeded by the flutter around them.

"What exquisite beauty!" cried one.

"Who is she?" cried another.

"Does no one know the name of this divine creature?" cried a third.

"I'm sure she's English," said a fourth.

"She's certainly a foreigner," said a fifth—in short, the aristocratic crowd was in commotion.

"What's the matter?" said the Duc de Rochechouart, who at that moment came out of the palace.

"The most incomparable beauty has just appeared," replied the Comte D'Armagnac; "and we cannot make out who she is."

"Where is she?" inquired the duke.

"There, just before," answered De L'Orme. "The man that accompanies her looks like a blackguard."

"She's provincial," said Rochechouart, eyeing her figure through his glass.

"She has no fashion, I admit," answered D'Armagnac; "but her face is divine."

"Let us see," said Rochechouart, calmly, and with the air of a man certain of accomplishing whatever he chose to undertake; and advancing hastily, close behind the colonel and his fair companion, he contrived slightly to entangle the hilt of his sword in the drapery of Miss Jones's dress.

"A thousand pardons!" cried he, taking off his hat in the most irresistible manner in the world; and exhibiting a head that Adonis himself need not have disowned; whilst under pretence of extricating the sword he took care to entangle it still further—"I am really in despair."

"Miss Jones does not speak French," replied the colonel, who easily penetrated the manœuvre; "or I am sure she would be happy to accept your apologies."

"You are extremely obliging," returned Rochechouart. "I have the happiness to speak a little English, having been ambassador in your country for a short time; but I did not make myself so much acquainted with the language as I might have done, which I always regret when I have the good fortune to meet any of your charming countrywomen. "Jons," said he, "Jons—I am sure I met a family of that name in England."

"Nothing more likely," replied the colonel. "Our name, if I may be excused for saying so, is pretty well known in most parts of the island."

"And you have very lately arrived in Paris, I presume?" said Rochechouart, "with this young lady, your daughter."

"Miss Jones is my niece," replied the colonel. "We arrived three days since, and are lodging at the Hôtel Marbœuf, Rue St. Honoré."

"Where I hope mademoiselle will permit me the honour of paying my respects," returned Rochechouart, handing his card to the colonel.

"We shall be particularly happy," returned the colonel; and with another elegant salutation, Rochechouart retreated, and joined his companions.

"Well!" cried D'Armagnac, "I'll bet you haven't learnt the name of this divinity."

"Then you'll lose," returned the duke. "Her name is Jons—she's the niece of the man that accompanies her—she arrived three days since, and she lodges at the Hôtel Marbœuf, where to-morrow I shall have the honour of presenting myself."

"The devil!" cried D'Armagnac; "and you have found out all that already."

"Just like him," muttered De L'Orme; "there's another hooked —they all go the same road."

In the meantime the travellers had studied the card with infinite satisfaction.

"A duke!" said Miss Jones. "I never saw a duke before."

"A duke he is, indeed," replied the colonel; "and one of the first dukes in France, I assure you. Young, handsome, and devilish rich, I've no doubt. What think you of him instead of the old marquis?"

"Perhaps he wont think of me," said Miss Jones.

"I'll answer for that," returned the colonel. "What is he coming to call on us for? Not to see me, you may take your davy."

The colonel held some debate with himself the next morning, whether it would be advisable to await the duke's visit, or to go out and leave Miss Jones to receive him alone; and after a due calculation of probabilities, he resolved on the latter. Miss Jones was extremely clever, indeed, for an extempore Miss Jones, and had a natural genius for her part; and though certainly she was singularly ignorant, and the duke singularly fascinating, he relied on her beauty to charm and her ambition to preserve.

"Monsieur le Duc de Rochechouart," said Grosbois, the French servant the colonel had engaged, as he threw open the door, and introduced the noble visitor.

"I am enchanted," said the duke, with the most captivating address.

Miss Jones rose and dropped him a curtsey.

"And is this the first visit of mademoiselle to Paris?" said he, seating himself beside her.

"Yes, sir," replied Miss Jones; "I never was here before."

"I flatter myself you'll be delighted when you see more of it," said Rochechouart. "There is nothing like Paris. You have not been to the Opera, I dare say?"

"I don't think I have," answered Miss Jones. "What sort of a place is it?"

"How!" exclaimed the duke. "You have never seen an opera?"

E

"I believe not," replied she. "What is it like?"

"Very extraordinary," said he. "Mademoiselle has probably been educated in a convent?"

"I was brought up at Mapleton," replied Miss Jones.

"Is Mapleton a convent?" inquired the duke.

"I'm sure I don't know," answered Miss Jones. "It's a village."

"She has not common sense," thought Rochechouart. "Handsome as an angel, but silly as a sheep."

"But what is a convent?" inquired Miss Jones.

"Ah! I remember," said the duke, "you have none in your country. A convent's a place where we shut up pretty young ladies, to prevent their falling in love."

"But that must make them more inclined to fall in love when they come out," said Miss Jones.

"Not quite such a fool either," thought Rochechouart. "It's ignorance. I believe it does, indeed," answered he; "but we don't let them out till they're about to be married,—and after that, they may fall in love as much as they like, you know."

"May they?" said Miss Jones, opening her eyes with astonishment.

"Certainly," replied he. "It's the custom; everybody does."

"Do they?" exclaimed Miss Jones, looking still more amazed.

"How can they help it?" said the duke. "There's no living without love, you know."

"Then it don't signify who one marries in this country," returned Miss Jones, "if one may fall in love with whoever one likes afterwards?"

"Precisely," replied Rochechouart; "a young lady naturally marries for an establishment—for a fortune or a title; and having secured that which is indispensable, she must of course console herself with a lover for the sacrifice she has made."

"But the people that have fortunes and titles are sometimes young and handsome themselves," said Miss Jones, looking at the duke. "How is it, then. Don't they marry?"

"Occasionally we do, certainly," replied Rochechouart.

"And don't your wives love you?" asked she.

"Sometimes!" said he, "a little; but it don't last."

"And what do you marry for? Is it for love?" asked Miss Jones.

"Sometimes," said he, "now and then; but more generally for an alliance, or a fortune. But, my fair lady," continued he, observing that Miss Jones looked rather disappointed at this avowal, "although we seldom marry for love, we very often love without marrying—marriage has nothing to do with love."

"But it has something to do with the establishment you speak of," answered Miss Jones.

"She attacks me with my own weapons," thought Rochechouart.

"True," said he, "and we sometimes sacrifice interest to love."

"Would *you*?" said Miss Jones, with the greatest simplicity imaginable.

The duke, experienced as he was, found some difficulty in answering the question. "Hem!—It's not impossible," he said. "I might, certainly, under great temptation;" and he darted a thousand loves from his beautiful black eyes.

It was a decided hit. Miss Jones cast down her beautiful blue ones, and a delicate blush suffused her fair cheeks.

"It's a crisis," thought the duke; "I must seize the opportunity to withdraw. I shall hope for the honour of seeing mademoiselle in my box to-night," said he, rising to take his leave. "One of my carriages will be wholly at your orders; and you will find it at your door at eight o'clock, to convey you to the theatre. As I am in waiting at the palace, and must dine at the king's table, I may be late: but I shall have the honour of attending mademoiselle the moment I'm released. Adieu! till the evening."

"It's very singular," thought he, as he drove away. "Her beauty is exquisite; yet she is without the slightest education, and has the manners of a peasant. I much doubt whether this man's her uncle. Why leave her alone to receive me? There is a mystery which I am determined to solve."

"Well, Rochechouart?" said D'Armagnac, when they met presently at the palace. "How do you like your goddess?"

"She's divine," answered Rochechouart, who had no idea of depreciating the value of his own anticipated triumph; and who was oftener urged to these pursuits by the silly ambition of outstripping his companions, and the desire to show them that he could accomplish whatever he chose to undertake, than by his own passions or inclinations. "She is charming, and her simplicity is as captivating as her beauty."

"I have been making acquaintance with the uncle," said D'Armagnac; "and he has invited me to visit him."

"Invited *you?*" said Rochechouart, looking not very well pleased.

"Why not?" said D'Armagnac.

"You will be nothing the forwarder," answered Rochechouart, "for she cannot speak a word of French, and you do not speak English."

"Bah!" said D'Armagnac, "what does that signify? Do you think I can't talk to a pretty woman without a grammar and a dictionary."

"Well," said Colonel Jones, to the young lady, when he returned home, "how do you like the duke?"

"I like him very well," replied Miss Jones.

"And did he tell you he liked you?" asked the colonel.

"I believe he's courting me," answered the niece; "but I'm not sure it's for marriage."

"Leave that to me," returned the uncle. "If you take care of yourself, we shall bring him to that, I warrant."

"I'll have nothing to say to him else," answered Miss Jones. "I would rather go on to Bordeaux directly to the old marquis. Mr. Gaveston said he was sure he'd marry me."

E 2

"May be he would, but there's no telling," replied the colonel.
"And, at all events, a young duke in the hand is well worth an old
marquis three hundred miles off. Besides, you will have dozens
of lovers, and may make your own terms. If one wont, another
will. There's one of 'em coming here to-morrow, the Count D'Armagnac, just such another swell."

Precisely at eight o'clock, an elegant equipage, with two pow-
dered laquais in gorgeous liveries, drove up to the door of the
Hotel Marbœuf.

"The Duc de Rochechouart's carriage for madame," said Grosbois; and the colonel presenting the young lady his arm, they entered it, and drove off.

"Limed, said the birdcatcher," murmured Grosbois to himself,
as he stood at the gate and looked after the carriage.

"Come in, come in, Monsieur Grosbois," said Madame Coulin,
as he passed the door of her entresol; "come in and take a glass
of something."

"You are very kind, madame," replied Grosbois, accepting the
invitation.

"There, Monsieur Grosbois," said she, handing him a glass,
"there's a drop of cherry-brandy of my own making. I flatter
myself it's not bad."

"It's excellent," said Grosbois. "There's nothing better."

"Take another," said Madame Coulin, "and I'll join you. Ah!
that's good! Well, Monsieur Grosbois," continued she, as they
sipped the liqueure, "they're going it nicely, I think, up stairs.
That was a duke's carriage, if I'm not mistaken."

"Rochechouart, the rogue," replied Grosbois; "he's really an
extraordinary fellow that! He devours the young girls like an
ogre."

"But the uncle!" said Madame Coulin, "how will he like it?
An officer, too—a colonel?"

"For the uncle," said Grosbois, "I don't exactly know what to
think of him; for to tell you the truth, I have discovered that he
has but three shirts; and even they bear decided marks of a very
venerable antiquity."

"Oh, heavens! Monsieur Grosbois!" exclaimed Madame Coulin,
"you've taken away my breath—but three shirts, and take my
first floor."

"It's too true," answered Grosbois; "and I even suspect that
the young lady's wardrobe is not too well provided."

"Gracious goodness!" cried Madame Coulin, "I shall certainly
faint! What opinion can one form of people so ill-provided with
linen?"

"Doubtless," replied Grosbois, "one cannot feel much respect
for a man who has only three shirts."

In the meanwhile, the uncle and niece were conveyed to the
theatre, and conducted to the duke's box by Dillon, his servant,
who was an Englishman, and therefore appointed to attend on the
young lady till the duke arrived: and if she was amazed at the

splendour of the scene to which she was for the first time introduced, her beauty, and her appearance in that situation, produced
no less effect on the audience. The honest citizens pitied *her*, and
the young exquisites envied *him*.

"What a pity!" cried the first, as they directed their glasses to
the box she was in,—"so young, so beautiful! And to all appearance, so innocent!"

"What a fortunate fellow that Rochechouart is!" cried the second. "Now, there's a young beauty that has been in Paris but
three days; whose existence was positively unknown to him a few
hours ago; and she's in his net already! He must have some
secret for fascinating them—they actually drop into his mouth."

"Boldness and promptitude—these are his secrets," said the old
Marquis de Langy. "He takes the fort, while you are looking
about for the pontoons and the scaling-ladders."

"That's true," said D'Armagnac. "We'd a fair start—there
was an open field for all; but whilst we have been discussing who
she is, and where she came from, Rochechouart pays her a visit,
and persuades her to accept his carriage and his box."

"He ought to make a capital commander, Rochechouart," said
De L'Orme.

"And so he would," answered De Langy. "I am old, and may
not live to see it; but you'll find that when Rochechouart has discharged the unhealthy humours that disfigure his character, he'll
be another sort of man. There are the germs of much good in
him; but they are stifled by his passions and his vanity."

"I have a mind to go round and introduce myself," said De
L'Orme, "before Rochechouart comes."

"You may as well remain where you are," said D'Armagnac.
"I've tried my fortune already, and that scoundrel, Dillon, literally shut the door in my face, declaring he'd the duke's special
orders to admit no one. 'I dare not, for my life,' said he; 'the
commands of monseigneur were absolute, and extend even to you,
Monsieur le Comte.'"

"Then he's not sure of his game, and it may not be too late to
enter the lists," said De L'Orme.

"Look! look!" cried several voices, "there's Rochechouart just
arrived; now we shall see how she receives him."

"That's capital! she has absolutely risen to salute him!" said
De L'Orme. "She has never been in any society, that is evident."

"Ah! she is charming!" said the old marquis. "It's not the
grace of a duchess, I allow; but it is the perfection of rustic grace
—the grace of a milkmaid."

"By the bye, that is the ballet to-night," said D'Armagnac.

"And trust me," said De Langy, "if the actress, who plays the
milkmaid, could only imitate the simple grace of that English girl,
the performance would be perfect."

"I will explain to you the argument of the piece we are about
to see represented," said the duke to Miss Jones. "It is called
La Belle Laitière—which means, the pretty milkmaid."

"Does it?" said Miss Jones, looking round at him.

"Yes," replied he, "it does. It has been very popular here all the season; and the danseuse who performs Nina, the heroine, is extremely clever—there she is now; that's her, appearing with her milk-pails. That youth who follows her is a shepherd, who is deeply in love with her—but she disdains his suit, See, he kneels, but she is inexorable. Now, observe the cavalier who enters at the back of the stage, and is watching them; that is a prince, who, captivated by her charms, has come in disguise to seek her."

"Does he intend to marry her?" inquired Miss Jones.

"Diable!" muttered Rochechouart. "You will see presently," said he. "Now, observe, he kneels at her feet, and vows eternal love. Ah! she says, you must prove it by making me a princess."

"And will he?" asked Miss Jones.

"Look! he says she shall be mistress of his heart, but that, being a prince, he cannot marry her."

"Then I wouldn't listen to a word more he has to say, if I were her," said Miss Jones.

"You think so," said Rochechouart; "but you wouldn't be able to help it."

"Indeed I should," replied the young lady.

"Not if you were in love," said he, tenderly.

"But I'm not in love," answered Miss Jones.

"That alters the case, certainly," said the duke. "It's very extraordinary," thought he: "she's not the least like any other woman I ever met with;" and he fell into a reverie, forgetting for a time to continue his explanations.

"He's gone," said Miss Jones.

"Who?" said the duke, starting.

"The prince," said she. "Has she dismissed him?"

"Yes," replied Rochechouart; "she has sent him away discomfited; and there is the shepherd returned to try his fortune again; but she can't bring herself to listen to him."

"I don't wonder at it," returned Miss Jones. "Who would, after being made love to by a prince?"

"I admire your sentiments," said Rochechouart, with animation.

"My lord," said Dillon, opening the box-door, "here is the Comte D'Armagnac, who insists on coming in."

"Had you not my positive orders to admit no one?" said the duke.

"True, my lord," said Dillon, "but the count is peremptory; he will take no refusal."

"You mean to say that he has just been slipping five guineas into your hand, I suppose?" said Rochechouart.

"Upon my honour, my lord," said Dillon, laying his hand on his heart.

"Well, I suppose he must be admitted," said Rochechouart.

"This is the gentleman I mentioned to you," said the colonel to his niece. "The Count d'Armagnac, Miss Jones."

D'Armagnac could not speak any English; but he was very handsome, and dressed bewitchingly; and if he could make no effective use of his tongue, he made amends with his eyes.

"But look," said Rochechouart, "we are forgetting the ballet all this while."

"There is the prince again at her feet," said Miss Jones; "and he has changed his dress."

"He hopes to be more successful in his present brilliant costume," said Rochechouart.

"But she's dismissing him again," said Miss Jones. "And see, she's accepting the peasant, after all. Then the prince wont marry her."

"No," replied Rochechouart. "He says he would, if circumstances permitted; but he can't."

"Well, I would never have married that shepherd, with his coarse clothes, and his crook, if he had knelt there for ever," exclaimed Miss Jones.

"To be sure not," replied Rochechouart. "I was sure you'd end by being in favour of the prince."

"I'm not in favour of the prince," said the young lady; "I should have blamed her much more if she had listened to him."

"How, then," asked Rochechouart, "what would you have had her do?"

"Wait for another prince," replied Miss Jones, glancing at D'Armagnac; "there are more princes in the world than one."

CHAPTER XI.

SUSAN FINDS ANOTHER SITUATION—THE LOST LETTER.

IT was with a sad heart that Susan knocked at her friend's door, and a humble, doubting knock she gave; for bad as had ben her situation when she wrote to Dobbs, it was now, from th loss of her clothes, and little stock of money, much worse; ard she felt mortified and ashamed at presenting herself before he in so destitute a condition.

Her first reception did not tend to encourage her; for the pert fotboy that answered the summons, on seeing who had rung, baged the door in her face, and told her to go down the *hary*. Ssan, who was not accustomed to cockneyisms, or London areas, ws looking about for the means of accomplishing his behest, when a well-known voice, bidding a butcher's boy not to forget the bef-steaks, drew her eyes in the right direction, and in a minute mre she had shaken hands with Dobbs, and was comfortably sated by the kitchen fire.

"As for losing your boxes," said Dobbs, "it's just my fault, and nbody's else. I should have told you to let me know what coach you were coming by, and have sent somebody to meet you. How should you know the tricks of the Lunnuners? Bless you, it takes a life to learn 'em! However, when things come to the worst, they'll mend; and what's done can't be undone; and so there's no use fretting about it. Now, I've got a place in my eye for you, that I think will do very well for a beginning. By and by, when all this here business is blown over and forgotten, you can look for something better; and I'll lend you a trifle of money, just to set you up in a few necessaries for the present, which you can pay me when you get your wages."

Grateful indeed was Susan for this kindness; but she still expressed some apprehension that the family, when they had heard her name, might object to take her.

"No fear of that," answered Dobbs; "they'll be quite satisfied with my recommendation, and ask no questions. Their name's Wetherall—he's a clerk, or something of that sort, in the post-office; and she's sister to our baker's wife; I meet her sometimes when I go to the shop, and that's the way I know her. They've been living hitherto in lodgings, where the people of the house did for them; but he's just got a rise, and so they've taken a small house in Wood-street, and mean to keep a servant. She asked me the other day if I knew one to suit her, and thinking how pat it would do for you, I said I did. You'll have everything to do, and the wages are low; but you mustn't mind that for a beginning."

Susan was too glad to get into any decent service, and thereby break the spell that she feared fate had cast over her honest exertions, to make any objections; and therefore, in the evening, as soon as Dobbs was at leisure to escort and introduce her, they started at once in quest of the situation, lest some other candidate should forestall them.

As Dobbs had foreseen, no difficulties were raised on the part of the lady; and as Susan made none on hers, the treaty was soon happily concluded, and she engaged to enter on her service the next day, which she accordingly did, after spending the intervening time with her friend, who was no less anxious to hear and speculate on the state of affairs at Oakfield, more especially all that regarded Harry Leeson and his fortunes, than she was to tell them.

It was impossible for any master or mistress to be more good-natured, and more disposed to be satisfied with her exertions to please them, than were Susan's. Mr. Wetherall was a little pursy man, with a very *enjouée* expression of countenance, although much marked with the small-pox; he delighted in a laugh, and was extremely fond of a pun or a joke, practical or otherwise; and was by no means sparing in the indulgence of his fancy. Mr. Wetherall was a handsome young woman about eight and twenty years of age, rather disposed to be fat, of an excellent temper, and extremely fond of her husband. Though their means had hitherto been restricted, their contentment and good spirits had helped to feed and clothe them, but now that their circumstances were improved, they proposed to indulge in a few amusements and a little society, to which they had both a natural tendency, and therefore, with a view both to profit and pleasure, they had arranged to take a boarder, a gentleman of the name of Lyon, who performed in the orchestra of one of the theatres.

"I don't doubt," observed Mr. Wetherall to his wife, "that we shall find Lyon a very agreeable acquisition. People in his situation see so much of life, and have so many good stories to tell, that they are generally the pleasantest fellows in the world. Besides, I dare say, he'll be able to give you tickets for the theatre sometimes; and though I can never have much leisure, I shall have more than I had, and I hope we shall enjoy ourselves a good deal."

"We've always been very happy," replied his wife, "and have no right to complain; but I certainly should like to be a little more gay than we have been; and as we have no children to provide for, I don't see why we need be too saving."

"Certainly not," answered her husband, "it would be folly not to make hay while the sun shines. Besides, things will improve, I've no doubt. There's poor Davenport with just one foot in the grave already; it's impossible he can hold out long, and that'll give me a step; and then when Bingham's father dies—and he has had two seizures, I know—that will be another; for Tom will never stick to the office when he's got a thousand a year and a nice house in the country. So I reckon our worst days are over, and that we shall get on now we're once set going."

"If we never see worse days than we have done," said his wife, smiling, "we shall have no reason to complain, either."

As Mr. Wetherall had foreseen, Mr. Lyon proved an extraordinary acquisition. He was not only a capital fellow himself, but he knew a number of other capital fellows, who were all as willing to be introduced to Mr. Wetherall as he was to them, and who unanimously agreed that Mr. Wetherall himself was also a capital fellow. The consequence was, that there were dinner parties on a Sunday, and supper parties four or five times in a week, at which the only contention that arose was, who should be the merriest, and say or do the funniest things. The visitors were mostly actors of an inferior grade, who, if they could make nobody laugh when they were on the stage, could keep Mr. Wetherall's table in a roar; and who, if they could not act themselves, had a particular talent for imitating those who could. The host was little behind them—he could bray like an ass and crow like a cock, and do a great many other humorous things; and as from the retirement in which he had lived, these talents had hitherto been much in abeyance, he was the more sensible to the honour and glory of exhibiting them now to actual professors in the art of being funny, more especially as the applause they drew was certain, loud, and long. It is so easy to please a set of capital fellows at your own table, when they have no other table to go to.

But, unfortunately, these delights, like most others, have their sting. It is impossible to entertain a set of capital fellows four or five days in a week without cost; and, however unaristocratic the nature of the potations, it is equally impossible to consume a great deal of liquor without liquidating a great deal of cash. After these things had been going their train for some months, the butcher and the baker began to be extremely importunate; and Mr. and Mrs. Wetherall took a particular dislike to single knocks at the door, and hated the sights of little bits of dirtyish-white paper that Susan was ever and anon forced to present to their notice. At the same time, the man that kept the public-house at the corner discontinued his morning salutation to Mr. Wetherall as he passed, and his evening commentaries on the state of politics and the weather; and it was not long before the clerk, who missed these civilities, turned to the left instead of the right when he quitted his house for his office, and preferred going farther about to meeting the cold eye of the once obsequious publican. When matters get to this pass without a very vigorous effort, they rapidly get worse; and as neither Mr. nor Mrs. Wetherall had the resolution to shut their door against their pleasant friends, nor to retrench the flood of their hospitality, their difficulties daily increased, and ruin stared them in the face.

It was in this crisis of affairs, that Susan, one morning when she was cleaning the parlour grate, found amongst the ashes some remnants of a letter, which appeared to have been torn up and thrown on the fire, but which the flames had only partly consumed before it had fallen beneath. She was about to thrust them in with her coals and wood to facilitate the operation of ignition, when the words "*Harry Leeson,*" caught her eye, and induced her to examine further. But except the first syllable of the word "Oakfield," and part of the address, which appeared to have been to Parliament-street, there was nothing more remaining that could throw any light either on the writer of the letter or its subject: but the writing of the few words she had found was a scrawl so remarkable, that Susan fancied she could hardly be mistaken in attributing the epistle to Mr. Jeremy.

But how could a letter from the worthy butler, addressed to Dobbs, have found its way under Mr. Wetherall's parlour grate, without her knowledge or intervention? It was not easy to imagine, unless Dobbs had sent it or left it at the house some day when she had been out, and that it had got amongst Mrs. Wetherall's papers, and been torn up by mistake. She finally decided that this must have been the case: and regretting that she had thus lost the opportunity of learning something about her much-loved Harry, she resolved to go to Parliament-street the first day she could get out, and inquire the particulars of Dobbs.

However, the distance being considerable, and her moments of leisure rare, some weeks elapsed without her being able to accomplish the enterprise; and at length one Sunday evening it was rendered unnecessary by the arrival of Dobbs herself.

"Here's a kettle of fish," said she, seating herself in Susan's kitchen. "You haven't heard frem Jeremy, have you?"

"No," replied Susan, "that's just what I wanted to speak to you about."

"About what?" asked Dobbs.

"About the letter from Jeremy," answered Susan. "Did you leave it here yourself, or did you send it?"

"Oh, then, you have had it!" said Dobbs.

"Not I," returned Susan; "I never got it at all; and I want to know who you gave it to."

"I don't know what you mean," said Dobbs, looking bewildered. "If you never got it, how do you know there was any letter at all."

"Just because I found some bits of it torn up, and half burnt, lying under the parlour grate," answered Susan. "Here they are;" and she handed Dobbs the remnants she had found.

"Well, that's the funniest thing!" said Dobbs; "that's Jeremy's hand, sure enough; but how in the world did it come here?"

"Did you send it?" said Susan.

"Not I," replied Dobbs. "I never had it, I tell you. I never so much as knew there had been a letter sent, till a few days ago, when a young man called and left a few lines from Jeremy, asking if I had received his letter; and expressing much surprise at your not having written immediately to acknowledge Miss Wentworth's kindness."

"Well, that's the strangest thing," said Susan, "I ever heard."

"The fact is," said Dobbs, "he must have directed the letter to you instead of to me by mistake."

"But still, as 'Parliament-street' is on it," said Susan, "it would have gone to your house, not here; and then you must have heard of it. No; I think it more likely that he sent it up by a private hand, somebody that knew I lived here, and who found it less inconvenient to leave it in Wood-street, than at the other end of the town; and thought it would do quite as well."

"That's not unlikely," replied Dobbs; "but how in the world it got under your grate, I can't conceive, without your ever seeing it."

"It must have been left here some time when I was out of the way, and got mixed up with some of my master's or mistress's papers," said Susan, "and been overlooked. But it's very provoking to have lost it."

"Jeremy'll write again, no doubt," replied Dobbs. "I sent him a line by the young man, who called for my answer next day, to say that I had received no letter, and to beg he'd write immediately, and tell me how he sent it, and what it was about. But at all events, we had better ask Mrs. Wetherall if she knows anything about it's coming here."

"She's not at home now," replied Susan, "but I'll take an opportunity of mentioning it to her to-morrow;" and after a little more chat, Dobbs said "Good night," and departed.

CHAPTER XII.

THE ALARM:

"IT's a very odd thing," said Mrs. Wetherall, when she was pouring out the tea, a day or two after the visit of Dobbs, mentioned in the last chapter, "Susan's been telling me something about a letter that was left here for her, and that must have got amongst our papers and been torn up. You didn't take it in, did you, Mr. Lyon?"

"No," replied Mr. Lyon; "I have never taken in any letter."

"And it isn't likely you should, Wetherall," continued the lady, "unless it was left on a Sunday. You didn't, did you?"

"What?" inquired Mr. Wetherall, looking up from the newspaper on which he was intent.

"You haven't at any time taken in a letter for Susan, have you?"

"Not I," replied Mr. Wetherall, helping himself to another slice of bread-and-butter, and resuming his perusal of the paper.

"Well," said Mrs. Wetherall, "it's a very remarkable thing! How it can have got here, I can't conceive. I'm sure I never saw it."

"Did it come by the post?" said Mr. Lyon.

"She don't know how it came," replied Mrs. Wetherall; "nor, indeed, is it clear that the letter was addressed to her at all. It appears to have been written to a friend of hers called Dobbs—"

"Dobbs?" said Mr. Wetherall, looking up suddenly from his paper.

"Yes, Dobbs," answered his wife—"that's the person that recommended Susan to me; she's housekeeper to a family in Parliament-street, and—"

"In Parliament-street?" reiterated Mr. Wetherall.

"Yes," replied his wife, "and there the letter was directed. But it seems Dobbs never got it, nor did she know a letter had been sent, till the man who wrote it sent a second to inquire for the answer."

"It was forwarded by a private hand and never delivered, probably," said Mr. Lyon.

"Well, but the most extraordinary part of the business is," continued Mrs. Wetherall, "that Susan found the letter torn up, and partly consumed, lying under the grate—Look, my dear Wetherall, you're dipping the paper into the slop-basin."

"She must have been very much gratified with the warmth of the epistle," said Mr. Lyon, facetiously. "But it's really singular."

"It certainly is," answered Mrs. Wetherall. "How it should have come here, being directed to Parliament-street, and who could have taken it in, I can't make out. My dear Wetherall, do come and finish your tea; you've no time to lose. What are you looking out of the window at?"

"He's looking for the lost letter," said Mr. Lyon.

"You don't know how late it is," said Mrs. Wetherall. But Mr. Wetherall, with his body stretched half out of the window, paid no attention to the summons.

"What the devil *are* you looking at?" said Mr. Lyon, giving his host a smart slap on the shoulder, and thrusting his own head out to ascertain what was to be seen.

"D—n it, I wish you'd keep your hands to yourself!" ejaculated Mr. Wetherall, turning round, at last, and discovering a face as white as the handkerchief that was round his throat.

To Mr. Lyon, who had seen a good deal of the world, and something of the indifferent part of it, this sudden ebullition of temper in a man usually so forbearing and patient of jests, combined with the altered hue of the complexion, was a flash of lightning.

"My dear Wetherall, you're not well," said his wife, rising, and concluding that he had been hanging out of the window to breathe the air.

"I'm very well," replied the husband; "give me another cup of tea, as strong as you can."

"I am sure you are not," said she, taking the cup and saucer from his hand, which were rattling against each other as he held them out. "Can't you eat your bread-and-butter?" said she.

"No," said he. "I'm thirsty, give me some more tea. I suppose it's time I was off," added he, as he tossed off the fourth cup.

"It is," replied Mr. Lyon, who had for the last few minutes been standing with his eyes fixed on him in a state of painful surprise. "As we're going the same road, I'll walk part of the way with you."

"I really believe I am not quite well," said Mr. Wetherall, as he staggered across the room to look for his hat; "have you any brandy in the house, Eliza?"

His wife fetched him a glass of brandy, which having swallowed, he said he didn't doubt but it would set him right; but in attempting to place the glass on the table, he set it on one side and it fell to the ground. "I feel giddy," said he, "and I have a dimness before my eyes; but it will go off when I get into the air;" and accompanied by Mr. Lyon, who, seeing the condition he was in, offered him his arm, he left the house.

"It's a singular thing about that letter," said Mr. Lyon, when they had walked a little way; "isn't it?"

"Letter?" said Mr. Wetherall, interrogatively.

"The letter found under the grate," replied Mr. Lyon. "I wonder how it came there, or indeed how it ever got to the house at all."

"Oh, servants' letters are so ill-directed that there are constant mistakes about them," said Mr. Wetherall.

"But it's being ill-directed wouldn't account for its getting under your parlour grate," returned Mr. Lyon; "it certainly was not directed there."

"No, it wouldn't account for that, certainly," answered Mr. Wetherall.

"Nor for its coming to the house at all, you know, when it was legibly directed to Parliament-street."

"No, it wouldn't," said Mr. Wetherall.

"I hope there was no money in it," observed Mr. Lyon.

"I dare say not," replied Mr. Wetherall. "Nobody said there was, did they?"

"I believe not," answered Mr. Lyon; "but we shall hear more on the subject, no doubt. But I must step out now, for I'm late; so good bye."

When Mr. Lyon left him, Mr. Wetherall was very near his office, but instead of going straight towards it he turned down towards Cheapside. He wanted a little time to compose his countenance and his demeanour before he presented himself to what he now apprehended would be the scrutinizing eyes of his fellow-clerks; for although it was but an hour and a half since he quitted them, who could tell what might have occurred in that brief space. No doubt the person who wrote the letter, as well as the one to whom it was addressed, would lose no time in applying to the post-office for an explanation; and it would be easily ascertained that it had passed through his department. To present himself with an agitated countenance was meeting discovery half way, and he felt that if he could only get over this—if he could but escape suspicion this time, no embarrassment; no temptation, however powerful, should ever again induce him to risk his soul's tranquillity on such a fearful cast.

But it is not easy for a man, with his hat over his brow, and his hands behind his back, to compose his thoughts in Cheapside, where he stumbled over a truck one minute, and was pushed off the pavement the next; and Mr. Wetherall, after making the experiment, found that he was staying away from his office, which was itself an offence, and might look suspicious, without any chance of regaining the requisite composure. So he braced his nerves as well as he could, and walked in.

"Mr. Wetherall!" cried one: "Mr. Wetherall!" cried another —"You're wanted directly—Mr. Russel wants you—you're to go to his room—he has sent out half a dozen times to inquire if you were come." More dead than alive, Mr. Wetherall turned his steps to Mr. Russel's room. "You're late, sir," said that gentleman, in a tone of displeasure. "I have been wanting you this half-hour to speak about a very unpleasant affair that has occurred in your department. But you're ill, sir," added he, observing that Mr. Wetherall had sought the support of the table to keep himself from falling.

"I am not very well," answered Mr. Wetherall, passing his hand over his brow.

"Then I had better put off what I have to say to another opportunity," said Mr. Russel.

"Oh, no, sir," replied Mr. Wetherall, somewhat relieved by this last speech, which seemed to imply that the thing was not so very important. "I feel better now. There's been no neglect in my department, I hope, sir?"

"There has been something very wrong in your department," replied Mr. Russel, "but I have got to learn who is the delinquent—but I see you're getting ill again, sir; you had better send for a coach, and go home. Here, Bingham," continued he, opening a door, "just step here and look to Mr. Wetherall a moment. You had better go home, sir; what I have to say will do as well at any other time as now."

So that all this agony of apprehension had been suffered about a communication that was of so little weight, that it would do as well at one time as another! Such a tyrant is conscience, and so does it play the bully with our fears!

However, relieved of his terrors for the moment, Mr. Wetherall declared himself better again, and forthwith addressed himself to the business of his office with what attention he could command.

On the same evening, not long after Mr. Lyon and Mr. Wetherall had left the house, Susan was surprised by another visit from Dobbs, who, accosting her as before, with "Here's a kettle of fish!" announced that she had had a letter from Mr. Jeremy, by which she learned that the former despatch had contained a present of ten pounds for Susan, from Miss Wentworth, who was to be married in a few days, and who had heard from Jeremy of the misfortune the poor girl had sustained on her first arrival in London.

"Now," said Dobbs, "that's a loss not to be put up with; and I'm going to the post-office to have it inquired into. But I thought I'd step round here first, to ask you if you'd mentioned it to Mrs. Wetherall?"

"I did," answered Susan, "but she knows nothing about it; and just now, when I was taking away the tea-things, she told me she'd been asking the gentlemen about it, and they know no more than she does."

"Well, then," said Dobbs, "there's nothing to do but to go at once to the post-office. There's nothing like going to the fountain-head, and the sooner it's done the more chance there is of the truth coming out."

"I should like to go with you," said Susan, "if Mrs. Wetherall can spare me. I think I'll go and ask her."

"Do," said Dobbs, "for as the money was yours, you've the best right to complain;" and Susan's leave being obtained, the two friends were soon on their way to the post-office, pausing only for a moment at the end of the street, to borrow an umbrella of Miss Geddes, the milliner, as it was just beginning to rain.

In the meantime, Mr. Lyon, when he left Mr. Wetherall, had proceeded to the theatre, and taken his seat in the orchestra, in a

state of mind little less agitated than his friend. He was a roué
sort of young man, of dissipated habits enough, but neither bad-
hearted nor ill-natured. He had never taken the trouble to consider whether the Wetheralls could or could not afford the
expense they were at in entertaining the pleasant fellows he had
introduced at their table, nor what might be the consequences if
they were exceeding their means; but now that these consequences burst upon his view, and that reflection told him he was
in a great degree the cause of the mischief, he was struck with
terror, remorse, and pity. From the condition in which he had
left Mr. Wetherall, he could not help fearing that the slightest
accident would make him betray himself; and he regretted very
much that he had not been bolder, and persuaded him, under the
pretext of illness, to stay from the office, till he had himself tried
what he could do by speaking to Susan on the subject, to prevent
an exposure.

Under these circumstances, it may be imagined that the instru-
ment he held did not contribute very much to the harmony of the
evening. He made all sorts of mistakes; played when he should
have rested, and rested when he should have played; threw the
leader into a passion, and drove an unfortunate debutante, whom
he was to accompany in "Water parted from the sea," almost
insane, by forgetting every direction he had given him at rehearsal. At length, finding he was of no use where he was, and
eager to learn what was going on at the post-office, he pleaded
indisposition, and obtained leave to retire.

"I'll make some pretence or another to go in and speak to
Wetherall," thought he; and, urged by anxiety, he walked at a
rapid pace towards the office. When he reached it, however, he
found he had not made up his mind under what plea he was to
excuse his unexpected appearance; for, as Mr. Wetherall believed
him at the theatre, he would naturally be surprised, and perhaps
alarmed, at so unusual a visit. Whilst he was considering this matter,
and as he did so, pacing backwards and forwards before the door,
two women passed him, one of whom held an umbrella. As he was
wrapped in reflection, and looking on the ground, he did not
observe them till the umbrella happened to come in contact with
his hat, which it nearly knocked off. "I beg your pardon," said
the woman. The voice struck him as familiar, and he turned to
look after her. The two women were just stepping into the office,
but the one that carried the umbrella turned round to shake off
the wet before she put it down—the light of a lamp at the door
fell upon her face, and he saw that it was Susan.

"Gracious heavens!" cried he, darting forward and seizing her
by the arm, "what are you doing here?"

"I'm only going to speak about a little business—about a letter,
sir," answered Susan, surprised by the vehemence of his address.

"Stop," said he, "I beg of you to stop a moment, whilst I
speak to you—who is this woman?"

"She's a friend of mine, sir, Mrs. Dobbs;" replied Susan. "The

SUSAN HOPLEY. 81

letter was sent to her, but there was some money in it for me, and we're going to mention that it has never come to hand."

"If you'll leave this business in my hands, Susan," said Mr. Lyon, "I will undertake to say you shall not lose your money. You'll oblige me very particularly if you'll not stir further in it at present—I can't explain my reasons to you now, but——"

"There's no occasion, sir," replied Susan, who, from the energy of his manner, and his evident agitation, began to suspect something like the truth; "we'll go back directly, and I'm very glad I met you: I'm sure I wouldn't be the occasion of anything unpleasant for twice the money."

"You're a good girl, Susan," said he: "and you shall lose nothing by it, depend on it. Say nothing on the subject to anybody, till you and I have had some conversation; and if you can persuade your friend to be equally cautious——"

"I'll answer for her," replied Susan, and thinking better of Mr. Lyon than she had ever done before, Susan turned her face homewards; whilst he, relieved from present anxiety, resolved not to disturb Mr. Wetherall at the office, but to speak to him after supper.

"They say there's many a slip betwixt the cup and the lip," said Dobbs, as Susan and she commented on what had passed, "and so I suppose there is betwixt a man's neck and the halter."

But all was not so secure yet as they and Mr. Lyon imagined.

CHAPTER XIII.

A CONVERSATION IN A MERCHANT'S COUNTING HOUSE, AND A NIGHT SCENE ON BLACKFRIARS BRIDGE.

On the same evening that Mr. Wetherall underwent all the horrors of anticipated detection, that we have described in the last chapter, and that Mr. Lyon's opportune intervention preserved him from the imminent danger that threatened him, in a certain counting-house in Mark lane, might be seen an elderly gentleman in deep cogitation over various letters and ledgers that were spread on the table before him. The room was one evidently devoted wholly to business; a couple of desks with high stools before them, shelves loaded with heavy account-books, two well-worn black leathern arm-chairs, and a table, also covered with black leather, on which stood a lamp, formed nearly all its furniture.

The occupant of the apartment—for there was but one—was a gentleman of about fifty years of age, of the middle height, rather stout than otherwise, and of a cheerful, agreeable aspect. He was attired in a full suit of brown, with gold buckles in his shoes, his hair well-powdered, and tied in a queue behind, as was the fashion

F

of the time, and with the wristbands of his shirt, which, as well as the handkerchief round his throat, were delicately white and fine, just appearing below the cuffs of his coat.

He was seated by the fire in one of the arm-chairs, with his left side to the table, on which rested his elbow, whilst he appeared to be deeply considering the contents of the papers, to which he ever and anon referred, comparing some of them with the ledgers, making notes, casting up columns, and balancing sums total. Most of the letters bore a foreign post-mark, but there was one which bore that of Mapleton.

Several times the gentleman looked at his watch, and listened, as if expecting somebody; and as the hour grew late, and he impatient, he frequently arose and took two or three turns about the room.

At length, towards ten o'clock, when a foot was heard ascending the stairs, he resumed his seat, thrust the letters under a ledger, and prepared to receive his visitor with composure.

"I'm afraid I'm late, Simpson, and have kept you waiting," said a tall, good-looking man, in a great coat, and comforter round his neck, who entered the room with the familiarity of easy acquaintance; "but I came up by that d——d coach, for Bess had taken a mash when I received your summons, and I couldn't bring her out."

"I'm afraid you are wet," replied Mr. Simpson, stirring the fire, and drawing forward the other arm-chair, whilst the visitor took off his great-coat and comforter, and hung them on pegs appropriated to such uses.

"But what's the matter?" said he; "there's nothing wrong, is there?"

"How's Miss Wentworth, sir?" inquired Mr. Simpson.

"Quite well," returned Mr. Gaveston, for it was he; "you know we're to be married in a few days, and she desired me to say that she hoped you would come down, and be present at the ceremony."

"I fear that will not be in my power," replied Mr. Simpson, with a sigh, and casting his eye on a handsome mourning-ring that he wore on his little finger.

"But what's the matter?" said Mr. Gaveston, without urging the invitation. "You must have had some particular reason for sending for me."

"I had, sir," replied Mr. Simpson, "a very particular reason." Here he paused, as if he found some difficulty in announcing the motive of his summons. "In short, Mr. Gaveston, I have made up my mind to resign my situation. I do not think I can be of any further use here; and I propose to retire, and end my days in the country."

"You don't think of such a thing, I hope, Simpson," replied Mr. Gaveston, with an unusual appearance of sincerity. "You have been conducting this business for many years to the entire satisfaction of everybody concerned with you; why should you leave it now?"

"Because, sir," returned Mr. Simpson, "I feel that I cannot henceforth conduct it to my *own* satisfaction; without which the approbation of others will be of very little avail to me."

"Why not, sir?" asked Mr. Gaveston, with a less complacent voice and countenance. "If you mean because after my marriage with Miss Wentworth I shall become sole proprietor of the concern, you need not throw up your situation on that account. I am very sensible that nobody can conduct the business as well as yourself; and I shall interfere very little with you, I assure you."

"Nevertheless," answered Mr. Simpson, "I must beg leave to adhere to my resolution. You may not propose to interfere with my management; but as sole proprietor, your power will be absolute; and things may happen that I may disapprove, without the means of controlling."

"Nonsense, nonsense, my dear Simpson," exclaimed Mr. Gaveston, assuming an air of frankness. "I dare say the truth is, you feel yourself ill-used—I ought to have proposed of my own accord to raise your salary—I know it's not equal to your merits."

"I have always been quite satisfied with my salary, Mr. Gaveston," answered Simpson. "If I had not, I had only to have mentioned the matter to Mr. Wentworth, and he would have met my wishes on the subject; but I had quite enough for any single man, and never desired more, whilst he lived—but circumstances are now changed."

"Well, then, what do you say to a couple of hundreds a-year in addition?"

"That it would not make the slightest difference in my determination. I should be exactly as much subject to the disagreeables I apprehend as I am now. In short, sir, to be more explicit, you will understand my motives better when I tell you, that I have received letters from Messrs. Râoul and Bonstetten, and also from the houses of Durand and Co., and the brothers Dulau, by which I learn that sums long ago intrusted to you by Mr. Wentworth to settle the accounts between us, have never been received; that we are in debt to those firms to a very large amount—so large, in fact, that they have begun to be apprehensive of our stability, and our credit totters at Bordeaux—the credit of a house, Mr. Gaveston, that was never impeached till now."

The annoyance and confusion betrayed by Mr. Gaveston at this unexpected intelligence, are not to be described. A few days more, and all would have been secure. From the precautions he had taken, he had reckoned with certainty on being able to accomplish his marriage before any stir was made in this business; and the ceremony once over, and he sole proprietor of Miss Wentworth's fortune, and the concern in Mark Lane, he would have had immediate means of discharging these debts, and of hushing up the whole affair. There were reasons of the most powerful nature, besides the care a man generally has for his own reputation, that made it of the last importance to him that this defalcation, this misapplication of sums intrusted to his faith, should not come under public discussion. Investigation, inquiry, gossip, once set afloat, who shall say into what port the wind may waft them? In what direction might suspicion, once raised, conduct the curious? It was a peril not to be encountered, and must be fought off at any cost—but how? He knew Mr. Simpson to be a sturdy, straightforward, upright man,—a man whom he feared was neither to be cajoled, bought, nor intimidated. Nevertheless, the case was desperate and urgent; and hopeless as he considered the experiment, he resolved to try the first; and if that failed, to have recourse to the second.

At Mr. Simpson's alarming announcement, Mr. Gaveston had risen from his chair, and during these reflections had been pacing the room with an agitated step, his hands in the pockets of his trousers, and his eyes bent on the ground. He now, however, reseated himself, and drawing his chair nearer to the worthy clerk, he said, " I will not deny that I had hoped these early imprudences of mine would never have become known to you. It was my intention to discharge those debts as soon as I had the means, which you know my marriage in a few days will give me. I shall still do so, and you need be under no apprehensions of similar follies recurring on my part. I have sown my wild oats, and intend henceforth to be a sober, steady man; and I trust, therefore, Simpson, for the credit of a concern you have so long conducted, and for the interest of Miss Wentworth and myself, that you will not refuse to keep your present situation. I will make any addition to your salary you desire."

Mr. Simpson shook his head. "Your intentions may be very good," replied he, "but you are yet a young man, and—excuse me—I have heard much addicted to the turf and high play. As long as you are sole proprietor, you may draw upon me for every shilling the concern yields, and I must answer your demands; till, at last, we shall not be able to pay our way, and the house will stop disgracefully. Now, I do not choose to involve my character nor my peace of mind in this perilous contingency. And as I am inclined to agree with you, that when I have left it, the concern will be even less likely to prosper than it is now, I intend recommending Miss Wentworth to dispose of it at once, without a day's delay, whilst it is in her power to do so. I have made up and balanced the accounts as they stand, debtor and creditor; and I have a purchaser ready to sign and seal the moment I get her consent."

"But she's not of age," returned Mr. Gaveston.

"I shall recommend her to defer her marriage till she is," replied Mr. Simpson—"or we can throw the business into Chancery till she can dispose of it."

"Consider the sacrifice," urged Mr. Gaveston—"such a business, such a connexion."

"The first loss is the least," returned Mr. Simpson. "If the concern gets involved, Miss Wentworth's whole fortune may go to pay the deficit."

"I see but one way," said Mr. Gaveston, after a pause, "since you are so mistrustful. Suppose you take a share in the business —a fourth, we'll say. I'll give you this, and leave the whole management of the concern in your hands."

A faint smile might have been observed stealing over Mr. Simpson's features at this proposal, but he hastened to convert the expression into a look of dissent.

"I should still be nearly as much at your mercy, sir," replied Mr. Simpson, "with the additional disadvantage of having the savings of my life perilled with the fortunes of the firm."

"What would induce you to remain, Mr. Simpson?" said Gaveston. "If my offer don't satisfy you, name your own terms."

"They are what you probably will not accede to, sir," replied Mr. Simpson, "therefore it would be useless to name them."

"Name them, nevertheless," returned Gaveston.

"Half the concern, sir, instead of a quarter; and that all payments and receipts of every kind whatsoever be permitted to pass through my hands. I dare say you do not doubt my honour; besides, you will be welcome to inspect the accounts whenever you please."

This was a hard morsel for Gaveston to digest. Again he started up and walked about the room, and bit his lips, and knit his brows; and as they trembled on his tongue, swallowed a volley of oaths that might have shaken the welkin; but exposure was ruin in every way—there was no alternative but to submit.

"As soon after my marriage as I can come to town," said he, when he had expressed his acquiescence in Mr. Simpson's demands, "I will settle this business to your satisfaction—in the meantime you can get a deed drawn up."

"That, sir," replied Mr. Simpson, "can be done to-morrow; and if this agreement between us is to stand, the whole affair must be arranged, signed, and sealed, before your marriage."

When the conference had terminated, the triumphant clerk conducted his visitor with great deference to the door, and then with a satisfied smile, and rubbing his hands with delight, he returned to his arm-chair, and prepared to write a note. I'll send a line to Olliphant immediately," said he to himself, "to beg he'll get the deed put into hand early to-morrow morning. He'll be as much surprised at my success as I am—I couldn't have believed he'd be so easily frightened, or that he'd have cared half as much about his reputation; however, since the poor girl's so infatuated that she'll listen to no advice, it's fortunate there's some hold over him, be it of what nature it may. I've half a mind," thought he, pausing as he was about to ring the bell, "that I'll take the note myself—the walk will do me good after that battle. By the bye, there's that letter of Jeremy's, too, I must attend to to-morrow— it's a disagreeable business, and one I'm not very fond of interfering in: I wish I knew the safest way of setting about it—but I don't know who to consult—" and thus soliloquizing, he put on

his great coat, and telling the porter he should be back presently,
he took his way to the solicitor's.

Nothing could exceed the rage that boiled within Gaveston's
breast at finding himself thus in the power of a man whom he at
once feared, despised, and respected. He clenched his hands as
he went down the stairs, and strode along the streets towards the
west end of the town, where he intended to sleep, figuring to himself the joy with which he could have closed them round the throat
of the man that had found the way to take such advantage of his
fears. He was astonished, too, as well as incensed—" He, too, with
all his parade of honesty," he said, " is to be bought—a fellow that
has no use for money—that will never spend it: but every man
has his price."

In this state of mind he felt it was useless to go to his lodging
with the view of sleeping; and when he drew near the river, the
cool air from the water blew pleasantly on his heated brow, and he
turned towards it. He wanted to think—to reflect if there were
yet no way of escaping his dilemma without such a sacrifice; and
when he reached Blackfriars Bridge, it looked so inviting for a noc-
turnal walk, that he directed his steps that way, and began pacing
backwards and forwards, reviewing the conversation that had
passed; anon regretting his own precipitation, and then again
rejoicing that even that way remained of escaping the éclat and
danger of an exposure.

It was now approaching to midnight, and his cogitations were
undisturbed by noise or jostle. But two human beings besides
himself were on the bridge—a woman who, with a child on her
lap, was sitting on a stone. She had a bonnet on, and a shawl,
the ends of which were folded round the infant; and she sat
silently rocking herself backwards and forwards, as if in trouble,
but she said nothing; and Mr. Gaveston passed her again and
again unheeded, till the words, "Mamma, I'm so hungry!"
reached his ears; and then he abruptly crossed over to the other
side to escape the interruption to his reflections.

He had not taken many turns here, before he heard the sound
of feet approaching from Bridge-street. The passenger was
advancing along the side that he had just quitted, and as he drew
near, he perceived it was a gentleman. There was something about
the air and carriage of the new comer that struck him, and he
retired into the shade to observe. A slight cough and a "hem!"
confirmed his suspicions; he had heard that voice too recently to
be deceived.—"It's Simpson himself!" said he. "He's going to
Olliphant's about the deed, I'll be sworn!" and he stepped lightly
after him to observe his movements. "He'll drop the letter in
the box and return," thought he, "and, now, if fortune favours
me——" and he grasped more firmly a stout stick with a thick
knob at the end of it, that he held in his hand—"one good blow,
and a heave over the parapet, and I'm at once revenged and
safe!"

In the meantime, the unconscious Mr. Simpson proceeded on

his way. He, too, was deep in thought, looking neither to the right nor the left, till the sound of a feeble moan from a child, followed by a groan from a more mature voice, attracted his attention, and looking back, he perceived the mournful group whose proximity had driven Mr. Gaveston away. "Poor thing," said he, feeling in his pocket for some silver, "I shall return in a minute, and then I'll give her something; I wish I'd done it at once: this is a dangerous neighbourhood for misery at midnight," and he hastened forward to Albion-place, which is just at the farther extremity of the bridge, dropped his note into the solicitor's box, and hurried back.

"Here he comes!" thought Mr. Gaveston, who, concealed in a recess, with his bludgeon poised, awaited his victim. On came Mr. Simpson, but just as he arrived at the spot where his enemy was lurking to take his life, the faint outline of a figure mounted on the parapet caught his eye. "Gracious heavens! it's that wretched creature going to drown herself," exclaimed he, and with a loud cry to arrest her desperate purpose, he darted across the road, whilst the weapon raised for his destruction descended through the unresisting air.

CHAPTER XIV.

THE RENCONTRE AND THE DISCOVERY.

GREAT was Mr. Wetherall's relief when the hour arrived that released him from his confinement, and from the importunate eyes of his fellow labourers. As he stepped off the threshold he turned his eyes back upon the building which he doubted he should ever enter again as a free man, and then with a slow and melancholy pace he sauntered onwards. He felt that he could not go home to encounter the anxious though unsuspecting inquiries of his wife, nor the scrutinizing questions of Mr. Lyon; so, instead of bending his steps towards Wood-street, he turned them in the direction of the river.

The streets were nearly empty now, and he could deliberate without interruption on the unhappy situation to which his folly and crime had reduced him. He was a man untried in affliction; for till that one fatal error had planted a thorn in his pillow, his days had passed in cheerful contentment and his nights in unbroken sleep. From that moment he had been restless, abstracted, and occasionally irritable; humours so unusual with him, that his wife had imagined him ill; he had denied it; but the moment was now come when concealment and denial could no longer avail; probably the next post, at all events a few hours, must tell her all, and expose him to the vengeance of the law and the scorn of mankind. It was true, there might be yet time to flee: if he mounted one of the earliest coaches, he might possibly reach the coast, and be across the channel, before pursuit could be commenced. But in the first place he had no money; in the second he felt remorse at the idea of taking care of himself and leaving his poor wife to bear the horror of the surprise, and the ignominy of the exposure alone; and thirdly, he hadn't energy for the enterprise. He was utterly cast down and depressed. What would be the use of escaping? he could never be happy. Even if he could find the means of supporting life, it would not be worth supporting; and, but for the disgrace and horror of a public execution, he would have preferred death.

As he sauntered forwards in this mood, he kept almost insensibly bending his steps towards the river; "there," thought he, as his eye glanced on the broad expanse, "there is a quiet bed where a man might sleep:" but then rose again the thought of his poor wife; it was so cowardly to desert her—to leave her to weather the storm alone. But on the other hand, would she not rather—would she not rather know him dead, and at rest, than see him dragged a prisoner from his home? than behold him a culprit at the bar, a criminal at the scaffold? "If we could only escape together—but the thing's impossible without money—and wouldn't this be the next best alternative for her interest, as well as for myself? She'd be deeply grieved—but time alleviates all grief when it's unaccompanied by remorse—and how much better it were, than to drag her from her home, her country, her friends, to pass her life in an exile of poverty and wretchedness, with a husband disgraced and broken-hearted—a criminal escaped from justice!" Thus he reasoned, and every glance of the river became more inviting, and every review of life, of such a life as must henceforth await him, too, less so.

"She, too, and the world, will see that I preferred encountering death to shame. My name will not stand in the calendar of crime, a disgrace to all connected with me. At first, they'll think I have fled—and there'll be a reward offered—and the police will seek me—and the coast will be on the alert—but, ere long, the body will be found and my fate ascertained—there'll be a little noise about it—a few remarks in the newspapers—and then the whole will be forgotten;" and so saying he quickened his pace, and walked briskly forwards towards Blackfriars Bridge. "That will be the best place," thought he; "a leap from the parapet, and all is done—and since my mind's made up, there shall be no pause—" he stepped upon the bridge—"since I am to die, hesitation will be weakness—and how much better is it thus to die a death of my own choosing, than to have my shame and my agonies made a scoff and a spectacle to assembled thousands!—Farewell, Eliza," he whispered, as he prepared to mount the parapet, "farewell, dear wife! Forgive me, and be happy!"

At that moment a cry reached his ears. Absorbed in his own reflections, he had looked neither to the right nor to the left—but, at the sound of a human voice, he lifted up his eyes and beheld on the opposite side of the bridge the figure of a woman exactly in the very act he had himself contemplated a moment before: she, too, had been for an instant arrested by the cry, and in that interval he rushed across the road and caught her by the dress.

He had scarcely lifted her to the ground, when a gentleman out of breath with haste, came running towards him from the further extremity of the bridge—"Thank God!" cried he, as soon as he perceived the group: "when I lost sight of her, I didn't know which side she'd gone down—I was afraid she was in the water—child and all!"

"I was but just in time," said Mr. Wetherall; "another moment and she'd have been gone."

"And I should never have forgiven myself," said Mr. Simpson, "that I hadn't stayed to relieve her the first time I passed."

During these brief words they were both supporting the unfortunate woman, who, either from weakness or agitation, appeared unable to support herself. "Give me the child," said Mr. Simpson, taking it from her arms.

"I'm so hungry!" said the little girl in a feeble voice.

"Oh, give her food!" cried the mother, "or let me die at once, for I cannot live and hear that cry!"

"She shall have food, and plenty!" said Mr. Simpson—"God! that such things should be! Have you a home?" he asked. "Where can we take you?"

"I've no home," replied she; "I've no roof to shelter myself nor my child, nor a bit of bread to give her!"

"Where can we take her?" said Mr. Simpson, abruptly. "She should go home with me, but I have no woman in the house—it's so late that no respectable place will be open; besides, unless they know us, they will object to let her in. I don't like to take her to the watch-house."

"She shall go home with me, sir," said Mr. Wetherall, carried away by his own good nature and the benevolence of the stranger. "I can give her shelter for to-night at least."

"God will reward you for it," returned Mr. Simpson. "After to-night she shall be no burden to you; I'll take her off your hands to-morrow. But I don't think she can walk—we must look for a coach."

This they had no great difficulty in finding; and handing her into it, Mr. Simpson still keeping the child in his arms, they proceeded to Wood-street; whilst Mr. Wetherall was so bewildered, and the current of his ideas so changed, that he almost forgot his own misfortunes and the dread he had entertained of meeting his family. Besides, the presenting himself, accompanied by the two strangers, under circumstances that would necessarily turn attention from himself, was very different to going home alone to be the subject of scrutiny and wonder.

The moment the coach stopped at the door, Mrs. Wetherall,

Mr. Lyon, and Susan rushed into the passage, the first expecting to see him brought home ill, the two last expecting something much worse.

"My dear Wetherall, how you have frightened us!" cried his wife. "Mr. Lyon was just going off to the office in search of you."

"Never mind me!" answered Mr. Wetherall, "but see what you can do for this poor woman."

"Whose life your husband has been fortunate enough to save, with that of her child," said Mr. Simpson, carrying the little girl into the parlour, where the mother was laid on a sofa by the fire, whilst the worthy clerk began rubbing the child's hands and feet, which were numbed by cold and starvation; and when, in a few minutes, by the active kindness of Mrs. Wetherall and Susan, food was placed on the table, he fed her like a young bird, bit by bit, lest the too hasty indulgence of her eager appetite should injure her.

In the meantime, the circumstances under which the party had met were narrated, and Mrs. Wetherall was loud in her wonder as to what could have taken her husband to Blackfriars Bridge at that time of night—"he that always comes home the moment he is released from the post-office! I dare say he never did such a thing in his life before. Did you, Wetherall?"

"I believe not," replied he; "but there were a great many letters to sort to-night, and I came away with such a headache that I thought a walk would do me good."

"Do you belong to the post-office, sir?" inquired Mr. Simpson.

"I do," replied Mr. Wetherall, casting down his eyes, for he said to himself, "you'll learn that soon from other channels."

"Well," said Mr. Simpson, "that is very singular! I have been all this day wishing I knew somebody connected with the post-office, whom I might consult confidentially about an awkward circumstance that has occurred; but it's a matter I shall not trouble you with to-night. To-morrow, if you will allow me, I shall take the liberty of calling, to make some arrangement for this poor woman and her child, and then we can talk it over at our leisure."

"But Wetherall is out all day," said the wife.

"I feel so unwell that I think I shall not be able to go to the office to-morrow," said Mr. Wetherall; for he felt, in the first place, that he could never go voluntarily to the office again, and, in the second place, he couldn't help feeling some curiosity to hear Mr. Simpson's communication.

Soon after this the worthy clerk took his leave, and the poor woman and her child were conducted to a comfortable bed that Susan had prepared for them.

"You don't remember me, ma'am?" said Susan to the stranger, after Mrs. Wetherall had left the room.

"No," replied the other.

"I have good reason never to forget you, ma'am," returned

Susan, "for you gave me food and shelter when I needed it as much as you did to-night."

"Oh, no!" replied Julia, "for you had no child! Ah, I remember you now," said she; "and I remember your words, too, when you refused the five shillings. I had never known the agony then of seeing Julia want bread."

"I went to Oxford-street, ma'am, to inquire for you the first moment I could, but you had left the lodging, and I couldn't learn where you were gone," answered Susan. "But I wont talk more to you to-night. Please to stay in bed till I come to you in the morning and bring you some breakfast. Please God, your worst days are over; for I think that gentleman, by his looks, means to be a friend to you."

During the progress of all this bustle and interest, Mr. Wetherall had scarcely leisure to remember that he was a criminal with the sword of the law suspended over him; and that probably after the post came in on the following morning, he should be torn from his home, and dragged away to a prison; but as soon as he lay down in his bed, and the world was quiet around him, whilst his wife slept the calm sleep of innocence, he, with burning hands and throbbing brow, was tossing from side to side in all the agonies of terror and remorse. How few people, if they had sufficient acquaintance with the nature of the human mind to calculate the sufferings consequent on crime, would ever commit it! and how necessary it must be to educate them into this acquaintance, and to dissipate the ignorance that veils the future from their view!

Now that the excitement was over, he looked back with regret at the interruption his design had met with—a moment more and all would have been over, and he at rest. The struggle was past, his mind was made up—in short, the worst part of the desperate enterprise was overcome; but it was not easy to work his resolution up to the same point: his sufferings returned on him with twofold force, but he had lost the energy necessary to flee from them. In vain, he painted to himself the horrors of being seized —the arrival of the police officers—the tears of his wife—the wonder of his neighbours—the ill-natured triumph of the discontented butcher, baker, and publican, as he was carried past their doors—the imprisonment—the trial—the execution. In vain he asked himself why it was too late to escape it all still by the very means he had intended—the river still awaited him; his wife slept soundly, and would never miss him from her side; but the rain was pattering against the windows, and the wind blew—and it is altogether a different thing to rise deliberately from a warm bed to jump into the water from the parapet of a bridge, to performing the same feat on the spur of a sudden resolution, and in the fever of excitement.

In this way, like one of Dante's wretched souls on the burning lake, he tossed and turned till morning dawned; then came brief and uneasy slumbers, filled with confused and dreadful visions

dimly figuring forth the fate that awaited him, till he opened his
eyes and found that it was broad day, that his wife had already
risen, and that he was now irretrievably tied to the stake, the hour
for escape being past. "Ere this," thought he, "the morning
mails are in—and they'll soon be here." And at every knock and
ring, and at every foot on the stairs, his heart sunk within him.
His wife brought him some breakfast, and told him she had requested Mr. Lyon to call at the office when he went to rehearsal,
and say he was ill; and willingly Mr. Lyon undertook the commission; for he thought no place so safe for Mr. Wetherall as
his bed, where he could not betray himself, until he had an opportunity of speaking to him in private on the subject of the ten
pounds; a thing he had neither had the means of accomplishing,
nor the resolution to attempt.

But time crept on—the hour for the arrival of the mails passed—
and an interval sufficient to admit of the discovery at the office, and
the police being sent in pursuit of him, elapsed also. The letter, then,
could not have reached the post-master, and there was another day
left at his disposal; and perhaps another night; and then he might
yet execute his first intention, and leave his shame and his sorrows
behind him.

Under these circumstances, towards the middle of the day, he
ventured to rise and come down stairs; and he had not been long
in the parlour, when his wife, who was standing at the window,
announced the approach of Mr. Simpson.

With a cordial and friendly salutation, the good man entered,
and was pleased to learn that the young woman and her child were
still in bed, which Mrs. Wetherall thought the best place for them
at present; "for," said she, "although I have made no inquiries
about her history yet, I am sure the poor things have been for
many days exposed to cold and want; and that a good warm clean
bed must be the greatest luxury they can enjoy."

"I love and honour you for your goodness, madam," said Mr.
Simpson. "How few of your sex there are, especially of the young
and handsome members of it, (and here by a bow, he appropriated
the compliment to Mrs. Wetherall,) would have admitted this
poor creature under their roof and given her a night's lodging,
until they had ascertained the cause of her destitution, and
whether her child was born in lawful wedlock. But you opened
your doors and administered food and shelter to the wretched,
without demanding that poverty should be perfect, or human
frailty, exposed to temptations that the prosperous never know,
exempt from error. Yours, madam, is real charity, and I feel
honoured in having made your acquaintance. With respect to
this poor creature, as you think she is not yet fit to be moved, and
are willing to give her another night's shelter, I'll not disturb her
to-day; and perhaps by to-morrow you may have learned something of her history, and in what manner I can best serve her.
That she is not altogether blameless, is extremely probable; but
young and pretty as, amidst all her wretchedness, she is, I am

inclined to think she need not have been reduced to the extremity in which we found her, if there had not been some virtue left in her; and her devotion to her child, to my mind, speaks volumes in her favour."

After this matter had been sufficiently discussed, Mr. Simpson, turning to Mr. Wetherall, reminded him that he wanted to speak a few words with him in private; upon which hint, the lady, having retired, he drew his chair closer to his host, and having given three taps on the lid of his gold snuff-box, and refreshed his nose with an ample supply from its contents, he drew a letter from his pocket, and opened the business as follows:—

" The affair that I want to consult you about is one of a very delicate nature; and I must premise, before I begin, that the communication I am about to make, must be upon honour, strictly private between us. It is not that I have so bad an opinion of human nature—and still less of yours, of whose character, as well as that of your amiable wife, I have formed the most favourable opinion— as to suspect mankind of wishing to injure and expose each other gratuitously; but there are contending interests and enmities, and Heaven knows what, in the world, that one must guard against; especially where the reputation and probably the life of a fellow creature are at stake. The fact is," continued he, unfolding the letter he held in his hand, " there has been something wrong about a letter—a money letter, sent from the country by a worthy friend of mine—at least he was the esteemed servant of a very dear friend, who is unfortunately dead—and he has written to me to request I will go to the post-office, and inquire into the business. The letter came from a place called Mapleton, and contained ten pounds; and it was addressed to a woman in Parliament-street. My friend Jeremy says, that he has no suspicion of the people at the country post-office, and that he put the letter in himself. He therefore feels assured that the delinquent is to be looked for in London; either at the office, or amongst the men that deliver the letters. Now, sir, no man respects the laws more than I do; and I am aware of the great importance in a commercial country of viewing breach of confidence as a capital crime. Still, I confess, I am one of those who think we are apt to make too free with human life. Very young men are sometimes placed in situations of great temptation: a single error, and perhaps the hope of a family—the only son of a widowed mother—a kind brother, or a beloved husband, perishes on the scaffold. I know the laws can- not afford to make these distinctions, nor descend to the detail of private suffering; but, as an individual, before I have recourse to the law, I think it my duty to weigh all these considerations. I dont know, sir, how far your views on the subject may accord with mine—" here Mr. Simpson, who had been hitherto bending for- ward, with his eyes directed to the letter in his hand, raised them to Mr. Wetherall's face. What he saw there, it would be vain to attempt to describe. Whatever it was, it occasioned him to draw himself up erect; for a moment his countenance was fixed in surprise—and then he stooped forward again, and bent his eyes on the letter more perseveringly than before—"What I mean to say, sir, is," continued he, "that I—I—should be sorry—I wouldn't for the world be the occasion of—of anything—" and he stammered, and got red in the face, and finally broke down in his oration altogether; whilst the unfortunate culprit before him laid his head upon the table and wept like a child.

Mr. Simpson arose and walked to the window—took out his handkerchief and blew his nose, and cleared his throat, and wiped away the tears that were gathering in his eyes. At that moment there came a loud double knock at the street door; Mr. Wetherall started from his seat, rushed to the door of the room, and turned the key, and then, trembling like a leaf in the autumn blast, he sank pale and breathless on a chair.

"It is only some women—visitors to your wife," said Mr. Simpson, interpreting his fear aright. It proved so; and Mrs. Wetherall being denied, they went away; but this little shock had broken the ice. Mr. Simpson turned round, and advancing to Mr. Wetherall, held out his hand, saying—"Come, sir, let us talk over this matter coolly;" and leading him back to his former seat, took one beside him—"Perhaps," said he, "you have some interest in the person who has been guilty of this breach of trust?"

But Mr. Wetherall was not a person to have recourse to a subterfuge on such an occasion. He understood the man he had to deal with; and he now opened his bosom, and poured out the whole truth, as he might have done to an earthly father, or to his Father in Heaven; and never was confidence better placed. "It was my first and my last crime," said he. "An urgent necessity, a pressing occasion for a few pounds, made me do it—but I have never known a moment's peace since. So confused, indeed, was I at the time, that it appears I didn't even destroy the letter; and it was found and recognised by our servant, who, strangely enough, happens to be acquainted with the woman in Parliament-street, to whom it was addressed. I am afraid, therefore, I am not yet even safe, in spite of your kindness and indulgence; for they will naturally speak of the circumstance, and endeavour to recover the money; and, God knows, I have not ten pounds in the world to replace it. In short, to confess the truth, such has been my imprudence, that I am in hourly dread of being arrested; in which case, whether the letter business is discovered or not, I shall probably lose my situation."

"How much do you owe?" inquired Mr. Simpson.

"I'm afraid, almost two hundred pounds," replied the other.

"Well, sir," said Mr. Simpson, "you shall not lose your situation for two hundred pounds. For your wife's sake, as well as your own, I'll lend you the money. You can pay me by quarterly instalments; and the habits of economy that this will require, will be beneficial in their effects, and bring you round to a more prudent way of living. With respect to this woman, your servant, if you'll give me leave, I'll speak a few words to her in private, and find out how she's to be dealt with."

With a heart glowing with gratitude, and lightened of a load of care, Mr. Wetherall thanked his benefactor, and retired to send up Susan to the conference.

Poor Susan entered the room with a very nervous feeling. She judged from Mr. Wetherall's disturbed countenance and agitated manner, that she was going to be interrogated about the letter, and with what intention she could not tell. Mr. Simpson, for anything she knew, might belong to the post-office, and her testimony might be of the most fatal importance to her master; and poor as she was, she would not have been instrumental in bringing him into trouble for a hundred times the sum she had lost.

"Come this way," said Mr. Simpson, beckoning her to advance, when she had closed the door. "You have a friend called Dobbs, I believe, who lives in Parliament-street?"

"Yes, I have, sir," replied Susan.

"I understand there has been some mistake about a letter addressed to her?"

"Has there, sir?" said she.

"So I understood," returned Mr. Simpson. "I thought you were aware of it?"

"No, sir," answered Susan.

"Come a little nearer," said he. "Are you not aware that a letter, containing a ten pound note, which was sent to this Mrs. Dobbs, is missing?"

"No, sir," persisted Susan, turning at the same time very pale.

"Excellent girl!" said Mr. Simpson to himself. "Then I am to understand," continued he, "that you know nothing at all of the affair in question?"

"Nothing in the world, sir," answered she, growing still paler than before.

"But your friend does, I suppose? This Mrs. Dobbs, I dare say, knows all about it?" said Mr. Simpson.

"I don't think she knows more about it than I do," replied Susan.

"Do you mean to say that you don't think she could give me any information on the subject?"

"I'm sure she couldn't, sir," answered Susan.

"Then it would be useless for me to question her about it?"

"Quite useless, sir," returned she.

"Well," said Mr. Simpson, nodding his head and smiling, "of course if anybody has lost any money it will be repaid. How long have you lived here?"

"About nine months, sir," said she.

"You appear to me a sensible, good-hearted girl," said he; "my name is John Simpson, and I'm a wine-merchant in Mark Lane."

"Are you, sir?" said Susan, thrown off her guard, for she recognised immediately who she was speaking to.

"Yes," returned he. "Why are you surprised at that?"

"I thought I'd heard the name before, that's all, sir," replied she; for she apprehended that the acknowledgment of who she was would not recommend her to the favour of her new acquaintance. "Then you don't belong to the post-office, sir?"

"No," returned Mr. Simpson. "What, you thought I did?"

"I didn't know but you might, sir," answered she, casting down her eyes, and blushing.

"No," replied he—"I'm a friend of your master's. But what I was about to say is, that my name is John Simpson, and that if I can ever be of any service to you, you may apply to me. I've taken a liking to you."

"Thank you, sir," answered Susan, curtseying, as she left the room. "Ah!" thought she, "I should soon lose his favour if he but heard my name."

"I can never be grateful enough for your goodness, sir," said Mr. Wetherall, when he learned the result of this interview; "and I think, considering my obligations, it would be wrong of me to conceal from you, that the same motive that took the poor woman, above stairs, to the bridge, took me there also."

"Merciful heavens!" exclaimed Mr. Simpson—"then my opportune midnight walk has been the means of saving three lives!"

Little did he or Mr. Wetherall imagine that Mr. Simpson's effort to save the life of another had been the means, under heaven, of saving his own.

CHAPTER XV.

MARRIED LIFE AT OAKFIELD—HARRY LEESON QUITS IT TO SEEK FORTUNE
ELSEWHERE.

When Mrs. Gaveston arrived at the age of twenty-one, she was not unmindful of the resolution she had avowed at the period of her father's death, when it was discovered that he had left no will—namely, to execute a deed in favour of Harry, as soon as she had the power, which should place him with respect to the property precisely in the situation he would have held had the will been forthcoming; for she had been fully aware of her father's intentions towards him, and the whole affair had been arranged with her entire concurrence.

Previous to her marriage she had made known her determination to Mr. Gaveston, who appeared perfectly to coincide in her views; and whenever she had occasionally adverted to it since, as he raised no objections, she interpreted his silence into acquiescence. Now, however, the time was arrived for fulfilling her intentions, and she opened the business to her husband one morning at breakfast, by observing that Harry would shortly be home for the summer vacation.

"What do you mean to do with that boy, Mrs. Gaveston?" inquired her husband. "He's now nearly fifteen, and it's high time he was put to something."

"That depends on what profession he selects, I suppose," replied the wife. "If he fixes on medicine, or the church, or the bar, he should go to college first, shouldn't he?"

"Nonsense!" answered Mr. Gaveston, "what should a chap like that do at college, that hasn't a rap in the world?"

"He'd stand in the greater need of a good education if that were the case," returned Fanny. "But I should be very sorry to think that was Harry's predicament. You know, Walter, I am now of age; and it has always been understood between us, that when that time arrived, Harry should be compensated for the loss he sustained by my father's having left no will."

"Nonsense! Fanny," replied the husband. "How can you be so absurd? You don't imagine I'm going to give away ten thousand pounds to a fellow that's neither kith nor kin to me."

"But he's both to me, Walter," said Mrs. Gaveston. "I love Harry as if he were my brother. Besides, I never could feel happy were I to neglect the fulfilment of my dear father's intentions."

"There is nothing so absurd, Mrs. Gaveston," returned the husband, "as arguing a point on which one's mind is perfectly made up. Now, I repeat, that I have not the slightest idea of doing what you propose. Therefore we may as well drop the subject."

"You never made any objections before," replied Fanny. "I'm sure I have named it to you twenty times, and you always appeared to acquiesce."

"Because I expected you'd grow out of your folly, and that opposition would be unnecessary," answered he.

"I shall never outgrow the folly of being just," replied Fanny.

Here Mr. Gaveston took up the newspaper which he had laid down when his wife commenced the conversation, and applied himself to its perusal with an air of perseverance, denoting that he did not intend to argue the matter further.

"I hope you will not interfere to prevent my doing that which I consider so," continued Fanny. But Mr. Gaveston remained silent. "An act," she added, "which is necessary to my peace of mind. I have had sorrows enough, Walter; don't add another to the catalogue."

"If you choose to coin sorrows out of every opposition to your will, I can't help it," said the husband. "When you are ten years older, you'll see the folly of what you want to do now, and thank me for preventing it."

"That I assuredly shall not," replied Fanny. "But I think it extremely improbable that I shall be in the world ten years hence to entertain any opinion on the subject. As you well know, my health has never recovered the shock it received at my poor father's death, and—"

G

"I thought it was agreed, Mrs. Gaveston, that I was at last to
have some respite from that eternal subject," said the husband,
throwing down the paper in an angry manner; and abruptly
pushing his chair from the table, he began to stride up and down
the room. "It's the sauce to my breakfast, dinner, and supper;
and I'm sick of it."

"You wrong me very much," answered his wife. "Painful as
silence very often is to myself, since you have forbidden the
subject, I never introduce it voluntarily—but in talking of such a
business as this, it's scarcely possible to avoid it. However,
consent to what I propose to do for Harry, and I'll give you my
word, Walter, I'll never mention it again in your presence."

"But you'll mention it behind my back, and complain that I
don't allow you liberty of speech, I suppose," said he.

"I am sorry you have no better opinion of my taste than you
have of my prudence," replied Fanny. "Whatever causes of
complaint I might have, I hope I shall not forget myself so far as
to entertain my friends with them. However, I will neither
mention the subject before your face nor behind your back, if you
will comply with my request in this one instance."

"As I said before," replied Mr. Gaveston, "there is no object
to be gained by arguing a point on which one's mind is perfectly
decided. If you are willing to have the boy put to some decent trade,
I'll go so far as to pay the fee of his apprenticeship; but as for
bringing up a beggar's brat like that to be a gentleman, or giving
him ten thousand pounds to make him one, I'll not do it; and as
you have now my definite answer, I beg I may never hear any
more on the subject," and banging the door after him, he quitted
the room.

As the door closed upon him, Mrs. Gaveston clasped her hands,
and ejaculated, "Oh, my father!" and then she relieved her heart
for some minutes, by showers of bitter tears. After this, having
composed herself as well as she could, she retired to her room,
and wrote a letter to her father's solicitor, Mr. Olliphant, inform-
ing him, that it had always been her intention to provide handsomely for her cousin Harry Leeson; and now she was of age, it
was her desire to do so still. That she had reason to apprehend
Mr. Gaveston did not acquiesce in her views; but she could not
feel that his dissent released her from her promise, and an obligation voluntarily assumed; and she therefore begged that he would
take the earliest opportunity of letting her know what was in her
power, &c. But, greatly to her disappointment, she had received
no answer to this letter, when the period of Harry's vacation
arrived.

As the academy was not far distant, Mr. Jeremy, who was sent
to fetch him, took Harry's pony with him, that the boy might
ride home; and as they jogged on together towards Oakfield, the
worthy butler told him what he called "a piece of his mind."

"Now, Master Harry," said he, "you're grown up to a fine
young gentleman, and it's time you learnt a little of what's what,

and who's who, and how you are yourself situated with regard to
these people."

"What people?" said Harry.

"A certain person," replied Mr. Jeremy. "There's some people,
that, like the devil, one ar'n't over fond of calling by their names,
lest one should see them looking over one's shoulder—but it's my
master I mean—that ever I should live to call him so!—but I
sha'n't call him so much longer; and would not now but for Miss
Fanny's sake."

"She's not Miss Fanny now," replied Harry. "I wish she was."

"You may say that, Master Harry," replied Jeremy, "and
nobody with more reason; and that just brings me to what I
wanted to say. As I observed just now, you're grown up a young
gentleman by this time, and old enough to understand something
of human natur, and that sort of thing—not that I think the person
we're speaking of has much of that sort of natur in him; but such
as he has, you must learn as well as you can to abide by it, and
make the best of it, for your own sake, and for the sake of Miss
Fanny—for as for calling her by any other name, it's a thing I
can't do."

"But what has he to do with me?" asked Harry. "I'm not
obliged to care for him."

"I wish you wasn't," returned Jeremy; "but he'll find the way
to make you care, or I'm much mistaken, which is a thing I never
was yet in man or woman. You see, sir, if your uncle had lived
the time that God Almighty intended he should, he'd have provided for you handsomely, I've no doubt; but them as curtailed
his life, curtailed your fortin; and that being the case, you must
cut your coat according to your cloth."

"But the money's all Fanny's, is not it?" said Harry.

"Not a bawbee of it," replied Mr. Jeremy; "and that's the
reason I want to give you a bit of a caution. If the money belonged to Miss Fanny, as it should have done, you might have
snapt your fingers at a person that shall be nameless, for it's little
you have to thank him for; but things being as they are, he can
make you or mar you, just as the fit takes him; and the bit of
advice I want to give you is this, just to keep in with him, and
put up as well as you can with his figaries and his insolence, and
what not, till you've got settled in the world in some way to do
for yourself—and then you may pitch him to old Nick for what I
care, which, according to my private opinion, is the place he com'd
from."

"Does he behave ill to Fanny?" inquired Harry.

"Does he!" ejaculated Mr. Jeremy. "If you'd been home this
last vacation you wouldn't need to ask that. He soon showed his
cloven foot, when the parson had joined them together for better
and worse. Lord love you! he's worse to live with than a Turk,
or a Jew, or a heretic!"

"Is he?" exclaimed Harry, alarmed by the force of Mr. Jeremy'
imagery.

"Her eyes that was as bright as diamonds, are dim with tears," said the butler, brushing a drop from his own eye with the cuff of his coat, " and the roses in her cheeks, that her father was so proud of—'s all washed out on 'em."

"Poor dear Fanny!" said Harry.

"He's no more heart than a flint," continued Mr. Jeremy, whose indignation made him eloquent; "and a tiger's whelp has more good-nature in his jaw tooth than he has in his whole composition! so Master Harry, mind your p's and q's till you can snap your fingers at him, that's all I want to say."

Jeremy's advice was excellent, but unfortunately not easily to be followed by a boy of fifteen, who had more spirit than prudence; and indeed it would have required a very considerable allowance of the latter quality to endure with patience Gaveston's tyranny and insolence to himself, and his hard and arbitrary behaviour towards Fanny. But as it is quite certain that the most forbearing demeanour Harry could have assumed would have been utterly unavailing towards placating Gaveston, whose hatred to him was ingrained, his failure made no great difference in the ultimate result.

As Mrs. Gaveston still hoped to find the means of providing for him, or at least of setting him well afloat in some profession, she took an opportunity of privately consulting him as to which he would select; and he told her that as his papa had been a soldier, he should like, if she had no objection, to be one too; and Fanny acquiesced willingly in his choice. It obviated the necessity of his going to college, which she much feared she might not be able to accomplish; and would remove him very much from Gaveston's path, which, greatly as she grieved herself to part with him, she saw was necessary for all parties.

One day at dinner, shortly after this decision, the conversation happening to turn on the army, Harry said that he hoped he should be a captain as young as his papa had been, for that it was when he was only nineteen, "and as I am only fifteen now," he added, "if I get my commission soon, perhaps I may."

"I hope you will, Harry," said Mrs. Gaveston. "I should like to see you with an epaulet on your shoulder."

"How can you fill that chap's head with such absurd notions, Mrs. Gaveston?" asked her husband. "How's he to get a commission?"

"By purchasing it, I suppose," replied Fanny; "I fear there's not much chance of getting one without."

"About as much chance as there is of getting one with, I fancy," returned Gaveston. "But it's really high time this sort of nonsense was put an end to, and that the boy was made to understand his real situation, which you take as much pains to blink from him as if you could prevent his learning it at last."

"I know I have no money," said Harry, blushing crimson. "There's no need to tell me that."

"And, pray, who do you expect will give you a commission, then?" said Gaveston.

Harry looked down upon his plate, and the tears swam in his eyes, for he did not like to say he expected Fanny would, lest he should turn the tempest upon her; whilst her face reflected all the poor boy's feelings; and as for Mr. Jeremy, who was standing behind her chair, he grasped the back of it, and clenched his teeth, to keep down the indignation he durst not give vent to.

"He expects I will," returned Fanny; "and with the best reason."

"Then the sooner he is undeceived the better," replied Gaveston, coldly. "What I am willing to do for him—and even that he has no right to expect—I have told you already; and if you did what's right by the boy, you would have endeavoured to open his eyes to the realities of life, instead of filling his head with these romantic and extravagant notions, which must end in disappointment. If he chooses to be put to some decent trade—a boot and shoemaker, for example—there's Wilcox that I deal with, I have no doubt would take him for a small sum—indeed, when I hinted the thing to him, he said he would, to oblige me—if you, young sir, can make up your mind to exchange the gold epaulet you've been dreaming about for a leathern apron, and the sword for an awl, I'll pay the fee of your apprenticeship. If you don't, you must shift for yourself as you can."

"Then I will shift for myself, sir," said Harry, rising from the table, and with a bursting heart he quitted the room.

"Oh, Walter!" said Mrs. Gaveston, "if you knew how I love that boy!" and she covered her face with her hands, to hide the tears that were streaming down her cheeks; whilst poor Jeremy, unable any longer to control his feelings, caught up a plate and disappeared.

From that moment Harry's mind was made up. He felt assured that Gaveston would keep his word where the thing promised was to make other people unhappy; and he felt moreover, young as he was, that after the insults he had received, he never could condescend to eat the bread that that man's purse had provided. "No," said he, "I'll keep my hands free, that, by and by, when he has broken poor Fanny's heart, as I am sure he will do, I may challenge him, and have a chance of punishing him for all his cruelty and his insults by blowing out his brains."

What Gaveston had said, had certainly the effect of opening the boy's eyes, as he called it, to his real situation. The darling of his mother, and then the darling of Mr. Wentworth and Fanny, poor Harry had never had occasion to learn what poverty and dependence were; but the lesson was instilled into him now with all its bitterness. He saw that his cousin had no power to protect nor to assist him; and that his presence was only aggravating the misery of her situation in every way. He comprehended what she suffered when she saw him oppressed and insulted; he found, that instead of being a comfort to her, he was only an everlasting source of irritation to Gaveston, and of dissension betwixt her and her husband.

It was not without many and bitter tears that poor Harry came to the resolution of leaving Oakfield, and throwing himself upon the world—dear Oakfield, where he had been so happy, and so beloved; and that he had felt to be as much his home, as if it had been the house of his father. He thought, too, of that noble and brave father, whom he well remembered; and of his sweet mother, and his kind good uncle—even Dobbs, and Andrew, and Susan—the memory of all that had ever loved him, rushed upon his heart, and swelled it almost to bursting.

But it was time to think of the future—that future which is the legitimate inheritance of youth, the field of their enterprise, the arena of their glory, of which it is so cruel to rob them, by substituting stern realities for vivid hopes, and mournful truths for bright delusions.

There was but one plan he could think of, and that was to go to London. He had been there once with his uncle, and had seen the morning parade of the guards at St. James's; and it occurred to him, that if he went there, he might possibly contrive to make the king acquainted with his situation, and that his papa had been a brave officer, who had fought many battles, and had died in his majesty's service. Then, thought Harry, "he couldn't do less than give me a commission." The first step is everything—having accomplished this, the rest followed naturally; his promotion would be rapid, his feats of bravery remarkable—they would inevitably reach his majesty's ears, and when he was summoned down to tea, he had just been commanded by the king to rise Sir Harry Leeson.

Engrossed by these visions, Harry felt himself at that moment quite independent of Gaveston and his insolence. He reckoned confidently on the day coming when he would be his superior, and be able to render back scorn for scorn, and insult for insult. Instead, therefore, of presenting himself in the drawing-room with the subdued and mortified air that Fanny had expected, he entered it with a bright countenance and an erect bearing. She was relieved, attributing it to the natural elasticity of youthful spirits that *would* rise again, and fling off sorrow; and she was particularly glad, because, in the interval between dinner and tea, two visitors had arrived whom she intended to take an opportunity of privately consulting about Harry and his fortunes. These were Mr. Olliphant, the lawyer she had written to on the subject, and Mr. Simpson, her father's old clerk, now a joint partner in the concern; she was anxious that they should form a favourable opinion of the boy, and it so happened that he never appeared to greater advantage. The laurel wreath he had so lately won was still upon his brow, his satisfaction at his majesty's gracious reception was still dancing in his eyes; and the glory of his martial deeds, and the pride of his well-earned honours pervaded his whole person, tinging his smooth cheek with a bright carmine, and lending firmness and dignity to his carriage.

"How can any one dislike that boy?" was the question that occurred to three of the party as he entered the drawing-room; as for the fourth, Mr. Gaveston, who had expected to meet him with a very different aspect, something like a glimmering of the truth suggested itself to him as the cause of the change.

"He has got some project in his head that's to make his fortune," thought he. "He has found some fool's ladder by which he expects to mount to wealth and fame in a trice; and he'll be cutting his stick and away, some fine morning, to seek them."

Harry had no intention of keeping him long in suspense. On many accounts, he felt, that if his project was ever to be executed at all, it could not be commenced too soon. He had read in the paper only that very morning, that the king, who had been staying at Weymouth, had returned to London, where he was to remain a fortnight, previous to going somewhere else. Thus there was no time to lose. Besides, the weather was beautiful, the nights clear, and the moon at the full. Then his pride spurred him on to the enterprise, and urged him away; and his fears were not much less active. He could not tell the moment that Gaveston would carry him off against his will, and consign him to some odious master, from whom it might be no easy matter to escape; and the very idea of finding himself in his enemy's power, away from Fanny or anybody that had any interest in him, was terrific. He saw clearly, that, for some reason or other, he was the object of his intense hatred, and a secret instinct told him that Gaveston's hatred was not to be despised. Since he had been older, and more capable of reflection and observation, some vague suspicions had arisen in his mind about the fall in the pond, and other accidents that he had been exposed to when in his company. The notions had first found their way into his head through some words dropped by Andrew and Jeremy; and now that the antipathy was so evident and so active, and that there was no one to stand between him and it, he shrunk instinctively from the idea of finding himself at his mercy.

The evening passed in general conversation, in which Harry, when the strangers addressed him, freely took his part; and many were the approving glances that passed between them at the answers and remarks he made. As the visitors had not arrived till after dinner, there was a supper, which Harry thought by no means inopportune. He could not tell when he might meet with another good meal; and as he had fared ill at the last repast, he determined to fortify himself for his journey, by making himself amends now.

His pride and his hopes kept up his spirits through the whole evening, till the moment came that he was to take leave of Fanny. Then, the feeling that it was his last *good-night*, his last kiss to her that he loved so much, and who so warmly returned his affection, almost overthrew his resolution. He left her, too, so unhappy; subject to all the humours and tyranny of her odious husband. "But my staying cannot mend that," he said to himself —"I only make it worse; and if I can suceeed in my project, and once write to her that I am comfortably provided for, I'm sure she'll be much happier, than in seeing me the victim of ill treatment she can't prevent."

Soon after the supper was removed, Fanny rose to retire; and he rose too. Gaveston took no notice of him, but the visitors shook hands with him kindly; and then he followed Fanny out of the room. They ascended the stairs together, and when they reached his room door, he threw his arms round her neck, and said, "God bless you, dear Fanny!" She thought his flushed cheek and unusual energy arose merely from the events of the day, and she returned his embrace with equal ardour. She longed to tell him that she hoped the visit of the two gentlemen below, would result in some satisfactory arrangement for him, and if he had appeared depressed, she would have risked doing so to raise his spirits; but as it was, afraid of awakening hopes she might not be able to fulfil, she thought it better to wait till she had had some communication with her father's friends in the morning.

When Harry had shut himself in his room, the tears he had suppressed in Fanny's presence, burst forth, and for some minutes the pang of parting with her seemed greater than he was able to encounter. Then once more he invoked the memory of all those who had loved him—his brave papa,—his dear, beautiful mamma, —his kind, indulgent uncle,—his good and faithful servants. The grief of a young heart is so bitter whilst it lasts, that it's a blessed thing it seldom lasts long. When the paroxysm, whose violence soon exhausted itself, was abated, he arose from his knees—for in that attitude, with his face leaning on the side of his bed, he had wept his last farewell to Oakfield, and recommended himself, a friendless orphan as he was, to the care of his Father in heaven— took up his little bundle, and softly descended the stairs. He knew that it would be much easier for him to get away unheard before the door was locked for the night, which in the summer was not done till Mr. Gaveston retired to his room; and he, with the two visitors, was yet at the supper table. So Harry gently opened the door, and stepped out upon the gravel walk that surrounded the house. Here he paused to take a last look at his once happy home, at the windows of the room that had been his uncle's, and at the light that showed Fanny's shadow as she moved about in her apartment. "Farewell, dear Fanny!" he whispered, and was about to move away, when it occurred to him that he should have left a few lines to account for his disappearance, and relieve in some degree the grief and alarm he was sure his departure would occasion her. He did not dare return into the house lest he should meet Gaveston, and his journey be impeded; so with his pencil he wrote a few words on a scrap of paper he found in his pocket, and folding it so as to attract observation, he placed it on the ledge of the drawing-room window, and secured it with a stone from blowing away. Then, without further pause or hesitation, he walked briskly down the avenue; and, climbing the park-gate, which was already locked, he leaped into the high-road.

When Mrs. Gaveston descended from her chamber in the morning to take her usual early walk, she found the two visitors already at the door with their hats on. The moment was convenient for the consultation she desired, for she knew her husband was gone to take a survey of some land he was proposing to purchase, and would not return till breakfast time. She, therefore, joined them; and opened the conference by inquiring of Mr. Olliphant if he had received her letter.

"It is that letter that has occasioned our visit," replied the lawyer. "We thought it was much better to see you than to write; and we should have been here before, but I was out of town when your letter arrived; and my clerk considered the business of too private a nature for him to interfere in."

"Well," said Fanny, "you have seen Harry—what do you think of him?"

"I never saw a finer lad," returned the gentleman. "And it would be a thousand pities that his prospects were blighted for want of a little money," added Mr. Simpson.

"Wouldn't it?" said Fanny; "and that was why I wrote to you, Mr. Olliphant. Unfortunately, Mr. Gaveston does not see him with our eyes; but in a case like this, where I know I should have my dear father's approbation, I shall venture to act for myself. What is there in my power that I can give to Harry?"

"Nothing," replied the lawyer—"not a stiver."

"Oh," exclaimed Fanny, in the greatest alarm, "you don't mean to say I can do nothing for him?"

"I do mean it, indeed," said Mr. Olliphant. "You must remember that before your marriage, I pointed out to you the consequence of marrying without settlements, or any arrangement of your property."

"I do recollect that when you were here immediately after my father's death," returned she, "you said something about it—but I was in such a state of mind that I never thought of it again."

"But when I understood you were about to be married, Mrs. Gaveston, I wrote to you on the subject," said Mr. Olliphant.

"Then I never received your letter," said she.

Mr. Simpson and the lawyer exchanged glances. "I said everything I could on the subject," continued Olliphant; "urged by my friendship for your father, and my regard for you. Besides, I had heard you say you intended to provide for this boy, and I thought it right to tell you, that if you did not do it before your marriage, you could not do it after."

"I assure you your letter never reached me," repeated Fanny; "though possibly, if it had, I might still have trusted to being able to do it afterwards, with Mr. Gaveston's consent; for I never expected he would oppose it. But you distress me very much—what is to become of poor Harry?"

"Though you can do nothing, my dear lady," said Mr. Olliphant, "here is somebody that's willing to do a great deal, if it will contribute to your happiness," and as he spoke, he laid his hand on Mr. Simpson's shoulder.

"Yes," said Mr. Simpson, blowing his nose, and clearing his throat, for he felt something there that almost choked his voice, when he looked at the wan cheeks, and listened to the desponding tones of the once gay and blooming Fanny Wentworth, the child of the man he had loved so much. "Yes, my dear," said he, "let no anxiety about your cousin Harry disturb your peace. Olliphant and I have foreseen this day, and have provided against it. I am aware that it was your father's intention to give Harry Leeson half the business and ten thousand pounds. The ten thousand pounds he shall have when I die; and the half of the business is his already. I obtained it not for myself—my salary has always far exceeded my expenditure—but for him. Everything I have in the world I owe to your father, and everything I have shall go to his children."

This was consolation indeed for Fanny; the warm pressure of her hand, and the tears that swam in her eyes, touched the honest man more eloquently than words. "I'll run directly," said she, "and bring Harry, that he may learn the good news, and thank you himself. I wonder he has not joined us before this; but perhaps he thinks we're talking of business. Harry, dear," said she, gently opening the door and peeping in, "Harry! what, are you not up yet?" for the curtains of his bed were still drawn—but as she received no answer, she stepped into the room. The bed had evidently not been slept in: she flew down stairs—"Who has seen Harry Leeson this morning?" No one. The truth flashed on her mind. "He's gone! He's gone!" she cried, rushing towards the portico.

"And here is his farewell," said Mr. Olliphant. "I was looking at the clematis by the drawing-room window, when this bit of paper caught my eye, and I took it up without reflection. It has evidently been placed there for you."

"Oh, how unfortunate!" exclaimed Fanny. "When he might have been so happy!"

"Never fear," said Mr. Olliphant. "We'll find him again. We'll publish a reward, and put an advertisement in the papers inviting him to return; and in the meantime, you had better send out some of your people on horseback to search the country for him."

"He's gone to Lunnun, as sure as my name's John Jeremy," said the butler—"all boys think they can make their fortin there."

The measures proposed were adopted, but without success. Harry Leeson was not to be found.

CHAPTER XVI.

JULIA BEGINS TO RELATE THE HISTORY OF HER PARENTS.

"I WILL tell you nothing but the truth," said Julia, in answer to Mrs. Wetherall, who, in compliance with Mr. Simpson's directions, had requested her to communicate as much as she might think proper of her history, in order that he might the better know how to serve her; "but to enable you to comprehend my story, I must first give you some account of my parents.—I almost fear to begin," she continued, after a short silence, and wiping away the tears that were gathering in her eyes—"you will repent of your charity, and of having sheltered such an one as I am under your roof."

"Indeed, I shall not," returned Mrs. Wetherall; "you have nothing to fear on that head, either from me or my husband. And if you had things to tell me twenty times worse than I am sure you have, I should still have reason to bless the chance that brought you here;"—for Mr. Wetherall, partly to relieve his own mind, and partly to engage his wife's co-operation in the plans of retrenchment that he projected immediately commencing, had, in the course of the evening after Mr. Simpson's visit, confessed to her his guilt, and acquainted her with his miraculous escape from detection, and with Mr. Simpson's generous offers of assistance; —"I mean, because it has been the occasion of our knowing Mr. Simpson," she added, observing that Julia looked surprised, "who, my husband says, is one of the best of men, and has already done us a great service. So proceed, and tell me whatever you please without apprehension."

"My father," continued Julia, "was the only son of a tradesman, who aspired to bring him up to the church, and with this view gave him the rudiments of an excellent education; but before this could be completed, or the young man ordained, misfortune, sickness, and death overtook the parent, and the son was left alone in the world to shift for himself.

"It happened that my grandfather had an acquaintance in the way of business at Nantes; and this person, who came over occasionally to make purchases of English merchandise for his trade, had been commissioned by a brother-in-law of his, who kept an academy, to look out for some young man who would be willing to undertake the situation of English teacher in his establishment; which was chiefly supported by the mercantile class, who, having considerable intercourse with this country and America, made it a point that their sons should be taught the language.

"On learning the death of his friend, and the overthrow of my father's prospects, this gentleman proposed the situation to him, and advised him to accept it; which, after consulting the few friends he had on the subject, he finally did, and accompanying the stranger abroad, was installed at once in his office.

"Here he remained for two years, with little to complain of, except that his salary was too low to allow him to lay by anything for future contingencies; but at the end of that period, the master of the establishment died, and poor Valentine (that was my father's Christian name) was thrown, once more destitute, on the pity of the world. He had, however, by this time, so far improved his acquaintance with the language, that he thought himself fully competent to undertake the office of French teacher in an English school; and he proposed to return to his own country with that view; but whilst his departure was delayed for the want of sufficient funds for the journey, a certain notary called Le Moine, a relation of one of his pupils, offered him employment. This gentleman, whose business lying amongst the merchants, frequently had deeds, agreements, and processes brought before him where a knowledge of English was requisite, wanted a clerk who understood both languages, and engaged my father at a comfortable salary in that capacity. Here he was well treated, and might have lived very happily, but that one circumstance interfered with his tranquillity.

"Monsieur Le Moine had an only daughter, of whom he was extremely fond and proud, for whom he destined the little fortune he was acquiring by his professional labours, and whom he aspired to see well married. My father, however, had not been many months under Monsieur Le Moine's roof, before he perceived that this young lady regarded him with a too favourable eye. Numerous were the excuses she made to visit the office to inquire for her father, when she knew he was not there, to get a pen mended, or to ask for a sheet of paper; and when Valentine was alone, she would linger on one pretence or another, drawing him into conversations and discussions, which she invariably contrived to turn on the subjects of love and marriage. However flattered the young man was by his conquest, as soon as he perceived her prepossession, he took every pains to avoid giving it encouragement, aware that it could only be to him a source of fresh misfortunes. He was quite certain, that so far from consenting to his union with his daughter, the very first suspicion of her attachment would be the signal for his immediate dismissal from Monsieur Le Moine's service. He was by no means in a situation to take a portionless bride, had he even been so much in love as to contemplate marrying the young lady without her father's approbation; added to which, the obligations he lay under to Monsieur Le Moine made him recoil from any such idea. It must also be admitted, that these good principles and prudential views were considerably fortified by an attachment he had formed for the youngest daughter of the lately deceased schoolmaster—an attachment which, though mutual, was scarcely likely to terminate more happily than the other, both parties being penniless, and the young lady's surviving parent utterly averse to the connexion.

The lovers, however, contrived occasionally to meet and walk together in the suburbs and remote parts of the town; and sometimes a little note or a confidential messenger would give Valentine a hint, that the mamma and sister were to be absent from home at a certain time, and that Ma'm'selle Aurore would be alone.

"The continued insensibility my father testified to the regard of the notary's daughter, together with some other circumstances, at length induced her to suspect that his heart was defended by a previous attachment; and being a girl of high spirit, and strong passions, her wounded pride and disappointed affection urged her to various stratagems to penetrate the secret; but as Valentine and his mistress were, from the necessity of their position, extremely cautious, her endeavours were for a long time fruitless. At length, however, accident seemed disposed to favour her curiosity. Monsieur Le Moine happening to be called to Paris on business, Julie was at liberty to indulge her inclination, by spending more of her time than usual in Valentine's company; and, one day, when, on some pretext or another, she was lounging in the office, a little boy entered, and gave the young clerk a note, on opening which, she observed him to blush and look confused.

"'Very well,' said he to the messenger, whom he seemed anxious to get rid of—'that will do—you may go;' and conscious of his own embarrassment, and that Julie's eye was upon him, he threw the note with an air of affected indifference amongst other papers on the desk at which he was writing, intending, the moment she left the room, to destroy it. But she had seen enough in his manner to awaken her suspicions, and she resolved not to quit her ground till she had satisfied them, so drawing her chair to a part of the room where she had full view of Valentine and the papers, she took down a volume of the *Causes Célèbres*, that, with other law books, stood upon the shelves, and seating herself, began to read, or at least to pretend to do so; her whole attention, in effect, being fixed on the young clerk and the note.

"In this way they had sat some time, he wishing her away, and she plotting how to get a sight of the billet, when a footman opened the door to say that Monsieur le Comte d'Emerange was below in his carriage, and begged to speak to Monsieur Le Moine or his clerk.

"There was no alternative—Valentine could do no otherwise than go on the instant; and he had neither courage nor presence of mind sufficient to destroy his note first, or to take it with him.

"No sooner had he closed the door, than like a hawk on her prey, Julie darted on the paper, and with an eager eye devoured the following words:—

"'Come to me when your office closes—I shall be alone to-night, and to-morrow night; Aurore——.'

"When Valentine returned, he found Julie sitting exactly as he had left her; and as he took his seat at the desk, he glanced his eye over the papers, and saw the note lying just where he had thrown it. 'I was mistaken,' he said to himself, 'she has no suspicion;' and he took up his pen and continued his work, whilst she, shortly afterwards, with an air of perfect indifference, left the room.

"It so happened, however, that on that particular evening, Valentine was unable to avail himself of his mistress's invitation, being under the necessity of preparing some papers of importance, for a cause that was to come on the next day. He therefore sent a note to her to that effect; at the same time promising to be with her on the following evening.

"In the meantime, Julie was eager with impatience, for the moment that was to satisfy her suspicions, and would, perhaps, moreover, afford her the means of revenging the mortification she had endured on her happier rival; for many indications led her to believe that the intercourse, of whatever nature it might be, was clandestine, and she did not despair of finding some way to break it off.

"When the usual hour for closing the office approached, she dressed herself in a black gown, shawl, and bonnet; and seating herself in an apartment that, with the door ajar, gave her an opportunity of seeing whoever went in or out of the house, she awaited Valentine's movements. But the usual hour arrived, and passed, and Valentine still wrote on. The clock struck again and again, till at length she counted twelve. 'He can't mean to go,' thought she, 'or has he any suspicion I am watching him?' and she arose softly and extinguished her light, that when Valentine opened the door, he might have no reason to imagine her up so much after her customary hour for retiring. It was some time past one, and Julie was beginning to think that she might as well go to bed in reality, as it must be too late for any rendezvous that night, when she heard the door bell ring violently, and saw Valentine, a moment afterwards, on the summons being repeated, pass through the passage to answer it. Who the stranger was she could not see, nor could she distinctly hear what was said; but the voice was a man's, and she fancied she distinguished the words, 'Come, come quickly!' At all events, they were but few, whatever they might be: the interview was momentary: Valentine returned hastily into the office, snatched up his hat and cloak, and accompanied the stranger from the house.

"'She has sent for him!' exclaimed Julie; and furious with jealousy, she rushed out after them. The feeble light of the street lamps only just enabled her to discern two figures moving rapidly away, and she ran lightly on, till she was sufficiently near to be in no danger of losing sight of them, trusting to her black dress and soft step, to protect her from observation. One walked rather in advance of the other, and as they were both about the same height, and both wore dark cloaks, she could not distinguish which was Valentine, and which the stranger—but she fancied Valentine was the last.

"On they went, so fast, that it was not without considerable difficulty Julie succeeded in maintaining her distance: through street after street they hurried, till they reached the outskirts of the town, and there they stopped at a small villa, the door of which being ajar, they entered and disappeared.

"'Here, then, she lives,' thought Julie, as she drew near to survey the premises—'the rest I shall easily discover—whether she be maid or wife; and she shall pay a heavier price for her pleasure than she dreams of! But now I must return, for Valentine will doubtless stay till morning, and I can't remain here all night;' and the excitement being somewhat abated, she began to contemplate with terror her lonely situation, the hour, and the distance she had to retrace.

"Just, however, as she was turning away, she was startled by the sound of a foot, and on looking round, she perceived one of the figures that had entered, come out again, close the door, and move rapidly back towards the town; but whether it was Valentine or the other she could not discern.

"'At all events, I'll keep near him,' thought she. 'It will be a protection, whichever it is—besides, if it is Valentine, I may be returning with half my errand, if I don't trace him further.' Whoever it was, he walked back even faster than he had come, and she was frequently obliged to run, to keep him in view. He returned by the same way, till he reached the heart of the town; he then turned down a narrow street, stopped at the door of a small inn or public-house, where there was still a light glimmering through the windows, knocked with his knuckles against the door, which being presently opened, he entered, and she saw him no more. Whilst he was waiting to be admitted, the town clocks struck three, and the commencement of a heavy shower of rain warned Julie to hasten away. 'That is not Valentine,' said she to herself—'he has remained at the villa with his lady—this was but the messenger that was sent to fetch him;' and she returned to her home, where Madeleine, the maid-servant, whose services she secured by a few francs opportunely administered, let her in. She went to bed, possessed with rage and jealousy; and passed the sleepless hours till morning, meditating plans of vengeance to be wreaked on her happy rival.

With the first dawn of light she arose. She felt an irresistible desire to return to the villa—to survey it by daylight—find out by whom it was inhabited, and perhaps detect Valentine in the very act of leaving it clandestinely. She dressed herself hastily, and having warned Madeleine not to be alarmed at her absence, she hurried along through the streets she had carefully marked the night before, and soon drew near the spot, where she did not doubt the man she loved was happy in the arms of her rival.

"The front of the house looked on the high road, the back into a garden; and on each side of the main door, there was a small door in the wall, which led into it. One of these was locked, the other, which opened into a little alcove, was not; and she lifted the latch to take a peep at the garden, and to observe if there were any outlet on that side, but there was none. The garden was not large, but it was carefully cultivated, and surrounded by a wall of middling height. 'He must, then, come out by the front,' thought she; and she took up her position in the recess formed by the garden door that was locked, determined to await Valentine's appearance. She had not waited long when she heard the door of the house open, but instead of the person she expected to see, there came out hastily two women, apparently servants, who being neither young nor handsome, had not the air of rivals to be feared. Whoever they were, however, they set off with all the speed they could command towards the town, and were soon out of sight.

"They had not been gone long, when Julie's attentive ears distinguished a sound, that appeared like the opening of a window at the back of the house; and presently afterwards, the sound of feet on the other side of the door she was leaning against—the latch was lifted, and an effort made to open it, which proving ineffectual, the feet retreated. She expected to see the person, whoever it was (and she had little doubt but it was Valentine), emerge from the other door; but in this she was disappointed. The feet continued to retreat, till the sound ceased altogether.

"If it were, as she suspected, Valentine taking his early departure, which way could he escape? She felt almost certain, from the short survey she had made, that there was no back-door. 'He has got out of the window, and will climb over the wall;' and, as the idea rushed into her mind, she darted to the other door and opened it. There, sure enough, she saw what she was looking for. Valentine was at the top of the wall: and before she could make a step towards him, he had leaped down on the other side. 'Perfidious traitor!—barbarous villain!'—every epithet of abuse she could think of, was lavished on him at this confirmation of her suspicions; forgetting, as ladies are apt to do on these occasions, that he had never made any vows to her. However, her objurgations were squandered on the vacant air. Valentine was beyond her reach, and she had only to debate whether she should return home the way she came, or remain where she was, till she had made some discovery with respect to the inmates of the house. After some deliberation, her desire to meet Valentine, to confront him, to hear what excuse he would make for staying out all night, determined her to the former measure, and she retraced her steps as fast as she could. When she reached home, he had not yet arrived; but secure that she should see him ere long, she desired Madeleine to bring her a cup of coffee, and sat down at the window to watch his approach, and meditate her plans of vengeance. But hour after hour passed, and no Valentine appeared; and to account for his absence, I must now relate his part in the adventures of the night.

"Anxious to finish the work he had in hand, he had sat up far beyond his usual hour, and was still diligently plying his pen through the concluding lines of the document he was preparing, when he was roused by the loud and hasty summons of the bell, which has already been alluded to. At first, imagining from the lateness of the hour, that it was either a mistake, or a piece of mischief of some wanderer of the night, he did not move; but a second peal, louder than the first, succeeding, he hastened to the door to inquire the cause of so unusual a disturbance.

"'Is this the house of Monsieur Le Moine?' eagerly asked a man who stood there, muffled in a blue mantle and a slouched hat.

"'It is,' replied Valentine.

"'Then come quickly,' cried the man, seizing his arm as he spoke—'the patient is dying of a wound—there is no time to lose —bring with you what is needful; and in the name of God make haste!'

"'I'll only fetch my hat and cloak,' said Valentine, who concluded that the service required was to draw up some testamentary document of importance, and that as Monsieur Le Moine was absent, he must supply his place as well as he could. Equipping himself, therefore, in haste, and thrusting a sheet of parchment in his pocket, without stopping to ask more questions, he set off after the stranger, who, at a rapid pace, conducted him to the house to which Julie had followed them, pushed open the door, and without even waiting to shut it, ascended the stairs by the light of a small lantern which he drew from under his cloak—unlocked a chamber-door, made a sign to Valentine to enter, which he had no sooner done, than he instantly closed it upon him, saying, 'You'll see what's necessary:' and turning the key, was heard descending the stairs as fast as he had mounted them.

"Alarmed by so strange an adventure, and fearing he had been lured into a snare by a villain for some desperate purpose, he used every effort to open the door, but in vain. He then rushed to the window, threw it open, and called as loudly as he could for aid, but no sound answered his appeal.

"Whilst he was still looking out of the window, endeavouring to discover by the imperfect light how he was situated, and whether there was any chance of escape that way, by letting himself down to the ground, he fancied he heard a slight movement in the room behind him, and turning suddenly round to investigate the cause, he, to his horror, beheld by the light of a night-lamp that stood on the table, a ghastly figure of a man in a bloody shirt and night-cap, peeping out between the curtains of the bed, who, the moment Valentine's eye met his, let go the curtain and disappeared.

"Transfixed with fear and horror, the young man at first stood motionless, staring on the curtains, from between which he expected again to see the fearful apparition emerge; but all remaining quiet, he presently ventured to cast his eyes round the room, to ascertain if there were any one else in it besides himself and the figure he had seen; but perceiving no one, he next summoned courage to advance towards the table, take up the lamp, and approach the bed.

"Valentine was young, and his situation was so extraordinary, that he may be excused for hesitating some time before he ven-

H

tured to withdraw the curtain; when, however, at length he did so, there lay the person he had seen, to all appearance, dead; at least, he would not have doubted his being so, had he not given signs of life so lately. His eyes were closed, his mouth open, his face of a ghastly hue, and both the sheets and his own person smeared with blood.

" 'In the name of God, sir,' exclaimed Valentine, 'what is the meaning of this, and for what purpose am I brought hither?' but the man not only made no answer, but he showed no symptoms of hearing that, or any other question Valentine put to him; and after contemplating the body for some time, he came to the conclusion, that the exertion the person, whoever he might be, had made in rising to look through the curtains, had been a last effort of nature, and that he was now really gone.

" But now again recurred the question, for what purpose had he been brought there to be shut up in a room with this dying stranger,—where were the friends, where the attendants that should have surrounded the bed? The bed, too, of ease and affluence; for there was nothing that indicated poverty or destitution. On the contrary, the house appeared a good one, and was situated in a respectable quarter; and the furniture of the apartment he was in, was not only handsome, but abundant. Had the occupant of the bed been murdered? But no; it did not seem probable, that, in that case, a notary of all persons should have been sent for, unless by the friends of the victim; and none such appeared: so that he rather concluded the stains about the linen proceeded from the patient's having been lately bled.

" Again he examined the room, the window, and the door; but without finding any means of escape. He remembered he had a clasp-knife in his pocket, and thought that by its assistance he might possibly pick the lock; but it broke in the attempt: so, having tried all he could without success, he saw nothing left but patience, and resolved to compose his mind as well as he could, and sit down quietly to await the events of the morning.

" In spite of his unpleasant situation, he had not sat long before he fell into a doze, from which he was aroused by what appeared to him some movement of the person in bed. Hastily he started up, and seizing the lamp, drew aside the curtain—but all was still as before. Again he spoke—but no sign of life was given; so concluding it had been fancy, he once more composed himself in an easy chair, where, fatigue soon overcoming him, he fell into a sound sleep, from which he did not awaken till he was aroused, some hours afterwards, by a knocking at the room-door.

CHAPTER XVII.

JULIA CONTINUES THE HISTORY OF HER PARENTS AS FOLLOWS.

" ' COME in,' cried Valentine, suddenly awakening, and at first unconscious where he was; upon which injunction the handle was turned, and efforts made to open the door.

" ' The door's locked, sir, and the key's inside,' replied a female voice.

" ' Locked!' cried Valentine, rousing himself, looking about, and beginning to recall the events of the night—' My God! I remember now—so it is. For Heaven's sake, get the door opened, and let me out!' He then heard the woman move away, and presently return with another; and by their conversation he made out that they were searching for the key, wondering what had become of it, and how the door should have been locked. After an interval they both assured him that the key must be inside, as they had sought for it in vain.

" ' My good woman,' exclaimed Valentine, 'I tell you I am locked in. I was brought here in the middle of the night, for what purpose I can't guess, and shut into this room. I heard the man that lured me hither turn the key; and all I beg of you is, to send for some one to break the door open, and let me out.'

" After this, he heard the women whispering and tittering together; and then they went away, and all was silent.

" Having waited some time in expectation of their return, he looked about for a bell; he found one, which he reached by mounting on a table, for the cord was cut short; but he rang it in vain. He then made a noise at the door, and tried to kick it open, but no sound indicated that there was any one in the house but himself. Desperate at the delay, and uncertain whether the women would return or not, he next rushed to the window, and threw it open, resolving to jump out at all risks, rather than longer submit to this mysterious imprisonment. Now that it was light enough to distinguish surrounding objects, the feat did not appear so difficult as he had imagined. The window looked into a garden, and immediately beneath was a flower-bed of soft earth, which would serve to break his fall; and, accordingly, he succeeded in reaching the ground uninjured. His next object was to get out of the garden, and he tried the only door he saw, but it was locked. Every moment his eagerness to escape increased—he could not tell what trouble and delay might await him if found where he was; so, without seeking further, he climbed over the wall. On the other side were fields which led by a back way into the town; and with all the speed he could command, he hurried across them, resolving to go straight to a justice of peace, and tell his story; aware of the importance, under such mysterious circumstances, of being first heard, and demanding an investigation himself.

H 2

"The way by the fields was shorter than by the road, and he preferred it, as there was less chance of his being met by any one before he had accomplished his object; but there were several dikes and enclosures in his path, and unfortunately, in leaping a wall, having failed to observe a ditch on the other side, he fell and sprained his ankle.

"The pain was so intense, that to move was impossible, and there he sat, cursing his hard fate, and as anxious to be discovered by some passenger, as he had been a moment before to avoid observation.

"A heavy half hour he had passed in this painful situation, when he was cheered by hearing the voices of persons approaching by the way he had come, and he made an effort to get upon his feet to ask their assistance; but before he could accomplish his purpose, a man suddenly leaped over the wall, who, the moment he set his eyes upon him, called out, 'Here he is, the rascal, crouching in a ditch,' and immediately seized him by the collar.

"'Bring the fellow along!' cried two others, looking over; and without mercy they roughly pulled him out of the ditch.

"In vain he attempted to explain his situation, and the accident he had met with; not a word would they listen to; but reckless of his expostulations and the pain they were inflicting, they dragged him over the wall, and back across the fields to the house he had so lately escaped from; where, flinging him into a dark closet, two of them departed, leaving the third to keep guard at the door, with strict injunctions rather to take his life than let him away.

"After making several fruitless efforts to induce the man outside to throw some light on the mystery that seemed to be thickening around him, he at length resigned himself to his fate, and stretching himself on the floor, in as easy a position as the limited dimensions of his prison would admit, he resolved to await the result with what patience he could.

"He had passed about two hours in this situation, when he heard the voices of several persons entering the house; and one of them having inquired of his gaoler 'if all was right,' and being answered in the affirmative, they proceeded up stairs. In about a quarter of an hour afterwards the closet door was thrown open, and he was desired to come out; but by this time, his leg being so swollen, that he was utterly unable to move, they placed him in a chair, and so carried him up stairs to the room in which he had passed the night.

"The occupant of the bed was still there; but though looking as ghastly as ever, he was not dead. He was sitting up supported by pillows, and on one side stood a gentleman, whom Valentine recognised as an eminent surgeon of the city, and on the other a priest. At a small table near the window, sat a grave, elderly man, in the costume of a justice of peace; and beside him, one younger, apparently his clerk, before whom were materials for writing. Two women, and the men who had pursued and brought him back from the fields, were also present.

"The chair in which Valentine had been conveyed up stairs was set down at the foot of the bed, amidst a general silence that bespoke the awe and wonder of the assistants. Every eye was turned towards him, and amongst them the glazed and lustreless orb of the apparently dying man. As he gazed on the features of the amazed and agitated youth, a faint and transitory flush passed over the blood-forsaken cheek, and for a moment the dead eye shone with an unnatural light; slowly and with difficulty he raised his feeble arm, and pointing his fore finger to Valentine, he exclaimed, 'That is the man!'

"'Bring him forward!' said the justice, and they lifted the chair and placed it nearer to the table. 'Now, sir,' continued he to the sick man, 'are you prepared to swear that that man is your assassin?'

"'I am,' replied the other.

"'Good heavens! sir,' eagerly interrupted Valentine.

"'Silence!' ejaculated the magistrate, 'and wait till you are interrogated. Write down, Bontems,' addressing the clerk, 'that the accuser swears to the identity of the criminal;' and then turning to Valentine, he inquired his name and address.

"'My name is Valentine Clerk, and I am employed in the office of Monsieur Le Moine, who resides in the Rue de Mousseline,' replied the prisoner.

"'That is true,' said the surgeon; 'I recognise the young man's face.'

"The justice then turning to Valentine, urged him, according to the then custom of French criminal jurisprudence, to make a confession, since the circumstantial evidence against him was so clear, that there could be no doubt of his guilt.

"'If by a confession you mean a relation of the events of the past night,' replied Valentine, 'and of the circumstances that have placed me in a situation I am quite at a loss to comprehend, I will willingly give you all the information I am able; and I trust, strange as it may appear, that you will listen without prejudice to my story. And you, sir,' he added, turning to the sick man, 'I beseech you to pause before you swear away the life of an innocent person. You are, perhaps, on the threshold of the grave yourself —do not, in your eagerness for vengeance or for justice, drag a victim with you thither, who, as he stands beside you, before the throne of the Almighty, will prove your last words to be a lie.'

"After this appeal to the consciences of his accuser and his judge, the young man recapitulated every circumstance that had occurred, from the summons of the stranger up to the moment of his being discovered in the ditch; but he had the mortification of perceiving that he was listened to by all parties with a perfect incredulity, which the examination of the witnesses that followed had no tendency to dispel.

"The two women-servants declared that no one slept in the house but themselves and their master; that he had gone to bed well on the preceding evening; that the house-door was shut, but not locked, and could not have been opened from without, but by picking the lock; the lock was picked; they had heard nothing unusual during the night; and the first that came down-stairs in the morning had stopped at her master's room to awaken him, as was customary; that on finding the door locked, she had called her fellow-servant, and searched vainly for the key; that they had first supposed it was their master that was speaking to them; but that on finding the house-door ajar, they were satisfied some one had got in during the night; and they had therefore both ran off to the town instantly for assistance, neither having courage to stay behind.

"The police officers then related how, on receiving the summons, they had hastened to the spot, and broken open the bed-room door; that there were evident marks of an attempt to force the lock, and part of the blade of a clasp-knife was found on the floor.

"Here the clerk interrupted the evidence to suggest that the prisoner should have been searched at the commencement of the investigation. This omission being repaired, they found on Valentine's person a purse, containing a few francs, a silk pocket-handkerchief, a note-book, containing memoranda of the business he had to do, and a clasp-knife, the broken blade of which exactly fitted the fragment the officers had picked up.

"Though Valentine had himself avowed his attempt to make his escape by picking the lock, yet, on the adjustment of the fragments, everybody in the room looked at one another triumphantly, and seemed to consider this coincidence as the indisputable condemnation of the prisoner.

"The officers then continued to say, that they had found no one in the room but the gentleman in the bed, who had desired them instantly to pursue the assassin, who had escaped by the window, which was open, and to fetch a surgeon; and concluded their evidence, by relating how they had found the prisoner hiding himself in a ditch.

"'Hiding myself!' exclaimed Valentine, indignantly. 'Look at this swollen limb, and you'll have no difficulty in conceiving why I was found in a ditch.'

"'Doubtless,' rejoined Bontems, the clerk, 'it was very unfortunate; but for that you might have escaped altogether.'

"'It was a special providence,' said the priest. 'The guilty man caught in the Almighty's snare!' and he crossed himself devoutly at the idea of this signal instance of Divine intervention.

"'Now, then, Monsieur Bruneau,' said the justice, turning to the wounded man, 'we shall be happy to hear your account of the affair. Imprimis, did you ever see the prisoner before?'

"'Never, till I saw him in my room last night,' replied Bruneau.

"'Did you see him enter it?' asked the justice.

" 'No,' returned Bruneau. 'I was asleep. It was the blow
which inflicted this wound (and he opened the bosom of his shirt
as he spoke, and displayed the bloody bandages that crossed his
breast,) which first awakened me; but I believe I fainted instantly.
When I came to my senses, I found myself bathed in blood, and
my first thought was to try and ring the bell. But when with
difficulty I had raised myself in the bed for that purpose, and
drawn aside the curtain, I saw the window open, and a man
apparently endeavouring to make his escape by it. I fancy it was
the cool night air from the open window that had recalled me
from my swoon. I believe he heard me move, for he turned suddenly round, and it was then for the first time my eye fell upon
the face of the prisoner. The fright and the exertion together
overcame me, and I fainted again. When I recovered the second
time, hearing the breathing of the assassin near me, and fearful
that if he found me alive, he might be tempted to complete his
work, I lay as silent and motionless as I could till I heard and
saw him escape by the window. Then I made another attempt
to ring the bell, but found the cord had been cut away, and that
it was out of my reach.'

" 'Which indicates premeditation and malice aforethought on
the part of the prisoner,' said the clerk.

" 'Can you form any idea of his motive for the crime?' asked
the justice.

" 'None, unless it be robbery,' returned Bruneau, 'as I never
heard of his existence before.'

" But not only was there nothing suspicious found upon Valentine, but, on examination, no indications of robbery, nor of an
intention to rob, could be discovered.

" 'Can you recollect any enemy who might have hired him to
commit the act?" inquired the justice.

" 'None,' returned Bruneau.

" 'Or any one who has an interest in your death?'

" A strange spasm seemed for a moment to convulse the features of the wounded man at this question; but he answered as
before, 'None.'

" Nothing more could be elicited, and here ended the investigation for the present. Valentine's appeals for justice and asservera-
tions of innocence, passed quite unheeded; and, indeed, he was
so overpowered himself by the body of circumstantial evidence
that had been brought against him, that he could scarcely expect
his accusers should listen to him; nor was he surprised to hear
the magistrate directing his clerk to draw up his committal, and
forthwith see him conducted to the gaol.

" Whilst the committal was preparing, the surgeon humanely
administered some relief to his hurt leg, the torture of which, but
for the greater torture of his mind, would have been almost insupportable. But the greater evil somewhat subdued the less.
His thoughts were so bewildered and distracted by the strangeness of his situation, that they could grapple with nothing—not

even his acute bodily pain could fix them; and he was placed in
a chair, and carried through the streets to prison, in a state of
unconsciousness almost amounting to an annihilation of the
faculties.

"'It is a very singular case!' said the justice, as he arose from
his seat, after Valentine was carried away—'One can hardly doubt
the young man's criminality—and yet—!' and he raised his
shoulders to his ears.

"'The evidence is certainly strong—but still—' said the surgeon, imitating the gesture of the justice.

"'If that man is not guilty,' said the clerk, striking the table
with his knuckles, 'I never saw a criminal!'

"'Gentlemen,' said the priest, as he crossed himself devoutly,
'behold the finger of God!'

"'What a pity!' said the women, walking away, arm-in-arm—
'he is really a pretty young fellow!'

CHAPTER XVIII.

CONTINUATION OF THE STORY OF JULIA'S PARENTS.

"It was not till towards mid-day, that, by the arrival of Bontems, and an officer, to search Valentine's chamber for proofs of
his criminality, Julie learned he was thrown into prison, for
having, on the preceding night, attempted to assassinate a gentleman of the name of Bruneau.

"'He has a daughter, that Monsieur Bruneau?' inquired she,
eagerly.

"'No,' replied Bontems, 'I believe not.'

"'A niece, then? or perhaps a wife? Some female connexion
living with him?'

"'Certainly not living with him,' replied Bontems. 'He is an
elderly man, and has no one in the house but two maid-servants.'

"'Mr. Valentine is a very respectable young man,' said Julie,
whose jealous ire was quelled by this last assertion of the clerk's.
'It is impossible he can be guilty. What motive could he have?'

"'That remains to be discovered,' returned Bontems. 'My
opinion is, that he has been an agent for somebody else.'

"'Bah!' cried Julie, indignantly. 'Valentine act the part of a
hired assassin! It would be easier to believe he did it on his own
account, than that. But what does he say himself?'

"'Ah! that will come out on the trial,' answered the cautious
Bontems.

"'I must know before that,' thought she: and equipping herself
in her bonnet and shawl, she started for the prison.

"'I don't know whether I ought to admit you, my pretty lady,'
said the gaoler; 'but as no orders are yet given to the contrary,

I'll venture to do it,' and he conducted her to Valentine's cell. There, with his elbows resting on his knees, and his head on his hands, she found the unhappy young man.

"'Julie!' cried he, starting, as he raised his head and saw who it was; 'is it possible I see you here?'

"'Certainly,' said she, calmly seating herself by his side on the ground. 'Do you not need assistance?'

"'What assistance can you give me, Julie?' said he, kindly, affected by her devotion.

"'We shall see,' replied she; 'time will show that. Meantime, tell me your story. You are innocent?'

"'As you are yourself,' returned he. 'But the evidence against me is so circumstantial that I see no possibility of justification.'

"After detailing to her all the occurrences of the night, 'You see,' he continued, 'all my chance of safety rests on the discovery of the stranger who fetched me. But what hope is there of that? I can give no clue; I should not know him if I met him in this room, for I never saw his face. It is not likely he'll come forward of his own accord, for he must doubtless either be the assassin himself, or be connected with him. No, there is no hope!' cried he, giving way to his despair; 'I must die the death of a murderer, and leave a blasted name behind me.'

"'You must depart immediately, madam,' said the gaoler, interrupting them; 'orders are arrived that no one is to be admitted to the prisoner.'

"'Adieu,' said Julie, as she took her leave, 'and trust to me.'

"All the circumstances Valentine had related corresponded so exactly with what she had herself witnessed, that she never doubted for a moment the truth of his story; but she saw that her evidence would tend nothing to his exculpation, although she were to brave the exposure of her motives by coming forward to give it. 'I must discover this man,' said she to herself, as she mused on the means of extricating Valentine; 'and then, then perhaps—if I could be the means of saving his life—myself—by my own courage and address—who shall say what might follow?'

"'Madeleine,' said she, shutting herself into her chamber with her confidante, 'I have a project in hand in which you must assist me.'

"'Well, mademoiselle,' said Madeleine, 'what is it?'

"'I want a suit of boy's clothes that would fit me. How can I get them?'

"'Boy's clothes!' said Madeleine; 'why, let us see. Mr. Valentine's would be too large, though he's not very big either, Monsieur Valentine.'

"'Much too large,' replied Julie; 'besides, I should prefer a more ordinary suit.'

"'Ah!' cried Madeleine, clapping her hands together, 'I've got it—you shall be a footman.'

"'A footman! The very thing!' replied Julie. 'Where can I get a livery?'

"'At my aunt's,' returned Madeleine. 'There's a little rogue there—he was page to Madame la Comtesse de Rodement, but he was turned off for his tricks, and he is lodging at our house. He has two suits, and no doubt will be glad enough to lend you one for a trifle.'

"'Go, then, directly,' said Julie, 'and fetch it, for there is no time to be lost;' and away went Madeleine, the interval of whose absence Julie employed in cutting off her hair.

"'Ah!' cried Madeleine, when she returned, staring at her; 'what a pity! all your beautiful hair!'

"'Never mind,' said Julie; 'what does it signify? It will grow again. You must cut it closer behind for me still, or it may spoil all.'

"'Oh, this love, this love!' said Madeleine, as she unwillingly clipped away the hair that Julie had not been able to reach. The page's suit fitted quite well enough for Julie's purpose, and when fully equipped she looked like a smart lad of fifteen or sixteen.'

"'Now,' said Julie, 'if I don't return to-night, or even to-morrow, you have no occasion to be alarmed. I am not going into any danger, I assure you; and if any one inquires for me, say I am gone to stay a few days with my aunt.'

"'Very well,' replied Madeleine, 'I will. But good heavens!' she exclaimed, as the suspicion struck her, 'you're not going to shut yourself up with Mr. Valentine in the prison!'

"'Not I,' said Julie. 'What good would that do?'

"'For you know, mademoiselle,' said Madeleine, 'that a young man will be a young man, whether he's in prison or anywhere else; and although you will be dressed as a boy, you will be a young lady all the same.'

"In spite of her eagerness to commence her enterprise, Julie had to wait upwards of an hour before she dared venture into the street; for till the evening had closed in she did not think it prudent to risk the chance of being seen to leave the house by her neighbours and acquaintance, lest any suspicion should be awakened; besides that, being a novice in her part, she preferred making her first appearance by candle-light. As soon, however, as the dusk of the evening gave her confidence, manfully she sallied forth, and took her way towards the little inn to which she had followed the stranger the night before.

"'May I come in?' said she, stepping into a small room or kitchen on the right of the passage, the door of which was ajar, and from which voices were heard to proceed—'may I come in?' and she took off her hat with a boyish grace that gave good earnest of her abilities for the part she had undertaken.

"'Come in, come in, my pretty youth,' said a withered, haggish-looking old woman, with an array of wrinkles that none but an old Frenchwoman could show, who sat knitting on one side of the large open chimney, where a brisk wood-fire was burning on the hearth; 'come in, you are welcome.'

" 'It rains like the devil,' said Julie, shaking the rain from her hat, considering *the devil* as part of her ' stage directions.'

" 'Make a corner for the youth,' said the old woman to those who sat round the fire—'don't you see he is dripping?'

" The seats were pushed a little aside, and a chair drawn forward for Julie, who had now an opportunity of seeing the faces of the company.

" There was no woman present but the one that had spoken to her, who was evidently the hostess ; the men were six in number, apparently of very low grade, with one exception.

" The first glance convinced Julie that not one of them could be the man she sought, unless it were he who formed the exception. The others had all the air and dress of artisans, mechanics, or labourers, but it would have been difficult to assign to this man his exact position in society. His dress was that of a gentleman, but it occurred to Julie that he was not its first wearer. He sat exactly opposite to the old woman on the other side of the hearth; he appeared quite at home, and it was he who had handed Julie a chair. The hostess called him by the name of Rodolphe; the others addressed him as Monsieur Rodolphe. As she had not seen the face of the stranger she had traced to the house on the preceding night, Julie had nothing to guide her but height, the figure even having been too much enveloped by the cloak to leave her any notion of it: but with respect to height, she thought, when he rose to give her a seat, that there was considerable resemblance.

" 'What weather!' said one of the company, as Julie seated herself.

" 'The vineyards are drowning,' said another, who appeared to be an agriculturist.

" ' We sha'n't get wine for our money, if this weather continue," observed an artisan.

" 'Messieurs,' said the hostess, 'the price is risen already a penny a bottle.'

" ' Worse luck,' exclaimed the last speaker.

" 'Wont you take something?' said the hostess to Julie, ' to keep out the cold? We have good beer, or brandy, if you like it better.'

" ' I should prefer wine,' replied Julie, who comprehended that to say *no*, would spoil her welcome.

" The old woman arose and produced the wine, assuring her that for the price there was none better in Nantes.

" ' Madame et Messieurs,' said Julie, ' will you pledge me?' and after pouring herself out a small quantity, she sent round the bottle, which returned to her emptied of its contents. The evidently favourable impression produced by this liberal proceeding, induced her to call for a second.

" ' Ah !' exclaimed one, 'there is nothing like wine, after all; it warms one's inside.'

" ' When will the moon change?' inquired another.

" ' She is in her last quarter, I think,' said the artisan.

" ' Pardon me,' said the labourer, ' we had a new moon last night.'

" ' A bad beginning,' observed a third, ' for I fancy it rained the whole night.'

" ' By no means,' said Rodolphe, 'you are mistaken, the weather was fine the first part of the night. *The rain began to fall just as the clock struck three.*'

" Julie's heart bounded—' It is him!' she said to herself.

" ' That is the Rodement livery you wear?' said the old woman.

" ' Yes,' said Julie, 'it's the Rodement livery.'

" ' You're in a good service,' added the old woman.

" ' I was,' replied Julie, shrugging her shoulders expressively.

" ' What! have you lost your place?' inquired the hostess.

" ' Worse luck,' said Julie, ' but I hope to get back again.'

" ' What did you do,' said the hostess.

" ' Tricks,' returned Julie.

" ' Bah!' said the old woman, 'young heads! young heads! what can be expected?'

" ' I wonder,' thought Julie, ' if this Rodolphe lives here, or is only a visitor like the rest; for I must, somehow or another, contrive to keep him in view, till I can be sure he is the man I seek.'

" The consequences of making a mistake she saw would be fatal, as it might give the real criminal, whoever he were, time and warning to escape.

" The conversation, after turning on a variety of subjects, was beginning somewhat to flag, when one of the company said, ' What is this story about a murder? does anybody know? I heard some shopman had stabbed his master, and was carried to prison.'

" ' Not his master,' said the artisan, ' a certain Monsieur Bruneau, a gentleman.'

" ' Bruneau!' exclaimed the old woman and Rodolphe at the same moment, in accents of astonishment.

" ' It's not him,' said Julie to herself. ' That surprise is genuine.'

" ' I think that was the name I heard,' said the artisan; ' I was passing the gaol as the criminal was carried in, and I inquired of the people that were standing by, what he had done.'

" ' And what was it?' said Rodolphe and the old woman together.

" ' Broken into the house of this Monsieur Bruneau, as I understood,' replied the artisan, ' for the purpose of robbing him, and meeting with some resistance, he attempted to murder the old gentleman, who, however, succeeded in securing the villain, and kept him fast till the arrival of the police.'

" The eyes of Rodolphe and the old woman met, and astonishment was depicted on the countenances of both.

" ' And this was last night?' inquired Rodolphe.

" ' Yes,' said the artisan, ' they were taking him to prison as I passed to my work this morning.'

"'What sort of person was the criminal?' inquired Rodolphe.

"'A little man—young—perhaps five-and-twenty,' returned the artisan.

"The old woman and Rodolphe were evidently anxious for more information, but nobody present could give any. The conversation, from this, turned upon murders and robberies, and the crimes that had been lately committed, in which the hostess and Rodolphe took very little part, the minds of both, according to Julie's observation, being occupied with what they had heard. She observed several expressive glances pass between them, and after a short time had elapsed, Rodolphe arose, and taking down his hat that was hanging on a peg against the wall, he said he was sorry to be obliged to leave the company, and went out.

"That he was gone for the purpose of investigating the report he had heard, was as evident to her as if he had told her so; and she felt quite satisfied that he not only knew something about Mr. Bruneau, but that he was, on some account or other, particularly interested in the intelligence he had just received. Still, that he was either the criminal, or concerned with him, she doubted. The emotion betrayed both by him and the old woman, was that of surprise, curiosity, and interest; not fear or confusion. But might not that confidence arise from his absolute certainty of not being known, and from his assurance that, by shutting Valentine up in the room with the wounded man, he had effectually shifted all chance of suspicion from himself? But, then, why should he be so astonished at the success of his stratagem; and would he not naturally have contrived some means, in the course of the day, of ascertaining the fate of his victim? Of one thing she felt assured, that she was on the right scent, and that whether the inn was his home or not, that he would return to communicate the result of his inquiries to the old woman; therefore, thought she, 'I must not quit my ground.' But the difficulty was, on what pretence to stay. The rain had furnished a very good excuse for entering; but unless she proposed remaining there all night, it was now time to think of moving—the rest of the company were dropping off one by one, she would ere long be left alone with the hostess. Would she be allowed to stay, too? That was another question, or were there means for her accommodation? Whilst she was pondering on these difficulties, the two last of the party rose to depart.

"'I think,' said one of them, walking to the window, 'the rain is over for the present, and we may take advantage of the opportunity.'

"'Adieu, messieurs,' said the old woman, and she spoke with an alacrity of tone that indicated she was not sorry to be relieved of their presence.

"Julie arose also, and taking up her hat, stood smoothing round the nap, which was ruffled by the rain, with the back of her hand. The men paused a moment, apparently thinking she meant to accompany them, but she seemed intent upon repairing the disarrangement of her hat, so saying once more, 'Adieu, madame! Adieu, monsieur!' they took their leave.

"The old woman raised her eyes from her knitting, and looked at her over her spectacles, as much as to say, 'Well! why don't you go, too?' But Julie stood still by the fire, turning her hat about in her hand, with an air of perplexity and depression.

"'Don't you return to the Countess of Rodement's to-night?' at length said the hostess,

"'Alas! no,' replied Julie.

"'But you have friends?'"

"'I have some,' returned Julie,—'but then—'

"'A mother?' inquired the old woman.

"'Alas! no,' answered Julie, despondingly.

"'How? Is it that you are afraid of your friends' displeasure, when they learn you have been turned away?'

"'That's the truth,' replied Julie.

"'Poor child!' said the old woman.

"'In short,' said Julie, 'to say the truth, I should be glad they did not learn it at all, till I have ascertained whether I have any chance of being reinstated; because, you know, if within a few days I should recover my situation, my friends need never know anything about the matter.'

"'That's true,' said the old woman.

"'If I knew anywhere to go—' continued Julie, hesitatingly.

"'What?—to sleep?'

"'Yes,' replied Julie, 'for a few days.'

"'You have money?'

"'Oh, yes,' returned Julie, 'enough to pay.'

"'You would not like to stay here?'

"'Yes, I should,' said Julie, 'if you have no objection.'

"'None in the world,' returned the hostess. 'Will you have a room to yourself?' continued she, 'that will be sixpence; or if you like to sleep with my son Rodolphe, that will be cheaper.'

"'I should prefer a room to myself,' returned Julie, with an involuntary shudder at the latter proposal—'I have been so long used to lie alone at the countess's, that I fear a companion would disturb me.'

"'As you please,' said the old woman. 'It's the same to me, since our spare room is unoccupied. Last night we had company, and I could not have accommodated you.'

"'Who was that?' thought Julie. 'Was it the person I seek? and where is he now?' She would have been glad to ask some questions about the lodger the old woman spoke of, but she did not know how to manage it.

"'They are mostly travellers, strangers, that you accommodate, I suppose?' she said.

"'Sometimes,' said the old woman, 'but oftener servants out of place, like yourself. Would you like some supper?'

"Julie had little inclination to eat, especially anything she was likely to get there: but her object was to make herself welcome, so she accepted the offer with all the alacrity she could assume.

"'He is your son, then, Monsieur Rodolphe?' said Julie to the hostess, who with more activity than she would have imagined her capable of, was preparing the repast.

"'Yes, he's my son,' replied the old woman; 'my only son.'

"'He is a fine looking young man,' observed Julie.

"'He's well enough,' returned the hostess, as she quitted the room to fetch some eggs.

"Julie felt a great desire to learn what might be the means or occupation that enabled Monsieur Rodolphe to live, and to maintain a style of dress that appeared so inconsistent with the situation of his mother; but she was afraid of giving offence by betraying her curiosity, or of awakening suspicion of her motives, if they really happened to have anything to conceal. However, the old woman seemed disposed enough to give her the information she wanted.

"'Yes, he's well enough, Rodolphe,' said she, as she broke her eggs into the stewpan; 'he was always fond of dress, and ambitious to be a gentleman; and we never could make him take to any trade that soiled his fingers—worse luck! So he has got a little employment in the town—but it's not the way to make money. Better work while he is young and able, than wear fine clothes, and lead an easy life, trusting to other people to keep him when he is old. I have little faith in promises, for my part.'

"'Whatever God's word may be,' returned Julie, 'the word of man is not bread.'

"'That's true,' replied the old woman, nodding her head approvingly; 'and now,' she continued, as she placed an omelette, with some bread and cheese and a bottle of wine, on the table before her guest, 'I'll go and prepare your bed whilst you eat your supper; and accordingly, after selecting a pair of sheets from a cupboard near the fire, she disappeared, and Julie presently heard her foot bustling about above.

"When the young heroine was left alone, she began to review her situation; and it was not without some surprise at her own temerity, that she reflected on the arrangement she had made to sleep under the obscure roof of this old woman, of whose character she knew nothing, and in the near neighbourhood of a man, whom she was by no means certain might not be the assassin she was in search of. Altogether, whether he were or not, her opinion of Monsieur Rodolphe was not very favourable; he had that nondescript sort of air that made it difficult to assign him to any class, and inspired the suspicion that he did not adhere very strictly to the duties of any.

"Of the old woman, however, she thought better. In spite of her haggish exterior, there was a certain degree of frankness and good faith in her manner; and many an honest parent, she reflected, has an idle and good-for-nothing son. It was true, no human being interested in her fate knew where she was; and she might

have disappeared from the face of the earth, if her hosts had a
mind to evil, without leaving a single trace of her destiny behind
her, unless a clue were discovered by her chance association with
the humble companions with whom she had passed the evening.

" 'However,' said she to herself, 'nothing venture, nothing
have! Is it not by the energy and courage I display in his cause,
that I hope to win Valentine's heart? and, after all, probably the
worst I have to fear is bad accommodation and an extortionate
bill.'

" She had just arrived at this comfortable decision, when the
door opened, and a man in a cloak entered, looking so exactly like
the one she was in search of, that she involuntarily started with
surprise.

" ' Don't be alarmed,' said he, throwing off his cloak, 'it's only
me;' and she perceived that it was Rodolphe, who, having made
that addition to his dress after he had left the room, was thus
changed in his appearance.

" ' Pardon me!' said she, endeavouring to assume as much tranquillity as she could, ' I did not recognise you at first.'

" ' It's the cloak,' said he, carelessly. ' Where's my mother?'

" ' Up stairs, preparing a bed for me,' replied Julie.

" ' You sleep here, then?' said he, in a tone that rather indicated
annoyance than satisfaction.

" ' Yes,' returned Julie, ' if you've no objection.'

" ' None at all,' replied he, ' it makes no difference to me.'

" ' He speaks as if he didn't think me worth killing,' thought
Julie; ' there's some comfort in that.'

" ' Will you take a draught of wine after your walk?' said she.

" ' Thank you,' replied he, ' presently,' and quitting the room,
she heard him ascending the stairs, and immediately afterwards
his voice reached her in earnest conversation with his mother.

" A great deal she would have given to overhear the dialogue, of
which she felt quite certain she knew the subject; but although
every intonation of their voices penetrated the rafters that formed
the ceiling of the room she was in, not a single word could she
make out. At length the door above opened, and she heard the
old woman say, 'It's very alarming, at any rate; and if Monsieur
Rodolphe does not send——'

" ' Hush!' said her son, ' we can talk it over by and by.'

" They then descended the stairs, and resumed their places by
the fire with Julie; who again invited them to take a share of her
bottle of wine. She felt a great desire to ask Rodolphe if he had
heard anything about the murder, and was besides particularly
anxious to learn whether Mr. Bruneau was dead, or likely to recover; but her dread of exciting suspicion or resentment, by introducing a subject in which she was assured they were somehow
or other more than commonly interested, made her voice falter
and her heart beat so much whenever she approached it, that she
was constrained to renounce her intention; so she sat slowly sipping her wine, and picking the crumbs of bread off the table-cloth,

conscious that her hosts desired her absence, but feeling every instant an increasing dislike, bordering upon horror, to the idea of retiring to bed under a roof, and amongst strangers, over whom there hung a mystery she could not penetrate. But the conversation flagged—the old woman nodded in her chair, and Rodolphe yawned audibly. 'Bless me!' exclaimed the former, starting out of a doze into which she had fallen, 'what o'clock is it?'

" 'It is very late,' replied Rodolphe. 'Would it be agreeable to Monsieur to retire?'

" 'Certainly,' returned Julie, 'I had really forgotten myself.'

"Upon this, the old woman arose, and lighting a bit of rush-light, said she would have the pleasure of showing Monsieur to his apartment. She accordingly proceeded up the narrow, creaking stairs, followed by her unwilling lodger, whose courage might truly be said to be 'oozing out at her fingers' ends.' On the land-ing-place at the top were three doors, the centre one of which she opened, and introduced Julie to a better apartment than might have been expected. The furniture was humble and coarse, but clean and decent, and, but for the fear that beset her, there was no reason why she might not be reconciled enough to the prospect of passing the night there.

" 'You'll sleep well there, my child,' said the hostess. 'It's a good bed—everybody sleeps well in it.'

"Julie looked sharply at her, for terror made her suspicious, and she thought the words sounded oddly.

" 'Why, now,' said the old woman, who seemed to be struck by her countenance; 'you're not afraid, are you?'

" 'Afraid! Oh, no!' replied Julie, 'what should I be afraid of?'

" 'If you are afraid of sleeping alone, you can sleep with my son,' continued the hostess.

" 'By no means,' replied Julie. 'I am quite satisfied.—Do you sleep near me?'

" 'I have a little closet close to you—here on the right,' said she, pointing to one of the doors, 'and Rodolphe, my son, sleeps on the other side of you. Oh, you'll be quite safe—fear nothing.'

" 'I shall sleep like a dormouse,' returned Julie, wishing to ap-pear at ease.

" 'To be sure you will,' replied the hostess, with a chuckling laugh, that seemed to Julie's excited nerves to carry some strange and sinister meaning with it; and, wishing her good-night, the old woman descended the stairs. As soon as she was gone, Julie's first impulse was to look under the bed, and examine the walls of the room, lest there should be any closet or secret door, but there was nothing to alarm her; and the only thing she discovered, which she had not observed on her first entrance, was a small portmanteau which stood on the floor in one corner.

"As nothing was unimportant to her in her present situation, and she could not tell what slight tokens might put her on the right track, and forward the object for which she was encountering so much an-noyance, she took her rushlight to examine it. It proved to be a

small black leathern portmanteau, just sufficient to carry a change
of linen, and the few articles for the toilet a gentleman might require in an expedition of a few days; it was locked, and on the
top were the initials, *R. B.* ' *R. B.*,' thought she—' that may be
Rodolphe something'—for she did not know the second name of
the persons under whose roof she was—' it is most likely his, as he
is so fine a gentleman. Well, I suppose I must go to bed—I wish
they would have let me sit below all night—I did not feel half so
wretched there in the chimney corner, with the bright fagots
blazing; but there's something terrific in a bed when one's frightened; it looks like a grave. However, I wont undress; I'll just
lie down in my clothes, so that if there's any alarm, I could be
ready to show myself in a moment.'

"There was a rude wooden bolt to the door, which she drew,
though without much reliance on its efficiency: it was enough for
honest people, but it would have made a feeble defence against
force. Just as she was about to lie down, another thought struck
her—' I shall presently be in the dark, and as I am sure I shall not
sleep, that will add greatly to my terrors.' It was but a few inches
of rushlight the old woman had given her, and that was fast burning down to the socket: so she drew back the bolt again, and
opened the door, resolved to go down and beg for more light from
those whom she still heard talking below. As she had taken off
her shoes preparatory to stretching herself on the bed, her step
was noiseless, and seemed to cause no interruption in the conversation between mother and son; and she was just placing her foot
on the first stair, when the words *Monsieur Rodolphe* again caught
her ear, but this time it was in the voice of her son.

" ' Again Monsieur Rodolphe,' thought she—' then this is not
Monsieur Rodolphe, or there are two,'—and she crept down a few
stairs more, as softly as she could.

" ' I admit I can't comprehend it,' she heard the old woman say;
' the thing's incomprehensible, but I'm not the less convinced that
my apprehensions are well-founded. He falls upon us here as if
he came down the chimney; nobody knows how or why, with a
cock-and-bull story, that means nothing—it's true I had my own
notions—I thought it was somebody—some intrigue or another,—
and then he's off again like the cork from a bottle of champagne.'

" ' But what should he have to do with this young Englishman?'
returned the son. ' I'm satisfied he knew no such man.'

" ' How can you tell that?' rejoined the mother—' you think
you're in all his secrets—but I doubt it.'

" ' We shall see,' replied Rodolphe; ' for doubtless the youth,
being taken, will confess everything when brought to trial. He
wont die with closed lips.'

" ' Not he,' returned the old woman: ' why should he? He'll
lose his recompence and his life—he'll have a good right to cry
out.'

" ' It appears to me,' said the son, ' that be the truth what it
may, it is of the last importance that we should inform Monsieur
Rodolphe of the capture of the young Englishman.'

" 'By no means,' replied the old woman, emphatically; 'are you going to involve *your*self in the business? Haven't you got the eyes of the police upon you already? Besides, where is he? Most likely not at home; and into whose hands might the letter fall? No, no; take my advice, know nothing, ask nothing, tell nothing. No one knows he was here but himself and us. None else need ever know it. The youth must die—he has but his deserts. Monsieur Rodolphe, doubtless, will take care of himself, and keep out of the way—if not, what do I care! I have had trouble enough about him, and through his means; and shall still, I dare say. Apropos! I wish he had taken his portmanteau away with him!'

"At this moment, Julie's rushlight, which, as her room door was open, afforded her some light, flickered and went out; and the darkness she was in was only relieved by the faint glimmer that shone through the half-open door below. Without loss of time, therefore, she crept back, and after making a noise with the the bolt sufficient to attract the attention of the speakers, she called out from the top of the stairs that her light was out, and begged for another.

" 'What!' cried the old woman, who ascended to her with a candle,—' you are not undressed yet?'

" 'No,' replied Julie; 'I sat down to think of my troubles, and to consider what I should do to get back to my situation again.— I believe I had fallen half asleep, when I was aroused by the light going out. But now I shall go to bed directly.'

" 'Go to bed, to be sure,' returned the old woman. 'Sleep, child, by night, and think of your troubles by day.'

"And Julie did go to bed, and to sleep too. She had heard enough to satisfy her of her own safety, and to convince her that she was on the right track, and had a very fair prospect of saving the life and the honour of the man she loved,—' and surely,' thought she, as she closed her eyes,—' he will love me, when he hears all I have done for him; he'll forget Aurore;—that is, he'll write to her and say, 'Mademoiselle, or Madame,—just as it may be, I regret extremely that circumstances of a very particular nature—particular nature—will preclude—my having the happiness —to—to unite myself—to you—in—in——' and here her drowsiness overcame her, and she fell fast asleep.''

CHAPTER XIX.

THE STORY OF JULIA'S PARENTS CONTINUED. }

" WHEN Julie awoke on the following morning, her eye immediately sought the portmanteau. 'You are my compass,' said she, as she looked at it, ' and I must not lose sight of you. I wish I could get a peep at the inside—who knows but I might make further discoveries. If I could but learn the name of the owner, it might not be difficult to discover in what relation he stands to

Mr. Bruneau. Bruneau!' she repeated, rising on her elbow as the thought struck her. 'R. B., Rodolphe Bruneau! Oh, heavens! then, perhaps, it's his son! How dreadful, if it be so—and for me to be the means of bringing such a tragedy to light! I tremble at the idea of moving further in the business—and yet Valentine must be saved, and vindicated, be the consequences to others what they may;' and with this determination she arose, and having adjusted her toilet as well as she could by a bit of broken glass that hung against the wall, she descended to the room below.

"Rodolphe was not to be seen; but the old woman was busily engaged preparing coffee for two of the men who had been there on the preceding evening.

" 'Ah, good morning, Monsieur!' said they on Julie's appearance, 'what! you have passed the night here?'

" 'And slept well, I hope,' added the hostess.

" 'Never better,' returned Julie. 'Your bed is a capital one.'

" 'Shall I give you some coffee?' said the old woman.

" Julie accepted the offer; and a basin of coffee with a slice of bread being placed before each of the party, they sat amicably sipping their breakfast around the hearth.

" 'Is there anything new this morning?' inquired Julie of the artisan.

" 'Nothing, that I have heard,' replied he.

" 'Nothing more about the assassination you mentioned last night?' said Julie: and before the words had passed her lips, she repented of her rashness, and resolved to allude to the subject no more: for she was conscious of blushing, and felt that the old woman's eye was upon her.

" 'Only that the assassin is an Englishman,' replied the artisan, 'and supposed to be the agent of another.'

" Her fear of exciting suspicion induced her to turn the conversation after this, and the subject was introduced no more. The men soon took their leave: other parties dropped in, and took their morning refreshment of a basin of coffee, and departed in their turn; whilst Julie still sat in the corner of the chimney, not knowing very well what to do next.

" In the first place she had a great objection to going out, and walking the streets whilst the daylight lasted, in her present attire; and in the second place, she was terribly afraid of losing sight of the portmanteau. On the other hand, sitting there all day might appear strange, and excite surprise; besides that, she was anxious to set on foot some inquiries about Mr. Bruneau and his connexions, which might forward her discoveries. But irresolution and fear conquered, and still she sat on; gazing into the fire, and feeling, rather than seeing, the glances of wonder and curiosity that the hostess cast upon her, ever and anon, as she passed backwards and forwards about her avocations.

" 'What!' said she at length; 'you don't go out, and the sun shining so bright?'

"Julie shook her head sadly, and answered, 'No.'

"'Bah!' said the old woman; 'take courage. You mustn't be cast down. If you have lost one situation, there are others to be had. You should be stirring, and look about you.'

"'So I shall,' replied Julie, 'if I find there are no hopes of getting back to the countess; but the truth is, I have a friend in the family, who is at work for me. To-night, when it is dusk, I shall go out and inquire what hopes there are. If none, I must then turn my thoughts elsewhere.'

"This explanation seemed sufficiently satisfactory, and no more was said on the subject, till about an hour after noon, when a hasty foot was heard approaching, and Rodolphe suddenly appeared, with a countenance that denoted considerable agitation. On seeing Julie, he stopped short at the door, and the words that were on his lips remained unuttered. He was evidently annoyed, and beckoning his mother into the passage with an impatient gesture, Julie heard him say, 'What! is that young jackanapes going to stay here all day?'

"'Never mind,' answered his mother; 'what does it signify? He has his reasons, poor child. But what's the matter?'

"'He is dead!' returned Rodolphe.

"'Jesu Maria!' exclaimed the old woman; 'is it possible?'

"After this the conversation was carried on in a lower key, and Julie only caught a few words here and there; amongst which, *Monsieur Rodolphe*, however, frequently recurred.

"The Monsieur Rodolphe of the inn dined at home with her and his mother. The meal passed in silence, except that now and then an ejaculation would burst unconsciously from the old woman, the offspring of her disturbed thoughts; whilst the son sat in gloomy abstraction, eating mechanically, without seeming to know what he was about, and only awakening from his reverie to cast, ever and anon, an impatient glance at Julie, whose absence would, evidently, have been much more agreeable than her company.

"The dinner over, after some further private colloquy with his mother, he departed; and when the evening arrived, Julie took up her hat, and telling the hostess she was now going to ascertain what chance she had of recovering her situation, and that she should return to sup and sleep, she sallied into the street.

"Her first business was to direct her steps homewards, in order to relieve the anxiety she did not doubt Madeleine was feeling, and to learn if there were any tidings of her father's return.

"'Oh, gracious!' cried Madeleine, as soon as she saw her, 'what a night I have passed! Do you know, that if you had not come back before midnight, I had resolved to go to the police, and send them in search of you.'

"'Beware of doing any such thing,' returned Julie. 'For my part, I have passed the night in a comfortable bed, and, I believe, under an honest roof, to which I am about to return. But those with whom I am lodging believe me to be what I appear, the

Countess of Rodement's discarded servant. Had they the slightest
suspicion of my disguise and of its motives, I cannot tell what
danger I might incur. I charge you, therefore, comply strictly
with my directions. I will return here every evening when it is
dark. If, however, three evenings should elapse without your
seeing or hearing from me, I shall give you leave to go to the
police, tell all you know of the causes of my disappearance, and
add, that all the information you can give to aid their researches,
is, that they may seek me at Monsieur Rodolphe's.'

" ' Stay,' said Madeleine, ' let me write that down.'

" ' There is no letter, nor tidings of any sort,' continued she, in
answer to Julie's inquiries; ' no one has been here but people to
the office. I have asked everybody for news of Mr. Valentine,
but can learn none. Being a foreigner, nobody seems to be
interested about him. Ah! by the by, I had forgotten,—there
was a young lady here last night—'

" ' A young lady!' exclaimed Julie; ' was she handsome?'

" ' Yes, she was,' returned Madeleine,—' a pretty, fair girl—'

" ' Fair, was she?' said Julie.

" ' Yes,' replied Madeleine,—' with light hair and blue eyes—a
mild, gentle, little creature—she wept bitterly, poor thing—'

" ' Ah!' said Julie, ' she'll weep, but she'll do nothing. But
what did she come for?'

" ' Simply to learn what we could tell her of Mr. Valentine.'

" ' But you could tell her nothing?'

" ' Nothing, but that he was imprisoned for an assassination,
which she knew before. Then she asked if she could see Monsieur
Le Moine, but I said he was from home; so she went away in
tears. Poor little thing!'

" ' Never mind her,' said Julie. ' But, Madeleine, where is my
father's little portmanteau? did he take it with him?'

" ' No,' replied Madeleine; ' he took the large one—the little
one is here.'

" ' Then fetch me the key of it,' said Julie.

" This done, Julie, having repeated her cautions and directions
to Madeleine, bade her good night, and took her way to the prison,
where she rang the bell, and begged to speak to the gaoler. The
man who had let her in the day before presented himself at the
gate, but he said all access to the prisoner was forbidden. ' But
you could take a message?' said Julie, slipping a piece of money
into his hand.

" ' Perhaps I might,' replied the gaoler, with a nod.

" ' Listen,' said Julie, in a low voice: ' I am page to a great
lady—a very great lady,' and she placed her finger on her lip, to
imply that there was a secret—' you understand?'

" The gaoler nodded his head significantly.

" ' If,' continued she, ' you treat your prisoner well, she will
remember you. In the meantime, tell him to keep up his spirits.
That those are at work for him that know he is innocent, and who
will not rest till they have brought the guilty to justice.'

"'With all my heart,' returned the gaoler; 'there is no harm in telling him that.'

"'None,' replied Julie; 'so good night. We shall rely on you. But, by the by, I forgot: has any one been here to see him?'

"'Yes,' answered the gaoler; 'there was a handsome young lady here.'

"'But she did not see him?'

"'Yes, she did,' answered the gaoler.

"'A fair girl, was she?' inquired Julie, eagerly; 'little, too.'

"'No, no,' returned the gaoler; 'a handsome brunette, tall and well made.'

"'Perhaps it was yesterday,' said Julie, beginning to perceive it was herself he spoke of.

"'Yesterday,' answered the gaoler, 'before orders came to admit nobody.'

"'Any one else?' asked Julie.

"'There came a man here last night,' replied the gaoler, 'to make inquiries who the prisoner was—his name, and where he lived, and so forth.'

"'A man in a blue mantle?' inquired Julie.

"'Exactly,' answered the gaoler; 'in a blue mantle, and a hat low on his brow. I couldn't distinguish his face.'

"'Adieu, and remember!' said she, as she turned away, adding to herself, 'that was Monsieur Rodolphe.'

"At that moment she heard a voice behind her say, 'Yes, it's him, assuredly. One can't mistake the livery.'

"She looked back to see who the words proceeded from, and caught a glimpse of two men crossing the street, but the imperfect light did not permit her to distinguish who they were.

"'Heaven forbid it should be Monsieur Rodolphe!' said she; but she did not think it was. Certainly, neither of the persons wore a cloak, nor did it appear to be his voice. 'Now to visit Monsieur Bruneau's,' she added, and forthwith directed her steps to the scene of the mysterious murder.

"'I am sent,' said she, her summons on the bell being answered by a female servant, 'to inquire how Monsieur Bruneau is.'

"'He's dead, poor man,' answered the woman, shaking her head. 'He died this morning from the effects of his wound—or rather from the fright; for the doctor says that the wound was not mortal, but that the terror, and getting no assistance for so many hours, has killed him.'

"'Poor man!' exclaimed Julie. 'How sorry my mistress will be!'

"'She knew him, your mistress?' said the woman.

"'Intimately, I believe,' replied Julie; 'at least, I judge so, from the concern she expressed. Ah! by the by, she also desired me to inquire about Monsieur—Monsieur—something Bruneau—Goodness me! I forget,—but it must be his son, I fancy.'

"'He has no son,' answered the woman. 'His nephew, perhaps, Monsieur Ernest.'

" 'That was not the name,' replied Julie—who felt that, some-how or other, there was such a mystery attached to the awful name of Rodolphe, that she could hardly shape her lips to bring it out. ' No,' said she, musingly, as if trying to remember, 'I'm sure that was not the name—is there not another—a Monsieur—Monsieur—Rodolphe.'

" 'I know of no other,' returned the woman. 'It must have been Mr. Ernest you were told to inquire for. He is sent for, and will be here to-morrow, we expect.'

" Julie's efforts to extract any information more to her purpose proved quite ineffectual—it was evident the woman told all she knew, and that she knew nothing likely to be of any service; so there was nothing left, for the present, but to return to the inn, and follow out her perquisitions there.

" Some of the visitors of the preceding evening were already seated round the hearth; and the old woman, who received her cheerfully enough, placed a chair for her in the corner as before. She had scarcely, however, thrown off her hat, and taken pos-session of it, before Monsieur Rodolphe entered the room. His eye darted on her with a scrutinizing glance, as he advanced and took his seat beside her; and there was that in his countenance that made her think of the words she had heard whilst she was talking to the gaoler. Her heart quailed at the possibility of his having overheard the conversation, and she turned away her face, that he might not read the confusion she was conscious it betrayed.

" The first words that were addressed to her were not calculated to diminish it. 'It was you, I think, we saw talking to some one at the prison gate as we came along,' said one of the men to her.

" ' Me? no,' said she, with as much firmness as she could com-mand; ' I have not been in that quarter.'

" ' That's odd !' said the man ; ' I could have sworn it was you.'

" ' And I too,' rejoined another.

" ' The livery perhaps deceived you,' said she ; ' but the countess has more pages than one.'

" ' No doubt that was it,' returned the man, appearing satisfied with the explanation.

" Julie stole a glance at the old woman, who went on knitting her stocking, seeming to take no notice of what had been said; but as Monsieur Rodolphe sat beside her, she could not look at his face without turning her head directly towards him, which she had not courage to do. However, he said nothing—indeed, he seemed, as far as she could judge of him, to be habitually a silent and abstracted man, and on this evening he was more than usually taciturn. She was silent, too, from anxiety, and the fear that she felt returning as night approached, and the mystery thickened round her. She called for wine, and shared it with the company as she had done the night before; the strangers and the old woman chatted familiarly over theirs, whilst she sipped hers, with her looks fixed on the log of wood that smouldered on the hearth; and ever and anon catching, from the corner of her eye, a side view of Monsieur Rodolphe's legs, which were stretched out and crossed before him in an attitude the immobility of which, combined with his rigid silence, filled her with awe.

"She felt a growing inclination to throw up her enterprise, and leave the house at once; but she had not courage to announce a resolution that, from its suddenness, must appear strange, and excite curiosity. She was yet meditating on the possibility of taking her departure with the other visitors, when they rose and took up their hats; she advanced to the table where her own lay, when she recollected that the preliminary step to going away was to pay her bill, and before she could have done that, or even have learned its amount, the strangers were gone, and she found herself alone with the mother and son.

"'Shall I get you some supper?' inquired the old woman.

"'Certainly,' answered Julie, with assumed cheerfulness; 'I am exceedingly hungry.'

"'And have you good news?' rejoined the hostess. 'Will the countess receive you again?'

"'I think she will,' returned Julie; 'I am to hear positively to-morrow.'

"'That's well,' said the old woman; 'I wish you joy;' and she broke her eggs, and tossed up her omelette, and spread her table, every now and then uttering an ejaculation, as she stumbled over Monsieur Rodolphe's extended legs; whilst he sat with his hands in his pockets, his lips compressed, and his eyes as fixed as if he were in a cataleptic fit; Julie the while walking about the room, catching stolen glances at his portentous face, wondering how she was to swallow the supper with a throat as dry as a dusty road in August; and, in spite of love and jealousy, ardently wishing herself safe at home with Madeleine.

"Many's the time that love has conquered fear, even in the most timid breasts, as it had thus far done in poor Julie's—she must be forgiven if fear for a short time gained the ascendant, and the heroine sunk into the woman."

CHAPTER XX.

THE STORY OF JULIA'S PARENTS CONTINUED.

"IT was on the morning of the fourth day after Julie's visit to Madeleine, the gaol, and Monsieur Bruneau's, as related in the last chapter, that a woman, bathed in tears, as she was described by those who saw her, demanded an interview with the lieutenant of police, and was admitted to the private sanctuary of that astute official.

"From the duration of the audience, her information was judged to be important; the more especially as, when she departed, the lieutenant himself conducted her to the door, and was overheard strictly charging her to observe an inviolable silence

till she heard from him: 'further,' said he, 'you will not come
here by daylight, but in the dusk of the evening, unless the communication you have to make is urgent, and then you will muffle
your head in a shawl, and avoid observation as much as possible.'

"She was no sooner departed than the lieutenant summoned
to his presence a man called Simon, whom he generally employed
on occasions that demanded particular adroitness or sagacity.

"'Do you,' said he, 'know of a house kept by a man called
Rodolphe?'

"'There is no such name in my list,' replied Simon.

"'I was afraid not,' said the lieutenant; 'the name is doubtless fictitious.'

"'May I ask what is the affair in hand?' said Simon.

"'It appears,' returned the lieutenant, 'that five days ago a
young lady—in short, the daughter of the notary in the Rue de
Mousseline, that the Englishman lived with, he who is in prison
for the assassination of Bruneau—'

"'Le Moine,' said Simon.

"'Exactly,' returned the lieutenant. 'Well, it appears that
five days ago this young person left her home in the disguise of a
page—she wore the livery of Rodement, which her servant, the
woman who was here just now, procured for her. On the following evening she returned, charged the servant to make no inquiries
about her, unless three evenings elapsed without her appearing—
that she might then come here and apply for assistance; but that
all the indication she could give was that she was to be sought
at Monsieur Rodolphe's. The woman thinks she would not be
more precise in her information, lest she, the servant, either from
curiosity or apprehension, should follow her to the place of her
concealment, and either betray her, or disappoint her plans.
Finally she went away, taking with her the key of a small portmanteau, and has not since been heard of. The prescribed period
having elapsed, the woman, who is naturally under the greatest
alarm, has come to give information of the circumstances.'

"'Does she know nothing of her motive?' asked Simon. 'Is it
an intrigue?'

"'That is the most curious part of the story,' replied the lieutenant. 'It appears that she is in love with the young Englishman, her father's clerk, and that her enterprise is somehow
connected with the accusation brought against him. The servant
says, that by certain words she dropped, she gathered that she, the
young lady, whose name by the by is Julie—Julie Le Moine, is
not only aware of the young man's innocence, but knows also who
is the real criminal; and it seems that on the night of the murder
she was absent from her home for some hours. The servant does not
know exactly when she went, being herself in bed, but she returned
soon after three o'clock; she then lay down, but arose at dawn
of day, went out again, and was absent about an hour and a half.'

"'That's strange!' exclaimed Simon, knitting his brows.

"'Now,' said the lieutenant, 'the first step is to discover the house she's gone to—probably an inn or public-house; but we must be cautious, for—'

" 'Undoubtedly,' said Simon, filling up the pause of his principal—'for they have probably found out that she knows too much; and if they have not silenced her already—which is to be feared—they will be apt to do it in the panic, if our perquisitions are heard of.'

" 'At the same time,' added the lieutenant, 'there is no time to lose; delay may be as fatal as too much precipitation.'

" 'Trust to me,' said Simon, taking up his hat. 'You'll be pleased to give me twenty francs.'

" The money was given, and Simon took his leave. 'At Mon—sieur—Ro—dolphe's,' murmured he to himself, as he directed his steps to his own lodging, which was hard by, and attired himself in the dress of a mechanic. 'First,' continued he, taking out his list of the numerous public-houses in Nantes, 'it is not *that*—they are honest people—I know them: nor *that;* nor *that;*' and so he ran his finger down the list till he came to the name of Lobau—Jacques Lobau, Rue de Maille. 'Ah,' continued he, 'I'll mark you, Jacques Lobau: I've observed Garnier, the sharper, and others of that fraternity, going in and out of your house very familiarly lately; and on Sunday last I saw Madame Lobau, as she calls herself, in a pair of ear-rings that were never purchased by the sale of sour wine and small beer.—Robineau—Pierre Robineau—a rogue, connected with smugglers and thieves—there's a mark for you, Robineau.—Grimaud—Mother Grimaud—a good woman, so report says. But stay: didn't I hear she had a son—marker at a billiard-table—a fellow that dressed above his means, and would never settle to anything?—he may demoralize the house; that must be looked to.' And having run through his list, and marked the suspected houses with a cross, Simon sallied forth on his mission of discovery.

" He had not gone far from the police-office, where he had called to ask some questions that had occurred to him with respect to Madeleine's evidence, when he was surprised by seeing advancing towards him the very person—at least, so it appeared to him—that he was in search of, a young lad of about fifteen or sixteen, with dark hair and eyes, and wearing the Rodement livery. The boy advanced straight to the police-office, and entered, followed by Simon, who had turned to watch his motions, and was close at his heels.

" 'I am come to make a complaint to the lieutenant of police,' said the youth.

" 'Then you will come this way,' said Simon, who immediately conducted him into the presence of his chief.

" 'You have succeeded already?' exclaimed the lieutenant to Simon.

" 'I believe so,' replied Simon; 'but it's by accident. I met this young person not a hundred yards from the door.'

" 'I am come,' said the lad, not waiting to be questioned, 'to

complain of a woman who borrowed of me a suit of clothes, for a
few hours, she said; but she has now had them nearly a week,
and I cannot get her to return them, nor give any account of
what she has done with them.'

" 'Ah! I understand,' replied the lieutenant, nodding his head
to Simon, who nodded his in return, as much as to say, he understood too.

" 'The worst of it is,' continued the lad, 'it was my best suit,
and I shall be ruined by the loss of it. The countess, my mistress, who discharged me about ten days ago in a fit of anger,
has agreed to take me back; but if I go without my new clothes,
which had been given me, they will think I have sold them; and
I shall be turned out of the house again, and lose my character
into the bargain.'

" 'I believe,' said the lieutenant, 'I know what is become of
your clothes, and shall probably find means to recover them for
you; at all events, I shall be able to satisfy the countess that your
story is true, and prevent any suspicion attaching to your character from the circumstance.'

" 'If,' said Simon, 'the youth would place himself at my command for a few hours, and abide strictly by my directions, I dare
say we might recover the clothes, and he earn twenty livres into
the bargain.'

" André—which was the name of the young page—willingly
acceded to the terms offered, the lieutenant becoming guarantee
for the payment of the money; and Simon once more set forth on
his expedition, accompanied by his new ally.

" 'All I require of you is,' said Simon, 'that wherever we go,
you speak as little as possible, only corroborating what I say, and
that you permit me to call you *nephew*. Above all, make no
allusion to the loss of your clothes, nor even to your being dismissed from your service; let it simply be understood that you
are in the countess's establishment, and leave the rest to me. I
shall have to call probably at various houses, at each of which I
shall offer you drink; but take as little as possible, lest your
head be affected, and you lose your discretion.'

" These preliminaries being arranged, Simon led the way to the
house of Pierre Robineau, where he found a goodly company,
many of whom he knew to be rogues, drinking, and playing at
dominoes, or morra, and other such games as form the diversion
of the lower classes. Pierre Robineau himself was amongst them,
and Simon fixed his eyes intently on his countenance as he entered
the room, followed by the page. But there was no emotion nor
surprise, nor did the appearance of the youth seem to excite the
slightest attention from any one of the party. 'It is not here,'
said Simon to himself; and having called for a small measure of
beer, they left the house, and proceeded to Jacques Lobau's.
Jacques himself was tipsy, and took little or no notice of them;
but madame, his wife, or who passed for such, fell to ogling the
handsome page, and was evidently bent on making a conquest of

him. She made them more than welcome; and Simon, who felt
satisfied there were no discoveries to be made there, had some
difficulty in getting away, and rescuing his companion from her
civilities.

"In this manner they visited, one after the other, the houses
that Simon thought most likely to be the scene of some mysterious
or illegal proceeding, but so far without the slightest indication of
succeeding in his object. 'Come,' said he, 'we'll try one more,'
and he turned down a narrow street, and entered the house of
Madame Grimaud.

"There was no one in the room but an old woman, who was at
that moment on her knees gathering up with a wooden spoon a
heap of barley seeds which appeared to have been accidentally
spilt on the floor. As she heard the sound of Simon's foot, she
looked round, and seeing, as she supposed, a customer—she said,
'Ah! your pardon, Monsieur, come in, and I shall be at your
service directly—I must just gather up these first, lest they be
trod on.'

"'Permit me to help you,' said André, who at that moment
emerged from behind his companion, and advanced towards her.

"'How!' cried, or rather screamed Madame Grimaud, 'you
have—?' and there she stopped, with her mouth open, and
her eyes fixed on André's face, which evidently puzzled and
confounded her.

"'Ha!' said Simon to himself—'right at last!'

"'Yes,' added he, aloud, addressing the old woman, apparently
willing to finish her interrupted sentence, 'yes, he is a good-
natured lad, my nephew, and not at all proud, although he's in a
high service. He was always taught to respect and assist the aged
—were you not, André?'

"'Yes, uncle,' replied André, as he industriously collected, and
poured into a basin the scattered seeds.

"By this time Madame Grimaud had recovered herself, and
saw her way. She remembered that the countess might have
more pages than one, or that this might be he who had replaced
her late lodger; so the seeds being gathered up, she arose from
her knees, composed her countenance, and inquired their pleasure.

"Simon threw himself into a seat like a man that was tired,
and called for something to drink.

"'I have walked hither,' he said, 'from Rennes to see my
nephew; and I am glad to find myself at my ease in a snug public-
house. Ah! Madame Grimaud,' added he, 'and you don't remember me now?'

"'No,' replied she, looking from one to the other of the visitors,
and visibly perplexed how to conduct herself—'No, I don't know
that I ever saw you before.'

"'I can't wonder at it,' answered Simon, 'for I should not have
known you if we had met under any other roof: but yet I have
drank many a good glass in this room—but it is long ago, before
I went to live at Rennes. And my old friend, Grimaud, how is he?'

"'Ah, you knew him? You knew my husband?' said the old woman, brightening.

"'To be sure I did,' returned Simon. 'How goes it with him?'

"'Ah! he is dead!' said she, shaking her head—'dead these seven years, come Martinmas.'

"'The deuce he is!' exclaimed Simon, with becoming indignation; 'how fast you drop off here! There's my sister, the mother of this child, and her husband gone too; and there's scarcely a person alive that I knew when I left it twenty years ago. And your children—you had children, I think; it appears to me that I remember a little lad—a little black-eyed rogue—?'

"'Yes, I had a son,' returned Madame Grimaud, in a more reserved manner than she had last spoken.

"'Had!' said Simon; 'I hope he is not dead, too?'

"'No—no,' replied Madame Grimaud—'oh, no; he is not dead.'

"'Then he stays to comfort your old age, I hope,' said Simon. 'I suppose he's the landlord, now. I shall be glad to see him.'

"'He has nothing to do with the house,' returned she, drily. 'Neither is he at present in Nantes.'

"'Uncle,' said André, according to the instructions he had received, that whenever he judged from the tone of Simon's conversation, that the object was attained, he was to find an excuse for going away, 'uncle—it is already evening, and I fear my mistress may require my services; I shall be chided if I am absent when she calls for me.'

"'Very true,' said Simon, starting as if suddenly awakened to the propriety of the boy's suggestion—'you had better go home immediately; and I will see you again to-morrow.'

"André took an affectionate leave of his uncle, made a bow to the hostess, and returned to the police office, as he had been previously directed, to communicate the result of their expedition to the lieutenant.

"As the evening advanced, some of the frequenters of the house dropped in, with whom Simon drank and conversed, carefully supporting his character of a stranger; but nothing was said that tended to throw any light on the mystery, except that one of the men inquired of Madame Grimaud if her son was still absent, and another who came in afterwards, repeated the inquiry, but instead of *your son*, said, *Monsieur Rodolphe.*

"When night drew on, Simon said, being tired, he did not wish to look further for lodgings, and proposed sleeping there; but the hostess said she could not accommodate him; so, having waited till the last of the company, he took his leave.

"As he passed up the street, he made signals to three different persons who were separately lounging about within sight of the door; one was a woman, the others had the appearance of workmen. Simon, by calling at a few of the houses where a billiard-table was kept, had no difficulty in ascertaining the one to which Monsieur Rodolphe was attached; and he there learned that the marker had been absent for two days, being, as they understood, summoned to the country by the death of a relation. He next presented himself to the lieutenant.

" ' If Mademoiselle Le Moine is alive, and still in the house,' he said, ' I believe her to be perfectly secure from any extreme violence; the old woman would never sanction anything of the sort. She will perhaps consent to her detention, or to any measures that would not endanger her life or do her bodily harm, if she thinks it necessary to the preservation of her son; but nothing more. But I doubt her being there. From any part of that house, which is very small, she could make herself heard—besides, I was there some time alone with Madame Grimaud, and observed nothing to indicate that there was any other person within its walls. This Rodolphe, who is probably either the assassin of Monsieur Bruneau, or concerned with him, has no doubt, on discovering Ma'm'selle Le Moine's suspicions, made his escape, or concealed himself. But what has become of her? It would be easy to seize the old woman and examine her; but I know them—we shall extract nothing from her that will implicate her son, unless she is certain he is beyond our reach. We can also search the house for the young lady, it's true; but if we raise the alarm, this Rodolphe may slip through our fingers altogether, or he may take desperate means to rid himself of her, in his panic. Altogether it's a ticklish affair.'

" ' The house is watched?' said the lieutenant.

" ' Strictly,' returned Simon; 'no one can go in or out unobserved: and I think I will therefore employ the next few hours in endeavouring to ascertain if any persons answering the description of this Rodolphe have been seen leaving the city. I have contrived to obtain a pretty correct description of his appearance from the billiard-rooms, without exciting any suspicion of my object, and I almost think I could clap my hand upon him if I met him.' "

CHAPTER XXI.

THE STORY OF JULIA'S PARENTS CONTINUED.

" About eight o'clock on the same evening that Simon paid his visit to Madame Grimaud, on the road from Le Mans to Nantes, and about ten miles from the latter city, two horsemen alighted to refresh themselves and their animals, at a small house of entertainment for travellers, whether man or beast, that stood by the road-side. The wayfarers were much of the same height, age, and complexion; and though there was no real resemblance of feature, there was a striking similarity in the appearance of the two men—a similarity which extended to their dress, both as to colour and form, both being wrapped in blue mantles, and wearing slouched hats that hung over their brows. The attire of one of them, however, was much fresher than that of the other, and he might be said to wear it 'with a difference.' To him, also, seemed to belong precedence and sway, his companion falling back to allow him to pass first, and evincing other slight marks of deference and consideration. They declined entering into the public room, but desired to be shown to a private apartment. There they took some slight refreshment, after seeing their horses attended to; and having rested about an hour, they again mounted their steeds, and proceeded on their way.

" 'I perfectly agree with you,' said he who appeared to take the lead, after they had ridden some yards from the inn in silence; 'I wish the thing could be avoided, but it cannot. Self-preservation is the first law of nature. I am quite clear, whatever may be his motive, that if I don't take his life, he'll take mine; and there can be little doubt, that somehow or other, though how I can't imagine, he is in possession of the truth, and has the means to do it. We may lay this salvo to our consciences, that it is not a death of our seeking, but of his own. Had he not thrust his head into our affairs, he might have lived on to the end of the chapter without harm or damage from me. The whole affair, I don't deny it, is unfortunate; and I regret it, from first to last. But since I cannot undo the past, since I cannot retrace my steps, I must wade on. I confess, of the two, I rather pity the other, the lad that's in prison, since his misfortune was not of his own seeking—this foolish boy's is; and he must take the consequences.'

" 'Setting his interest aside,' said his companion, 'and to return to our own; it is certainly peculiarly unfortunate that he was seen by so many people at our house. The livery is remarkable, and if he should have any friends that think it worth their while to inquire for him, he will, doubtless, be traced to my mother's, through the evidence of those men.'

" 'We shall probably be away before any steps of importance are taken, if ever they are,' replied the first. 'According to what you gathered from the countess's porter, he is a young rascal that nobody cares for, and without friends. He has probably some connexion with this English lad; but *he's* bound hand and foot, and will never see daylight again, except it's on his way to the galleys or the scaffold. Besides, when a thing must be done, there's no use in anticipating the consequences, or calculating the difficulties. As I said before, I am sorry; but I have a choice of two evils, and I have not the slightest hesitation as to which I shall select. I prefer my own life to his, twenty to one; and I see no means of securing the one without taking the other—therefore, he must die, and the sooner the better. You will then look to your own safety by instant departure; and I will not fail to meet you at the appointed spot, as soon as I have had time to receive my share of the inheritance, and convert it into money. We will afterwards set out, and range the world together, turning our backs on this cursed city for ever.'

" 'I am of opinion, now,' said the same speaker, when they had reached a spot where the road divided, within two miles of the

city, 'that we should separate, and enter the town by different
avenues. We shall excite less observation. It will also be better
for me to avoid any communication with your house, or even with
you. In short, I—I don't see anything that need keep you here
above an hour—nothing so weak as delay or deliberation in these
affairs—few men would face a battery, if they paused to contemplate the act in all its bearings—so of this, or any other feat that
demands resolution—let it be done, and away. Just send me a
line to the Golden Lion, where I shall put up, to say that all is
right. Not in those terms, though—they're suspicious, if seen or
intercepted—say, ' Sir, the papers you required are safe, and shall
be produced whenever you desire it,' and sign it merely by initials
—not your own though; any others you please. That can lead to
nothing. Thus, if the boy is inquired for, you'll be away, and no
connexion can be traced between us. As for your mother——'

" ' My mother, sir,' said his companion, ' as you well know, will
never say a word to betray either you or me. I own, I—I have
feelings about my mother. She has spoiled me—perhaps ruined
me—at least helped to do it—but I—I couldn't bite off her ear at
the scaffold for all that——' and the voice of the speaker faltered.

" ' You're growing sentimental, friend,' said the superior—
' touching on the confines of the pathetic. Bah! nonsense.—Do
you repent? Do you wish to retract?' continued he, after a pause,
finding his companion made no answer to his last exhortation—
' because if you do, now's your time to say so. Two alternatives
will then remain for me—I must go on, and change places with the
young Englishman; or I must turn my horse's head and get beyond the borders of France as soon as I can—I shall then be condemned in my absence, my flight will confirm the evidence of the
two lads, I shall be outlawed—lose my inheritance, and be doomed
to poverty for the rest of my life. As for you, you'll wear fustian,
and live on onions and black bread for the remainder of yours.
Make your choice.'

" ' I have chosen,' said his companion, doggedly, ' and have no
intention of retracting.'

" ' Good,' replied the other; ' then we will say no more about it.
And now,' continued he, drawing his rein, ' here we will part.
You to your business; I to mine. Let the future be our motto—
Forward! the word; and remember, that the beginning, middle,
and end of our drama must be action—action—action! Adieu!
we meet again at Philippi!'

" ' Adieu!' cried the second, as he turned his horse's head away,
slowly pursuing the right-hand road — ' Adieu!—But for the
future,' and he drew in a long breath—' who can foresee it!'

" ' It's natural—perfectly natural!' murmured the first, turning
round on his saddle to look after him—' he has neither so much to
lose nor to gain as I have. Poor Rodolphe! Besides, he has a
mother, whilst I have not a human being in the world to care for,
or who cares for me, unless it be himself.'

" We will here leave the travellers to pursue their separate ways,

K

and return to the police office, where Simon, fatigued with his peregrinations, arrived about one o'clock in the morning, having spent the intermediate hours in an unsuccessful endeavour to discover whether Julie had been conveyed out of the city. His conclusion, however, was, that she had not; the livery she wore being sufficiently remarkable to have excited attention. But with respect to Monsieur Rodolphe, there was no saying—his appearance being much less distinctive.

" 'There is no intelligence,' asked he, ' of any importance?'

" 'Only that Blase was here just now, to say that a man in a blue cloak and slouched hat was seen to enter Grimaud's house about midnight. He let himself in with a key.'

" 'Was the lieutenant informed of it?' said Simon.

" 'The lieutenant was gone—but Blase says he can't escape them; there are three watching the house; and they will not lose sight of him if he comes out, but will send some one to let us know.'

" 'Good,' said Simon, 'the bird's limed, then; which being the case, I'll take an hour's rest, and a snatch of something to eat, for I'm devilish tired. He has been conveying the girl away somewhere or other,' thought he; 'drowning her in the river, I shouldn't wonder; and now he's returned, thinking all's safe, poor fool! They're always so—they never see an inch before their noses, but walk right into the noose. It's their fate, and they can't help it.'

" It formed part of Rodolphe's plan not to arrive at home till there was a tolerable certainty of his mother not only being in bed, but asleep. It is true, she had lent herself to his plans up to a certain point; but he was certain that her compliance would stop short of any violence being offered to Julie. In short, he could not have proposed such a thing to her. He had won her consent to what she considered only a temporary confinement and inconvenience imposed on the young page, by representing that it was indispensable to the safety of one they both loved—he more than she, certainly: but still there was ' one part of her heart' that would have been sorry for her son's friend and namesake, for he was her foster-child—Rodolphe's foster-brother; and that is a bond of attachment, that amongst the lower orders of Frenchwomen, as with the Irish, is rarely broken. He had caused her much woe, for he it was who had enticed Rodolphe from the sphere and occupations to which by birth he was destined, made him discontented with his home and his fortunes, led him into vice and ill company, and given him habits and desires that could not, in his station, be honestly satisfied; yet she could not learn that his life was in danger, without feeling that she loved him still. His mother had died in her arms within the hour that gave him birth, and up to the age of seven years the children had equally shared in her care and affection. At that period, Rodolphe Bruneau was sent to a distance to be educated, whilst the parents of the little Grimaud proposed to give their son such instruction as accorded with his situation and prospects: but from the moment of the departure of his playfellow and companion, the child pined visibly—he had always been of an unusually grave and taciturn disposition for his age—but now he renounced all diversion, fled from all fellowship, neglected his whip, and his ball, and his hoop, and passed his hours seated on a little stool, in one invariable corner of the room, silent, still, and sad.

"'This will never do,' said Robert Grimaud to his wife, one day, when he had been quietly smoking his pipe in the chimney corner, and contemplating the melancholy child—'the boy will sink into an atrophy—this separation has struck upon his heart. We are not so ill to do but we may afford to give our Rodolphe an education too, as we have no other child; and perhaps make a priest of him, or let him study the law—why not?'

"Madame Grimaud saw no reason why not—the house was then a flourishing concern; her vanity was flattered at the idea of making her Rodolphe a gentleman, and the child was accordingly sent to join his companion. But although Rodolphe Bruneau was educated and maintained with considerable liberality at a distance, he was never suffered to return to Nantes. The late Monsieur Bruneau had had two sisters, on whose male heirs his property devolved, if he himself died without children. Rodolphe was the son of the sister he most loved; but she had made a marriage degrading in itself, and odious in the eyes of her brother, who extended the hatred he felt for the father, to this sole offspring of the inauspicious union. When his age made it necessary for him to choose a profession, the youth selected that of an advocate, whilst his humble and still constant companion fixed on a lower walk in the same line—but the selection was only in word, not in deed. Rodolphe Bruneau was idle, dissipated, and vicious; Rodolphe Grimaud had a morbid craving for excitement, was irresistibly fascinated by gaming of every sort, and never happy when he was away from his friend. Thus they journeyed on the road to ruin together. Grimaud sometimes came back to see his parents, and got what money he could of them: and Bruneau, whenever he was in funds, shared them liberally with his companion.

"At length an awkward transaction in which they were both involved, but the chief discredit of which fell on Grimaud, caused a temporary separation, and an apparent, but *only* apparent alienation. Grimaud returned to his mother, who had by this time been some years a widow, and was reduced to poverty by his extravagance. He got a situation as marker at a billiard-table, the only thing he was fit for, and lodged at his mother's; soothing himself with the prospect of rejoining his friend when circumstances should be more propitious.

"In the meantime, affairs went ill with Rodolphe Bruneau. His uncle turned a deaf ear to his applications for money, and he was without resources. His exigence was so great, that he even ventured to break through the condition upon which maintenance had hitherto been afforded him. He came to Nantes and presented himself to the old man; but so far from the enterprise proving successful, the sight of him seemed only to augment the

K 2

dislike that had been coeval with his birth. He returned with rage in his heart; matters became worse, and he desperate. He was aware that at his uncle's death, the one half of his property must devolve to himself. He arrived suddenly one night at Grimaud's, announcing he was come on business of a very private nature; and having left his portmanteau, [and borrowed a dark lantern, he went out, saying he should return shortly. Some time afterwards, he did return, apparently much agitated, and declaring he had got into a quarrel, and must leave Nantes immediately, lest his uncle should hear he had been there. He started within ten minutes, on foot, leaving his portmanteau behind him. More than that, the Grimauds knew not; but when the story of the assassination reached them, they naturally believed that Rodolphe Bruneau was involved in the guilt, and that Valentine was his agent.

"But it happened, by a singular coincidence, that on the evening Julie called at home to comfort and encourage Madeleine, and for other purposes of her own, that Rodolphe was standing at the window of a gaming-house, exactly opposite, led thither by a certain curiosity to contemplate the house where the young Englishman, who had become so singularly mixed up with the fortunes of his friend, had resided. The glaring colours of the livery caught his eye. He saw her enter—watched her out, and followed her; learned what she had said to the gaoler, who saw no motive for concealing it, pursued her to Monsieur Bruneau's, and easily extracted the same information from the maid. It needed no more to convince him that his friend was in danger; and upon this he acted; placing the page in a durance from which he judged he could not escape; and departing himself in pursuit of Rodolphe Bruneau, whom, however, he met on the road, making his way towards the city, summoned thither by a letter, which informed him of the old man's having been assassinated by an Englishman; and that his presence was necessary to the arrangement of the affairs. On hearing Grimaud's story, he comprehended at once the mistake he had made, and the importance of silencing the page; and was, moreover, extremely anxious to secure, if possible, his share of the inheritance before the trial came on. There was, therefore, no time to lose; and instead of turning back on learning his danger, he only hastened forward with the greater speed.

"In pursuance of his plan to avoid an interview with his mother, Rodolphe Grimaud contrived not to reach his own door till after midnight. He was certain she would long ere that have retired to her bed, and in all probability be asleep; and as she was somewhat deaf, and he had the means of entering the house without her assistance, it was not very likely that his stealthy pace would disturb her slumbers; and it having been agreed between them that no nightly lodger should be harboured during his absence, he had no other interruption to fear.

"The streets were nearly deserted by the time he turned into that narrow one wherein his mother dwelt. One or two persons, apparently hastening to their nightly rest, crossed him as he passed down. Softly, softly, he inserted the key and turned it in the lock—at that moment a man in the dress of a labourer came hastily by—'Can you tell me,' said he, 'if it be past midnight?'

" 'Midnight has struck,' answered Rodolphe.

" 'Good night,' said the man, as he moved on his way, and Rodolphe entered, and gently closed the door. He turned into the room where Julie had first seen him, and which served the purpose both of kitchen and parlour. It was empty, as he expected, and all within the house seemed silent. He took up a piece of wood that lay upon the hearth, and raked back the ashes with which the old woman had covered the smouldering logs to keep in the fire till morning; then he took a rushlight out of a drawer, lighted it, and sat down in his mother's chair. He felt that the deed once done, he must fly, and that all the pause he had was before. He knew that he should never see his mother again, and after some reflection, he resolved to write to her, and leave the letter where she would find it in the morning. So he wrote, not saying why he had returned, nor alluding to Julie; but giving her his last farewell, and bidding her not curse him. Then he arose, made a strong effort to call up the man within him, and cast off the soft-ness that the thought of his mother had gathered round his heart, walked firmly to a drawer where knives were kept, examined them deliberately and artistically, rejected them all, saying—'No, a razor is more sure,' and taking off his shoes, proceeded up stairs to his own bed-room to fetch one. He placed his ear to his mother's door, but no sound reached him: 'She sleeps sound,' he murmured, 'that's well;' and he descended the stairs again. Before he put on his shoes, he passed the razor over the sole of one of them to clean the edge; then he took off his coat, tucked up his shirt sleeves above the elbow, and with a candle in one hand, and the razor in the other, he left the room, proceeded along a narrow passage which led to the back of the house, put the razor into his mouth, and the candle on the floor, whilst he raised a trap-door which formed the entrance to the once well-filled cellar, where they still kept the small quantity of liquors their humble trade demanded. There was a bolt to the trap which should have been drawn—it was not; but Rodolphe's mind was too much absorbed to observe the neglected caution. The panel being raised, a ladder appeared, by which the descent was to be made; but being almost perpendicular, it was necessary to turn round and go down backwards. Rodolphe did so, cautiously and softly, for he would have been glad that his victim were asleep: step by step he descended, the razor still in his mouth, and the candle in his hand —he reached the last round of the ladder; the next step was deeper—he stretched out his foot to place it firmly on the ground —he trod on something—it was not the earth—it gave way beneath his weight—he stooped the rushlight and looked down, and saw he was standing on his dead mother's breast! Horror seized him —he dropped the razor and the light, rushed up the ladder, and fled amain."

CHAPTER XXII.

THE STORY OF JULIA'S PARENTS CONCLUDED.

"CROUCHING in the corner of the cellar, in darkness and in terror, sat Julie, the intended victim. In truth, she had suffered enough within the last few days to have turned many a stronger brain.

"She had gone to bed on the night we last left her, beset with fear from the strangeness of Rodolphe's manner, and yet willing to persuade herself she had no cause, from her confidence in the old woman. Long and earnestly she heard the son and mother talking below—the voices for the most part reached her but faintly; but now and then a sudden burst in a louder key betokened the energy of the debate. But the door of the kitchen being closed, no word passed through the rafters with sufficient distinctness to throw any light on the subject of the colloquy.

"'It cannot be about me,' at length she said. 'They have enough to talk of, there's no doubt of that—and if they had any suspicion, they would surely never let me stay here to be a spy on them;' and, comforting herself with this conviction, she went to bed, but, as she had done the night before, without undressing. 'As I know all I want *now*,' thought she, as she laid her head on the pillow, 'to-morrow I'll go to the police office—tell everything I have discovered, and leave the rest to them.'

"At first she thought she should not sleep; but gradually her eyelids became heavy, her thoughts wandered, and she dozed. A slight sound at her chamber-door aroused her. She lifted up her head, and saw through the wide chinks and seams of the old shrunk wood, that there was some one on the other side with a candle, who with the blade of a knife thrust in, was endeavouring to withdraw the wooden bolt. The feat was soon accomplished, the door opened, and Rodolphe entered the room. Julie started from the bed, trying to make for the door; but he seized her arm with a powerful gripe, and holding the knife he still held in his hand to her throat, he said in a low but firm voice, 'Obey me, and you shall suffer no harm—but if you resist, or seek to raise an alarm, you die!' He next tied a handkerchief over her eyes, and led her down the stairs; at the bottom, the voice of the old woman said to her, 'Fear nothing, you shall not be hurt'—then conducting her along the passage, going himself first, he guided her steps to the bottom of the ladder. There he took off the handkerchief, and repeated his injunctions and threats; whilst his mother went up stairs to fetch the mattress and blankets, which she handed down to him. This done, after making her bed on the ground, they both retired, enforcing again that her life depended on her silence, and, closing the trap-door, left her in darkness and alone. After that, the old woman regularly brought her her food, and seemed willing to relieve her discomforts as much as she could; but though she saw no more of Rodolphe, she never doubted his being in the house—indeed, his mother, at every visit, assured her he was close at hand.

"A few hours before Rodolphe's arrival, when Simon left the house, Madame Grimaud, having prepared Julie's supper, proceeded to descend with it as usual to the cellar. The panel was heavy, and being old and rather feeble, she had always some difficulty in lifting it; but on this occasion, whether from want of caution or want of strength, she let go her hold a moment too soon, and falling forwards into the cellar, pitched upon her head and broke her neck; whilst the trap, dropping back, closed over the scene, before Julie had time to discern who it was that had made this sudden irruption into her prison. At first, she momentarily expected the person, whoever it might be, to speak or stir; but as minute after minute passed, and all remained motionless and silent, fear and surprise grew into horror—she was no longer alone, she knew she had a companion, though to her invisible; who was it? what was it? was the visitor alive or dead? 'Perhaps,' thought she, 'it's a corpse; some murdered bleeding wretch they have flung down here!' and she crawled farther and farther away, and squeezed herself closer and closer to the cold damp wall, her living, creeping flesh scarce less damp and cold than it. From this horrid trance she was at length aroused by the lifting of the trap-door a second time, and seeing Rodolphe slowly descending the ladder with the razor between his teeth. That he came to murder her she felt assured: but in an instant, before she had time to discern the cause of his precipitate retreat, the light was suddenly extinguished, and he was gone. When the house was entered shortly afterwards by the police-officers, the trap was found open; the old woman lying cold and stiff at the foot of the ladder, with the candle and razor beside her; and Julie sitting of a heap, with her face buried in her lap, utterly speechless.

"In the meantime, Rodolphe Bruneau arrived at the Golden Lion, which was a small and obscure inn in the suburbs, and not far from the residence of his late uncle, attributes which accorded especially with the views of one who desired to avoid observation, and have as little communication with the town as possible.

"Having supped and slept, he presented himself on the following morning to his co-heir and the legal gentleman engaged in the settlement of the affairs, to whom he had been hitherto a stranger, and by whom he found himself very coolly received. He returned coolness for coolness—declined any discussion of the late catastrophe, saying that, as from his earliest childhood, he had been condemned to be an alien from his uncle and his house, he could not be expected to feel a very vivid interest in the event; and that as he was wholly unacquainted with his affairs and connexions, it was impossible he could form any idea with respect to the motives of the assassin. He also represented, that being called to a distant part of the country, by business of an urgent nature, which might occupy him an indefinite time, he wished his claims on the estate to be settled, and discharged as soon as possible. The attorney answered, that the affairs being perfectly understood and arranged, he had only to affix his signature to certain documents, and appoint some one on the spot to receive, and give a discharge for the money, and he might depart immediately: but Rodolphe, having powerful reasons for hastening the payment, could not agree to this; but obtained a promise that, by the third day, he should be released with the money in his pocket, the attorney himself consenting to advance it for the consideration of a certain sum which he was to be permitted to retain to repay himself the interest. Thus, as the assizes were not held till the following month, Rodolphe considered the matter satisfactorily arranged, and he waited as patiently as he could the moment that was to set him free.

"One thing, however disturbed him; he did not receive the promised intimation from Rodolphe Grimaud. Had the heart of his ally failed him, and had he permitted the page to live? The silence was perplexing; and when the eve of his departure arrived, the attorney having appointed an early hour on the following morning for the payment of the money, he could no longer restrain his anxiety, but resolved to go to the Rue St. Jacques, and endeavour to find out what was doing at the inn.

"Accordingly, when the evening closed in, he wrapt his cloak about him and set forth. The house, when he reached it, looked much as usual—the outer door was open, and a light in the kitchen shone through the chinks of the shutters; so he stept in. Two men were sitting by the fire smoking, who instantly arose and laid their hands upon his shoulders.

"'There he is!' exclaimed one of them; 'did I not say he'd come back? Trust me, I know their ways; they never can keep out of it—it's their destiny—they can't help it. Come, Monsieur Rodolphe,' continued he—'for I think you wont deny that you are Monsieur Rodolphe?'

"'I cannot deny that my name is Rodolphe, certainly,' replied the young man, whose conscience gave him every appearance of guilt; 'but by what authority, or for what reason, you treat me thus rudely, I am at a loss to comprehend.'

"'Doubtless,' returned Simon—for it was he who had spoken—'persons in your situation generally labour under a like difficulty of apprehension. However, it is not my business to enlighten you; that is the affair of my superiors. Meanwhile you will have the goodness to accompany these gentlemen and me;' and so saying, assisted by two other of their fraternity, who were in the street watching the door, without further explanation they led him away to prison.

"On the following day he was brought up for examination before the magistrate; who, with Bontems beside him, and a copy of Valentine's deposition on the table, was prepared to find in the prisoner the confederate of the young Englishman. As for the prisoner himself, confusion and terror were depicted in his countenance; he concluded that Grimaud had, somehow or other, allowed the young page to escape, whose information, however obtained, would be sufficient to convict him, and that he was a lost man.

"But the very commencement of the interrogatory overthrew the conjectures of both parties.

"'Your name,' said the justice, 'is Rodolphe Grimaud?' and Bontems had written, 'name, Rodolphe Grimaud,' before the magistrate had completed the question.

"'No, it is not,' replied the prisoner.

"The justice and clerk looked at each other, and raised their eyebrows; whilst Simon, who was standing behind, smiled contemptuously.

"'What name do you profess to answer to, then?' said the justice.

"'To my own name, Rodolphe Bruneau,' returned the prisoner.

"'It makes no difference,' replied the magistrate. 'I fancy you are not the less the person we are in search of, whether you choose to call yourself by one name or the other.'

"Rodolphe very much feared that in that respect the justice's notions were correct.

"'You are, at all events, the son of the woman calling herself Grimaud, who lately kept a certain inn in the Rue St. Jacques?'

"'No, I am not,' replied the prisoner.

"'But you have passed for her son, and lived with her under that character?'

"'Never!' returned the prisoner.

"'Do you mean to deny that you have been dwelling under her roof, calling her mother, whilst she addressed you as her son?'

"'I do deny it,' replied the prisoner. 'I cannot deny that I have been in the house of the woman you speak of; but I never either eat or slept under her roof since I was seven years old. As a child I may have called her mother, because she was my nurse, and the only mother I knew; but I have never done so since. In short, it is evident that you mistake my identity—you take me for another person. I am altogether ignorant of the motive of this inquiry, or of what crime I am suspected; but that I am not the person you take me for I can easily prove.'

"'When we seized you in the house you made no attempt to convince us of our mistake,' said Simon, who felt considerable vexation at the turn affairs were taking. He was a man who prided himself extremely on his dexterity and astuteness in matters of this nature, and he had been greatly annoyed at the escape of Rodolphe Grimaud, who, under the influence of the horror which had seized him when he left the cellar where his mother lay, had rushed out of the house and through the street with such rapidity, that he was away and out of sight before the persons who had been set to watch the door, and who were not prepared for such an explosion, had had time to lay hands on him.

"'I did not deny that my name was Rodolphe,' replied the prisoner, 'which was all you asked me—why should I?'

"'What took you to the inn at all?' inquired the justice.

"'I have been here for a few days on business,' replied the prisoner; 'in short, I am one of the co-heirs of the late Monsieur Bruneau; and I wished, before I departed, which had I not been detained I should have done ere this, to pay a visit to Madame Grimaud, who, as I have explained, was my nurse, and whom I had only seen once since I was seven years old. In short, I never was in Nantes since that period, except about two years ago, and then it was only for a few hours, till within the last three days, when I was summoned hither by letters, which informed me of the death of my uncle, and that my presence was required. If you will take the trouble of sending for Monsieur Ernest Bruneau, and a certain attorney called La Roche, you will be satisfied that I speak the truth.'

"Accordingly a messenger was despatched for these two gentlemen, who shortly appeared; and on being asked if they knew the prisoner, answered without hesitation that he was Monsieur Rodolphe Bruneau, and corroborated the account he had rendered of himself.

"The magistrate rose from his chair and apologized; Bontems wiped his pen on his coat-sleeve, and replaced his papers in his portfolio; whilst Simon, crestfallen and disappointed, left the room.

"'But may I be permitted to inquire,' said the attorney, 'the meaning of all this? On what grounds has this gentleman been arrested, and why have we been called upon to speak to his identity?'

"'Gentlemen,' replied the justice, with an ingratiating suavity of manner, 'I owe this gentleman, Monsieur Rodolphe Bruneau, as he has satisfactorily proved himself to be, an explanation. Do me the pleasure to be seated for a few minutes; and I will have the honour of relating the circumstances that have occasioned the mistake he has so much right to complain of.'

"Thereupon he narrated all he knew of Julie Le Moine—her motives, and her adventures; with the reasons they had for imagining that she was in possession of some material evidence with respect to the assassination of Monsieur Bruneau, and that Rodolphe Grimaud was implicated in the crime. 'But, gentlemen,' added he, 'the poor girl is incapable of giving her testimony; and it is even doubtful whether she will ever be in a condition to do so. She was found in the cellar speechless, and has remained so ever since; in short, her life is despaired of, and it is too probable that the secret will descend with her to the grave.'

"To the whole of this story the attorney listened with an attentive ear, moved by curiosity at first, but as the narrative proceeded, enchained by a stronger interest; whilst ever and anon, as the circumstances were unfolded, he darted, from his small grey eyes, over which the wrinkled forehead and bent brows portentous hung, glances that shot through the soul of Rodolphe Bruneau.

"When the voice of the magistrate ceased, Monsieur La Roche took out his snuff-box, and deliberately patting the lid, and furnishing his finger and thumb with an ample provision, which he slowly transferred to his nostrils, he said, 'It must be admitted that the affair is embarrassing, and that it is not easy to see one's way through it. In short, there is a mystery. What interest, for example, could this Rodolphe Grimaud have in the death of my late friend and patron? Possibly you, sir,' and here he faced round upon Bruneau, 'who have always been so intimately connected with him, could throw some light on the affair.'

"'Really,' answered Rodolphe, with a voice and countenance that betrayed an agitation he could not control, 'it would be impossible for me to conjecture—human motives are often inexplicable. But I must say, that it does not appear to me by any means evident that Grimaud has had anything to do with the affair at all. It was not him, but the Englishman, that was discovered escaping from the house, and that my uncle recognised as his assassin.'

"'That's true,' said the attorney; 'and it is certainly possible that the suspicions which have led this young lady to the house of the Grimauds *may* have been misplaced. But, if there was nothing to conceal, if her testimony was not apprehended, why was she confined in the cellar? That Grimaud must have had some interest or other in keeping back her evidence is clear, and a powerful one too; since the razor that was found at the foot of the ladder furnishes a strong presumption that security for himself and his confederates was to be purchased with her life. Did you ever see this Grimaud?' added he, turning to Ernest. 'What sort of person is he?'

"'I never saw him,' replied Ernest.

"'Here's the deposition of the young Englishman,' said Bontems, taking a paper from the portfolio, 'in which he describes, as far as he was able to distinguish it, the appearance of the man, whom, he affirms, conducted him to the villa, and shut him up there; and we are left to presume, if there is any truth in his story, which, till these late circumstances came out, nobody supposed there was, that that man was Grimaud.'

"At that moment the door of the room was gently opened by Simon, who, putting in his head, made a signal to Bontems that he desired to speak to him. Bontems arose, and handing the paper to the attorney, left the room; whilst the latter slowly drew his spectacles from his pocket, slowly released them from their shagreen case, which he as slowly returned to the same pocket, before he, with the like deliberate measure, fixed the glasses on his nose; which process being at length accomplished, he commenced reading aloud that particular part of Valentine's deposition, pausing every now and then, and casting his eyes up at Rodolphe, as if comparing his person with the description set down.

"The truth was, La Roche was at a loss how to proceed without committing himself, if his conjectures should happen to be erroneous; and his object was to gain time for reflection, and if possible to turn the magistrate's suspicions in the same direction as his own. But this was not so easy. The justice was altogether unacquainted with the circumstances on which the attorney's distrust was founded—namely, Rodolphe's previous character and conduct, and his intimacy with Grimaud, which were perfectly well known to La Roche, who had been for many years the legal adviser of Monsieur Bruneau; and in addition to these presumptions against him, there was his extraordinary haste to secure his inheritance and depart, even at the sacrifice of a pretty considerable sum; the circumstance of several urgent applications for money having been found among the murdered man's papers, some of a date immediately previous to the catastrophe; and, finally, the palpable terror and confusion he evinced on the present occasion. 'If he be really guilty,' said the attorney to himself, 'once out of this room, he'll be off and away out of the kingdom—but on what pretext to detain him?'

"As for Rodolphe, his desire to go was evident, but that very desire tied him to his chair, so much he feared to betray it.

"At this juncture the door opened again, and Bontems entered, followed by Simon; André the page, and a stranger; the first holding in his hand a torn letter and a key, and the second a small portmanteau. Hereupon, Rodolphe Bruneau arose, took up his hat, made a bow to the justice, who courteously returned his salutation, and moved towards the door.

"'I beg your pardon,' said Bontems, gently placing his hand against his breast, to arrest his egress—'I beg your pardon; but this business concerns you. Have the goodness to resume your seat:' and he again drew forward the chair Rodolphe had previously occupied, who saw no alternative but to take it.

"'What have we here?' said the justice. 'What portmanteau is that?'

"'It has been found in the house,' replied Simon, 'where the young lady was confined, and is marked by the initials R. B., by which we judged that it might possibly belong to this gentleman.'

"At the announcement of this supposition every eye took the same direction, and turned towards Rodolphe Bruneau; whilst the attorney said, with animation, 'Bravo! the interest of the drama is increasing;' the justice, too, who began to perceive that there was something more in the matter than he had suspected, polished his glasses before he put them on, in order that he might have a clearer view of the scene that was acting around him.

"'Here is a key, too, which fits the lock,' said Bontems.

"'Has the portmanteau been examined?' inquired the justice.

"'It has been looked into at the police office,' returned Simon, 'in the presence of the lieutenant; but the contents are left exactly as they were found.'

"'Let us see them,' said the justice. Upon which, the portmanteau being opened, they discovered, rolled up, and lying on the top, a shirt which had evidently been worn, and which, on being unfolded, exhibited stains of blood upon the wrist. There were also a few other articles of dress, and necessaries for the toilet, one of which was wrapped in a letter, which on examination proved to be in the writing of the late Monsieur Bruneau, and was addressed to Rodolphe, at Le Mans. It was evidently an answer to an application for money; and conveyed, with many reproaches, a positive refusal. The post mark was on it, and it appeared to have been duly sent and received. But when Simon shook out the shirt, another piece of paper appeared, which had been wrapt in it. It was the half of a letter, also in the hand of Monsieur Bruneau, and clearly addressed to the same person as the other—and there was enough of it legible to decipher that it contained a proposal, on certain conditions, of making an addition to his annuity of four thousand francs. There was no post mark on the paper, nor did it appear that it had ever been forwarded.

"'That letter,' said the attorney, 'must have been written on the very evening previous to the assassination, and taken out of the house by the assassin, whoever he was; for it was on that very afternoon, that Monsieur Bruneau spoke to me on the subject, and proposed this means of shaking off an annoyance that kept him in a constant state of irritation.'

"'Do you admit that the portmanteau is yours?' said the justice to Rodolphe.

"'I admit that it *was*,' replied he, 'but I presented it some time since to Grimaud.'

"'With its contents, I presume?' said the attorney, ironically.

"'With respect to the key,' said Bontems, 'it was found by this lad, André, in the pocket of the dress when it was returned to him this morning.'

"'And I intended taking it to the woman who borrowed the dress of me,' said André, 'but before I had time to do so, the tailor that I had sent my clothes to, that he might repair the lining that was unripped, brought me this letter.'

"'Which I found concealed betwixt the lining and the cloth,' said the tailor.

"'So I thought it better to take them both to the lieutenant of police,' added André.

"'Gentlemen,' said Rodolphe, 'the plot is cunningly laid, certainly; and the object of it is evidently to transfer the crime, and its penalty, from the shoulders of the young Englishman to another's. But allow me to ask, how should this girl, Julie Le Moine, who has been playing so extraordinary a part in this

drama, have become honestly possessed of the key of a porman-
teau, which, whether it be mine, as you seem to suspect, or
Grimaud's, as I assert, assuredly was not hers?'

"'That I can answer for,' said Simon.   .' The key is not that of
your portmanteau, but of a similar one belonging to the young
lady's father ; and she procured it from her own servant the night
she called at home.'

"'Still,' rejoined Rodolphe, 'it must have been for the purpose
of opening what did not belong to her—and in all probability her
object was, by placing the letter taken by the assassin, in the box,
to fix the crime on Grimaud.'

"At this suggestion the attorney, Simon, and Bontems, all
shook their heads incredulously ; whilst the justice desired to hear
the contents of the letter the tailor had found ; which proved to
be the other half of that which had dropped from the shirt, and
contained the offer of the augmented annuity, on the condition
that Rodolphe quitted the kingdom, and never returned to it
during Monsieur Bruneau's lifetime, nor troubled him with further
applications.

"'It is my opinion,' said the attorney in a low key to the
justice, 'that the young lady has opened the portmanteau, and
there found the torn paper ; or she may have divided it herself
with some view of her own.'

"'It is not exactly easy to perceive how she obtained her information ; but the direction in which her suspicions turned is plain
enough.'

"'And correct enough, I fancy,' said Bontems. 'The others
may have been agents and confederates, but I suspect this is the
principal.'

"'I confess,' said the attorney, 'I find myself rather inclining to
believe in the young Englishman's story, only that it is impossible
to discover what motive could have induced the assassin to take
him there.'

"'Perhaps to fix the crime on him,' said the justice.

"'It's not impossible,' replied the attorney ; 'but I doubt its
being simply that. There was more danger likely to accrue from
the proceeding than advantage to be gained by it. But meantime,
what is to be done next?'

"After some further consultation, in which the attorney did
not hesitate to give it as his decided opinion that Rodolphe was
implicated in the crime, it was judged prudent to commit him to
prison, till it was seen whether Julie recovered so far as to be able
to give her evidence, or till the affair could be otherwise further
inquired into.

"From this moment La Roche, who had been the intimate
friend of the late Monsieur Bruneau, devoted himself with energy
to the investigation of the truth. He offered a reward for the
discovery of Grimaud, who, however, never appeared; and he
obtained that a pardon should be promised to any one who, not
being a principal in the crime, would come forward and give evi-

dence on the subject. But nothing was gained by this measure either.

"He also procured permission to visit Valentine in the prison; and after hearing the young man's story from his own lips, came away strongly impressed with the truth of it; and satisfied that the stranger who had conducted him to the villa, and left him there, was either Bruneau or Grimaud; but as Valentine was unacquainted with the features of the men, the personal description and dress answered as well for one as the other.

"In the meantime the period for holding the assizes had arrived, and its business was drawing to a conclusion, whilst there appeared little prospect of Julie's being in a condition to communicate the information she had suffered so much to obtain.

"Much, therefore, to La Roche's annoyance, it seemed likely that the trial of the prisoners would be postponed; and although he was himself fully persuaded of Rodolphe's guilt, he was beginning to despair of procuring such proofs as should vindicate Valentine and set him free, when an advertisement caught his eye, from the host of an obscure inn in the suburbs, distinguished by the name of the Red Mullet.

"The advertisement was to the effect, that if the gentleman who left his horse on a certain night in the stables of the Red Mullet did not return to claim him, he would be sold to reimburse the host for the expenses of his keep. The date struck La Roche—it was the very night of Monsieur Bruneau's assassination.

"Now the attorney had taken considerable pains to find out if there were any traces of Rodolphe Bruneau's having visited Nantes on that night, but without success. He had written to a friend at Le Mans, and had, through his inquiries, ascertained that he was not there at that particular period: but although he had inquired at the coach offices, and interrogated the different drivers, he had found no indications of him on the road.

"'Come!' said he, after reading the advertisement, as he took up his hat and walked out of the café—'we'll try the Red Mullet.'

"'Monsieur,' said he to the host, 'I have seen an advertisement of yours, about a horse that was left here. Perhaps you'll permit me to see him, for I have a notion I am acquainted with the owner.'

"'Willingly,' said the landlord; who straightway conducted him to the stable.

"'Did you receive the horse of the gentleman yourself!' inquired La Roche.

"'I did not,' replied the host; 'it was the lad in the stable who took him. Gilles,' cried he to the ostler, 'show this gentleman the brown gelding.'

"Having ascertained that the traveller had arrived on that particular night, and gone away again after committing the horse to the charge of the ostler, without entering the house, the attorney inquired if they had also the saddle.

"'To be sure we have,' said Gilles; 'we have not only the

saddle, but the whip. I believe he left that by mistake; for he
ordered me to unstrap the portmanteau which was fastened on the
saddle, and took it with him.'

" The heart of the attorney bounded at the word portmanteau.

" ' Should you be able to recognise the owner of the horse if
you saw him?' inquired he.

" ' Undoubtedly,' replied Gilles; ' the rather that I happened to
see him again on the same night.'

" ' Indeed!' said the attorney. ' Have the goodness to explain
how that happened.'

" ' Why,' returned Gilles, ' on that night my poor mother was
very ill—she is since dead, God rest her soul! She died of spasms
in the stomach. Well, they had sent to say she wished to see me,
and I was just going, when the stranger arrived. I was obliged
to stay to put up his horse, and I rubbed him down and fed him as
carefully,' added Gilles, glancing at his master, ' as if my mother
had been already in her coffin.—However, that done, I hastened
to her bedside, to give her what comfort I could; but she got
worse, and I went out to a certain shop where they sell drugs, in
the Rue de Mousseline, to ask for a cordial. It was late, but they
opened the door when I rang, and gave me what I wanted.
Whilst the man was mixing it, the gentleman who had left the
horse entered precipitately, and inquired if there was a surgeon
to be found in the neighbourhood; and they directed him to
Monsieur Le Moine's, hard by——'

" ' Is there a surgeon of that name in the rue de Mousseline!'
interrupted the attorney.

" ' There is,' answered Gilles; ' and the gentleman hurried
away to fetch him. I suppose he came to Nantes to see some sick
friend. I don't think he observed me, but I recognised him immediately.'

" Here ended the mystery. Not only Gilles, but the man in
the druggist's shop, swore to the person of Rodolphe Bruneau,
who, when he found further subterfuge was vain, admitted his
guilt. There was, however, one saving clause in the dark story
which mitigated his sentence from death to the galleys. The
crime was no sooner committed, than remorse seized him—he had
hurried out of the room and the house, carrying with him the
letter he had seen lying on a table by the bed-side, addressed to
himself, and which by the light of the lantern he bore he contrived to read. Then it was he hastened in search of a surgeon,
by whose assistance he thought his uncle's life might yet be saved;
certain, that as the blow had been struck when the old man was
asleep, he himself had not been recognised, and quite satisfied
that the Grimauds, the only persons who were in the secret of his
having visited Nantes, would never betray him. It had been his
original plan, the murder once committed, to remount his horse and
return with all speed to Le Mans; but the apprehension and dismay that instantly took possession of his mind, confounded his
arrangements. He, therefore, after he had shut up the supposed

surgeon in the wounded man's room, which, by the way, he locked lest Valentine should pursue and trace his own steps to the inn, hastened thither himself, ascended to the chamber above, where he changed the stained shirt for one he had provided himself with in case of such an emergency; and then, without disclosing the truth to the Grimauds, or bearing about himself any signs of guilt, instead of returning to the Red Mullet to fetch his horse, the doing which he feared might make it more easy to trace him, he hastened out of the town on foot. Thus did the very precautions he used, lead to his detection; and thus may we say with Simon, ' 'Tis their destiny, which they cannot escape.' "

CHAPTER XXIII.

WHICH CONTAINS THE STORY OF JULIA.

" THUS you see," said Julia, when the story of her parents was concluded, "my earliest misfortune was that I had a speechless mother—for the heroine of this strange adventure did not die. She recovered her health and her memory, though not her speech; and it may easily be imagined that her devotion and her sufferings left Valentine no alternative but to offer her his hand. But the object she had taken so much pains to attain brought her little but sorrow and disappointment—the union was not a happy one. She felt that her husband had married her from gratitude, not from love; and she could never dismiss from her mind that he had preferred another. The consciousness, too, of her own affliction irritated her temper, and rendered her suspicious. She might have trusted that the recollection of its origin would be sufficient to endear her to a generous mind; and perhaps she would have trusted had she known herself to have been the object of Valentine's free and uninfluenced selection: but she was not, and that bitter drop in her cup empoisoned all the rest. Her husband did his best to reassure and make her happy; but his efforts were vain, and when experience convinced him that his endeavours were useless, he resigned the struggle. Kind, reasonable, and patient, he continued; but he no longer tried to give her confidence in an affection that she was determined not to believe in.

" Her father had consented to the match, though not without many pangs of disappointment; but after all that had happened, and the publicity of the history, there was no alternative. He was still a poor man, for he had not long been established in business on his own account, and had had but little time to make money: but what he could do for them he did. He took Valentine as a partner, with the view of qualifying him to become hereafter his successor; and he made arrangements for the young couple to live with him at a much cheaper rate than they could have done with a separate establishment. But all these advantages were counteracted, and finally rendered of no avail, by Julie's temper and jealous suspicions. Aurore, the fair and gentle Aurore, of whom she had truly predicted, ' she will weep, but she will do nothing,' was still a dweller in the city of Nantes. She did weep the loss of her lover for some time; but she had the consolation of feeling that she could not blame him; and that he was guilty of no premeditated or voluntary infidelity to her. She herself could not have advised him to act otherwise than he did, and—Aurore was a woman—she knew that she still lived in his heart; and that still, were he free, she would be his choice; so the thing was bearable; and after a reasonable measure of time and of tears, she gave her fair hand to another.

"But this so far from improving the case, rather rendered it worse; as, according to the manners and customs of the city of Nantes, and indeed of the French nation in general, a married woman was a much more dangerous rival than a single one. Like other people, Aurore was to be seen at the promenades, the gardens, the theatres, and the festivals—and the sight of her was death to Julie, and the sound of her voice was worse. If she went to these places she was wretched; and if she stayed at home she was wretched too, unless Valentine was by her side; for she believed every hour he spent away from her was passed in the society of Aurore.

"At length the disquiet of the unhappy couple reached such a climax, and became so annoying to Monsieur Le Moine, that he consented, and advised Valentine to consent, to what Julie had long been urging; namely, to return to England, and either establish himself as a French teacher, or set up a school; his acquaintance with the language, an accomplishment, at that time, far from general, giving him a fair prospect of success.

"'This plan,' continued Julia, 'was finally executed; and my father and mother quitted Nantes and removed to England, bringing me, then a child of four years old, along with them.'

"But it is easier to change our country than our character; and matters did not go much better in England than they had done in France; for Julie brought her misfortunes with her. The temper and the passions which had always been violent, indulgence and the absence of restraint had rendered uncontrollable; and if, during the first month of their marriage, Julie could not believe that her husband loved her, still less could she believe it now, when she was conscious she had done so much to alienate his affections, and to efface the obligations he owed her.

"The poor man made his first essay as a French teacher in his native town, where, as the neighbourhood was large, he might have done well enough, if his wife would have permitted him to stay there; but she became jealous of a lady, who having been a companion of Valentine's in his childhood, and since prosperously married, was anxious to be kind to him, and do him what services she could; and after committing many minor offences, she at length, in a fit of passion, struck her supposed rival in the street. Shame and vexation at the exposure she had incurred, rendered the place odious to her, and she never rested till she had won her husband's consent to leave it. But the next experiment succeeded no better. There were ladies everywhere; and where there were not female friends, there were female pupils. Every ebullition of passion or folly reacted on her own temper, and produced a fresh crop of suspicion and violence, till she rendered herself obnoxious to everybody. People began by wondering, and ended by fearing and avoiding this tall, tremendous dark, dumb woman; and though they compassionated the fate of the unhappy husband, they could not venture to employ or associate with him, under the almost certain penalty of being annoyed and insulted by his wife. Thus was the unfortunate Valentine driven from place to place, growing poorer instead of richer, being obliged to expend for their daily support and frequent transmigrations, the little money his father-in-law had given him; till his energies were exhausted, his spirit broken; and hopeless, sad, dejected, he gradually relaxed in his exertions, and resigned himself patiently to the wretchedness and poverty he saw no means of avoiding.

"The only pleasure that remained to him, in short the only object or occupation that seemed capable of rousing him from the lethargy of disappointment and despair that was overgrowing his faculties, was the education of his little girl. She had been from her birth extremely pretty, rather resembling her father than her mother; and in spite of her hereditary claims to violence in the female line, she was gentle, mild and amiable, but timid to excess. In short, her passions, whatever they might have been by nature, had been frightened out of her.

"Julie Le Moine was born with the spirit of a heroine, the passions of a Medea, and the temper of a vixen; and the circumstances of her youth had rather tended to foster than subdue these dangerous endowments. But the training of her child was exactly the reverse of her own. Fear, privation, and suffering were the earliest lessons of the little Julia. During her infancy, whilst her father was engaged and called .from home by his business, she was left wholly to the charge of her mother, who loved her as love could only exist in that heart of fire, passionately; but, unhappily, the only sentiment she inspired in the bosom of her child was awe; an awe which time and circumstances augmented into terror.

"Thus the poor girl advanced from childhood to womanhood, beautiful in person, not uncultivated in mind, but a stranger to enjoyment; without energy, without hope, and steeped in poverty to the very lips.

"At length the small, very small earnings of the father proved inadequate to the support of the family; and it was found necessary to put Julia in a way of adding something to their resources. They were at this time residing in a small lodging in the suburbs

of London; and after looking about for some weeks, they succeeded in getting Julia employed in a ready-made linen warehouse in the city. Here she worked early and late, returning
home only to sleep; and for scanty wages and indifferent food,
performed tasks as monstrous, irksome, and dispiriting, as the
labours of a galley-slave.

"She had been some time chained to this weary captivity, when,
one day, a foreigner entered the shop to order a set of shirts; and
as he spoke English with difficulty, Julia, who had been taught
French by her father, was called from the back room, where the
tired fingers plied from morn till night, to act as interpreter. The
stranger was evidently struck with her, and on some pretence or
another he repeated his visit on the following day; but this time
he came not alone: he was accompanied by an Englishman, younger
than himself, and of a much more showy exterior. At the first
difficulty of apprehension that arose betwixt the mistress of the
shop and the foreigner, the Englishman was about to explain;
but the other making him a signal not to interfere, requested the
assistance of the young lady who had served as interpreter on
the preceding day; adding, in a low tone, to his friend, 'I am
going to show you a pretty girl.'

"Julia was again called forward; and if the Frenchman had
admired her, the Englishman seemed to admire her much more;
at least his admiration was much more openly exhibited, and
from that day he neglected no means of making an impression
on the heart of the young sempstress. He almost daily returned
to the shop with his friend, who had first introduced him, or with
other foreigners; and although it was evident to Julia that he
spoke French with facility, he always declined exercising this
accomplishment, and requested her assistance. His next step
was to hover about the door at night, till the hours of labour
were expired, and the poor prisoners set free; and then he would
accompany her home. At first the timid girl was as much
frightened as flattered; but gradually the attention of her admirer
gained upon her, till at last her daily toil was cheered by the
prospect of her evening walk.

"But, as may be imagined, this devotion on the part of the lover
was by no means disinterested. He looked to be rewarded for
his pains; and lost no opportunity of dilating on the wretchedness of the life she was leading, and of pointing out how much
happier she might be, if she would throw herself on his protection, and allow him to provide her with all the appliances of ease,
comfort, and leisure, to which she was so much a stranger, and
which her beauty and merit so fully entitled her to enjoy.

"Poor Julia was not gifted with much power of resistance, and
the serpent charmed her wisely, for she was wearied to the very
marrow of the life she led; but there was one link that held her
still, and that was her father. She loved him and she pitied him;
and she knew that to leave him, was to extract the last drop of
cordial from his cup

"One night she had been kept at her work later than usual, and when at length she was released, her usually constant attendant was not to be seen. She concluded he was weary of waiting, and had gone away, so she hastened home through the cold, wet, foggy streets as fast as she could; for it was winter, and she was anxious to gain the shelter of her own humble lodging, and the warmth that her scantily furnished bed-clothes could supply.

"She rang the door bell, expecting her mother, who was in the habit of sitting up for her, to open it—but no one came. She rang again and again. At length, a window above opened, and a voice, which she recognised as that of the owner of the house, inquired who was there.

"'It's me,' replied Julia; 'is my mother gone to bed?'

"'Your mother!' exclaimed the woman, in an angry tone, 'your mother's gone to gaol, and your father too; and I recommend you to go after them. It's the fittest place for them, beggarly French folks as they are! I only wish they'd been there long ago, instead of living in my parlour floor for nothing, for I've not seen the colour of their money this six months, I'll take my oath. Putting me off from day to day with promises: till at last down comes Giblet the butcher, this morning, and arrests them, and I'm left in the lurch; for all the rags they've got put together ar'n't worth twenty shillings; curse 'em!'

"At the close of this oration, the excellent woman shut down the window with a bang; and left Julia standing in the street bewildered with fear and surprise. Had she known more of the world, she would not have been astonished at that happening at last, which had been long threatening. But she knew wonderfully little. Her speechless mother had been unable to teach her anything; and her poor, dejected, disappointed, hopeless father, though he gave her such education as he had the means of communicating, seldom or never conversed with her on general subjects; but lived on in a sort of dreaming existence, appearing to take no part in the affairs of a world in which so scanty and bitter a portion had been allotted for him. Friends or acquaintance they had none—they were too poor to make any in a respectable station; and Julie was too proud, and Valentine too indolent and indifferent to seek, or accept of others: so that their daughter grew up singularly unacquainted with all worldly affairs. She knew they had very little money, but she did not foresee that that little would be reduced to none; they never told her so; and as she left home early, and returned to it late, she had neither seen nor heard anything of the daily struggles and difficulties her parents had to contend with; and had continued in happy ignorance of the weekly menaces of the butcher and baker, and the hourly objurgations of the landlady.

"She waited some time, thinking it impossible the woman could intend to shut her out, and expecting every instant to hear her foot in the passage; but she was overrating the hostess's benevolence. That worthy woman, on closing the window, had straight-

ways returned to her bed, drawn the blankets comfortably round
her shoulders, and whilst Julia was shivering at the door below,
was gradually subsiding into an easy doze.

"At length when waiting seemed vain, the poor girl turned off
the step, and stood looking through the hazy atmosphere up and
down the street, at a loss which way to go, or where to apply for
shelter.

"'If I knew where my father and mother are confined,' said she
to herself, 'I'd go there and try to get admittance;' and she be-
thought herself of addressing her inquiries to the butcher. But
when she reached the spot where she had been often sent for a
pound of coarse beef, or a few bones of the scrag of mutton, she
recollected that the man had only a stall there, and had his dwelling in some neighbouring street—where, she knew not. She
could think of but one other alternative; it was to go back to
the shop where she worked, and try to get shelter there.

"Perhaps as she tramped back through the weary way she had
trod but an hour before, when she believed she was hastening to
her parents and her bed, she contrasted the *then* and the *now ;* the
former state appearing, now that it was lost, so much better than
she had imagined it—the present seeming worse if possible than
it was; and she felt how, in the depths of poverty and wretchedness, there is a lower deep remaining still—and, perhaps, she
thought of her lover.

"With a faint heart she approached the door, for her mistress
was a hard woman, and would doubtless be angry at being disturbed at so late an hour—her hand was upon the bell to ring it,
when an arm was thrown round her waist, and a well-known and
too welcome voice, said, ' Julia, my love, what are you doing here
at this time of night?'

"'I'm going to ask Mrs. Walker to let me sleep here, sir,' replied
she; for the timid Julia had never got beyond *sir*.

"'On what account?' inquired he. 'Why don't you go
home?'

"'I have been home, and they wont let me in, sir,' answered
Julia.

"'Your father and mother wont let you in!' ejaculated he, with
surprise.

"'It is not my father and mother, sir,' returned she, unwilling
to expose the real cause of her dilemma—'they're not at home—
it's the woman of the house.'

"A glimmering of the truth broke on the mind of the young
man, who, by the way, had made himself known to her as Mr.
William Godfrey; and the opportunity seemed too favourable to
be lost. He soon extracted from the simple girl all she knew of
her parent's situation: and he then eloquently represented to her
the probable abuse and insult she would draw upon herself by an
application to Mrs. Walker; whose stock of compassion being far
too limited to divide betwixt the twenty poor young sempstresses
she employed, each of whom had miseries enough to have en-

grossed the whole of it, had prudently closed the avenues of her heart to all their sorrows and sufferings at once, thus sparing herself pain, and them disappointment.

" ' Then,' continued he, ' even if she were to take you into the house now, which, as I said before, she wont, what are you to do to-morrow night, and the next night, and for months that your father 'll be in prison—perhaps for his life ?—Nothing more common, I assure you, than these sort of events. You can't earn enough to pay for lodging, fire, and so forth for yourself and your mother ; and she can do nothing, by your own admission. How much better trust to me. You shall have every comfort yourself, and something to assist your parents. Come, Julia, be advised,' and he wound his arms with tenderness about her, and pressed her to his heart—' come, my Julia, come, and put your trust in me.'

" She did put her trust in him ; and the remainder of poor Julia's story may be too easily anticipated.

" When the father was arrested, the owner of the lodging unhesitatingly turned the mother out of doors; at all events, Julie would have wished to accompany her husband, for extremities of that sort called forth the best part of her character; so she hastily wrote a line to her daughter, desiring her to beg shelter for that night of Mrs. Walker ; and in the event of its being denied her, she directed her where she would find her parents, intrusting the letter to a neighbour who promised to deliver it. But the ambassadors of the poor are apt to be negligent; the duty was at first deferred, and at last forgotten, till it was too late to be of any avail. On the following day the mother sought her child at the linen-warehouse ; but Mrs. Walker knew nothing about her : and after seeking her wherever she thought it possible she might have taken refuge, she returned amazed and disconsolate to her husband.

" In the meantime Mr. Godfrey was by no means willing to run the risk of losing his conquest whilst it had yet the charm of novelty. He placed Julia in a lodging a little way out of town, as remote as possible from the direction in which she had formerly lived. Timid, inexperienced, irresolute, and knowing nothing of London but the ground she had been daily in the habit of walking over—in fact, a mere child of sixteen, it required a degree of energy far beyond anything she could command, either to find her own way to her parents, or to insist on being conducted to them. She ardently desired to see her father, and urged her wishes frequently on her lover ; but he put her off on one pretext or another ; and in some degree satisfied, or at least relieved her mind, by enclosing small sums of money in letters which she wrote, and which he assured her should be duly delivered to her parents.

" He was indulgent and kind ; whilst she enjoyed many comforts that she had never known before ; and as he was occupied by business and other engagements, the hours he passed in her company were too few to give rise to satiety, or afford time for ill

temper. She became gradually reconciled to the separation from
her parents,—a separation, indeed, which as far as regarded her
mother had never been very painful: and when at the end of a
twelvemonth the little Julia came to awaken a new interest in her
heart, and furnish an occupation and amusement for the many
hours she had hitherto been doomed to spend alone, she might be
said to be really happy, for she was too unknowing and inexperienced to foresee the reverse that awaited her.

"Shortly after the birth of the child, Mr. Godfrey announced
that he was going on a journey, and should probably be absent
about three months: but he left her in the charge of a friend,
who was to call frequently and see that she was well taken care
of; and he arranged with the people of the house to provide her
with board and lodging during the interval.

"The friend, who called himself Dyson, endeavoured, as is the
custom of friends, from time immemorial, on the like occasions, to
make an interest for himself in the heart of his fair charge; but
Julia was incorruptible. Without being violently in love with
Mr. Godfrey, she liked him, and felt grateful to him for the protection and comforts he had afforded her; and she was moreover
bound to him by her passionate affection for the child. It was the
first vivid sentiment that had been awakened in her heart, and it
rushed over it with the spring and vigour of a newly opened
fountain—filled it to the brim, and inspired her with a new life.
So she sought no further—her full content was in the cradle of
her babe. The only favour therefore she accepted of Mr. Dyson,
amongst the numerous attentions offered her, was, that he would
find out where her parents had been conveyed, and conduct her to
see them; a request to which he most willingly acceded. But
when they arrived at the Fleet, where Valentine had been confined, they learned that, about six months before, some wealthy
foreigner, who had visited the prison, having been touched by the
story of the poor French teacher and his dumb wife, had paid
their humble debt and set them free. Whither they were gone no
one could tell, nor did Mr. Dyson's inquiries in the neighbourhood
of their former lodging throw any light on the subject.

"Thus Julia lost all traces of her parents, as they had previously
done of her; for as for the letters their daughter had intrusted to
Mr. Godfrey, they never advanced further on their way to the
Fleet than the first convenient fire he came to; and thus was she
thrown wholly on the tenderness or compassion of her lover.
But alas for the tenderness and compassion of a libertine!

"At the end of a few months, Mr. Godfrey returned, and appeared for a little while to take some interest in her and her child;
but gradually the interest became weaker, the visits more rare, and
the means of maintenance less liberally furnished. Julia was not
very speedily alive to the change; for she did not expect it, in the
first place; and in the second, her affection for Mr. Godfrey was
not of a nature to render her either jealous or susceptible. But at
length, after a gradual alienation of some months, he disappeared

altogether, leaving her a letter, in which he strongly recommended her to have recourse to the protection of his friend Dyson : and promising, provided she followed his advice, to pay her a weekly maintenance for the child.

"The poor girl saw no alternative but to walk the streets with her baby in her arms—one lover had forsaken her, and the other swore she should never want a home whilst he had a guinea in his pocket—her heart was with neither of them ; it was with her child—so she took him at his word, and accepted his protection.

"After some months Mr. Godfrey again returned, and, from that time, he used frequently to visit Mr. and Mrs. Dyson, as they were called. The two gentlemen often went out together at night, and not uncommonly, made excursions of several days into the country.

"This state of things lasted some time, but at length Mr. Dyson's funds seemed to be on the decline, and Julia was often put to sad shifts to furnish the necessities of her scanty table. She was beginning to dread that the time was not far distant when he would actually not have a guinea in his pocket, and that she would be again thrown upon the world with nothing to rely on but the compassion of her first seducer.

"Suddenly, however, the scene brightened; at least, as far as regarded the pecuniary department. Mr. Dyson declared that he had won a large bet at Newmarket ; and careless and profuse of money, Julia's wants were now as liberally supplied, as if the sum were inexhaustible. But with this access of good fortune, came other changes less agreeable. Mr. Dyson was an altered man. His spirits were much more unequal than they had been ; his temper much more irritable. He had strange fits of gloom ; was suspicious, nervous, restless ; curious about things which appeared to Julia of no consequence, and was seized with an unaccountable mania for changing his lodgings.

"In the meantime the money fled ; and that at such a rate, that in a very short time their circumstances became as straitened as before the last access of fortune ; and poverty stared them in the face. Just at this period Mr. Godfrey called one day, and said, that he had the charge of a young woman from the country, who was on her way to the continent ; that she was taken extremely ill, and had imbibed such an inveterate aversion to the persons he had placed her with, that she talked of giving up her journey altogether, and returning to her friends. He therefore begged Julia to go and see her, and endeavour to reconcile her to waiting patiently where she was, till her health should permit her to travel. Accordingly, Julia visited the young lady, whose name she learned was Miss Jones, and who was suffering from the effects of a neglected cold, caught, she said, on her journey to London ; Mr. Godfrey having neglected to call in medical advice, till she was so bad, that the servant of the house she was lodging in, had one night taken fright, and ran out for an apothecary, of her own accord, when he was absent.

"Miss Jones disowned any sort of attachment to Mr. Godfrey; was quite indignant at Julia's natural suspicion that he was her lover; and declared that she was on her way to the continent to be married. She was otherwise by no means communicative; and Julia neither learned where she came from, nor whither she was going.

"In due time, by the care of the apothecary, she recovered, and Julia was informed that Mr. Godfrey being unable to accompany her abroad, the charge of escorting her to her destination was to devolve on Mr. Dyson.

"Accordingly they departed; and in a very short time, as Julia had foreseen, the woman of the house, when she found that the ostensible husband did not return, gave the wife warning to quit within twenty-four hours; adding, that but for the sake of the child, whom she had grown fond of, and whose pretty playful ways might have melted a heart of marble, she should certainly have seized her clothes to pay the arrears of rent. In this dilemma Julia might naturally have applied to Mr. Godfrey for assistance; but with Mr. Dyson's departure, the visits of the friend had ceased: and where to seek him, or to address a letter to him, she could not tell; for, from the very commencement of their acquaintance, he had carefully abstained from giving her any information on the subject. Like the wind he came and went—she neither knew whence nor whither.

"Fortunately, her wardrobe was tolerably furnished by the liberality of Mr. Dyson; and she had a few trinkets that he had given her in the flush of his fortunes. These she pawned; and after taking a very humble lodging in Holborn, she next proceeded to the shop of her former mistress at the ready-made linen warehouse, and requested to be supplied with work which she might do at home, where the care of her child confined her. She obtained a little employment, and by the aid of what she thus earned, and the gradual disposal of her wardrobe she contrived for a time to pay her rent, and purchase food for herself and her infant. But in process of time the wardrobe was exhausted—next, the little girl was seized with measles and hooping-cough, and was very ill: some money inevitably went for drugs, and much time was spent in nursing and attendance. Matters became daily worse and worse: the child recovered from the maladies, but remained weak and helpless; pining for want of air and exercise, and craving for food which could not be supplied. The love for the infant, which had hitherto given her energy, and enabled her to support this hard struggle, now that she saw the struggle was in vain, and could no longer be maintained, only added a thousand-fold to her despair.

"At length the dreaded night arrived, that found her houseless, penniless, without a friend to turn to, or a hope to cheer; and with the fearful agony of those cruel words, 'Mamma, I'm so hungry,' for ever wringing at her heart.

"For several hours she wandered through the streets, the inhospitable streets, that furnish nothing to the penniless wretch that cannot beg—amongst crowds of busy and incurious strangers, hurrying on their several errands and rudely brushing with their elbows, as they passed, the fainting mother and the starving child; —on she wandered. Ever and anon the broad, gray sheet of the gloomy river, with its sable canopy of fog hung over it, appearing betwixt the divisions of the streets, and reminding her that beneath its dark waters there was a last refuge for the destitute—a bed wherein once laid, no sound can wake them, no cold can shiver them, no hunger tear their entrails, nor cries of starving infants pierce their hearts.

"Who shall condemn her that she sought its rest?"

CHAPTER XXIV.

WHICH NARRATES THE PROGRESS OF HARRY'S JOURNEY ; AND HOW HE FELL
INTO UNPLEASANT COMPANY.

IT was a fine moonlight night when Harry Leeson leaped over the park gate of Oakfield into the high road, and he walked on bravely —bravely for fifteen. It can't be denied that there was something heavy at his heart ; that he thought of what his life and his prospects had been ; of his uncle and the happy days at Oakfield when he was alive, and all the world wore smiles for Harry—of Fanny, kind, gentle, affectionate Fanny, that, although she could not protect him, still loved him as much as ever. It must be confessed, too, that he occasionally thought of the comfortable bed he had left behind him ; and that when, by dint of walking, and the fresh night air he got an appetite, the alluring picture of the hot rolls, and the well-spread breakfast table in the library, would, in spite of his heroic efforts to despise all such considerations, present themselves to his imagination in a too fascinating form.

Then, though Harry would not have admitted to himself that he was afraid, or that there was anything to be afraid of ; yet ever and anon, when there was a dark turn in the road, or a mysterious looking shadow of some old tree with its arms waving in the wind fell across it : or some restless bird of night fluttered from amongst its branches, and with its ominous cry sailed slowly through the air, there would be something fluttering, too, within poor Harry's breast. But presently would come the brisk rattle of revolving wheels, the lively smack of the coachman's whip, and one of the mails would dash past him ; or a heavy wagon would crawl by, and a "good night, master," from the wagoner, would put him in heart again.

Thoughts, too, of the future would intrude. It was not *quite* certain that he would be admitted into one of his majesty's regiments of the line, rise to be a general, and be knighted,

although it was highly probable—and if this did not happen
exactly as Harry had planned, he did not very clearly see what
else could. His whole arrangements had been entirely made on
this supposition; his castle with all its towers and battlements
raised upon this foundation—if it slipped away, there was nothing
left—like the fall of the Rossberg, it carried everything else with
it. Occasional doubts as to whether he had really done the very
best thing in the world for himself, would intrude; and once or
twice he wondered whether he had been missed; and whether if
he walked straight back as fast as he could, and presented himself
at the breakfast-table at the usual hour, the adventure might
not remain wholly unknown. But he did not turn back; and as
the hours advanced, and the distance from Oakfield increased,
the experiment became impracticable; and therefore there was
nothing left but to walk forward.

As the morning dawned, and human beings began to be
stirring, another Gorgon presented itself to Harry's imagination,
which filled the place of all those which had been only visions
of the night, and were now melting away in the bright beams of
the rising sun. This was the fear of being overtaken, and carried
back in triumph by Gaveston; to be taunted, jeered, insulted,
laughed at; and finally forced, without the means of resistance,
to accompany him wherever he pleased to take him, and conform
to whatever arrangements he chose to make for him.

"No!" said Harry, with a swelling heart, "never! I'd rather
do anything in the world! I'd rather be a common soldier, if I
can't be an officer—I'd even rather get my living as a servant in
some nice family, where the people would be kind to me, perhaps
when they found I was a gentleman—I'd submit to anything,
anything in the world, so that I can feel I'm my own master,
and not dependent upon that fellow! And by the by," thought
he, "surely, now that it's daylight, I'm very wrong to be walking
along this high-road, where I may be traced so easily if they send
in pursuit of me. I'll strike off across the country instead of
keeping the direct line to London, and find my way thither by
some other route."

Upon this, Harry leaped over the first stile he came to, cut
across several fields, till he found himself in a very rural district,
amongst hop gardens and pretty farm houses; and on arriving at
a neat little village, where he saw a pink horse standing upon
three legs over a door, he entered and inquired if he could have
some breakfast.

A clean, healthy, honest-looking woman answered him in the
affirmative; and showing him into a neat little sanded parlour,
furnished with wooden chairs, deal tables, and adorned with
whole-length portraits of the Marquis of Granby, the Duke of
Cumberland, and other worthies, she soon set before him an
excellent breakfast of brown bread, sweet butter, new milk for
his tea, and a smoking rasher of bacon for a relish.

Harry did justice to his fare, and felt himself an emperor. It was a capital commencement to his adventures; and it was the first breakfast that had ever been served at his own command, and paid for from his own pocket. In short, it was the first independent bread and butter Harry had ever eaten, and he relished it accordingly.

The woman was so civil, too; and after breakfast, having refreshed himself by dipping his head in some cold water, and having had his clothes brushed, he strolled into the little garden behind the house, where she invited him to make free with the fruit; in fine, the quarters were very agreeable, and Harry had walked all night; the village, moreover, was in a sheltered nook, quite off the direct road, where it was very unlikely he would be sought for; so after some consideration, he resolved to remain there till the next morning.

An excellent dinner of eggs and bacon and hasty-pudding made an agreeable diversion in his day's amusement; after which, throwing himself across a row of wooden chairs that stood against the wall, he fell fast asleep—and, as soundly as if he had been on a bed of down, slept till his hostess came to inquire if he would have any tea. The tea, with its due accompaniment of bread and butter, being swallowed in a sort of somniferous medium between sleeping and waking, he immediately afterwards retired to the humble but clean bed that had been provided for him; and there, in a state of complete oblivion of all the joys and sorrows of this world, passed the hours till morning. Poor Harry! it was too good a beginning to last.

He awoke the next morning in a condition of perfect comfort; and having devoured a second edition of the good breakfast, and made some inquiries about his road, he started again on his journey; and in this manner he continued to travel, keeping as wide as he could of the high road from Oakfield to London; walking by day and resting by night, till he had arrived within twenty miles of the great city. And so far he reached without any adventure worth recording. The small country inns he put up at, afforded him all the accommodation he needed; the guests he met at them were chiefly the honest farmers of the neighbourhood; the hosts were civil, the charges low, the weather fine, and the country pleasant; no one asked him whence he came or whither he was going; and Harry indulged himself with easy stages by day and sound sleeps by night.

It was about seven o'clock on the evening of his last day's journey, for he looked to make his entrance into London on the following morning, that he stepped into a small inn by the road side, which, not only with respect to its situation, but in its appearance also, bore a less rural and inviting aspect than those he had hitherto put up at. The sign was "The Admiral;" and exalted on a high pole about three yards from the door, swung a rude representation of Admiral Jarvis. There was a trough for watering horses on one side of the house, and a set of ill-conditioned looking stables on the other. The echo of rude

voices resounded from within; and a powerful odour of beer and
tobacco exhaled through the open door.

Harry hesitated a little, for none of his senses were invited by
the tokens they detected; but he had already extended his walk
an hour beyond its usual limits in the hope of meeting with some
desirable resting-place; but these he perceived became more rare
as he approached London. The character of the small inns
became less rural, the hosts less simple and civil; and the company he met, less unobjectionable. However, he was tired; and
reflecting that by going farther he might fare worse, he resolved
to content himself with such accommodation as "The Admiral"
afforded.

"How now, master?" said a big bluff man, who advanced from
an open door on the right, with a pewter porter pot in his hand,
and wearing a blue apron, one corner of which was turned up and
tucked into the waistband—"What's to say?"

"I wish to know if I can have some supper, and a bed here,"
replied Harry, rather abashed by the rude address.

"There's little doubt of that," replied the host, taking a deliberate survey of Harry's accoutrements, "if so be that you can pay
the score."

"Certainly I can," answered Harry, not a little offended at the
doubt expressed. "I don't expect you to feed me, nor lodge me
either for nothing."

"No offence, master, no offence!" cried the rude host; "but
it's as well to be on the safe side: we get all sorts here."

Harry felt a great inclination to turn round and walk out; but
he was afraid that, if he did so, the man would be insolent to
him; so he followed him into a small back room that looked on
the stable yard, where he requested he might have some tea;
which the host promised should be forthcoming immediately.

The room itself was evidently one reserved for such select
visitors as preferred being alone to joining the smokers and
porter and grog consumers that assembled in the other. The
walls were covered with a dull-looking paper that appeared to
have once been blue, but in which now neither pattern nor colour
was discernible; numerous stains of liquor, and sundry bare
places where long stripes had been peeled off, testified that the
occupants of even that choice apartment did not always confine
themselves within the limits of temperance and decorum. A
small square bit of carpet with torn edges that laid traps for the
toes, and of as nondescript a hue as the paper, was spread in the
middle of the room, and over it stood an old battered, shattered,
leaf and a half of a mahogany dining-table, scored, scratched, and
blotted with all manner of disfigurements. Four ancient chairs
with high backs, and black hair seats which had once been
stuffed, but from which the chief part of the contents had either
been consumed by moths, or abstracted through the large holes
that appeared in the hair cloth, completed the furniture of this
best apartment of the inn at B——. The window was exceedingly

dirty, and cut all over with plebeian names, and coarse rhymes; and a bit of torn, faded, green stuff of an open texture, affected, in the form of a blind, to shut out the view of the stable-yard from the eye of the genteel customer within; or to defend him from the obtrusive curiosity of the profane vulgar without. The window appeared never to have been opened within the memory of man; and the odour of the apartment, in which there was no chimney, perfectly corresponded with its other attractions. The wretched appointments of the tea table, the battered tray, the cracked cup and saucer, the black pot with the remnant of a spout, the notched and broken knife, the stale, dirty-looking, ill-baked bread it was to cut, the strong, yellow, salt butter, the coarse dingy lump sugar, and the pale blue drop of milk in a broken black ewer, were all in accordance. It was Harry's first introduction to the ungraceful adjuncts of poverty and humble life. Till now the experiences of his journey had not disclosed to him their vulgar and offensive side. The rural inns, with their clean whitewashed walls, their sanded floors, their chairs and tables of well-scrubbed deal, their neat gardens filled with cabbages, and French beans, and gooseberry and currant bushes, mingled with pinks, and sweet peas, and hollyhocks, with a venerable apple-tree in one corner, and a little arbour twined with honeysuckles and sweet-brier in the other—all this was lowly and simple, but not vulgar. Nothing that is pure and simple can be vulgar; but the dirty, stained paper, the faded, ragged carpet, and the mahogany table and chairs, in the select room of the inn at B——, were all essentially vulgar, for they were intended to be genteel.

Harry's high hopes and the exaltation of his spirits fell with his fortunes. Here was already a reverse; a taste of the future, always supposing he was not made a general and a grand cross of the Bath; the certainty of which events varied with the height of the quicksilver in the barometer of his comforts. It is delightful to be independent, and feel that one is master of his own actions; but Harry found it impossible to enjoy these privileges to their full extent in the best room of the inn at B——; so, tired as he was, when he had taken enough of his uninviting repast to appease the most urgent calls of his appetite, he went to the door to get a breath of fresh air; but the vulgar merriment, and the vulgar odours from within, still assailing his ears and his nostrils, he walked across the road, and swung his legs over a gate that led into a turnip field.

In this position he sat some time, when he observed two men approaching from the London side, who on reaching the house, having taken a survey of its exterior, turned in. They both wore shabby black coats, and hats with very small brims; and had that undefinable appearance of belonging to no recognised class, that led the beholder to imagine that they lived by no acknowledged means, but upon such means as accident or the exercise of their own enterprise or dexterity might furnish.

Harry thought no more of them, but turned his reflections on his own affairs; till they again attracted his attention by appearing at the door together. They seemed in close consultation; and one of them held a printed paper in his hand to which they occasionally referred, whilst they cast their eyes so frequently across the road to where Harry was sitting, that he began to feel uncomfortable, and to fancy they were speaking of him.

So much did this notion prevail, that, at length, he descended from the gate on the other side, and walked up the field, which was divided by a path in the middle. When he had moved a little way, he could not help turning his head to see what the men were doing; and he perceived that they were both leaning over the gate he had just left, and were looking after him.

Harry felt exceedingly annoyed, and began to be assailed with unpleasant suspicions. It occurred to him, could they be emissaries of Gaveston? They looked men fit for any mischief or ill service; and their attention was certainly singularly directed to him. At the extremity of the field was a stile which gave access to another; he crossed it; and when he did so the men leaped over the gate, and walked up the turnip field, as if resolved to keep him still in view.

This was so disagreeable, and he felt so much averse to the idea of finding himself in their company remote from the house, that when he had crossed the second field, instead of going further, he seated himself on the stile: upon which they drew up, and seated themselves upon the opposite one.

It was too evident to Harry that they were watching him; and a host of apprehensions and suspicions rushed into his mind with the conviction. Either they were sent in search of him, or they were induced, by perceiving he was a young gentleman, alone and unprotected, to form some evil design against his person or his pocket.

" Perhaps they suppose I have money, and they mean to rob me," said he; " and if they take what little I have, what am I to do when I get to London?" And as the evening was drawing on, he thought he should be safer near the house; " and there's my bundle, by the by, in that parlour; somebody may walk off with that too," he added, as he jumped off the stile and turned his steps towards the inn.

When the two men saw him move, they followed his example; and lounging slowly back, " marshalled him the way that he was going"—Macbeth's dagger could not be more disagreeable.

Harry, to avoid them, walked straight into the house, and into his odious parlour; where, however, he found the pocket handkerchief that contained all his worldly goods, quite safe. He was hungry, and would have been glad of some supper; and tired, and would have been glad to go to bed; but he distrusted both the supper and the bed. He doubted the roof he was under being an honest one; and of all places in the world, bed is the least inviting where such a suspicion prevails—even according to the landlord's

own admission, " he got all sorts there;" and the sample Harry
had seen, slight as was his experience of mankind, unpleasantly
confirmed the assertion. So as he felt he must do something, for
it was impossible to sit in the wretched room doing nothing, he
decided on the supper as the least evil of the two.

The supper, when it appeared, promised better than the tea—it
was more in the line of business at " The Admiral," where such
" thin potations," were seldom called for; and the remains of a
cold round of beef, the loaf he had at tea, and a pint of porter in
a pewter pot, graced the dirty and scanty table-cloth.

Harry had just cut himself a slice of meat and a corner of the
loaf, and was preparing to make himself some amends for his
previous fast, when the door opened, and the landlord ushered in
the two odious men in black—announcing that the gentlemen requested permission to join the young gentleman at supper.

Banquo's ghost was not a more unwelcome visitor. Harry
coloured to the eyes, and looked confused and annoyed, but he
had not courage to object. In fact, he had a notion that his objections, had he made any, would have been of very little avail:
so he went on eating his supper as composedly as he could, without raising his eyes from the plate, or taking any notice of his
company. The landlord brought them knives, and forks, and
plates, and a pot of porter; and they straightway helped themselves, and began to feed like ostriches.

" Here's to you, sir," said one of them, raising the pewter vessel
to his lips. Harry bowed.

" You don't feed, sir," continued the man. " One 'ud expect a
youngster like you'd be more peckish after your walk. And this
here round's capital."

" I've eat very well," replied Harry, who might have added,
" the sauce has spoiled the supper."

" I take it, now, you've trudged some miles since sunrise?"
pursued the man.

" Not far," answered Harry, wishing to imply that he rather
belonged to the neighbourhood, than came from a distance.

" How many miles can you do in a day now, without knocking
up?" continued the questioner.

" I really don't know," replied Harry, " I never tried."

" Perhaps twenty?" said the man.

" Perhaps I might, if I tried," said Harry.

" Twenty a day, keeping on for four or five days running, is
enough for a youngster at your age," observed the man who had
not before spoken.

Harry thought the speech singular: for it was just five days
since he left Oakfield; and the twenty miles a day had been much
about his rate of travelling.

" How does the country look downwards?" inquired the first
speaker.

" I've not seen much of the country," said Harry. " I believe
it's looking very well."

M

"Hops looking pretty smartish?" asked the man.

"Odd again," thought Harry. "How should he know that I have come through the hop districts?" "I don't know, I'm sure," he answered.

"You're making direct for Lunnun, I take it?" said the second man.

"To be sure he is," said the other, perceiving that Harry was not disposed to answer. "That's the place to make a fortin' in. Isn't it, sir?"

"I don't know, indeed," said Harry, sulkily; "I never was there."

"No, no, you arn't there yet," said the man, with a sneer; "but you're going, you know. I take it, now, you reckon upon being there to-morrow : don't you?"

"I'm by no means sure I'm going there at all," replied Harry, whose cheeks were by this time crimson with vexation and annoyance, and whose countenance plainly denoted his feelings.

"Oh, you shouldn't balk yourself," said the man, in an ironical tone; "in for a penny in for a pound—neck or nothing. I'm always for carrying things through, I am. You'll be off, I s'pose, by times in the morning?"

To this inquiry Harry made no answer.

"I wonder what o'clock it is," said the second man. "Have you a watch, Larkins?"

"No, I ha'n't," replied Larkins. "Perhaps you can tell us what o'clock it is, sir?" added he, addressing Harry, and directing his eye to where the boy's little chain and seals hanging out betokened that he had a watch within.

Harry did not know how to evade answering the question, so he unwillingly drew out poor Fanny's present, for it was a watch she had given him on his birth-day; and his initials and crest were engraven on it.

"It's half-past nine," he answered; and was about to replace his timepiece in his pocket; when the man nearest him stretched out his hand, and without violence, but in a manner that denoted he was determined to have it, took it away from him.

Harry started up, for he thought they intended to rob him.

"Sit down, sir, sit down; don't be flurried," said the man. "No harm's meant. You shall have your watch again directly; I only want to look at it."

"Rale metal," observed Larkins, as he and his companion examined the watch; observing the initials, the engravings on the seals, and opening it to read the maker's name; after which they handed it back to Harry; and asked him if he'd join them in a glass of brandy and water; to which polite invitation he answered in the negative, and said he was going to bed. They admitted that he couldn't do better, as he'd be the fitter for his next day's journey; so with that encouragement, he rang the bell, and asked to be shown to his bed-room.

A dirty drab of a girl brought him a flaring bit of tallow candle in a tall, crooked, copper candlestick, and desired him to follow her.

"I'll take care to lock my door," thought he, as he took leave of his friends, "and I'll be off by daylight in the morning, that I may escape them, if possible;" but he didn't feel very sure that it *would* be possible; for he still believed that, for some purpose or another, they were watching his proceedings.

CHAPTER XXV.

HARRY MAKES AN EFFORT TO PART COMPANY WITH THE TWO GENTLEMEN
IN BLACK; AND MEETS WITH ANOTHER ADVENTURE.

"WELL," exclaimed Larkins, when Harry had closed the door, "ar'n't this prime luck?"

"It's the right covey," said the other, taking a printed paper from his pocket. "No mistake."

"Read it," said Larkins.

"'Fifty pounds reward,' said the other, spreading the paper on the table before him. 'Left his home, on the night of the 15th, from the neighbourhood of Mapleton—a young gentleman, five feet three and a half in height, figure slight, fair complexion, hair brown, eyes dark, features handsome. He wore a blue jacket with a velvet collar, a black silk waistcoat, iron-gray trousers, and a black ribbon round his neck; and is supposed to have carried a small bundle, in a red silk handkerchief. He had also a silver watch, on which were engraven the letters H. L. and a crest. Maker's name Grierson. Fifty pounds will be given to whoever will bring the above young gentleman safely to No. 7, Mark Lane: or give such information as shall lead to his discovery.'"

"All right," said Larkins, "ev'ry partick'ler."

"D'you think he smokes us?" said the other, whose name was Gomm.

"He don't like us," said Larkins, "but that's nat'ral. Thinks we want to pluck him."

"All he's got about him, watch and all, wouldn't fetch ten pounds," answered Gomm.

"No, no," said Larkins: "t'other's the go: all safe too."

"Let's have another jorum," said Gomm—"the covey 'll pay the tick," so they called for another edition of brandy and water, and invited the landlord to give them his company.

"You're in luck, gentlemen," said the host, when he heard their story. "It might have fell to me, if I'd seen the bill; for I'd a notion from the first he was on a lark, and had a mind to ax him a few questions; but he held up his head, and war'n't over communicative."

"It was just an accident," said Gomm, "that I see'd it. We were coming through Southwark yesterday, and I spied a man afore us sticking the bills; so I stopped to read one on 'em—and

M 2

I said, says I, to Larkins, that 'ud be a fine fish to catch, if we could light on him—"

"Let's get his marks, says I," said Larkins, intersecting the course of his friend's narration, "who knows but we may light on him? The road we're going's as like as any for him to take, if he's making for Lunnun; as they all do, when they go upon a lark."

"So I ax'd the fellow for a bill," said Gomm; "and sure enough what should I see as we come down the road but the very identical covey."

"*You* see'd him?" exclaimed Larkins, "*I* see'd him, if you please. You'd ha' walked on, and never stopped till we got to Rochester, as we'd fixed on, if I hadn't twigged him."

"I had my eye on him," said Gomm, "afore ever you spoke, and had been surweying him for some time."

"Why didn't you say so then?" asked Larkins.

"Cause 'twas no use speaking till I was sure," answered Gomm; "besides he was looking at us, and I didn't want to set him a suspecting of anything till we had him safe. He might ha' been off afore we'd time to see his marks."

Upon this Mr. Larkins contradicted Mr. Gomm, and asserted that he was sure he had not seen him till he had himself drawn his attention to the lad swinging on the gate. Mr. Gomm swore that he had; and added that if he hadn't first observed the billsticker in Southwark, Mr. Larkins would never have known anything about the fugitive at all; and thus, from less to more, they quarrelled as to who had contributed most to the discovery, and who had a claim upon the largest share of the fifty pounds. In short, each felt that he could have accomplished the business as well by himself, and was not disposed to admit a partnership in the reward. When they had quarrelled sufficiently, the host interfered, and succeeded in bringing about a reconciliation; upon which they called for more liquor, and sat drinking far into the night.

The bed-room to which Harry ascended, was not raised more than half-a-dozen stairs above the ground-floor, and appeared to be a small offset from the house built over the stable-yard. It contained two beds standing near together, each furnished with blue checked curtains, and a red worsted quilt. The rest of the appointments consisted of two chairs, which had once had straw seats, but had now scarcely any seats at all; a rickety painted table, with an old looking-glass on it, that being cracked across the middle presented to the eye of the curious two half faces that did not appear to have any connexion with each other; a washing stand, with the legs tied, to keep them from a disunion which would have been fatal to the security of the whole body, together with that of the cracked basin and ewer which it supported.

"Is there a key to the door?" inquired Harry of the girl, as he examined the lock.

"A key!" said she, "no; what do you want with a key?"

"To lock the door," replied Harry, "to be sure."

"Lock the door!" exclaimed the girl, looking at him with astonishment at so unreasonable a proposition, "how be the other company to get in, if you locks the door?"

"Other company!" said Harry. "What other company? You mustn't put anybody else into this room."

"Mustn't I?" said the girl. "Where be the gentlemen to sleep then, when we ha'n't no other room?"

"What gentlemen?" asked Harry.

"The two gentlemen as supped in the best parlour," answered the servant. "They've bespoke this here t'other bed."

"I won't let anybody sleep in my room," said Harry.

"What for?" said she, contemptuously, "you can't sleep in both beds yourself, can you! Where's the harm of having two Christ'ens to sleep in the room with you?" and without waiting to hear further objections to an arrangement that appeared to her so unobjectionable, she walked out of the room.

Harry stood aghast! To sleep in the room with the two odious men in black! The thing was impossible! There was not only disgust, but an overpowering sense of danger—"Then that was why they gave me back my watch," said he, "because they can take it in the night, and perhaps they mean to murder me too!"

Whether Gaveston had sent them to find him out, or whether their object was plunder, that they had evil designs against him he felt assured. How was he to escape them? Should he throw himself on the protection of the landlord? But he was by no means certain that the landlord was any better than his customers. He still heard the voices of the noisy topers in the front room below, that echoed with their rude merriment, and vulgar songs; but if he addressed his apprehensions to them what could he expect but insult and laughter? Harry, like other boys, had read strange stories of treacherous hosts and murdered travellers; and he searched about for the trap-door through which his body was to be conveyed away when they had murdered him; and, oh, horror! he found it! There was actually a trap in the floor. Here was the confirmation of his worst suspicions! He had fallen into a den of thieves and murderers, and was doomed to die the death of his poor uncle; to be murdered in an inn! Oh, how he arraigned his folly! How he wished himself back under Fanny's roof! There danger could not reach him; and whilst she knew where he was, Gaveston dared not have touched his life. But now, no one knew where he was; he was without defence, without protection; and with little peril to his enemies he might be put out of the way and his destiny never discovered.

He softly opened the door, and listened to the voices below. He not only heard those in the front room, but he distinguished those of his friends in the back parlour. He thought there was a third amongst them; and on venturing a little nearer, he discovered it was that of the landlord. The front door of the house stood wide open the while, and looked very inviting. The door

of the parlour was shut, but that of the front room was partly
open; he discerned the light shining into the passage. Should
he be able to pass unobserved? Or, if the occupants of the room
saw him, would they stop him?

He was yet debating these essential points when the door of
the parlour opened, and the landlord came out. Harry had
barely time to retreat out of sight. The host passed into the
front room, and said something to the people in it. Harry gently
closed his room door that the light within might not betray him;
and then concealing his person behind a projection of the
wainscot, he watched the proceedings below. Presently the
landlord came out again, and went into his bar, which was on
the opposite side of the passage to the best parlour, and in a few
minutes he descried Sal, the maid-servant who had turned such
a deaf ear to his expostulations, bearing a tray into the front
room, on which were sundry pewter pots, jugs, and glasses. She
then returned to the bar; and, anon, the landlord himself
appeared, loaded with a fresh supply of liquor, which he carried
into the back parlour, and shut the door; and ere long, he
heard his voice mingling with that of Larkins and Gomm in loud
debate.

"Now," thought Harry, "is my time. They'll none of them
stir till they've drunk that, at all events;" and he stepped back
into his room and fetched his bundle and hat; which last article,
in the heat of his suspicions of the gentlemen in black, he had
fortunately brought up stairs with him.

He came out softly; and after waiting an instant to take a final
survey, he had just set his foot on the first stair, when, to his
dismay, Sal the maid came out of the bar, and banged to the
front door; after which she again returned into her den.

Here was a catastrophe! His last hope cut off; for it was
utterly impossible he could open the door without being heard.
He returned to his room, and sitting down on the side of his
miserable bed, he burst into tears. He was, then, doomed to die
in that wretched place; and he wondered if his poor mamma
was looking down from heaven in pity for his melancholy fate.
Her sweet gentle face rose up before him—so did the image of
his kind uncle, and all the friends who had ever loved him. His
poor heart swelled as if it would burst with the agony of these
tender memories and regrets; and the bitter contrast betwixt the
past and the present.

When the paroxysm had a little abated, he again rose and
looked out; all below was as it had been; the outer door still
closed. Suddenly, he thought of the window; it could not be
very high, for the room was but little raised above the lower floor.
He shut his door again, and examined the window. It was in
the lattice fashion, consisting of small three-cornered pieces of
glass, united by leaden bands, and opened in the centre with a
latch.

He unfastened it, and looked out—the distance from the ground was nothing to an active boy, more especially one who was flying for his life. The only thing to be feared was, that there might be some one yet stirring in the stable-yard; but all seemed quiet. He stepped back and closed the curtains of his bed all around; untied his bundle and threw the red handkerchief conspicuously across the back of a chair by the bed side; extinguished the candle, and set that also on the chair, as if it had been put out after he was in bed; and then, without further pause or deliberation, he let himself down from the window, hanging by the sill with one hand, whilst he closed it after him with the other. All was as quiet as he could desire. He stepped softly past the window of the best parlour, and heard the voices of his dreaded companions apparently raised in anger; they were just then in the crisis of their dispute, as to whom belonged the merit of first discovering Harry. He was afraid there might be a dog; but there was none; and he passed under the little archway into the high road; crossed it, and fled across the fields that he had walked over in the evening. He remembered to have seen smoke rising from a chimney somewhere in that direction; it might be from a farmhouse where he could claim protection; and, at all events, he thought his enemies would be more likely to pursue him, if they chose to do so at all, along the high road than across the country.

For some time Harry walked on very fast, occasionally varying his pace with a run; and in the energy that his terror lent him, forgetting that he was tired.

At length, however, his legs took the liberty of reminding him that they had been going all day; and he would have been very glad to have found an open barn-door, or some sort of shelter where he might have obtained a few hours' rest; but nothing of the sort presented itself. Indeed Harry was approaching a neighbourhood where people leave nothing open that they can keep closed—he was drawing near to Gravesend.

Delicately nurtured as he had been, he was afraid to lie down and sleep upon the damp grass; and afraid, too, lest his pursuers might steal upon him whilst he slept; but he was too exhausted to go further without some respite, and he looked about for a seat that would afford him a place of repose. The moon that had lighted him from Oakfield was waning now, but the night was clear; and the purple canopy above him was spangled with countless gems. The field he was in was the last of a series that he had been crossing, and led into the high road by a stile; the only seat he could discern was the step of the stile, a desirable one enough in his circumstances, since it afforded the convenience of resting his back against the bars; but it had the fault of being conspicuous. However, there was no choice—he was now far away from the odious inn, and he sat down upon it, resolving to trust to his ears to warn him, in time, of approaching danger.

But his most vigorous efforts could not defend him from falling into a doze, which would, doubtless, ere long have terminated in a sound nap, had he not, in his imperfect sleep, dreamed that he was in bed at the inn; and that he heard the voices of the gentle-men in black as they were ascending the stairs, consulting as to what manner of death they should inflict upon him. He started awake with the horror that seized him—and he fancied he heard them still—a moment more and he was sure of it; at least, he was sure he heard footsteps and voices approaching, although he could not distinguish what they were saying.

His first impulse was to jump over the stile into the high road; but just as he was about to do so, a moving shadow falling across it, caught his eye, and showed him he was going the wrong way; the persons were approaching by the road; his only resource was to crouch down under the hedge; which he did instinctively; although, as the strangers were coming from an opposite direction, he had no particular reason to fear them, nor to suppose they were in pursuit of him.

They gradually drew near, walking very slowly, and speaking so low, that Harry could not catch a word of the conversation. He listened intensely to ascertain if the voices were those of Larkins and Gomm; but he could not be certain. At length, however, when they reached the stile they stopped, and he was afraid they were about to cross it; but instead of doing so, they drew up, and placing their backs against it, they continued their colloquy.

"There's no danger of our being suspected," said one of the persons. "Every man on 'em thinks we are at sea in the Halifax. They don't know we got ashore again at Scilly. How should they?"

"I take it she's sure to drop down with the tide to-morrow," said the other.

"Sure enough," answered the first. "But s'pose she didn't she'll be down next tide."

"But then she might be off next morning, and that wouldn't do, no how."

"She'll be down to-morrow," said the first. "Bill Jones heard the captain say so for sartain."

"Is Bill sure of the second watch?"

"Sartain," said the other. "If all's right, he'll hang a white flag over her starboard. If we don't see the white flag, we're to keep off. If so be it's as clear as it is to-night, we should see it from the shore; but a cloudy sky would suit better."

"There's no fear but what he's got the chest aboard with him, I s'pose?" said the second speaker.

"Sure to have it," replied the first; "promised to take it out with him this voyage, 'cause the girl's to be spliced, and wants it. Bill heard him order his own servant to fetch it. The only fear I know is, that he may sleep ashore. He does sometimes, but not often."

"It'ond be the easier done," answered the second; "there'd be no difficulty then whatsomed'ever."

"And let him off?" exclaimed the first. "Not if I can help it.

Whatever you may think on't, I'd sooner have his life than the jewels, if so be I could only have one on 'em,—b—t him !"

" The sun'll be up in another hour," observed the second ; " we'd better be moving off."

" We'll keep ourselves snug at the Pretty Polly till nightfall," said the first, as they moved away—" we shall see her coming down along——" and the remainder of the sentence was lost to Harry. " Villains too," said he to himself, " but they are not my villains, at any rate. However, it's fortunate I hid myself, for they might have robbed me, if they'd done nothing worse."

Lest he should fall in with them, Harry thought it advisable to remain where he was till the sun was above the horizon ; and then, his valour fortified by the broad light of the day, he jumped over the stile, and directed his steps to the westward, which he knew must be the side London lay on.

He had scarcely advanced a mile, when he was cheered by the sight of a large town, with the thin smoke of the newly-lighted fires curling up through the atmosphere, and the tall masts of numerous vessels, some with their blue-peters waving in the breeze, appearing at intervals between the chimneys.

With renewed vigour he quickened his pace ; and having passed through the suburbs, where he remarked several inns that bore a striking resemblance, hosts as well as houses, to the one he had fled from in the night, he soon found himself at the entrance of a long, decent-looking street ; where perceiving an elderly man taking down the shutters from a respectable shop, he requested he would recommend him to an inn. The man pointed out one two doors off, where he assured him he would be very comfortable ; Harry, following his advice, addressed himself to a sleepy-looking waiter he saw standing at the door, who forthwith introduced him into the coffee-room ; there, after a reasonable interval, he procured some breakfast, and then, weary and exhausted, he went to bed.

CHAPTER XXVI.

HARRY MAKES A NEW ACQUAINTANCE, AND PROVES HIMSELF A HERO.

IN a blessed oblivion of the two gentlemen in black, and of all his other troubles, Harry spent the day succeeding the eventful night —the history of which we have detailed in the last chapter—and he might possibly have slept for twelve hours more, but that the chambermaid, whose good-will had been won by his handsome face and pleasing manners in the morning when she conducted him to his room, took the liberty of putting in her head to investigate the cause of his protracted silence and eclipse. He was still fast asleep, and she walked up to his bedside to look at him.

Harry opened his eyes, and beheld the round, good-humoured
face of the woman leaning over his pillow.

"Is it time to get up?" said he, not recollecting at first the
circumstances that had brought him there.

"You need not get up if you don't like, my dear," said she:
"but you'd better let me bring you some tea. You've had no
dinner; and you'll be starved."

"I think I should like some tea," said Harry, sitting up in
the bed.

"I'll bring you some," said the woman: "what would you like
to eat?"

"I think I'll get up," said Harry, beginning to shake off the
drowsiness of his long slumber. "I believe I've had sleep
enough."

"You must have walked a great way to be so tired," remarked
the chambermaid. "Had you been travelling all night?"

"A great part of it," replied Harry. "And, besides that, I'd
a sad fright. I put up at an inn where I'd reason to suspect
they'd some bad designs against me, and I ran away."

"Lawk, my dear," said the chambermaid, "sure they would
not hurt such a lamb as you!"

"I don't know," replied he. "I can tell you I'm very glad I
got away. The chambermaid was such a wretch too—very unlike you, I assure you."

This last compliment completed Harry's conquest: and Jenny
having satisfied herself that he was provided with everything he'
wanted in his room, proceeded down stairs in order to use her interest with the waiter, that he might have a comfortable meal prepared for him against he was dressed.

The contrast between the comforts of his present situation, and
the terrors and miseries of the preceding evening, was a most
agreeable one to Harry; and the kind solicitude of the chambermaid, and the civility of the waiter, as they hovered about his
tea-table, quite warmed his heart, and cheered his spirits.

"What ship was that came down along just now?" asked
Jenny of the waiter."

"The Fire Fly, Captain Glassford," replied he: "bound for
Jamaica. I should not wonder if we have him up here to supper
by and by. He most times gives a supper before he sails."

"Perhaps, my dear," said Jenny, "you never saw any
shipping?"

"No," replied Harry, "I never did."

"Well, then," said she, "I'm sure it would be worth your
while to walk down to the shore. You'll see a sight of it there,
and it ar'n't two minutes' walk."

Harry said he thought it would do him good after sleeping so
much; so he took her directions, and set off.

It was really an interesting sight to him, and he stood gazing
with wonder and admiration at the forest of masts, and the monstrous hulks, heaving to and fro on the waves; and thinking he

should like to go on board some of them, and be initiated into the
mysteries of the interior. One particularly attracted his attention. It was a beautiful vessel, with a fine gilt figure-head that
glistened in the beams of the setting sun ; and she was just in the
act of lowering her white sails and throwing out her anchor.
Harry thought it would be very pleasant to go to sea in such a fine
ship ; and wondered whether, if he did not succeed in getting into
the army, he might not possibly be more fortunate with the navy.

As soon as she had dropped her anchor, Harry, who continued
to watch her motions with the curiosity of a boy to whom such
scenes were new, observed them lowering a boat, into which, as
soon as it touched the water, leaped several men in white jackets.

"It's the captain's gig," observed some of the bystanders.
"He's coming ashore."

The long, narrow boat vaulted over the waves, impelled by the
regular strokes of the oarsmen, and soon touched the strand ; and
a handsome-looking, middle aged man, with rather a stern expression of countenance, stepped out.

"Shall we lay to, sir?" asked the steersman, touching his hat.
"No," replied the captain, "I shall sleep ashore ;" and he walked
quickly away ; whilst Harry still stood watching the progress of
the graceful boat on her return to the ship.

After he had strolled through the principal parts of the town,
when he at length returned to the inn he found the house in some
bustle. Captain Glassford had arrived, and, as the waiter expected, had ordered supper for himself and friends. Harry
thought he should be as well out of the way ; and as he felt that,
in spite of his day's rest, sleep was still in arrears to him, he went
to bed.

It was late when he descended to the coffee-room the next
morning, where the waiter had placed his breakfast. He had tied
up his little bundle before he came down, intending to start for
London without further delay ; and with a feeling of regret he sat
down to eat his last meal where he had met so much civility and
good treatment.

Whilst he was waiting for his tea and toast, a gentleman who had
been seated in one of the recesses with a newspaper in his hand,
arose, and walked over to the hearth where Harry was standing
warming himself by a little fire that had been just put in the grate
on account of the frostiness of the morning.

"A bit of fire is not unacceptable," observed the stranger,
whom Harry recognised as the captain of the vessel he had seen
dropping her anchor on the preceding evening, and who had
afterwards come ashore in his gig.

Harry said it was very cool ; but he thought it must be colder
in a ship ; and he asked if there were fires on board ; and made
some other inquiries with respect to the internal arrangements of
a vessel ; so that from one thing to another they fell into conversation, and the captain proposed that they should eat their breakfast at the same table ; an offer which Harry gladly accepted, and

by which he was much a gainer; for the captain ordered a luxu-
riant breakfast, of which he urged his young companion freely to
partake, and for which he would not permit him to pay any share
of the expense.

"If you never saw the interior of a ship," said the captain,
" suppose you go on board with me this afternoon. The novelty
will amuse you for some hours; and my gig shall put you ashore
at night. I shall sleep on board myself, as I intend sailing with
the morning's tide."

Harry hesitated a little, for he thought he ought not to lose
more time; besides that his funds were daily reducing, and he was
dreadfully afraid of their being exhausted before his objects in
London were accomplished. Still the temptation was great—
" Besides," thought he, ",I should like to see the inside of a ship,
and how people live in one; for who knows but I myself may be a
sailor some day?" So he finally resolved to defer his journey
another day, and accept of Captain Glassford's invitation.

" If you'll meet me at four o'clock," said the captain, " where
you say you saw me come ashore last night, I'll take you off in my
gig."

When the breakfast was ended the captain went out; and
Harry, who found the shipping the most attractive object, walked
down to the strand and seated himself on the edge of a boat,
where he could be amused with watching the proceedings in the
various vessels that were anchored near the shore. The Fire Fly
lay farther out than some of the others, but yet not so far but he
could see the crew moving about, apparently washing and cleaning the decks. One man he observed come to the side, shake a
white cloth over several times; and once or twice he left it hanging there for some minutes as if to dry.

The morning passed quickly enough in a scene so new, and after
returning to the inn to take some dinner, Harry repaired again to
the strand to keep his appointment.

Punctual as the hour the captain appeared, and the gig was as
punctually there to meet him; and, rapidly borne over the waves
by the light boat, a few minutes saw Harry on board the Fire Fly.

Having first taken him to his own cabin, and shown him everything there, Captain Glassford called one of the officers and committed him to his care.

" You'll find plenty to amuse you," he said, " for two or three
hours. I've got some letters to write; but when tea's ready I
shall send to you."

There was amusement enough, and Harry found so many questions to ask, and the young man, whom Captain Glassford had
selected for his intelligence, was so willing to give information,
that the afternoon passed rapidly away. At seven o'clock he was
invited to tea with the captain, who treated him with great kindness, and showed him his arms, and a variety of curiosities;
amongst others a small red snake preserved in spirits.

" It's a beautiful creature," said Harry; " is it venomous?"

"Deadly," replied the captain. "It was nearly the cause of my death, and that's why I keep it."

"Did it bite you?" inquired Harry.

"No," said the captain, "it did not, or I shouldn't be here to show it to you. But it was intended to do so; and I had a very narrow escape."

Harry felt considerable curiosity to hear how the serpent could have been designed to bite the captain; but he forbore to ask farther questions, lest he should appear impertinent; and between eight and nine o'clock he was put ashore.

It was not without a good deal of regret that he parted with his new friend. He was in a situation that naturally inclined him to cling with eagerness to any one that showed him kindness. Poor fellow, he was so much in need of friends! "I've none," he thought, "that can help me. Fanny's but a slave herself; and Jeremy, and Dobbs, and Susan, though they all love me, they can do nothing for me." He half regretted that he had not told his story to Captain Glassford, and asked his advice—"but then," said he, "perhaps he'd have blamed me for running away: everybody's ready to think a boy that run's away is in the wrong; and perhaps he mightn't believe Gaveston's as bad as he is—so it may be better I held my tongue."

He watched the gig on its return till he saw it heaved upon the deck; and then bidding farewell to the Fire Fly, and its captain, he walked into the town. In passing the corner of a street he observed several people standing round a door, and many others were making their way to the same spot; so Harry, supposing there was something to be seen, took the same direction.

"What is it?" he asked of one of the crowd.

"It's the playhouse," replied the man. "There's the great Mrs. Siddons, from London, acting to-night."

Harry had read plays, and he had heard of the great Mrs. Siddons, but he had never seen either.

"Can I go in?" said he.

"Certainly," replied the man, "as soon as it's half price, which will be in a few minutes."

Harry inquired the price of admission, and having ascertained that it was a sum within the compass of his means, he resolved to treat himself with so rare a sight; and accordingly pushed forwards with the rest of the aspirants, and succeeded in obtaining a seat in the pit.

Here, for about three hours, he sat rapt—first entranced by the glorious tragedy, and the glorious actress, and then thrown into fits of uncontrollable laughter by the humours of the farce. The past and the future were alike forgotten—it was the unveiling of a new world, the opening of a mine of pleasures unconceived; and when, at a little past midnight, Harry found himself in the street, his mind was in such a state of excitement and bewilderment, that he hurried on after the crowd, without knowing or pausing to reflect, whether he was pursuing the right road to "the Crown" or not.

He was, at length, brought to his recollection by finding himself at the water-side; and when awakened to a consciousness of the scene before him, he did not regret his mistake. The twinkling stars and the waning crescent of the pale moon served enough to show the large hulks with their bosoms resting on the now nearly motionless waters; whilst their tall masts looked dim and shadowy in the dreamy and uncertain light. All was still and quiet—no sound proceeded from those giants of the deep, nor from the many hundred living beings they contained.

Harry looked for his friend the Fire Fly—she was conspicuous, for she lay rather apart from the others, and, as he fancied, had moved somewhat farther out since he left her.

He now recognised where he was, and when he had gazed sufficiently on the fairy scene before him, he turned in the direction of his lodging, still, however, keeping by the shore, by which for a certain distance he could approach it as well as by the street.

In his course he passed several low public-houses, in which he could see and hear the noisy revellers of the night, drinking and smoking within; and occasionally the echo of a boisterous song, or a loud burst of laughter, or the cry of a woman's voice, testified to the coarse nature of their merriment.

He was just on the point of leaving the strand for the street, when, as he approached one of these houses that stood a little remote from the others, he heard the voices of persons in conversation proceeding from an open window; and on looking up, he perceived two men with their heads out, one of whom was holding a glass to his eye.

"There's Bill Jones, by G—!" exclaimed one of the voices at the very instant Harry was passing beneath the window—"all's right! come along!" and they pushed back their seats and disappeared.

"Bill Jones," thought Harry, as the name struck on his ear— "Bill Jones," and he looked about, but saw nobody near him. "Bill Jones!" again he repeated, "that was the name those fellows mentioned in the night—they certainly said something about Bill Jones. What was it?" and he tried to recall what he had heard, which, partly from the pre-occupation of his own fears, and partly because he did not understand their phrases, and had caught but disjointed bits of the dialogue, had not made much impression on him.

"There was something about Bill Jones—and the Pretty Polly —I wonder if this is the Pretty Polly!" and he looked up at the sign that was slung on a pole, but he could not discern what it was—"and the captain sleeping on board, and a chest that they were going to steal, I suppose—I hope it wasn't my captain, by the by;" and he turned his head back to look at the Fire Fly—and he discerned something—he was not at first sure, and he strained his eyes to see—yes, there was a glimmering light that appeared to proceed from a lantern held or slung over her side, and by that faint light, on the dark hull of the ship gleamed a white flag.

On the instant. the whole truth flashed upon Harry's mind; and without pausing to reflect what would be most advisable to do, he turned back, and ran with all the speed he could along the strand to where he had parted with the Captain's gig some hours earlier; but just as he reached the spot, he saw a boat push off with two men in it, whom he could not doubt were the villains upon their desperate expedition.

"Oh, what shall I do?" thought Harry. "If I go to the inn, by the time I've told my story, and got assistance, it will be too late. They'll have murdered him before that—who can I apply to? Perhaps the people in these public-houses are all rogues too, and wouldn't help me if they could—but I must try them," and so saying, he set off towards the nearest house in which he saw there was a light.

The door was open, and in rushing into the passage Harry ran against a man that was coming out.

"Hallo, my hearty?" cried the man. "What quarter's the wind in now?"

"Oh," cried Harry, seizing the hard hand of the bluff sailor, "will you help me?"

"To be sure I will," replied the man. "What's the row?"

"Can you get a boat?" said Harry. "We can do nothing without a boat."

"What," said the man, "ashore without leave? In plain clothes, too? Whew!" and he gave a long whistle, as much as to say, "I see."

"Oh, come along!" cried Harry, pulling him by the hand; "come along, and get the boat, and you shall be paid anything you like; only make haste!"

"What ship is it?" said the sailor, jerking up his trousers, and preparing to accompany Harry.

"It's the Fire Fly," replied he. "Where's your boat?"

"What, Captain Glassford!" said the sailor, and he gave another long whistle—"He's a taut hand too. Don't stand no gammon."

"Where's the boat?" reiterated Harry.

"Hauled up here close by," replied the man. "This is her;" and he began pushing the little boat into the water; Harry, in his eagerness, helping with all his might and main. They were soon in it and away.

"Give me an oar," cried Harry. "Perhaps I can help you;—you must row for your life."

But Harry had never used an oar, except on the pond at Oakfield; and the quick eye of the sailor soon detected him.

"Y' ar'n't used to handle an oar, master," said he. "You pull like a landsman."

Harry was conscious that the man misunderstood the object of his haste, and uncertain of the sort of character he had to deal with, he was afraid to disclose it, lest he should refuse to proceed. "I never could row," said he, "but never mind that. Pull away as fast as you can;" and still, though his exertions did not

advance the boat an inch, he tugged at the oar with all his might
and main.

"I wish I knew whether he's an honest man," thought he, as
they neared the ship. "He might advise me what to do."

"Avast rowing there! The captain 'll hear you, and you'll get
a wigging," said the good-natured tar, taking away the oar that
Harry was splashing and dashing the water with to no purpose,
and laying it quietly across the thwarts; whilst he himself, as
softly as possible, and with a scarcely perceptible motion of his
arm, urged the boat forwards.

"Will you help me?" said Harry, again, who thought the
good-nature of the man towards himself testified in his favour.

"Arn't I helping you?" answered the other.

"But will you stand by me?" said Harry; "will you come
aboard and help the captain? There are thieves and murderers
aboard, and I'm going to try and save him."

"You!" exclaimed the sailor, amazed, and beginning to think
the boy was out of his senses, or had been drinking.

"Yes," replied Harry, "there's no time to explain—only follow
me aboard and stand by me—that's all I ask."

"I'll do that," replied the sailor, "with all my heart. But I
hear no stir aboard—all's quiet."

"Yes," said Harry, "and the greater the danger the captain's
in, because they'll attack him in his sleep. But I don't see anything of the boat the thieves were in, though I saw them push off
just before I met you."

"Mayhap she's round o' the larboard side," answered the
sailor.

The lantern and flag had also disappeared; and there was not
the slightest symptom that anything unusual was going on
aboard the Fire Fly. "Can I be mistaken?" thought Harry—
but no; everything had corresponded so exactly with the conversation he had overheard in the field, that it was scarcely
possible he could have misinterpreted the intention of the men.

"Is there a public-house called the Pretty Polly, a little way
up the strand, in that direction?" inquired he of his companion.

"There is," replied the man, "and a blackguard place it is."

"Then I'm right," said Harry, "for that's the place the thieves
named."

"We'd better keep to the starboard," said the sailor, "if you
think the rascals are o' t'other side. Shall I call somebody to
hand us over a rope?" added he, as they touched the side of the
ship.

"No, no," answered Harry, "only help me up and follow me
as quickly as you can."

"I'll only stop to make her fast with an end of a rope I've got
here," answered the sailor, as he hoisted Harry upon his shoulders,
"and be after you in a twinkling."

When Harry set his light foot on the deck he cast a rapid
glance from one end of it to the other. There was but one person

to be discerned: and that was a man who was hanging over the larboard side, apparently speaking to a boat below; and whose back consequently being turned, and his attention deeply engaged, he had not been disturbed by the noiseless approach of the new-comers.

Harry only paused to ascertain thus much, and then he darted forward to the companion, and was in the captain's cabin in an instant.

"Wake!" he cried, throwing himself upon the cot, "wake, and get up: your life's in danger!"

Captain Glassford, a man long inured to peril, was upon his feet in a moment; and in another his hand was upon his pistols, which he always kept loaded.

"Give me one," said Harry, elevated into a hero by excitement and enthusiasm, and elated by the success of his enterprise —"give me one—I can fire."

"What's the matter?" said Captain Glassford, now that being prepared for the peril, whatever it might be, he had time to inquire.

"There are thieves coming to attack you—to steal some chest you've got here, and to murder you," replied Harry. "Their boat's by the side now, and there's a man talking to them."

"You must be mistaken, my dear," said Captain Glassford—"such a thing's not likely."

"Have you a man on board called Bill Jones?" asked Harry.

"Yes," answered Captain Glassford, "it must be his watch now."

"Then I'm not mistaken," said Harry—"he's a villain too. Hark—listen—" and he lowered his voice—"they're coming now —don't you hear footsteps?"

"There is some one coming," whispered the captain, and he placed himself opposite the cabin door with a pistol in each hand; whilst Harry, with glowing cheeks and sparkling eyes, raised by his feelings far above the sense of danger, stood fast beside him with another. "Don't fire unless I tell you," said the captain.

The cabin door was still open, and the shoeless feet softly descending were distinctly heard. The experienced officer, calm and collected, cast a glance at his young ally. "Noble little fellow!" he said to himself, "I was taken by his countenance the first moment I looked at him. Who could have thought—?" but the appearance of a head at the door, immediately followed by two others, arrested the train of his reflections.

The men, who had expected to effect their object without noise, and to make their escape before the alarm was given, were not provided with fire-arms; and were therefore taken aback on perceiving the preparation made for their reception. The foremost stepped back upon the others, and they were about to retreat precipitately up the stairs, in the hope of being over the side and away, before they could be overtaken, when they found their

N

progress arrested by a pair of sturdy arms stretched across their path.

"How now, my hearties?" said Harry's boatman, for it was he who was the new ally, "whither so fast?"

The alarm was given; the villains were quickly surrounded and disarmed, and Harry had the satisfaction and the glory of having saved his friend.

"What!" said the captain, when he approached to examine the men after they were secured, "my old enemies—Tyler and Strickland, by heavens! Why, rascals, I thought you were both at sea in the Halifax?"

"We swam ashore by night when she was off Scilly," replied Tyler, "and they put to sea afore they missed us."

CHAPTER XXVII.

A CONSIDERABLE IMPROVEMENT IN THE ASPECT OF HARRY'S AFFAIRS.

HOLDING out his hand, "Well, my dear fellow," said Captain Glassford to Harry, when the bustle and confusion had a little subsided, "you've in all probability saved my life; but how you managed the business I cannot possibly imagine. How did you find out the villains' designs? And how did you contrive to arrive here in the very nick of time?"

"I heard them planning it all in a field last night," replied Harry; "but I didn't understand then very well what they meant to do; nor who it was they were going to rob; nor where the attack was to be made; and when I got here, I was so tired and worn out, that I went to bed and thought no more about it, except that it was lucky they didn't see me, as they would perhaps have robbed me too. And I never should have made out exactly what they meant, if it hadn't been for the mention of Bill Jones, and the white flag;" and then Harry narrated to the captain the conversation he had overheard in the field, the accident that had conducted him to the strand at so late an hour, and all that had followed.

"They are great villains," said Captain Glassford, after he had warmly expressed his acknowledgments to his young preserver; "and this is not the first attempt they have made against my life. This time you've saved me; on the last occasion I owed my preservation to a worthy old friend of mine, to whom I introduced you last night."

"The officer that drank tea with us?" inquired Harry.

"No," replied the captain; "honest old Tycho!"

"What, the old grey terrier?" exclaimed Harry.

"His very self, I assure you," said Captain Glassford; "and as you must stay on board with me to-night, we'll have some supper and a glass of negus, and I'll tell you the story."

Harry made no objections to so agreeable a proposal; and his boatman, after receiving an ample reward for his services, was directed to call at "the Crown," and inform them that their young lodger was safely disposed of for the night—"for I'm sure that good-natured chambermaid would be uneasy about me."

"I believe she would," replied Captain Glassford, "for, to tell you the truth, it was Jenny herself that was the original cause of our acquaintance. I called her in when I was dressing yesterday morning, to sew on a button for me; and happening, by way of saying something, to ask her who was in the house, she took occasion to name you, and to expatiate on the good qualities she had discovered in you. So that, when you came into the coffee-room afterwards, I laid down my paper to take a look at Jenny's favourite."

The captain did not add what Jenny had done, "that she thought the poor little fellow was in some trouble; and that it would be a great kindness in any gentleman to take a little notice of him."

"So you see," continued he, as they sat down to supper—

"'What great effects from trifling causes spring.'

"And here's my friend Tycho, come to listen to his own exploits. It was on my last voyage to Jamaica that those two villains, Tyler and Strickland, were on board my ship. They came to us with very bad characters; but men were scarce, and we were ordered to sea in a hurry, so that I'd no time to be nice, but was obliged to take such as I could get. I gave directions that a strict eye should be kept upon them, and though they were very trouble-some, the rest of the crew being decent, well-behaved men, they couldn't do much mischief during the voyage.

"When we're in port, it's usual to let the men go ashore by turns; but I was very unwilling to let these fellows out of the ship, fearing they'd get into some mischief. However, they begged hard; and though I'd an ill opinion of them, they hadn't done anything bad enough to justify a refusal; so I gave them leave.

"It was a standing rule that no man should be absent from the ship after eight o'clock without a special permission; by which means I kept a taut hand over those I couldn't depend upon, although I never refused reasonable liberty to the steady men.

"The morning after these fellows had had their leave, however, when the second lieutenant came ashore to make his report, he informed me that nothing had been seen of Tyler and Strickland since they left the ship the preceding morning. Upon which I ordered that they should be sought for, and carried aboard directly; and that if they gave any trouble they should be put in irons. The search, however, was vain; we couldn't make out what was become of them.

"I think it was on the third morning of their absence, that we learned a gentleman's house in the interior had been broken into in the night, and robbed of some valuables: and I confess I no sooner heard of it, than I suspected my villains had a hand in the business; and I despatched some of the crew that I could depend upon to look for them in that direction.

"Presently afterwards, however, there came tidings from the ship that Tyler and Strickland were returned. Their story was, that they had wandered far away into the woods to see the country; and that there, Strickland being thirsty had eaten of some fruit or berries he had plucked, which had produced the most violent indisposition; and that Tyler, thinking every moment was to be his last, had been afraid to leave him. To prove the truth of their story, they produced some specimens of the fruit of a very pernicious shrub; and certainly, Strickland had every appearance of having been extremely ill.

"Nevertheless, I doubted their story. I suspected that Strickland had eaten the fruit for the express purpose of accounting for their absence. I knew they'd been in the island before, and the chances were that they were acquainted with the shrub; and I ordered that they should be searched, and be kept close to the ship during the remainder of our stay. Nothing, however, was found upon them; and having no proof that they were guilty, I could not punish them any further.

"After this, they made repeated applications for a day's liberty on shore, which was always denied them; till just before we were about to sail, when they became so urgent, that as they had been conducting themselves better for some time, I yielded to their entreaties, but on the condition that they should not go together, but be each coupled with one of the steadiest of the crew.

"This arrangement evidently annoyed them, and they pleaded hard to go together, promising faithfully to return before eight o'clock, under pain of any punishment I chose to inflict; and representing that it was not pleasant to go ashore with those I had appointed, who were not on friendly terms with them.

"But I was inexorable, suspecting that they had no good motive for their urgency; and, at all events, satisfied that I had no right to let loose such a couple of rascals on the island.

"Strickland went first; and we learned from the man who had accompanied him, that he had made several attempts to give him the slip, and get away into the woods, but that he was too sharp for him.

"It was only a couple of days before we sailed that Tyler had his liberty under the same restrictions; and the companion that had been allotted to him described his attempts at evasion to have been as evident as those of his friend. He even offered a considerable bribe to the man to let him off for a couple of hours, promising faithfully to return at the expiration of the time; but all his efforts and persuasions were unsuccessful, and he was brought back boiling with rage and malignity. In short, it was evident to everybody that they had been prevented from accomplishing some object or another that they'd set their hearts upon, and that they were both grievously disappointed.

" On the following day I came on board myself, and a few hours afterwards we put to sea; and as there was no further possibility of the two fellows getting away, the vigilance with which their motions had been observed was somewhat relaxed.

" I had, and have still, a custom of going upon deck of a morning in my dressing-gown and slippers to look at the weather, and returning to my cabin afterwards to finish my toilet.

" On the morning in question, the first after we had put to sea, when I came below, after my visit to the deck, I found old Tycho lying in the cabin with his fore paws stretched out, and his eyes intently fixed on my boots, which my servant had placed ready for me to put on.

" I patted and spoke to him as I usually did, and asked him to what I was indebted for the honour of such an early visit, for Tycho rarely made his appearance below till breakfast time. He licked my hand, but still his attention appeared more engaged by the boots than by me. However, I thought nothing about it, and presently afterwards I took up one of the boots and drew it on; a proceeding to which Tycho made no manner of objection. But when I stretched out my hand for the other, he barked, and very significantly expressed his disapprobation, and the more I persisted, the more violent became his opposition.

" I could not imagine what the dog meant; and being rather amused at what I considered his eccentricity, I jested with it for some time, stretching out my hand towards the boot, and then drawing it back, as if in submission to his protestations; till at length, having no more time to waste, I resolutely took hold of the boot and prepared to put my foot into it.

" But Tycho was resolved I should do no such thing; and he renewed his opposition with so much energy and determination, that, at last, it grew to a perfect scuffle between him and me which should have the boot, he pulling it one way, and I the other, really disabled from exerting a sufficient degree of force to vanquish him, from the violent fits of laughter he threw me into.

" But fortunately for me, just as I was about to give him a kick and put an end to the nonsense, the battle was decided in favour of Tycho. By a sudden jerk, he wrenched the boot from my hand, and flung it to the other side of the cabin; and, with the impetus of its fall, out flew that beautiful little red snake you so much admired last night.

" Poor fellow! his instinct, or reason, or whatever faculty it may be that Providence has endowed him with, had saved my life."

" But how did the snake get there?" asked Harry. " Are there snakes on board a ship?"

" Not unless they be brought there," replied the captain; " and from subsequent investigation we had every reason to believe that Tyler had contrived to procure the reptile from a negro the day before when he was on shore, brought it on board in a bottle, and conveyed it into my boot whilst I was upon deck.

"His motive was revenge for the severity I had shown him and Strickland; and the disappointment I had inflicted by not letting them go on shore alone. For shortly afterwards, the jewels that had been stolen on the occasion of the robbery I mentioned, were found concealed in the woods; and though it could not be proved, there is little doubt but that they had committed it, and had hidden their plunder, intending to seize some favourable opportunity of securing it when their persons were not likely to be searched. And now, my dear fellow," said the captain, when he had finished his narrative, "we must think of going to bed; and to-morrow, for I must remain here another day to make arrangements about those rascals, we will, if you'll give me leave, have a little conversation about your affairs; and you must explain to me by what strange chance you happened to be concealed under a hedge in the middle of the night—certainly, about the last place I should expect to find you in."

Harry, who had now good reason to feel that he had made a friend, declared his readiness to relate all his adventures; and accordingly, the next morning at breakfast, he communicated to Captain Glassford, without reserve, the whole history of his birth, parentage and education; together with his subsequent misfortunes and disappointments in consequence of his uncle's death and Fanny's marriage; and concluded by disclosing the hopes and views with which he had fled from Oakfield and had directed his steps to London.

"My dear child," said Captain Glassford, when Harry had finished his story, "all that's moonshine in the water."

"What is?" asked Harry.

"Your hopes of getting a commission in the way you propose," replied the captain.

"Is it?" said Harry, with a face of dismay.

"I fear so," replied Captain Glassford; "and as for your entering the ranks with the view of promotion, it mustn't be thought of. You little know the sort of life and company you would be subject to—at your age it would be perdition."

"Could I get into the navy, then?" asked Harry.

"I could very likely get you appointed to my own ship as a midshipman," answered the captain, "but the misfortune is, that I have no interest, and without some very favourable chance, you might remain a midshipman all your life, and die a beggar at last. But are you entirely bent on the army or navy? Couldn't you be satisfied with some other mode of life?"

"I should have liked the army," answered Harry, "because papa was in it; but I could be happy in any profession that was fit for a gentleman."

"Then I think I can do better for you," returned the captain, "than in getting you into either the land or sea service, where I have no means of pushing you on. You must stay with me for the present, and consider my ship your home. We can talk the matter over at our leisure; and I'll write to my brother on the subject. Does that proposal suit you?"

"Oh yes, sir," replied the much contented Harry, "I'm very much obliged, indeed."

"Then the thing's settled," returned the captain. "And now, my dear fellow, you'd better go ashore with me. You must be provided with a few little matters that we can easily get here; and you must go and take leave of your friend Jenny at 'the Crown,' to whom I think we both owe our thanks, and something more. We shall return on board to sleep, and sail to-morrow, if possible."

The honest Jenny was liberally rewarded; Harry furnished with everything he required; and relieved from all his cares, grateful and happy, he sailed with Captain Glassford for Jamaica.

CHAPTER XXVIII.

SUSAN FINDS ANOTHER SITUATION, AND MEETS WITH AN OLD ACQUAINTANCE.

As it formed part of Mr. and Mrs. Wetherall's plan of economy to give up their house, and resume their former mode of living in lodgings, without a servant of their own, until they were free from the embarrassments they had incurred, it became necessary for Susan to look out for another situation.

This she found in the family of a Mrs. Aytoun, whose husband, being engaged as a foreign traveller for some great mercantile house, was frequently absent for several months at a time. They had a comfortable small house in one of the streets leading from the Strand down to the water; keeping two female servants; one of whom attended to the cooking department, and cleaned the lower part of the house; whilst the other, who acted as housemaid, had charge of the upper rooms, and was required to wait at table. These last were the duties that devolved upon Susan. Without being affluent, Mr. Aytoun's salary was sufficient to enable them to live respectably; and the little establishment was altogether kept on a very comfortable footing.

The marriage, also, seemed a fortunate one. It had been a union of affection, formed about a year before Susan entered her situation; and the husband and wife appeared very well calculated to make each other happy. Mrs. Aytoun was a pretty, cheerful, animated young woman, who had just entered her one and twentieth year; fond of dress, and fond of company; neither of which tastes, however, she allowed herself to indulge to any criminal extent. She was, indeed, much too fond of her husband to stand in need of any constant succession of other people to divert her; and if she were occasionally guilty of any little extravagance for her toilet, it was prompted much more by a desire to please him than to be admired by the world. And Susan thought him well worthy of the pains she took. He was both handsome

and agreeable; his age, perhaps thirty, and his tastes very much
in accordance with his wife's, to whom he also seemed passionately
attached. But it was impossible to be long in his company without perceiving that he had one foible; and that was a too sensitive
pride and an over-susceptibility as to what the world would say
on all subjects connected with himself and his family. Many a
time when Susan was waiting at table she heard his wife jesting
upon this weakness, the existence of which, silly as he admitted
it to be, he never denied.

"I cannot help it, Alicia," he said one day; "I know it's a
folly, since it is utterly impossible to prevent the world saying a
great many things that are not true; but to fancy people are
whispering or talking about us, or that we form a subject for the
gossip of the neighbourhood, would make me miserable; perfectly
wretched."

"What would you do if you'd a wife like poor Mr. Morland, I
wonder," said Alicia, "who thumps her servants every now and
then, and gives them black eyes?"

"Oh heavens, don't mention it!" cried Mr. Aytoun.

"Or Mrs. Parsons, that they say drinks gin, and very near set
the house on fire the other night, when she was in a state of in-
toxication. Or Mrs. Bloxham, that the baker asserts alters his
figures in her book that she may cheat him out of a loaf or two a
week?"

"I'll tell you what I should do, Alicia," he answered. "I should
blow my brains out. However, I don't think," he added, laughing, "you'll ever put me to so severe a trial. But at the same
time, my love, I cannot forbear, now that I am going to leave you
for a few months, warning you to be very careful. Your situation
is peculiar, Alicia. Young, gay, well-dressed, and I dare say you'll
excuse me for adding, pretty, you are left a great part of your
time without protection, and, therefore, necessarily exposed to
much more close observation than you would be if I were always
with you. You'll find people will be ready to take hold of the
slightest thing—trifles that would never be observed in another
woman."

"But you know I never flirt with anybody, Arthur," replied his
wife. "Who could they connect my name with? Besides, you
know my opinion of married women who flirt. I think a woman
who risks her own reputation and her husband's respectability for
the indulgence of her vanity is virtually much more criminal than
the unfortunate creature who has been led astray by a passion she
could not control. Besides, if a woman chooses to behave as if
she were guilty, who's to tell whether she is or not? She cannot
expect the world will take the trouble of penetrating the truth;
and she may be well assured, that a portion of it, at least, will put
the worst construction on what they see. No, no, my dear Arthur,
you need never fear me. I love and revere my husband a great
deal too much to peril our happiness and respectability at such
foolish play as that. Besides, there, I confess," she added, laugh-

ing, "I should be as susceptible as you are. I couldn't bear to be pointed out wherever I went as Mrs. So-and-so, that has an affair with Mr. So-and-so."

"Heaven forbid!" exclaimed her husband; "but I merely mean to put you on your guard. I know very well you would not flirt, but I would avoid everything that was the least particular—many things you might do, for example, when I am here—I'd dress more plainly too, if I were you."

"That advice I shall have no difficulty in following," replied Alicia, affectionately. "The motive for dressing will be wanting."

Shortly after this, Mr. Aytoun set out on an expedition which engaged him about three months, and nothing could exceed the cautious conduct of his wife during his absence. Other journeys ensued at intervals; but the time he passed at home was always a period of unalloyed happiness.

In this manner three years had elapsed since Susan entered on her situation without any occurrence worth recording, when she learned that Mr. Aytoun was about to start on an expedition that would probably occasion an absence of ten or twelve months.

The parting was a great grief to the young couple, and the last evening they spent together Alicia shed showers of tears. "I used to think two or three months' absence a great hardship," she said; "but this is dreadful. I don't know how I shall ever get through it."

"Time will fly," said her husband, "faster than you imagine."

"Ay, with you," she replied, "who will be always moving, and have plenty of amusement and occupation. But think how different it will be with me, living here alone."

"But you need not always be alone, my love," answered Mr. Aytoun. "You have plenty of acquaintance, and need not want society. At the same time I would not, under present circumstances, engage in too much of it," he added, "or the world will be apt to say that you are gayer when I'm away than when I'm here;" and upon this ensued several other cautions of the like nature; in short, with slight variations, a repetition of the conversation we have above detailed.

Mr. Aytoun had been gone but a very short time when his wife found herself in the family way; a discovery most gratifying, for they had both ardently desired to become parents. "I'll not tell Arthur yet, though," she said to herself, "for fear there should be a disappointment. I declare, I've a mind not to tell him at all, but keep it for a surprise to welcome him home"—and she continued to write letter after letter without giving the slightest hint of the important secret. Neither did she communicate it to her acquaintance; she had no female connexions, nor no very confidential friend. Her home had been in the country, where Mr. Aytoun had first met with her; she settled amongst strangers, and the society they had, had been chiefly formed since their marriage.

Of course, there were great preparations for the expected baby,

and many discussions with Susan, who was in the secret, about
caps, frocks, pinafores, and so forth.

About four months of Mrs. Aytoun's pregnancy had elapsed,
when she called at a shop where she occasionally dealt, to purchase some fine lace, cambric, and other articles, together with
some silk to make a dress for herself. As she did not find it altogether easy to make a selection amongst the multitude of things
presented to her notice, nor was quite certain of the quantities
required, she at last desired the shopman to send her a choice of
the different articles to her house, which were accordingly laid
aside for that purpose. This being arranged, she turned to go
away; and as she did so, took up her handkerchief and purse
that had been lying on the counter, and was thrusting them into
her pocket as she moved towards the door; but before she reached
it, she felt a hand laid on her arm, whilst the man who had been
serving her said, "I beg your pardon, ma'am, but you are not
aware that there is a piece of lace attached to your handkerchief."

She looked down, and saw that she had unconsciously taken up
a remnant of fine lace, and that the end of it was hanging from
her pocket. A circumstance of this sort is always extremely
unpleasant; and it is so difficult to distinguish between accident
and design, that shopkeepers are naturally suspicious. However,
in this instance the man was civil enough, and said nothing that
implied a doubt of her innocence. Nevertheless, Alicia blushed,
and looked confused, as most people would do under the like
circumstances; especially when she saw the heads of several persons turned to look at her; and she hurried out of the shop with
a very uncomfortable feeling, saying to herself, "Heaven be
praised, Arthur was not with me! I believe he'd have fallen into
a fit on the spot."

On the following morning, the things she had desired to look at
arrived; but Mrs. Aytoun having a visitor at the moment,
requested the man to leave them, and call again by and by. He
accordingly went away, and returned in about a couple of hours.
She then selected what she chose, he measured and cut off the
quantities required, and carried away the remainder.

About an hour had elapsed, and she was sitting in her parlour
inspecting her purchases, which were spread out on the table,
when she heard a loud ringing at the bell, and presently Susan
ushered in Mr. Green, who desired to see her immediately.

"I am sorry, ma'am," said he, in rather an insolent tone, "to
be obliged to trouble you; but there is a whole piece of lace missing from the parcel I sent here, besides some yards of another.
The silk returned, also, is short of the measure it ought to be, by
several yards."

"Good heavens, sir!" said Alicia, quite alarmed, "I'm very
sorry; but your man himself measured and cut off what I kept."

"No doubt, ma'am," replied Mr. Green; "I'm aware of that.
But the goods were left here some time by your desire; and the
thing looks very awkward."

"You don't intend to imply that I have your lace!" exclaimed Alicia, indignantly.

"I don't know who else can have it," returned Mr. Green; "unless you have any reason to suspect your servants."

"No," replied Mrs. Aytoun, "I do not suspect my servants; and indeed I am quite sure they were neither of them in the room whilst your goods were here."

"I'm very sorry to do anything so unpleasant, ma'am," said Mr. Green, "but you must permit this gentleman to search your person;" and upon that he called in an officer that he had brought with him, and who was waiting in the passage. Alicia's horror and indignation may be conceived. She rang the bell furiously for Susan, who suspecting nothing of what was going on, had returned to the kitchen after showing in Mr. Green.

"Susan!" she exclaimed, bursting into tears, "this man accuses me of having kept back some of his goods, and insists on having me searched."

"Lord, sir!" cried Susan, almost as much shocked as Alicia, "I'm sure my mistress wouldn't keep your things. How can you think such a thing?"

"Unfortunately," replied Mr. Green, "this sort of thing happens too often. I'm sure three hundred a-year wouldn't cover my losses by the dishonesty of the ladies who frequent my shop; and I'm determined to pursue the thing with rigour that it may be a warning to others. So if you please, ma'am, searched you must be." And accordingly the officer proceeded to fulfil the unpleasant duty.

Nothing however was found upon Alicia, nor in the room, every part of which they examined. They next proceeded to search the other parts of the house, drawers, servants' boxes and everything; but with equal ill success.

Nevertheless, Mr. Green still affirmed that the goods had been abstracted by somebody in that house; that he wouldn't mind taking his oath of it in any court of justice in Europe; and he insisted that Mrs. Aytoun should accompany him and the officer to a magistrate.

"I may never recover my goods," said he, "for I know how easy it is to conceal these sort of articles, or get them conveyed out of the house—I don't recover one time in ten; but, as I said before, I'm determined to pursue this business—I'll follow it up, I'm resolved, just to let ladies see these things can't be done with impunity."

"I'll pay you the price of the things, Mr. Green," said Alicia. "Heaven knows I hav'n't got them, nor do I know anything of them; but I'd pay for them twenty times over rather than submit to this degradation."

"I dare say you would, ma'am," returned Mr. Green, "but that wouldn't answer my purpose. I once did let a lady off in that manner; but though I did it really out of good-nature, because she cried, and screamed, and went into hysterics, and de-

clared she'd make away with herself, and so forth; what did she
do afterwards, when she found the danger was over, but spread
a report that I had frightened her into paying for things she
never had, by accusing her of purloining them.—No, no; it wont
do—it's a magistrate's business, and to a magistrate we must go.—
I suppose you'd prefer having a coach to walking? If so, I'll run
myself and get one."

"Of course, if I'm to go, it must be in a coach," replied the
terrified Alicia, sinking into a chair, and giving way to a fresh
burst of tears.

"I'll be back with one in a moment," said Mr. Green. "You'll
stay here, Jackson," added he, nodding to the officer as he went
out.

"Never fear me, Mr. Green," replied Jackson, with a significant look.

"Was there ever anything so dreadful?" exclaimed Mrs.
Aytoun to Susan, who stood crying by the door. "What am I
to do?"

"I was thinking if I were to run for some of the neighbours,
ma'am," said Susan. "Sure Mr. Green can't have a right to
treat a lady in this way."

"Mr. Green's o' the right side o' the law," said Mr. Jackson.
"You may depend upon that. There's ne'er a man knows better
what he's about than Mr. Green do."

"What do you think of my running to see if Mr. Morland or Mr.
Parsons is at home, ma'am?" said Susan, "and just begging
them to step in?"

"Oh no, no," said Alicia, "that would only be making the
thing public. It would be all over the town before night. If I
must go, the more quietly it's done the better."

"I'd better go with you, I think, ma'am," said Susan.

"Do, Susan," said Mrs. Aytoun; "and I'll go up stairs and put
on my bonnet at once, that the coach mayn't be kept at the door;"
and she rose to leave the room.

"You must give me leave to go out with you, ma'am," said
Jackson, following her—"I hope you'll excuse me; but in these
here cases my orders are never to lose sight of a person we've
got in custody."

Sobbing as if her heart would break, poor Alicia resumed her
seat, and bade Susan fetch down her bonnet and shawl, and at
the same time put on her own; and by the time they were ready,
Mr. Green arrived with the coach, and handing them both into it,
he stepped in after them, telling the shopman, who was in waiting
at the door, to run forward and meet them at the office; whilst
Mr. Jackson mounted the box, and desired the coachman to drive
to Bow-street.

As Mrs. Aytoun was utterly ignorant of the ways of a police-
office, and had no one with her to claim the little indulgences and
exceptions that are usually granted to the feelings of people
moving in a respectable station of life, she was at once shown

into the public room, where the magistrate was sitting, receiving the deposition of a gentleman, who was accusing two women of ill character of having, on the previous evening, purloined his watch and purse.

There were many other people in the office—pickpockets, street-walkers, chimney-sweepers, coal-heavers, dustmen, receivers of stolen goods, and others of the dregs of society, amongst whom Alicia and Susan were introduced.

" You had better come over here," said Jackson, making a way for them through this mass of vice and corruption, to the other side, where there was a bench; for it's like enough you'll have a pretty time to wait. There's a good many to have their turn afore you." So the two abashed women took their seat, with Mr. Green beside them; Alicia with her veil drawn close over her face, and her pocket-handkerchief to her eyes; whilst Mr. Jackson drew himself up in an easy position, with his back against the wall, in order that he might listen in perfect luxury to what was as interesting to him as a new tragedy to an amateur.

The two women, pretty-looking young creatures, who seemed to have been designed by nature for better things, declared that the watch and purse found upon them (one having been found possessed of the watch and the other of the purse) were their own; and had been given to them by a gentleman, who they admitted was not quite sober, in the early part of the evening. Shortly afterwards, they said, they met their present accuser, who accompanied them to an oyster shop; where they had imprudently shown him the presents they had received. He had examined them very curiously; opened the watch to look at the maker's name, and counted the money in the purse, before he returned them. After which they all came out together, and walked arm in arm for some time, till he saw an opportunity of giving them into custody, upon which he had, to their great astonishment, accused them of robbing him.

The gentleman, who was a foreigner, swore on the contrary, that the things were his own. He said he had arrived in town in the morning, and having dined with some friends, had taken a little too much wine: and on his way home, had fallen in with the prisoners, who had persuaded him to accompany them to the oyster shop. That there, under pretence of romping, they had examined his pockets, and taken out the watch and purse, which after inspecting, they returned: he having given them a guinea each out of it; and that afterwards, whilst walking beside him in the street, he had felt them picking his pockets, but had forborne to speak till he saw an opportunity of giving them into custody, lest they should run off, and he lose his property. He concluded by saying, that there was a gentleman present who could testify that the watch and purse belonged to him, and that he had seen them in his possession a few hours before. This witness was then called forward, and swore positively to the truth of what his friend had asserted.

During the progress of their examination, Susan occasionally listened to the evidence, and at other times devoted her attention to her distressed mistress; but the affair being brought to a conclusion, and decided by the magistrate in favour of the accuser, there was a general move, and falling back of the crowd, in order to make way for the party to come out.

"By Jingo," she heard Jackson exclaim, suddenly, "I'm blow'd if that 'ere ar'n't Nosey! I ha'n't seen him this four or five year, I b'lieve; I thought he wer' dropt off the hooks."

Her attention attracted by Jackson's exclamation, Susan turned to look at the retreating party, whose yet uncovered heads just appeared above the crowd. The first was a handsome dark man, with a quantity of black hair, mingled with gray, on his head and face, who had perhaps seen forty years. The second, apparently about the same age, was of a lighter complexion; the crown of his head was quite bald; and his profile being turned to Susan, the cause of the nickname by which Jackson had designated him appeared in prominent relief. It was a nose, once seen, not to be easily forgotten; the bridge had evidently been broken, either by a blow or an accident, and a projection which gave a singular expression to the feature had been the consequence. Susan felt she could have sworn to having seen that nose before, and she started to her feet under the influence of her emotion.

"Sit still, sit still, my dear," said Jackson, patting her on the shoulder, "it ar'n't your turn yet by a good many;" and as the strangers disappeared through the door, Susan sank again into her seat.

"No," said Jackson, continuing the conversation that Susan's movement had interrupted—"No, I don't know t' other swell; he can't ha' been long upon town—newly imported, I suppose—"

"Genuine," interrupted his companion, with a knowing leer.

"Be sure o' that," returned Jackson. "As for that 'ere Nosey, his perboscis, as some on 'em calls it, was familiar enough on the turf and the ring; and he was well enough known at all the hells about the West End—but he disappeared all on a sudden. I suppose, by the pal he's got, he's been across the water."

"Pray, sir," said Susan, "do you know the name of the gentleman you're talking of?"

"I never heard him called by no name but Nosey, my dear," answered Jackson, "and that was the best name to know him by, if ever we wanted him, 'cause one saw it in his face. A chap may shift his name as easy as his shirt, but he couldn't get rid of his nose, no how, you know."

"I dare say, after all, the girls' story was true," remarked the other man.

"You may take your davy o' that," replied Jackson. "Them there ar'n't the flats that gets their pockets picked. I'd defy the cleverest hand on the town to get anything out on 'em."

Several other cases followed and were disposed of; during which time Susan sat wrapt in her own meditations, and unconscious of everything around her; even her mistress's troubles were, for the moment, effaced from her memory by the flood of vivid recollections and absorbing feelings that the sight of that face had conjured up. Her mind had always been impressed with the notion that the visit of the stranger, whom she now felt certain she recognised as Nosey, made at the back door of Oakfield House two nights preceding Mr. Wentworth's death, was somehow or another connected with that catastrophe. Many a time in the silence of night, or of an evening, when her work being done, she was seated in her clean cap and apron, quietly by her kitchen fire, did the circumstances of those eventful days pass in review before her. Especially her dream—that strange and significant dream, which even then appeared to her more like a vision than the unstrung bubbles that usually occupy the brain of a restless sleeper; and which now, followed up as it had been by such singular coincidences, was daily, more and more, assuming in her mind, form, substance, and reality. But these speculations always terminated in the depressing sense of her own helplessness, and a thorough conviction of the impossibility of persuading anybody else to give credit, or attach any importance, to circumstances which had so much weight with her. "No," she would say, as she wiped her eyes with the corner of her apron, at the conclusion of her cogitations, "no, I can do nothing—nothing in the world. I should only be stirring up enemies for myself without doing a bit of good. If ever poor Andrew is to be justified, it will be through the goodness of God; and I do think he, in his own good time, will bring the truth to light yet."

These reflections of Susan's were at length interrupted by Jackson's saying, "Now, Mr. Green; now, ladies, your turn's next. Please to step this way;" and thrusting aside the staring mob, whose curiosity was excited by the appearance of Mrs. Aytoun and Susan, he made room for them to advance towards the bench.

"What have we got here, Jackson?" inquired the magistrate.

"A case of shop-lifting," returned Jackson, "at least the purloining of goods that were sent home on sight."

Mr. Green was then called upon to tell his story. He averred that he had measured the goods himself, both before they were sent out and when they returned; and he had been the more particular in doing so, because he was not wholly without his suspicions with respect to the lady in custody.

At this avowal the unfortunate Alicia raised her head and looked at him with unfeigned astonishment.

"I don't meant to say," continued Mr. Green, in answer to the surprise he saw depicted in her countenance, "I don't mean to say that it's a thing I could swear to as having been done intentionally; but this I must say, that it had a very suspicious look about it; and that many a one has been brought up to this office upon quite as little a matter; though at the time we passed it

over, as we make it a rule not to be too hasty in these cases."
He then mentioned that Mrs. Aytoun, on the preceding day,
had been detected in the act of putting a piece of lace in her
pocket that was wrapped up and partly concealed in her handker-.
chief; and it may be imagined that this unlucky circumstance
had considerable influence on the minds of the audience, and
seriously aggravated the peril of her position.

The shopman next testified to his having received the goods
from Mr. Green, after seeing them measured, and the precise
quantities noted down; that he had himself delivered them to
Mrs. Aytoun in the parlour, where she was sitting in conversation
with a lady—that she requested him, as she was then engaged,
to leave them, and call again; that he had accordingly done so;
and on returning to the shop with the goods, he had delivered
them at once into the hands of Mr. Green himself, who had
immediately measured them and found the deficiencies stated.

Mr. Jackson then explained his part in the business; adding,
that the search had been ineffectual; but that there had been
quite sufficient interval for Mrs. Aytoun to have removed the
goods, or transferred them to somebody else; and that therefore their ill success could not be accounted in her exculpation.

Mr. Green then gave the strongest testimony in favour of the
character of the shopman. He was his nephew; a young man of
unexceptionable morals and conduct; and he had been selected, in
this particular instance, to carry the goods on that very account.

Poor Mrs. Aytoun was then asked what she had to say in her
own defence. She raised her head, threw back her veil, clasped
her hands in a beseeching attitude, and answered, " Only that I
am innocent! I know nothing of the things said to be missing.
I looked over what was sent, and laid aside those I wished to
keep—but God is my witness, that till the shopman returned,
not a single article had been removed from the table where he
left them, nor a single yard of anything cut off. I am utterly
unable to explain or throw any light upon it. I recollect that I
went to my bed-room to fetch a yard measure; but no one, in the
interval, could have entered the room without my meeting them."
She testified freely to the character of her servants, and gene-
rously exonerated them from any suspicion.

The evidence against her was certainly strong, and the unlucky
accident of the previous day had made a powerful impression.

" I fear, madam," said the magistrate, "we must commit you;
unless you can find bail."

Alicia, without answering, hid her face in her handkerchief,
and sobbed as if her heart was bursting; whilst Susan wept with
her for sympathy. They had neither of them a very clear idea
of what was required; but whatever it was, it was certain to
lead to an exposure amongst her friends and acquaintance;
besides that she felt she had scarcely that degree of intimacy or
confidence with any one of them to select him on such an emergency.

"If the lady will permit me the honour of doing her this little service," said a gentleman, taking off his hat, and approaching her respectfully, "it will give me great pleasure; and relieve her from the annoyance of further detention. You will not object to my bail, I presume?" added he, turning with a smile to the magistrate, whose acquaintance he appeared to be, and to whom he had occasionally addressed a few words during the course of the previous examination.

"Oh, certainly not—certainly not," replied his worship, with a sly and significant look at his friend, "if it's agreeable to the lady."

Alicia had no time for reflection; all she saw was the advantage of immediate release, and the means of avoiding an application to any of her acquaintance—she thanked the stranger, and accepted his offer.

A few minutes sufficed to conclude the business, and set her free. Mr. Green and the shopman departed; whilst her new found friend, who was a handsome, well dressed, elegant looking man, of about forty, with very polished manners, gallantly advanced to offer her his arm, and conducted her to her coach, which was still waiting. Having placed her in it, he stepped in after her, saying, he could not think of permitting her to return alone in her present state of agitation and distress; and when they reached her door, after handing her out with the same deferential courtesy, he gallantly lifted his hat from his head, as she ascended the steps; and took his leave, with the announcement, that he should do himself the honour of calling, on the following day, to inquire after her health.

CHAPTER XXIX.

WHICH EXHIBITS A SPECIMEN OF THE SYMPATHY OF FRIENDS, AND THE INCONVENIENCE OF OBLIGATIONS.

"That of all the people in the world, this misfortune should have fallen on me!" exclaimed Mrs. Aytoun, as, in an agony of tears, she flung herself on her own sofa! "If Arthur hears of it I'm undone—not that he'll believe me guilty—but the disgrace will break his heart. And he must hear of it, if this dreadful man continues his accusation. Heavens and earth!" she exclaimed, clasping her hands, "how cruel it is that an innocent woman should be plunged into all this wretchedness, and perhaps the whole happiness of her life destroyed, by an accident that no caution could have foreseen or avoided."

The evening that followed was a wretched one for Alicia. The faithful Susan, whose sympathy and commiseration was all the consolation she had, spent the greater part of it by her side, offering her humble tribute of advice, and aiding her mistress in suggesting and canvassing all the possible accidents that could have occasioned the deficiency of the goods; or the means, practicable or impracticable, of eliciting the truth, and vindicating her reputation.

Great as her misfortune appeared whilst she was discussing it in her parlour with Susan, the aspect it assumed when she reconsidered it in the silence and solitude of her chamber, was ten times more terrific. Hour after hour the weary clock chimed on, whilst she lay tossing on that couch, till now so peaceful and so blest, in the restless fever of fear, anxiety, and mortification; weeping over the past, wondering at the present, and trembling at the future; till towards morning, imperfect slumbers, interrupted by sudden starts and dreadful awakenings, varied the incidents of the miserable night.

Though unable to sleep, she was yet unwilling to rise, for daylight brought no pleasure to her; and it was near twelve o'clock before she descended to her parlour. She had not been seated there many minutes, and her untasted breakfast was yet beside her, when Susan hastily entered the room, saying, she had just seen Mrs. Morland and Mrs. Bloxham coming down the street apparently with the intention of calling, and begging to know whether they were to be let in. Mrs. Aytoun first said *no*, and then *yes*; adding, "If I am denied, and they find out I am at home, they will only be the more spiteful when this story reaches their ears."

People who are conscious that they have made themselves the subject of their neighbours' gossip, which happened to be the case with these two ladies, are generally particularly glad to find any of their friends getting into the same dilemma; upon the principle, perhaps, that as the power of human tongues is limited, and they can only get through a certain portion of scandal in a day, the more multitudinous the victims, the more moderate must be the dividend allotted to each.

Any one who had observed the lingering pace with which the two visitors advanced along the street, with their arms linked, their closely approximated heads bent forwards—the frequent pauses, when at some interesting point of the conversation they drew up, and looked each other steadily in the face, might, without difficulty, have predicted that they were engaged on some very fresh and attractive piece of scandal. At length, after a more protracted pause, and a final summing up of the chief heads of the discourse at the door, they ascended the steps, rang the bell, and inquired if Mrs. Aytoun was at home. A significant glance, shot from one to the other when Susan said *yes*, showed that they had entertained some doubts of being admitted; and as they proceeded along the passage they endeavoured to subdue the animated and pleased expression their countenances had assumed under the influence of the late discussion, to the sad and solemn tone of sympathy that became the occasion.

"My dear Mrs. Aytoun," they both exclaimed with one voice, as they entered the room, "how *do* you do?"

"Quite well, thank ye," answered the pale and agitated Alicia, with as much firmness as she could command.

"How late you are with your breakfast," observed Mrs. Bloxham; "you that used to be so early. One might see Mr. Aytoun wasn't at home."

"I wasn't very well, and stayed in bed later than usual," said Alicia, forgetting that she had just said she *was* very well.

"Have you heard from Mr. Aytoun lately?" inquired Mrs. Morland. "Do you expect to see him soon?"

"I had a letter the day before yesterday," replied Alicia; "but he said nothing about returning."

Here there was a pause, and the dialogue flagged; as dialogues always do, when people are thinking of one thing and talking of another. Mrs. Morland, who was the most impetuous of the two, was dying to treat the subject after the epic fashion, and plunge *in medias res;* but Mrs. Bloxham, a more deliberate and cool-headed person, wisely reflecting that that would be spoiling sport, and running down the game before she had well started from her cover, had enjoined her to be cautious, and leave the management of the affair in her hands.

"It's such a lovely morning; I wonder you don't go out," observed Mrs. Bloxham.

"I believe I shall, by and by," replied Alicia.

"What a sweet silk that is you've on," remarked Mrs. Morland, who was eager to draw near the subject.

"I'm sure you must have seen me wear it a hundred times," said Alicia. "It's quite old and faded now; it *was* pretty."

"A good silk wears so long," remarked Mrs. Bloxham, "and looks well to the last. They're the cheapest things in the end."

"Indeed they are," returned Mrs. Morland. "Do you remember that puce silk I used to wear last winter?" added she, addressing Mrs. Aytoun.

"I don't think I do," replied Alicia; which, by the way, was not only an extremely imprudent answer on this particular occasion, but is so under all circumstances; because people feel a natural astonishment and indignation at your not remembering their puce silk; and under the excitement of those passions, are apt to enter into lengthy details with respect to the article in question, and elaborate eulogiums on its merits, which are sometimes less interesting to the hearer than to the speaker. Accordingly, Mrs. Morland exclaimed, "Well, I'm surprised you don't remember it! for the very first time I put it on was to come and dine with you—at that dinner, you know, that the roast beef was so underdone, that you had it cut into slices and sent out to be broiled; don't you remember it, Mrs. Bloxham?"

"To be sure I do," answered Mrs. Bloxham; "I remember it perfectly."

"I remember that," said Alicia. "We were very unlucky about our dinner that day."

"Well then, I'm surprised you don't recollect my puce silk!" reiterated Mrs. Morland, "for it was so much admired. I remember Mr. Aytoun was quite struck with it. Well, after wearing it for two years as a best gown for company, it lasted me the whole blessed winter for the streets, and very handsome it looked—didn't it, Mrs. Bloxham?"

"Very," returned Mrs. Bloxham, who hadn't the most distant recollection of ever having seen it.

"And now," continued Mrs. Morland, "I've turned it, and made it into a frock and spencer for Maria; and I'm sure nobody could tell it from new. By the bye, she had it on last Sunday at church: Mrs. Bloxham, you must have observed it."

"Was it *that* Maria had on?" exclaimed Mrs. Bloxham, in the accents of wonder and admiration that the occasion called for. "I never should have thought it."

"Well," continued Mrs. Morland, recurring to the motive with which she had introduced the subject, and which her indignant feelings at Mrs. Aytoun's oblivion had caused her for the moment to forget—"Well, I gave just four shillings a yard for that silk, twelve yards—two pound eight the dress came to; and six shillings I paid Miss Geddes for making it up; there was a trifle for lining too, and tape—eighteen pence, I think—I know I thought it a dear gown at the time; and Morland made a long face at it. But see how cheap it's been in the end! Always buy good things, I say; and that's why I like to deal at Green's; you're sure there to get your money's worth. Don't you agree with me, Mrs. Bloxham? I know you deal there."

"Yes," answered Mrs. Bloxham, with a distinct and deliberate enunciation, and a countenance as fixed and unmoved as a stone idol; "yes, I always do deal there; and I was there last night to get some buttons for a new set of shirts I'm making up for Bloxham."

"And *I* was there this morning," said Mrs. Morland, "just before I called upon you."

Here the conversation languished again. The ladies had rather expected to have found Mrs. Aytoun in hysterics, or to have thrown her into them by their innuendos; but Alicia, though pale and depressed, and really suffering agonies at heart, contrived to preserve an exterior of decent composure; and they had hoped to draw her into a full and detailed narration of her adventure; but conscious that she should meet with neither sympathy, sincerity, nor good counsel from them, she intrenched herself within a cautious silence; resolved, that unless they broke the barriers, she would not; and the only part she took in the conversation, was occasionally to fill up the pauses in their dialogue, by polite inquiries after the health, educational progress, and general welfare of Miss Morland, and the Masters Bloxham.

Finding that their visit was not likely to turn to any very good account, the ladies were beginning to think they might spend their time more profitably and agreeably in a succession of calls about the neighbourhood, where they would have much to tell, and something to hear; together with the incalculable advantage of having had an early interview with Mrs. Aytoun, which would entitle them to an enviable precedence in any convocation of gossips they might meet with; and enable them to describe, with the minuteness of an entomologist, every particular of her looks, bearing, and demeanour.

At this interesting crisis, just as a certain telegraphic communication had been exchanged between the visitors, which being interpreted, implied, " I suppose we may as well go," there was heard a startling knock at the door. The summons bore such a decided character, such an undoubting assurance of welcome, and of a claim to be admitted, and was, altogether, so unlike the timid, half-hesitating, bourgeois knocks usually heard in the neighbourhood, that it sent the blood into Mrs. Aytoun's cheeks, and caused the ladies immediately to recompose themselves in their seats.

"Mr. Seymour," said Susan, announcing and ushering in the elegant stranger of yesterday.

" I hope Mrs. Aytoun will excuse the earliness of my visit," said he, advancing towards her with great eagerness and a most graceful address; "but I was so extremely anxious—" here his eye caught sight of the two ladies, who, being partly concealed by the door, he had not at first perceived—" anxious," continued he, in a more calm and reserved tone, " to learn if your cold was better, that I could not defer the honour of making the inquiry."

"It is better, I thank you," replied Mrs. Aytoun, blushing intensely at the awkward consciousness of having a secret understanding with a man who was almost a stranger to her.

Without dwelling farther on personal matters, the accomplished Mr. Seymour, who thoroughly knew the world, and comprehended his situation at the first glance, immediately directed the conversation into other channels; talking of theatres and exhibitions, parks and parties; and without any appearance of display, but as of things to which he was perfectly accustomed, of high people and high places.

No very elegant man ever entered a society of women without producing more sensation than the sex would be generally willing to confess; and when to his other advantages, he adds that towering one of belonging to a circle much more exalted than the company he has fallen amongst, he has it in his power to create a revolution in the minds of half the ladies present. He can make the unamiable, amiable; the malignant, charitable; and the good-humoured, dissatisfied and envious. Few, indeed, are exempt from his influence, but the women whose hearts are already in the bosom of another.

Accordingly Mrs. Morland and Mrs. Bloxham, who were very far from belonging to the last category, were carried off their feet by the grace, suavity, and conversational powers of Mr. Seymour.

They were all smiles and dimples; and the malicious triumph they had come to enjoy over Mrs. Aytoun, was wholly forgotten in their pleasure in his society, and their desire to appear amiable and agreeable in his eyes.

Most unwillingly, and prompted rather by an apprehension of seeming ill bred, and ignorant of the usages of the world, than by any better feeling, they at length took their gracious leaves: affectionately, of Mrs. Aytoun; and with a fascinating amenity, of the stranger.

He had no sooner bowed them out, and closed the parlour door upon them, and before Alicia had time to resume her seat, than Mr. Seymour, still gracefully and respectfully, but yet with the assurance of an accepted friend and confidant, advanced from the distant chair he had hitherto occupied, and tenderly taking her hand which he raised to his lips, was beginning to say, "My dear Mrs. Aytoun, now those afflicting persons are gone—" when the door opened, and Mrs. Bloxham putting in her head, cried, "I beg your pardon, but I've left my scarf somewhere—Oh there it is, fallen down behind the chair I was sitting in."

In all ages of the world *revenans** have been found extremely incommodious visitors. When people are once gone, whether out of the world, or out of a room, their departure should be final. Coming back upon any pretence whatever, whether it be to point out buried gold, or to seek a silken scarf; whether to disclose a secret, or to pry into one, is altogether inexcusable, and a thing not to be tolerated. And, certainly, as regards themselves, their intrusion is extremely impolitic, and apt to be punished, by a verification of the old adage, that "listeners seldom hear any good of themselves."

So thought Alicia on the present occasion; but Mr. Seymour, nothing daunted, and probably esteeming the accident rather favourable to his views than otherwise, as it reduced the standard of Mrs. Aytoun's independence and self-esteem "by a chopine," picked up the scarf, and after presenting it to the lady, and once more bowing her out with the same deference as before, returned, and drawing a chair close to Alicia, resumed the thread of his discourse. "My dear Mrs. Aytoun," he continued, "I was about to say, now those afflicting persons were gone—but people of that sort never *are* gone—but I am most anxious to hear how you really are after your most annoying adventure. I hope you have not suffered the affair to make more impression on you than it merits."

"More impression than it merits!" said Alicia, giving way to the tears she had suppressed in the presence of her tormentors— "can it make more than it merits? Isn't it the most dreadful imputation that ever was cast on a respectable woman? And how am I to throw it off? How am I to recover my reputation? How am I to vindicate my innocence? Oh, Mr. Seymour, imagine what it must be, to be accused, insulted, searched like a common thief;

* French word for ghosts, and for those who return where their company is not desired.

dragged to a police-office like a felon, and there, amongst the very dregs of society, the low, the abandoned, the vicious, to be threatened with a gaol. Oh, my God!" she exclaimed, clasping her hands in agony, "is there no way of shaking this horror from me? must it for ever cling to me, till it drags me to my grave, as it surely will? Tell me, Mr. Seymour, advise me, is there no help? can nothing be done to clear me from the stigma?"

"My dear Mrs. Aytoun," answered he, drawing his chair a little nearer, and again taking her hand, for Alicia was very attractive in the energy of her despair; "I really scarcely know how to advise. You see the misfortune of doing anything in these affairs, unless you are quite sure of success, is, that every movement one makes only further disseminates the scandal and adds to the publicity; and if once the newspapers get hold of you, you may as well carry your misfortune inscribed upon your back; there is no corner of the world to which you can escape from it."

"Good heavens!" cried Alicia, struck with a new terror, "perhaps, even now, they may put it in the paper amongst the police reports!"

"Why," replied Mr. Seymour, "to confess the truth, I was apprehensive that might be the case; and therefore yesterday evening, instead of going to a dinner at Lord H——'s, to which I was engaged, I took a coach, and drove round to the different publishing offices, where I found means to secure their silence."

"How can I thank you sufficiently!" exclaimed Alicia, warmly impressed with the extent of the obligation. "It would have been the climax of my misery to see my name in the paper."

"Which it would have been, I fear," returned Mr. Seymour, who had no intention of detracting anything from his own merits and services—"and it is that that leads me to think, that if the affair could be hushed up—if, in short, we could induce this Mr. Green to let the thing drop, and satisfy him in some way or another—that is, make it his interest to pursue it no farther, that it would be the most prudent mode of proceeding."

"But he wont give it up," said Alicia. "I offered to pay him the value of the things from the beginning; but he wouldn't take it."

"No, not the mere value of the things, I dare say," returned Mr. Seymour. "But he may not be able to resist the temptation if the bribe offered be large enough."

Alicia was silent, for she had no means of offering a bribe considerable enough to answer the purpose.

"At all events," said Mr. Seymour, "I'll take an opportunity of seeing him, and hearing what he says. With respect to yourself, I'd advise you to have no communication with him whatever. The more independent and fearless you appear, the better chance there is of my success. And pray," he added, with an appearance of the deepest interest, "keep up your spirits in the meantime; do not suffer the circumstance, annoying as I admit it to be, to press too much on your mind: but rely on my exertions, and if I may

venture to use the term on so short an acquaintance, my regard, to
extricate you from your dilemma."

It may easily be conceived that Mr. Seymour found motives or
excuses for visiting his fair friend every day; and how was she, enchained by a confidence and an obligation of such a nature, to shut
her door against him? Besides, he contrived to make his visits so
interesting; he had always something to tell, or something to
suggest. And then he was the only person in the world, except
Susan, with whom she permitted herself to speak of what was for
ever the subject of her thoughts; so that daily his knock at the
door became more welcome, and his visits more protracted.

Her neighbours and acquaintance, at first paid her visits of curiosity; but finding that her obstinate silence disappointed them,
they gradually relaxed in their assiduities, contenting themselves
with watching her door to ascertain how often Mr. Seymour called,
and how long he stayed; endeavouring, at the same time, to persuade themselves and others, that their alienation was occasioned
by a virtuous horror of her heterodox proceedings.

However, as time advanced, it became too evident to Mrs.
Aytoun that Mr. Seymour's visits were by no means disinterested.

He permitted himself gradually to betray all the symptoms of a
decided passion; dropped them out one by one, with such a well-
acted air of inadvertence and absence of design, that it would have
been impossible for Alicia to have doubted his sincerity. Indeed
he was sincere enough for the moment. Alicia was a very attractive woman; and he a man who made it a point to give way to all
his susceptibilities, and never relax in his pursuit of an amour till
he was satisfied success was utterly hopeless. He held that

"The proper" bus'ness " of mankind is" love;

and he conceived it highly improbable, considering his own advantages, and the nature and amount of his services, that Alicia's
heart should remain untouched; and next to impossible that, en-
tangled as she was in a complication of embarrassing circumstances,
her person should escape him.

But Alicia wore a shield over her heart that all the Seymours,
Somersets, and Fitzroys that ever shone in the galaxy of fashionable life could not have penetrated—she loved Arthur Aytoun;—
and when she became thoroughly aware of Mr. Seymour's views,
she resolved to fly the danger—danger to her reputation, not to her
affections—and by leaving town, without giving him any intimation of her design, she hoped to convince him that his pursuit was
vain. And, indeed, she had other inducements to abandon the
scene of her mortification. Unwilling to expose herself to the
curious eyes of her neighbours, she had made her house her prison;
and had debarred herself from air and exercise, which in her situation were especially necessary, till her health was affected by the
privation. So, one day, she despatched Susan, in whose prudence
she could rely, by the coach to Hammersmith; with directions to
engage a small lodging for a month, in an agreeable situation;

and in two days afterwards, with no companion but this faithful servant, she departed with her baggage in a hackney-coach; leaving directions with her cook, that if anybody inquired for her, she was simply to answer she was out of town, without communicating her address.

CHAPTER XXX.

WHICH SHOWS THAT AGREEABLE SURPRISES DO NOT ALWAYS PROVE SO AGREEABLE AS MIGHT HAVE BEEN EXPECTED.

BUT Mrs. Aytoun had exceedingly underrated the power of her own charms, or the limits of Mr. Seymour's perseverance, when she imagined that her removal to Hammersmith would be of the slightest avail towards slackening the ardour of his pursuit. On the contrary, he no sooner found she was gone, than the affair assumed a piquancy that it had not before. Had she exhibited no inclination nor power to resist, there would neither have been excitement in the pursuit, nor triumph in its success; but nothing could be more agreeable to him than the interesting occupation she had furnished for his mornings, by her flight.

Finding the cook faithful to the instructions her mistress had given her, and not being able to make out anything satisfactory by his description of the lady at the coach-offices; he next addressed her a note, on some matter connected with Mr. Green's affair, requesting an immediate answer; and left it with the servant, desiring it might be forwarded without delay, as it was on a matter of importance.

"How soon," said he, "can I have an answer, do you think?"

"I'll put it in the post directly, sir, and the answer will be here to-night I dare say," replied the woman.

And so it was; and upon that hint, Mr. Seymour took to mounting his gallant horse every morning, riding through all the towns and villages adjacent to London, and making inquiries at all the inns, libraries, grocers' shops, and so forth: with a success certainly indifferent as to the main point, but with infinite benefit to his own health, spirits, and good looks.

In the meantime poor Mrs. Aytoun, whether from the anxiety and agitation she had undergone, or from the previous undue confinement and privation of air which had debilitated her frame, had not been two days in the country before she was taken ill; and she found the hopes she had so fondly cherished were doomed to be disappointed. She suffered much, her recovery was extremely slow, and her return to London consequently deferred much beyond the period she had proposed.

At length Mr. Seymour's patience of research beginning to be somewhat exhausted; by way of bringing things to a crisis, he wrote to tell her that either some way must be found of inducing Mr. Green to drop proceedings, or her unfortunate affair would be very shortly brought before the public; and he added, that it was absolutely necessary he should see her, as it was impossible to discuss the matter to any purpose by letter.

"I must see him, I suppose," said she to Susan; "and yet I am extremely unwilling to let him come here; for when he has once ascertained where I am, I'm afraid he'll never be out of the house."

"Suppose you were to go to town for a few hours, ma'am," said Susan, "and see him at your own house. You could easily come back by night."

"I could certainly," replied Alicia, "but you know the eyes of the whole street will be watching me; and what a strange appearance it will have to go to town on purpose to meet him. I was thinking of saying that I'm staying at a friend's house where I can't receive him; and proposing to meet him somewhere else."

"That may do very well, ma'am," replied Susan, "if you could be sure nobody 'll see you. But if they should, it would have a worse appearance than the other."

"It would, certainly," said Alicia, "but it's hardly likely anybody should see me. It is but for once. I think I'll appoint a time to meet him in Kensington Gardens. You and I could go by the coach as far as the Park gate; and I could walk to a seat, and there wait for him. What do you think?"

"Just as you please, ma'am," replied Susan, who had nothing better to advise; and who being one of those people who, thinking no evil herself, was not sufficiently aware how prone the world is to think it.

This plan was accordingly decided on; and the following morning, which happened to be Tuesday, appointed for the meeting.

By activity on his own part, spurred on as he was by an ardent desire to return home, and by a union of some fortunate circumstances, Mr. Aytoun, who had reckoned on being absent at least ten or twelve months, found his business concluded, and himself at liberty to repair to England, before the expiration of seven. He had hinted, occasionally, in his letters to his wife, that he entertained hopes his absence might not be so protracted as they had expected; but had forborne to name any probable period for her seeing him, uncertain as he was himself; and preferring to give her an agreeable surprise, to the risk of occasioning a disappointment. He had yet to visit a considerable trading city in Germany, where he expected to be detained some time; when he received letters from the house he travelled for, saying, that a sudden emergency having occurred, which obliged them to despatch a special messenger to that quarter, he was at liberty to return as soon as he pleased; and on the Monday evening, the very day on which Mrs. Aytoun and Susan had agreed upon the plan of meeting Mr. Seymour in the Gardens, Mr. Aytoun arrived at his own door.

He was in a hackney coach, having parted from the stage by which he had travelled up from the port he landed at; and as the lumbering vehicle slowly rolled down the street, he put out his head to catch the first glimpse of his own dear home. Alicia herself might have been visible; she might have been going out, or coming home—and he so longed to see her. No Alicia, however, appeared; but instead, a gentleman whom he observed coming out of the door; and who, after pausing a minute or two to say something to the servant who had opened it, deliberately descended the steps, and walked up the street, reading with a smiling countenance a letter which he appeared to have just received. "Who the devil's that?" said Mr. Aytoun to himself, as the handsome and elegantly dressed stranger passed the coach. "I'm sure it was my door he came out of. Open the door, coachman," he cried, the moment the carriage stopped, and jumping out he vehemently pulled the bell and knocked at the same time, making the cook, who was in the act of descending the kitchen stairs, say, as she turned to come up again, "Lord! I could have sworn that was master himself if I didn't know he was abroad."

"Well, Betty," said the eager husband, as the woman surveyed him with astonished eyes; "is your mistress at home?"

"Lord, sir," answered Betty, "we never expected you so soon. My mistress don't know a word of your coming, I'm certain."

"I know she doesn't," replied Mr. Aytoun, turning into the parlour; "where is she?"

"My mistress is out of town, sir," answered the maid, "and we expect her back the latter end of next week."

"Where the devil has she gone to?" inquired Mr. Aytoun with surprise.

"Only as far as Hammersmith, sir," replied Betty; "she's in lodgings there, and has got Susan with her."

"What made her go there?" asked Mr. Aytoun. "Was she ill?"

"My mistress has been very poorly since she's been there, I hear, but she's better now," returned Betty, whose communicativeness was considerably checked by not knowing exactly what she should tell, and what she should not; and, indeed, her own acquaintance with the state of affairs was but imperfect; since neither Mrs. Aytoun nor Susan had given her any information; and what she had picked up of the gossip of the neighbourhood was such a distorted and exaggerated mass of incongruities, that it tended rather to puzzle than enlighten her.

"Very odd she didn't write," said Mr. Aytoun. "I've been wondering I didn't hear from her. It's too late for me to go to Hammersmith now," continued he, looking at his watch—"the coaches must all be gone; besides, I must contrive to see the Messrs. Karl this evening, or early to-morrow morning. I'll just run over and ask the Parsons about her; I dare say they can tell me more.—By the by, Betty," added he, as he was leaving the house, "who was that I saw calling here just now?"

"A gentleman was it, sir?" said Betty, borrowing a little time for reflection.

"Ay, to be sure; just as I drove up—who is he?"

"Oh, sir," said Betty, "that's Mr. Seymour."

"Seymour!" reiterated Mr. Ayton, "what the deuce brought him here?"

"I'm sure I don't know, sir," returned Betty, whose caution augmented with the delicacy of the crisis.

"But you know what he came for," responded Mr. Aytoun. "Who did he ask for?"

"He didn't ask for anybody, sir," answered Betty.

"Well, but what did he say?" persisted Mr. Aytoun. "He didn't come to rob the house, did he?"

"Oh Lord! no, sir, he's quite a gentleman, entirely. I believe he's an Honourable, or a Right Honourable, or something of that sort."

"Well, what did he say?"

"He only asked for a letter, sir," answered Betty, finding further equivocation was useless.

"A letter! I saw him reading a letter as he went up the street. What letter was it?"

"A letter from my mistres, I believe, sir."

"From your mistress!" exclaimed Mr. Aytoun, looking sharply round at the woman. "Is he an acquaintance of your mistress's, then, this Mr. Seymour?"

"Oh, yes, sir, my mistress knows him very well indeed, I believe," replied Betty.

"Oh, does she?" said Mr. Aytoun, in a tone of greater indifference than he felt; for he saw clearly that the woman was upon her guard, and that there was something to be concealed. "Does he come here often, then?"

"Pretty often—sometimes, sir," said Betty.

"How d'ye do, Mr. Aytoun?" cried a voice from an open window on the opposite side of the street. "Do step over and tell us how you are, and take a cup of tea."

"Thank ye; I will," replied Mr. Aytoun, and he walked across the way, and knocked at the door of his neighbour's house, with an odd sort of uncomfortable feeling about his heart, that made him scarcely sorry that he was not to meet his pretty wife till the next day.

"Here we're all assembled, as if we'd known you'd been coming," exclaimed Mrs. Morland, as he entered the parlour. "The Bloxhams called on us, and proposed that we should walk down together, and see if Mrs. Parsons was at home; and could give us a cup of tea, and make up a loo table."

"Well, Aytoun," said Mr. Parsons, "why, you've come back before your time. How's that?"

"I got through faster than I expected," returned Mr. Aytoun; "and I was not obliged to go to Frankfort at all; which alone made three weeks difference. But I find an empty house. My wife's in the country, Betty tells me."

"Yes, she's been away some time, I believe," replied Mr. Parsons, "hasn't she, Jemima?"

"Hem!" began Mrs. Parsons, clearing her throat; "I fancy

so. I think it must be near two months now since you and I were standing at the window, Maria——"

"No, mamma," interrupted Maria, "it was I was standing at the window;—you know it was the day you cut out the curtains for the new bed; and you were cutting them in the back parlour, when I called you to see Mrs. Aytoun's things put into the coach."

"So it was; I recollect now," said Mrs. Parsons; "and that'll be eight weeks come Monday. I remember it, because, in the evening, I said to Parsons, says I, 'Let us go and give the Morlands a call——'"

"And you came; and I sent for Mrs. Bloxham to join us," said Mrs. Morland.

"And I did," said Mrs. Bloxham—"it'll be just two months, come Monday, as Mrs. Parsons says. I know it from a particular circumstance."

"But why did Alicia go?" inquired Mr. Aytoun, who was more curious about his wife than about Mrs. Bloxham's particular circumstance, "was she ill?"

"I'm sure I don't know," answered all the ladies together.

"But what reason did she give?" asked Mr. Aytoun.

"I never heard what her reason was," returned Mrs. Parsons. "Did you, Mrs. Morland?"

"Never," returned Mrs. Morland.

"Nor I either," added Mrs. Bloxham.

"Didn't she say she was going?" inquired Mr. Aytoun, getting a little impatient.

"Not that I ever heard," replied Mrs. Parsons. "Did you ever hear of it, Mrs. Morland?"

"Never," answered Mrs. Morland.

"Nor I," added Mrs. Bloxham.

"The first I heard of it," said Mrs. Parsons, "was just Maria calling me to the window to see the luggage put into the coach. 'La! mamma,' said she, 'I do think Mrs. Aytoun's going away somewhere; for only look at the band-boxes and things Betty's putting in;' and presently, sure enough, out came Mrs. Aytoun herself, and stepped into the coach, and Susan after her; and away they drove."

"And the first I heard of it," said Mrs. Morland, "was when Mrs. Parsons came up to us in the evening. 'Lord, my dear,' says she, 'what do you think? Mrs. Aytoun's gone to rusticate a bit in the country.'"

"And I'm sure I'd never heard a word on the subject till you sent for me to tea that evening," said Mrs. Bloxham, "I declare I was quite surprised."

"This is very peculiar," thought Mr. Aytoun, who felt as if he were treading on enchanted ground, and was afraid to take another step, not knowing whither it was to lead him. He was dying to learn more, and yet did not like to ask questions, lest his curiosity should be interpreted into suspicion.

"Then you've not been down to see her?" said he, after a pause.

"Oh dear, no," replied the ladies.

"Indeed," added Mrs. Morland, "we couldn't, had we been inclined; for we didn't know where she was."

"Betty could have told you," said Mr. Aytoun.

"She said she didn't exactly know the address, when I asked her," replied the lady.

"And so she told me," said Mrs. Parsons.

"And me too," said Mrs. Bloxham.

"Well, ladies," said Mr. Aytoun, unable to bear these strange, significant sort of innuendoes any longer without betraying his impatience; "I must wish you good evening. I am obliged to see the Messrs. Karl before I can go to Hammersmith to Alicia; and I shall try to obtain an interview with one of them to-night, that I may be free to set off in the morning."

"To Hammersmith! so that's where she is?" exclaimed the ladies.

"My wife's no further away than Hammersmith," replied Mr. Aytoun, calmly. "She went there for her health," and he took his departure leaving the ladies to enjoy their tea and scandal at their leisure.

Mr. Aytoun did not succeed in obtaining an interview with his employers on that evening, and could not therefore start so early in the morning as he had desired; but the moment he was free, he hastened to Piccadilly, where, mounting the box of one of the Hammersmith coaches, he was soon in a fair way of having the uneasy feelings that, in spite of himself, the evident mystery of his wife's conduct had inspired, either dispersed or confirmed.

As the coachman was rather behind his time, he drove at a good round pace; but as they passed the Park gates near the Kensington turnpike, Mr. Aytoun observed a hackney-coach in waiting, and the coachman holding the door open as if the party to whom it belonged were approaching. Without knowing why, he turned his head to look at them as they came out of the gates. It consisted of a gentleman, a lady in a yellow shawl, and a plainly dressed person in a straw bonnet and black cloak, looking like a servant maid. There was something in the air of the first, that put him so much in mind of the stranger he had seen leave his own door on the preceding evening, that he continued to watch the party till a turn in the road hid them from his view.

However, he had time to see him hand the females into the carriage, though not to ascertain whether he also got in himself. The lady, too, had very much the figure of Alicia; but he had never seen her wear either a bonnet or shawl like those she had on—but she might have bought them during his absence. It struck him, also, that the third person was very like Susan; but he struggled against his own persuasion.

"It's those d——d women that have put this nonsense in my

head," said he to himself. "I ought to know them well enough
not to mind anything they say; and yet I'm such a fool I can't
help thinking of it."

However, on they went; and at the entrance of the town of
Hammersmith, he got off the coach, and inquired his way to
Prospect-place, whither he repaired on foot. It consisted of a
neat row of small houses, evidently constructed to attract the eye
of the dwellers in cities; having showy little verandahs overgrown
with creepers, small flower-gardens in front, and being adorned
with a profusion of green and white paint.

On inquiring if Mrs. Aytoun lived at the house he had been
directed to, the girl who answered the door said she did; but
that she was not at home. She believed she was gone to Kensington; but that as she dined early, she was momentarily
expecting her back.

"I'll wait for her then," said Mr. Aytoun. "Her servant's
with her, I suppose?"

"Yes, sir," answered the girl. "They went out together."

Mr. Aytoun ascended to the little drawing-room which was the
apartment occupied by his wife. His temples beat audibly; and
his heart felt too big for his bosom. He threw himself on the
sofa, where lay her netting box, and a volume of "Clarissa," that
she appeared to have been reading. "Alicia!" he said, pressing
his hand on his forehead, "Alicia! Wife! What is it that's awaiting me? What strange and unknown fear is this that's creeping
through my veins? Can it be possible, that in less than eight
months her whole character can be changed? Can she have forgotten the principles on which I had so much reliance? Can the
heart I thought so securely mine be already given to another?
Oh, it's impossible," he exclaimed, endeavouring to rouse himself,
and shake off the terror that was getting possession of him—"quite
impossible. I'm a fool to believe it. Don't let me run to a conclusion, and make myself wretched without anything to go upon.
She may have had very good reasons for leaving town; and though
I certainly do think that it was her I saw with that d——d fellow
just now, I'll wait till I hear what she has to say. Perhaps the
very first sentence may clear up the whole mystery, and show me
what an ass I am to suspect her."

With this prudent supposition, Mr. Aytoun endeavoured to
compose his mind; and it was not long before the sound of wheels
stopping at the garden gate announced the arrival of his wife.

"There's a gentleman in the drawing-room," said the maid; "he
said he should wait till you came home."

"A gentleman!" said Alicia, "who in the world can it be?"

"A tall gentleman," replied the maid.

"Good Heavens!" said Alicia to Susan, "depend on it, it's Mr.
Seymour, who has found out the house from the coachman, and
contrived to get here before us. He said his horse and groom
were waiting."

Susan thought so too; and they ascended the stairs with the

firm conviction that they should behold the gentleman they had so lately parted with.

It would have been natural, instead of waiting till his wife came up, that Mr. Aytoun should have run down to meet her the moment the coach stopped; but he felt he could not do it. Try as he would, he could not assume the glad, free, joyous bearing with which he had been accustomed to embrace her after an absence; and he stood in the middle of the room, listening to her foot as she ascended, rather like a man who was awaiting an enemy than the wife of his bosom.

"Good Heavens!" cried she, stopping short as she entered the room, "Arthur! is it you?"

"It is me, Alicia," said he, advancing towards her—"how are you?"

Now, if Mr. Aytoun had acted naturally and ran down to the door to meet her, she would have thrown herself into his arms with exactly the same fervour and affection she had done on all former occasions; but the coldness and constraint of his manner was reflected in hers. It brought the consciousness of all he had yet to learn, that she knew would be so displeasing to him, full upon her mind; and thus they met, not like parted lovers as they were, but like persons merely on civil terms of acquaintanceship.

The thing was too unnatural not to be deeply felt by both. Each attributed it to the other; he fancied that she was annoyed at his return; and she, that he had heard something of her affair at the police office; and as neither had resolution enough to ask for an explanation, their constraint, instead of diminishing, increased every moment.

"Where have you been, Alicia?" said the husband, looking at the yellow shawl, which he immediately recognised.

"Susan and I went to take a walk in the Gardens," she replied. "I thought a little change would do me good."

"You don't look well," observed he.

"I have not been well," she replied. "I had hoped, Arthur, to have some good news for you against you returned—but I have been disappointed."

"What do you mean?" said he.

"I have been in the family way," said she, blushing, and really, from his odd manner, feeling as abashed as if she were telling the thing to a stranger.

"In the family way!" he reiterated, in a tone that testified much more surprise than pleasure.

"Yes," answered she, her confusion momentarily augmenting; "soon after you went I found that was the case; and about two months since, not feeling very well, I came down here; and only two days afterwards, I was taken ill."

"You never mentioned a word of such a thing to me in your letters," said the husband, regarding her with scrutinizing eyes.

"No," replied she; "I wished to give you an agreeable surprise; and after my disappointment I was not able to write for some time;

but I sent a letter to Frankfort, about a fortnight ago, wherein I told you all about it."

"I have not been to Frankfort," replied he. "Then you came here because you didn't feel well," he continued, after a pause; "was that the reason?"

"Yes," said she, "that was the principal reason," and her cheeks crimsoned at the recollection of the other reason, and the apprehension of his knowing it. "When did you arrive, Arthur?" said she.

"Last night," he replied, "about eight o'clock."

"Did you see anybody besides Betty?" said she.

"I saw the Parsons, and the Morlands, and the Bloxhams; they were altogether at tea, and called me over."

"I suppose they were not very well pleased at my not telling them where I was coming to?" said Alicia, curious to discover what had been said.

"They seemed to think it odd, certainly," returned Mr. Aytoun, "and so I thought it myself."

"They're such tiresome, gossiping people," said Mrs. Aytoun, "that not being well, I was not in a humour to be troubled with them."

And in this sort of strain the conversation was carried on, without affection, without confidence; each hiding their heart from the other; his suspicions and her fears every moment augmenting; till, at last, to her relief, though very much to her surprise, Mr. Aytoun, about a couple of hours after dinner, suddenly arose, and saying he had business in the city which called him to town, bade her good evening, and walked away, intending, as he said, to get upon the first coach that overtook him on its road to London.

"Shall you be here to-morrow?" asked Alicia, following him to the top of the stairs.

"Most likely," he replied; "I can't say positively;" and the next minute the door closed on him and he was gone.

Alicia threw herself on the sofa and wept; whilst he, far from thinking of getting on a coach as he had said he intended, strode along the road at the rapid pace that men are wont to walk who desire to walk away from themselves and their own thoughts. He couldn't have commanded patience to have sat in, or on, the fastest coach that was ever drawn by four horses. The motion of his own limbs seemed indispensable to his very existence. Had he been forced to sit still—had the engine been stopped, and he debarred from applying to bodily exercise the superfluous energy of his passion, he felt as if the vapours of wrath that were boiling within him, must have rent his heart in twain.

When he reached the Park gates where he had seen the coach in the morning, he turned in, and stopped for an instant to look around, as if he still expected to see the handsome stranger lurking near.

"I wonder if she meets him here every day!" said he to himself. "I shall be sadly in their way, I'm afraid." The hour was between

P

four and five; and the Park was thronged with gay equipages and
fashionable equestrians. When he reached the Piccadilly extremity of the walk, he was obliged, with many others, to draw up
for a minute or two to wait for an opportunity of crossing. Leaning with their backs against the rails, and patting their shining
black boots with their ebony canes, or silver-mounted riding
whips, was a row of fashionable young men, who having finished
their ride, had dismounted, and were grouping together to talk
over the affairs of the day, and remark on the beauties and cele-
brities as they slowly rounded that crowded corner, where the
crossing and jostling of carriages entering and leaving the Park,
the access to which was far from being as wide and commodious at
that time as it is at present, obliged the emulous, struggling, and
impatient drivers to slacken their pace.

"I say, Seymour!" cried the thin voice of a very young man,
who, still mounted, had drawn up his horse by the rails, close to
this group of exquisites—" Seymour, I say!"

"Well, what do you say?" asked the rich, deep voice of Seymour.

"I've been calling to you this half hour," said the other. "I
want to know who that woman was I saw you with in the gardens
this morning."

"You don't expect I should tell you, do you?" said Seymour,
carelessly.

"She's devilish pretty," said the youth.

"She is pretty," returned Seymour.

"I only ask for the reversion," said the young man; who being
but just turned loose upon the world, was anxious to show himself
already initiated into all the profligacies of high life. "You owe
me something for my forbearance," continued he, "for I might
have spoiled sport if I'd liked, and flurried your bird before you
came up."

"How so?" inquired Seymour.

"Why," said the other, "I am aide-de-camp in waiting, you
know, this week; and I had to go to the palace with a message;
so I got off my horse at the gate to walk across the gardens; and
just as I'd crossed the broad walk, I caught a glimpse of a bright
yellow shawl glancing amongst the trees, evidently wishing to keep
out of sight—ladies should never wear yellow shawls when they go
to a rendezvous, they're so devilish conspicuous—so I pushed
through the copse, and presented myself right in front of her."

"D—d impudent of you," said Seymour.

"You know, my dear fellow, I couldn't tell she was waiting for
you," replied the boy, "or I should have kept off; I never poach
on my friends' manors. However, I got a capital view of her face;
and a devilish pretty one it was."

"But how did you know she was there to meet me?" returned
Seymour.

"Because I saw you with her as I came back," said the youth:
"I passed through the trees close to you, attracted again by the

yellow shawl. You were coming it strong, I fancy, Seymour, eh? She'd got her handkerchief to her eyes; and you were squeezing her hand, and laying it on like the old serpent himself, I've no doubt. Don't forget I'm for next turn," cried the beardless boy, as he cantered away; thinking he had shown a manhood that might have become Julius Cæsar himself.

"What an insufferable coxcomb that is!" said Seymour, looking after him.

"Shocking puppy!" echoed the others, shrugging their shoulders; and finding the conversation reverted no more to the yellow shawl, Arthur Aytoun walked on.

CHAPTER XXXI.

THE CHALLENGE.

ON the following morning Mrs. Aytoun received a few lines from her husband, saying that he was detained in town by business, and should not be able to see her on that day.

Alicia was relieved; she had hopes that that morning was to see her free from her embarrassments, and release her from the dangerous and inconvenient necessity of further interviews with Mr. Seymour. He had informed her on the preceding day, that since he had written to her, he had had another conversation with Mr. Green, on whom he thought he had, at last, made some impression.

"I am to see him again to-night," continued he, "when I am to have his final answer; and if you will allow me the honour of meeting you to-morrow at the same hour—here, if you *really* cannot receive me where you are staying, I shall be able to tell you the result; and give you any advice that the circumstances may render necessary:" and Alicia, eager to be released from the terrors that hung over her, and if possible extricate herself from the whole *imbroglio* before her husband's return, had consented to meet him; fully determined that it should be the last time. She doubted very much Arthur's having received any hint of Mr. Green's accusation, and of the police-office story; for she thought if he knew it, he could not have forborne to have mentioned it instantly; and it was her ardent desire, dreading as she did the effect it would have on his susceptible pride, that he never should hear of it. She rather concluded, on reflection, that his coldness had proceeded partly from the surprise he felt at her leaving town without telling him; and partly, probably, from her own embarrassment and confusion, which must have made her appear as cool to him as he did to her. "Once free from this odious business," she said to herself, "I should soon regain my spirits, and be myself again: and Arthur would think the difference he observed in me

P 2

had arisen from my illness. As for Mr. Seymour, I am very much
obliged to him; but I can't sacrifice my own happiness and my
husband's to his gratification; and I am quite sure Arthur would
never tolerate his visits for a moment. I shall tell him I am sincerely grateful, which I am; but that Mr. Aytoun is returned;
and that if any suspicion of our acquaintance reached him, it
might occasion the most distressing consequences to all parties:
and I shall throw myself on his honour and generosity not to seek
any further interviews or correspondence. If he is the gentleman
I take him to be, he can't refuse; and, indeed, I don't know why
he should; for he must have clearly seen, by my avoiding him as
I have done, that any other termination to the adventure is not to
be looked for."

But Mr. Seymour saw no such thing; on the contrary, he
looked with confidence to a termination much more flattering and
agreeable. The price of Mr. Green's forbearance was to be five
hundred pounds. He had hinted nothing of the sort to Alicia,
lest she should take fright at the magnitude of the obligation, and
refuse to incur it; but the money once paid, and irrevocably en-
closed in the hard fists of the grasping haberdasher, he considered
that she would be so completely involved in his toils, that she
would have no alternative but to purchase her immunity by the
sacrifice of her honour.

At the appointed hour, accompanied by Susan, as before, Alicia
repaired to the rendezvous; and never did any unfortunate
woman incur the appearance of guilt with less inclination to commit it, than herself. Her whole heart was with her husband; and
all Mr. Seymour's graces and fascinations had made no more impression on her, than if they had been squandered on the effigy
of the chaste Diana. Indeed the more assiduity he evinced, the
more he was repelled. Nothing can be so abhorrent to a woman
really in love with one man, as the slightest approach to tenderness or familiarity from another. In a chaste and delicate woman's
heart there can exist no partnership; and the mere pressure of
a hand, if it is not the one hand she loves, sends back the blood in
her veins with the cold chill of disgust. There are, doubtless,
many unhappy circumstances that may force a most virtuous
woman to give her hand where she cannot give her heart; but
where she gives her heart, she gives her hand *indeed;* not meta-
phorically, according to the newspaper ritual, but according to a
ritual that nature has established in her own breast. Her whole
and entire self is the property of the one beloved, even where the
love is unrequited and disowned; and the most distant attempt
at an encroachment on the rights with which it has pleased her
generous and devoted affection to invest him, is recoiled from as
a profaning of the holy temple dedicated to the pure worship of
the idol she has set up.

Mr. Seymour was at the rendezvous before her. He thought it
not unlikely that the young coxcomb who had seen her on the
preceding day, might be again crossing the Gardens on his way to

the palace; and he did not choose that the woman for whom he designed the honour of being seduced by himself, should be insulted by another.

"I flatter myself," said he, "I have been successful at last with that fellow; and I think you may now consider yourself secure of hearing no more on the subject."

"I am most grateful to you," she returned. "I cannot describe the obligation you have conferred on me. Mr. Aytoun is, of all persons in the world, the one the least able to endure that the slightest reflection should be cast upon his wife, or anybody belonging to him. His susceptibility on such subjects is quite morbid; and I assure you, innocent as our acquaintance has been, I tremble lest it should reach his ears. He would so entirely disapprove of my having permitted your visits in Craven-street, that nothing but a full explanation of all that led to them would exonerate me from his displeasure. I fear, therefore, after thanking you most sincerely for a service I can never cease to remember with gratitude, that I must request, as a last favour, that you will permit our acquaintance to terminate with this interview."

"Is it possible?" returned Mr. Seymour, "that in requital—I will not say of the service I have had the happiness to render you, for that is its own reward; and if it had cost me five thousand pounds, instead of five hundred, I should have thought the pleasure cheaply purchased—but is it a fair requital for the regard that prompted my exertions, to banish me from your presence the moment I cease to be useful?"

Mr. Seymour had expected that his allusion to the money would have awakened Alicia's curiosity, and alarmed her delicacy; and he was surprised that she had not interrupted him on the instant to demand an explanation; but Alicia's eyes, and thoughts, and whole soul were bent on a figure she dimly discerned, hovering near them, through the trees; and his eloquence was squandered on unheeding ears.

The person, whoever it was, was evidently watching them, and concealing himself. As they advanced, and their change of position would have exposed him to their view, he retreated, hiding himself first behind one tree and then another; but still keeping near enough to observe their motions. A cold fear crept through Alicia's veins, and her heart sunk heavy within her, for she thought it was her husband. It was not so much from the intelligence of her eyes that she judged, for she had seen the figure too imperfectly to recognise it; but some other sense, like that which warns the ghost seer that a spirit from the grave is near, whispered that it was Arthur. Like one, too, in the presence of some such fearful apparition, her speech forsook her, her voice died away in her throat, her knees bent under her, and she laid her hand on Mr. Seymour's arm, partly to prevent herself from sinking to the earth, and partly in the design of drawing his attention to the person that was dodging them.

But Mr. Seymour, who was carried away by his own eloquence,

and occupied with his own views, having seen nothing of what
alarmed his companion, mistook the motive of the action. He
imagined she was overcome by the announcement of the price at
which he had purchased her immunity; that she was vanquished
by his generosity, and that her reserve was melting in the beams
of its splendour; and under that persuasion, he suddenly flung
his arm about her waist, and pressed her, half fainting as she was,
and almost incapable of resistance, even had there been time for
it, with fervour to his heart.

Like lightning, quicker than words can speak it, the figure
Alicia had descried darted upon them from behind a neighbouring
tree; with one hand he tore her from the arm that encircled her,
and flung her off with such force, that she fell to the earth at a
distance of several yards from the spot where the impulse had
been received; whilst, with the other, he dealt Mr. Seymour a
blow across the face that in an instant deluged his whole person
with blood. Pale and gasping with passion, and with a countenance in which revenge sat glaring at her victims, Arthur Aytoun
stood before them.

Mr. Seymour was quickly upon his feet, and whilst wiping the
blood from his face, he looked with almost as much astonishment
as resentment at the author of so unexpected an assault. Alicia
had not yet told him of her husband's return; and his first notion
was that he had been assailed by a lunatic; but Mr. Aytoun's
first words undeceived him.

"Villain!" cried the enraged husband, "cowardly, sneaking
villain, infamous seducer of honest men's wives, when you think
their absence ensures you impunity—wretch, not worthy to breathe
the pure air of heaven that you pollute with your adulterous vows
—you perhaps don't know me? But you shall learn to know me
to the peril of your body, that I'll tear piecemeal; and of your
soul, that I'll send to hell! I am that woman's husband!"

"Sir," replied Mr. Seymour, with a command of himself that,
considering the situation he was placed in, was truly surprising;
and which nothing could inspire but that great usage of the world,
which, if it does not subdue, most assuredly tempers the rage of
angry passion, and gives man the power of moderating the expression of its violence, "Sir, under the circumstances in which
we are mutually placed, words of any sort are worse than useless.
No explanation I could make could appease your resentment;
and even if it could, no apology on your part could efface the
affront I have received. Blows, sir, unless from a person I could
meet on no other terms, I never return. These," and he held out
his hands, "these are not the weapons I am accustomed to use.
Here is my card—make your arrangements to-day; and at as early
an hour to-morrow morning you please to appoint, and at whatever spot you choose to name, you will find me punctually awaiting you."

As Mr. Seymour concluded these words, he picked up his hat
that was lying on the ground, and having smoothed round the nap

with the cuff of his coat, he cast a pitying glance at Alicia, who, with her head supported on Susan's lap, was still stretched, in a state of insensibility, on the earth; and then bowing calmly, and with perfect grace and self-possession to Mr. Aytoun, he walked deliberately away to where he had left his horse and groom.

Mr. Aytoun looked after him for a moment, and then, without even casting his eyes in the direction where his wretched wife was lying, he turned his back towards the path Mr. Seymour had taken; and like a chafed lion, striding through the wildest and most unfrequented parts, he crossed the gardens, and issuing from them by the Bayswater gate, he returned by that road to London.

For some time Susan sat on the ground supporting her mistress, afraid to leave her, and unable to remove her. At length, catching a glimpse of a man at a little distance, she called to him. He proved to be one of the rangers, and with his assistance she contrived to get the unfortunate Alicia conveyed to the lodge. There, after a while, they succeeded in restoring her so far, that Susan ventured to have her carried to the coach; and bidding the driver make all the speed he could, they soon reached Hammersmith; where, yet but imperfectly remembering what had occurred, Mrs. Aytoun was lifted out of the carriage, and conveyed to her own bedchamber.

CHAPTER XXXII.

THE DUEL.

Some hours elapsed before, by means of restoratives and a reclining position, Alicia revived sufficiently to recal the scene she had witnessed. From repeated fainting fits she had sunk at length into an uneasy slumber, and Susan had ventured out of the room for a few minutes, to direct that some tea should be prepared for her against she awoke, when she was summoned to return by the violent ringing of Mrs. Aytoun's bell; and, on rushing up stairs, she found her mistress standing on the landing-place, half undressed as she had left her, with cheeks as white as the muslin peignoir that was flung around her person, and looking rather like one lately risen from the grave, than an inhabitant of the earth, but supported on her limbs by the flame that was raging within her.

"Susan!" she cried with vehemence, as soon as she descried her faithful attendant,—"oh, Susan, why did you let me rest? I must be up and stirring, girl, or I have rested my last rest on earth. Send off instantly for a post-chaise, and while they are fetching it, come you and get me ready—we must away to London."

Susan obeyed without a word; she thought it better she should go. She might do good, but even if she did not, to have denied her the relief of, at least, attempting to do something, would have been cruel; the feelings that urged her, had they found no vent in action, might have destroyed her reason.

"Tell me," said she, whilst Susan assisted her to dress, "tell me everything that passed—every word you heard. For myself, I saw nothing after I was flung to the earth—the last thing I remember was seeing Mr. Seymour's face streaming with blood. Of course there was a challenge; did you hear when they are to meet?"

"To-morrow morning, early," replied Susan, who thought the danger much too serious to risk anything by diminishing its imminence; "but the place was not fixed. Mr. Seymour gave master his address, and left him to settle it as he pleased."

"And where was the address, Susan?" asked Alicia, eagerly.

"It was a card he gave, ma'am; he didn't mention it," returned Susan.

"Oh, that he had!" exclaimed Alicia. "Perhaps he would take pity on me if I could see him; but I have no idea where he lives. I think I once heard him say he lodged, when he was in town, at an hotel; but how am I to discover which; and so little time to do it in?"

The chaise was quickly at the door, and a very short time sufficed to convey them to Craven-street.

"Is your master here?" cried Mrs. Aytoun, anxiously, as soon as Betty appeared at the door.

"No, ma'am," replied the calm and unconscious Betty. "Master has not been here since he left yesterday morning. I thought he was with you at Hammersmith."

"What!" said Mrs. Aytoun, as she threw herself on her sofa, "didn't he sleep here last night?"

"No, ma'am," replied Betty; "I've seen nothing of him."

"Then he must have been told something before he came to me," said Mrs. Aytoun.

"Master went over to Mrs. Parsons," said Betty, who perceived that there was something wrong.—"And oh! I forgot, master saw Mr. Seymour, ma'am, when he called for your note the night before last. He was just at the door when master's coach drove up—"

No further explanation was necessary; Alicia saw it all; and her only hope lay in the chance of finding her husband, and inducing him, by a timely explanation, to make an apology to Mr. Seymour, and forego the meeting. Susan ran for a coach; and they were soon started on a chase, unfortunately not very likely to prove successful. Alicia knew nothing of her husband's haunts; or rather he had none to know. His home had been his haven; and he was seldom away from it, except when engaged on business. The hours for business were passed, for it was already between eight and nine o'clock; and she almost feared she should find no one at the office of the Messrs. Karl, where she first proceeded; and it proved, indeed, that every one had left it but the porter.

"Mr. Aytoun has not been here, ma'am," said he, in answer to her inquiries, "since yesterday morning. I am quite sure of it; because I know Mr. Karl has been expecting him all day; and waited at home for him several hours; and he desired me, if he came, to beg he would be here by ten o'clock to-morrow."

Alicia next directed the coachman to the private residences of the Messrs. Karl; and, in succession, to the house of every other acquaintance she could think of; but with the same result. No one had heard or seen anything of Arthur Aytoun.

"Oh, how like him," she said; "my poor, poor husband; he's hiding his unhappy head that he thinks I have covered with shame; whilst I, his wretched and innocent wife, am seeking in vain to undeceive him."

Her endeavours to find her husband proving fruitless, her last hope was in obtaining an interview with Mr. Seymour; but how to discover his residence? She only knew that he was the Honourable Mr. Seymour, and that he generally lodged at an hotel. Armed with these feeble indications, she set forth on this new quest; and after inquiring at the door of a vast number of hotels at the West End of the town, she at length learned that there was an Honourable Mr. Seymour lodging at one in Grosvenor-street; and thither she immediately drove.

It was now near midnight; but the door of the house was partly open, and she saw a light in the passage. The coachman rang the bell, and the summons was quickly answered by a waiter.

"Does the Honourable Mr. Seymour lodge here?" asked Alicia.

"Sometimes, ma'am," replied the waiter. "He always keeps a room here, and we take in his letters."

"Is he here now?" said she.

"No, ma'am," returned the waiter. "He hasn't been here since the morning; he called then to give some orders; but he said he should not return to sleep."

"Oh, my God!" cried Alicia, unconscious of the insolent curiosity with which the waiter was surveying her, "and can't you tell me where he's to be found?"

"No, ma'am," returned the man, who could have told her very well if he had pleased; for Mr. Seymour had been there on his return from the Gardens, to say that he expected some letters of consequence; and that they must be forwarded to the house of his friend Colonel Alleyn, the moment they arrived. But the man had some doubts how far the visits of a lady, in a hackney coach, at twelve o'clock at night, might be agreeable to the Honourable Mr. Seymour. He remembered some visits of the like sort before, which had terminated in tears and reproaches from one party, and sundry smart oaths addressed to himself from the other, for not having prevented the interview: so, on this occasion, he resolved to be prudent; and, having given what he intended should be his final answer, he turned on his heel, and re-entered the house.

"Where now, ma'am?" asked the coachman.

"Where shall we go, Susan?" said Alicia. "I shall go mad if I return home, and sit there doing nothing but count the hours till the dreadful morning."

"Suppose we were just to drive there, and see if master's called since we came out, ma'am," said Susan, by way of proposing something to pacify her. "There's no telling, you know; he might wish to leave some message, or a letter, or something."

"So he might," replied Alicia; "and in that case he wouldn't go till night, lest the neighbours should see him. Tell the man to drive home instantly," she added, impatiently.

"Go back to Craven-street directly," said Susan; and the slow and burly coachman, encumbered with great-coats, gradually ascended to his box.

"Good Heavens!" said Mrs. Aytoun, "I wish he'd make haste; every moment is precious. I may miss seeing Arthur by the delay," and she thrust her head out of the window to bid him be quick.

At that instant the door of the hotel opened, and a gentleman, stepping out, walked rapidly away. Mrs. Aytoun, whose attention was engaged by the coachman, did not observe him till he had moved two or three yards from the door, but then, whether he had heard her voice, or from whatever cause it might be, he turned his head and looked back. Imperfect as the light was, she was quite sure it was her husband.

"Let me out!" she cried to the man, who had just succeeded in getting his horses to move on—"let me out. Or drive after that gentleman as fast as you can."

"Which shall I do, ma'am?" asked the man, with imperturbable coolness, and making no attempt to do either.

"Oh, let me out," she cried, struggling with the handle of the door.

"Let me, ma'am," said Susan, "I can open it;" and in a moment more Alicia had jumped out, and was in full chase of her husband; Susan, of course, following with all the speed she could.

But Susan being last, she had not gone many steps before she found her progress arrested by the stout arm of the coachman; whose natural apathy being overcome by the peril of his fare, had contrived to tumble off his box much quicker than he had mounted it; and now demanded to know what they meant by bilking him.

"It's no use your stopping me," said Susan, impatiently, "for I have but a couple of shillings in my pocket—you may have them, if you choose, and if you'll call to-morrow at Craven-street, where you took us up, you shall be paid as much as you please. Only let me go now, that I may overtake my mistress, for I believe she's going out of her senses."

"She seems maddish, sure enough," replied the coachman; and won by the liberal promise of being paid as much as he pleased, he let go her arm; and giving a view halloa after her as she set out, he remounted his box, and drove to a neighbouring public-house; where, considering the two shillings as extra money, and no part of his fare, he converted them into copious draughts of porter, and hot brandy and water.

In the meantime, Susan, who had lost sight of her mistress by the delay, and only knew that she had run towards Bond-street, followed in the same direction; but, when she reached the corner, she was uncertain which way to take; till a watchman, who was passing at the moment, said he had just seen a lady cross the street, and run towards Hanover-square.

Away went poor Susan, crossing the square, and through street after street, fancying at first she saw her mistress before her: and afterwards running on, more from her alarm and confusion than from any rational hope of overtaking her; till she found herself in one of the streets leading out of Soho. She then recognised where she was; which before, so erratic had been her course, she had not very well known; and she slackened her pace to consider what she should do.

"My mistress will surely go home," thought she, "whether she overtakes Mr. Aytoun or not; and the best thing I can do, is to go there too."

She had just arrived at this decision, and was thinking which was the most direct way to reach the Strand, when a powerful grasp was laid upon her arm, and a man, in the dress of a sailor, said—"Give me what money you have about you, or I'll take your life."

"For God's sake, don't hurt me," replied Susan. "I hav'n't a farthing in my pocket, I do assure you."

"Have you a watch?" asked the man, sternly.

"No," answered Susan. "I never had such a thing belonging to me. I'm only a poor servant; pray let me go!"

"I'll see if you're telling me a lie," said the man, and he put his hand to her side to feel her pocket.

"I'm telling you the truth," said Susan. "I'd rather give you my money, if I had any, than be kept here. Pray let me go!"

"Go, and be d—d!" said the man, as he dropped her arm, and hastened away in the direction of Oxford-street: whilst Susan took the opposite one.

"I've seen that man before, I'm certain," said she to herself, "but I can't think where;" and as she walked on at a rapid pace to Craven-street, she reviewed all the situations and circumstances in which it was possible she might have met with him; but without being able to assign either time or place to the recollection that had struck her.

When she reached Craven-street, her dismay was great at finding Mrs. Aytoun had not arrived; but as she did not know in what direction to seek her, she concluded that the most advisable thing she could do, was to wait there till she came.

However, the night passed without any intelligence of her;

and it was not till between eleven and twelve o'clock on the following day, that a man arrived from Hammersmith with a message, saying that Mrs. Aytoun had been brought to Prospect-place
early in the morning, having been found in the Gardens in a state
of delirium. It appeared that she had passed the night in searching for, or imagining she was searching for her husband; and the
lodge-keeper at Kensington said, that when he opened the gates
in the morning, he had found her waiting there in a hackney
coach; and had let her in, thinking she looked strange, but not
aware that there was anything wrong. After waiting upwards of
two hours, the coachman, whom she had not paid, spoke to the
keeper, and mentioned how he had taken her up at the dawn of
day in Piccadilly, and said that he had some suspicion that she
was out of her senses; which inducing the keeper to search for
her in the Gardens, she was found lying on the ground exactly
on the spot where her husband and Mr. Seymour had quarrelled
on the preceding day. She was extremely unwilling to be taken
away, alleging that she was waiting there to prevent her husband
being killed in a duel. Finally, however, they had succeeded in
removing her; and the keeper, who on the previous day had
learned her address, had sent her to Hammersmith in the coach,
accompanied by his wife. Susan lost no time in repairing thither
also: and to her great relief she found her already in bed, and
under the care of the medical man who had attended her in her
late illness.

Where was Arthur Aytoun the while? Alas! Arthur Aytoun
was in custody for the murder of Mr. Seymour. Never doubting
his wife's guilt, and mad with passion, he had written to Mr.
Seymour, that he should take no second to the meeting, and that
the contest must last till one of them fell. Mr. Seymour, who
knew that Mr. Aytoun was not so much injured as he imagined,
and only waited till, by an exchange of shots, the affront he himself had received should be wiped away, to tell him so, did not
think himself bound to comply with the conditions demanded.
He, therefore, went to the ground accompanied by his friend.
But Mr. Aytoun refused to listen to anything Colonel Alleyn had
to say, or to submit to any of the regulations established for such
occasions. He said he came there with the determination to kill
Mr. Seymour, or to be killed himself; and scarcely waiting till
the ground was measured, and before any signal could be given,
he fired, and Mr. Seymour fell, shot through the heart, having
only time to say, "It was my own fault," before he expired.

Mr. Aytoun made no attempt to escape; on the contrary, he
kept his ground sullenly, till the officers arrived to take him into
custody; avowing, that he came there with the intention of taking
Mr. Seymour's life, and that they were very welcome to take his
in return.

CHAPTER XXXIII.

SUSAN MAKES A VISIT TO NEWGATE.

A DANGEROUS fever, accompanied by delirium, confined Mrs. Aytoun for many weeks to her bed; and during the wanderings of her brain, her thoughts unceasingly ran on the events of that dreadful day and night. Sometimes she would imagine herself kneeling at her husband's feet, and in the most affecting terms would assure him of her innocence; and swear that she loved him a thousand times better than her own existence. At others, she would fancy herself still pursuing him through the streets, whilst he fled from her; and then again she would speak of it to Susan as a thing past.

"Wasn't it cruel of him," she would say, "to make me follow him all the livelong night, and yet never let me overtake him? The faster I ran, the faster he ran: and yet I could see him all the time. Sometimes when I was tired, I slackened my pace, and then he turned and beckoned me to come on—and when I couldn't go any further and sat down upon a step to rest, I heard his voice calling to me *Alicia! Alicia!* he said, *Come on! come on!*"

The first symptom she gave of her returning senses was, that one day when she had been asleep, and Susan was sitting by her bedside at work, she suddenly awoke, and raising herself on her elbow, she drew aside the curtain that concealed Susan from her view, and looking steadily in her face, she said, "Is Arthur dead?"

"No, ma'am," replied Susan, "master's alive and well."

Alicia then fell back on her pillow, and went to sleep again, and it was not till the next day that she made any further attempt at conversation.

"Susan," said she, on the following morning, "I believe I've been very ill."

"You have, ma'am," replied Susan; "but, thank God, you're better."

"That's not it," said she, putting her hand to her head—"it's something else."

Susan was afraid to suggest what she might probably wish to ask; lest the recollection of the late events should be too much for her.

"I dare say you wish to ask after master, ma'am," said she; "he's very well; but you're not to see him till you're stronger."

"Who says so?" asked she.

"The doctor says so, ma'am," replied Susan.

"Oh, very well," she said; and after that she appeared satisfied, and her health rapidly improved.

But as her strength returned, so did her memory; and by degrees she extracted from Susan, question by question, an

account of all that had happened, except the death of Mr. Seymour and Arthur's imprisonment. Those two circumstances,
which she herself had learned from the medical man, Susan
thought it prudent to withhold.

At length, one day, when Mrs. Aytoun was considerably
recovered, though not yet strong enough to leave her bed, Susan
said to her, "I've been thinking, ma'am, that perhaps if you
would give me leave to go to town and try to see master, I might
do some good."

"I'm afraid he wouldn't listen to you, Susan," said Mrs.
Aytoun. "Depend on it, Mr. Seymour has told him I'm guiltless; for though he's profligate enough to have desired to seduce
me, I do not believe him so wicked as to let me lie under an
imputation that he knows I don't merit. And yet, you see,
Arthur would let me die deserted and broken-hearted before he'd
stretch out a hand to save me."

"Nevertheless, ma'am," said Susan, who had heard that Mr.
Seymour had died before he had time to enter into any explanations, and who was aware that Arthur couldn't come if he would—
"nevertheless, ma'am, if you've no objection, I should like to go.
It is your duty to do all you can to clear yourself—if master wont
listen to the truth, God forgive him!"

"Go, Susan!" said Alicia, "go, my honest girl; and may the
blessing of Heaven go with you!"

Accordingly, on the following day, Susan left Hammersmith
by one of the early coaches; and having ascertained that her
master was confined in Newgate, thither she proceeded at once,
and was admitted without difficulty.

"I'd better go and tell Mr. Aytoun you wish to see him," said
the turnkey. "He's not very fond of company, and most times
sends people away."

"If you please, don't tell him," said Susan to the man, beseech-
ingly. "I come from his poor wife, that's breaking her heart
about him; and if I go back without seeing him, it will be such
a cruel disappointment!"

"Oh, well," said the man, "if that's the case, come along at
once: I'll say nothing about it—there," added he, "that's where
he is; go in;" and Susan found herself in the presence of her
master.

Mr. Aytoun, who, when she entered, was pacing the room like
the restless denizen of the jungle when torn from his native wilds,
and condemned to waste the fiery energies of his fierce nature in a
prison of six feet square, started and turned hastily round to see
what unpermitted visitor had dared to intrude on his desolation.
When he saw who it was, the wrath that seemed at first kindled
by the unexpected interruption, changed to an expression of the
coldest and haughtiest contempt. He crossed his arms, and
looked at her in silence.

Nothing dismayed was Susan, for she knew she came armed
with truth.

"If I were what you think me, sir," said she, "you'd have a right to look at me so, for I should deserve it; but it's hard to be condemned unheard."

"I don't condemn you, woman," said he. "You must earn your bread."

"Honestly, sir, I must," replied Susan; "but I'd rather want it than do a thing against my conscience."

"Conscience is very accommodating," he said, coldly.

"Mine is not, sir," returned Susan.

"What brings you here?" inquired Mr. Aytoun. "If it's to justify yourself, it's unnecessary. Your conduct can be of no importance to me; nor can my opinion, henceforth, be of any to you."

"You're mistaken, sir," returned Susan. "I can't remain quiet and know myself unjustly suspected; and, in Christian charity, you're bound to listen to what I have to say. If you don't believe me when I have done, I can't help it. I shall at least have the comfort of knowing that I have done my duty to myself."

"Well," said Mr. Aytoun, "what is it you want to say? Make haste, and let me hear it as concisely as possible."

"Thank ye, sir," replied Susan, dropping a curtsey. "I wont keep you long,—but, you know, sir, I can't speak of myself without, perhaps, betraying things—about other people."

"Never mind, never mind, go on," said Mr. Aytoun; who, though he would not have condescended to ask, or even to listen, had he been invited to do so, to any details on the subject of his wife and Mr. Seymour, was nevertheless not sorry to have some light thrown on the mystery of their intimacy.

"Well, sir," said Susan, "you hadn't been gone more than four or five weeks, when my mistress mentioned to me, one day, when I was taking up her breakfast, that she began to think she was in the family way."

"Four or five weeks after I went away?" said he.

"Yes, sir," returned Susan. "I'd observed that my mistress looked poorly, and couldn't eat her breakfast of a morning—so that when she told me, I wasn't so much surprised. Of course, I said how pleased you'd be, sir; and she said you would; 'but,' says she, 'Susan, I wont tell him yet, for fear of a disappointment.' Poor thing! I'm sure she thought more of the pleasure it would give you, than of her own."

"Well, go on," said Mr. Aytoun, impatiently, afraid of betraying the tender memories that Susan's words had awakened.

"Yes, sir," continued she. "Well, my mistress, as you may suppose, naturally took to preparing for the little one she expected; and a great amusement it was to her: and all the while I used to be waiting on her at breakfast, or dinner, or dressing her, we never talked of anything else but what it was to have; and how she hoped she should be able to nurse it herself; but still when I asked her if she had mentioned it to you, she always said, 'No, Susan, I hav'n't said a word about it yet. I should so like to keep it for a surprise for him; and presently, after he comes back, just quietly to ring the bell, and desire you to bring down the baby. Poor, dear Arthur! I can just fancy I see his dear face, when I put it into his arms, and told him it was his own.'"

"You'd better sit down, Susan," said Mr. Aytoun, turning away to draw forward a chair. "You'll be tired with standing so long."

"Thank ye, sir," said Susan, quietly seating herself. "Well, sir, all this went on very well for about four months; and then a thing occurred that has caused all these misfortunes."

"What was that?" inquired Mr. Aytoun, with evidently awakened curiosity; and thereupon Susan narrated all the particulars of Mr. Green's affair, and the visit to the police-office; Mr. Aytoun the while listening with the most intense interest.

"But what was Seymour doing at the police office?" inquired he. "Are you sure, Susan, he did not go there to meet her? She must have known him before, depend on it."

"I'm certain, sir, as I'm sitting here, that it was the first time she ever saw him. As for his being at the office, I heard him say in the coach, as we came home, that he was a friend of the magistrate's, and that he had gone there to speak to him; indeed, he said that he often dropt in there of a morning, when he'd nothing to do, because he liked to see human life. Neither my mistress nor I heard what his name was till he called the next day; and we did not know he was the 'Honourable,' till Betty learned it from Mrs. Parsons' maid. Mrs. Parsons had heard it from Mr. Green."

"But why, instead of encouraging the visits of a profligate man of fashion like Mr. Seymour," said Mr. Aytoun, "didn't Alicia send for me? She knew that at any risk or loss I would have flown to her assistance."

"Ah, sir, there she was wrong; that was her mistake, sir. She thought you'd be so angry, and so unhappy, and think it such a disgrace; and Mr. Seymour always advised her to hush it up, as it was impossible she could prove her innocence, unless she could produce the real thief."

"And who could be the real thief?" said Mr. Aytoun.

"God himself knows, sir," answered Susan. "I have sometimes had thoughts about it I shouldn't like to speak unless I was sure. Besides, there's no telling whether the things ever came right out of Mr. Green's shop."

"You don't suspect Betty?"

"Oh, no, sir! To my certain knowledge, Betty never was out of her kitchen whilst the things were in the house."

"But to return to Seymour," said Mr. Aytoun; "Alicia must have known very well what his motives were from the beginning. She couldn't suppose he was taking all that trouble for a stranger, without looking for his reward."

"I believe, sir, at first she thought it was all good-nature and pity," replied Susan, "but after a little while she did begin to see through him; and then it was that she began to talk of going away to the country."

"She told me it was for her health," said Mr. Aytoun.

"Because she was afraid to tell you the truth, sir," answered Susan. "But she was ill too, with fretting, and shutting herself up in the house so much; and that was the cause of what happened directly after we arrived at Hammersmith."

"Did anybody attend her?" inquired Mr. Aytoun.

"To be sure there did, sir," answered Susan. "Mr. Perfect, the first doctor in Hammersmith. And he's been attending her again now; and saved her life, I believe; for it went very hard with her."

"Has she been ill?" inquired Mr. Aytoun, with assumed indifference.

"All but dead, sir," replied Susan.

"However, Susan," said Mr. Aytoun, "you've certainly accounted for a great deal that I couldn't understand—at least if I'm to believe your story—"

"And I'm sure you do believe it, sir," returned Susan.

"It's of very little consequence whether I do or not," said he; "because, at all events, it can neither excuse nor account for what happened afterwards; the confirmation of which, you know, I saw with my own eyes. She could have no motive but one in having private meetings with him in the Gardens, when she could either have received him at home, or communicated with him by letter; and when a married woman permits any other man than her husband to throw his arm round her waist, her virtue, if it's not already lost, is scarcely worth the keeping."

"All that's very true, sir," answered Susan, "except the motive: her motive for meeting Mr. Seymour in the Gardens was, that he mightn't find out where she was; and I'm satisfied that he died without finding it out, though he took great pains about it. Poor thing! she thought to get Mr. Green's business settled without your knowing anything of it; and then to break off all acquaintance with Mr. Seymour, before your return."

"She couldn't suppose he'd consent to that," said Mr. Aytoun, "when she had accepted such obligations from him."

"She did suppose it, sir," said Susan. "She mayn't know the world as well as you do; but, she said, he must see that there was no use in his courting and troubling her; and that therefore she thought, when she told him so, he'd give it up. As for his putting his arm round her waist, I never saw him do such a thing before; and why he did it then, I don't know, nor she neither. She says, she saw you amongst the trees, and took hold of his arm to make him look at you; and perhaps he misunderstood her meaning—but that's gone with him to his grave; and we can never know it."

"And what then has been the object of your visit to me?" said Mr. Aytoun, after some reflection.

Q

" To tell you the truth, sir," answered Susan.

" And to persuade me that my wife is innocent; and that I have taken the life of a fellow-creature without provocation?" and Mr. Aytoun rose from his seat, and walked hastily about the room.

" The innocent must be justified, sir," said Susan, " come what will of it."

Still Mr. Aytoun traversed the room with an agitated step, and his countenance betrayed the conflict within him.

" Why her very manner of receiving me on my return," at last he said, suddenly stopping opposite to Susan, and fixing his eyes on her fiercely, " was enough to proclaim her guilt. Why, woman, she couldn't look me in the face."

" Very likely, sir," replied Susan, calmly. " She knew she'd a secret that she was afraid of your finding out: and that's enough to make any wife tremble before her husband, except she's used to deceive him. Besides, sir, what reason you had I don't know; but you were no more like yourself than she was. She fancied you'd heard something about Mr. Green ; and to say the truth, so did I."

" Great God!" exclaimed Mr. Aytoun, after an interval of violent emotion, " if she is innocent, I am a murderer !"

Susan, who had admirably maintained her firmness during the whole interview, was now ready to weep with him. " Nevertheless, sir," said she, " the sin *must* be taken away from the guiltless, and laid where it is due."

" Where is my wife?" said he, sobbing like an infant.

" At Hammersmith, sir, in her sick bed, where she has lain these six weeks, between life and death." And then Susan resumed her story from the time the two gentlemen had left her in the Gardens, up to the present moment; simply and naturally narrating all Alicia's anxiety for her husband's safety; and her eager pursuit of him in the hope of convincing him of the truth, and preventing the fatal meeting : and finally how she had been found in the Gardens, and conveyed to the lodgings.

There was such an impress of truth in all Susan said, and his previous experience of her character gave so much weight to her assertions, that conviction stole upon Arthur Aytoun's mind, in spite of the obstinate and passionate incredulity with which he had begun to listen.

" Leave me," he said, holding out his hand to Susan, after a violent fit of weeping ; " leave me! for I've a heavy account to settle with my conscience. Go to her—go to Alicia—to my wife—my poor wronged—injured woman : tell her I must try first to make my peace with God; but that when I'm sufficiently calm, and she is well enough to come, I'll see her—and before I presume to take her in my arms, and press her to my heart, I'll kneel down at her feet, and ask her to forgive me, and to remember me when I am gone—as I soon shall be, Susan, for I shall be condemned to death, as I deserve—to remember me with pity, and to believe, that it was my great love for her that, when I thought I'd lost her, made me mad."

CHAPTER XXXIV.

THE PLEADING.

Susan returned to Hammersmith, the herald of comfort; but it now became necessary to account for Mr. Aytoun's continued absence; and his unhappy wife had to learn that he would, in all probability, pay the forfeit of his hasty suspicion by the sacrifice of his life.

She abandoned her country lodgings the moment she was well enough to be removed to London; and after the first painful interview with her deeply repentant husband was over, melancholy as was the prospect before them, her grief was soothed by the conviction that she had recovered his esteem; and his, by the certainty of her unfailing affection.

But now poor Arthur Aytoun was less willing to die. It is true, his crime sat heavy on his conscience; but he was a young man, in the prime of life and health; and the reckless despair that had made him seek to sacrifice his life on the altar of his lost happiness, was now converted into horror at the image of the ignominious death that awaited him; and a mournful regret at the idea of prematurely parting with his young wife, with whom he had looked to live so many happy years.

Poor Alicia, too, had not only the pain of so cruel a separation in perspective, but had to support, in addition, the terrible consciousness, that though guiltless in act and thought, still her own imprudence had been the cause of the catastrophe.

She procured the best advice she could on the management of her husband's case; but it was the universal opinion that his conduct had been of so violent and aggravated a character, that there was little hope of his escape, unless the friends of the late Mr. Seymour could be induced to forego the prosecution; a result scarcely to be looked for, from the indignation they loudly expressed at the unfair advantage Mr. Aytoun had taken.

Mr. Aytoun's solicitor waited on Colonel Alleyn, who was married to a sister of Mr. Seymour's; and urged every motive he could think of to induce forbearance: but without success. Colonel Alleyn said he considered it a duty he owed, not only to his brother-in-law, but to the world in general, to make an example of a man who, regardless of the laws of honour, and of the rules established for the benefit of all, had shot his adversary like a dog, without taking the risk of a shot himself.

"If conduct like Mr. Aytoun's," he said, "were permitted to pass with impunity, no gentleman could go to a meeting of the sort, without the chance of being murdered; the whole structure of modern society, as it at present stands, would be overthrown, and people would end by shooting their adversary on the first convenient opportunity without warning or witnesses."

The period for the trial was fast approaching, and there was but one resource left—one feeble hope; it rested in the possibility that the appeal which had failed from the lips of the lawyer, might be more prevailing from those of the heart-broken wife. Alicia resolved to make the experiment.

She arranged her dress of plain white muslin, and her neat straw bonnet, with all the care she could; and took as much pains to look pretty, as she had been used to do in her maiden days when she expected a visit from Arthur; for she felt she was about to enter on a conflict wherein no weapon should be neglected.. She selected an early hour, and without any previous announcement of her intention, lest she should be denied admittance, she presented herself at Colonel Alleyn's door; and the servant, having received no orders to the contrary, ushered her at once into the spacious and richly-furnished drawing-room.

On a sofa, at one end, with a newspaper in his hand, lay Colonel Alleyn himself—an elegant and distinguished-looking man of about forty years of age. His wife, a handsome young woman apparently about thirty, was seated at a round table in the middle of the room, on which lay, in careless profusion, a number of splendid trifles; together with a beautiful inlaid desk, on which, with a golden pen, she was writing diminutive notes on black-edged paper. On the richly flowered carpet, which vied in its glowing hues with a parterre of bright tulips, sat a lovely little girl, on whose fair head perhaps seven summers might have smiled, with her arms twined round a beautiful Blenheim spaniel that was lying by her side. On another sofa, at the opposite extremity of the room to Colonel Alleyn, sat an elderly lady of a grave and dignified aspect, occupied at an embroidery frame. The whole party were in deep mourning.

As Mrs. Aytoun was announced, Colonel Alleyn and his lady both rose from their seats in evident surprise, and, without advancing, each stood, he with his paper, and she with her pen in her hand, as if uncertain how to receive their visitor; whilst the old lady, with her needle arrested in the air, looked over her frame with equal astonishment at the new comer.

The first sensation over, Colonel Alleyn moved a few steps forward, and said, "Allow me the honour of offering you a seat," and advanced a chair for Alicia, not far from the sofa which he had previously occupied, and on which he again placed himself. Mrs. Alleyn also resumed her seat, and drew her paper towards her as if she considered that she had no part in the visit; and the old lady once more slowly set her needle in motion, though with her attention evidently rather fixed on the scene that was about to be acted, than on her own employment. The little girl, too, whose antics with the dog had been for a moment arrested by the general disturbance, again threw her arms about its neck, and turned her back to the stranger.

"I am come, sir," said Alicia, perceiving that Colonel Alleyn sat with a grave countenance, in which the rigid determination not to be influenced by anything she had to say, might be easily deciphered—"I am come to ask for mercy—a wretched wife, to implore the life of her husband—of the dearest, best, and kindest of husbands, sir, whose love for me has been the cause of his offence; and who, till the belief of my unworthiness drove him from his senses, never had a reflection cast upon his character, nor was ever guilty of an action that the most scrupulous man of honour could arraign."

"We must the more regret, madam," replied Colonel Alleyn, in a low tone of voice, and with an unmoved countenance, "that his first deviation should have been of so fatal a character, that it is impossible to find either exculpation or excuse."

"Oh, sir," returned Mrs. Aytoun, "don't say that! never venture to assert that there is no excuse, till you have been yourself placed in a like situation."

But Alicia had no sooner pronounced these words than the thought occurred to her, which had not struck her before, "Is Colonel Alleyn aware that I am innocent?" If not, the speech she had made was certainly ill calculated to appease either himself or his wife; and, indeed, the very idea of having intruded herself into their drawing-room, whilst they imagined her otherwise, overwhelmed her with dismay. Her cheeks crimsoned at the supposition, and she added hastily, "But, perhaps, sir, you believe me guilty?"

"Oh, no," cried Colonel Alleyn, with more warmth than he had yet evinced; whilst his wife and the elderly lady each raised her head from her occupation and echoed the "Oh, no!" at the same moment. "Oh, no," repeated the colonel. "My unfortunate brother-in-law did you full justice, and effectually vindicated your character in his conversation with me the day before the meeting."

"I thought he would not wish to leave me under so cruel an imputation," replied Mrs. Aytoun, "and I have always believed that, had he lived long enough to do it, he would have justified me to my poor husband."

"Certainly, he would," returned Colonel Alleyn. "I was not aware that Mr. Aytoun had entertained any doubts on the subject."

"Oh, yes, sir," replied Alicia. "Many things tended to mislead him, and appearances were much against me. I have been most unfortunate," she added, weeping, "for in the first instance the whole thing originated in an accusation as extraordinary as it was unfounded, and from which, to this hour, I have never been able to clear myself, and perhaps never may."

"Had I been aware," returned Colonel Alleyn, "that Mr. Aytoun entertained any doubts of your innocence, I should have esteemed it my duty to remove them; and if any remain, I shall be most ready to do so still. That he might consider your conduct imprudent, I could, of course, conceive."

"Yes, sir," replied Alicia, firmly, "in one point of view I was very imprudent. I had much better have braved the publicity of

the first accusation than have incurred the appearance of worse
guilt. But I was not imprudent in the sense in which, I believe,
you used the word; and my husband's persuasion of my guilt
arose out of his conviction that I never could be so. He perfectly
well knew my opinions on subjects of that nature, and he knew,
also, that he had left me an attached and devoted wife, whom
nothing but the most entire alienation and perversion could have
induced to consent to clandestine meetings with any man. Oh,
sir, there was much excuse for him; there was indeed! He came
home after a long absence, elated at the prospect of seeing me;
and he found me, as he believed, the debased minion of a stranger.
A most unhappy combination of circumstances tended to deceive
him—my unexpected removal into the country, for one—"

"And the whole of this unhappy combination, he, without
pausing for inquiry, made Mr. Seymour pay for with his life,"
rejoined Colonel Alleyn.

"No doubt, he should have paused to inquire, sir," returned
Alicia; "but is it unusual for men who consider themselves
injured to lose their reason in their passion? And with respect to
making Mr. Seymour pay for the combination of circumstances
that gave me the appearance of guilt, pardon me for saying, that
Mr. Seymour's own conduct was, in effect, the chief cause of that
fallacious appearance. It was to avoid Mr. Seymour's too obtrusive attention that I quitted my home; and it was to prevent his
knowing my address that I agreed to meet him in the Gardens,
instead of receiving him at my own house."

"I cannot deny, madam," replied Colonel Alleyn, "that the
motive of quarrel was quite sufficient to justify Mr. Aytoun in
demanding satisfaction; but I think you will yourself find it difficult to offer any excuse for his conduct on the ground."

"None, sir, but that he was not in his senses," replied Alicia.

"Which is an excuse every criminal may offer for every crime,"
answered Colonel Alleyn.

"They may, sir, certainly," replied Alicia; "and it would
therefore, I am aware, in a court of justice be dangerous to admit
it. But in private, sir, when one human being sits in judgment
on another, every extenuation should be listened to. I know
that by the laws of every civilized country in the world, my husband would be pronounced worthy of death; and that the violence
of his passion could not be admitted in mitigation of his sentence.
But my visit is to implore you, sir, not to look on his offence with
the eye of the law, but with the eye of a fellow-creature—of a
fellow-creature liable to the same passions and to the same errors.
The judge, whilst he is pronouncing sentence on a criminal, may
be conscious in his heart, that under the like degree of temptation
he would himself have fallen into the same crime; but it is his
duty to be guided by the laws established; and he is not called
upon to make his own conscience the standard of his judgment.
But is it possible for you, sir, to pursue my poor husband to his
grave, without asking yourself how you might have acted under
the same provocation?"

"I cannot believe, Mrs. Aytoun," replied the colonel, "that under any circumstances, however aggravating, I could be so unmindful of the laws of honour, as to take the unfair advantage that Mr. Aytoun did."

"Oh, sir," said Alicia: "but remember that it was not with the view of killing his adversary and escaping himself, that Arthur did it. His eagerness to lose his own life, was quite as urgent as his desire to take Mr. Seymour's. All he seems to have aimed at was the certain death of both. Arthur's natural feeling was, that if he himself fell and Mr. Seymour survived, the injured would suffer and the offender escape; which, considering that his adversary was a much more practised shot than himself, was the probable result. If you could lay aside resentment, sir, and consider the case quite impartially, I think you might perceive such extenuations as would make you hesitate to take a life in cold blood, in revenge for one taken in passion. You have time to reflect, sir: Arthur had none. Besides, to address myself to your compassion, think of the heavy chastisement your are inflicting on me. I admit it is cruel that Mr. Seymour should have paid so dearly for his fault; though his was a fault committed knowingly, and with intention; for I fear that his views, from the first, in the assistance he gave me, were not honourable. But how much heavier will be my penalty for an error committed from ignorance and timidity! How much better were it to fall as Mr. Seymour did, than to die the slow death of the broken-hearted—or to drag on a wretched existence, a prey to repentance and regret."

Here Mrs. Alleyn took out her pocket-handkerchief and wiped her eyes; whilst the old lady, blowing her nose sonorously, attracted the attention of the child, who looked about to see what was the matter.

"Oh, listen to me, sir," said Alicia, clasping her hands; "be merciful, and spare my poor husband's life! If you knew the tender love we've borne each other—how happy we always were, without a sorrow in the world till this sad misunderstanding came upon us; and if you could conceive his remorse—if you could imagine what he has suffered since he has been convinced of my innocence—how he hourly accuses himself as a murderer, and says he deserves to die! Oh, Colonel Alleyn, you may safely leave his chastisement to his own feelings. Don't imagine that if his life is spared, he is escaping with impunity. I know that years of remorse and bitter regret are before him—but oh, don't take him from me! Madam," she said to Mrs. Alleyn, who she saw was not unmoved, "plead for me! I know you are injured, too, even more deeply than Colonel Alleyn—but oh, forgive! forgive! and if ever sorrow overtakes you, the remembrance of your mercy to the poor imploring wife that kneels to you to beg her husband's life, will help you to support your afflictions!"

As Alicia uttered these last words she fell on her knees, and with uplifted hands and streaming eyes, awaited her sentence from Colonel Alleyn. Mrs. Alleyn sat with her pocket-handkerchief to her face, but she said nothing; whilst the child, who had been gradually creeping towards Alicia, softly stole her little arm round her neck and imprinted a kiss on her cheek.

"Don't cry," she whispered; "papa will. He always forgives me when I'm sorry for being naughty; and he says it's everybody's duty to forgive when people are sorry: so don't cry," and she gave her another kiss.

Alicia, quite overcome by the sweet words of the innocent child, and grateful for the force of her artless pleading, threw her arms round her, exclaiming, "Oh, angel, ask him yourself! Beg for me—he never can refuse you!" and the child, climbing on her papa's knee, threw her soft arms about his neck, and with a loving kiss, whispered, "Do, papa! forgive her this time: I'm almost sure she'll never do it again!"

"Archibald, my son," said the elderly lady, who had crossed the room during the latter part of the colloquy, laying her hand on Colonel Alleyn's shoulder, and speaking in a calm, dignified tone that denoted the influence she still retained—"Archibald, my son, we must forgive and spare. We mustn't take this poor young creature's husband from her. She has suffered more than enough; and we owe her a reparation for the wrong our kinsman sought to do her, in the guise of a service. Beware, lest *we* should be seeking our revenge in the guise of justice."

"Papa's going to forgive now," whispered the child to Alicia, slipping off Colonel Alleyn's knee, and kissing her cheek; "so you needn't cry any more. I always know when he's going to forgive by his face."

When the day appointed for Arthur Aytoun's trial arrived, the court assembled, and the jury were sworn—but neither prosecutor nor witnesses appeared: and he was acquitted.

CHAPTER XXXV.

THE RECOGNITION.

ON the evening preceding Mr. Aytoun's trial, Susan was sitting at the gate of the prison in a coach, which she had been desired to have in attendance; for the purpose of bringing away certain of his clothes, and other articles which had been conveyed there for his use. Everything had been put in, and she was waiting for her mistress to come out and join her, when she observed a man in a sailor's jacket pass and repass two or three times before the gate. Since the night of her attack in Soho-square, she had never met a person in the same costume without turning to have a second look at him, and she now thrust her head out of the window to endeavour to catch a view of the face of the person in question. When he came opposite the coach, he also looked up at her. On his part there appeared no recognition, for he pursued his walk as before; but she felt satisfied that it was the same man that had demanded her money on that occasion. It was not only from her recollection of his face on that night that she recognised him, but her memory was aided by some previous recollection, to which she could assign neither time nor place.

After taking several turns, he at length stopt and rang the bell, and the summons being answered by the gaoler, some words passed between them, which Susan was unable to distinguish; after which the man went away.

"Can you tell me the name of that person?" inquired she of the gaoler, "or who he is?"

"I don't know," replied he. "I never seen him afore to my knowledge, but once; and then he came to leave a message for Tim Swipes, as is in here for larceny."

"And what did he come for now?" inquired Susan.

"He come for the same thing," returned the man. "Just to leave a word for Tim."

The Messrs. Karl, Mr. Aytoun's employers, thought they could not do him a greater service than to supply him immediately with some active occupation, which should perforce direct his mind from himself, and take him away, for a time, from the scene of his troubles; they therefore informed him that they had some urgent business in Russia, which they wished him to undertake; and accordingly, within a fortnight after his liberation, he again started on his travels.

Mrs. Aytoun, too, was not sorry for this arrangement. She ardently desired to leave the neighbourhood they had been living in, and she thought it better that all the bustle and inconveniences of removal should be spared to Arthur in his present state of nervous excitability. It was therefore arranged that she should fix on another house as remote as possible from the scene of their disasters; and that when the important matters were concluded, and nothing remained but what might devolve upon Betty, that she and Susan should go down to Brighton for a while, to enjoy a little change of air and recreation.

This plan was accordingly executed, and Mrs. Aytoun took a small first floor, consisting of two little bed-rooms and a sitting-room, in the house of a Mrs. Richards, on the West Cliff, who informed them that her parlours were let, for a month, to a young gentleman, who, with his wife and child, had come down from London a few days before.

The day after Mrs. Aytoun was established in her new lodgings, Susan happened to see the little girl who belonged to the occupants of the parlour floor playing with her doll in the passage; and being a lover of children, she seated herself on the lower stair, and called her to come and show her her doll. The child was shy at first, and needed a little coaxing, but after a while, she was won by Susan's good-humoured face, and sidled up to her.

"What a nice doll!" said Susan. "Who gave it you?"

"Papa," she said; "he gave it me on my birth-day. Look, she's got a new frock on."

"A very handsome frock indeed it is," replied Susan, surveying it with some curiosity.

"And who, my dear, gave you the frock?"

"Mamma gave me the frock," said the child. "We went out in a boat upon the sea the other day, and the sea came into the boat and spoilt mamma's bonnet; so she made dolly a frock out of it yesterday. Isn't it a nice one?"

"It is, indeed," replied Susan, still examining the frock; "and what's your name, my dear?"

"Nancy," replied the child.

"But your other name?" inquired Susan. "You've another name besides Nancy"—but before the child could answer the question, the parlour door, which had not been previously quite closed, was suddenly thrown open, and a showily-dressed young woman coming out, seized the child angrily by the arm, and dragged her into the room.

"I'll ask their name of Mrs. Richards," thought Susan—"though, to be sure, there must be many pieces of silk made to one pattern, so I don't know why I should think anything of it."

The truth was, Susan's attention had been attracted by observing that the doll's frock was of the exact pattern and colour of the piece of silk which had been brought to Craven-street from Mr. Green's; and of which sundry yards were asserted to be missing. The silk which Mrs. Aytoun had had cut off by the shopman, and which she designed for a dress, was still lying in her drawer unused—so great an aversion the circumstances connected with it had inspired; and Susan, when packing up, had seen it only the day before they left London. It was an expensive silk, of French manufacture, and remarkable both in pattern and colour. She made no remark, however, on what she had seen to Mrs. Aytoun; both because the coincidence was too trifling in itself to notice, and because she made it a rule never to allude to the unpleasant circumstances connected with that period; but the little girl was no more seen in the passage.

On the day following this slight adventure, Susan and her mistress went out together; the latter was going to bathe, and the former to attend her. They had not got three yards from the door, when Susan recollected that she had omitted bringing some article that Mrs. Aytoun would require, and she turned hastily back to fetch it. As she did so, she caught a glimpse of two heads over the parlour blinds, one of which—the gentleman's —disappeared the instant it met her eye. The lady, who was the same person that had fetched in the child the day before, continued to watch them as long as they were in sight. "I wonder why he don't like to be seen," thought Susan. "I'll certainly not forget to ask Mrs. Richards his name."

Susan rose the next morning betimes, intending, after she had got the drawing-room ready, and laid the breakfast things, to run into the town and endeavour to procure some fresh eggs for Mrs. Aytoun, whose still delicate health required a nourishing diet. She had just finished her household affairs, and was crossing the landing-place to her own little room to put on her bonnet, when she heard a voice below saying, " Mind you cord that trunk well," which induced her to stop for a moment to look out of the staircase window, which was immediately over the door.

In front of the house stood a porter's truck, and jumping round about it was the little girl of the parlour, with her doll in her arms (no longer, however, adorned with the new silk frock), and her bonnet and pelisse on. The child appeared in a high state of excitement, as children usually are when something new is about to happen—running in and out of the house, and chattering to the people in the passage.

Presently the owner of the truck himself appeared, carrying out a largish hair trunk, which he placed on his machine; and having successively fetched out a portmanteau and a band-box, which he added to his burden, he put his wheels in motion and moved off, followed, at the interval of a few yards, by the child and her parents, who a minute afterwards issued from the door, habited for a journey. The lady had a good-sized basket in her hand, and the gentleman a couple of cloaks thrown over his arm.

As they walked away, with the child skipping joyfully before them, the wife made some observation to the husband, and as she did so, turned her head and looked up at Mrs. Aytoun's window, as if her remark had some relation to the occupants of the drawing-room. Susan was still looking out, wondering what could have caused their hasty departure; the lady evidently perceived her, and, as it appeared to Susan, mentioned the circumstance to her husband. He did not, however, turn his head to look at her; but, with a hasty and apparently involuntary impulse, he abruptly pulled his hat over his eyes, and quickened his pace.

"Very odd," thought Susan, again; "I should like to know something more about them." She then put on her bonnet, and set forth in search of her eggs, towards a street where she had seen announced in a window, " New-laid eggs sold here."

The shop happened to be situated only two doors from an inn; and at the inn door stood a coach, apparently on the point of starting; and beside it, the identical porter and truck that she had seen leave the lodging a few minutes before. Susan stationed herself at the shop door to watch their proceedings, for she felt an indefinable desire to get a view of the gentleman's face; more, perhaps, because she fancied he sought to conceal it than from any other motive.

"Hand up that 'ere trunk, now," cried a man who was packing the luggage on the roof of the vehicle.

"Put your best leg foremost, Joey, will you?" said the coachman, coming out of the inn; "we're 'hind time already. Now
gemmen," continued he, "now ladies, if you please," addressing
the passengers that were standing by, and cramming the six in-
sides into the small door of the vehicle; whilst the outsides
ascended as they could to the roof.

The porter looked up the street—"Here's three more coming,"
said he, "what belongs to the luggage I brought;" and the lady
and gentleman appeared hastening towards the inn; the former
dragging the child onwards by one hand, who in the other held a
bun, which she was too intent on eating to be disposed to quicken
her pace. They had evidently, from the appearance of their
basket, been purchasing a little provision for the journey, which
had retarded their arrival.

As they reached the coach, the impatient Jehu seized the lady's
arm, and hoisted her up to the back seat, and then handed up the
child to her; whilst the gentleman was engaged settling the demands of the porter.

"Now, sir," said the coachman, "we're off," as he advanced to
ascend his box, whilst the passenger set his foot upon the wheel.
Susan stepped forwards, determined to get a look at him as the
coach drove past.

"You're sure that portmanteau's in the boot?" said he, leaning
forwards and addressing the porter, whilst the coachman was
adjusting himself on his seat.

"Sure of it, sir," replied the man.

"Lord A'mighty!" ejaculated Susan, as she caught a view of his
face.

"All right!" cried a voice, and away went the coach; and as it
dashed forwards, the gentleman looked down and descried Susan—
their eyes met, and the mystery was unveiled. Mr. James Hurley,
for such she had learned from Mrs. Richards, on the preceding
evening, was the name he went by—Mr. James Hurley was the
shopman who had brought the fatal goods from Mr. Green's; and
who had given evidence against Mrs. Aytoun at the police-office:
more than that; she felt also perfectly assured that Mr. James
Hurley was also the sailor that had attacked her in Soho-square,
and whom she had afterwards seen inquiring for Tim Swipes at
the gate of Newgate.

She had never seen him in his character of shopman, except on
that fatal day; and the disguise he wore on the other occasions,
had so far perplexed her memory, that though she remembered
the features, she could not recal where she had seen them. But
now, dressed as he had been in the first instance, the truth struck
her at once; the recognition was perfect.

Her surprise was so great, that she stood for some moments
staring after the coach, mute and motionless; and feeling as if the
four horses were bearing away Mr. James Hurley from her sight
for ever, just at the instant he had assumed an inexpressible degree
of importance in her eyes.

"Did you want to go by that 'ere coach, my lass?" said the ostler of the inn, perceiving the interest with which she was looking after it. "You're just a bit too late."

"What coach is it, sir?" said she; "where's it going to?"

"It's the Portsmouth coach," answered he. "Is that the one you're waiting for?"

"No: I'm much obliged to you," she replied. "I was only looking at it;" and she turned into the shop to bargain for her eggs.

The combination of circumstances struck Susan as most singular. "This man, then," she said to herself, "that Mr. Green says is his nephew, and a person of most excellent character, is a thief that walks the streets by night, in disguise; and that associates with Tim Swipes, who is confined in Newgate for larceny! And what, in the name of goodness, has sent them off in such a hurry, I wonder!" and she hurried home, impatient to learn what Mrs. Richards might have to tell her on the subject.—"Yes," said the worthy landlady, "they're off with a flea in their ear; but, hows'-ever, they've paid me my month, though they've only been in the lodgings ten days; so I've no right to grumble."

"But how came they to go in such a hurry," asked Susan, "when they'd engaged the rooms for a month?"

"I knew nothing of it till ten o'clock last night," replied Mrs. Richards. "But when they came in to supper, they sent for me into the parlour, and said they'd heard of some relations of theirs that were staying at Margate, and that they wished to go and join them; and asked me if I'd let them off for a fortnight's rent. But I couldn't do that, you know, when I'd turned away an old lodger of mine, because I couldn't take him in, only the day before yesterday—I hope he's not fixed yet, by the bye—I've just sent Jemmy to inquire for him at 'the Ship'—so they paid me my month without more ado; and off they went. She's a dressy sort of body, Mrs. Hurley," added Mrs. Richards; "but I couldn't make out what they are. I asked the child one day if her papa kept a shop, and she said, 'No.' He's some sort of a clerk, I take it."

"Very likely," returned Susan. "Does the Portsmouth coach go to Margate?"

"Bless you, no," cried Mrs. Richards. "They're the opposite ends of the world—Margate's that way, and Portsmouth the other," said she, pointing east and west.

"They're gone by the Portsmouth coach, however," said Susan.

"No!" exclaimed Mrs. Richards, incredulously. "What makes you think so?"

"Because I saw them off, not a quarter of an hour ago," replied Susan; "they went away from the inn next to where I was buying my eggs; and I asked what coach it was."

"That's a good joke," said Mrs. Richards. "They've made a mistake, depend on it, and got on the wrong coach."

But Susan had her own reasons for thinking otherwise; indeed,

she had a very strong suspicion that they not only had sought to
conceal their departure, and the direction of their travels; but she
believed that it was nothing else in the world but Mrs. Aytoun's
arrival that had routed them. However, for the present, she resolved to keep her thoughts and her discoveries to herself. She
did not wish to agitate Mrs. Aytoun, or to revive unpleasant
recollections, unless she was tolerably sure of attaining some satisfactory result. "I'll endeavour, when we go back to town, to find
out something about this Mr. James Hurley," said she to herself;
"and then, if I find it's worth looking into, I'll mention it to
master when he returns."

CHAPTER XXXVI.

SUSAN INTRODUCES HERSELF TO AN ACQUAINTANCE OF THE READER.

Mrs. Aytoun and Susan, after remaining a month at Brighton,
returned to London by the coach. When they reached Croydon,
a slight accident occurred to one of the wheels, and the passengers
took refuge in the inn till the damage was repaired.

There were several newspapers of various dates lying about the
room they were shown into, and Susan have taken up one of them,
the following paragraph met her eye:—

"The young man suspected of being concerned in the late
robbery at Mr. Green's, having been brought up for the third time
before Mr. C——, has at length been finally committed to take his
trial at the approaching session."

Anything relating to Mr. Green's shop, more especially since
her late recognition of Mr. James Hurley, had assumed an interest
in Susan's eyes; and her curiosity was immediately excited to learn
something more of the robbery in question.

"What," thought she, "if it's Mr. James Hurley himself?
I should not be surprised; but I'll find that out, I'm determined, as soon as I get to London." And accordingly, a few days
after her arrival, having obtained leave of absence for a couple of
hours, she went straight to her friend the gaoler at Newgate, with
whom she had picked up a little acquaintance during the term of
Mr. Aytoun's detention there, and telling him she had a particular
reason for the request, begged him to give her a sight of the young
man that was imprisoned for Mr. Green's business.

"Do you know anything of him?" said he, as he led her along
to the room where the prisoner was confined.

"I can't tell till I see him," she replied. "What's his name?"

"The name we've got him by is Tomkins," returned the gaoler;
"but I believe he has several aliases."

"Then he's not a young thief?" said Susan.

"He's a young man," replied the gaoler: "and we never had

him in here before; but they say he's been at it some time. He was shopman to Mr. Green, who turned him away a little while ago, because he suspected him of robbing the till; but he couldn't prove nothing against him, so he got off. But it seems this here robbery's been a put-up business—somebody on the premises, or as knew them well, has been concerned in it; and Mr. Green, nat'ral enough, suspects this here chap. That's he," said he, pointing to a youth about twenty, who was tossing up a halfpenny for heads or tails, with one of his companions.

"Then it's not the person I suspected," said Susan, disappointed. "Does he confess he did it?"

"Not he," replied the man; "he says he'd no hand in it whatsomever. But that goes for nothing, you know."

Susan had got a little time to spare, before she was obliged to return home, and she resolved to employ it in a visit to Mr. Green's shop. She had never been in it since the accusation brought against her mistress, nor, indeed, above once before in her life; and she thought it most likely that Mr. Green would not recognise her. She was curious to ascertain if Mr. James Hurley was still in the haberdasher's service, and whether that was the name he went by in London as well as at Brighton; so she resolved to spend a couple of shillings in tapes, buttons, pins, and needles, which being articles that required some nicety in the selection, would afford her time to look about.

The shop being very full, and she in no immediate hurry, she seated herself in a convenient position whence she could take a survey of the different young men behind the counter; but amongst them she could not descry Mr. James Hurley. She was disappointed again; but, however, he might be out, or not yet returned from his country excursion; so she bought some trifling articles, and left the shop, resolved to look in again some day when opportunity offered.

But she was destined to meet with Mr. James Hurley in the place of all others she would have least thought of looking for him. Mrs. Aytoun permitted each of her servants alternately to spend the Sunday out; and Susan had appointed with a friend that the first time it was her turn they would go to the evening service at the Foundling, which having at that time the attraction of a most eloquent and powerful preacher, was drawing immense congregations, amongst whom were to be found many, of both sexes, of the highest rank and fashion.

The crowd was very great, and the contest for places almost as warm as in a theatre on the night of a new play; but Susan's friend had a sister who was one of the nurses, and by going early, and addressing themselves to her, she gave them seats in the gallery amongst the servants of the establishment.

Susan was a devout person, and during the prayers, in spite of the temptation, she looked very little about her; but whilst the organ was playing, she ventured to take a survey of the scene below her. The aisles were full as well as the seats, and standing in the midst of the throng, immediately under her, who should she see, to her astonishment, but Mr. James Hurley!

"Well," thought she, "of all the places in the world, what should make him come here!" and in spite of herself, during the remainder of the service, Mr. James Hurley and the suspicions she had connected with him, drew more of her attention than the admonitions of the preacher.

As soon as the entertainment they expected is over, people are generally as eager to get out of a place of this sort as they are to get into it; and so it proved on this occasion. The moment the service was concluded, and the congregation, having finished their last silent orison, had risen from their knees, there was a rush made towards the door by the most impatient, who sought to get away before they were impeded by the throng. But too many were of the same mind, and consequently a considerable degree of confusion ensued; but of all the eager and vehement strugglers below, nobody appeared to Susan to be in such a violent hurry as Mr. James Hurley. And yet, in spite of his pushing and jostling and working with his elbows, he did not seem to make so rapid a progress as might be expected. His efforts seemed rather to retard the progress of other people than to advance his own; and, at all events, they materially added to the general confusion and inconvenience. In process of time, however, the mass of human beings was pushed or struggled through the doors, and the church was nearly empty; but Susan and her friend stayed behind awhile to look at the children, and have some conversation with the nurse.

Presently, whilst they were yet standing in the gallery and looking about them, several persons were seen re-entering the doors below, whilst the vergers and seat-keepers appeared, all at once, under a considerable degree of bustle and excitement.

People ran to the places they had occupied, and stooped down to look under the benches; whilst the officials rushed up and down the aisles and through the nave, as if they were in a state of delirium; and the cry went forth that several of the congregation had been robbed.

"Lord A'mighty!" murmured Susan to herself, as certain suspicions crossed her mind; but they were only suspicions, and therefore she said nothing. "There are more thieves in the world than Mr. James Hurley," thought she; "but I'll go to Mr. Green's again to-morrow, if I can get time, I'm determined;" and she did go, for she was commissioned to make some purchases for her mistress; and, as Mr. Green could not know who they were for, she considered that, in spite of the feud, her motive was sufficient to justify her in making them there without hinting her intention to Mrs. Aytoun.

As usual, the shop was very full, and the young men very busy; and, as before, she was disappointed in her expectation of seeing the person she was looking for amongst them.

However, when her purchases were completed, and she tendered a note to pay for them, the man who had served her, and who had scribbled the amount on a scrap of paper, said, "If you'll walk backwards and show this at the desk, they'll hand you the difference."

Susan obeyed; the top of a man's head appeared above a high desk, over which he was stooping—"Will you please to take this bill?" said she, holding up her money and the amount; the man deliberately finished the column he was casting up, and made a note of the amount at the bottom of the page—and then he lifted up his head, and displayed to Susan's admiring eyes the features of Mr. James Hurley.

Whatever emotion Susan's face might indicate, the gentleman's certainly indicated no less. He turned first very red, and then very pale, whilst with a trembling hand he took the money and returned her the change. His eye quailed before hers, and she read in it the guilt that sat upon his soul.

Susan had now to reflect what she should do next. Had Mr. Aytoun been at home, she would not have hesitated to acquaint him with her suspicions, and the circumstances that had given rise to them; but she was unwilling to disturb her mistress's tranquillity till she had something more certain to go upon. Alicia had never been strong since her former illnesses, and she was now again in a situation to require peculiar delicacy and consideration. "I'll go," thought Susan, after due reflection, "and tell it all to master's lawyer, Mr. Olliphant, and hear what he thinks about it;" and accordingly she went.

Mr. Olliphant had heard the whole of the circumstances connected with Mr. Green's accusation from Mr. Aytoun, when he waited on that gentleman to consult about his case, in Newgate, and he had entertained a suspicion that coincided exactly with the one Susan had hinted to her master on the day she had pleaded so efficiently for her mistress. The notion of both parties was, that the lady visitor who was in the parlour when the goods were left, and who was no other than Mrs. Bloxham, must be the real criminal; and Alicia herself, when the idea was suggested to her, inclined very much to the same opinion, for no particular reason except that the lady's reputation was not quite unspotted in the matter of honesty, and that the character Mr. Green had given of his nephew, put him out of the category.

"All you tell me," said he, when he had listened to Susan's narrative, "is very striking indeed; and it would be a most desirable thing for poor Mrs. Aytoun and her husband if we could remove the thing entirely from her shoulders, by bringing it home to somebody else; but I don't exactly see how we are to proceed, except we attack him for his attempting to rob you in the street; and now that's so long ago, and there being nothing but your word for it, I am afraid the character the uncle will give him will be too strong for us; and they'll say it's a plot to clear Mrs. Aytoun, and so make her case worse than it is now. However strong the presumptions are, you can't swear that the doll's frock was cut off the same piece of silk; nor if it were, that they came by it dishonestly. Neither can you assert that he robbed the people at the Foundling; though in all probability he was one of the gang, from the confusion you saw him creating."

"No, I can't," replied Susan. "Besides, the thing would be to find some of the articles upon him."

"Well," said Mr. Olliphant, "I'll think over the business, and see what's best to be done; and if I require your assistance, I'll send you a penny-post letter. What's your name?"

"Susan Hopley, sir," she replied.

"Hopley, Hopley," reiterated he. "I've heard that name before. Hopley! What is there connected in my mind with the name of Hopley?"

Poor Susan's cheeks crimsoned, and if the lawyer had looked in her face at the moment, its expression might have recalled what he was seeking to remember; but he did not. He was making notes in his memorandum book of her address, and of what she had told him; and by the time he raised his eyes to dismiss her, she had recovered from her confusion. "How hard it is," thought she, as she walked home, "to be obliged to blush for one's name, when one has done nothing to disgrace it!"

CHAPTER XXXVII.

THE JUSTIFICATION.

On the following day a gentleman presented himself to Susan's friend, the gaoler at Newgate, and requested an interview with Abraham Tomkins, who was in for Mr. Green's business.

"Abraham Tomkins," said he, when he had led the youth away from his companions, "I don't know whether it may be possible for me to convince you that I speak the truth—but for private reasons of my own, it is my desire to undertake your defence in the trial that's about to ensue."

Abraham Tomkins on this announcement looked a little incredulous, and very much puzzled.

"If you are guilty," said Mr. Olliphant, "I can only defend you according to the technicalities of the law, taking advantage of whatever accidents or obscurities may be in your favour; and that I will promise to do, to the best of my abilities. If, on the other hand, you are innocent, I think there is little doubt I can prove you so; but the condition of my having anything to do with the business at all is, that you tell me the precise truth. You must be aware," added he, "that I can have no ill design against you in seeking your confidence. Even if I were your enemy, and sought to entrap you, it would be useless. I dare say you know that you will be judged according to the evidence, and not according to any private confession I might extract from you."

"I know that, sir," replied Abraham; but still looking suspicious.

"And observe," rejoined Mr. Olliphant, "I don't pretend that I am interfering in this business for your benefit. I do it for ends of my own, though you will be the gainer. My object is to ascertain the truth, which I have a particular interest in knowing; and I make it your interest to tell it me, by engaging to undertake your defence, to the best of my abilities; and you know it is impossible for me to do that effectually, unless I am acquainted with the facts."

"Are you a lawyer, sir?" inquired Abraham.

"Yes," replied Mr. Olliphant, "and it is for the benefit of a client of mine I am acting."

"I'd no hand in it, sir," said Abraham.

Mr. Olliphant looked sharply in the lad's face, and he thought he was speaking the truth.

"I hadn't, indeed, sir," replied the young man; "and I could prove an alibi; only the witnesses I have to bring forward wouldn't be believed."

"You were in bad company, then?" said Mr. Olliphant.

"It warn't very good," replied Abraham.

"But I may contrive to make their testimony available," rejoined the lawyer; "so tell me where you really were."

"At Isaac Lecky's, the Jew," replied Abraham.

"You might have been in a better place, assuredly," returned Mr. Olliphant; who from this unreserved avowal was the rather disposed to think the young man was telling the truth.

"I was there from eight o'clock in the evening till ten the next morning," added Abraham; "and I never heard a word of the business, till Isaac himself told me of it."

"And does Isaac know who did it?" inquired Mr. Olliphant.

"No, he doesn't," returned the lad. "And yet, maybe, he does; there's no saying. He swore he didn't; but he made me drunk, and kept me there all night; and perhaps it was that I mightn't be able to prove an alibi."

"Is he acquainted with any of the young men in Mr. Green's establishment?" inquired the lawyer.

"Not that I know of," answered Abraham; "but there's no telling who he's acquainted with."

"Do you think I could get anything out of Lecky if I were to go to him?" asked Mr. Olliphant.

"If you could make it his interest," replied the lad. "But it's more like to be his interest not to peach, when there's no suspicion. He might blow up a walable hand by it. He'd ask a pretty round sum before he'd sing, I take it."

"Have you any suspicion yourself who did it?" inquired the lawyer.

"I can't say I have," replied Abraham.

"Are there none of the young men in the shop that keep bad company?"

"Not one, that I know of," answered the lad. "Mr. Green's the partick'lerest master as is about his young men. He turned

R 2

me off for next to nothing, and that it was threw me out of employment; else I shouldn't be here on suspicion now."

"I thought you robbed the till?" said the lawyer.

"The till had been robbed before I touched a stiver out of it," answered Abraham; "but I just borrowed half-a-crown to go half-price to the play, and so I got the credit of taking all that had been missed."

"Then there's undoubtedly a thief on the premises?" said Mr. Olliphant.

"That's certain," said Abraham; "but he's a close 'un, whoever he is.—You might go to Isaac," added he, after a little consideration, "and try him; he might peach; there's never no telling."

"I will," said the lawyer, "and before the trial, you shall see me again."

Mr. Olliphant felt no doubt of the lad's having told him the truth; and everything he had heard tended in his mind to the confirmation of Susan's suspicion. There was, as Abraham said, a thief on the premises, "and a close 'un," who, shielded by the confidence reposed in him, had been committing the most daring robberies; and every circumstance pointed to Mr. James Hurley as the criminal.

Isaac Lecky, who was a known receiver of stolen goods, and connected with half the thieves about London, was a man who nevertheless kept up a tolerable outside of honesty in his front shop, which was situated near St. Martin's-lane, and had the appearance of a decent pawnbroker's. No man was more plausible; and his character amongst his customers, who were in the habit of pawning their Sunday clothes on Monday morning, to redeem them on Saturday night, was that of a fair-dealing man. But there was a certain back-door, opening on an obscure court, known to customers of another description, that, had it a tongue to speak withal, could have told many a curious tale.

Thither, at all hours of the night, stole visitors apparently of the most various grades. Gentlemen, dressed in the very extreme of the fashion, with large whiskers or moustaches, shirt-collars that almost reached their eyes, and gilt chains round their necks, to which nothing was appended. Then there were demure-looking, silent, and tolerably well-dressed men, who appeared to belong to no class at all; but who did a little business in a quiet way, and picked up a great deal of useful information. Their grave and respectable appearance rendered their testimony to the exemplary virtues of any of their acquaintance who happened to be unpleasantly situated, especially valuable and efficient. Footmen in shabby worn-out liveries, whose last place had unfortunately spoiled their characters; and now and then, one in more gorgeous attire, who, like the golden chrysalis, was in a state of transition. Beggars, sailors, dustmen, chimney-sweepers, were all to be seen in their turns at Mr. Lecky's back-door, and occasionally, though less frequently, women. But they were customers to whom the cautious Jew gave little encouragement; as many as pleased were welcome to his front-door, but he preferred reserving the more secret entrance for visitors of harder metal.

Isaac Lecky was a man who looked like an anasarcous tallow candle—so puffy, so featureless, so white. As unlike as possible to Duncan, "who had so much blood in him," Mr. Lecky appeared to have none at all—his arteries and veins seemed to be filled with serum. His hair was of a dirty-looking shade of light brown; his eyes gray, small, and piggish, whilst his diminutive nose, and small pursed-up mouth were scarcely discernible between the pair of colourless tumid cheeks that bordered them. In short, Mr. Lecky, though still calling himself a Jew, and adhering pretty closely to his own people, as he professed to consider them, had so deteriorated from the type of his ancestors by the frequent alloy of Christian blood they had grafted into the stock, that he had lost all the distinguishing characteristics of those generally handsome infidels; whilst nature, probably thinking that he could make out no good title to the features of any other sect, had evaded the difficulty by giving him an assortment that would have been unanimously repudiated by every denomination whatsoever. His dress, consisting of a well-brushed, but rather thread-bare black coat, with drab continuations and gaiters, had an air of being put on with great precision; and the handkerchief round his neck, which considering the region wherein he dwelt, showed a paler tinge of yellow than might have been expected, was folded over his breast with particular neatness, and attached to his shirt by a paste pin, that many of his front-door customers venerated as a real diamond.

When Mr. Olliphant stepped into the shop, Isaac, who was standing behind his counter sorting his tickets, cast upon him a glance of curiosity; for the well-attired, well-fed, cheerful-looking lawyer had by no means the air of a person likely to have dealings with the pawnbroker.

"You're Isaac Lecky, I presume?" said Mr. Olliphant.

"The same, sir, at your service," replied Isaac.

"Mr. Lecky," continued the lawyer, "I've a little business with you of a private nature; but I should like to be out of the way of interruption whilst we talk it over. But perhaps you've nobody to take care of your shop."

"Oh yes, sir," answered Lecky, "I can get my daughter to do that for me;" and on his opening a door and calling "Jessy," a handsome girl of about eighteen or twenty, with features of so decidedly Jewish a type, that it was impossible to look at her without entertaining the most painful doubts respecting the prudence of the late Mrs. Lecky, descended from an upstairs apartment, and, in spite of her green silk dress, and large gold ear-rings, unhesitatingly placed herself behind the counter.

"This way, if you please, sir," said Mr. Lecky, bowing, and with a very demure aspect preceding Mr. Olliphant into the small parlour that was behind the shop, and from which it was separated by a glass-door; a view through which he insured for himself by the seat he selected, after presenting one to his visitor.

As soon as he was seated, he placed his hands between his knees, which he closed firmly on them to hold them fast, as if it were necessary in the presence of good company to suppress any evil habits they might have acquired, or restrain their propensity for picking and stealing; and then with his body bent forwards, his mouth pursed into its smallest dimensions, and his small gray eyes inclined to the earth, but still catching ever and anon a glance at Mr. Olliphant's features, he waited silently till that gentleman should be pleased to open his communication.

This was not instantly; for the lawyer, though well acquainted with Isaac Lecky's reputation, had never seen him before; and he could not help surveying with some curiosity and interest the strange blank face he had before him, so unlike what he had expected; and he had also to consider what was the most likely way of gaining his point without doing mischief; for he did not wish to betray his own suspicion of Hurley, unless he were pretty sure of Isaac's co-operation, as such a disclosure might only serve to put the other on his guard.

"The fact is," said Mr. Olliphant, "to come to the point at once—you have it in your power to do me a service, Mr. Lecky—whether you will be willing to oblige me, remains to be seen."

Mr. Lecky bent his person slightly forward, but it was a cautious bend that took care not to promise too much.

"The case is this. There is a young lad in trouble about a robbery, with which I happen to know he had no concern. For reasons it is not necessary to explain, a client of mine is deeply interested in the fate of the boy, and has committed the charge of his defence to my management.—You know the lad I mean, of course?"

Mr. Lecky, however, called up an unconscious look.

"Abraham Tomkins," said Mr. Olliphant, and paused for an observation from the other side; but Isaac preserved his attitude and his silence.

"Now, as I know, as you do also, Mr. Lecky, that the young man is innocent, I am desirous of doing the best I can in the business, and I want you to assist me. Have you any objection?"

"None, sir; no objection whatever," replied Mr. Lecky; "but what can I do?"

"In the first place, you know the boy was here on the night the robbery was committed, from eight at night till ten the next morning."

"Was he, sir?" said Mr. Lecky, "that's more than I know, I'm sure; but I don't say he wasn't; for it's a thing I'm not likely to keep in my mind so long; the human faculties being so imperfect."

"He most assuredly was," returned Mr. Olliphant, nodding his head significantly, as if he knew more than he avowed; "that I have found the means of ascertaining—to my own satisfaction, at least. But I own I'm not so clear of being able to satisfy the jury on that point, unless you'll give me your assistance."

"What can *I* do, sir?" said Mr. Lecky, again; "I'm sure I couldn't take upon myself to swear to such a thing. It's at least three months ago now, since it happened; and I couldn't charge my memory with what took place on any particular night. I've so many people coming here, backwards and forwards, that I couldn't undertake to say the next week, let alone months, on what night I saw them. It's not possible, sir. You must see that yourself—the human faculties being so imperfect, sir; that of memory in pertick'lar; and since the late Mrs. Lecky's death, I can't say mine has ever been what it was afore."

"That's to be regretted," gravely answered Mr. Olliphant. "However, there are circumstances which don't easily escape the most treacherous memory; and as you first informed the lad of the robbery yourself, the morning after it was committed, you must have been perfectly aware at the time that he was not the thief. Now, though the exact date might escape you, I should think that circumstance could not."

"Lord, sir," replied the Jew, "you forget that I may have mentioned the same thing to twenty people, at least, within an hour after I heard of it myself. It was natural I should speak of it to whoever I saw, a thing like that—that was making a noise. I couldn't pretend, I'm sure, to say who I mentioned it to, and who I didn't."

"Then you really can't give me any information on the subject?" said Mr. Olliphant.

"None whatever, sir," said Isaac. "I wish I could, I'm sure. But the human memory, as I observed before——"

"I'd give anybody fifty pounds that would put me in the way of finding out the truth," said Mr. Olliphant, taking up his hat, and speaking rather to himself than addressing Isaac; and so saying, he arose to take his leave.

"Cash down, sir?" said Mr. Lecky, without changing his attitude, or moving a muscle of his countenance.

"Cash down," replied the lawyer.

"And nobody know where you got your information?" said the Jew. "All close?"

"All close," said the lawyer.

"Sit down, sir, if you please," said Isaac.

Affairs had reached this crisis, when, through the glass-door, a woman with a parcel in her hand was seen to enter the shop.

"Excuse me a moment, sir," said the pawnbroker, "but my daughter's not used to the shop; I must just step and see what that person wants;" and he arose and quitted the room, closing the glass-door after him.

He had scarcely done so, when Mr. Olliphant heard some one knocking with their knuckles at the back door, which was immediately beyond the room he was sitting in, and only separated

from it by a very narrow passage. The summons not being
answered, it was repeated more impatiently; upon which the
lawyer arose, and opening the door of the room, looked out.

"Why the devil don't you open the door?" said a voice without.
"Don't you know the bell's broke?" And Mr. Olliphant, who
had no objection to being a little initiated into the mysteries of
Isaac's establishment, obeyed the summons; and by drawing back
a couple of strong bolts, and turning a heavy key, gave admission
to the stranger.

"What the h— do you keep one so long at the door for?" said
a man, entering abruptly. "I tugged at the bell last night till I
broke it." But having by this time reached the room, where it
was lighter, he perceived that he was addressing his objurgations to
a stranger. "I beg your pardon," said he, looking surprised at
the sort of person in whose company he so unexpectedly found
himself.

He was rather a genteel-looking young man, about five or six
and twenty; wearing a blue coat, gray trousers, and spotted waistcoat; and on finding that it was not Isaac who had admitted him,
he stood in the middle of the room, as if uncertain what to do.

But before there was time for further explanation, the glass-door
opened, and the Jew himself returned, with an apology in his
mouth for detaining his visitor; but on perceiving the new comer,
the words were arrested on his lips. He looked at one, and at the
other, and at the door of the room which Mr. Olliphant had shut
after letting in the stranger; and seemed to think that the person
he saw before him, was either but the semblance of a man, or must
have ascended through the floor.

"I wanted to speak to you particularly," began the young man.

"Mr. John Brown," said Isaac, hastily interrupting him as he
was about to speak, "I'm at this moment particularly engaged.
Call to-night, to-morrow, next night—there's no use fixing a
time."

"But I must speak to you," said the young man. "I was here
last night tugging at the bell for an hour. I suppose you were
out."

"I was," replied the Jew. "It was a festival; and I and my
daughter supped from home. But, my dear sir, Mr. Brown, as I
observed before, I'm particularly engaged—some other time—some
other time—" and he urged the stranger towards the door.

"I must speak one word to you," said the young man, keeping
fast hold of Isaac by the breast of his coat; and they vanished
from the room together and closed the door.

The conference was not long, and having dismissed his visitor,
Mr. Lecky returned, casting up his eye as he entered to the broken
wire of the bell, which he appeared not to have before known was
disabled.

"Now," said Mr. Olliphant, getting impatient to settle his
business with the Jew, and be gone—"as we had agreed, fifty
pounds—cash down—and nobody know who gave the information."

"I'm sure, sir," said Mr. Lecky, resuming his former attitude, "if it had been in my power, I should have been most happy. But as I said before, the human faculties are so imperfect, especially that of memory, that it's not possible to remember the particulars of a thing that happened so long since."

"But my good Mr. Lecky," said Mr. Olliphant, smiling, "we had got over that stage of the business some time ago; and had advanced far into the next. You know, when you were called away, you had just agreed to give me the information I want, upon the above-named conditions. Cash down, and all close."

"I sir!" exclaimed Mr. Lecky, with apparent astonishment. "Not I, sir. How could I agree to tell what I don't know? I'm sure, sir, I know no more about the business than the babe unborn."

Mr. Olliphant began to suspect that the Jew's memory really was in some degree defective; for that he had been on the point of communicating the secret when he left the room, he could scarcely doubt. So he renewed his offer, and described his object more explicitly; but by no effort could he bring Isaac Lecky up to the point he had got him to before. There certainly appeared to exist some strange hiatus in his faculties: and the lawyer finally quitted the house, uncertain whether the Jew had altered his mind, or whether he had mistaken his intentions; and having only gained one step by his motion, which was a more confirmed belief in Abraham Tomkins's innocence.

It wanted now but two days to the trial; and in order to fulfil his promise to Abraham, he put his case into the hands of a barrister of his acquaintance, with a request that he'd do what he could for him; and he desired Susan to be in attendance, in case anything should occur to make her testimony desirable. "But I fear," he said, "there's nothing to be done. Mr. James Hurley is, I dare say, what you take him to be; but we have nothing but your suspicions to advance, and can show no sort of grounds for an accusation. However, he'll dish himself in time, no doubt; and then the truth about Mrs. Aytoun's business, if he'd any hand in it, may perhaps come out."

When Abraham Tomkins learned that the Jew refused to remember that he had passed the night of the robbery at his house, he said, "Then he's been concerned in the business; or at any rate knows who was; and that was what he kept me there for, and made me drunk."

The circumstantial evidence against Abraham Tomkins produced on the trial was but slight; but the presumption against him was very strong.

He had been, for some time, suspected of keeping bad company; articles of value were frequently missing from the shop, in a way nobody could account for, and the till had been repeatedly robbed, to a greater or less amount. At length, he was detected in abstracting half-a-crown, and consequently pronounced guilty of all the other defalcations; but nothing was found on him. However, he lost his place and his character, and he had been heard to say, "that as Mr. Green had taken the bread out of his mouth, he would make him pay for it." A maid-servant of Mr. Green's also asserted, that he had been tampering with her to let him visit her of an evening, and that she had told her master she was sure Abraham Tomkins had some bad design: and that if any robbery were committed, she should know who did it.

One of the first witnesses called was Mr. Green himself, but the court was informed that being dangerously ill of a fever, he was unable to attend; but that his nephew, who was his book-keeper and foreman, and who knew more of the business than he did himself, was in court, and ready to appear for him.

Mr. Edward Green was therefore called into the witness-box, and to Mr. Olliphant's astonishment, the young man whom he had himself admitted through Isaac Lecky's back-door, only two days previously, answered to the summons. "Mr. John Brown!" said he to himself, "Mr. John Brown, then, turns out to be Mr. Edward Green!"

"Here's a bit of paper for you, Mr. Olliphant," said a man, tapping him on the shoulder—"a woman gave it me that's waiting outside."

It was a request from Susan that he would come and speak to her.

"That's him, sir," said she, "just gone in."

"Which do you mean?" inquired he.

"The last witness they fetched in, sir," said Susan. "That's Mr. James Hurley."

"You're certain?" inquired Mr. Olliphant.

"Quite positive, sir," said Susan.

"Did he see you?" inquired the lawyer.

"No," replied Susan; "I took care he shouldn't; and that's why I wouldn't send in to you before."

"It's all right," said the lawyer. "I think we have him now."

And they had: presently afterwards, when the counsel for Abraham Tomkins was called upon for the defence, his first step was to demand that the late witness, Mr. Edward Green, alias James Hurley, alias John Brown, should be taken into custody, and a warrant of search immediately granted.

In a lodging near the Haymarket dwelt the lady who went by the name of Mrs. James Hurley, and the little girl that Susan had seen at Brighton; and there was discovered quite enough to establish Mr. Edward Green as the delinquent, not only with respect to the affair immediately under investigation, but in several others, especially the robbery lately committed at the Foundling. The doll's frock, the remnants of a bonnet splashed with sea-water, and a spencer still in tolerably good repair, were also found, and sworn to by Mr. Green and his shopmen, to be cut from the identical piece of silk that had been sent to Mrs. Aytoun.

Finally, she was triumphantly vindicated by the criminal's confession, and Mr. Aytoun had the consolation of feeling, that however much he had to lament the consequences of his own precipitation, not the faintest cloud remained to obscure the brightness of his wife's reputation.

"It's plain enough," said the lawyer to Mr. Aytoun, when on that gentleman's return they discussed these strange events—it's plain enough what it was that confounded the worthy Isaac's human faculties. By the bye," added he, "that's a capital girl, that servant of yours—Hopley, Hopley—I always forget to ask her where she came from."

CHAPTER XXXVIII.

A GLANCE INTO THE INTERIOR OF DON QUERUBIN DE LA ROSA'S DOMESTIC ESTABLISHMENT.

"Look at that beautiful woman," said the Marquis de la Rosa to his wife, as they were seated in a box at the Théatre Français; "I think she is an Englishwoman."

"What is it to you if she is?" answered the marchioness.

"One is never tired of admiring beauty," replied the marquis, appropriating the compliment to his lady by a bow.

"Content yourself with what you have," returned she, sharply. "It's more than your due."

"My dear Dorothée," replied the marquis, "that is not a pleasant way of speaking."

"I have a right to speak as I like," returned the marchioness.

"Not to me," answered the marquis; "neither do I merit such ungracious observations. Do I not comply with your desires in everything? What can I more?"

"Leave me alone," replied the lady, turning her white shoulder to the marquis and her face to the stage.

The advantage of this arrangement was, that Don Querubin could indulge himself with the contemplation of the English beauty as much as he pleased. The object of his admiration was not only young and extremely beautiful, but she was also splendidly attired. Nor was elegance sacrificed to splendour; brilliant as were the jewels she wore, the graceful form of her white satin robe, and the inimitable fall of the rich scarf that was thrown over her shoulders, were not less attractive.

The power of her beauty was perhaps rather enhanced than diminished by an air of languor, almost amounting to melancholy, that shaded her lovely features. During the early part of the evening, she was alone in her box, and she sat in one corner of it, with her white arm, round which was entwined a jewelled bracelet, leaning on the velvet cushion in front, and her eyes fixed on the scene, where a tragedy of Racine's was representing, which seemed wholly to absorb her attention. Many an admiring gaze was fixed upon her; and as the lenders of opera-glasses passed between the rows of the pit, crying, "Who wants a spy-glass?" many more were borrowed for the purpose of being directed at her than at Ma'm'selle Duchesnois. But she appeared either unconscious of, or indifferent to, the admiration she excited; till, later in the evening, a very elegant man, apparently of the highest fashion, entered the box, and took his seat beside her, after which some others joined them; and she occasionally took a part in the conversation, though still preserving the same air of languor and indifference.

"Criquet," said the marquis, when he found an opportunity of confiding to his faithful valet the impression made upon him by the lovely stranger; "she is adorable."

"I don't doubt it," replied Criquet.

"And between you and I, Criquet, I think she looked at me."

"It is possible, certainly," answered Criquet.

"We must find out who she is," continued the marquis.

"That will not be difficult," returned Criquet.

"By no means," rejoined the marquis; "since I am satisfied she is a person of the first distinction."

"And when we have discovered who she is," said Criquet, "what then?"

"We'll procure an introduction, Criquet. Being a marquis, she cannot refuse."

"And the marchioness?" said Criquet, raising his eyebrows, and folding in his lips.

"Ah!" said Don Querubin, slightly shrugging his shoulders.

"She'll stand no gammon," observed Criquet.

"That's true," replied Don Querubin, with a considerable elongation of visage. "I thought to have contented her by bringing her to Paris—but alas!"

"You thought to have contented her!" cried Criquet, with an air of astonishment.

"No doubt," replied the marquis; "wasn't it what she was always urging me to do?"

"There is no denying that," returned Criquet, "but you know—"

"I know what?" said Don Querubin.

"There are some people in the world that are never contented," observed Criquet.

"That's true again," answered the marquis. "But you must admit, Criquet, that she's very handsome?"

"Oh, no doubt of that," replied Criquet.

"Beautiful as an angel," added the marquis.

"Hem!" said Criquet; "I never saw one."

"But to return to the beautiful stranger—" said Don Querubin.

"A more interesting subject, certainly," observed Criquet.

"We must find out who she is, and then procure an introduction."

"Those are two different things," remarked Criquet. "With respect to the first, I undertake it."

"About it, then," said the marquis; "we have no time to lose."

"That's as true as gunpowder," replied Criquet, as he left the room.

"Monsieur," said Madame de la Rosa, flinging into the marquis's dressing-room shortly afterwards, "that servant of yours is detestable."

"How?" said the marquis; "is it Criquet?"

"Certainly," replied she; "his assurance is insupportable."

"But, my love—" said Don Querubin, in a tone of expostulation.

"Hold your tongue!" said the marchioness, "and don't defend him."

"I don't defend him," returned the marquis, "if he is wrong."

"Wrong!" ejaculated the marchioness; "of course he's wrong; but you, you'll never admit it."

"But what's the matter now?" inquired the marquis.

"It is," said the marchioness, "that I desire to have my carriage drawn by six horses at Longchamp, and he says it's impossible."

"He is quite right," replied the marquis.

"I knew you'd say so!" exclaimed the lady.

"I only say what is true," rejoined Don Querubin; "the thing's impossible."

"Possible or impossible," replied the marchioness; "I'll have them."

"But, my dear," rejoined Don Querubin, "it cannot be. No carriages will have six horses but those of the royal family. Others must content themselves with four."

"I shall have six," rejoined the marchioness.

"You'll be turned back," answered Don Querubin; "you'll not be permitted to advance."

"But I will advance, though," answered the marchioness.

"But, my lovely Dorothée!" said the marquis, "listen."

"I will not listen," replied the lady. "I know very well that you and Criquet combine to impose upon me; but you'll not find it so easy as you imagine."

"I never thought it easy," answered Don Querubin. "I have a better opinion of your understanding."

"I dare say!" returned the marchioness, with a contemptuous curl of the lip.

"But with respect to the horses—" rejoined the marquis.

"I shall have them," interrupted the lady; and she flung out of the room, as she had flung into it.

"Ah, heavens! Criquet," exclaimed the marquis, when he was next alone with his faithful valet; "I am in despair!"

"What's the matter!" inquired Criquet.

"I shall be insulted—my carriage will be turned back—she insists on appearing with six horses at Longchamp!"

"Give yourself no uneasiness on that score," replied Criquet, with inimitable composure; "I have just been to the livery stables—they'll tell her they're not to be had."

"That's well," said Don Querubin, greatly relieved. "It's to be regretted, Criquet, that she is not more reasonable on certain points."

"Doubtless," replied Criquet.

"Because, really, at bottom, she is a good woman."

"That may be the case," answered Criquet.

"I am sure of it," rejoined the marquis.

"I am glad of it," replied Criquet.

"And I am convinced of her attachment to me," continued Don Querubin.

"That is certainly satisfactory," answered Criquet.

"Though, it must be granted that her temper is not always perfect," added the marquis.

"That is a fact which admits of no contradiction," replied Criquet.

"But, come," said Don Querubin, recalling his spirits, and shaking himself free of the marchioness; "what news have you learnt of the fair stranger?"

"Ah, by the bye!" said Criquet, "thereby hangs a tale."

"What is her name?" inquired the marquis.

"First," said Criquet, "what was the name of the lovely Englishwoman—the beautiful girl that rascal Gaveston was to send you, and who never arrived?"

"Ah!" answered Don Querubin, with an involuntary sigh; "which was the cause of our marriage; for I believe if Mademoiselle Dorothée had not been incited by jealousy, that we should not have obtained the avowal of her attachment."

"That is extremely possible," replied Criquet.

"We might even never have known it, Criquet."

"I am disposed to think we never should," answered Criquet. "But to return to the beautiful Englishwoman—what was her name?"

"Ah," said Don Querubin, let us see!" and he took out his tablets to search for the name—"here it is, here it is, Mademoiselle Amabel Jons!"

"Then it's herself!" cried Criquet, hitting the table with his fist.

"How?" exclaimed the marquis.

"I tell you it's her," answered Criquet—"her very self—Ma'm'selle Amabel Jean! I have heard her whole history from Madame Coulin here below; and from Truchet the tailor. She lodged, on her arrival in Paris, at this very hôtel."

"You pierce my heart!" exclaimed Don Querubin, falling back in a sentimental attitude.

"Listen," continued Criquet. "It was exactly at the very period we expected her at Bordeaux, that she appeared here under the guardianship of a man that called himself her uncle—but he was a sharper—a black leg. He called himself Colonel Jean or Jons—lodged here for a month—got clothes for himself and for her—was visited by the young men of the highest fashion, who swarmed about her like bees round a honey-pot: they say she was a simple creature—knowing nothing of the world—credulous as a child. At the expiration of the month, they went away one evening in the carriage of the Duc de Rochechouart—she was seen no more for some time. At length, after several months, she returned as the Duc de Rochechouart's mistress. But the report is, that she was deceived by a false marriage, in which that old villain Dillon, the Duke's servant, officiated as priest; and we know how probable that is, since it was the office they did me the honour to design for me."

"Just heaven!" cried Don Querubin, lifting up his hands; "what villany there is in this world!"

"You may well say that," answered Criquet.

"But does she still live with the duke?" inquired the marquis.

"Still," answered Criquet. "What could she do?—she had no means of subsistence—her hopes of making an advantageous marriage were annihilated. Besides, they say the Duc is very much attached to her—that she is the first woman that has fixed him."

"What a history!" exclaimed Don Querubin. "Do you know, Criquet, I must see her—I must, indeed."

"I don't object," answered Criquet. "But we must look about for an introduction."

"I have rather a mind to write," said the marquis, "and tell her who I am; probably she'll not refuse me an interview, which I shall solicit in the most respectful terms."

"It's not amiss;" said Criquet; "write, and I'll endeavour to deliver it into her own hands."

"Good," replied Don Querubin. "Give me my portfolio at once, Criquet, that I may compose something suitable to the occasion. Now let us see, how shall we begin?"

"MADAME,—There was a time when I had hoped to have been invested with the privilege of addressing you by a dearer title— [that will doubtless awaken her curiosity, and she'll cast her beautiful eyes to the bottom of the page, to ascertain the signature]—but some adverse destiny, which I am unable to comprehend, disappointed my expectations, and plunged me into eternal despair.

"For the purpose of augmenting my agonies, the cruel fates have decreed that I should not remain ignorant of the charms that I once hoped would have completed my bliss, and rewarded the most faithful and devoted of lovers. I was doomed to behold them, for the first time, last night at the Théatre Français; and having ascertained by my inquiries, at least by Criquet's, which is the same thing—[Exactly, remarked Criquet,]—that the possessor of so much beauty is no other than the lovely Englishwoman I had hoped to lead from the altar as Madame la Marquise de la Rosa y Saveta, I venture to petition for the honour of being permitted to throw myself at your feet, in order that I may have an opportunity of expressing my despair, and at the same time the unceasing adoration with which I shall remain, Madame,

"The most humble and devoted of your admirers,
"DON QUERUBIN, MARQUIS DE LA ROSA Y SAVETA."

"It's perfect," said Criquet.

"You like it?" said Querubin, with a gratified air.

"Nothing can be better," replied Criquet. "I shall wait upon her without delay. But take care,—not a word to my lady."

"No, no," said the marquis, "that poor little heart of hers would burst with jealousy."

CHAPTER XXXIX.

THE FOUNDATIONS OF THE WICKED BEGIN TO TREMBLE.

CRIQUET, who by the way thought himself quite as much injured as his master, by the adverse fortune which had somehow or other turned the fair Englishwoman's steps in the wrong direction, and thrown them both under the tyrannical dominion of the imperious Dorothée, charged with Don Querubin's missive, proceeded to the hôtel of the Duc de Rochechouart, and requested the honour of delivering a letter into the hands of Madame Amabel Jons; and no difficulties being cast in the way of his admission, he was speedily introduced into an elegant boudoir, and found himself in the presence of its lovely inhabitant.

The hangings of the room were of pale blue satin, ornamented with a rich gold fringe; and the chairs and ottamans were covered with the same material. The panels of the walls and of the doors were adorned with beautifully executed arabesques, and finished with superb gold mountings; the carpet was of velvet; the tables of the most curious inlaid woods; the slabs of the finest marble, supported by richly gilt figures of cupids, and bearing vases of the most delicate china, filled with rare flowers. A splendid or-molu clock was on the mantelpiece; and a variety of equally splendid nothings scattered about the room. Books and music lay on the table; and beside them a guitar, on which the lady appeared to have been playing. Her own dress was in a style of simple, but refined elegance; and her excessive beauty appeared, to the curious eye of the valet, fully worthy of the splendour by which she was surrounded.

Supposed to have considerable influence over the duke, and by his liberality towards her having the command of a great deal of money, she was accustomed to receive many visits and applications, of one sort or the other—petitions for her interest, her patronage, or her charity; and she therefore received Criquet and opened the letter he brought without the slightest curiosity or emotion. But as she perused Don Querubin's epistle, the colour mounted to her fair cheeks; and as she finished it, there was some confusion in her manner, when she said: "I have not the honour of knowing the Marquis de la Rosa."

"That, madame," answered Criquet, "is our misfortune; and it is in the hope of in some degree repairing it, that I have done myself the honour of waiting on you. My master, Don Querubin, earnestly solicits the honour of throwing himself at your feet, as the only consolation that now remains to him."

"I scarcely know," replied the lady, "what purpose can be answered by such an introduction; but if the marquis desires it, I have no objection to receive him. If he will present himself here to-morrow at this hour, he will find me at home."

It is possible that Criquet's mission might not have been so successful, but the lady's curiosity pleaded powerfully in his favour. She could not help desiring to see the man who was willing to have raised her to the rank she had so much desired, and to have an opportunity of comparing what she had gained with what she had lost; and certainly, when the figure of Don Querubin presented itself to her eyes, it required either an excess of virtue, or of ambition, to regret the exchange she had made, in becoming the mistress of the elegant and accomplished Rochechouart, rather than the wife of the honourable, but extremely ugly old Spaniard.

The marquis, who considered her not only a most lovely, but from what Criquet had related to him, a most injured woman, approached her with as much deference as if she had been a goddess; and he would have literally thrown himself at her feet, as he had threatened in his letter, but that Criquet not being at hand to help him, he somewhat distrusted his own alacrity in rising again; so he contented himself with raising her fair hand to his lips, and bowing to the ground.

"Madame," said he, "you see before you the most disappointed of men; and whatever regret I may have hither felt, its poignancy will be from this moment tenfold augmented. You are doubtless acquainted with the hopes I was led to entertain, and which for some months I refused to resign."

"Your disappointment, sir," said the lady, "did not originate with me; or, at least, if it did do so in any degree, it was only my excessive inexperience that was in fault. I was conducted to Paris, while I thought I was on my way to Bordeaux; and after my arrival here, circumstances occurred which changed all my prospects. The person to whom I was intrusted took advantage of my ignorance of the world, and I had no means of extricating myself from his toils."

"I have heard something, madame," replied the marquis, "of an odious imposition being practised upon you; and, from a circumstance known only to me and Criquet my valet, I am too much disposed to believe the report well founded; and I have requested the honour of this interview, madam, not only that I might enjoy the privilege of contemplating your divine beauty, which I had once hoped to call my own, but also to offer myself as an avenger of the wrongs you have received. I here lay my sword at your feet; and I shall never consider myself worthy of wearing it again, unless you'll permit me to draw it in your cause."

g

"You are very good, sir," replied Madame Amabel, calmly; "but it is much too late to think of avenging my wrongs, whatever they may have been. I don't deny that I was deceived; but my own foolish ambition aided the deception; and though the person to whom I was entrusted betrayed me, he was a villain, unworthy the sword of an honourable man. Added to which, even were it desirable, I could not tell you where to find him. After he had received the price of his villany, he disappeared, and I have never seen him since."

"And is there no other person, madame," inquired Don Querubin, "who merits your reproaches?"

"None, sir," replied the lady. "At least, whatever resentment I may have entertained against any one else, has long since expired. The truth is, sir, as you seem interested in my fate, that for nearly three months I believed myself the wife of the Duc de Rochechouart; and when, at the end of that time, I discovered the deception that had been practised upon me, I had become too much attached to him to desire to part. I married him from ambition, but I live with him because I love him. He leaves me nothing to wish for, but his name, that it's in his power to bestow; and that, now that I know the world better, I am aware I ought never to have aspired to. I don't deny that I am disappointed, and that my situation is not what I would have chosen; but it can never be mended now, neither do I desire to change it. It is, therefore, useless to speak more on the subject. Do you still correspond with Mr. Gaveston, sir?" she added. "Do you know if he is married?"

"The rascal!" replied Don Querubin, clenching his teeth; "the scoundrel! to betray such an angel. I correspond with him! Never! But he is married, I learn from Monsieur Râoul. He married the daughter of his principal—the poor man that was murdered."

"Murdered!" cried Madame Amabel. "Was Mr. Wentworth murdered? By whom?"

"By his servant, I heard," replied the marquis; "but I never learnt the particulars; it was somewhere on the road, when he was travelling, I think."

"And how long is it since this happened?" inquired the lady. "Is it lately?"

"Oh no!" returned the marquis. "Let me see; we heard of it in Bordeaux, about the time I was looking for your arrival. I remember I had sent Criquet in to make inquiries at the Quay, and at the coach-office, for I didn't know which way you proposed to travel, and there he saw Monsieur Râoul, who mentioned that he had just got a letter from Monsieur Simpson, to say his principal was dead."

"And that he was murdered?" said Madame Amabel.

"Assuredly," replied Don Querubin.

"I should like to hear the particulars," said the lady. "Can't you recal them?"

"I forget," returned the marquis; "but perhaps Criquet may recollect: he is in the ante-room, if you'll permit me to call him in and question him."

"Pray do," said Madame Amabel; and Criquet was summoned.

"Oh, yes," said he, on being interrogated. "I remember very well what Mr. Râoul told me. He was travelling, the poor gentleman, returning from the sea to his own house, and he was murdered at an inn on the road, by his own footman."

"By his own footman!" exclaimed Madame Amabel; "did you hear his name?"

"If I did I have forgotten it," replied Criquet; "the English names are difficult."

"But are you sure it was about the time you were expecting my arrival at Bordeaux?"

"Quite sure," said Criquet. "It was to inquire for your ladyship that I went to Bordeaux, by the marquis's orders; and I called at Monsieur Râoul's, to ask if there were any letters, and it was then he told me of it. He had just received the news."

"And it had just happened, had it?" inquired Madame Amabel. "Then it must have been after Mr. Gaveston's marriage?"

"No, no," replied Criquet; "it had happened sometime before, I think; and for that villain, Gaveston, he was not married till some time afterwards. We had him in Bordeaux after the old gentleman's death; but he was not married then."

"It's very singular," said Madame Amabel. "I wish you could tell me more about it. Was the footman taken?"

"Oh no," answered Criquet. "I remember now—he was not taken, and it was for love he did it. Gaveston himself told Monsieur Râoul so, when he came to Bordeaux—for, for our parts," added Criquet, looking at Don Querubin, "we never spoke to him."

"The wretch!" exclaimed the marquis; "never shall he set his foot within the Château de la Rosa."

"But go on," said Madame Amabel; "and tell me all you can remember—you say he did it for love?"

"Ay," answered Criquet; "so said Gaveston. It appeared that he was in love with one of the servants of the house—a very handsome girl, but she was a bad one, and she would not have him because he'd no money. So he robbed the poor old man, and murdered him, and they both went off together."

"What! the footman and the dairymaid?" exclaimed Madame Amabel.

"I can't say whether she was the dairymaid," answered Criquet; "but I know it was one of the servants of the house, and that they both disappeared after the murder, and had not been heard of since."

"Heavens and earth!" exclaimed Madame Amabel. "And it was Gaveston who told this story?"

"It was himself," replied Criquet. "I didn't hear him, be-

s 2

cause, as I said before, we don't speak to him; but I had it from
Mr. Râoul, to whom he related the particulars."

"Gracious heavens!" again exclaimed the lady.

"But he's a scoundrel, that Gaveston," added Criquet, observing
that for some reason or other she was very much affected by the
intelligence; "he's not to be believed. Perhaps there's not a word
of truth in the story."

"The fact of the murder cannot be doubted," said the marquis,
"because the news came from Mr. Simpson, who is an honest
man."

"But why do you doubt Mr. Gaveston's word?" inquired Madame Amabel; "have you any particular reason for doing so?"

"Because he's a villain," answered Criquet.

"It's too true," rejoined the marquis; "read that letter, and
you'll be convinced of it;" and he handed her Gaveston's letter,
which he had brought with him.

"Good heavens!" once more exclaimed Amabel, who seemed
quite overwhelmed with these discoveries. "What could be his
motive?"

"We never could conceive his motive, madame," replied the
marquis, "to tell you the truth. Could we, Criquet?"

"Never," answered Criquet. "Had it not been for that infamous clause at the termination of the letter, we should have
supposed that you were some young lady, perhaps a relation of
his own, for whom he wished to obtain an advantageous settlement;
and that he had proposed the alliance from knowing my lord the
marquis's predilection for the ladies of your country."

"It was so I understood it," returned Madame Amabel. "The
fact is, Mr. Gaveston desired to make love to me on his own account; but, aware that he was engaged to Miss Wentworth, I
wouldn't listen to him. He then pretended to be my friend, and
told me that he was acquainted with a nobleman at Bordeaux, who
had commissioned him to look out for an English wife for him,
and that he would send me there, only that I must mention to
nobody where I was going; and he himself arranged everything
secretly for my journey."

"It is quite true that I had said to him that I wished he would
find me a beautiful English bride," returned the marquis. "But
it was a villanous thing of him to propose a false marriage, and I
cannot conceive his motive for doing it."

"I think I can," said Madame Amabel. "He thought that my
ambition would inspire me with a desire to visit England as a
marchioness. I remember hinting something of the sort, for I
was very vain, and as silly as a child: and he wished to put
that out of my power. But are you sure he married Miss Wentworth?"

"He married the daughter of the murdered gentleman, beyond
a doubt," replied Don Querubin; "since which, he no longer takes
an active part in the business. The correspondence of the firm is
carried on through Mr. Simpson."

"That was the clerk, I think?" said Madame Amabel.

"He was," replied the marquis; "but he is now a partner."

"I should be happy to have his address," said the lady, "if you could give it me."

"I can procure it from Mr. Râoul," replied the marquis. And he and Criquet took their leave, charmed with Madame Amabel, and with permission to repeat their visit.

CHAPTER XL.

SUSAN VISITS HER OLD ACQUAINTANCE.

THE injury Mrs. Aytoun's health had sustained proving of a more permanent nature than was expected, she was at length recommended to try the effect of travelling for a year or two; in pursuance of which advice, their little establishment was broken up, and their servants discharged. She accompanied her husband to the continent, and Susan found a situation as housemaid, in the family of a Mr. and Mrs. Cripps, who resided in the neighbourhood of Clapham.

Mr. Cripps had formerly been a grocer in the city, and had retired from business with a very considerable fortune, a wife, and three daughters. He lived in a handsome house, with iron gates, and a carriage-drive up to the door in front, and a large garden with graperies and hot-houses behind; and he maintained his establishment and his table on a liberal and hospitable footing.

The day before Susan quitted London to undertake her new service, she paid a visit to her friend Dobbs, who was still living in Parliament-street; and also to Julia, who, by Mr. Simpson's kindness, had been settled in a small neat shop at Knightsbridge, as a haberdasher; where she was doing very well, and making a decent maintenance for herself and her child.

Harry Leeson's disappearance, which they had heard of, at the time it occurred, from Jeremy, had been a source of extreme unhappiness both to Dobbs and to Susan: and though now several years had elapsed since his departure, their anxiety had experienced but little alleviation. Mr. Simpson had made every effort to discover him for some time, by means of advertisements and handbills; but Harry, who knew nothing of the friend he had in his uncle's old clerk, believed that the invitations to return were only lures held out by Gaveston to get him again into his power; and as he soon found himself, through the friendship of Captain Glassford, in a comfortable situation, with a fair prospect of independence in view, his pride and resentment made him resolve never to present himself before his enemy till he had attained an age and station that should be a check upon his insolence.

To relieve Fanny's anxiety, he had written her a few lines from one of the West India Islands, assuring her that he was safe and well provided for, and that, in process of time, she should see him again, but giving her no clue by which he might be traced. This he had done during his voyage in the Fire-fly, soon after his departure from Oakfield; and from that time nothing had been heard of him. The general apprehension amongst his friends was that he had gone on board some ship as a seaman; and this notion gained strength when years elapsed without farther intelligence.

On this, the most interesting subject to Susan, Dobbs had no news to give; but she had heard from Oakfield that Mrs. Gaveston was no longer residing there, but had quitted her husband, and was living with a sister of her father, at Brighton. He led her such a life, Jeremy said, that Mr. Simpson had advised the step, and had made all the necessary arrangements for her. Jeremy himself had taken a small inn in the neighbourhood; for that retaining his situation after his mistress was gone, was out of the question. Gaveston he described as insupportable; growing daily more gloomy, arbitrary, and tyrannical, and above all, suspicious; and that the minister of the parish had been heard to liken him to certain tyrants of old, called Di and Ishus, who had false ears made so large that they could hear what everybody said of them. "More fools they," as Mr. Jeremy justly observed. He concluded his letter with some affecting remarks on the declining state of Mrs. Jeremy's health; observing, at the same time, in a manner that Dobbs thought rather significant, that deplorable as such a loss would be, it was quite impossible he could live without a wife, and that he should be under the melancholy necessity of immediately looking out for another.

"Bless the man," said Dobbs; "does he think I'd have him?"

"Why not?" answered Susan. "He's a good man, comfortably to do, and much of an age for you."

"That's all true," said Dobbs, with a laugh that Susan fancied did not augur ill for Mr. Jeremy's hopes—"but the world would make such a joke of it, if I was to get married at this time of day. But, by-the-by, Susan, there's a bit of news in the letter about an old friend of yours."

"About William Dean, is it?" asked Susan, with a slight blush.

"'Deed is it," answered Dobbs, "and I scarce know what to say for him. I didn't think William would have done so."

"What has he done?" inquired Susan; "nothing wrong, I hope?"

"It's not what's right," replied Dobbs, "after what passed between him and you. Jeremy says he's keeping company with Grace Lightfoot, Mabel's sister."

"I don't blame him for giving up thoughts of me," answered Susan. "I always told him he would be very silly to keep from marrying for my sake; and it is time William thought of settling; but I almost wonder at his fixing on Grace, though, to be sure, she's very pretty."

"I'm afraid it's not for her beauty so much as for her riches," answered Dobbs, "at least so Jeremy says; but perhaps that's in anger."

"Her riches!" exclaimed Susan.

"Ay," replied Dobbs, "you may well stare. But it seems that every Christmas, for some time back, Grace has received a present of money as regularly as the Christmas came, without ever being able to make out who sent it till lately; and then there came a letter from Mabel."

"From Mabel!" cried Susan, eagerly; "and is there anything about Andrew?"

"Wait, and I'll tell you," answered Dobbs. "The letter begins with hoping she has regularly received the money every Christmas, and that she is well and happy. Then it says that she, that is Mabel, has heard by chance that Mr. Wentworth is dead, and that he was supposed to have been murdered by his footman; and she desires to learn all the particulars—what footman it was, and when it happened—and whether the man was taken. She adds, that she never can believe it could be Andrew, who was so much attached to the family; and was, besides, such a good young man."

"Then she doesn't seem to know anything about Andrew," said Susan.

"Nothing in the world," answered Dobbs. "But then, as Jeremy says, that goes for nothing; because if she does know, of course she wouldn't own it."

"But then she needn't have written to ask what she knew already," said Susan.

"But to find out what people thinks about it, perhaps," said Dobbs. "However, there's no saying; for my part, I never believed that she went away with Andrew, and I don't believe it now."

"But where is she?" inquired Susan. "I'll go to her, and find out the truth, if I beg my bread along the road."

"Ah! there's the thing," replied Dobbs; "nobody knows; and she doesn't say a word about herself from the beginning of the letter to the end of it; and there's no hint of where she is, nor who she is, married or single. The only thing that makes them think she's married is, that she advises Grace to be satisfied with her own station, and not to be looking for a match above herself, as she always had done; for that pride of that sort is sure to meet with a fall, and bring people into trouble. So they think that she has married somebody that treats her ill."

"And where is Grace's answer to be sent?" inquired Susan.

"To a banker's here in Lunnun," responded Dobbs; "and Grace wrote to the banker to beg he'd tell her where her sister was; but the answer came, that he had received the commission from one of his correspondents, but that he knew nothing further on the subject."

"And William's keeping company with Grace, is he?" said Susan.

"He is," answered Dobbs. "It seems he has had a liking for her for some time; but people believing her sister went away with Andrew, and was somehow concerned in the murder, made him fearful of making up to her. But now this letter's come, he says it's clear Mabel knows nothing of Andrew, and that he don't see why Grace should suffer for what she'd nothing to do with, anyway."

"I don't see why she should, either," replied Susan; "and I don't blame William at all. He would have taken me when I was in the midst of my troubles, with scarcely a creature to speak to, except Mr. Jeremy; and that's what few men would have done. Grace was always a very nice girl, and I never heard anything against her."

"Nor against Mabel either, till she went away, except her pride," observed Dobbs.

"Nothing else," answered Susan; "and I wonder people didn't see how improbable it was that her pride would let her go off with a poor lad like Andrew, without even being married to him. She'd refused many better offers than Andrew; that everybody knew. And is that all the news from Oakfield?" inquired she.

"Yes," answered Dobbs; " except that Mr. Gaveston's got himself made a magistrate for the county, and is making himself very busy; Jeremy says, meddling with everything. There's talk of a new road being made somewhere, and Jeremy says that Mr. Gaveston wants it one way, and the rest of the magistrates another; and they are all at sixes and sevens about it; Gaveston's so tyrannical and obstinate."

After giving Dobbs her address, and requesting her to send her any information she might get either about Mabel or Henry, Susan took her leave, and proceeded to pay her visit to Julia.

Julia had nothing very particular to relate, except that she had seen Mr. Dyson. "I happened to be standing at the door," she said, "when he was passing on the outside of one of the Bath coaches, and saw me. He called to the coachman, and got down directly. He said he'd been abroad sometime; and that ever since his return he'd been looking for me."

"But you wont have anything more to say to him, sure?" said Susan.

"Oh no!" replied Julia, "never, depend upon that; neither does he desire it, I fancy. What he wanted, was some deed, or will, or something of that sort, that he says was left in the lodging we were living in, when he went away; and I do remember his once showing me such a thing, and desiring me to take care of it; but that was some time before, and what became of it I can't think. When we fell into such distress, after he went away, I parted with everything by degrees, and the parchment may have been amongst some of the things; I couldn't say, Heaven knows! I may have lighted the fire with it some day, when Julia was so ill; for I often didn't know what I was doing, my mind was in such a distracted state. But he says it's of value, and would bring him money; and he wants me to try and find out what became of it; so the first evening I can spare from the shop, I'll go to the lodging, and inquire if such a thing was found; but I don't expect to hear anything of it."

"I wouldn't encourage his acquaintance, if I were you," replied Susan. "If he's seen coming here, it may get you an ill name in the neighbourhood."

"I wont let him come here," answered Julia. "The only reason I was glad to see him, is, that I have no other way of sending a message to Mr. Godfrey. Now, he says, though Mr. Godfrey has been married some years, he has no children, and if he shouldn't happen to have any, perhaps if he were but to see what a nice little girl Julia is grown, he might do something for her, which would be a great relief to my mind."

"I wouldn't look to any such thing, if I were you," replied Susan; "but I'd bring Julia up to get her living in some decent way; and above all, never give her a notion that she has a rich father. From his past conduct I shouldn't expect anything from him; and if it ever comes, it wont be the less welcome for coming unlooked for."

CHAPTER XLI.

THE READER IS INTRODUCED TO A PERSON OF DISTINCTION.

On the following day. Susan proceeded to Virginia House, the residence of Mr. and Mrs. Cripps, and was installed in her new situation.

Mr. and Mrs. Cripps were in many respects an extremely happy couple. They were rich, good-tempered, and fat; and had three daughters, whom they thought not to be equalled by any daughters that ever were born. The eldest, Miss Caroline, was a beauty; she had very fair hair, that flowed in a profession of soft ringlets over a very white neck; her person was *petite*, and her features extremely small and unmeaning. Miss Livia, the second, was less remarkable for her personal charms; but she was of a very inquiring turn of mind, and extremely anxious to be well informed on all subjects. As her papa justly observed, "Let Livy alone; she'll never let anything go by without asking the meaning of it."

As for Miss Jemima, the youngest, she was, as her mamma assured everybody, a pro*gidy*. Nothing came amiss to her. She always knew her lessons, although nobody ever saw her looking in a book; she had such an ear for music, that having heard a tune once, she was sure to be humming it the whole day afterwards; her dancing-master said she was his best scholar, although she had only, as Mrs. Cripps observed, been at it a quarter: " as for drawing," said the admiring parent, " she has such a turn for doing things after nature, that I wont have her taught, for fear it should cramp her genius. For as dear Mr. Cripps remarked, when she showed him a ship she'd done after nature, when we were at Margate, ' Anybody can draw if they're taught; but the true test of talent is to do it without.' "

With respect to education, beyond reading and writing, two faculties which she very sparingly made use of, Miss Caroline never had any; because, being a beauty, she thought, and her parents were of the same opinion, that learning was quite unnecessary. Added to which, her constitution being delicate, might have been injured by application. A few abortive attempts had been made to educate Miss Livia in her childhood: but they were soon abandoned, not only being found ineffectual, but superfluous; the young lady's desire for information being sufficiently active to supply all that was required; and her preference for oral instruction as decided as was her aversion to whatever was presented to her in a literary shape. Miss Jemima was yet a child; but it appeared to her parents as unnecessary to educate her as the others, because she was evidently determined to educate herself. As Mr. Cripps observed, " Teach Jemmy her A, B, C, and leave the rest to her." This was accordingly done, and apparently with great success; as at nine years old Jemmy was found to have read a great deal, and to be acquainted with many things that were utterly unknown to the rest of the family.

All this was very gratifying; and Mr. and Mrs. Cripps would have been a very happy couple, but for one drawback; which was, that the people in the neighbourhood of Virginia House, whose dominions were no larger than theirs, and whose fortunes were generally not near so large, did not visit them. Unacquainted with the manners of polite life, they had themselves, on their first settlement there, made some rather indiscreet advances, which had been ill received, and had probably operated against them, and been sufficient, combined with other slight objections, to obstruct their entrance into society, so that they lived alone in their glory. This was strange, as Mr. and Mrs. Cripps justly thought, where there were three such daughters in a family, each of whom had the prospect of fifty thousand pounds; and it was extremely mortifying to the parents; who, although they would have been content with inferior society themselves, were ambitious for their children, whom they had hoped to see exalted into another sphere by marriage; and who had, with that view, dropped all communication with their former acquaintance when they retired from business. It was a great misfortune to them, that the most fashionable young man of the neighbourhood, he whose example all the rest followed, had declared decidedly against them. He could afford to do it, because he was engaged to be married to a young lady with thirty thousand pounds already, who had reasons of her own for wishing to exclude the Crippses from society; and the others, who were not equally independent, and to whom the fifty thousand pounds would have been very acceptable, turned their backs on Virginia House, because no one amongst them had courage enough to set up for himself, and follow his own inclinations.

Their isolation formed also a considerable obstruction in the way of Miss Livy's education; limiting her opportunities of inquiring, and restricting her means of information.

In order to compensate in some degree for these disadvantages, Mr. Cripps took his family every year to the sea-side, where they could attend the public assemblies and breakfasts; and sometimes succeeded in making an acquaintance who was willing, after their return home, to accept of the hospitalities of Virginia House.

At the period of Susan's location in the family, they had just returned from one of these annual excursions; and it was rumoured amongst the servants, that the expedition had resulted in a very fair prospect of a high alliance for Miss Caroline. The lady's maid, who had accompanied them from home, narrated, that a foreign gentleman of distinction had been struck with Miss Carry at a ball, and was remarked to take up his glass whenever he met her; that some days afterwards, she had herself been introduced to his servant, a tip-top sort of man, at the races; and that when his master rode past, and took up his glass to look at Miss Carry, who was in the carriage, he had observed, not the least knowing that she belonged to the family, that that was the young lady his master was in love with.

"Why don't he tell her so then? said I," continued Mrs. Gimp, the abigail in question; "who knows but she might take a fancy to him?"

"How do you know but he has told her?" responded George, the count's servant.

"Because I know he has not," answered Gimp. "If he had, I should have heard of it, because I belong to the family."

"Upon that," observed Gimp, "the man seemed quite struck, for it was evident he'd no idea who I was. 'Oh!' said he, then, eyeing me from top to toe; and I had on a pink spencer, and a pea-green bonnet, as good as new, that Miss Carry herself had only just given me; 'Oh!' says he, quite surprised, 'then it is a genteel family, after all.'

"'A genteel family,' says I, 'to be sure it is. Why, that's their own carriage and horses they're riding in.'

"'Is it?' says the man; 'I declare you perfectly astonish me. We heard they were nothing but tradesfolks from London, and that was why my master, the count, refused an introduction; for, of course, persons of his rank are exceedingly particular who they make acquaintance with at these sort of places.'—'No doubt,' says I; 'and so are we very particular, who we make acquaintance with, I assure you. But as for tradesfolks from London, my master is Mr. Cripps, of Virginia House, as handsome a place as you'd wish to see; a gentleman with two hundred thousand pounds, if he's worth a farthing.'

"'God bless me!' exclaimed the valet; 'it's really a pity the count refused an introduction, on the young lady's account. It might have been a fine thing for her.'

" 'And for him too,' says I. 'I suppose he'd have no objection to fifty thousand pounds?'

" 'No,' says he; 'I suppose he'd have no objection—nobody has; but it wouldn't be any consideration, with all his estates. Lord bless you! he's one of the richest noblemen in Europe.'

" 'You don't say so!' says I.

" 'He is,' says he; 'why, don't you know who he is?'

" 'Not I,' says I: 'Miss Carry couldn't tell us his name.'

" 'Oh, then,' says he, looking sly, 'Miss Carry did speak of him?'

" 'Did she?' says I, 'to be sure she did. I don't know but what she was as much struck as he was; only it's no business of mine to say so, she being a young lady, unless he'd spoke first; so of course you won't tell him.'

" 'Oh, no,' says he, 'honour bright!' laying his hand on his breast.

"I knew he would tell, in course," continued Gimp; he'd ha' been a fool not. 'But,' says I, 'you was going to tell us his name, and who he is.'

" 'Why, Lord,' says he, 'I thought everybody knew that! Why he's the famous Count Ruckloony, to be sure; the greatest proprietor in Europe. In course, Mr. Cripps must have heard of him in his travels.'

" 'I dare say he has,' says I; 'and I am sure it's a pity such a handsome couple as they'd make, that they shouldn't be acquainted. He's so dark, and she's so fair, that they'd make a beautiful match.'

" 'It's a pity, certainly,' answered the man; 'but I'm afraid it's too late now, for the count will only be here one more ball. After that, he must go up to London, to pay his respects to the king, that's expecting him on a visit.'

"Well," continued Gimp, "you may be sure Miss Carry went to the next ball; and beautiful she looked, in her blue and silver; and the count was introduced by the master of the ceremonies, and danced with her: and they say the whole company stood by to see them, they danced so beautifully. After that, he called several times, and paid great attention to Miss Carry; and he's coming to Virginia House, as soon as the king can spare him away from the palace."

It was probably from sympathy with Miss Carry's feelings, or with the count's impatience, but the king did spare him sooner than was expected; and one fine morning the count arrived on horseback, to make a call.

He appeared, as far as it was possible to distinguish his features, a handsome man, of about forty, or thereabouts; but his face was provided with such a plentiful crop of dark hair, which was suffered to grow wherever there was the slightest excuse for it, that it was not easy to discover exactly what sort of ground it covered. His figure was good, and his dress extremely fashionable; but with some additions of foreign ornament and splendour, not general amongst English gentlemen at that period.

With respect to his manner, it was grave, deliberate, and self-possessed. He was by no means a great talker, rather the contrary; but Miss Livy found him an invaluable acquisition, as he was prepared to answer all her questions, never being at a loss upon any subject whatever. He spoke English fluently, and with very little accent, sometimes, indeed, with none at all; a peculiarity of which Miss Livy very naturally inquired the reason; and he informed her, that it arose from his having acquired the language from two different masters. One was himself a foreigner, and taught it him with a foreign accent; the other was an Englishman, and taught him without any; and the result was, that he sometimes spoke like one of his instructors, and sometimes like the other; which, Mr. Cripps observed, was "extremely natural;" recommending him, at the same time, to "stick to the Englishman, and cut the parlez-vous." But Miss Carry, on the contrary, preferred the accent; on which account it probably was that he continued to vary his mode of speaking in a manner that alternately satisfied each. Finally, to complete the count's description, he never laughed, or even smiled; his gravity was imperturbable; a peculiarity which, as may be easily conceived, gave him an air of dignity and superiority to the rest of mankind that was truly imposing.

This distinguished person having alighted from his horse, and followed the footman to the drawing-room, who announced him as Count Ruckalony, presented himself with his usual calm demeanour, which formed a striking contrast to the excitement and eagerness with which he was received.

"It's so good of you to remember us so soon," exclaimed Mrs. Cripps. "We were half afraid you'd have forgotten the direction; and dear Mr. Cripps was thinking of enclosing a card to the king's palace, where we supposed you must be staying."

"It's impossible I could forget," answered the count, with a significant glance at Miss Carry.

"So Livy said," replied Mrs. Cripps. "'For,' says she, 'how could he have so much information on every subject, if he couldn't keep such a trifling thing as a direction in his mind?'"

"Miss Livy's observation was extremely just," returned the count. "I make it a rule never to forget anything."

"We hardly expected his majesty could have spared you so soon," observed Mrs. Cripps.

"Why," replied the count, "to say the truth, my visit has been curtailed by a circumstance that, situated as I am, I cannot help exceedingly regretting;" and here he cast another expressive glance towards Miss Carry.

"Nothing unpleasant, I hope?" said Mrs. Cripps.

"Only inasmuch as it will oblige me to quit this country sooner than I had intended," answered the count. "The fact is, I am summoned to the court of Austria on particular business."

" Good gracious !" exclaimed Mrs. Cripps and Miss Livy;
"how unfortunate !" Whilst Miss Carry said nothing; but as
she walked to the window and took out her pocket-handkerchief,
it was presumed that she was considerably affected by the
intelligence.

"But you'll come back to us ?" said Mrs. Cripps, affectionately.

"Should it be in my power, I shall be too happy to do so,"
returned the count. "But these things do not always depend
upon ourselves. We are unfortunately not so independent of our
sovereign as you are in this country. He sometimes interferes
in our family affairs, in a manner that crosses our dearest
inclinations."

"Goodness !" cried Miss Livy, "what does he do ?"

"Proposes an alliance, for example, which we are not at liberty
to decline. Or, perhaps, forbids one that we have set our hearts
upon."

Here Miss Carry, who still kept her place at the window, with
her back turned to the company, raised her handkerchief to her
face and appeared to be wiping her eyes.

"There is nothing of that sort likely at present, I hope," said
Mrs. Cripps, as she rose and presented her vinaigrette to Miss Carry.

"I trust not," replied the count; "but I confess I am not without apprehensions; it is one of the misfortunes attending large
possessions that we are not always permitted to bestow them as
we would desire. There is a niece of the emperor's at present of
marriageable years, and they will naturally be looking for suitable
alliance for her."

Here Mr. Cripps, whom the servants had been sent in search
of, made his appearance in the drawing-room, and after exchang-
ing greetings with the count, was informed of the threatened
calamity ; while Miss Carry's emotion became so uncontrollable,
that her mamma recommended her quitting the room, which she
incontinently did.

"What !" exclaimed Mr. Cripps, "would the Emperor of Hungary, or whatever he is, go to marry a chap at your time of life,
whether he will or no ! By jingo ! that's a pretty go !"

"It's shocking tyrannical," said Mrs. Cripps, "and very affecting;" and she put her hand in her pocket for her handkerchief,
but unluckily she had left it up-stairs.

"I know what I'd do," said Miss Jemmy, who had hitherto
been a silent listener to the conversation, "if I was as big as the
count, and anybody wanted to marry me against my will."

"What would you do ?" inquired Mrs. Cripps.

"Why I'd marry the person I liked directly, before the emperor
could hinder me; and then he couldn't make you marry twice,
could he ?"

"Certainly not," replied the count; "if I were so fortunate as
to have time to follow your advice, Miss Jemima, I should esteem
myself a happy man. But the orders of the emperor are peremptory. I must depart almost immediately."

"How soon?" inquired Miss Jemmy.

"In a fortnight at furthest, I fear," said the count.

"And can't people be married in a fortnight?" asked Miss Jemmy.

"No doubt, if everything had been previously settled," replied the count, "but when one has not procured the lady's consent, or even dared to make known one's wishes, I fear it would be presumption to entertain a hope."

"Not at all," said Mrs. Cripps; "if the lady likes you, I don't see why things can't be as well done in two weeks as in twenty."

"But I am not so happy as to be certain that the lady does like me," answered the count, with an air of great modesty.

"Oh yes she does," said Miss Jemmy.

"Jemmy!" exclaimed Mrs. Cripps, "fie! child; how can you talk so? You don't know what you're saying."

"Yes I do, ma," replied Miss Jemmy. "Isn't Carry saying she adores the count all day long? I'm sure she said so this morning to Gimp, when she was dressing her hair; and she asked Gimp if he wasn't a sweet fellow."

"Oh my goodness!" cried Mrs. Cripps, putting her hands before her face; "get out of the room, Jemmy; your a very naughty child to talk so. Pray excuse her, count, and don't attend to what she says. She's such a very precarious child, that it's quite impossible to keep her back—quite a pro*gidy*, I assure you."

The count, however, taking advantage of the young lady's communication, pressed for further information; when Mrs. Cripps, with all due reluctance and reserve, admitted that she was afraid he had made a deep impression on poor Carry's heart.

"To be sure he has," added Mr. Cripps. "What's the use of mincing the matter? The girl's as fond of him as she can stare."

The count's modesty being thus reassured, and such signal encouragement given to his suit, he declared that he had no further hesitation in avowing the most decided passion for Miss Carry; whose charms, he confessed, had touched his heart from the first moment he beheld her, but that some malignant reports had prevented his seeking an immediate introduction; now, however, he was too happy in being allowed to lay his title and fortune at her feet.

Nothing could exceed the satisfaction of the family at this consummation of their most ambitious hopes, and the triumph it would afford them over their proud and scornful neighbours. Even the necessity for so early a union as the count's peculiar circumstances rendered necessary, appeared to them far from objectionable. From what they had gathered from Gimp, and from the few words the count had dropt about "malignant reports," and "declining an introduction," they were not without apprehensions that a discovery of the very recent date of their transmigration from the shop in the city to Virginia House, might operate against them in the aristocratic mind of Roccaleoni; and that therefore the shorter the interval before the ceremony the better. Once married,

as the happy couple were to start for the continent immediately,
it was not likely that the count's prejudices would be disturbed
by hearing anything of the matter.

The preliminary arrangements were soon satisfactorily arranged;
but as much remained to be discussed, the count was requested
to pass the rest of the day at Virginia House, to which he conde-
scendingly acceded.

It would be advisable, he said, to keep their intentions as secret
as possible till the ceremony was over, lest any rumour of what
was impending should reach the court of Austria.   News travelled
apace; and of course he had enemies—all great men have—and
there were those connected with the Austrian embassy who would
not be sorry to do him an injury with the emperor. Mr. and
Mrs. Cripps had not the slightest objection to this precaution.
They were also afflicted with that inseparable symptom of great-
ness—they too had enemies, who would be envious of Miss Carry's
high fortune; and who might, in the hope of interrupting the
alliance, be disposed to volunteer some communications about the
shop and the city.

Thus the views and wishes on both sides perfectly coincided,
and nothing could be more harmonious than the negotiations of
the contracting parties; more especially as Mr. Cripps declared
that, on the wedding-day, he should be prepared to transfer fifty
thousand pounds consols to the bridegroom's account.

"On my part," said the count, "our mode is somewhat different
—you'll allow me to settle a little estate on the young lady. I
wish I knew which of those I possess would be most agreeable to
her taste. It's important; because, in the event of her being left
a widow, it would be desirable that she should have a residence
that suited her; and it is perfectly immaterial to me which it is."

Of course Miss Carry put her handkerchief to her eyes, at the
word widow; and Mrs. Cripps murmured an emphatic "God
forbid!"

"Roccaleoni," pursued the count, "from which I derive my
title, is naturally entailed on my eldest son."

"Ha! ha!" said Mr. Cripps, jogging Miss Carry's elbow; "we
shall be having a young count soon;" at which Miss Carry said,
"Don't, pa—for shame!" and blushed very becomingly.

"And it is there," added the count, "that I chiefly reside."

"Where is it?" asked Miss Livy.

"It's in Transylvania," replied the count.

"Is it a pretty place?" said Miss Livy.

"Rather splendid than pretty," answered the count. "The
castle is very ancient."

"How ancient?" inquired Miss Livy, who, elated with the
exaltation of her sister, was beginning to be in train.

"It dates from the reign of Nero," answered the count.

"Was he the king of Transylvania?" asked Miss Livy.

"He was," replied he.

"Well," said Miss Jemmy, "I've a large sheet of paper, with

the pictures of all the kings upon it; and there it says he was the Emperor of Rome."

"That was his brother," said the count.

"What's the English of Roccaleoni?" inquired Miss Livy.

"It means the rock of lions," replied he.

"Are there lions there?" asked Miss Livy.

"We meet with one or two occasionally," answered the count. "Formerly they were very numerous, as well as the bears; but we have extirpated them by degrees."

"My goodness!" exclaimed Miss Carry; "I hope I sha'n't meet a lion when I'm out walking in Transylvania."

"I don't think it very likely," answered the count; "every precaution will be used to prevent it."

"Well," said Miss Jemmy, "look here; in my book of animals, it says there are no lions except in Asia or Africa."

"Well," said Mr. Cripps, "how do you know but Transylvania's there too?"

"Is it?" inquired Miss Livy.

"No," replied the count, "it's in Europe."

"And the book says there are no lions in Europe," said Miss Jemmy.

"The information in books is not to be depended on," answered the count; "on which account I never read them."

"Nor I," said Miss Livy; "they go such a round-about way to tell one anything, and make so many words about it, it's quite tiresome."

"It is," observed Mr. Cripps; "and they're so full of lies. What was the name of that book I read, Jemmy?"

"It was 'Gulliver's Travels,'" replied Jemmy.

"Ah!" said Mr. Cripps, "he must take us for gulls to believe him. Lord bless you, such a farrago of lies!"

"Entirely false," said the count. "I've been in those parts myself, and know that his account is not to be depended on."

"If you never read books," said Miss Jemmy, "how do you know so many things?"

"Entirely by observation," answered he; "and by asking questions, as Miss Livy does. As for geography, orthography, and the use of the globes, I learnt them all by travelling, and making use of my eyes."

"And how did you learn history?" inquired Miss Livy.

"By visiting the countries themselves, and talking to the people," replied he. "For example, when I wanted to learn the Roman history, I went to Rome, and questioned the Romans about it. Of course they must know their own history best."

"The devil's in it if they don't," said Mr. Cripps.

And in this sort of improving discourse, the afternoon passed very agreeably; till in the evening the count took his leave, with a promise of returning on the following day to dinner.

T

CHAPTER XLII.

SUSAN MAKES A DISCOVERY THAT CHANGES HER PLANS.

As there were many purchases and preparations to be made in the short period that intervened before the wedding, Mrs. Cripps and the young ladies spent the succeeding morning in London. Amongst other wants, it was discovered that the bride would require a maid to accompany her abroad. The count had given his opinion, on this subject being mentioned, that it was unnecessary, as English maids were useless on the continent, and he could easily procure an accomplished foreign one as soon as they had crossed the Channel. But Miss Carry had always been accustomed to the services of Gimp, and was, moreover, a remarkably helpless young lady; and she avowed her utter incapability of dispensing with the attendance of a femme-de-chambre; besides, she said, she could not speak French, nor understand it either, and that it was therefore useless for her to engage a foreign servant till she had acquired that accomplishment.

Mrs. Gimp was therefore applied to, and a proposal made to her to accompany the bride; but that prudent lady declined to make any change in her situation. She knew when she was well off, and preferred the luxuries and comforts of Virginia House to the prospective accommodations of an ancient castle in Transylvania. Besides, she entertained a decided aversion to old castles, which, she justly observed, were apt to be haunted; and with respect to Transylvania, or any such outlandish place, it might be all very well for them that liked it, but England was good enough for her.

Susan, who had been accustomed to wait on her former mistress, and was a very handy person, was next applied to; but she also declined; because, knowing nothing of the count, and thinking Miss Carry a fool, she did not choose to embark herself with their fortunes. It therefore became necessary to look out for some one else to fill the situation.

In the meantime, Roccaleoni arrived duly to dinner every day, and continued liberally to satisfy Miss Livy's curiosity, and to store her mind with a variety of agreeable information. But Mr. Cripps's hospitality revolted at seeing his future son-in-law mount his horse of an evening to return to town, especially if it happened to rain; and he therefore proposed to the count to establish himself at Virginia House, and remain there till the wedding.

The count said he should be exceedingly happy to do so, and that he would send down his servant on the following morning with his portmanteau. Mrs. Cripps inquired if the man could speak English.

"Oh yes," answered he; "he is an Englishman. I have no foreign servant with me at present. This is a very valuable fellow, that I have had some time. I engaged him on the continent for the purpose of exercising myself in speaking English before I came here; and he has been travelling with me through France and Italy, in a tour I've been making to look after my estates in those countries. He's a very superior sort of person for his situation in life; when we were in Rome, the Romans were struck with his resemblance to Julius Cæsar."

"Well," said Miss Jemmy, "I've got a picture of Julius Cæsar amongst my kings, so I shall be able to see if he's like him."

"Julius Cæsar was very bald," observed the count, "and George is very bald."

"Wasn't Julius Cæsar a great warrior?" inquired Miss Livy.

"He was," replied the count.

"My book says he conquered Britain," remarked Miss Jemmy.

"Whew!" said Mr. Cripps, "that's a good un."

"Absurd!" said the count.

"Them books of yours is full of lies, Jemmy," said Mr. Cripps; "you should burn them. The man that dares to say any d——d frog-eating Frenchman ever conquered Britain, must be a rascal."

"Julius Cæsar wasn't a Frenchman, pa," answered Jemmy; "he was a Roman."

"It's all one," observed Mr. Cripps. "A Frenchman and a Roman's all the same thing. They neither on 'em ever conquered Britain, nor ever shall." And Mr. Cripps brandished his knife and fork in a manner that evinced his determination to prevent it.

"Did Julius Cæsar lose his hair in battle?" inquired Miss Livy.

"He did," answered the count. "It was singed off by a cannon-ball that passed immediately over his head."

On the following morning, Susan was preparing the best bed-room for the count's accommodation, when one of the coaches which passed the house, drew up, and deposited that great man's servant and portmanteau at the gate.

"Oh!" said Miss Jemmy, running into the room with a large sheet of paper in her hand, "look here, Susan; I've brought my pictures of kings, that I may see if George is like Julius Cæsar, as the count says. That's Julius Cæsar, and here's George coming up stairs with the portmanteau;" and accordingly the living transcript of the Roman emperor, conducted by the footman, entered the room.

"Well," cried Miss Jemmy, "I declare he is like him. Turn round, George, and let me see if you are bald. Look, Susan, isn't he like him?" And she took hold of her to invite her to a nearer inspection of the new-comer. But Susan stood transfixed, staring at the man with no less astonishment than if Julius Cæsar himself had actually stood before her—for George, the count's servant, was no other than the man with the crooked nose.

"Who is it I'm like?" said he. "What are you looking at me so for?" apparently more surprised than pleased at the sensation he had created.

"It's to see if you're like Julius Cæsar," replied Miss Jemmy; "and now I see you are, I shall go down and tell Livy, that she may come and look at you too;" and away she ran.

"Well!" said the man, in an impatient tone, to Susan, who, speechless with amazement, still stood with her eyes fixed on his face; "what the devil are *you* staring at? Is this the count's room?"

"Yes," answered Susan, endeavouring to rouse herself. "Are you his servant?"

"To be sure I am," replied he. "Did you never see a gentleman's servant before, that you can't take your eyes off me?"

"It's only the likeness I was struck with," answered Susan; "the child had been just showing me the picture."

"It's a joke of my master's," said he, partly recovering his good humour. "You seem to have a comfortable house here."

"Yes," replied Susan, "it's a comfortable house, and everything comfortable about it. I hope Miss Carry wont change for the worse where she's going?"

"Bless you!" cried he; "this is nothing to Roccaleoni. Why, our pigeon-house is well nigh as large as this. She'll be astonished when she gets there, I fancy."

"Comfort and grandeur don't always go together," observed Susan.

"Well," said George, "if Roccaleoni's too large for her taste, she may go to one of the other estates; there's plenty to pick and choose from."

"I hope she'll be happy," said Susan, with a sigh; for her recognition of George had very considerably abated her respect for his master. Indeed, an idea occurred to her that never had presented itself before—she had a notion that the count was the very man she had seen at the police-office, with Nosey, the day she was there with Mrs. Aytoun, and had overheard Jackson's remarks upon their evidence about the watch and purse.

On that day she had only caught a side view of his face as he went out, and had seen little more than she had yet seen of the count's—namely, that it was very much overgrown with dark hair. But that coincidence, coupled with the appearance of the servant, awakened some unpleasant suspicions in her mind.

It is true, she knew nothing in the world against George's character herself. She had never even seen or heard of him till he rang at the back-door of Oakfield two nights before Mr. Wentworth's death; and she had no rational grounds for putting an ill construction on so slight a circumstance; nor did she find that anybody else to whom she had mentioned it, was disposed to do so. Her dream, if dream it was, could have no weight with anybody but herself; and therefore all the ill she could have advanced against him, was comprised in the few words Jackson had uttered; which, after all, did not amount to much more than that his person was familiar in places not over respectable—but direct accusation there was none. Still she could not help auguring ill of the count, and of Miss Carry's prospects; and had Mr. and

Mrs. Cripps been a different sort of couple, she would have felt inclined to have imparted to them the doubts she could not banish from her mind; but being what they were, she was quite certain that anything she could allege, had she had ten times as much evidence to adduce, would have no weight in the world against the count's plausibility.

However, as far as her private interests were concerned, she was by no means sorry to have this opportunity of making the man's acquaintance, and discovering his character. She had always anxiously desired to learn something about him; and now that the occasion offered, as she feared she could do no good in Miss Carry's case by interfering, she resolved to use it for her own satisfaction—to be silent and observe.

With respect to George, his displeasure appeared to subside when her inspection ceased; and he conversed with her and the other servants familiarly enough, answering all their inquiries about his master by magnificent accounts of his wealth and grandeur.

In the meantime, the days flew rapidly by, and it wanted but three to the wedding. Mrs. Cripps and Miss Carry were gone to town on their shopping affairs, and Mr. Cripps to transact some business at the bank; Miss Livy was embroidering a green cat in the drawing-room, and Miss Jemmy was in the coach-house, drawing the new barouche " after nature ;" whilst the count, who now seldom left the villa, lest he should be seen by anybody connected with the Austrian embassy, remained behind.

Susan had gone into the garden at the cook's request, to pick some herbs, and was stooping down behind a row of raspberry bushes, when she heard footsteps and voices approaching; and peeping between the leaves, she perceived they proceeded from the count and his man George.

They were walking slowly, side by side, with their arms thrown behind their backs, the servant apparently quite as much at his ease as the master, and in earnest conversation. She could not resist her curiosity to overhear something of the dialogue, and she therefore preserved her attitude, and remained as quiet as she could.

" But it's too late," said the count. " You should have thought of it before."

" Not at all too late, if you manage it well," replied George. " They'll agree to anything you'll propose—they're such fools!"

" I don't know that," answered the count. " Perhaps she wont consent herself. She's a d——d fool, certainly; but she's got a will of her own, for all that."

" Well, try it," said George. " There's no harm in trying it—" and here the course of their walk took them out of Susan's hearing.

Presently, however, they approached again. " Of course," said George, in answer to some observation of the other's, which had not reached Susan; " of course, I should give up that claim entirely; and therefore it's your interest as well as mine."

"It's a devilish pity you didn't think of it before!" observed
the count, who appeared to be moved by the last suggestion to
take a more favourable view of his companion's proposal, whatever it might be. "There's so little time left; only three days to
do it in."

"Time enough," answered George. "Propose it to-day at
dinner, you can say it's only for a few weeks; depend on it, she'll
do it, and leave the rest to me."

"I'll go and sound her about it now," said the count,—and
with that they turned off and left the garden,

The words she had heard amounted to little or nothing: she
could not tell what they meant; they might mean evil or they
might not; but the familiarity, the strange tone of equality, that
seemed to subsist between master and man, struck Susan as most
extraordinary. "If I had but sensible people to deal with," she
said to herself, "I'd speak, although it does want but three days
of the wedding—but they're such fools; by-the-by, that was what
George said, and certainly he was right there."

On the following morning, after breakfast, Susan was summoned
to an interview with Mrs. Cripps. "Susan," said the lady, "we
hav'n't been able to find a maid yet, to accompany the countess
abroad, and now we have but three days before us. All the
women we've seen have objected to go, because the family is not
coming back."

"Indeed, ma'am?" said Susan, "that's a pity."

"It's very inconvenient," answered Mrs. Cripps; "and, perhaps, if we had decided before on letting Livy and Jemima go
with her sister, there wouldn't have been so much difficulty;
because the woman, whoever she is. could return with them."

"Is Miss Livy going too, ma'am," said Susan; "and Miss
Jemima?"

"Yes," answered Mrs. Cripps; "they're both to go; it will be
much better and pleasanter for Carry, as the count says—he's all
kindness and consideration, I'm sure; a perfect angel of a man,
he is, as ever lived. Carry 'll be a happy woman, as I'm always
telling her. However, as I was saying, Livy's to accompany her
sister, just for a few weeks; and by that time the countess might
get a foreign servant; and whoever goes with them might return
with Livy and the child. But we've no time now to look about
for anybody that would suit."

"Wont Mrs. Gimp go, ma'am?" said Susan. "No, she wont,"
answered Mrs. Cripps; "I've just been asking her. But, perhaps,
as it's for such a short time, Susan, and it would be such a convenience to us, you would?"

Many thoughts flashed through Susan's mind at this proposal.
In the first place, her curiosity about George was yet by no means
satisfied. He talked away fluently enough amongst the servants,
and gave them many amusing accounts of his travels, the places
and people he had seen abroad, and the ways and customs of
foreign nations—but nothing ever transpired about himself per-

sonally, and he was singularly reserved with respect to all his former experiences in England. No interrogations elicited from him in what families he had lived previous to his taking the count's situation, nor what parts of the country he was acquainted with. His very name she was yet ignorant of; in short, she knew no more of him than she did on the day they first met in the count's bed-chamber, and she was unwilling to lose sight of him till she had made better use of her opportunity.

Then she recalled the conversation she had overheard the day before in the garden. She now suspected that it regarded Miss Livy; what it meant she could not tell, but she inclined to think it was no good. "If I go," thought she, "I may be of some use to the poor foolish thing, if any harm's intended her." "Well, ma'am," answered she to Mrs. Cripps, "as it's only for a few weeks, I've no objection. I'll go with the young ladies."

CHAPTER XLIII.

SUSPICIOUS CIRCUMSTANCES.

THE count having, to Mr. Cripps's infinite satisfaction, announced himself a member of the Protestant Church, the happy couple were married, by special licence, at Virginia House; and the mutual desire for secresy still prevailing, no one was present at the ceremony but the family themselves, and their servants; and, as soon as the ladies had exchanged their white robes for their travelling dresses, the bride and bridegroom, with Miss Livy, started in their new barouche, with George and Susan in the rumble; the four horses and two postilions decked with white favours, announcing to the envious neighbourhood, and to the admiring world, the auspicious event that had taken place.

They slept the first night at Rochester, the second at Dover, and on the following morning they crossed the channel to Calais; during which interval, Susan remarked nothing very particular in the conduct of her companions, unless it was the peculiar empressement with which George handed Miss Livy in and out of the carriage, and attended to all her wants; taking upon himself, also, the duty of occasionally answering her questions, when the count did not seem disposed to do it himself: which induced the young lady to observe, that she found George a very well informed person for his situation in life.

When they got over the water, however, the scene in some respects changed. George, who, from the beginning, had been dressed in plain clothes, and might have passed for one thing as well as another, being a sort of flashy, swaggering man, instead of acting as he had hitherto done, looking after the luggage and doing the duty of an attendant, assumed a different tone, com-

mitting the charge to others, and calling about him with an air of
authority and independence; and instead of offering to conduct
Susan, to whom he had hitherto been civil enough, up to the
hôtel, he desired her to follow with the porters, who were bringing the luggage, and walked away himself with the rest of the
party. Neither did he assist in unpacking the dresses and articles
for the toilet that were required; but, having his portmanteau
placed in the bed-room he had selected, he arranged his attire to
his own satisfaction, and then, without saying anything to anybody on the subject, he went out.

Susan's curiosity being considerably excited by these unusual
proceedings, she took an opportunity of asking Miss Livy, in the
evening, what was become of him. "Oh!" said the young lady,
"the count says we shall see him again in Paris, where we're
going to-morrow."

"I thought we were going to the count's castle in Transylvania?" said Susan.

"So we are, afterwards," replied Miss Livy; "but we're going
to Paris first, where the count says we shall meet a particular
friend of his, called Colonel Jones, that he is as fond of as if he
were his brother."

With a mind by no means at ease, Susan started, with the rest
of the party, for Paris, on the succeeding day. The strange conduct and disappearance of George formed a serious addition to
the previous amount of mystery, and she could not but apprehend
that "worse remained behind." If the servant had been assuming a false character, the chances were that the master had been
doing the same; and she could not avoid certain misgivings with
respect to the estate in Transylvania, and all the other estates;
especially that in the south of France, where, she had one day
heard the count assuring Miss Livy, in answer to her inquiry
"whether echoes ever spoke first?" that a phenomenon of that
nature was to be found. The only encouraging circumstance
was, that Roccaleoni continued to treat them kindly; she could
perceive no difference in his behaviour, and the young women appeared perfectly satisfied and happy in his company.

On their arrival in Paris, they took up their abode in the best
apartments of a handsome hôtel; and the count lost no time in
introducing them to the usual round of spectacles and amusements; even Susan, for the first week, much as her suspicions
were awakened, observed nothing uncommon or unsatisfactory in
his proceedings.

One day, however, about the eighth or ninth after their arrival,
when she happened to be in the salon, receiving some directions
from the ladies, the laquais-de-place entered, and announced
Monsieur le Colonel Jones; and, to her infinite astonishment,
though apparently creating none in the minds of the rest of the
party, George, the late valet, presented himself, attired in the
height of the fashion, and with all the ease and confidence of an
old acquaintance.

"Ah! mon cher,"* said the count, who, now that he was in France, occasionally garnished his conversation with a few foreign phrases, "vous voilà, enfin !"† Do you know that we have been expecting you these three days, with the utmost impatience? That is, I and my dear little countess here—as for Miss Livy, of course she had no desire for your arrival; none in the world— had you Livy?"

"I am very sorry to hear that," replied the colonel, taking a seat beside Miss Livy, who laughed and blushed, and looked extremely conscious; "and, had I known it sooner, I might have extended my visit to the duke for another week, as he urged me to do. But my impatience would not permit of a longer stay; and I ordered my horses to the door this morning before he was up, and left a note excusing my sudden departure."

"And how did you find the duchess, and all the family?" inquired Roccaleoni.

"Surprisingly well," answered the colonel; "with the exception of the young marquis, who had a fall from his horse the day before I arrived, and had broken the small bone of his arm. However, he's doing very well."

"Was there much company at the château?" asked the count.

"A great deal," answered the colonel. "There was the Duc de Rochechouart, the Prince of Tarentum, all the Armagnacs, the Marquis and Marchioness de Beauregard, and several others. But, nevertheless, they are extremely anxious for a visit from you and the ladies; and begged I would urge you to fix an early period."

"That I will," replied the count, "as soon as we have seen a few more of the sights of Paris; but, as the weather is so fine at present, I wish to take advantage of it, to show my dear little Carry the environs of the city. To-morrow we propose spending the day at Versailles. Perhaps you'll give us the pleasure of your company?"

To this polite invitation the colonel acceded; and shortly afterwards, a walk to the Thuilleries being proposed, they all four started together, Roccaleoni giving his arm to his wife, and the colonel his to Miss Livy.

"Well," thought Susan, as she looked out of the window after them, "it may be all right—I hope it is. But why Colonel Jones should pretend to be the count's servant, I can't for the life of me make out; and, for all his fine clothes and great talk, I don't feel clear in my mind that he's not the servant yet."

In the meantime, the colonel and Miss Livy proceeded down the street, for some minutes in a silence which being only interrupted by the sighs which ever and anon proceeded from the o'ercharged breast of the former, was infinitely more moving and expressive than the most eloquent oration could have been; especially as each "suspiration of forced breath" was accompanied

* My dear fellow. † Here you are at last.

by a corresponding pressure of the fair arm he supported, every pressure augmenting, by a regular gradation, in tenderness and intensity.

At length, "unable longer to conceal his pain," the enamoured colonel ventured to murmur, "Can you forgive the follies that my unhappy passion has made me commit?"

"I can't think why you did it!" answered Miss Livy, who by no means approved of "silence in love," and who was extremely glad to have her tongue set free, and her curiosity satisfied.

"Hasn't the count explained my motives?" said he.

"No," said she, "he told us you'd do it."

"D—n him!" murmured the colonel, in an inaudible whisper. "I am sorry for that," he continued aloud; "for it's a delicate subject for me to enter upon, especially when my feelings are so apt to overpower me. I'm sure you must have often perceived my agitation when I approached you."

"But what did you do it for?" reiterated Miss Livy. "Why didn't you come as Colonel Jones at first?"

"Alas!" replied the colonel, "the smallness of my fortune compared to the count's, and my not having a title to bestow, like him, made me fear you would scorn my pretensions, and drive me from your presence unheard. And I fancied if I could only introduce myself under your roof, and perhaps, in my disguise, make some impression on your heart, I might have a better chance of success afterwards. It was very absurd, no doubt; but you know love makes men commit all sorts of follies: and mine, I believe, has almost overpowered my reason;" and here the colonel's voice faltered, and he appeared exceedingly affected.

"When did it come on?" inquired Miss Livy, whose gratification, great as it was, by no means quelled her curiosity.

"The first time my eyes beheld you," he replied; "you were walking with your sister, the present countess, and Roccaleoni and I were together, arm in arm. 'Heavens!' I exclaimed, 'look at that lovely woman!' 'Which?' said he; 'she in blue?' 'No,' I answered; 'the other, in green. Observe her countenance; see what mind there is in her face!' However, he persisted in admiring your sister most, whilst I couldn't take my eyes from you. From that moment I was a lost man; and when I found that my friend was about to pay you a visit at Virginia House, I besought him to introduce me under your roof as his servant."

"Well, it's very odd," said Miss Livy; "but papa and mamma would have been very glad to see you, if you'd said you were Colonel Jones."

"Perhaps I was wrong," replied the colonel; "and on that account, if I am so happy as to make an impression on your heart, I should request, as a particular favour, that you would not expose the folly that my passion led me to commit. I shouldn't like to be laughed at."

"But they'll know you when we go to England," said Miss Livy, jumping at once to the conclusion.

"But I shall not mind that," answered he, "if I am only so happy as to secure your hand first. But I fear if they should discover the imposition I practised on them before I have obtained their consent to our union, it may operate against me."

"It's very funny," said Miss Livy; "but papa said I should be sure to get a husband in Transylvania."

"Then you consent to my wishes?" said the colonel; "and I may consider myself the happiest of men?"

It had not entered into Miss Livy's mind to oppose them; she had that sort of weak good nature that would have inclined her to accept anybody that had offered; and a man of the colonel's rank and figure, a particular friend of the count's, one who visited dukes and marquises, and who had performed such a feat as disguising himself, and appearing in a false character, in order to win her affections, combined every recommendation she could desire.

Miss Livy's consent, therefore, was soon won; but that was not enough for the colonel, who declared himself quite incapable of taking her, without the approbation of her respected parents; but lest the attachment should appear too sudden, it was arranged that a way should be paved for his application for her hand, by a few preliminary letters, wherein his name and qualifications might be advantageously introduced. Thus Miss Livy wrote—

"MY DEAR PAPA,—I told you in my last letter that we were expecting to be joined by the count's particular friend, Colonel Jones. He has been with us now some days; and a charming man he is! I'm sure you'd be delighted with him, he's so full of information; I really don't know which is the cleverest, he or the count; and you know I was always naturally fond of clever people. Jemmy likes him exceedingly; and so does Carry. It makes it very convenient for Carry and me, and saves us a deal of trouble, as we don't understand French, and the men who show the sights can't speak English; so the count and the colonel tell is what everything is, and who painted it. We went yesterday to see the catacombs where they bury the dead here, not like our churchyards, but large places underground; but it's not disagreeable, because they've no flesh on. The colonel says they are all boiled first, till the flesh turns into fat, and they make wax candles of it, which is the reason they're so much cheaper here. There was a picture of a lady in blue satin, and a Spanish hat, so like mamma, that the count talks of having it copied: the colonel says 'It's the mother of the Gracchi, by Sir Christopher Wren;' but he couldn't remember her name. The skulls are all piled up one above another in rows, and you walk through them with a bit of candle in your hand; but sometimes the candle goes out, and then you can't go out, for every one of them's exactly the same. We went to see the Goblins at work; but the colonel says 'they've worked it all on the wrong side,' which is a pity. There was a very grand piece, large enough to cover one end of the drawing-room at Virginia House. The colonel told us it was 'a battle between Alexander the Great and Louis the XIV.; but he could not recollect which beat. But I think one of the most beautiful things we've seen, is the king's palace at Versailles, which is entirely full of water-works, that sprinkle you all over with gold-fish; and such loads of crimson satin I never saw! But at the theatre they don't act in English, which makes it not very amusing to Carry and me; but the colonel tells us what it's about, and I'm certain you'll be delighted with him. Carry is, and says I'm a fortunate girl; and believe me, dear papa,

                         " Your affectionate daughter,

                                " LIVY CRIPPS."

" P.S. We saw a beautiful picture of Queen Cleopatra, committing suicide with a large pearl. The colonel says ' it stuck in her throat, and choked her.' But the picture that pleased me most, was a large one that contains all our royal family; there's King George and Queen Charlotte, and the Prince of Wales, and all the princes and princesses; and beautiful likenesses they are. The colonel says ' it was painted by Vandyck.' I'm certain you'll be surprised when you see the colonel. You'd never guess who he is, if you were to guess from now till Christmas."

After a few epistles of this nature had been forwarded to England, a proposal in form from the colonel, strongly supported by the recommendations of the count and countess, was despatched, with a request for an early answer, as it was desirable the marriage should take place before the party quitted Paris for Roccaleoni, which they intended doing shortly; and as no doubt was entertained by the ladies of Mr. Cripps's compliance, every preparation was made for the ceremony.

However, to their surprise, the answer, instead of the expected consent, contained a decided refusal; and an intimation, moreover, that Mr. Cripps was about to start immediately for Paris.

On the morning after this intelligence reached them, the travelling carriage appeared at the door, and the count, countess, colonel, Miss Livy, and Susan, started for the castle in Transylvania.

CHAPTER XLIV.

THE CHANCES OF ARRIVING AT ROCCALEONI APPEAR RATHER AT A DISCOUNT.

FOR two days the party travelled without adventure; and as the three women were all equally ignorant of the language and of the country, they had no further means of knowing where they were going, than what they learned from the gentlemen who escorted them.

On the third evening, after passing for some hours through a country thinly inhabited and little cultivated, the carriage drew up at a small lone inn on a barren heath, and the two gentlemen alighting, handed out the ladies, and conducted them into the house.

"Take out the ladies' travelling bags, and whatever they will want for the night," said the count to Susan; "but leave everything else in the carriage."

"Are we to stay in this lonely place all night?" inquired the countess.

"It's inevitable," returned her husband; "there is no other inn within a considerable distance."

As they entered the narrow passage that led to the interior of the house, they were met by a tall, dark-complexioned woman, apparently about fifty years of age; and who, although she had still the remains of much beauty, had also, what Susan thought, a most sinister expression of countenance. She wore a dark-coloured linen bed-gown, which only descended to her knees, below which appeared a red stuff petticoat; on her feet she had blue worsted stockings and wooden shoes; and on her head, a yellow handkerchief, in the form of a toque. Her hair, which straggled from beneath it, was perfectly grey, and formed a striking contrast to her black brows and jetty eyes, which were still lighted by the fiery temperament within, and from which glances of distrust and suspicion were darted on all that approached her.

On meeting the party in the passage, she made a sort of salutation to the gentlemen, which seemed to imply a previous acquaintance, but she said nothing; whilst they addressed a few words to her in a low voice, in French.

She then silently preceded them into the kitchen, and drawing a wooden bench towards the chimney, she wiped off the dust with her apron, and, by pointing to it, invited the ladies to sit down.

"Am I to sit down in the kitchen?" inquired the countess, with some indignation.

"There is no alternative," said the count; "there is no other room in the house except the bed-rooms; and, besides, the evening is chilly, and it is the only one with a chimney."

With some remorse for their elegant silk pelisses, the ladies accommodated themselves to the necessity of the case, and seated themselves, giving Susan a corner beside them. The kitchen, which was paved with red bricks, was scantily furnished: shelves with a few cooking utensils, a deal table, and some wooden seats, forming the whole of its contents, with the exception of a very old, large arm-chair, covered with what had once been red damask, which stood on the other side of the chimney, and which was occupied by a man who appeared to Susan (the most observing of the party) as well worthy of attention as the woman. Not that he had the same sinister expression of countenance; on the contrary, the expression he bore was that of a deep and fixed

melancholy—of a melancholy that seemed to have imprinted itself
there under former circumstances, and in other times, and of which
the type still remained, although the griefs were no longer remembered, nor the feelings yet in existence which had engraven
the lines. The face was long, and very pale; and the well-formed
features testified had once been a very handsome one. His person
was on a smaller and slighter scale than that of the woman;
and, although he looked much older, to an observing eye the
marks of age appeared rather the result of trouble than of time.
He sat with his body bent forward, his arms resting on the two
elbows of the chair, and his face turned almost invariably to the
embers which flickered on the hearth, and on which his eyes
seemed to fix themselves, as if he traced in the bright sparkles
that successively shone their short moment of existence, and then
set in darkness, the image of his own transitory pleasures and
extinguished hopes. His dress, which consisted of a loose coat of
grey flannel, with trousers of the same material, and a black
velvet cap, was respectable and very clean, as indeed was that of
the woman; and altogether he had the air of having been designed
for something better than the situation in which he now appeared.
When the party entered the room, he rose slowly from his chair,
and made them a profound and respectful salutation, after which'he
reseated himself, without saying a word, and resumed his contemplation of the fire, testifying no further consciousness of their
presence.

Whilst Susan was making these observations, and the young
ladies were mutually expressing their impatience to reach the
elegant accommodations of Roccaleoni, the woman and the two
gentlemen left the room together, and were absent some minutes.
When she returned, she brought in some eggs, and immediately
set about preparing a repast for the company, in which office she
was aided by an odd, rough-looking, red-haired boy, in a blue
blouse, perhaps about fourteen years of age, whom she appeared
to have summoned from some other occupation to her assistance.

During this process, the gentlemen walked about before the
door, in deep conversation, pausing now and then to hold a consultation with the postilion, who still remained there with the
carriage. The horses were then taken out, and the vehicle
wheeled under a shed, whilst they re-entered the house, and partook of the refreshment prepared for them. When they had
finished their meal, the woman drew the table into a corner, and
spreading the board with humbler fare, she and the postilion and
the boy took their evening repast; but before either herself or
the others were served, she appropriated a portion to the occupant
of the arm-chair, whose wants she appeared sedulously to attend to.

"Is that the master of the house?" inquired Miss Livy.

"Yes," answered the count; "but he's almost childish, and
takes no part in the management of it."

The remainder of the time that elapsed before the ladies retired,
passed dully enough. There was something depressing in the

desolate air of the place, and the imperturbable silence of its inhabitants; for not a sound from any of their lips had yet reached
the travellers. The man still sat gazing at the fire, the boy quietly
cleared away the supper things, and the woman went and came
about her household affairs. The countess appeared languid and
tired; Miss Livy's active mind found little subject for inquiry;
Miss Jemmy was so sleepy she could not keep her eyes open; and
the two gentlemen appeared very much occupied with their own
reflections.

As for Susan, she did not feel in any respect comfortable or
satisfied. She had many reasons for being displeased at their
hasty departure from Paris, and suspicious as to its motive. She
distrusted all she saw and all she heard; and she watched the
motions of the strange silent people, under whose roof they were
to pass the night, with an uneasy feeling of curiosity.

"I think," said the count, at length, "you had better go to
bed. Is the room ready?" he added, addressing the woman, who,
bowing her head in token of assent, immediately lighted a candle,
and stood ready to conduct the ladies.

"As for us," said he, "we must pass the night by the fire here;
for, unluckily, there is but one room in the house, besides what
the people themselves occupy. However, it's but a few hours,
and we shall do very well."

The room to which the woman conducted them was up-stairs,
and like the rest of the house, poorly furnished, but clean. It
contained two beds, each originally designed but for one person;
but on this occasion it was arranged that the countess and Miss
Livy should occupy one, and Miss Jemmy and Susan the other.
After waiting a moment, as if to ascertain if there were any further commands, the woman bowed her head and departed.

The young ladies, whose minds were neither suspicious nor
anxious, undressed and went to bed; where, after a few observations on the coarseness of the sheets, and the inferiority of the
accommodation, they soon fell fast asleep. Susan went to bed
too, and after a time, to sleep; but her mind being less tranquil
than the others, her sleep was less sound. She dreamed uneasy
dreams about her brother and Gaveston, and the strange, silent
woman; then she thought the melancholy-looking man in the
arm-chair was Andrew, and that the count and the colonel were
going to murder him, and that she interfered to save his life.
This crisis woke her, and she opened her eyes. The room appeared
light, although there was no candle burning, and she raised her
head to look at her companions. They appeared in a calm sleep;
and without reflecting whence the light proceeded that enabled
her to see them, she turned round, and tried to go to sleep again.
But before she had sunk into forgetfulness, she was again roused
by a sound that seemed to proceed from beneath the window:
there were voices and wheels—probably some travellers arrived—
then the sound of horses' feet; and at last the smart slam of a
carriage door, the smack of a whip, the wheels rolled away, and

the room was dark. Susan almost involuntarily jumped out of bed and ran to the window. It looked to the front, and there was neither curtain nor blind to impede her view; but all she could discern was two fast-receding lights, evidently the lamps of a carriage. "Travellers stopped to bait their horses," thought she, and once more settling her head on her pillow, she fell into a sound sleep that lasted till morning.

It was near eight o'clock when she awoke, and she arose and dressed herself that she might be ready to assist the ladies. Soon afterwards Miss Jemmy, who was by much the most lively and active of the three, lifted up her head and announced that she was ready to rise and be dressed; and as was her custom, as soon as this ceremony was accomplished, she ran out of the room to see what was going on below; and Susan soon saw her, from the window, amusing herself with some fowls, that were pecking about in the front of the house.

When the ladies were nearly dressed, Miss Livy opened the window, and called to Jemima to request the colonel would give her a certain parcel that he would find in the pocket of the carriage.

"I don't know where he is," replied the child.

"Isn't he in the kitchen?" said Miss Livy.

"No!" answered Jemima; "I've been looking for them, and they're not there. I think they must be gone for a walk."

"Well, then, try and get it yourself," said the countess. "Make somebody open the door for you."

On this injunction the child disappeared, but presently returned, saying that she could not find the carriage, and that she could not make any one understand what she wanted. The article required was therefore dispensed with; and the ladies, having finished their toilet, descended to the kitchen, where they found everything precisely as on the preceding evening. There was a small wood-fire on the hearth; the man in the arm-chair sat gazing at it as if he had never stirred or turned his head since they left him, and the woman was making preparations for their breakfast. The ladies stood before the fire warming themselves—for although it was yet early in the autumn, the mornings were already chilly—and wondering where the gentlemen were; but as they had never yet made any attempt at speaking the language, their two cavaliers having always interpreted for them, and given them no encouragement to acquire it, they were shy of making the inquiry.

When Susan had closed her travelling bags and finished her business up stairs, she descended; and on entering the kitchen, the first thing that struck her eye was the breakfast table. On it were three basins of coffee at one end; and at the other, removed from the rest, there was another basin placed for her, as had been done at the supper the night before; but there appeared no breakfast for the gentlemen. However, it was rather late, and they might have breakfasted already.

When everything was prepared, the woman touched Susan's

arm, and pointed to the table; and then, without explanation or comment, she quitted the room, and busied herself with her other affairs.

"Shall I call Miss Jemima in to breakfast?" inquired Susan.

"Do," answered the ladies; "but isn't it very odd where the gentlemen can be?"

"I'll see if I can find them," said Susan; and after sending in the child, she hastened with some anxiety to see, not exactly if she could find the gentlemen, but if she could find the carriage—but no such thing was visible; neither carriage, horses, nor postillion, could she discover a vestige of.

"Then they're gone!" said she; "and that was the carriage I heard last night! Gone, too, without explanation, or announcing their departure, soon after we left them!" and Susan could not help auguring from this that they had probably no intention of returning.

The carriage, which had been built expressly for the journey, and formed to contain a great deal of luggage, was altogether no despicable prize. There were there, not only the expensive wardrobes of the ladies, but some very valuable jewels, which Mr. Cripps had given his daughter in honour of the high alliance she was contracting; and so low had Susan's opinion of the count and his friend fallen, that she had no difficulty in believing them capable of any stratagem to avoid meeting Mr. Cripps, and to appropriate the property.

However, as this was only her own conjecture, and if correct, the ill news would be known soon enough, she kept her thoughts to herself.

In the meantime, when the breakfast was despatched, the ladies became very impatient to depart; and Jemima, who had more notion of putting a few words together than the others, pulled the woman by the gown, and inquired as well as she could, where the gentlemen were. The hostess looked surprised at the question, but without answering pointed to the east.

"Ask if they'll soon be back," said the countess. But this was an interrogation beyond Jemima's capabilities, and they were therefore obliged to be satisfied without further information.

But the day wore on, and nothing was seen of them; neither did any other travellers arrive to break the mysterious stillness around them. The only voice they heard, besides their own, was that of the boy, who spoke occasionally to the woman, but in a patois that would have been perfectly unintelligible to any stranger. As for the hostess herself, it became pretty evident that she was either dumb, or under a vow of silence, as all her communications were conveyed by signs. Altogether, nothing could be less encouraging than their situation. The man and the boy took no notice of them at all; the woman none beyond serving them their meals, which she did unasked; and though they all watched the road as anxiously as ever did Bluebeard's wife and her sister Ann, they could "not see anybody coming."

U

Jemima played with the fowls and the ducks, and kept up her spirits well enough; but her sisters, overcome by ennui and the weariness of expectation, gave way to their tears. Not that they had any suspicion that they were abandoned. They were too simple, and had been too completely deceived, to entertain any such notion; Susan alone penetrated the truth, and she saw very clearly that with her alone must rest the remedy for their misfortune.

But the difficulties before her were many. In the first place, she was well aware that beyond a few francs there was no money amongst them. The gentlemen had kept that, as well as everything else, in their own hands, and the simple girls scarcely knew the denominations of the coin of the realm. Then, she had not the slightest idea where they were, and she could not conceive any means of ascertaining. She judged that they must have deviated from the high road, because, before arriving at the lonely inn, they had travelled a vast distance without passing through any but the meanest villages; the stages had been very long, and the places where they had changed horses merely posting stations where relays were kept.

Nevertheless, as she was satisfied they were abandoned, and that every chance of escaping from their present disagreeable situation rested with her, she set herself seriously to consider what was to be done, after having allowed a fair interval for the yet possible, but as she considered, very improbable, return of the husband and the lover.

CHAPTER XLV.

SUSAN FINDS HERSELF IN AN UNEXPECTED DILEMMA.

WHEN three days had elapsed, which interval the ladies bestowed in tears, and in watching the road to see if "anybody was coming," Jemima in playing with the ducks and fowls, building towers of stones, and watching the boy in his out-of-door occupations, and Susan in reflection on their situation, and the means of extrication, she ventured for the first time to suggest her suspicions. The countess and Miss Livy were at first indignant at the idea—especially the former, whose husband had hitherto, for ends of his own, behaved very well to her; but Susan's representations, and the lapse of a couple more days, brought them pretty much to her way of thinking; and, utterly unable to act for themselves in such an emergency, they applied to her to decide what was to be done. Too weak to be much affected by the lamentable imposition of which they had been the victims, they mourned their desertion much less than their danger. The loss of the husband and the lover, and the rank and splendour expected to be derived from them, made but little impression; all such regrets were merged in fears for the present, and in anxiety to escape from their dilemma, and find themselves once more in the drawing-room at Virginia House; and to the attainment of this desirable object, they entreated Susan, with tears and clasped hands, to direct the whole of her energies.

"My dear young ladies," said Susan, "it's what I am as anxious to do as you can be, and I have been thinking of nothing else all these days we have been here. But as for any particular danger, I see no cause for fear. If the people here meant to harm us, they might have done it before now. But the thing that puzzles me most, is what we're to do for money; for if we saw an opportunity of getting away, we hav'n't enough, I'm afraid, even to pay what we've had here, much less for the expenses of a journey."

This set them to reckoning the amount of their funds, when it appeared that all they could raise between them was only about thirty livres.

Susan's first proposal was, that they should prepare a couple of letters, one addressed to Virginia House, and the other to Mr. Cripps, addressed to the hotel they had been lodging at in Paris; as, if he came in search of them as he had intimated, it was there, of course, he would inquire, and thus the letter might reach him. But the difficulty was how to forward them when written. During the five days they had been in the house of Monsieur Le Clerc, for such was the name inscribed over the door, they had seen but one stranger, and that was a man who arrived one evening with a large, shaggy-haired dog, and who had disappeared before they came down stairs in the morning: but whence he came, and whither he went, they had no idea. Susan, in fact, wondered how the people contrived to keep the house upon the profits of such scanty custom; and the more she thought of the dumb woman, the silent man, and the odd, half-witted boy—for he appeared little removed from an idiot—the more mysterious she thought their way of life and their means of supporting it.

The only symptom she had observed that indicated there was an inhabited place at hand, was, that on the morning after the man with the dog had been there, the boy was missing, and did not appear again until evening, when he brought home a basket on his arm, containing various articles of provision. Thus she concluded there must be a town, or village, or at least a shop, within such a distance as he could walk, and therefore attainable by her; and she saw no hope for them but in her attempting the enterprise. She might thus, at least, find some means of forwarding the letters, if she could do no more; and even this would be much gained, as she had already explained, as well as she could, to the woman and the boy, that she wanted them conveyed to the post, in the hope that they might direct her which way to find a post town; but they had only shaken their heads, and given her to understand that they knew no means of sending them. She would also, probably, discover where they were, so that their friends might learn

where to seek them : the only direction for that purpose they were
at present able to insert in the letters, being, that they were in an
inn, kept by a Mr. Le Clerc, three days journey from Paris.

But when Susan proposed setting out on this expedition, the
young women were seized with terror at the idea of being left
alone, even for a day, and still more at the possibility which suggested itself of her meeting with some danger or accident which
might prevent her return. She was their whole stay and reliance;
they had just sense enough to perceive that she had more than they
had, and on her they cast their cares. In her, they knew, lay their
whole chance of release; for they might have remained at Mr. Le
Clerc's inn to the day of judgment, before their own energies or
invention would have effected their restoration to their friends :
but like the weak creatures they were, they had not resolution
to encounter the inconvenience of losing her for a day, for the sake
of the ultimate benefit to be derived from her absence. They
imagined themselves surrounded by all manner of perils, from
which her presence alone protected them ; and "what shall we do,
if anything happens while you are gone?" was their constant
answer to her proposal of departure. They would even have preferred accompanying her, and encountering the unknown dangers
of the expedition, to remaining without her; but that was out of
the question, as neither their feet nor their shoes were calculated
for walking, and a couple of miles would have entirely exhausted
their pedestrian capabilities. The only one that agreed to her
proposal was Jemima, who, though but a child of twelve years old,
had a great deal more sense and character than her sisters. She
saw the necessity of it, laughed at their notions of danger, and
when she found that they would not give their consent, she advised
Susan to go without it. "Just set off," she said, "some morning
before they're up, and I'll tell them where you're gone." And
after duly considering the case, Susan resolved to follow her recommendation.

Accordingly, with a few francs in her pocket, the two letters,
and a slice of bread, that she contrived to secure the night before,
Susan started one morning from the solitary inn on her adventurous
journey. She had nothing to guide her as to the direction she
should take ; but recollecting, that on the road they had travelled
over there had been no town for many miles, she resolved to take
the opposite one.

It was about six o'clock, on a fine autumn morning, when she
set forth, her departure exciting no observation on the part of the
hostess, as she had made a practice of walking out before the
ladies were up, in the hope of effecting some discovery in the
neighbourhood that might be useful. For several hours she
trudged along the road without meeting a single human being;
and she judged that she must have gone over at least ten miles,
when feeling tired, and observing a fine clear spring of water
gushing from the bank, she sat down to rest, and refresh herself
with a draught of the cool element and her bit of bread.

Whilst she was yet sitting, she observed two figures approaching, not by the road, but across the common, immediately in front
of her, where there was no apparent path. At first she thought it
was a man and a child, but as they drew nearer she saw it was a
man with a large dog; and ere long, she discerned that it was the
very man and dog that she had seen at the inn some evenings
before.

When he arrived within a few yards he seemed also to recognise her, and advancing straight towards where she was sitting,
he said a few words in French, to which, not comprehending them,
she could only respond by shaking her head. He then pointed in
the direction of the inn, and mentioned the name of Le Clerc,
which she interpreted into an inquiry whether she was not living
there, and she therefore nodded in sign of assent; upon which he
took off one of his shoes, lifted up the inner sole, and taking out a
letter, handed it to her, pointing again towards the inn, and saying
something which she construed into a request that she would convey it there; and perceiving that it was actually addressed to
Madame Le Clerc, she testified her readiness to undertake the
commission.

The man upon this gave her to understand that he was obliged;
offered her a drink from a flask he carried in his pocket, which, on
tasting, she found was brandy; and then, whistling to his dog, he
turned round, and retraced his steps across the common; whilst
presently afterwards Susan resumed her journey.

She had walked nearly a couple of hours more, and was beginning to get a good deal alarmed at the space she was placing
between herself and the unfortunate girls she had left behind,
fearing that if she went much further she should find it impossible
to return that night, when she was cheered by the sight of a town
at no great distance. A pretty considerable one, too, it appeared;
and she stept forwards with a lightened heart, thinking that if she
derived no other advantages from her expedition, there was every
probability of her finding the means of forwarding her letters.
Some little way in advance, however, between her and the town
she was making for, there stood a single small house by the road
side, round the door of which she saw lounging several men; some
in uniform, apparently soldiers, and others in plain clothes.

"Stop!" cried one of them, as she was about to pass on—
"Where are you going?"

Susan, who was utterly ignorant of custom-houses, and barriers,
and passports, and the precautions used at particular times and
places on frontier towns on the continent, imagined, from the man's
insolent tone of voice and evident design of impeding her progress, that he intended to insult her; and instead of stopping, she
quickened her pace, and endeavoured to avoid him.

"Stop!" he cried again in a loud voice, as she slipt past him;
"stop, or I'll make you;" whilst a roar of laughter amongst the
lookers-on testified their diversion; when Susan, alarmed at the
augmented violence of his manner, and never doubting but some

insult was designed, converted her walk into a run, and fairly took to her heels. But her efforts to escape were vain. She soon felt her arm in the rough gripe of the angry soldier; and then apprehending resistance would only make matters worse, she quietly suffered herself to be led back to the guard-house; volleys of oaths and abuse being showered on her on the way, which, however, she had the happiness not to comprehend.

Next followed a series of interrogations, addressed to her in an angry tone, to all of which she could only answer by a silent shake of the head, being utterly ignorant of their purport, and of the nature of her offence.

"Come!" cried the man, with increased irritation, and forcing her at the same time into the house, a measure which she thought so suspicious, that she opposed it with all her strength, "Come, let us see what you've got about you."

Exceedingly alarmed, and her imagination running quite astray as to their intentions, Susan wept and entreated as they conducted her into a back room of the guard-house; and when, with a rudeness approaching to brutality, they proceeded to search her person, she resisted their efforts to lay hands on her with all the strength she could exert.

But her opposition availed nothing, except to augment their violence; and they speedily extracted the contents of her pockets, to the examination of which they had first directed their attention, and amongst them drew forth the two English letters, and also the one she had undertaken to deliver to Madame Le Clerc.

On perceiving the address of the latter there was an evident sensation amongst the men; they turned it all ways, peeped through it, endeavouring to make out something of its contents, and appeared to hold a consultation whether or not they should open it; a question, however, which seemed to be ultimately decided in the negative.

Gradually, Susan's first apprehensions subsided. She comprehended that they were searching her person for some purpose or other, and she regretted exceedingly that she was unable to understand or answer the interrogations they continued to put to her; more especially as she perceived that considerable importance was attached to the letter they had found upon her, and she would have been happy to explain in what manner it had fallen into her hands. But unfortunately this was impossible; and all she could do was to await the unravelling of the mystery in silence, and with what patience she could. With respect to the last, indeed, it appeared likely enough to be called into exercise; for when their search was over, instead of restoring the letters and setting her free, they locked her in the room by herself, and carried the papers away with them.

Unconscious of evil, and concluding that ere long she would be released, Susan, as regarded herself, would have felt no great uneasiness, nor perhaps considered her situation much worse than it was before; but when she thought of the helpless creatures she had left behind her, and the alarm they would feel if she did not return by night, she was seriously distressed at the obstruction thus placed in her way, and the delay it would occasion.

After enduring a confinement of a couple of hours, during which time she heard, by the clatter of knives and forks and plates, that the guards were at dinner, the door was opened; and being summoned forth, she was given to understand that she was to accompany two of them to the town, a proposal to which she was far from objecting; and they therefore set out immediately at a brisk pace, one walking on each side of her.

After some conversation between her guards and others that were stationed at the gate, she was conducted through the streets to the Court-house, where a great many people were assembled, whose attention appeared to be engaged by some matter of public interest. Making their way through the crowd, the men that had charge of her led her into an anteroom, where, mingled with soldiers and police-officers, were several persons, some of whom seemed, like herself, to have been brought there not wholly by their own consent. The latter were mostly seated on wooden benches that were placed against the wall; and on one of these she also was invited to rest herself. There was a constant hum and buzz of conversation amongst the officers on the one hand, and amongst the questionable-looking people on the other; and some observations were addressed to her, which, however, finding she only answered by a shake of the head, were soon discontinued. So she sat quietly watching the scene before her, wondering at the singularity of her own situation, and lamenting over the alarm of the poor helpless girls she had left behind her at the inn. Occasionally, the scene was varied by the opening of a pair of large folding-doors at one end of the room, and the appearance of some persons from an inner apartment, or by some of those who were in the outer being called in; but Susan's astonishment may be imagined, when on one of these occasions, a sudden rush of several people through the doors having awakened her attention, she lifted up her head, and beheld, first the count, and secondly the colonel, each surrounded by guards, and evidently in custody; and presently afterwards a second rush, when there came out, attended by several gentlemen, apparently of distinction, a very beautiful and elegant person, attired in deep mourning, and seemingly in great distress, in whom, at the first glance, she recognised *Mabel, the dairy-maid*.

The first party she only followed with her eyes as they were conducted through the room; but when the second appeared, thrown off her guard by the surprise, and her anxious wish not to lose the opportunity she had so long eagerly desired, she suddenly started to her feet, and made an effort to follow them. But ere she had advanced two steps, a sturdy arm arrested her progress, and she found herself forced back into her seat, with a stern command to be quiet, and not create a disturbance; whilst the brilliant company passed on, and disappeared through the door at the other end.

Her thoughts wholly abstracted from her own situation by this unexpected vision, unconscious of the lapse of time, and indifferent to all that surrounded her, even to her own detention, except inasmuch as it prevented her following Mabel, Susan sat for some time longer, whilst several of those about her, having been summoned into the inner apartment, got their business settled, and departed, either freely or otherwise, as it might happen.

In the meantime the hours advanced; evening was drawing on; and, at length, the folding-doors were again thrown open, and the contents of the inner room, amongst whom appeared magistrates, officers, and other persons in authority, pouring out, announced that the business of the day was over.

A certain number of Susan's companions then departed at their leisure; but others, and amongst them she herself, were led away by the guards that had charge of them, and being conducted to a place of confinement near at hand, were locked up.

CHAPTER XLVI.

TWO PERSONAGES APPEAR ON THE SCENE WHOM THE READER WILL
RECOGNISE AS OLD ACQUAINTANCE.

ON the following morning Susan was again conducted to the court-house, and in her turn was introduced into the inner apartment, and placed before the magistrates, accompanied by the guards who had brought her there.

"Who is this woman?" said the magistrate.

"We believe her to be Julia Le Clerc," replied the serjeant.

"Does she admit that she is that person?" said the magistrate.

"She is dumb, your worship," answered the serjeant.

"And deaf?" inquired the magistrate.

"No, not deaf," answered the other. "She is said to have lost her speech from fright many years ago."

"What is your name?" inquired the magistrate of Susan.

But Susan remained silent, for as the whole dialogue was conducted in French, she comprehended nothing that was going on.

"Can you write?" said the magistrate.

Susan shook her head in token that she did not understand the question.

"She can't write," said the magistrate. "How are we to interrogate a person who can neither write nor speak? On what charge have you brought her here?"

"Her house, as your worship knows," replied the serjeant, "is a well-known resort for smugglers; and we have been long on the look-out to get some proof against them."

"And have you any?" inquired the magistrate.

"Not exactly," answered the serjeant. "But yesterday we

caught her endeavouring to slip past the barrier, and she made violent resistance when we attempted to search her person."

"That's suspicious, certainly," observed the magistrate. "And what did you find?"

"Here are the contents of her pockets," replied the man, "consisting of three letters, five francs, a pocket-handkerchief, and a small box, containing an English half-crown and two shirt studs."

"But there's nothing criminal in that," said the magistrate.

"No," answered the serjeant; "but her coming into the town at this particular period is of itself suspicious, as she has never been seen here before. It is probable that she wished to find some means of communicating with the prisoners."

"Very likely," answered the magistrate, whose head appeared rather a recipient for other people's ideas than a magazine of his own.

"Perhaps the letters may throw some light on her designs," said the clerk.

"I shouldn't wonder," replied the magistrate; "hand them up. ' A Monsieur Creeps en Angleterre,'" said he, reading the address of the first.—"' A Monsieur Creeps à Paris,'" turning to the second. "And another to ' Madame Le Clerc ;' come, we'll take a peep at the inside of this one!" and thereupon, throwing aside the two first, he broke the seal of the third, and read as follows:—

"Madame,—This is to inform you that I have at length discovered the persons you have so long desired to find. I have been on their track for some time, but circumstances were unfavourable. Your intelligence was in all respects correct. They are free traders on the coast, and will be willing to undertake any business you propose, on satisfactory terms. They are inseparable, and undertake nothing but in concert. They will arrive at your house shortly after the receipt of this, which I send by Jacques Ménin.—Yours to command, LOUIS GROS."

"That's odd," said the magistrate. "I don't very well understand it."

"One thing in it is evident," observed the clerk; "these men are wanted to carry on some illicit traffic."

"That's clear, certainly," said the magistrate; "what shall we do with her, Drouet?"

"Detain her, I should recommend," said Drouet; "at least, for the present, and set a trap for the villains she expects. But suppose we see the contents of the other letters."

"Ah!" said the magistrate, when he had opened them, "they're in English, Drouet, which I don't comprehend; but it appears to me they're of no importance. They're signed "Leevy Creeps,' and seem to be addressed from a child to her papa: see, there is the word *papa* legible enough."

"Letters she has been entrusted to put in the post, probably," said the clerk, throwing them aside.

"Take her away," said the magistrate, and bring up somebody

else. We'll consider what's to be done with her by and bye." And Susan was accordingly led back to her previous place of confinement, and again locked up.

In the meantime, when the two ladies arose on the preceding day, and learnt from Jemima that Susan had already been gone some hours, they were seized with dismay at the idea of being left at the mercy of the fearful dumb woman, who was to them an object of the greatest terror. Every danger, possible and impossible, presented itself to their imaginations; they proclaimed their conviction that she would never return; or that, if she did, they should never live to see it, as, doubtless, the hostess would take advantage of the opportunity to rob and murder them: and the day was passed in tears and lamentations, which, as the hours drew on without any signs of her reappearance, became more and more violent. Jemima, on the contrary, passed the day in her usual amusements, and neither participated in their fears nor their distrust. She had as much confidence in Susan as they had; but, young as she was, she was a much more reasonable being. She had no doubt that she would return the moment she had effected the object she went for; and she entertained no apprehensions of the dumb woman, because she knew that Susan entertained none; and that, if she had, she would not have gone away and left them at her mercy. "Perhaps it's a great way to a post-office," said the child to her weeping sisters, when, as the night approached, their terrors became every moment more uncontrollable. "She said she would return this evening, if possible; but that we were not to be frightened if she didn't, as she couldn't tell how far she might have to go. I'm sure if Susan thought Mrs. Le Clerc would hurt us, she wouldn't have gone at all."

"How can Susan tell what Mrs. Le Clerc means to do?" said the countess. "I heard her say herself, when first we came, that she thought the woman had a very bad countenance."

"But if she wanted to hurt us, she might have done it when Susan was here," answered Jemima. "How could she have helped it? She's not a man to fight for us."

"Hold your tongue, Jemmy," said Miss Livy; "you're only a child, and don't know anything about it."

"Oh, yes, I do," said Jemima. "I know what Susan told me, and she said there was no danger, and that she'd come back as soon as she could;" and away she ran to see Rauque, the boy, feed the chickens.

At her usual hour Jemima went to bed; but the other two, having barricaded their room-door as well as they could, only lay down in their clothes, agreeing that one should sleep whilst the other watched; but terror kept them both awake, and they passed the weary night in fancying they heard stealthy footsteps approaching the door, or low whisperings outside of it, or a hand softly trying the lock; and, in short, in imagining all those mysterious and fearful tokens that presage the approach of danger.

However, the morning dawned, and found them alive, but not

relieved. They were still confident that Susan would never return; whilst Jemima, who had slept the sound and healthy sleep of childhood, awoke gay and refreshed, and as confident as ever that she would.

The hostess, who from the moment of their arrival had always appeared extremely indifferent to their presence, and little curious about their proceedings, serving them their meals at stated hours, and performing requisite services unasked, but lavishing on them not a grain of extra civility or attention, nevertheless seemed to feel some surprise at Susan's disappearance. She placed her cover, as usual, at breakfast, dinner, and supper, and was evidently perplexed that she was not forthcoming. She interrogated Rauque on the subject, with whom she was in the habit of communicating by the finger alphabet used by dumb people; but he shook his head, and declared he knew nothing about it. This very curiosity on her part, rational as it was, served only to augment the terror of her lodgers. They observed her eyes fixed on them whenever they happened to look towards her, and fearful eyes they were, certainly—bright, black, fierce, and suspicious; and they persuaded themselves that she was watching their movements.

"I'm sure," said Caroline to her sister, after they had eaten their breakfast, "that we should be safer anywhere than here; and I wouldn't pass such another night as the last for anything in the world. Suppose we go out as if we meant to take a walk, and see if we can't find some house, or somebody that would protect us. Perhaps, if Susan's coming back we may meet her; and if she don't come back, I'm sure I'd rather run any risk than remain in the power of this horrid woman."

Livia willingly acceded to the proposal; all she feared was, that the hostess would lay violent hands upon them, and confine them to the house; but Jemima objected; urging, that if Susan returned during their absence she would be seriously alarmed. But this argument had no weight with the sisters. Susan's alarm they represented couldn't equal theirs; she had a great deal more courage, and was better able to take care of herself; besides, the woman wouldn't think it worth while to hurt her: in short, they were resolved to go, whether Jemima accompanied them or not.

"Perhaps she'll be less likely to stop us if we leave Jemima," suggested Caroline. "She'd think we're coming back. Besides, she'll never think of hurting such a child as that."

"And she likes her better than she likes us," observed Livy. "She always gives her the best of everything; and the other day when her feet were wet, she would change her shoes and stockings for her."

"And then when we reach any place of safety or get to Paris, we can easily send for Jemmy," said Caroline; "and as she's not frightened, it's no hardship to her to stay behind."

"And as we've got so little money, it will be better not to be too many; it will last longer for two than for three."

So "laying this flattering unction to their" selfish " souls," they
arrayed themselves in their bonnets and shawls, and with an air of
as much indifference as they could assume, walked out; having the
satisfaction to find that the hostess made no effort to impede their
intentions, nor seemed to entertain any suspicion that they were
taking their final departure. As the road they had come in the
carriage was the one that led to Paris, they turned their steps in
that direction; and having sauntered on in a careless manner as
long as they were near the house, lest the hostess should be watching them, as soon as they were out of sight they accelerated their
pace, and advanced over the ground with as much speed as their
ill-exercised limbs permitted.

In the meantime, as the day advanced, the little girl became extremely anxious for the return of Susan; not that she was alarmed
for herself, but because she wearied without her, having no one to
speak to; and because she feared Susan might have met with some
accident.

When the dinner was served, and no one appeared to eat it but
the child, the woman seemed extremely surprised, and inquired of
her by signs, as well as she could, what had become of the rest of
the party. Jemima, who had picked up so much French as to know
that *marcher* meant to walk, pronounced that word; upon which
the hostess patted her kindly on the cheek, and invited her to eat,
at the same time setting by the dinner of the other two to be kept
till their return. But when the evening arrived without anything
being seen of them, her astonishment was evidently considerable,
and seemed to be accompanied by some uneasiness. She talked
a great deal to Rauque with her fingers, and apparently sent him
in search of them, as he went out and was absent for some time.
He returned, however, shaking his head, and giving her to understand he brought no intelligence. Still her surprise and anxiety
did not by any means take the form of displeasure to Jemima.
On the contrary, she treated her with a degree of kindness and
attention she had never done before; for, hitherto, whatever sen-
sibility her soul seemed capable of, appeared to be solely reserved
for the helpless being in the arm-chair. His wants and comforts
were never neglected; his meals were regularly prepared and
placed before him, ere anybody else was served; the fire was
maintained the greatest part of the day merely with a view to his
convenience, and she carefully moved his chair nearer or farther
from it as the temperature of the room directed; and at a certain
hour she always lighted a candle, and assisted him out of the room
to his bed.

It was this singular devotion that had so far redeemed her in
Susan's eyes, as to counterbalance in a great degree the unpro-
mising expression of her countenance, and the mystery that seemed
to hang about her. She could not help judging mercifully of a
woman who was capable of such a devoted and constant affection
to one, who, whatever he might formerly have been, was certainly

now only an object of pity; and Jemima had intelligence and natural tact enough to be inspired with confidence from the same source. Thus she received Madame Le Clerc's little advances with cheerfulness and good-humour, and although she wished very much for Susan's return, she was under no apprehensions for her own safety. When the child's usual hour for retiring arrived, the hostess attended her up stairs, saw her comfortably laid in bed, and as she patted her cheek when she left the room, there was a relaxation of the white compressed lips that almost amounted to a smile, where smiles for many a long year had never beamed. The next day passed as this, without events; nothing was seen of the sisters, nor of Susan. Jemima began really to fear something had happened to her, and she would have been very much relieved if she could have expressed her apprehensions to Madame Le Clerc in words; but that was impossible. All she could do, she did; she took hold of her hand and looked in her face with an expression of anxiety; and the dumb woman patted her head encouragingly, made the same feeble approach to a smile she had done the night before; and on one occasion, went so far as to take her head in her hands and kiss her forehead.

It was on the evening of the day after the sisters' departure that the four inhabitants of the lonely inn, the man, the woman, Rauque, and Jemima, were assembled in the kitchen at rather an earlier hour than usual. The afternoon had been wet and cold; the child had been driven in from her out-door amusements, and Rauque from his occupations; the fire was fed with an additional log, the old man's chair pushed close to the chimney corner, and Madame Le Clerc, seeing Jemima was in want of amusement, had given her a large hank of blue worsted, and asked her, by signs, if she would wind it for her.

Altogether, there was an air of comfort in the apartment that might have deceived a stranger into the belief that it was the abode of cheerful contentment: the fire blazed, the invalid watched the flickering flames, Rauque cut out wooden pegs for fastening the linen on the drying lines, Madame Le Clerc was employed with her knitting-needles, and Jemima in winding the worsted. All at once, the sound of heavy feet was heard at the outer door: all lifted up their heads, except the man, in whom it appeared to excite no attention. Madame Le Clerc and Rauque rose, and the latter went out to open the door; whilst Jemima, letting the ball of worsted roll from her lap, anxiously watched to see whether it was Susan, or her sisters, or their perfidious seducers, that had returned.

It was neither of them. Rauque entered the room preceding two men, who would neither of them have been very remarkable alone, but who were remarkable from their singular resemblance of air, manner, and dress. They were, as nearly as possible, of the same age, height, and complexion, the latter being extremely dark by nature and become more so by exposure to the weather; the hair of both was for the most part grey, a few black ones here and there remaining to show what it had been; they wore broad oil-skin hats, and were coarsely attired as sailors.

They advanced towards Madame Le Clerc with a salutation somewhat more polished than might have been expected from their appearance; and Jemima, who was observing the scene, looked up at her to see how she returned it. But she did not return it—she was standing like a person transfixed, with her face the colour of marble, and her eyes glaring on the men with an expression that inspired even the child with terror. Gradually, this fixed and ghastly expression relaxed, the usually compressed lips parted, and a smile succeeded—an unnatural and fearful smile, which denoted neither pleasure nor benignity, but which, accompanied as it was by the still vengeful glare of the eye, and the malignant extension of the nostrils, rather resembled the grin of an hyena, than a token of satisfaction.

Both expressions, however, were transitory; a moment or two, and the face of the hostess had resumed its usual appearance; except that it continued, perhaps, paler than before, and that a sterner resolution than common sat upon the brow. She seemed, too, to feel that she had not received her guests well; and she endeavoured to make amends for her inhospitality by an extraordinary degree of assiduity. She stirred the fire into a brighter blaze, drew a bench close to it, and, with remarkable alacrity, placed a table with refreshments and liquors before them; whilst the men, who seemed nothing loath, lost no time in availing themselves of the entertainment prepared for them.

A few words, remarking on the state of the weather and the season, formed all the discourse that accompanied the meal; but when they had done eating, and filled their glasses, the visitors seemed disposed for further communication.

"Ah," said one of them, "it's singular to be dumb and not deaf."

"Those things arise from illness occasionally," answered the other; "sometimes from a fever."

Here Madame Le Clerc, who heard what they were saying, looked up from her knitting, which she had resumed, and appeared, by her eyes, to take part in the conversation. "Has she been dumb from her birth?" asked the first man of Rauque, who was removing the supper things from the table.

At this question Madame Le Clerc touched Rauque on the arm, and drew his attention to herself before he had time to answer; "Tell them," said she, "that I lost my speech in a fright at sea, when I was like to be drowned;" and Rauque did as he was desired.

"That's likely enough," observed one of the men to the other. "You know it was said Julie Le Moine lost hers from the fright."

"No doubt she did, for some time," replied the other; "her evidence was given in writing. But I think she recovered it; it was only temporary, I fancy. Somebody cured her in England, where she went to reside with her husband."

"Well," said the first, "I think we'd better proceed to business, and learn what's required of us. Doubtless, madame," continued he, addressing the hostess, who, although she appeared to be engaged with her knitting, was lending an attentive ear to their discourse, "doubtless you have been expecting us, and it is needless to say who we are, or what has brought us here?"

"I presume," answered Madame Le Clerc, through Rauque's interpretation, "that I see before me the brave foster-brothers of Nantes, whose deeds are celebrated along the whole coast from Calais to Brest?"

"Precisely," answered one of them; "we are the two Rodolphes of Nantes, at your service; and are here ready to undertake any enterprise likely to be beneficial to ourselves and our friends."

"You have been wanted here for some time," replied Madame Le Clerc. "The fact is, we want an entire change of tactics, a wholly new organization. Everything's known, or at least suspected; and if it wasn't for the dogs, we shouldn't pass twenty louis' worth of lace in a month. You must be doubtless sensible of the difference yourselves. You must get much less to transport than you used?"

"Trade languishes, certainly," replied one of the men, "and we shall be willing to do our utmost to regenerate it. But we understood it was for some specific purpose you had desired to see us?"

"It was," replied Madame Le Clerc, "one I have long desired to accomplish;" and as Rauque interpreted her words, she fixed her eyes with a peculiar meaning on the two strangers.

"And what is it?" inquired the men.

"That," she replied, nodding significantly, "you will learn by and by; but you must receive the communication from myself. In the meantime, drink and be welcome."

The visitors were by no means slow to accept the invitation; and appearing content to wait her own convenience for the explanation she promised, they turned the conversation into another channel.

"This is an awkward affair," they observed, "that has just occurred; and had we heard of it before we reached this neighbourhood, we should have deferred our visit; for it sets the country on the alert, and makes travelling difficult."

"What is it?" inquired Madame Le Clerc.

"Is it possible you are not aware of it?" said they.

"I have heard of nothing," answered she; "we have had nobody here this week. The last was Jacques Ménin, and I expected him again yesterday, but he didn't come."

"Probably prevented by the circumstance we allude to," replied one of the visitors. "Listen: it appears there have been two men—interlopers—not belonging to us—who have been attempting something on a great scale—with a carriage and four

—provided with passports, too—passing for foreigners—they are,
indeed, proved to be English—they had been to Malines, Brussels,
and other places, and were on their return, well charged; the
whole inside of the carriage, which was English built, and therefore the less suspected, had a false lining—capitally done, they
say—never would have been discovered; in short, when they
passed through into Flanders about ten days ago, they were
taken for persons of the highest distinction, as their passports
represented,—it is supposed they transported goods to an immense
value on that occasion. Well, all went well till they got near
Lisle on their return—then fortune changed!—about five miles on
the other side of the barrier, they met three persons on horseback, a gentleman and lady, followed by a groom. The gentleman
was the Duke de Rochechouart, who, it appears, knew them both
—one, indeed, had been his own servant; and the other he had
become acquainted with in some unpleasant transaction—what it
was didn't transpire—however, the parties recognised each other.
It appears, that for some reason or other, the duke wished to have
some communication with them, and he desired his groom to
follow them into the town and observe where they put up. Probably they misunderstood the manœuvre, and fancied their enterprise was suspected; however that may be, when they perceived
that the man persisted in following them, they shot him dead on
the spot. The duke, on hearing the shot, galloped up to see what
was the matter, and a second pistol stretched him on the earth
beside his servant. In short, they were both killed. The postillions
then turned the horses' heads, put them into a gallop, and they
fled for their lives. A little more, and they had reached the
frontier; but the lady was at their heels—just in time they met a
troop of cavalry—she cried to them to stop the murderers—they
did so—they were turned back again and brought into Lisle, where
the lady—the duchess I suppose she is, gives evidence against
them. The whole town is in commotion—the duke was there
with his regiment, and very much beloved."

"I know the men perfectly," replied Madame Le Clerc, who had
listened to the narration with great interest: "they stopped here
on their way, and the child you see there belongs to them; and,
in short, I have goods of value of theirs now in my hands, which
we want your aid in transporting across the channel. You shall
see them by and by. You didn't come through Lisle?"

"No, no," replied one of the Rodolphes; "we never pass
through gates when we can keep on the outside of them. But
who are these men? Have you known them long?"

"They have been here two or three times before," answered the
hostess. "The first time I saw them was several years ago; they
had then not only passports, but a letter of recommendation to
the authorities, from this very Duke of Rochechouart, whom one
of them had found means of obliging. They have never attempted
anything but under the most favourable circumstances, and have,
hitherto, been very successful."

CHAPTER XLVII.

A DOMICILIARY VISIT.

ON the morning after the appearance of the two Rodolphes, as
described in the last chapter, the quiet of the inhabitants of the
lowly inn was disturbed at an early hour by the arrival of a party
of police from Lisle, who, entering the house with considerable
bluster and noise, announced that they were come in search of
the two men who had arrived there on the preceding evening.

"They are gone," replied the hostess, through the interpretation
of Rauque. "They departed with the dawn of light."

"That is not true," replied the chief of the party; "we know
that they are still on the premises."

"You are mistaken," answered Madame Le Clerc; "you will
not find them here."

"We'll try, however," returned the officer. "Do you remain
here," continued he to one of his party, "and let no one leave the
room while we search the house. We shall find them concealed
somewhere, I have no doubt."

A rigorous search was then instituted; every part of the house
was examined; every bed turned down, and looked under; every
closet opened; and the outhouses and stables were visited with the
same strictness; but the men were not forthcoming. In short, the
officers were beginning to be shaken in their convictions, notwithstanding that those who had been employed as spies, and had
watched the men into the house, positively affirmed that they had
never left it. They returned to the kitchen, however, without
having found the slightest trace of the persons in question. Rauque
was interrogated, and an attempt was made to interrogate Jemima
and the invalid in the arm-chair. Jemima, they soon found, did
not understand them; and as for Monsieur Le Clerc, all their
efforts were vain to rouse his attention sufficiently to extract any
information from him. Though he was very deaf, his ears were
by no means impervious to sound; and although his organs of
speech were in a great degree paralysed, and very rarely exercised,
they would have been yet available, if his memory had served him
sufficiently to put a sentence together. But it did not; and
neither were his powers of attention equal to taking in the scope
of a question. He would turn his head to the speaker, and appear
to listen to the first word or two, when an effort had been made to
rouse him; but before a sentence could be completed, the mind
had sunk again into forgetfulness, the eyes were again fixed on the
sole object of his attention, the fire on the hearth; and a repetition
of the experiment, how often soever made, invariably led but to
the same result.

As for Rauque, he declared he knew nothing about the men.
He said, "that when he went to bed on the preceding evening, he

X

left them with Madame Le Clerc in the kitchen, and that when he rose in the morning they were gone."

"Since this is the case," said the officer, "you must accompany us into the town, to be examined by the magistrates, and the hostess must go with us also. For this poor invalid, it appears useless to disturb him."

"Tell them," said Madame Le Clerc to Rauque, "that he cannot be left. Where I go, he must go. Who is to feed him, and give him a fire, and put him to bed? They wouldn't leave a child in the cradle; neither must he be left who is as helpless."

"But we have not the means of transporting him," answered the officer. "He can't walk, I suppose?"

"If our going is inevitable," said Madame Le Clerc, "you can attach one of your horses to the cart that's in the shed; it will serve to take us that far."

"And this child," said he, "who is she? She must accompany us, too."

"She's an English girl," answered Madame Le Clerc, "left here for a few days by some travellers, who will probably return shortly in search of her."

The cart was then drawn from the shed, a horse of one of the officers selected to draw it, and arrangements were made for the departure of the whole party, with the exception of two, who were to stay behind and watch the house.

Whilst this was doing, Madame Le Clerc, who saw there was no alternative and that opposition would be vain, busied herself in preparing her husband for the journey, and also gave Jemima to understand that she must accompany them; and the child, who was getting heartily weary of her situation, now that Susan and her sisters were gone, rejoiced in the prospect of a change.

When all was ready, and they were about to leave the house, the men asked Rauque for something to drink before starting; upon which he proceeded to a small cupboard, which opened by a sliding panel in the wainscot, where the liquors were kept.

"That is a place we overlooked," observed the officer; "but it is too small to conceal a man."

"It is," answered another, who was putting his head into the cupboard, and examining it; "it's full of bottles—ha, ha! good brandy—no doubt capital; it's in these places one gets it good. But let's see—what have we here?" and he drew out two small knapsacks, with straps attached to them, and inscribed with initials; R. B. on one, and R. G. on the other. They each contained a blue checked shirt, a couple of pairs of stockings, and one or two other small articles.

"Those knapsacks belong to the men we're in search of," said the officer to Rauque.

"That may be," answered Rauque.

"May be?" replied the officer; "you know it is so."

"I don't say to the contrary," returned Rauque.

"But do you admit that they do?" persisted the man.

"It's extremely possible," returned Rauque.

"But I say it's not only possible, but true," said the officer.

"Very likely," answered Rauque.

"But you wont admit it?" said the officer.

"I don't deny it," said Rauque; "doubtless you know better than I do."

At this point of the conversation Madame Le Clerc, who had been out of the room preparing for her departure, returned, and was asked if the knapsacks didn't belong to the men in question.

"Undoubtedly," she replied; "but they went away this morning without them; probably intending to return shortly."

The officers shook their heads incredulously—they even went over the house again, and examined it, if possible, more closely than before, but with no better success; and finding further delay unavailing, they placed Madame Le Clerc, her husband, Jemima, and Rauque in the cart, and started for Lisle.

When they arrived there, and were produced before the magistrate, there was some surprise created at the appearance of a second dumb woman; who was, however, easily identified as the real Madame Le Clerc, both by her own admission, and the testimony of others.

"That other person has been detained under an error, then," observed the magistrate; "she must be released immediately."

With respect to the men, Madame Le Clerc and Rauque, when interrogated, persisted in the same account they had given before. They admitted freely that they were the two Rodolphes of Nantes, the notorious foster-brothers, by which name they were known all over the kingdom; and she admitted, also, that she had employed people to invite them to visit her house. But she affirmed that they had left it early in the morning; and Rauque declared that he had neither seen nor heard anything of them since he went to bed on the preceding evening; while the officers who had been employed to watch them, as positively asserted that they had assuredly never left the premises.

Being informed that Jemima was an English child left at the inn by some travellers, who would return and claim her, which was either all Madame Le Clerc knew, or all she chose to say, a person was sent for who could speak a little English, and she also was interrogated about the men; but her account coincided with Rauque's: she had left them in the kitchen when she went to bed, and had not seen them since.

"Ask her if it's true that she was left at the inn by her friends," said the magistrate.

"Yes," answered Jemima.

"And do you expect them to return?"

"Yes," replied the child, who, forward as she was, was both abashed and frightened at the forms and ceremonies of a judicial interrogation; the more as, not comprehending any of the previous inquiry, she did not know what it all meant.

"What's your name?" said the interpreter.

x 2

"Jemima," answered she; which being a name entirely unfamiliar to French ears, was conceived at once to be a specimen of
the barbarous and unpronounceable English surnames.

As nothing further could be elicited with respect to the foster-
brothers—about whom some information had been received which
rendered their capture desirable; especially just now, when the
death of the Duke de Rochechouart, and the discovery of the real
character of the travellers in the English barouche, had set the
world on the alert, and had shaken some of the officials in their
seats, who expected nothing less than a sharp reprimand, if no
worse, from the higher powers—the Le Clercs and Rauque were
remanded for the present, and placed in confinement; whilst
Jemima, at the recommendation of the magistrate, was lodged
with a respectable person, to be taken care of till her friends
claimed her.

Whilst this scene was acting in the court-house, Susan, whose
natural philosophy had enabled her to endure her detention with
more patience than might have been expected, all at once found
herself set free, and turned into the street with as little ceremony
as she had been captured; "Go, you are free," being all the explanation offered on the subject.

If she had had the means of expressing herself, and had known
who to apply to, she would, before she left the town, have sought
some information about Mabel; but the difficulties that stood in
her way, from her ignorance in both respects, and her impatience
to return to the young people at the inn, whom she considered
wholly under her protection, and whose terrors at her absence
she easily comprehended, induced her to set forth on her way
back, the moment she was released. Added to which, there was
barely time for her to perform the journey on foot before dark,
and she neither liked the thoughts of being benighted on the road,
nor of seeking a lodging in the town.

"When once all this trouble is over, and we have got back to
Paris or to England," said she to herself, "I shall easily find the
means of learning all I want about Mabel. I'll go to Mr. Simpson, and tell him who I am, and all about it; and as she must be
well known here, no doubt he'll be able to discover her." And
staying the appetite of her impatience and curiosity by this resolution, she started on her way back to the inn.

CHAPTER XLVIII.

MR. OLLIPHANT RECEIVES AN UNEXPECTED VISIT FROM ISAAC LECKY,
THE JEW.

ONE morning, whilst Mr. Olliphant was engaged in his office,
he was informed that a person desired to speak with him on particular business; and on repairing to his private room, in obedience

to the summons, he was surprised to see his old acquaintance, Isaac Lecky, the Jew.

"How now, Mr. Lecky," said he; "do you want a little Christian law to settle the difference betwixt you and some of your tribe? Can't you get on upon the old rule of an eye for an eye, and a tooth for a tooth?"

"Ah, Mr. Olliphant, sir," replied Isaac, "we poor Jews are scoffed and scorned; but sometimes we do you Christians good service for all that."

"That's when there's more to be got by serving us than cheating us, Isaac," answered Mr. Olliphant. "But sit down; what's your business now?" And Isaac seated himself in his old attitude, with his hands tightly packed between his knees, which were inclined inwards to hold them fast.

"Well, Mr. Olliphant, sir," said Isaac, "my business regards a bit of parchment, that has somehow or other fallen into the hands of a friend of mine—indeed, I can't say that he's much of a friend either—just an acquaintance—a person I know to speak to, when we meet at the synagogue."

"Well, but the parchment!" said Mr. Olliphant. "What about that?"

"Well, sir, as I was observing," continued Mr. Lecky, "there's a bit of parchment fallen into his hands that, I take it, may contain something of more value than the skin—at least, if the right parties could get hold of it."

"What is it?—a deed?" inquired the lawyer.

"It is a deed," answered Isaac.

"What sort of a deed? a settlement? a will?"

"It's a will," said the Jew.

"Probably some old copy of a will of no value," said Mr. Olliphant.

"It's attested," said Isaac; "signed and witnessed in due form."

"Still it may have been but a duplicate copy," said Mr. Olliphant. "What makes you think it's of value?"

"I have my own reasons for thinking that," answered the Jew.

"I should like to hear them," said Mr. Olliphant.

"Well, sir," said Isaac, "the truth is, that a person has been inquiring for it."

"The right owner?" asked Mr. Olliphant.

"The person that brought it to me—that is, to my friend—but not the right owner, I'm certain."

"How then?—was the will left in pledge?" inquired the lawyer.

"No," answered Isaac; "it was found in the breast-pocket of a coat, that was pledged some years ago, with several other things which have never been redeemed."

"And now the will's inquired for?"

"Exactly," replied Mr. Lecky.

"And why don't you give it up?" said the lawyer.

"It's not me," answered the Jew; "it's my friend."

"Well, why don't your friend give it up? There can be no difficulty in ascertaining to whom it belongs," said Mr. Olliphant.

"None in the world," replied Isaac. "But you know, sir, a thing of that sort, that's of value, can't be expected to be let slip for nothing, particularly when it turns up in this here sort of way, years afterwards, when everybody must naturally have concluded it was lost and gone, past recovery."

"Then you want me to treat with the parties that the deed belongs to," said Mr. Olliphant; "in short, to negotiate between them and you, and get a price for you? Is that it?"

"Something of that sort," answered Isaac.

"Humph!" said Mr. Olliphant. "That's business very much out of my line. At the same time, if this document is really of value to somebody who has been defrauded of it, it should be restored one way or another. But, in the first place, I must see it; I must judge of its value and authenticity; and learn who the parties are to whom restitution is to be made. Have you it with you?"

"You know, sir," said Lecky, "the will is not mine—I'm only acting for another person, and I must either return the parchment or the price of it to my friend."

"Very well," said Mr. Olliphant; "all I can say is, that if the deed proves to be of value, I'll endeavour to obtain a suitable reward for the produce of it. But unless you'll trust it in my hands, it's useless prolonging this interview, as we're both losing our time;" and Mr. Olliphant rose impatiently from his seat.

"Here it is, sir; here it is," said Isaac, who was a timid man, and began to fear he had exhausted the lawyer's forbearance. "You see, sir," said he, still holding it folded as it was—"there are marks upon it—stains, sir, of blood—of bloody fingers. I remember the business well enough; it was thought to be a put-up affair betwixt the footman and the dairymaid—you remember it, sir? Wentworth—Mr. Wentworth, of Oakfield, the great wine merchant?"

"Good God!" exclaimed Mr. Olliphant, as he examined the document; "who did you get this from, Mr. Lecky?"

"From a woman," answered Mr. Lecky, who, in the excitement of the moment, here dropped his friend out of the transaction. "Most likely the dairymaid herself—a pretty creature, a very pretty creature, indeed, she was when she used to come first to my house; that's now perhaps seven or eight years ago. She'd a child, too, as pretty as herself; but I fancy the man, whoever he was—the footman, probably—that was concerned with her, left her; for she fell into great distress, and stript herself, little by little, of everything. Amongst the rest, there came a box of men's clothes; I sold them all but one coat, but that I never could get off. It was stained, very much stained and spotted; it often struck me it was blood, and now I don't doubt it. I don't know how it was I overlooked that pocket, for we always examine the pockets—but it was concealed in the breast, which was padded, and it wasn't easy to feel there was anything there. However, lately she came back, for I hav'n't seen anything of her for some years—but she came back to inquire for the parchment; but I told her I knew nothing of it, and that the things were all sold—and, indeed, I thought they were, for I had clean forgotten the coat, which had been thrown aside as unsaleable. But some time afterwards, a poor creature, one of our own people, came to me for assistance—he was starving, and had no clothes to his back; and as I was looking about to see if there was anything I could spare, what should I light on but this here coat. So, as I'd had it so long, I thought it wasn't wronging myself nor my daughter to clothe him in it; for, indeed, the moths were getting into it, and there was more like to be loss in keeping it than in giving it away. But whilst I was pointing out to him what a comfortable thing it was, and how warm it would keep him across the breast, all padded as it was, I thought I felt something that made me look a little closer, and what should I find but the pocket, and this here deed in it."

"And has the woman returned to make any further inquiries?" asked Mr. Olliphant.

"No," replied Isaac; "I have never seen her since."

"But doubtless you know where to find her?" said Mr. Olliphant.

"Why, no," answered Isaac, after a little consideration; "I don't think I do, and I don't expect to see her again. In short, to say the truth, I wonder at her risking the thing at all; for if I'd found the will before she came, it might have led to her detection. I might have stopt her, you know."

"Distress, I suppose, drove her to it," replied the lawyer. "People will do anything for bread. But we must find her out, Mr. Lecky; and I think it will be worth your while to help us."

"And the will?" said Isaac, anxiously.

"I will undertake to say that you shall be fairly rewarded," returned Mr. Olliphant; "but in the meantime you must trust to my word, and leave it with me. Moreover, it is desirable that the thing should be kept as private as possible till we see our way. Don't mention the circumstance to anybody."

"Except to my friend—my principal," said Isaac, who just then recollected him.

"Oh, your friend, of course, is an exception," said Mr. Olliphant, laughing, as he saw him to the door.

CHAPTER XLIX.

MR. SIMPSON AND THE LAWYER PAY A VISIT TO OAKFIELD.

WHEN Isaac Lecky said that he did not know where the woman was to be found who had pledged the articles amongst which the will was found, he happened to speak the truth. He neither

knew her residence nor her name, and thus the progress of the
investigation, which Mr. Olliphant was eager to prosecute, was
arrested. Isaac did not doubt that she was the dairymaid who
had eloped with the footman; and Mr. Olliphant and Mr. Simpson, to whom the affair was communicated, entertained the same
opinion.

However, the recovery of the will was in itself important.
There could be no doubt of its authenticity; it had been drawn
up in Mr. Olliphant's office, and sent down, with a duplicate, to
Oakfield, to be attested. The signatures of Mr. Wentworth and
the witnesses were attached to it; and, from the stains of blood
that appeared on it, the probability was, that Mr. Wentworth had
had it with him on his last fatal journey, and that it had been
taken from the portfolio which was found open and rifled after
his death. What had become of the other copy, which the same
witnesses affirmed had also been signed and attested, yet remained
a mystery.

As Mr. Gaveston's situation in regard to the property was entirely
changed by the recovery of this document, by which the bulk of
it was vested in trustees for the use of his wife, and as Harry
Leeson's right to his legacy was also established by it, as well as
the claim of the servants and others to various small sums which
Mr. Wentworth had bequeathed to them, it became necessary to
communicate the event to that gentleman without delay; and for
this purpose Mr. Simpson and Mr. Olliphant resolved to make a
visit to Oakfield. "I can be of no use, I believe," said Mr.
Simpson; "but it's a good while since I was there, and I should
like to see what's going on, and how he receives the intelligence."

"Not very gratefully, you may be assured," returned Mr.
Olliphant. "It will diminish his importance a good deal, and he
wont like that now that he's such a great man in the county."

"It's curious how, in some respects, his character appears to
be changed," observed Mr. Simpson. "It's true, he was always
eager for money; but formerly it was to squander it at the
gaming-table, or with a parcel of blackguards on the turf; but
now all that sort of thing's given up, and his whole ambition
seems to be to acquire influence, and to domineer over everybody
about him."

"Which he does with a vengeance, I understand," rejoined Mr.
Olliphant. "I'm told that his behaviour on the bench, since he
has been a magistrate, is quite unbearable; insomuch that two or
three gentlemen who were in the commission have resigned, because they wouldn't act with him."

"I don't wonder at it, I'm sure," replied Mr. Simpson; "from
the account I heard from old Jeremy, who came up to town lately
to settle some affairs on the death of his wife. But the great
offence he has given appears to be about the new road; and it's
curious how he seems to have got the better of them all. He
actually stood alone in his opinion; everybody but himself were
perfectly agreed as to the direction it should take; and Mr.

Franklin, who was anxious to keep it off a little estate he has lying in the line, thought the thing secure; but whether out of enmity to him, because he had interfered between him and his wife—Franklin says he's sure it's that—but whatever it was, he set to work to oppose them all; and, faith! he carried the day, and the road has been cut right through Franklin's property."

"It's singular," said Mr. Olliphant, "that Mrs. Gaveston should have attached herself to a man of such a character. One would think it impossible, seeing so much of him as she did, that she should not have found him out before she married him."

"He spared no pains to deceive her," replied Mr. Simpson. "And although they were cousins, and had known each other from childhood, yet they were never long together at a time. Then, it must be admitted, he had considerable powers of entertaining, and he excelled in all those sports and exercises which show a man to advantage and attract the attention of women. He deceived me for a long time, and Mr. Wentworth for longer. But he, poor man, had begun to dislike him very much before he died, and I had found him out a good deal earlier."

"Well, this bit of parchment, as my friend Isaac calls it, will take the shine out of him, I fancy," said Mr. Olliphant, "and will make poor Mrs. Gaveston independent and comfortable. And as for that little fellow, if we could find him——,"

"He'll turn up some day," answered Mr. Simpson. "You know that Mrs. Gaveston received a letter from him soon after he went, assuring her he was in a fair way of doing well; and it's extremely possible he may have written others, which being addressed to Oakfield, now she's no longer there, would naturally fall into Gaveston's hands, and never be heard of more."

The two gentlemen, on reaching Oakfield, were informed that Mr. Gaveston was at that moment engaged in the library with a person on business, and were therefore shown into the breakfast-room adjoining, and requested to wait till he was at leisure.

The rooms were divided by folding-doors, which were closed but not latched; and consequently the travellers, who were standing silently contemplating a picture of their old friend that hung over the chimney-piece, found themselves involuntary confidants of the conversation that was going on in the next apartment. The first words that reached their ears were, "That damned road!" upon which their eyes met, and a significant smile was exchanged between them, for it was the voice of Mr. Gaveston that gave utterance to them.

"But you know, sir, it was your own will," replied the other person. "You insisted the road should take that direction. I always told you from the first that it wasn't the best line; but you wouldn't listen."

"But you never told me you were going to take it through Maningtree," said Mr. Gaveston. "Why didn't you tell me that?"

"It followed of course, sir; there was no other way of doing it,

provided we took your line," replied the other. "If you would
only have looked at the plans I sketched, you'd have seen it yourself; but you wouldn't, you know, sir; you said you were resolved
it should go through Peach Mill, and no other way."

"Damnation!" muttered Mr. Gaveston. "Well, but, Borthwick, can't you turn it a little to the right or the left, and keep
clear of that place?"

"What place, sir?" said Borthwick; "Maningtree?"

"No, no, not Maningtree; you say that's impossible."

"Impossible!—to be sure, sir; why we're within a mile of it
now."

"Well, but that house—those grounds, I mean; can't you clear
them?"

"What, the old Manor House, sir?"

"Ay, ay," said Mr. Gaveston, impatiently; "the old Manor
House, or anything else you like to call it."

"Lord, sir," said Borthwick, "what would be the use of sparing
that? Why it's just a nuisance to the neighbourhood, and the
people are glad enough to get rid of it from before their eyes, particularly the inn; it's just an eyesore to them and their customers.
If it's not taken down, it'll tumble down; for there's never been
five shillings laid out in repairs these thirty years, nor ever will
again; for since that affair of Mr. Wentworth's, you know, sir,
it's never even been used for travellers, as it was before."

"Well, sir, but if I wish it spared?" said Mr. Gaveston,
fiercely.

"But it's too late, sir," replied Borthwick. "The bargain's
made with the agents for the property, and glad enough they were
to strike it; and so will the principal, for he never looked to get
sixpence an acre for it; and we've given a pretty round sum—
more than it's worth, in my opinion. But that's no business of
mine."

"But it is of mine, sir," replied Mr. Gaveston, arrogantly. "It's
my business to see that the public money's not thrown away, and
improperly squandered; and I wont agree to the bargain. I wont
stand to it, sir. As one of the trustees of the roads, and as a magistrate for the county, I've a right to object, and I will object.
Pray, sir, why wasn't I consulted before such a prodigal arrangement was made?"

"Lord, sir, you were present, you know, when the gross sums
for the different estates was voted; but you never objected to the
amount, nor inquired into the particulars, except about the com-
pensation for Peach Mill, to Mr. Franklin. Certainly you did
object to that, I remember, and said it was too high; and you got
a thousand pounds knocked off. And this other business was
settled the same day, sir; but I believe you were so much engaged about Peach Mill, that you didn't attend to the rest."

Here a pause of some minutes ensued. Mr. Gaveston was
forced into the conviction, that if the thing he objected to had become inevitable, or nearly so, he had nobody to blame but himself,

which formed a very considerable aggravation of his annoyance;
and he was engaged in thinking if there were no possible expedient left by which the error he had committed might be remedied.

"There's nobody in the line that could be brought to object,
Borthwick, is there?"

"Not one, sir," answered Borthwick. "Nobody ever did object; that is, none of the landlords nor proprietors that we proposed to cut through, except Mr. Franklin. All the rest found
their account in it too well; but it was a heavy loss to him, no
doubt, and a disappointment, too. But we've been through Peach
Mill these six months, so it's too late for him to object now."

"But suppose the proprietor wont ratify?" said Mr. Gaveston.

"Well, sir, if he wouldn't," answered Borthwick, "that might
cause a good deal of trouble and delay, certainly; and we might
be obliged to turn the road a bit aside; but it would be a pity, a
great pity! It would spoil the line altogether; for it cuts as
straight as an arrow through them Remorden grounds."

"Damn the line!" said Mr. Gaveston. "But if the proprietor
objected to ratify, there's time enough yet to turn it, is there
not?"

"You must be quick about it, sir," answered Borthwick;
"there's not a day to lose. Indeed, if it hadn't been that he's
abroad, we should have been at work there now, pulling down the
house. For some time the agents couldn't ferret him out; and at
last, when they did, they found he'd just started for the continent.
But they've sent after him, and it's likely the thing wont hang on
hand, for the money'll be welcome enough. They say he'd run
through everything he had at the end of the first two years, and
has been living on his wits ever since."

"Who are the agents?" said Mr. Gaveston.

"Their names are Wright and Greyling, sir, I believe," replied
Borthwick; "but the solicitor that acts for them is called Glassford, and he lives in the Temple. He'd be the proper person to
apply to, I should think."

"I believe he would," replied Mr. Gaveston, musingly; "but,
perhaps, Borthwick, you could get the address of this Mr. Remorden; you say he's on the continent, but that's a large field.
The thing is, to know the spot, the exact spot, or one may lose a
great deal of time."

"I'll try and find out, sir, if you wish it," said Borthwick.

"Do, Borthwick, and lose no time," returned Mr. Gaveston;
"and let me know the moment you hear."

"I will, sir," said Borthwick, taking his leave.

"Good morning, Borthwick," said Mr. Gaveston, in a friendly
tone; "and, Borthwick, you'll hang back a little—don't put on too
many men; and you needn't get the stones brought up so fast,
you know. Give us a little time to look about us. There's no
hurry; none in the world. The longer the road's making the
better for the poor people that are at work on it. It'll be a bad
day for them when they lay the last stone."

"It will, sir," said Borthwick, "no doubt, sir."

"So, Borthwick, don't hurry, take it easy. By the by, that bit of land you wanted—I think it's about an acre and a half?"

"Just about, sir," answered Borthwick.

"Well, I think we shall be able to come to an agreement; I have been considering about it—but we'll speak of that another time. Good morning, Borthwick."

CHAPTER L.

WHICH CONTAINS THE RESULT OF THE VISIT TO OAKFIELD, AND THE DEPARTURE THENCE OF MR. SIMPSON AND THE LAWYER.

MR. BORTHWICK having made his exit immediately into the hall, without passing through the breakfast-room, Mr. Gaveston arose, and not knowing any one was there, threw open the folding doors, in order to extend the space in which he was about to walk himself down a little; for like many other people, when he was vexed or excited, or wanted to collect his ideas, or calm his mind, he found exercise a great assistant in the operation. But what he saw, when he opened the doors, did by no means tend to arrange his ideas, or augment his placidity. He saw the two men, whom, of all others in the world, he most feared and hated; for he knew they despised him, and yet he did not dare to show his resentment. He could not but be aware that there were many who held no better opinion of him than they did; and he was on ill terms with a great proportion of his neighbours, for his arrogance and irritability were almost unbearable; but then he eased his mind by thwarting their plans, opposing their opinions, and showing them as much contempt and insolence as one gentleman dare show another without the risk of getting his brains blown out for his impertinence. But somehow or other he never could feel at his ease, nor give way to his natural temper in the presence of these two men. They had been Mr. Wentworth's most intimate and attached friends, they had been mixed up with all his affairs, they were the defenders of his daughter, and ready to be the protectors of his nephew. He knew that they were still as eager as ever to discover the truth, and to penetrate the mystery that hung over the fatal night at the Old Manor House; and he was aware that if even a link was found to guide them, they would never let it go till they had followed out the whole chain: and as the lawyer was shrewd, and Mr. Simpson was wealthy, they were extremely likely to succeed. In short, nothing but the disappearance of Andrew and Mabel, which fixed suspicion on them till it had grown into a certainty, had prevented the most active investigations on the part of the two gentlemen in question. But, beguiled by that circumstance, they had directed all their exertions to the discovery of Andrew and his supposed paramour, instead of to the ascertaining whether they were actually the guilty parties or not. But the moment might come that should start them in a new direction, and who should say what might follow? Then, they had outwitted him; they had taken advantage of his fears, without even knowing the power of the weapon they were wielding, to wrest from him one half of the lucrative business in the city. He had since found out Mr. Simpson's motive, and seen through the manœuvre, which he did not doubt the lawyer was at the bottom of; he was aware it was not for his own profit he had worked; but that, distrusting him, he had done it for the sake of the daughter and nephew of his friend and benefactor; but he did not like him the better for that, but the worse. Such men are to be feared, for they are untractable. Altogether, there were no two men whom he less desired to see at Oakfield, or anywhere else indeed, more especially in a moment of irritation and embarrassment, like the present; and certainly there were none whom he would have less desired to make the confidants of his conversation with Borthwick; and yet the probability was that they had heard a great part of it, if not all; how much, he could not judge, for he did not know how long they might have been there.

Under all these circumstances, it may be conceived that the surprise was not an agreeable one, and that the first involuntary expression which passed over his face, denoted anything but pleasure. But he "called up a look" as quickly as he could, and threw the blame of the first on his astonishment at so unexpected a rencontre in his breakfast-room, and on his not instantly recognising who his visitors were.

"Have you been long here?" said he.

"Nearly half an hour, I dare say," replied Mr. Olliphant, who felt a particular gratification in annoying him; "but hearing you so earnest in conversation, we wouldn't interrupt you, of course."

"It's that d——d road," replied Mr. Gaveston. "There's always something going wrong with it; and I've more trouble about it than enough. I find, because I didn't happen to be in the way to attend to it, they have been squandering the public money in a shameful way—giving five thousand pounds for an estate not worth two, when by turning the road only a few hundred yards to the left, they might have cleared it altogether, merely cutting through two or three small farms, where the people must have taken what they could get."

"They must have been fairly compensated," said Mr. Olliphant, "whether their farms were small or large; and probably the two or three small farms would have cost more to buy up than the single estate, because usually each proprietor takes care to ask something more than his property is really worth; and amongst them you might have found some extremely unreasonable. Besides, what's a thousand or two of pounds in making a road of such importance as the one in question. Surely, you wouldn't turn it out of its line for such a consideration as that!"

"Why, not if it were detrimental, certainly," replied Mr.

Gaveston; "but in my opinion, it wouldn't injure the line a bit to give it a little bend at that particular spot."

"And as for that cursed old place," continued Mr. Olliphant, "nothing in the world would give me greater satisfaction than to have it razed off the face of the earth. I'd have had the house pulled down, and the grounds ploughed up the very next day, if I had had my will."

"Would you?" said Mr. Gaveston, hanging his head a little on one side, and endeavouring to look sentimental. "Well I own I entertain a different feeling. I wouldn't have the place disturbed, but rather let it stand as a memorial—"

"Of a d——d, coldblooded, rascally murder, of one of the best men that the Almighty ever turned out of his hands!" exclaimed Mr. Olliphant, with vehemence. "God! a man must have a singular taste in memorials who would wish to spare the place on that account."

"But come into the library and sit down," said Gaveston, "whilst I desire Mitchell to bring some refreshments;" and he left the room hastily, in order to get the opportunity of gulping down a little of his vexation, and also that he might vent some of it on the unlucky Mitchell for having shown the two gentlemen into the breakfast-room instead of the drawing-room, which would have placed them beyond the hearing of his private conversation with Borthwick.

"When did you leave town?" said he, as he re-entered the room: you have had charming weather for the journey."

"We have," replied Mr. Simpson, "which induced us not to hurry; so we drove down quite leisurely, and have been three days on the road. This is Olliphant's idle time, and he wanted a little country air."

"Nothing like it," answered Mr. Gaveston, somewhat relieved by their last speech; for he had been wondering what could have procured him the honour of this unexpected visit, a curiosity that was not unaccompanied by anxiety; and he was glad to find that it was nothing but the desire of recreation that had brought the gentlemen from London. But they were only deferring the communication they had to make till Mitchell had cleared away the refreshments; and therefore, without hinting a word of it, they turned the conversation on general topics, whilst they were discussing the luncheon.

"What do you say to a walk over the grounds?" said Mr. Gaveston, who affected as much hospitality as he could contrive to throw into a voice and manner which indulgence and irritation had rendered rather indocile; "it will give you an appetite for your dinner."

"We shall have time for a walk, I dare say," replied Mr. Olliphant; "but before we move, we've a little business to talk over with you, if you'll give us leave."

"Assuredly," said Mr. Gaveston, reseating himself, with an uneasy air; "we can discuss the business, and have a walk too, before dinner."

"Hem!" said Mr. Olliphant, clearing his throat, as he settled himself in his chair. "You know one of the circumstances connected with our lamented friend's death, that has always created the greatest surprise and curiosity, was the disappearance of the will."

"Or rather, that no will was found," said Gaveston.

"Disappearance!" reiterated the lawyer, in a decided tone; "disappearance of a thing which was known to have existed—known not only to me, but to others."

"Well," said Gaveston, in the tone of a man who gives way without being convinced. "As you please: but go on."

"And not only one copy, but two," continued Mr. Olliphant; "which made the circumstance the more remarkable, as it left no room for attributing the loss to accident."

"Well!" said Mr. Gaveston, with some impatience.

"And therefore," added the lawyer, "I had the less hope of ever recovering the lost documents; as I naturally concluded that whatever motive had occasioned the theft, would also occasion their destruction."

"No doubt," answered Gaveston, whose countenance was every moment getting more and more beyond his control.

"However, strange to say," pursued Mr. Olliphant, "that does not appear to be the case; for at this present moment I've got the will in my pocket;" and he clapped his hand to his side with a decision that denoted not only his satisfaction at finding it, but his assurance of its validity.

Mr. Gaveston attempted a smile of incredulity, but it was a failure; the lips trembled, and his features, drawn from their natural position by the struggle between their own will and the power he was endeavouring to exert over them, gave a hideous expression to the face.

"Nothing was ever more true, I assure you," replied Mr. Olliphant, in answer to the doubt he perceived Mr. Gaveston wished to insinuate. "And alas!" he added, as he drew it from his pocket, and presented it to the horror-struck eyes of the wretched man before him; "alas! it bears but too melancholy marks of its authenticity—the bloody fingers of the murderer bear witness for it!"

Mr. Gaveston, apparently too much amazed and bewildered to know what he was doing, involuntarily held out his hand to take it; but Mr. Olliphant, feigning not to observe the movement, still grasped it tightly. It might be an excess of caution; but there was a fire in the room, and there is no accounting for the impulses of a desperate man.

"The provisions of the will," pursued the lawyer, "I have before acquainted you with. They correspond exactly with the rough draught I showed you after Mr. Wentworth's death; and, in short, were framed upon it—for after I had taken his instructions, I threw them upon paper, and submitted the sketch to him, before I filled it up with all the requisite formalities."

"Gentlemen," said Mr. Gaveston, making a strong effort to recal his scattered spirits, and as he spoke, he rose hastily, and walked across the room, in order to escape from the close inspection he felt himself under as he sat: "this is a very extraordinary communication—very extraordinary, indeed—and you cannot be surprised at my being rather shaken by it—it's a thing no man could hear without some degree of agitation, however strong his nerves might be—and it's not a trifle that shakes mine, I assure you. But are you really satisfied—are you really certain of what you affirm?"

"So certain," replied Mr. Olliphant, "that I'll give you leave to try the authenticity of this deed,"—and he clapped his hand upon it with the most determined air of conviction—"in every court of judicature in the three kingdoms; and more than that, I'll stake my whole fortune on the result."

"And so would I," added Mr. Simpson, quietly, but firmly.

"Oh!" said Mr. Gaveston, and there was an evident faltering of the voice; "I—I don't mean to dispute—I have no desire to—to question—if you are convinced—I certainly shall submit—there's no necessity for trying the thing before any court whatsoever, but the court of our own consciences, gentlemen."

"Any other appeal would be useless, certainly," replied Mr. Olliphant, who, as well as Mr. Simpson, was perfectly amazed at this submissive acquiescence, for they had both come prepared to encounter a storm of passion, a resolute denial of all belief in the authenticity of the will, and, in short, a regular declaration of war.

It was singular that the question that would naturally have first presented itself, and which, either to a person interested or uninterested in the result, would have most excited curiosity, Mr. Gaveston forbore to ask. He did not say, "How was it recovered?" but Mr. Olliphant volunteered the information.

"You must be naturally curious to know," said he, "by what accident the thing has turned up, after so many years, and when, despairing of success, we had long ceased all inquiry. But it's singular how documents of this sort do survive, and come to light when they're least looked for. Old Time's a great redresser of wrongs, and works out many a good cause and establishes many a right, in his own quiet way, where our most strenuous endeavours have failed. The way we got this is odd enough. There's a certain Jew, a pawnbroker, that lives in the neighbourhood of St. Martin's-lane, by name Isaac Lecky. A woman with whom he formerly had dealings, went to him lately to inquire if, amongst certain articles pledged some years since, and never redeemed, he had found a will. Isaac said he had not, and that the things had all been sold long since. However, not long afterwards, in looking over his stores, what should he stumble upon but a coat, which he remembered to have got from her, and which, being much stained —with blood, he thinks—had been found unsaleable, and thrown aside. The worthy Jew, of course, according to the maxims of his tribe, began to reckon what might be made of the accident; and as I had had occasion to see him formerly about some little matters, who should he fix on but me to bring the will to, with the view of engaging me to make a bargain for him with the persons to be benefited by his discovery."

During this communication, Mr. Gaveston stood at the window with his back to the gentlemen, and more than once, as he proceeded, he wiped the perspiration from his brow.

"And the woman?" he gasped out: "what became of her?"

"Oh! the woman," replied Mr. Olliphant, "he could give no account of. He neither knew her name nor her address; but for my own part, I have little doubt of its being Mabel, the dairymaid. He describes her as young and pretty, and says that she had with her a little girl, as pretty as herself. However, I have set him to ferret her out, and promised to reward him well if he succeeds; so that in all probability we shall soon come at the truth of the whole affair. In the meantime, with respect to the will——"

"Oh, with respect to the will," interrupted Mr. Gaveston, "there need be no trouble, no dispute—none in the world. I shall not oppose anything that is right, you may rely on it."

The two friends looked at each other with amazement. The man so violent, so obstinate, so selfish, and, as they believed, so unprincipled, seemed all at once subdued, complying, disinterested, and just. They could scarcely credit their ears or their understandings. Mr. Simpson, naturally benevolent and forgiving, began to feel his heart softening towards the being he had long despised and detested. But the lawyer, a man of sterner stuff and shrewder discernment, and whom much intercourse with the world had made intimately acquainted with human nature, saw something in this apparently sudden change of character that perplexed him. He had looked for the most pertinacious incredulity, the most vigorous opposition; and even if the thorough conviction of their inefficacy could be supposed to induce their forbearance, at the best, a submission to inevitable necessity, deformed by an exhibition of the worst passions, was the most favourable result he expected.

Strange thoughts crept into his mind—a chilling of the heart he had never felt before, made him shudder to the very marrow in his bones. He sat gazing at the profile of the man that stood at the window, as he might have gazed if a being of another world had suddenly presented itself before him. There was a dead silence: Mr. Gaveston *felt* the eye that was upon him, and was transfixed to the spot. Mr. Simpson cleared his throat, and tried to speak; but he was awed by the bearing of his companions, and could find nothing to say.

This sort of paralyzation of the party lasted some minutes, and might have lasted longer; for Mr. Gaveston could not move, and Mr. Olliphant had sunk into such a state of abstraction, that he was unconscious of the lapse of time. At length Mr. Simpson

made a desperate effort to shake off the petrifaction that he felt
was beginning to be infectious; he pushed back his chair, and
rising, said, "Well, gentlemen, shall we walk?"

Mr. Gaveston turned round; his cheeks and lips were of an
ashy whiteness; his mouth was contracted; the whole face drawn,
as if he had actually suffered from a stroke of paralysis: he walked
forward with an infirm step, and appeared to be looking about
for his hat. Mr. Olliphant rose too, but he moved like a man in
a dream.

"Our hats are in the other room, I believe," said Mr. Simpson;
and he walked forward to fetch them, followed by Mr. Olliphant.

When they had passed through the doors, Mr. Gaveston stopped
short in the centre of the room, clapped his hand to his forehead,
and held it there for a moment with a forcible pressure, whilst he
divided his pallid lips, and clenched his teeth, till his face assumed
an expression perfectly demoniacal. Then, as if the boiling agony
within was somewhat relieved by the energy he had wasted, he
made a strong effort to recal himself: and as the gentlemen were
returning into the room with their hats in their hands, he threw
open the door, and preceded them into the hall, where his own
was lying, and from thence stepped out on the lawn. They
followed; and seldom perhaps have three people commenced a
walk, avowedly of recreation, under more singular circumstances.

It may easily be conceived that, with all the efforts Mr. Gaveston could make—and he made most vigorous ones—the conversation was not very lively. As they walked through the gardens,
he tried horticulture; and as they walked through the fields, he
tried agriculture; and when they got into the road, as roads were
not exactly in the present state of affairs desirable subjects, he fell
upon politics and the state of the country. But besides that Mr.
Simpson was profoundly ignorant of the two first, and not very
well versed in the last, he was so struck by the singular bearing of
Mr. Olliphant, so unlike the cheerful, loquacious, but at the same
time firm and decided manner of the free-hearted, honest, and
prosperous lawyer, that he could not collect his ideas, nor direct
his attention to what the other was saying; whilst Mr. Olliphant
himself had the air of a person who had been exceedingly frightened by some very extraordinary or supernatural event, and
whose whole faculties were benumbed by the shock.

So they walked on from field to field, and from garden to
garden, till the hour of dinner drew nigh; when Mr. Gaveston,
who piloted the way, directed their steps homewards, and they
withdrew to their separate rooms to arrange their toilets.

"Olliphant, my dear fellow," said Mr. Simpson, entering the
lawyer's room when he was himself dressed, "what is all this?—
what, in the name of wonder, has come over you?—Why, you're
not dressed, man, and there's the dinner bell!—why, you've not
even unstrapped your portmanteau! Are you ill?"

"I am not well," replied Mr. Olliphant; "indeed, I feel extremely unwell. I'll thank you to say so to Mr. Gaveston. I
couldn't eat any dinner if I were to sit down to table. Excuse me

as well as you can. I shall go out and take a stroll; and if I am not better, perhaps you'll not see me in the drawing-room to-night. To-morrow morning, my dear Simpson, if you've no objection, we'll start for London, at sunrise. Our business is concluded, and we have no object in delaying here. We can then talk over this affair at our leisure."

Mr. Olliphant appeared no more that evening. Before he lay down in his bed, he carefully fastened the door, and placed the will under his pillow; and on the following morning, the two gentlemen started for London.

CHAPTER LI.

MR. GAVESTON LEAVES OAKFIELD FOR LONDON, AND PAYS TWO VISITS THAT ARE LITTLE EXPECTED.

No sleep blessed Mr. Gaveston's eyes during the night that lodged the two friends under his roof, and with the first dawn of light he arose and dressed himself; but he did not quit his room till he heard the wheels that were bearing away his inauspicious visitors, rolling from the door. Then he descended, ordering his breakfast to be instantly served, and his horse to be saddled; whilst he dispatched one of the servants forward to Borthwick's house, to desire he would be in the way, as he intended calling on him, as he passed, on his way to town.

The lawyer and Mr. Simpson had scarcely been gone half an hour, when Mr. Gaveston was mounted, and galloping down the lawn and along the road at such a rate that old Jeremy, who, roused by the clattering of the hoofs through the paved street of Mapleton, thrust his be-night-capped head out of the window of the Green Dragon, to see who was frighting the town from its propriety at that early hour, swore, that in the cloud of dust he kicked up, he saw the devil at his heels, urging him forwards. "He's riding to h—l," said he, "as sure as my name's John Jeremy, and there goes Old Nick after him!"

Old Nick, however, on this occasion, happened to be personated by Mr. Borthwick, who, having started early about some road business, had been met by the servant, and was now in chase of Gaveston.

The pre-occupation of his mind, and the noise his own horse was making, prevented his at first hearing the clatter of his pursuer; but the bay mare did; and accordingly the faster Borthwick followed, the faster she fled, till at length her augmenting speed and excitement drew the rider's attention, and turning his head, he perceived him of the roads urging on his steed to overtake him; upon which he drew in his rein, and waited till the other came up.

"I was just starting for Maningtree, sir," said he, "to see how things were going on, when I met your servant; so I turned my horse's head this way, and rode after you."

"Quite right, Borthwick," said Gaveston. "The fact is, I am called away suddenly on particular business, and it was necessary I should see you before I go. In the first place, with respect to that man's address—Remorden's, I mean."

"I've written for it, sir," answered Borthwick; "the letter went last night; but, at the same time, I don't feel altogether sure of getting it. He's most times in hiding from his creditors, as far as I can learn, and is not over fond of letting people know where he is. And I have heard that he's done more than a thing or two, that makes it awkward for him to answer to his name; so that he claps on an alias here, and another there, insomuch, that if you don't happen to know his person, you hav'n't much chance of lighting on him."

"But that attorney you spoke of—what's his name? He that's agent for the property?"

"Glassford, sir—Glassford of the Temple," replied Borthwick.

"He knows where he is, of course, because you say they had written, or were going to write to him, to ratify the agreement."

"Yes, I fancy they know, sir," answered Borthwick; "at least they have some way of getting at him, because he had long ago desired the estate should be sold if a purchaser could be found; and therefore he took care they should have some means of communicating with him on the subject, in case they got an offer. But it's not so certain they'll give the address. Very likely he may have forbidden them to do it; and they'll probably propose to convey any letter or message themselves."

"That's not impossible, certainly," answered Gaveston. "However, the moment you get an answer, of whatever nature it may be, forward it to me at Laval's, and I'll leave directions where it's to be sent, in the event of my being gone. And now, Borthwick, remember what I said yesterday—don't push forward too fast. Take off some of the men from that spot, and put them on somewhere else. Hang back as much as you can, till you hear from me on the subject."

"I will, sir," said the obsequious Borthwick, "you may depend on it, sir. We shall have no difficulty in stopping a bit for want of stones, and that sort of thing. Besides, two of the quarrymen were killed by an explosion yesterday, and another had his leg broke, which will make us rather short of hands for the present."

"That's fortunate," observed Gaveston. "Well, then, now Borthwick, I must get forward a little, for my business is urgent."

"You hav'n't thought any more of that little field," said Borthwick, "have you, sir?"

"Oh, the field!—to be sure I have," said Mr. Gaveston. "What could make me forget to mention it! It was exactly one of the things I wanted to see you about. You shall have it, certainly, Borthwick, on the terms you propose. You may pull down the cottage that's on it to-morrow, if you please, and go to work your own way. If you like to draw up a bit of an agreement, do so, and send it after me. I'll sign it, and return it immediately. It may be more satisfactory to you, perhaps."

"Thank you, sir," said Borthwick, agreeably surprised at this unexpected compliance, and little dreaming that Mr. Gaveston was giving what was no longer at his own disposal. "I will, sir, since you're so good. It's safer to clap things on a bit of paper, in case of accidents to either party."

"Well, then, Borthwick, good bye," said Mr. Gaveston, as he put his horse into a trot. "You shall hear from me as soon as I can make out this man. Till then—you understand?"

"Oh, perfectly, sir," said Borthwick. "Good morning, sir; pleasant journey to you!" And the well-pleased surveyor turned his horse's head in the direction of his newly-acquired field, where he forthwith gave orders for the immediate destruction of the cottage, the repairing of the hedge, and sundry other little matters of personal interest; after which he trotted briskly homewards, put his horse in the stable, and set himself to work to draw up the deed that was to bind Mr. Gaveston to his word; muttering to himself as he did it, "Fast bind, fast find; he's in a devilish good humour just now, certainly; but the wind may blow from another quarter when he comes back; and as for his word, I wouldn't give that for it!" and he squirted the ink out of his pen on the floor. "No, no; fast bind, fast find, I say; so here goes. I don't see very well, for my part, what his object can be in clearing them Remorden grounds. As for the price, that's all my eye! He care for the public money!" And Mr. Borthwick chuckled inwardly at the extravagance of the notion. "However, it's no business of mine; I've got the field by it, and that's enough for me. It's an ill wind that blows nobody any good—fast bind, fast find;" and so, alternately soliloquizing and writing on a subject, in itself so agreeable, the worthy surveyor pleasantly passed the hours till dinner-time, at which repast he indulged himself with a few extra glasses, in honour of his new acquisition; and then, after a comfortable nap, he finished the evening with a game of double dummy with Mrs. Borthwick, wisely leaving the roads to take care of themselves.

In the meantime, Mr. Gaveston hastened on his way to London with all the speed he could; and if the devil was not urging him on from behind, as Mr. Jeremy had asserted, he was urged on by something in his own breast, not a whit less complacent and agreeable. As he did not wish to fall in with the travellers that had left his house that morning, he made a little circuit through some bye-lanes, and then cut into the high road a couple of miles in advance of them, making up the extra distance by the speed of his mare; and when her limbs began to tire, and her pace to slacken, he left her in the care of a trustworthy ostler, where he was in the habit of baiting on less urgent journeys, and mounting the outside of one of the coaches, proceeded by that conveyance to London.

Although it was late when he arrived, he had no sooner dismounted, than he proceeded to a certain ready-made linen warehouse, near Temple Bar; and knocking at the private door—for the shop was already closed—he inquired if he could see Mrs. Walker, and being answered in the affirmative, he entered, and

was shown into a back parlour, where he found that lady refreshing herself with a dozen of oysters and a pint of porter, after her
fatigue.

"Mrs. Walker," said he, "your obedient servant. How are
you?"

"Lord, Mr. Godfrey!" exclaimed the lady, shading her eyes
with her hand, that she might get a clearer view of his features;
"who in the world would have thought of seeing you?"

"It's some time since we've met, certainly," replied he. "How
have you been doing since?"

"Tol lol, Mr. Godfrey," replied the lady; "no great things,
nor not much amiss either. But lauk, sir, you've grown a deal
fatter than you used to be."

"An idle life, Mrs. Walker, I believe; I don't take so much
exercise as I used to do. But I called to ask you if you can tell
me anything of a person that I am ashamed to say I have not
heard of for some time; but really circumstances of one sort or
another have prevented my doing exactly what I wished in that
quarter. You know who I mean, of course?"

"Julia Clark?" answered Mrs. Walker.

"Exactly," said he. "I'm afraid she must have been badly off.
Have you heard anything of her lately?"

"Why, yes, I have," replied Mrs. Walker.

"At least about twelve months ago or so, it was that I chanced
to light on her, for she has left off calling here for these three or
four years back. For some time she used to look in to inquire if
you had left anything for her; but as we heard nothing of you,
she gradually ceased coming; and I was wondering what had become of her, when one day last summer, as I was walking down
to Brompton to see a sister of mine that had taken a lodging there
for the sake of a little country air, after an illness she'd had, who
should I see standing at the door of a shop at Knightsbridge but
Julia Clark."

"What was she doing there?" said Mr. Gaveston. "Does she
live there?"

"Ay, does she," replied Mrs. Walker, "and has got as tidy a
shop of haberdashery and such like as you'd wish to see on a
summer's day; and very well she's doing, she told me. And as
for the child—"

"But who the devil put her into the shop?" interrupted Mr.
Gaveston. "She couldn't have any money herself."

"Oh, none in the world," replied Mrs. Walker. "Things went
very bad with her, and she was reduced to the utmost distress, I
know, before she got settled there; for she used to come here and
beg me to give her a little needlework to do, such as she could take
home with her, for she couldn't come out on account of leaving the
child. In short, it was as much as they could do to keep body and
soul together; but, as people say, when things get to the worst,
they must mend; and so it was with her. For, at last, being
actually driven to desperation, what should she do but go to one
of the bridges, and attempt to jump into the water, with her child

in her arms. But it was not to be. Some gentleman or another caught her just in time, and saved them both from a watery grave."

"And took her to live with him for his pains, I suppose," said Mr. Gaveston.

"No, no," replied Mrs. Walker; "nothing of that sort, I fancy; but she told him her story, and he took compassion upon her, and set her up in the shop, where, as I said before, she's doing very comfortably for herself and the child."

"Humph!" said Mr. Gaveston, folding in his lips, for he would rather have heard a less favourable account of Julia's circumstances. "And there she is still, then?" said he.

"There she was the last time I passed that way, and I have no doubt you'll find her there now," replied Mrs. Walker. "She seemed very happy and contented, and said that her friend, Mr. Simpson, was going to send her little girl to school for her."

"Mr. Simpson?" reiterated Gaveston; "who's Mr. Simpson?"

"That's the gentleman that saved her life, and set her up in the shop," answered Mrs. Walker.

"Simpson!" again repeated Mr. Gaveston. "What Simpson is it?"

"I don't exactly know who he is," replied Mrs. Walker. "She said he was an elderly man and a merchant. I'm not sure, but I've a notion she said he was a wine-merchant somewhere in the city."

Mr. Gaveston pushed back his chair, and, hastily rising, took up his hat.

"Lord, sir! what hurry!" exclaimed Mrs. Walker, who enjoyed a bit of gossip over her supper exceedingly. "Sit down, and perhaps you'll take a glass of something warm?"

"Not to-night, thank ye," replied Mr. Gaveston, in a hurried manner. "It's late, and I've business to do. Good night, Mrs. Walker. On the right hand side, you said?"

"Yes, sir, on the right; just about half way between the turnpike and the barracks. Nearer the barracks, I'm thinking, than the toll, though.—Lord, sir, wait till I light you—don't be in such a hurry; you'll be tumbling over the cat in the passage!" A prediction which a loud scream from the cat immediately afterwards announced to have been fulfilled ere it was well delivered.

"Bobby! Bobby! poor Bobby!" cried Mrs. Walker, rushing with the candle after Mr. Gaveston; who, utterly unmindful of her and Bobby both, darted out of the house, and slammed the door behind him, before she was well out of the parlour.

"Bless the man!" cried Mrs. Walker, "one ou'd think he'd a bogle behind him! Poor Bobby!—did he tread on Bobby's tail?" and lifting up the cat in her arms, she carried him into the parlour, where she solaced him with soft caresses and some chopped liver, and herself with a comfortable glass of hot gin and water.

It was less than half an hour after his precipitate exit from the linen warehouse, that Mr. Gaveston might have been seen striding through the turnpike at the west end of Piccadilly, at a pace that would have seemed to justify the hypothesis of either

Mr. Jeremy or Mrs. Walker; and the expression of his countenance, had there been light sufficient to peruse it, would indubitably have tended to its confirmation. As it was, the few passengers that passed him turned their heads with wonder, to see what strange vision it was that had darted past them with such extraordinary velocity; and if a gleam of a lamp happened to fall upon the face, something very like fear was superadded to amazement. His coat and waistcoat, which he had unbuttoned to relieve himself from the heat his agitation of mind and violent exercise occasioned, flew back, as he advanced against the air, displaying the broad breast of his shirt; whilst in one hand he carried his hat, and in the other a white pocket-handkerchief, with which he every minute or two wiped the perspiration that was dropping in showers from his forehead.

"It's a maniac escaped from some madhouse," said the people as they passed. "It would be a charity to send some of the watchmen after him; for he'll most like do himself, or somebody else, a mischief."

When he had proceeded beyond the dead wall, and had reached the spot where a row of small shops bordered the road, he slackened his pace, and began to examine the names over the doors, in order to decipher, by the imperfect light, which was the one he wanted; and he was not long in making out the words, Julia Clark, Haberdasher, inscribed over a shop front, where he had also the satisfaction of perceiving a light shining from the window of an upper apartment. It was a low, small house, consisting only of the shop, with a parlour behind it, and two small apartments above. The shutters of the shop were closed, as were those of the door, the upper half of which was of glass; to the windows above, where the light was seen, there were no shutters, but a low muslin curtain served somewhat to shade the interior from the intrusive eyes without.

"I wonder if she lives alone," thought Gaveston; and for a moment he paused to survey the exterior of the house, and then he lifted the knocker, and gave a single loud summons. Presently the light disappeared from the window above, and immediately afterwards a voice within was heard inquiring who was there.

"Open the door, Julia, and you'll see," replied Mr. Gaveston.

"Mr. Simpson!" she exclaimed, on hearing a man's voice addressing her by her Christian name—for her neighbours were accustomed to call her Mrs. Clark—"La! sir, is it you at this time of night?" and so saying, she drew back the bolts and unlocked the door.

Mr. Gaveston stept in, and pushing back the door behind him, stood before her.

"Good heavens! Mr. Godfrey!" she exclaimed.

"Yes, Julia," replied he; "you may well look surprised—it's me, indeed;" and he took her hand affectionately between his as he spoke.

"It's so unexpected," said she, leaning against the wall, "that I'm—I'm quite overcome—;" and she placed her hand before her eyes, whilst the involuntary tears that sprang from them testified to her emotion.

"Come," said he, supporting her with his arm, "come in and sit down. We've a great deal to talk over;" and thus saying, he led her into the parlour behind the shop, and placing her in a chair, sat down beside her.

"You must have thought me very unfeeling," said he, "for a long time past; and, indeed, although I have more excuse for my apparent neglect than you are aware of, I cannot altogether exonerate myself from blame. But the world, Julia, the world, has so many claims on men in my situation; we are so drawn this way and that way, and every way but the one that our inclinations lead us, that we often appear to women who don't, and indeed can't, allow for this sort of thing, much worse than we are. But there comes a time, I believe, to every man, when, either from age and reflection, or from disappointment and weariness, he is awakened to a sense of the hollowness of worldly friendships and worldly people; and feels inclined to fall back upon his early attachments as the best and truest solace for his declining years."

At the words "declining years," Julia lifted her eyes to his face, for Mr. Gaveston was yet in the prime of life.

"You look surprised, my dear Julia," said he, "to hear me talk in that strain; but the truth is, that though I am not old, I have seen a great deal of life, and have met with many vexations and crosses in my progress through it, which has exactly the same mellowing effect on a man's character as the lapse of years. However it be," he added, and he threw his arm around her waist, and drew her towards him—"whatever be the cause, and we need not waste our time in searching for it, the effect you see—it has brought me back to you."

To this eloquent oration Julia could only answer by her tears. All he said might be very true; she knew too little of the world to decide whether it was or not, but at all events it was extremely affecting. He was her first and only love (for she had been thrown into Mr. Dyson's arms by necessity and the manœuvres of Gaveston, and by no means by her own inclination), and he was the father of the child she adored, who had been the blessing of her past years of poverty and desertion, and who now, in her more prosperous days, was the pride and delight of her heart.

"Oh!" she exclaimed, "how I wish Julia was at home!"

"She's not at home, then," said Mr. Gaveston, looking about him.

"No, she's at school," answered the mother; "at a very nice school at Putney, where a good friend of mine has placed her."

"A friend, Julia!" said Mr. Gaveston, with an air of surprise, tinged with a shade of jealousy. "I hope it's not a lover?"

"Oh no," she replied; "he's quite an elderly steady man, quite different to that; but he's one of the best of human beings. He put me in this shop, and has been as kind as a father to me; and he has promised that if anything happens to me, he'll take care of Julia, which is such a comfort; for I often used to think what was to become of the poor child if I died, without a friend in the world to help her."

"Don't say that," answered Mr. Gaveston, reproachfully. "She has a father to help her, and shall never need the assistance of this Mr. Si——, what did you say his name was?"

"I didn't mention his name," said Julia.

"Didn't you?" said he. "I thought you did. What is it?"

"He's called Simpson," answered she; "John Simpson—he's a wine-merchant in the city."

"Have you seen him lately?" inquired he.

"Not for some time," she replied; "and it was partly that made me think it was him when you spoke; though I never knew him come so late. But I shouldn't wonder if he's here to-morrow. When he does call, it's generally on a Sunday; and I should like so much to introduce you to him."

"To-morrow, Julia, I shall be many miles from here," replied Mr. Gaveston, "and that brings me to the object of my visit. I am going abroad, perhaps for some time, and I came to ask you to accompany me."

"Me!" exclaimed Julia, astonished.

"Yes," he replied. "You. Surely you wont refuse me?"

"But your wife?" said she. "Mr. Dyson told me you were married."

"Mr. Dyson!" exclaimed Mr. Gaveston; "when did you see Mr. Dyson?"

"Not many months ago," she replied. "He saw me as he was passing on the outside of a coach, and got off to speak to me. He said he'd been abroad ever since he went away that time with Miss Jones: and it was he told me you were married."

"And is that all?" inquired Mr. Gaveston. "Tell me every-thing he said to you."

"I asked him about Miss Jones," continued Julia.

"Well?" said Mr. Gaveston, anxiously. "What did he say?"

"Oh, that he'd got her off capitally; married her to some great man—a duke, I think he said, in Paris."

"A duke in Paris!" reiterated Mr. Gaveston.

"Yes," replied Julia. "Didn't you know it?"

"No," answered Mr. Gaveston; "I never could make out what was become of her. I never heard either of her or Dyson from the hour they started; and I believed them to be still together somewhere. And what else did he say?"

"The principal thing he wanted," answered Julia, "was a will that he said was left by mistake amongst some of his old clothes; and he desired me to try and find it. But I can't; the man I'd pledged the things to had sold them, and could give no account of it."

"And do you know where Dyson is now?" inquired Mr. Gaveston.

"He's abroad again," she said. "He called here one day just before he went, to know if I'd found the will: and said he was just starting for Paris, and that if I heard anything about it, I was to write to him, addressed to Colonel Jones, at the post-office there; and he desired me to tell the pawnbroker that if he could find it, he should be handsomely rewarded."

"And have you?" eagerly inquired Gaveston.

"Not yet," said she. "It's so seldom I can leave the shop. But I mean to go the first time I can get away."

"And you can't tell me the name of the duke that he said Ma— Miss Jones, I mean, was married to?"

"No," replied Julia. "I don't think he mentioned it."

Here there was a pause in the conversation, which interval was occupied on Gaveston's part in reviewing his situation, and in making as close calculations as the time would admit, of the advantages and disadvantages of the different lines of conduct that were open to him.

One thing was quite evident—which was, that by some means or other, Julia herself must be put out of the way. The links that connected her with the concern by himself, Mr. Dyson, Mabel, Mr. Simpson and the Jew, were all too many not to render her existence perilous in the extreme to his own. With respect to attempting to secure her silence, it was a risk not to be ventured. In the first place, he could not purchase it, even were he quite assured of her acquiescence, without explaining the interest he had in the bargain, a confidence too dangerous to be thought of. A surer way would be, by attaching her to himself through kindness to her and the child; but he could not rely on his own temper and perseverance in a line of conduct so alien to his nature. Besides, in either case, she might by some evil chance or another be identified by Isaac Lecky, and her evidence be extracted from her in a court of justice, however unwillingly given. Had he been aware of her intimacy with Susan, he would have perceived yet stronger reasons for putting an effectual seal upon her lips; but of this he yet knew nothing.

"What!" said he, after a time; "do you live alone here?"

"Yes," she replied, "quite alone, now that Julia's gone to school. I miss her sadly."

"Then there's nobody in the house with you now at all? Nobody here but our two selves?" said he, casting his eyes round the room.

"Not a creature," said she. "Why do you ask? Do you want anything?"

"No," he replied; "only our conversation might be overheard."

"That's impossible," answered she.

Mr. Gaveston arose, and walked about the room; and as he did so, he shut the door that led from the parlour to the shop. The decision he felt himself called upon to make was difficult. There was no time to be lost—not an hour; he could neither afford to linger in town himself, nor could he venture to leave Julia behind him. For his own part, he had to set out instantly in search of the owner of the manor-house, and endeavour to prevent his ratifying a bargain which he had the greatest interest in annulling; and if he allowed her to remain where she was, the

next day, for anything he knew, might produce some accidental
concurrence of circumstances that might be fatal.

Two expedients remained; either to avail himself of the present
moment, or to induce her to depart with him at once for the continent, and afterwards be guided in his disposal of her by circumstances.

In favour of the first, there were many arguments. There
were but two persons in the world that were at the same time
aware of his connexion with Julia, and of his real name and situation, and they were Mabel and Mr. Dyson; either, he imagined,
little to be feared. Mabel, if what he had heard were true, was
never likely to return to England; or if she did, there was little
probability of her penetrating the fate of so obscure a person, and
so slight an acquaintance as Julia; and with respect to Mr. Dyson,
there were motives of sufficient force to keep him quiet. The
hour, the loneliness, all favoured him; no one could have traced
him to the house; and, indeed, no one knew of his being in town,
except the people at the hotel, and Mrs. Walker. But then, Mrs.
Walker did know it, and knew moreover that he was seeking
Julia's address. It's true she only knew him as Mr. Godfrey;
but she was well acquainted with his person, and there was no
telling what accident might enlighten her further; and therefore
this impediment had to be weighed against the other facilities.

With regard to the second expedient—the carrying Julia
instantly abroad with him, there were many difficulties to be got
over;—the necessity for immediate departure, the inducing her to
leave the child behind her, the natural aversion she would feel to
going away without explaining the circumstances to Mr. Simpson,
her acquaintance with his marriage; and finally, the obstacles
that might be in the way of disposing of her abroad, more especially after he had been seen, as he inevitably must be, in her
company. And all these important considerations had to be
weighed, and his decision made, in so short a time.

Whilst he was thus pacing the room, Julia too had fallen into a
fit of abstraction. She was thinking of his proposal to accompany
him, wondering what he meant by it, if he would repeat it, and
what she should say; and she was balancing in her own mind the
very arguments against the plan that he was foreseeing.

She sat with her face towards the fire-place, where a few red
ashes, not yet quite extinct, were lying in the grate; the only light
there was in the room, besides, was the candle she had brought
from above, when she came down to open the door, and which
now, with a flaring wick, that was eating a channel down one side
of it, stood upon the table, on which also rested the arm that supported her head. Young, and still very pretty, and in spite of all
the wrongs she had met with, yet most unsuspicious and confiding,
it was a savage heart that could think of taking the poor life that
had long been at odds with so many sorrows, and at last found a
little haven of peace to rest in—that could think of pouring out
her blood on her own hearth, and leaving the yet warm body
stretched in death that he had so lately pressed to his bosom.

But time urged; at each turn he took his eye fell on her—he put his hand in his pocket, and drew out a razor and his pocket handkerchief—he took the handkerchief in his left hand, and the razor in his right, and at every turn he imperceptibly approached nearer to her chair,

She never stirred, for she was still deep in thought, weighing the effect her consent or refusal might have on little Julia's future fate.

"The next turn," thought he, and he drew still nearer. At that moment a hand was heard on the latch of the outer door, which after Mr. Gaveston's entrance had not been bolted. Julia started from her chair—Mr. Gaveston hastily replaced the handkerchief and the razor in his pocket. "Whose there?" cried she, opening the parlour door.

"It's I, Mrs. Clark," said the watchman, stepping in with his lanthorn in his hand. "Since that 'ere robbery, I tries all the doors every night when it strikes twelve. Yours arn't locked. But I beg pardon," he added, perceiving Mr. Gaveston; "I did'nt know you had company."

The ensuing day, being Sunday, the shutters of Mrs. Clark's shop remained closed, as a matter of course; but when Monday and Tuesday came, and they were not taken down, the neighbours began to wonder; and at length the house was entered, and her absence being ascertained, an investigation was instituted as to what had become of her.

Nobody could throw any light on the affair but the watchman; and all he knew was, that he had seen a gentleman with her on the previous Saturday night at twelve o'clock; and that between that and two, he had met a man and woman walking at a rapid pace in the direction of Hyde Park-gate, whom he was inclined to think were Mrs. Clark herself and the gentleman in question.

Further inquiry elicited nothing more satisfactory on the subject; and the disappearance of Julia Clark served for a nine days' wonder, and a perpetual mystery to the worthy inhabitants of Knightsbridge.

CHAPTER LII.

MR. CRIPPS MAKES AN UNPLEASANT DISCOVERY, AND STARTS FOR PARIS.

WHEN Mr. Cripps found that his second daughter, Miss Livy, was about to follow her sister's example, and ennoble his family by another distinguished alliance, he reflected that such honours are not to be had for nothing, and that there would be another fifty thousand pounds to be paid for the distinction.

A hundred thousand pounds subtracted from his property in so short a period, would make a serious reduction in his income, and must lead to some arrangements about which it was necessary he should consult with his solicitor; and happening to be in town on

the day he had received his daughter's letter, requesting his consent to her union with the colonel, he took the opportunity of
calling at the Temple to discuss the subject.

"Another wedding in the family!" exclaimed Mr. Glassford;
"and so soon! Why, you're a fortunate man, Mr. Cripps. I've
got three daughters to dispose of, but I don't find they go off at
that rate."

"It never rains but it pours, you know," observed Mr. Cripps.
"It's a pity Jemmy arn't old enough for a husband. I dare say
the count would be able to find one for her amongst his great acquaintance."

"Oh! the gentleman whom Miss Livy is about to make happy,
is a friend of the count's, is he?" said Mr. Glassford.

"Partikler," answered Mr. Cripps; "they're just like brothers,
Livy tells me."

"That will be extremely pleasant for all parties," observed the
lawyer.

"Very," said Mr. Cripps; "as soon as the wedding's over,
they are all to go together to the count's castle in Transylvania."

"Where?" said Mr. Glassford.

"In Transylvania," replied Mr. Cripps.

"Bless me! that's a long way off, indeed!" said Mr. Glassford.

"Somewhere about Italy, arn't it?" said Mr. Cripps.

"Not exactly," answered Mr. Glassford. "It's on the borders
of Hungary;" a piece of information which did not by any means
tend to enlighten Mr. Cripps with respect to the locality of his
son-in-law's castle. "May I ask what is the count's tile, for I did
not happen to see the marriage announced in the paper!"

"It was in the papers," said Mr. Cripps; but not till after it
had taken place; for the count was afraid the Emperor of Austria
would have interfered to prevent it, because he wanted him to
marry one of his own relations."

"Indeed!" said Mr. Glassford; "and his name?"

"He's called Count Ruckalooney," replied Mr. Cripps.

"Of course—you'd settlements?" hinted Mr. Glassford.

"Oh! yes, in course," replied Mr. Cripps; "the count settled
a beautiful estate upon her—somewhere or another—I don't
exactly know where."

"I should think that was probably of little consequence," observed the lawyer. "And may I ask who drew up the deed?"

"A friend of the count's," answered Mr. Cripps. "We were
obliged to keep the thing so quiet for fear of the Emperor of
Austria, that he wouldn't allow anybody else to be let into the
secret."

"And your daughter's fortune, I dare say, you paid down?"

"On the nail!" answered Mr. Cripps, triumphantly. "No
shilly-shally, but forked out at once."

"Hem!" said Mr. Glassford; "and this other gentleman is a
friend of the count's, and perhaps a subject of the Emperor of
Austria, also?"

"No, no," answered Mr. Cripps, "he's an Englishman, I take

it, by his name ; or likely a Welshman. I never thought to ask
Livy. He's called Colonel Jones."

"Colonel Jones?" reiterated Mr. Glassford. "Of what
service?"

"I never heard," replied Mr. Cripps. "The reg'lars, I suppose."

"The name's so common," observed Mr. Glassford, "that it's
no guide at all. What sort of man is he?"

"Bless you, I don't know," replied Mr. Cripps. "I never set
eyes on him. Livy's met with him in Paris."

"In Paris!" said Mr. Glassford. "Colonel Jones! Excuse
me, but I really should like to learn a little more of this person
before you give your consent to the match. The fact is, there is
a man of that name, or rather who chooses to assume that name,
that we've had the misfortune to have had much dealings with.
Now I happen to know that he is at present in Paris, and I confess I cannot help wishing you would allow us to make a few
inquiries before this affair is carried any further."

"But the count's friend," observed Mr. Cripps. "He must
know him, you know."

"Hem!" replied Mr. Glassford. "But it is possible the count
himself might be deceived."

"That's true," answered Mr. Cripps. "He might, certainly."

"You can give me no further indication by which we might
ascertain whether or not it is our Colonel Jones!" said Mr. Glassford. "Miss Livy hasn't sent you his miniature to see how far you
may approve the physiognomy of your new son-in-law?"

"No," said Mr. Cripps. "She says I shall be surprised when
I see him, and that I little think who he is, and seems to hint that
I *have* seen him ; but she don't say where. Perhaps he used to
come to the shop."

"The person I allude to," observed the lawyer, "is sufficiently
remarkable to be identified easily. His name wont assist us much,
but his person will. He's a man that was known for some time
about town by the name of Nosey, owing to a peculiar formed
nose he has, from a blow he got in a brawl some years ago. By
means of that, and his bald head, we can easily describe him to
one of our correspondents in Paris."

"Nosey! reiterated Mr. Cripps. "Nosey! He warn't like
Julius Cæsar, was he?"

"I don't know that he was," answered Mr. Glassford, laughing.
"But he's very bald—that's the principal resemblance I know of."

"Bald!" again reiterated Mr. Cripps. "A stoutish man?
Fair complexion?"

"Exactly," replied the lawyer.

"The Lord look down upon us!" cried Mr. Cripps. "Is he a
rogue?"

"I fear a greater doesn't exist," answered Mr. Glassford.
"But you know him, then?"

"Know him!" exclaimed the astonished grocer,—"why he's
the count's servant!"

"As much as he is Colonel Jones," replied Mr. Glassford. "Rely on it he is neither one nor the other."

"And who the devil is he ?" inquired Mr. Cripps.

"His real name is Remorden," answered Mr. Glassford, "and he's a gentleman by birth. But what little property he had he ran through within a year or two after he came to it; and since that time he has been living by his wits. Latterly he has been very much abroad, where, I suppose, he found it easier to carry on his schemes than here."

"But the count," said Mr. Cripps, with a faltering voice; "how could he be so deceived?"

"We must hope he was deceived," replied Mr. Glassford. "But I cannot conceal from you that the account you have given me does occasion some misgivings. However, we must hope for the best. But with regard to the other fellow, there can be no doubt in the world of his being as consummate a rascal as ever breathed."

"What shall I do?" inquired Mr. Cripps, with a bewildered air.

"Set off for Paris instantly, and fetch back your two un-married daughters. They'll be getting a husband for Jemima else, rely on it, young as she is. As for the eldest, you must be guided by circumstances when you are there; but if the man's an impostor, as I suspect, a confederate of Remorden's, bring her away by all means."

"And my money ! my fifty thousand pounds!" cried Mr. Cripps.

"Forget that you ever had it," replied Mr. Glassford; "and be thankful another hundred thousand isn't gone after it."

Here was a fall! "Oh, heavy declension!" After the pride and glory of having outwitted the Emperor of Austria himself! And as for going to Paris, it was a thing Mr. Cripps contem-plated with absolute horror; it was worse than the loss of the fifty thousand pounds; and he returned to Virginia House to consult his wife, in a state bordering on distraction.

"To go to France to be fed on frogs and *soupe maigre*, and live amongst a set of fellows that wore wooden shoes, and talked an outlandish jargon that nobody could understand !"

The poor man hadn't resolution to set about it, so he wrote to Livia to say he was coming, and to forbid the banns; and then resolved to allow himself a little while to make up his mind to the enterprise.

A few days after this, Mr. Glassford, who never doubted his having instantly departed, drove down to Virginia House, and inquired for Mrs. Cripps, whom, on being introduced into the drawing-room, he found in tears.

"I hope no new misfortune has occurred?" said he. "Nothing worse than I learnt from Mr. Cripps last week, is there?"

"We've heard nothing since," replied the lady, sobbing; "but dear, dear Mr. Cripps is going to set off to-night for Paris; and I'm afraid I shall never see him again. I'm sure he'll never come back alive!" And a fresh burst of tears testified the violence of her affliction and the extent of her fears.

"Bless me! What, isn't he gone yet?" exclaimed the lawyer.

"We couldn't bring our minds to it," sobbed Mrs. Cripps. "His things have been packed up these three days, all ready; and we even had the sandwiches cut, and everything—but when it came to the point, he couldn't do it. Think what it is, at his time of life, Mr. Glassford, with a full habit of body, to go and encounter the dangers of a stormy ocean, full of sharks and whales and porpuses—we used to see them floundering about at Margate, ready to devour anybody they could get hold of; and he that wouldn't be able to understand a word they said to him!—what chance would he have amongst them?"

"Not much, if his safety depended on his eloquence, I'm afraid," replied Mr. Glassford, smiling.

"There was one of them we used to meet walking on the pier at Margate," added Mrs. Cripps; "and sometimes he'd try to get into conversation with my husband; but, Lord! they could make nothing of it."

"I should imagine not," said Mr. Glassford. "But really I cannot help feeling some uneasiness about your daughters from this delay."

"Oh! Mr. Cripps has written," said the lady, "to forbid the marriage; so a few days can't make any difference, you know."

"We can't be so sure of that," answered the lawyer. "But, however, would you have any objection to Mr. Cripps going, if he had a companion?—one who speaks French well, and would be able to take care of him?"

"That would be a great comfort, certainly," replied she.

"Well," said he, "a young man from my office, my head clerk, indeed, starts for Paris to-morrow upon some business we have in hand; and the object of my visit to-day, was to learn if he could carry any message, or be of any use in your affairs. Now, since Mr. Cripps is not yet off, what do you say to their travelling together?"

This proposition was gladly acceded to; and on the following morning Mr. Cripps and the young gentleman in question started on their adventurous journey; and having escaped the monsters of the deep, and the perils of the road, arrived in due time at Paris; where, after changing their dress, and taking some refreshment, they lost no time in seeking the Hôtel Dangeau, in the Rue de Richelieu, whence Miss Livy's letters had been dated.

But, alas! they were too late. Count, countess, Livy, Jemima, and Colonel Jones, had all departed together a week before, on their way, as the mistress of the hotel understood, to the count's castle, which was situated a long way off—where, she never rightly understood; only she was sure it was a place she'd never heard of in France.

Here was a sad blow; and if Mr. Cripps had been alone, as a journey to the unknown regions of Transylvania was quite out of the question, he would have stepped into the next diligence he met with, and returned straightway to England. But the young clerk took a different view of the case. z

"We must find out which road they've taken," said he, "and whither they're bound. Betwixt the police and the passport office, there's little doubt but that we shall arrive at the truth on those points, and then we must consider what's next to be done."

Accordingly, after some inquiry, it was ascertained that the party had started with passports for Brussels; and the authorities at Brussels were written to, to ascertain if such persons had been seen there. The answer was, that two gentlemen, whose names and description corresponded with those sought for, had been at Brussels for a day or two, but were unaccompanied by ladies; and had themselves left the city, on their way back to France.

"No ladies," said the young clerk; "then they must have left them somewhere on the road;" and although he was unwilling to communicate his own apprehensions to poor Mr. Cripps, he could not avoid feeling considerable uneasiness as to the fate of the unfortunate girls; and he proposed that, with as little delay as possible, they should both set out on the road to Brussels, and endeavour to trace the fugitives as they went along. A suggestion to which Mr. Cripps, who found himself well taken care of by his young companion, and in little danger either from sharks or Frenchmen, and who had also discovered that there was something better to eat in France than frogs and *soupe maigre*, made no objection.

CHAPTER LIII.

MYSTERIES UNVEILED.

IT was on the second day after his return from Oakfield, that Mr. Simpson received a note dated from an hotel in Brooke-street, requesting him to call on a person there who had something of importance to communicate, and directing him to inquire for Monsieur Courtois.

Conceiving the communication was about something relating to his foreign trade, the worthy wine-merchant lost no time in obeying the summons; and on asking at the door for Mr. Courtois, a Frenchman immediately came forward, and in tolerable English begged to know if his name was Simpson; and being answered in the affirmative, requested the honour of conducting him up stairs.

Monsieur Courtois was an elderly, respectable-looking man, with his thickly-powdered hair dressed in the fashion of the old court, and attired in deep mourning; and he preceded Mr. Simpson up stairs with much deference and politeness, but at the same time with a slow and dignified step, that well became the gravity of his appearance.

On reaching the first floor, he threw open a door, and announced "Monsieur Simpson," advancing at the same time to place that gentleman a chair before he retired.

The apartment to which Mr. Simpson found himself introduced, was a handsome and well-furnished drawing-room, evidently the best in the hotel.; and on a sofa, at one end of it, sat a lady, who, as he approached, arose with the utmost grace to receive him. She, also, was attired in deep mourning; and the extraordinary beauty of her face and figure almost dazzled the eyes of the staid visitor, who came all unprepared for such a vision of loveliness; whilst her attractions were rather augmented than diminished by the air of exceeding languor and deep melancholy that pervaded her countenance and manner.

"I have the pleasure," she said, " of seeing Mr. Simpson of Mark Lane?"

Mr. Simpson bowed assent.

"The intimate friend," she continued, "of the late Mr. Wentworth?"

"I had the honour to be so, madam," replied Mr. Simpson, with a sigh.

The lady sighed too; and drawing forth a delicate cambric handkerchief, she held it for a moment to her eyes.

"Come nearer," she said, pointing to a seat on the sofa beside her. "Will you have the goodness," she continued, when Mr. Simpson had obeyed the invitation,—" will you have the goodness to relate to me all the circumstances of Mr. Wentworth's death— as far, at least, as they ever came to light?"

"Certainly, madam," replied Mr. Simpson; and wondering intensely who his fair friend could be, and what the interview was to lead to, he proceeded to narrate all the particulars that were known regarding the tragedy in question.

The lady listened to his tale with undeviating attention, occasionally interrupting the progress of the narrative to ask questions which evinced her intimate knowledge of the persons and localities connected with the drama. When he had concluded, she again held her handkerchief to her eyes, appearing deeply affected; and a silence of some moments ensued.

"And from that time to this, sir," she said, at length, "no further light has been thrown on the mystery? Andrew has never reappeared, and he and Mabel the dairymaid are still supposed to have eloped together?"

"That, madam," answered Mr. Simpson, "is still the general conviction;" for he did not think it advisable to communicate the events of the last few days, and the suspicions they had awakened in Mr. Olliphant's breast, and consequently in his own, till he was better acquainted with the person he was speaking to. He wished to hear her story first; and for this she did not seem disposed to keep him long in suspense.

"Well, sir," she said, "it is in my power to prove its fallacy; and you will now perhaps have the goodness to listen to my history: the which, in order to render it more comprehensible, I will commence by avowing, that I myself am Mabel the dairymaid— by name, Mabel Lightfoot."

z 2

Mr. Simpson could only look his surprise—he had too much delicacy and good breeding, the good breeding that springs from generosity and benevolence, to make any comments on the confession.

"You may well look astonished," she continued, "but such is the fact. With respect to my own history, previous to my going to live at Oakfield, I have little to tell. My parents were poor, but respectable, each springing from families that in former times had belonged to the gentry of the county; and this circumstance, slight and unimportant as it may seem, has been the origin of my errors, and the foundation of my fortunes, good and ill; for my mother could not forget it; and when she saw that I was likely to be endowed with some charms of person, she neglected no opportunity of instilling into my mind the hope and the desire of improving my situation by a prudent marriage. With this view, she carefully guarded me from any intimacy with the young people of my own sphere, especially the men; and I grew up without a friend or a confidant but herself. But at the age of fifteen, I lost her; my father had died before; and both I and my sister Grace were thrown upon the world, and obliged to go to service.

"For my own part, I selected the situation of dairy-maid, because I thought it less menial than household service, and because it entailed the necessity of less communication with the other servants; for my mother's precepts had been sown in a fruitful soil. I was by nature as ambitious as she could desire me, and at the same time as ignorant of the world, and its ways, as if I had been born in another planet. I had been taught reading and writing, and had a tolerable notion of grammar; acquirements which my mother had taken some pains to procure me, as being important elements in my future establishment. But I had no access to books: indeed I was scarcely acquainted with any but the Bible; and as I avoided the conversation of my equals, and had no opportunity of enjoying that of my superiors, my mind was little more enlightened than that of an infant.

"Nevertheless, in spite of my ignorance and my pride, I had innumerable lovers, for I was considered the beauty of the village; but I treated them all with the utmost disdain and indifference. The only one I ever felt the slightest disposition to favour was Andrew Hopley, who was in many respects very superior to the other young men of his class; but his station and livery were an effectual bar to the indulgence of my inclination, and I carefully repressed it.

"Now, sir, comes the period of my story in which you will find yourself interested.

"I had not been long at Oakfield, before Mr. Gaveston found me out, and seemed disposed to pay me particular attention. At first he accosted me with the freedom and familiarity with which gentlemen permit themselves to address young women in my situation; but soon finding that I was only offended and repelled, he changed his tactics, and affected to entertain a violent passion for me; and ignorant as I was, it is extremely possible that I might have fallen into his snares, had I not known that he was engaged to be married to Miss Wentworth—but that circumstance preserved me; and therefore, although he lamented the vows that fettered him, and swore that he loved me a thousand times better than he did her, yet, as I was aware that he could not promote the objects of my ambition, I turned a deaf ear to all his protestations.

"At length, one day—it was not long before Mr. Wentworth set out on his excursion to the coast, from which you tell me he never returned—Mr. Gaveston took an opportunity of joining me early when I was going to milk my cows, before the rest of the family were about.

"'Mabel,' he said, 'I find that my unfortunate engagement to Miss Wentworth, which it is impossible for me to break, must for ever preclude my obtaining from you a return of the passion you have inspired me with; but my disappointment, great as it is, cannot diminish the interest I must ever feel in your happiness; and since it is not in my power to promote it myself by making you my wife, I feel the greatest desire to do it by some other means. In short, I can't bear to see you here milking cows, and performing menial offices so far beneath the station for which nature designed you; and I have been casting about in my mind what I can do to raise you into the sphere that you would adorn.

"'Now, you must know that I have an acquaintance in the neighbourhood of Bordeaux, which is in France, who is the greatest admirer of beauty in the world, and who is exceedingly anxious to obtain a handsome English wife; but as there are few Englishwomen there, and none that happen to be very lovely, he has hitherto found it impossible to satisfy his taste. When I took leave of him the last time I came away, he asked me if I would choose a wife for him, and send her out; and without thinking seriously at the moment of what I was saying, I promised I would. Now what do you say, Mabel, to marrying my friend, and becoming a marchioness?'

"'A marchioness!' I exclaimed. 'Is he a marquis?'

"'Yes,' said he; 'he is, I assure you, a marquis of a very ancient and noble Spanish family; and he has, besides, a handsome estate, and a good fortune. It's true, he's not very young; but if you can overlook that one defect, I promise you he'll make you an excellent husband. He'll fall desperately in love the moment he looks at you; and you may manage him completely, and have everything your own way. What do you say to my proposal?'

"I answered, that I didn't care the least whether he was young or old if he would make me a marchioness, and let me live like a lady.

"'Oh!' he said, 'you'll have carriages and servants at your command, and live like a princess.'

"'Then,' I said, 'I should like it very much. But how am I to go to him?'

"'Leave that to me,' he answered. 'But one thing, remember, you must keep the whole business a profound secret from every-body; for if it were to reach Mr. Wentworth's ears, he'd be writing off to the marquis to tell him you were only a dairymaid, which there's no necessity in the world for his ever knowing. I shall tell him you are the daughter of a particular friend of my own. All you have to do is to keep the thing to yourself, and be ready to start at a moment's notice.'

"Soon after this conversation, Mr. Gaveston was suddenly summoned abroad by particular business, and the marriage, which was to have taken place immediately, was consequently delayed; and Mr. Wentworth, his daughter, and Andrew, went down to the seaside to await his return.

"Well, sir, two nights before the family were expected back, as I was in my room, about eleven o'clock, preparing to go to bed, I heard a slight tap at the window. I must observe that my room was on the ground-floor, adjoining the dairy, and that there was a door which led from it into the other parts of the house. At first I took no notice of the signal; but when it was repeated, I went to the window and inquired who was there.

"'Open the door,' said a man's voice, speaking close to the glass; 'I've a letter for you, if you are Mabel the dairymaid.'

"'I am Mabel,' I said; 'but I'm not going to open the door unless I know who you are.'

"'I come from a good friend of yours,' returned the man; 'and the letter's about a certain marquis at Bordeaux. But open the door, and I'll explain everything.'

"On hearing this, I thought there could be no danger in open-ing the door, as whoever the man was, he must be a messenger from Mr. Gaveston; so, after fastening the other door that led into the house, lest we should be interrupted, I let him in.

"He was a stoutish man, dressed in a drab coat, with a red handkerchief round his throat, and over his chin; and he'd a face that, once seen, was not easily forgotten. He appeared to have been formerly extremely good-looking; but a strange twist of the nose, and a remarkable rise across the bridge, gave his features a peculiar expression.

"'Here,' said he, handing me a letter, 'are a few lines from Mr. Gaveston, which he has sent that you may be satisfied I am acting by his authority; but as I have no time to lose, I'll deliver my message, and leave you to read them after I am gone.

"'What he desired me to say is, that on the third night from this you are to hold yourself ready to start for London, on your way to the continent. He and I will be here to fetch you away; and to prevent any disappointment, the thing must be managed so quietly that you shall not be missed till the following morning. You are to take care to admit nobody into this part of the house; and we shall let you know we are here by the same signal I gave just now. Will you be ready, and are you willing to go?'

"'Yes, I am,' I replied.

"'Very well,' said he; 'that's a brave girl; I admire your

spirit. And that much being settled, there is no necessity for my lingering here. Remember, you are to take no clothes, nor anything with you, of any description whatever. Mr. Gaveston will supply you with all that is necessary.'

"Having said this, he went away, and I opened the letter; which, however, contained nothing more than a request from Mr. Gaveston that I would be guided by the directions I should receive from the bearer, who he assured me was his particular friend.

"Well, sir, the intervening time past without any unusual occurrence, and the night appointed for my departure arrived. No hour had been mentioned, and I was therefore uncertain how soon I might expect to be summoned; so I retired early to my room, which, as I was little in the habit of associating with the other servants, excited no observation; and having bolted the door of communication, I sat down with my bonnet and shawl on, to await the arrival of Mr. Gaveston.

"I had no watch, but I think it must have been about two hours after midnight that I was aroused by a noise at the window; for being quite unused to sitting up so late, I had fallen asleep in my chair; and I started up hastily and opened the door.

"'Why, Mabel,' said Mr. Gaveston, who entered, followed by the man who had brought me the letter three nights before, 'we thought you had forgotten the appointment; we have been trying to make you hear this quarter of an hour. However, make haste now, for we have no time to lose. You must disguise yourself in this dress,' he said, opening a bundle which the other man held in his hand, and which contained a suit of boy's clothes. 'Put them on quickly, whilst we step into the house for a minute or two. I want some papers I left in my room when I was here last;' and so saying, they passed through the door of communication with the house, and left me to change my dress.

"They were not gone many minutes, and I was but just ready when they returned. 'Now, come,' said Mr. Gaveston, taking me under his arm, and we stepped out; but just as I was closing the dairy-door, he said, 'By-the-by, I don't think we fastened the door of communication. We'd better do so, or somebody may get in and rob the house.' So he re-entered my room for that purpose, and when he came out he called me back.

"'Here, Mabel,' said he, pointing to the bonnet and shawl, and other clothes I had just taken off, and which, in my haste, I had left lying on the floor, 'pick up those, and tie them in a bundle; they must not be left there.'

"I did so, and he carried them out, and handed them to his companion. He then gave me his arm, and we walked away across the park, whilst the other man went round to the front of the house, where he said they had left their horses, which they would not bring to the back, because the servants' bed-rooms were all on that side, and there might be some danger of being heard.

"The horses met us at the park gate, of which Mr. Gaveston had a private key, to enable him to enter if he came home late at night when he was staying at Oakfield; and there, the gentlemen having mounted, I being placed on the saddle behind Mr. Gaveston, after stopping to re-lock the gate, we took the high road to London, for about ten miles. We then turned off, and had ridden for about five miles further across the country, through by-lanes and fields, when Mr. Gaveston suddenly stopt at a spot where two roads met.

" ' Now,' said he, 'Mabel, here we must part for the present, and you must continue your journey to London with my friend, who will take every care of you; and in less than a week I shall join you there. You are now within a couple of miles of a town, where you will find a conveyance; and so far you must walk, as I must take the horses away with me.'

" Upon this, they lifted me down; and Mr. Gaveston, taking the bundle containing my clothes, which he said he knew how to dispose of, we parted, he riding one way, and we walking the other.

" As he had predicted, we soon came in sight of a pretty considerable town, which we entered, after my companion had warned me that I was not to speak, but to hold my handkerchief to my eyes, as if I were in great distress. Walking briskly through the streets, which were nearly empty, for it was yet but early morning, we reached an inn, where the ostler and a few of the servants were already stirring.

" ' We want a chaise and a pair of horses as quickly as possible,' said my companion to a waiter, who was yawning at the door.

" ' First turn out, directly,' cried the man, and away ran the ostler to obey the orders. 'Please to walk in and take some breakfast, sir,' added he, ' whilst they put to.'

" ' We'll just step into a room for a moment,' answered my friend; 'but we must not stop for breakfast. We are on an errand of life and death. This young gentleman's father has been seized with a fit : and we're afraid, if we don't make the greatest speed, all will be over before we get there.'

" Upon this, according to my instructions, I pretended to cry very much, and the good-natured waiter ran out to hasten the post-boy's preparations. 'They'll be round directly, sir,' said he, as he returned; and in a couple of minutes more, the chaise was at the door; my companion handed me into it, and we were galloping along the road.

" For three stages we got on as fast as we could, my friend always urging the same motive for speed, and then we stopped to breakfast; after which we started again, and stopped no more till we reached London; having taken nothing but a biscuit and a glass of wine on the road.

" It was the middle of the night when we arrived; and just before we entered the town, my companion called to the driver to stop, and having asked him his fare, he paid him, and dismissed him, saying he needed him no further; and then giving me his arm, we entered the town, and walked at a rapid pace through a great many streets—I remember we crossed a bridge, and that is all I know of the course we took.

" At length, having arrived at what appeared to me a shabby

part of the town, my friend stopped at a house that looked rather better than the others, and rang the bell; and almost immediately, which made me conclude we were expected, an elderly, decently-dressed woman opened the door.

" ' Here we are, Mrs. Davis,' said my companion. And then turning to me, he said, ' This is your home for the present; you'll find yourself very comfortable under Mrs. Davis' care till your friend arrives. Good night!' and shaking me by the hand, he turned off, and walked away."

CHAPTER LIV.

MABEL CONTINUES HER STORY.

" WHEN the companion of my journey departed," continued Mabel, " Mrs. Davis, taking me by the hand, led me into a parlour, where I found a comfortable fire with a kettle of boiling water on the hob, and the tea-things ready upon the table.

" ' I thought,' said she, ' you would prefer a cup of tea to anything else after your journey; there's nothing so refreshing; and you can eat a bit of cold meat with it if you are inclined.'

" I thanked her and accepted her offer. She was extremely civil; but asked me no questions, speaking only of the weather, the fatigues of travelling, the comforts of tea, and so forth. I however knew that she was aware of my sex; as my companion, whose name I afterwards learnt was Dyson, had informed me that I was to be conducted to the house of a friend of Mr. Gaveston's, who had been told I was a young lady on my way to the continent with the intention of uniting myself to a gentleman to whom I had been some time attached, but whose alliance was not approved by my friends. I had also been instructed that I was to call myself Miss Jones; and that Mr. Gaveston was only known to Mrs. Davis as Mr. Godfrey.

" ' Now,' said Mrs. Davis, when tea was over, ' I dare say you'll be glad to go to bed; and I recommend your lying till I bring you your breakfast in the morning. You should take a good rest after such a journey.'

" ' But what am I to do,' I said, ' for clothes, when I do rise? I hav'n't a single article with me.'

" ' Oh!' said she, ' leave that to me. I'll supply you with clothes. If they don't exactly fit, never mind that. You'll see nobody here, and they'll do very well till Mr. Godfrey arrives.'

" Accordingly, the next morning, after I had taken my breakfast, she brought me a dark silk dress, and other indispensable articles, which seemed to have been made for a person about my size, and which she said belonged to her daughter; and when I was ready to leave my room, instead of taking me down to the parlour I had been in the night before, she led me into a room adjoining my bed-chamber, which looked only on a back yard, and which she said it was necessary I should inhabit for the

present; as, if I went below, I might be seen by people coming to
the house, and discovered.

"The first day I was so tired that I did not care much about
this confinement; but when I had recovered my fatigue, I began
to pine for air and exercise, and I begged Mrs. Davis to take me
out. But this she positively refused, alleging that it was absolutely contrary to Mr. Godfrey's orders. In every other respect
she was very obliging, giving me books to read, and doing what
she could to amuse me. But still I found my time dreadfully
tedious; and when at the end of a week Mr. Gaveston came, I
earnestly entreated that I might commence my journey immediately. 'That,' however, he said, 'was impossible, for that there
had been many inquiries made about me; and that I should be infallibly traced and taken back to Oakfield, if I showed myself out
of doors yet;' and so simple was I, that I gave credit to all he
said. 'Depend on it,' he added, 'the moment it's safe for you to
move, you shall. In the mean time, I must return to Oakfield,
lest I should be suspected of having any hand in taking you off.'

"It was fully a month before he appeared again, by which time,
between weariness, and a confinement to which I was so unaccus-
tomed, I was getting extremely unwell. Still he urged it was too
soon to move; and the only relief I got was, that two or three
times he took me out to walk of an evening, after it was dark.
But I could not help observing, that the more impatient I became,
the more closely I was watched; and I began to see that I was
little better than a prisoner.

"All these causes together, combined, I believe, with the effects
of a cold I had caught on my journey, at length overthrew my
health and spirits completely, and I fell extremely ill. Mrs.
Davis and a maid-servant that was in the house, attended me
assiduously enough; but no medical advice being called in, I continued to get worse and worse, till I was at death's door; and I
believe I should actually have died (which I have since believed
would have been exactly what Mr. Gaveston desired), had not
the servant taken fright one day when Mrs. Davis was out. I
happened to faint whilst she was standing by my bedside, and
finding it impossible to recover me by any means she had recourse
to, she ran out of the house and fetched in an apothecary that
lived in the neighbourhood.

"After this the man was suffered to attend me; and Mr.
Godfrey, as he was called, also brought a young person of his
acquaintance, to see me, called Julia Clark—"

"Who?" said Mr. Simpson, hastily interrupting the discourse.
"Did you say Julia Clark—"

"Yes," replied Mabel, "Julia Clark was the name of the lady.
A very pretty young person she was, and very kind to me. Do
you know her?"

"I rather think I do," answered Mr. Simpson. "But excuse
my interruption. Pray go on."

"Well," continued Mabel, "I gradually got better; and
Julia's visits helped me to bear my confinement; and when I was

sufficiently recovered to travel, Mr. Gaveston announced that everything was ready for my departure ; and that as he could not go with me himself, Mr. Dyson had undertaken to conduct me safe to Bordeaux.

" Accordingly, early one morning, to my infinite joy, I bade adieu to Mrs. Davis and her dreary apartments, and we proceeded to Portsmouth, and from thence to Harfleur ; where only stopping one night, we took places in a diligence, which I imagined was to convey us to Bordeaux.

" But my companion, Mr. Dyson, or rather Colonel Jones, for that was the name he assumed on the journey, had other views ; and instead of conducting me to the Marquis de la Rosa, my intended husband, as Mr. Gaveston had charged him to do, he took me to Paris, where, after engaging apartments in a handsome hotel, and providing himself and me with fashionable habiliments, he introduced me into public as his niece.

" It is easy for a young Englishwoman there, who is tolerably good-looking, to attract notice ; and I was soon surrounded by a crowd of admirers ; amongst whom, the most urgent and persevering was the Duc de Rochechouart, who was at that time considered the most dissipated and profligate man about the court— at least, where women were concerned. In other respects, his character was never arraigned.

" Well, sir," pursued Mabel, " not to detain you with a detail of the arts that were used to deceive me, it is sufficient to inform you that I was led to believe the duke was addressing me with honourable views ; and after a few weeks, having been conducted to one of his castles, at some distance from Paris, I was imposed upon by a false marriage—in short, sold. The ceremony was performed by a servant of the duke's, an Englishman, called Dillon, who pretended to be a clergyman, and read the marriage service from the prayer-book ; and Colonel Jones, my pretended uncle, having received a considerable sum of money for his treachery, afterwards took his leave, and left me to discover the deception at my leisure.

" For some months I believed myself the wife of the duke, and every pains was taken to keep up the delusion ; but, at length, an accident disclosed to me the truth. At the period of my supposed marriage, I was utterly ignorant of the French language ; and as the duke could speak English tolerably, having once been ambassador here, I found little inconvenience from my want of knowledge. But believing myself the Duchess of Rochechouart, and anticipating the time when I should be introduced at court and into society, I thought it right to acquire the language of the people I was to live amongst. I therefore privately engaged a master, and applied myself assiduously to the study, with the intention of some day surprising Rochechouart with my unexpected accomplishment ; and urged by this motive, and perhaps rather a natural facility, I made considerable progress in a short time. But this newly acquired talent was the accidental means of opening my eyes to my real situation.

"One day that I was sitting alone in my boudoir, with a door ajar that opened into the drawing-room, I overheard a conversation between the duke and one of his friends, which, although I was not a sufficient adept in the language to understand thoroughly, undeceived me completely with respect to my own position.

"The subject of the conversation was an alliance which had been offered to the duke, and which he had declined; and the visit was for the purpose of urging him to reconsider a proposal that was, on many accounts, esteemed highly desirable. But the duke was firm in his refusal; and I comprehended enough to learn that he mentioned me as the motive. The gentleman urged, 'that there would be no necessity for parting with me;' but the duke confessed, that he feared whenever I discovered the deception he had practised, I should leave him; 'and assuredly she will,' he said, 'if I marry.' In which conviction he was perfectly correct; for I certainly should.

"You may conceive, sir, what a blow this was to me. However, I commanded my feelings sufficiently to remain quite quiet till the visitor was gone; but when Rochechouart returned from seeing him through the ante-chamber, and I attempted to rise from my chair to speak to him, intending to express my indignation, and then immediately quit the house, I had only time to clasp my hands, and give him one look of reproach, before I sank to the ground in a state of insensibility. But that one look was enough. It told him that I was undeceived; and as soon as I recovered, and was able to listen to him, he entered on his exculpation; explaining to me the difficulties that lay in the way of an alliance between a person in his situation and one in mine—the opposition he should have experienced from his connexions, and the court more especially, as it was easily perceived that the pretended Colonel Jones was a mere sharper, who had brought me there to make money of, and that I was not his niece, as he had asserted; and finally, he made known to me how I had been actually sold; and that it had been merely a contest between the young noblemen I was introduced to, which should have me; Colonel Jones standing out for the highest price.

"'Thus, Amabel,' said he, 'you would not have escaped, rely on it; and if you had not fallen to me, you would to Armagnac, or De l'Orme, or some of the others, who probably would not have loved you half so much as I do. The conversation you have just overheard, must, at least, have convinced you of my attachment.'

"It certainly had; and that was the only thing that supported me under my disappointment and mortification. When I first encouraged the duke's attentions, and accepted the offer of his hand, I confess that I was actuated solely by ambition; and it would have been perfectly indifferent to me whether I attained my object through him, or through any of the other gentlemen who were contesting the prize. But my feelings were now wholly changed. Without affecting to undervalue the luxury, and indeed magnificence, in which I lived, or pretending to assert that it would not have required an extraordinary effort of resolution to have resigned them and fallen back into my original situation, yet, I can truly say, that the affection Rochechouart had inspired me with formed a much stronger obstacle to my leaving him, than his splendid castles and gorgeous liveries, or than my own sumptuous attire, gilded chariot, and elegant boudoir.

"I really loved him; and, the deception he had practised on me aside, I had certainly every reason to do so. His kindness and indulgence to me were unvarying; and as for his own qualities, he was universally admitted to be the handsomest and the most agreeable man about the court.

"You may imagine the result, sir: I consented to remain; and the duke immediately made a handsome settlement on me, which secured me in affluence for the rest of my life, whether I left him or not; and I must do him the justice to say, that never, till the hour of his death,"—and here she burst into a passion of tears that almost choked her utterance—"never to the hour of his death did he give me reason to repent my acquiescence!

"Indeed, I am sure that if I had urged it much, he would have privately legalized our connexion; but I never did; because I felt that I was not worthy to become his wife, and that, in many respects, I should have been doing him a great injury. It is true I was deceived, and so far innocent; but, on the other hand, I could not forget that I was not blameless. I had sought to deceive him also. I had acquiesced in Colonel Jones' imposition, and attempted to pass for what I was not; besides, my own motives were base and unworthy. I saw they were so, as my mind improved by education; and I felt that I deserved the degradation I suffered.

"I therefore made up my mind to the penalty I had incurred. I knew I must look to pass my life without any society but the duke's; and that when we returned to Paris, his numerous engagements would not leave him much time to bestow on me; and I also felt, that however unwilling he was to part with me then, I might not always retain the same power over his affections.

"Under these circumstances I could not look for much happiness; but I saw that one means of improving my situation, both present and future, was within my reach. I perceived that by repairing the deficiencies of my early education, I should not only render myself more agreeable to Rochechouart, but that I should be supplying myself with a resource during the life of solitude and abandonment that lay before me. To this object I therefore devoted myself; and as I was yet young, and could command all the advantages that money could purchase, I made considerable progress in the studies I undertook; and soon learned to find in my books and my music the best consolation for my lonely hours and degraded condition.

"In this manner my life passed, without any particular occurrence to interrupt its even tenour, till about six months since, when I received an unexpected visit from the Marquis de la Rosa, the gentleman for whom I had been designed by Mr. Gaveston. How he discovered me I do not know, but he wrote to me to say he was in Paris, and to desire an interview; and I believe it was more curiosity than anything else, that made me grant his request. But his visit led to disclosures I little expected.

"From him I first learned that Mr. Wentworth was dead; and although his information was imperfect, I gathered enough to ascertain that my removal from Oakfield had been somehow or other mysteriously connected with the catastrophe; and I was the more confirmed in this persuasion, by his showing me a letter of Mr. Gaveston's, wherein he proposed to the marquis to practise upon me exactly the sort of deception to which I had fallen a victim through the villany of his friend; namely, to deceive me by a false marriage.

"I must observe that the marquis had no idea that I was the dairy-maid; he only had heard of me as Miss Jones; neither had I ever confessed to Rochechouart that I had once filled so humble a situation; nor had I courage to do it yet. But for that remnant of silly pride, I should have immediately written to you on the subject of what I had learnt, for I obtained your address from Bordeaux; and perhaps the calamity which I have now to deplore might not have occurred.

"I fear my sad history must weary you, sir," continued Mabel; "but the regard you bore Mr. Wentworth will give you an interest in it; and I shall not detain you much longer.

"About two months ago, the duke's regiment, which had been for some time on a foreign station, having returned to France, and being quartered at Lisle, he thought it right to join it for a few weeks; and he proposed to me to accompany him. Of course I consented; and thither we immediately proceeded, attended by our horses, servants, and equipages.

"One of my favourite recreations was riding on horseback; and as I had but few pleasures, Rochechouart did all he could to make this agreeable, by supplying me with beautiful animals, and accompanying me himself whenever he could.

"Well, sir, one day, about ten days since, we were taking our usual exercise, accompanied only by a groom, when we perceived a handsome English carriage approaching at a rapid rate; and we slackened our pace in order to get a better view of the travellers within. But you may imagine our surprise, when, as the vehicle drew nigh, we distinguished, reclining in the opposite corners, our old acquaintance, Colonel Jones, and Dillon the duke's former valet!

"The moment I recognised Colonel Jones, I felt a vehement desire to obtain from him some information regarding the mystérious affairs at Oakfield; and I intimated to the duke that I had a particular reason for desiring to speak to him.

"'Go,' said he to the groom; 'ride after that carriage, and observe where they put up; we'll follow more leisurely, and meet you at the entrance of the town.'

"The man immediately set spurs to his horse, and had nearly overtaken the travellers, when, to our horror and astonishment, we heard a shot, and saw him fall to the ground.

"Incensed at this unprovoked attack, without a moment's deliberation, and deaf to my cries, the duke threw his horse into a gallop, and pursued the murderers. Whether they knew him, or whether, being in uniform, they mistook his intentions, I cannot tell—for we found afterwards that the carriage was loaded with contraband goods—but when they found he was gaining upon them, they fired another pistol, and shot him dead on the spot. They then immediately turned their horses' heads, and instead of pursuing the road to Lisle, they endeavoured to make the best of their way back across the frontier.

" But their escape, I, at least, had the consolation of preventing. Mounted on a very fleet horse, and in a state of too much excitement to think of danger, I pursued them at my utmost speed; and, fortunately, just at the moment they were beginning to fancy themselves secure, being met by a troop of the duke's regiment who had been out on a foraging expedition, I succeeded in having them arrested, and brought back to Lisle. Why they did not shoot me also, I cannot tell—perhaps they had no more ammunition—for I scarcely think they would have spared me from better motives.

" I will not detain you, sir," said Mabel, who, when she reached this part of her story, was almost unable to proceed, from the bitterness of her grief; " I will not detain you with an account of my feelings; those I leave to your imagination. I will only trouble you with such further particulars as you are likely to be interested in.

" The two criminals were of course placed in confinement; and as soon as I was able to appear in court, they were brought before a magistrate, and my evidence was given against them.

" For their own parts, they neither confessed nor admitted anything; but the contents of the carriage were quite enough to explain the motives of their expedition, and the origin of their fears.

" It was, as I said, lined with contraband goods of the most valuable description; and there was every reason to believe, that on their previous passage through Lisle, shortly before, they had taken as much out of France as they were now bringing into it.

" Finding, when I had given my evidence, that my presence would not be again required for a few weeks, and that I was in the meantime at liberty to depart where I pleased, I resolved to employ the interval in an endeavour to penetrate the mystery of Mr. Wentworth's death, and to clear myself from the suspicion that my absence had drawn upon me; and I felt the greater necessity for doing this without delay, because there can be no doubt that these men will be condemned to expiate their crimes on the scaffold, and with Colonel Jones will probably expire all chance of discovering the secret.

" With this view I started for Paris without delay; but I was destined, before I reached it, to be made acquainted with another instance of their villany. On the morning I quitted Lisle, as we were passing through a small village, I observed a number of

A

country people assembled round the door of a hut; and as we drew nearer, I perceived two ladies, apparently in a very exhausted condition, seated on chairs at the door, to whom the by-standers were administering such simple refreshments as they had to give. The singularity of the circumstance awakened my curiosity; and besides, there was something in the appearance of the young women that led me to believe they were English.

" I therefore stopped the carriage, and desired Courtois, who was with me, to inquire if anything had happened in which my assistance could be useful; and he presently learnt from the peasants, that the two ladies I saw there had crawled into the village shortly before, apparently quite exhausted and worn out by fatigue and want of food—that they were foreigners, who could speak no French—and that whence they came or whither they were going could not be discovered.

" Upon this, I alighted; and making my way through the crowd, I addressed them in English, saying, I was afraid they had met with some unpleasant accident, and offering my services.

"Poor things! if a voice from Heaven had reached them they could scarcely have seemed more relieved. All I gathered from them, however, at that moment, was, that they had fled from some place where they considered themselves in danger, and that they hoped to find their father in Paris, where they besought me to take them.

" To this request I of course assented; and they were immediately assisted into the carriage. They were so exhausted, that I found it necessary to give up travelling on the following day; and we therefore rested at Abbeville, where I first learnt the circumstances that had brought them into the strange predicament in which I found them.

" I will not detain you now with the details of their melancholy story. It is sufficient to say that the two men, Colonel Jones and Dillon, had contrived to impose upon their parents and themselves —one of them, indeed, was married to Dillon, who had received with her a large sum of money—and having brought them to France, had, for some reason or other which they were unable to comprehend, conveyed them to a lonely inn some miles from where I found them, and there abandoned them.

" On reaching Paris I made immediate search for their friends at the hotel they had lodged at; but although it appeared that two gentlemen had inquired for them, we could not ascertain who they were, or where they were to be found.

"Under these circumstances, urged also by my desire to assist in exposing the crimes of these villains, I resolved, instead of writing to you, as I had proposed, to accompany the young ladies to England; and at the same time restore them to their friends, and seek a personal explanation with yourself.

" On reaching Clapham, where my protégées reside, I learnt that their father had set out for Paris in search of them about ten days before."

CHAPTER LV.

MORE LIGHT.

It may be supposed that Mr. Simpson lost no time in communicating the substance of Mabel's story to Mr. Olliphant, who immediately requested an interview with her, in the course of which he perfectly satisfied himself that the suspicions Mr. Gaveston's strange deportment at Oakfield had first awakened, were but too well founded.

In the meantime, Mr. Simpson hastened to Knightsbridge, to assure himself of what there was scarcely room to doubt—that the Julia Clark. whose life he had saved, and she who had been introduced to Mabel, were the same person.

But, to his amazement, he found the shop shut, and the house uninhabited; and was informed by the neighbours, that two nights before, Mrs. Clark had departed, as was believed, in the company of a gentleman, and had not been heard of since.

This was "confirmation strong" of previous suspicions. There could be little doubt that the gentleman was Mr. Gaveston; and Mr. Olliphant at once detected his motives, He saw that not only were Gaveston and Godfrey the same person, but that Julia Clark was the woman that had pledged the clothes to Isaac Lecky, and had since been employed by Dyson or Jones, whichever his name might really be, to endeavour to recover it; and that Gaveston. having recognised her from their account of the circumstances, had sought her out for the express purpose of placing her evidence beyond their reach.

"But if human exertions can defeat his plans," said Mr. Olliphant, " he shall be disappointed. But in order to make assurance doubly sure, let us pay a visit to that Mrs. Wetherall, to whom you say Julia Clark related her history in detail, of which you only heard the outlines. From her we may learn whether the name of her seducer was Godfrey."

It is needless to say that Mrs. Wetherall's testimony fully corroborated their suspicions; and there could be no doubt left of the identity of the parties.

"Now," said the lawyer, "there is one thing more I should like to be certain of; which is, whether Gaveston followed us to London. To ascertain that, we must write to Jeremy, I suppose; unless you know where he's in the habit of putting up?"

"At Laval's, in Bedford-street, generally, I fancy," replied Mr. Simpson. " I know he preferred it, because it was a French house. It will be worth calling there, at all events."

"Yes, sir," answered the waiter, to their inquiry. " Mr. Gaveston was here on Saturday night for a few minutes. I fancy it might be between ten and eleven o'clock. He seemed in a great hurry, and only called to say that he expected a letter to be sent here for him, and that we were to forward it immediately to the post-office at Paris."

"It is exactly that letter we have called to inquire for," said Mr. Olliphant. "Mr. Gaveston requested us to procure it, and send it after him, as he changed his route after he was here."

"Here it is, sir," said the waiter; "it only came this morning."

Mr. Olliphant paid the postage and walked away with the letter. "Now," said he, "we at least know where we shall hear of him; for he'll either go to Paris, or he'll direct them where to forward the letter; for no doubt," observed he, peeping into it, "it contains something of importance, or he would not have taken so much trouble to get it. I should like vastly to know what is inside of it."

"And you mean to know, I suppose," said Mr. Simpson, smiling; "for else why did you bring it away?"

"It was the impulse of the moment," replied the lawyer; "but there are various reasons why this letter may be important; and I think there are sufficient to justify me in opening it. We are, in the first place, in pursuit of a criminal—for of Gaveston's guilt I now entertain no more doubt than I do of my own existence—and we must avail ourselves of whatever means may promote his detection. In the next place, to confess a truth, I do not feel quite easy with respect to the fate of that unfortunate woman he has carried off; and I'm inclined to lose no time in rescuing her from his gripe, and securing her evidence. Ha!" exclaimed he, as, compressing the sides of the letter, he again put it to his eye; "by Jove, here goes!" and he proceeded to break the seal.

"What is it?" inquired Mr. Simpson.

"I see a name," answered Mr. Olliphant, "that would make me break through a stone wall, with as little ceremony as I break this wax—there's something about that other fellow, Jones, in it. And see, it's from Borthwick, I declare; what can he have to do with the business?"

"Let us hear," said Mr. Simpson; and Mr. Olliphant proceeded to read as follows:—

"Sir,—In obedience to your commands, I write to inform you that I got an answer from the agents by return. They believe Mr. Remorden to be at present in Paris, and have orders to enclose to him, under cover to Colonel Jones, post-office, there.

"With respect to the little lease you were kind enough to mention, I have prepared it, and submitted it to lawyer Brice. Tomorrow I shall forward it, per coach, to be favoured with your signature.

"And I have the honour to remain,
"Your humble servant,
"Gregory Borthwick."

"A thousand thanks, Mr. Gregory Borthwick," said Mr. Olliphant; "your letter is invaluable; though there is something about this house and road business that I cannot understand. But this much I remember perfectly; that at the time of Mr. Wentworth's death, Franklin told me that that cursed old Manor House formed part of an estate that had been many years in the Remorden family, who were formerly amongst the most affluent and influential people in the county; but that a series of misfortunes, that almost seemed like a fatality, had fallen upon them, till the property was greatly reduced, and the family nearly extinct. The last possessor had died abroad, where he had gone in pursuit of some woman; and the remnant had then fallen to a nephew, who was the only surviving scion of the family. I well recollect Franklin's adding, 'he was a profligate, good-for-nothing fellow, who soon ran through the little he had; and not being disposed to live at the Manor House himself, nor able to let it, because it had fallen so completely out of repair during the absence of the last tenant, the place was shut up, till the innkeeper offered to pay a trifle for the use of the lower rooms during the full season. As for Remorden himself,' he added, 'he hasn't been seen in the country for years. It was said he'd taken to the turf, and was spending his life between the knowing ones at Newmarket and the hells in London.' Now, what will you bet me that Remorden, Dyson, and Colonel Jones are not all one and the same person?"

"Upon my word, it does not seem very improbable," answered Mr. Simpson.

"And what do you say to a journey to Paris? I can spare a week or two now in such a cause; and thus much I'm sure, that till I have come to some understanding of this business, I shall not be fit for any other. If that fellow, Colonel Jones, is going to have his head taken off, he'll very likely be disposed to make a clean breast of it before he mounts the scaffold. Besides, he'll have a natural desire to take his friend Gaveston with him for company in the other world, and thus we shall get at the truth. Added to which, and as I said before, I don't think it a thing to be neglected, we may find out what has become of Julia Clark."

Mr. Simpson needed no urging to accede to the proposal; but he begged leave to make one amendment, which was, that if it were agreeable to her, they should travel in company with Mabel, for whom he admitted himself to be not a little interested.

"There were all the elements of virtue in her," he said, "alloyed by ignorance and ill-directed ambition. Born in another station, and rationally educated, she would have been a noble creature; and she is a noble creature now, in spite of her errors."

"And you've only to look in her face, and you'll forget them all," said the lawyer, slyly.

"She's a beautiful creature," answered Mr. Simpson, warmly; "and it must be a heart of adamant that wouldn't pity and forgive her!"

"It is not mine, I assure you," said Mr. Olliphant, more gravely. "I do both: and I shall be most happy to travel with her, and serve her too, if any means of doing so lie in my power."

Very willingly Mabel accepted the proposed escort. Like most other people that sat an hour in Mr. Simpson's company, she was disposed to feel an affection for him; and she was so glad to make friends! Life is so heavy without them! It must be one of the most grievous penalties incurred by women who stray from the

A A 2

paths of virtue, that they can rarely have a friend. Few men are
generous enough to be to them disinterested ones; the virtuous of
their own sex cannot and dare not; and amongst the vicious there
can exist no true friendship.

———

CHAPTER LVI.

THE DEVICES OF THE WICKED MAN SHALL FAIL.

ALTHOUGH Mr. Gaveston could not venture to delay his departure from London long enough to receive the information he
had employed Borthwick to obtain for him, he yet resolved to
make straight for Paris, on many accounts. One was, that he
looked to find the disposal of his unfortunate companion a matter
of more easy accomplishment there than in a smaller place; and
the other, that according to the address Remorden had given
Julia, he hoped either to find him there, or at least learn his address
at the post-office.

He therefore travelled night and day till he reached the capital;
and when there, after stopping one night at an inn in the neighbourhood of the coach-office, he located his companion on the
following day in a mean lodging in the Fauxbourg Montmartre,
whilst he took up his own residence in a more cheerful and
fashionable part of the city.

As one of the most urgent motives of his journey was to obtain
an interview with the owner of the Manor House, he lost no time
in inquiring at the post-office for Borthwick's letter, and for the
address of Colonel Jones; but he could obtain no intelligence of
either. Borthwick's letter, for reasons the reader will have no
difficulty in divining, had not arrived; and with respect to Colonel
Jones, letters had been lying there for him for some days, but
they had not been inquired for. This was a serious disappointment; and as it might occasion considerable delay, a source of
much annoyance. There was no telling how to interpret it, or
whither to direct his researches. The man might not have reached
Paris, or he might have left it, or he might actually be there,
having only neglected to ask for his letters. He was aware that
at the passport office he might probably learn what he desired to
know; that is, if Remorden was actually travelling under the name
of Jones; but in the present state of affairs, and with the projects
he had in hand, he did not wish to make himself conspicuous in
that quarter, or to draw attention to himself, which he might do
were he by his inquiries to publish his connexion with a man who
was probably marked as a person of suspicious character, or worse,
for anything he knew; for how he had been living, or what he
might have done to draw the eyes of the police on him since his
residence abroad, was much more than he could guess.

He therefore employed the interval of inevitable delay in visiting
the gambling houses about the Palais Royal, and such other
resorts, where he thought there was a probability of meeting with

Remorden if he were in Paris; and in forming projects, and in balancing the difficulties attending the getting rid of Julia in some way that should remove her effectually from his path, and render her evidence inaccessible. But it was not easy to discover any way but one; and that one, setting remorse, pity, and all such feelings out of the question, (of which Mr. Gaveston, like other bad human beings, try what he would, could not wholly divest himself,) was one of very difficult accomplishment.

In order to induce her to accompany him, after the interruption of the watchman had rendered the atrocious act he was on the point of perpetrating dangerous to himself, he had persuaded her that his wife was dead, and that he had been for some time seeking her with the view of repairing her early wrongs by marriage; and there was no difficulty in adducing many reasons, plausible enough to satisfy her simple mind, for performing the ceremony privately abroad; nor any in persuading her, on their arrival in Paris, that propriety and prudence required, till he could introduce her as his wife, that she should reside apart from him, and in as obscure a situation as possible.

So far all was easy; and she, as ever humble, obedient, and unsuspecting, quietly submitted to the restraints he imposed, and awaited in patience the fulfilment of his promise. But now came the difficulty. He thought sometimes of actually marrying her, (she was already a Catholic, and he had no objection to a *pro tempore* conversion,) in the names of Mr. Godfrey and Mrs. Dyson, under which they had travelled, and afterwards confining her in a mad-house, a thing at that time easily effected; but then she might escape, or get a letter conveyed to England. Then there was the river, convenient and inviting—and there was poison.

There was a fourth way, which being less extreme and more secure than any other, death excepted, he would have preferred; which was, to put her in the hands of some fanatical or unprincipled priest, and either by persuasion, terror, or force, get her shut up in a convent. But there were two impediments in the way of this project; one was, the existence of the child, which would be an effectual bar to her taking such a step with her own consent; and the other was, that it would require time, and Mr. Gaveston had none to spare.

He had been some days in Paris, and was yet in this state of anxious uncertainty, when happening to drop into a coffee-house on the Boulevards, and chancing to take up a newspaper that was lying on the table beside him, his eye was attracted by the name of Colonel Jones; and on perusing the paragraph, he found it contained an allusion to the approaching trial of that worthy and his colleague, at Lisle, for the murder of the Duc de Rochechouart and his servant.

Mr. Gaveston's heart bounded at the news. Of the two persons he most dreaded, the life of one was in his power, and that of the other was about to be sacrificed to the laws; and if he could only successfully dispose of the first, and obtain an interview with the other before his execution, he fancied he might defy the fates and dismiss his fears.   True, Mabel probably yet lived; but if, as Julia had heard, she had made a prosperous marriage in France, it was not very likely that she would ever hear of the Oakfield tragedy at all; or if she did, that she would risk exposing herself for the sake of penetrating the mystery.

But the necessity for reaching Lisle with as little delay as possible became urgent; and he was called upon to decide at once upon his line of action.   He laid down the paper, placed his two elbows on the table, and resting his face on his hands, he sat for some minutes in deep meditation.   He then arose, buttoned up his coat, and taking his hat in his hand, moved towards the door.

"Give me a glass of brandy," said he to the waiter, pausing on the threshold; and having tossed off the dram, he stepped out, and at a rapid pace took the way to the Rue du Fauxbourg Montmartre.

"Yes," said he to himself, as he went along, "no one can ever trace her, if ever, which is not likely, anybody should take the trouble of trying to do it; and the people of the house neither know where she came from, nor who she is; nor, provided they are paid their money, will they ever concern themselves to learn what is become of her.   To-morrow morning I'll start for Lisle; and if I can get an interview with Remorden, I think I shall be able to persuade him.   What the devil difference will it make to him when he's dead? and I can be back to Oakfield almost before I'm missed."   And comforting himself with these cheering reflections, he walked briskly forward.

In the house where Julia lodged, and on the same floor, there happened to dwell a young artist, a dawning genius, struggling through poverty and obscurity to fame.   The door of his apartment was immediately opposite hers, and he had thus frequent opportunities of seeing her; and he had also several times met Gaveston on the stairs, and had chanced to be present when he bargained with the proprietor for the rooms she occupied.   The countenances of both had very particularly struck him; and, seizing on the idea they suggested, he had transferred them to paper, with the intention of introducing them into a picture he was designing of a man killing an innocent wife in a fit of unfounded jealousy.

Previous to the Duc de Rochechouart's unfortunate expedition to Lisle, this young man had obtained a recommendation to his notice, and earnestly solicited his patronage; and, at Mabel's persuasion, the duke had consented to his taking his portrait. The work was begun, but not completed, when their departure interrupted its progress; and when, after the duke's death, Mabel returned to Paris, she sent for the artist to inquire if he thought he could finish it from memory.   He said he thought he could, and promised to make the attempt.

As she possessed no likeness of Rochechouart, this was an affair that went very near Mabel's heart; and on the very day she arrived in Paris with her two friends, Simpson and Olliphant, she sent Courtois to the young man to desire he would bring her the portrait, that she might judge of his success, and have an opportunity of pointing out any misconceptions she might observe.

The artist lost no time in obeying the order; and, collecting a few sketches that were lying on his table that he thought might give a favourable notion of his talent, he put them in his pocket, and with the picture proceeded to the hôtel that had been indicated to him.

The resemblance gave great satisfaction, and drew many tears from Mabel, whilst the two Englishmen warmly expressed their admiration of the remarkable beauty of the original.

After a visit of some length, the young man, elated with the commendations he had received, and the permission he had obtained to exhibit the picture in the Louvre, which he hoped might prove a stepping-stone to better fortune, took his departure; leaving behind him his bundle of sketches, which he had thrown on the table when he entered, but had forgotten to exhibit.

He had been gone some hours before they were observed; but when they were, divining the intention with which they had been brought, they were unrolled and examined.

"Look here," said Mr. Olliphant, holding out one of them to Mr. Simpson; "wouldn't you really imagine that Gaveston had sat for that head? The likeness is really extraordinary."

"So it is," said Mr. Simpson; "wonderful! But, good heavens! the head of the woman is assuredly meant for Julia Clark—the very way she dresses her hair, too. This is most singular. One might have been accidental, but surely both cannot!"

Mr. Olliphant had never seen Julia, and could not therefore judge of the resemblance; but Mabel saw it distinctly, and was as much convinced as Mr. Simpson that the heads were actually portraits. What made it more remarkable, too, was the design; the heads were finished with some care, but the remainder, though only roughly sketched, plainly showed that the man was armed with a knife and was about to kill the woman.

"I'll send Courtois instantly to fetch him back," said Mabel, ringing the bell.

"Do," said Mr. Simpson. "I shall not rest till I get an explanation of the mystery."

"Rather let us go ourselves, with Courtois to show us the way," said Mr. Olliphant. "We may otherwise wait here the whole evening for him."

"With all my heart," replied Mr. Simpson; and Courtois having received his orders, they all three started for the Rue du Fauxbourg Montmartre.

It was about eight o'clock when they set out; and as they had to traverse the city from one end to the other, and as both being nearly strangers they made many stoppages from curiosity, the clocks were striking ten when they reached the artist's dwelling.

They found him at home busy with the duke's picture, availing himself, whilst they were yet fresh in his memory, of Mabel's suggestions; and, after apologising for their intrusion, the visitors, unfolding the sketch, requested to know if those particular heads were not portraits.

"They are," replied the young man. "The lady lodges in this house—she is my opposite neighbour. The gentleman is her friend, I suppose; he is not her husband, and does not reside with her. I was so struck with the singular contrast of the two countenances, that I could not forbear appropriating them for a design I have in my head for a large picture."

"How long has she lived here?" inquired Mr. Olliphant.

"But a few days," answered the painter. "I happened to be in the saloon of the proprietor when they first called. The gentleman took the lodging for a week, and paid the rent in advance, saying they expected to be called away suddenly by business, and it would prevent delay if the proprietor were absent."

"And have you seen much of them since?" inquired the lawyer.

"I frequently meet her on the stairs," replied the artist, "as she goes backwards and forwards from the porter's lodge, to whom she applies for what she wants; and I see him here sometimes, chiefly of an evening."

"Does she go out?" said Mr. Olliphant.

"I believe, never," replied the young man. "She told the proprietor, I understand, that she was to be married shortly to the gentleman that visits her, and that he did not wish her to be seen till after the ceremony."

"Gracious heavens!" exclaimed Mr. Simpson. "Poor thing! Do you know if she's at home now? Do you think we could see her?"

"I'll show you her door," answered the painter. "That's it, just opposite, and there's a bell that you can ring."

The bell was rung, but no notice was taken of the summons, nor when it was repeated did any sound from within testify that the apartment was inhabited.

"She must be out," said the lawyer.

"Or gone to bed," observed the artist. "She sleeps in an inner room, and it is possible may not hear."

After ringing for some time with no better result, the artist proposed applying to the porter, who would be able to inform them if she was out.

"Yes," replied the last-named functionary. "She is gone out. There is her key, which she left as she passed."

"Was she alone?" inquired Mr. Olliphant.

"No; she had her friend with her," answered the porter. "It is just about half an hour ago."

"It's useless to wait, then," said Mr. Olliphant. "Probably, too, he may return with her; and it would be much better we saw her alone first."

"We might leave a line to put her on her guard," said Mr. Simpson. And this gentleman would perhaps have the goodness to deliver it to her the first thing in the morning."

This was accordingly done; and having recommended Julia to

be cautious, and promised her a visit on the following day, the two
gentlemen set out with Courtois on their return home.

In order to reach the Rue de Vaugirard, where they had taken
up their abode, they had to cross the river; but, as the night was
fine, and Courtois had something interesting to tell them of the
different localities as they passed, instead of doing so, they continued their way along the Quai des Tuileries and the Quai de la
Conference, intending to cross lower down, and return by the
Quai d'Orsay.

"You have a vast number of suicides in this river, have you
not?" said Mr. Simpson.

"A great many," answered Courtois. "Especially at particular
seasons. It seems either to be a fashion or an epidemic. I have
seen six bodies lying together at the Morgue."

As they made these observations, they had drawn up preparatory to crossing the bridge, and were standing looking over the
parapet.

"Gentlemen," cried a little beggar boy, approaching them
hastily from the direction of the Quai Debilly, "there is a woman
in the water a little lower down, and I can't pull her out. Help
me, in the name of God!"

"Where?" cried they, eagerly setting off in pursuit of the
child, who flew along before them the way he had come.

"There! there!" cried he; "look, don't you see? She is
keeping herself up still with my faggots." And as they approached
the spot they distinguished a woman near the bank, endeavouring
to sustain herself by holding on to a large bundle of sticks.

"Save me!" she cried; "oh, save me! I can't hold any longer."

What was to be done? The bank was steep, and none of the
party could swim.

"Listen!" said the beggar boy. "You have handkerchiefs, and
you have a stick. Tie them together, and fasten the stick to the
end, and throw it towards her. Perhaps she'll reach it."

Almost as soon as spoken this was done. The stick fell across
the faggot. The woman seized it, and as they steadily drew in
the handkerchiefs, the faggot floated to the bank, she still grasping
both that and the stick. As soon as her hands were within reach,
they easily succeeded in drawing her out.

"Oh, my faggot! my faggot's floating away!" cried the boy, as
soon as he saw the woman was safe.

"Stay," said Mr. Simpson; "we'll try and save it," and he once
more threw the stick across it and drew it back.

"Thank ye, sir," said the boy, picking it up and throwing it
across his shoulder. "Your servant!" And, with a nod, he was
about to take his departure.

"Stay, my lad," said Mr. Simpson; "I'm not going to part
with you yet. Tell me first of all, how came your faggot in the
water?"

"When I heard the woman cry for help," said the boy, "I ran
forward and tried to reach her with my arms, but I could not.
Luckily, I was coming in from the country, where I had been all

day gathering sticks; and I thought perhaps they would help to keep her up till I got help, so I threw them to her."

"You're a fine fellow," said Mr. Simpson, with great satisfaction, as he patted the boy's head. "How do you get your living?"

"As I can," answered the boy. "I could get my own easy enough, for I don't want much: but I've my mother's to get, too, which is more difficult. But God helps us."

"You deserve that he should," said Mr. Simpson, "since you help yourself, and others too: here is a louis d'or for you, and if you will come to-morrow to the Hôtel Vaugirard, and ask for Mr. Simpson, I may do something else for you."

"Mr. what?" said the boy. "I fear I shall not remember the name."

"Well, then, ask for the English gentleman," said Mr. Simpson; "that will do as well."

"Ha! you are English!" said the boy. For Mr. Simpson had passed much of his youth at Bordeaux, and spoke French well. "She is your countrywoman, I think," added he, pointing to the woman, who was walking on before, supported by Mr. Olliphant and Courtois.

"Is she?" said Mr. Simpson, who, in the excitement of the moment, had not remarked that the woman had cried for help in English.

"She is certainly not French," said the boy.

"Did you see her fall in?" inquired Mr. Simpson.

"No," replied the little fellow. "As I said, I had been picking sticks in the country all day, and I had just come in by the Barrière des Reservoirs; and I was cutting along the quay as fast as I could—for I've got to go as far as the Quai de la Grève, where my mother lodges—when I heard a cry. I thought it came from the water, and I ran forwards. Just then a man rushed past me. I cried, 'Stop! stop! there is an accident!' But he only went the faster. Then I saw the woman, and threw her the faggot, as I told you. Adieu, sir, my mother's expecting me, and I must hasten home!" And the bare-footed urchin was out of sight in a moment.

Mr. Simpson's heart felt exceedingly warm and comfortable; and there was a certain moisture about his eyes that he brushed away with the back of his hand. Then he rubbed his two hands briskly together—took out his handkerchief and blew his nose—smiled, and gave himself two hearty thumps on the breast—and then he walked quickly forwards to overtake the rest of the party.

"What are you going to do with her?" said he to Mr. Olliphant, when he came up to him.

"Courtois is going to find some place to put her in,' replied the lawyer. "She is too feeble to give any explanations: but she says she lives a great way off. I wish we could meet with a fiacre; for I'm in momentary fear she'll faint."

"We shall, presently," said Courtois. "It's curious she can't tell the name of the street she inhabits."

"The boy says she is English," said Mr. Simpson.

"Yes," replied Mr. Olliphant, "by her speech, she is."

At this crisis the woman sank to the ground, unable to move a foot further. They looked in all directions, but they saw no house at hand that promised assistance; for it was now past midnight, and few, except in the upper stories, still showed light from their windows.

"Wait here!" said Courtois. "I'll be back with a coach in five minutes;" and away he ran.

The woman in the meanwhile lay extended on the ground, and the two gentlemen stood beside her.

"I believe we'd better take her home with us," said Mr. Simpson, "especially as she's English: we may be looking all night for a proper place to put her in."

"I think so, too," replied the lawyer. And when the coach arrived, she was lifted into it, and they drove to the Hôtel Vaugirard.

"See, madame!" said Courtois to the lady of the house, as they carried in the still insensible woman, "here is our first day's fishing."

"Bless me! you have fished to some purpose," said the lady. "What, is she drowned? You should have taken her to the Morgue."

"She must be immediately undressed, and put into a warm bed," said Mr. Simpson, approaching to unloose a straw bonnet she wore, and which had all this time been flapping over her face. "And pray, Courtois, run for a doctor instantly. Great Heavens!" cried he, as he threw off her bonnet and discovered her features— "It's Julia herself! It's poor Julia Clark!"

CHAPTER LVII.

A MIDNIGHT ADVENTURE.

As it was late in the afternoon when Susan set out from Lisle on her way back to the lone inn, the night had already set in when she came in sight of the sign-post, which stood on the opposite side of the road, and on which hung a rude daub of a woman with her finger on her lip, intended as a representation of the dumb hostess.

Relieved to find herself so near her resting-place, for she was both tired and rather alarmed at the lateness of the hour, in a country with whose morals and manners she was so little acquainted, and eager to ascertain the safety of the young ladies, and to set their minds at ease with respect to her own, she quickened her pace, and stept out with renewed energy, as her eye caught the harbinger of shelter swinging in the wind.

Whether from the honesty of the inhabitants of that part of the country, or from the fearlessness of the inmates of the inn, there were no shutters to the house, and the door usually stood open till the family retired to bed. The parlour or kitchen. which was the common resort of all, and indeed the only sitting-room in the inn, and the only one that had a fire-place, happened to be on the right side of the door—that is, towards Lisle; and Susan had to pass the window of that room before she could enter.

A light gleaming across the road showed her that the family had not yet retired, and she naturally approached the window to take a survey of what was going on within before she presented herself. But her surprise may be imagined, when, instead of Monsieur and Madame Le Clerc, Rauque, and her young people, she saw the room was occupied by three men—two in uniform, and one in plain clothes. Of the two in uniform, one was sitting in M. Le Clerc's arm-chair, and she recognised him at once as one of those who had treated her so roughly at the station-house, on her way to Lisle; the second was seated with his back to her, and she could not get a view of his face; and of the third, the one in plain clothes, as he sat with his face to the fire, she could only discern the profile.

It was that of a youth, apparently not much more than twenty, or at the most two or three and twenty, of exceedingly beautiful features; and, as far as it was possible to judge, of a very pleasing expression. The forehead was high, the nose finely formed, the upper lip short and impressed with a lofty character, the corners of the mouth sweetly curved, the complexion of a clear brown, with a roseate hue in the cheeks; the hair dark, and the shadows that fell from under the long dark lashes betokened that the eyes were of the same colour. The figure appeared light, graceful, and active; and he was attired in a blue coat, leathers, and top-boots. He sat with his legs stretched out upon the hearth; and, indeed, the whole three seemed very much at their ease. There was a bottle with jugs and glasses upon the table, with some remnants of a supper; and an animated conversation appeared to be maintained between the parties.

There was something in this change of occupation that perplexed Susan extremely. She looked up at the upper windows, but no light appeared from them. Then she remembered that Rauque slept in a sort of out-house in the back yard, and she crept round the house in order to ascertain if he were there. There was no light, and after listening a little while at the door, she ventured to lift the latch; the place was deserted. What interpretation to put on all this she could not tell. She felt pretty well assured that not one of those she had left there were still inmates of the inn. What could have taken them away? Whither were they gone? From seeing the two soldiers there, she was disposed to think they had been removed by authority, or arrested for some crime; and it occurred to her that possibly some search had been instituted by the family of the young ladies, and that suspicion had fallen on Monsieur and Madame Le Clerc, as accessaries to their detention.

"If that is the case," thought she, "they would probably be taken to the town I have just left; or, who knows, perhaps to Paris! And what in the world am I to do?—or how shall I find out?"

She felt more at a loss how to proceed than she had ever done in her life. But besides her perplexity on these points, there was another, for the moment more urgent, that troubled her much; and this was, whether or not to enter the inn, and present herself to the persons she had seen through the window.

From the manners of the soldiers at the station-house, and the treatment she had experienced in the course of her expedition, she had not formed a very favourable opinion of their habits and characters; and helpless and unprotected as she was, she felt a considerable aversion to placing herself, in this lonely place, and at this late hour, so entirely at their mercy. Certainly, she was disposed to place more confidence in the handsome young stranger; but still, looks were not an unerring guide; and if the others were disposed to ill-treat her, he might not be able, even were he willing, to protect her. They were not only much stouter and older men than he, but they were armed and he was not. Then the disadvantage of not being able to explain who she was, nor why she had come, was discouraging; and the more she considered it, the more she shrunk from the encounter. Still, weary and fatigued as she was, it was very disagreeable to pass the night without a resting-place; and she was neither able, nor had she courage to attempt to retrace her steps to Lisle.

Weighing these matters, and reflecting on what she should do, she crept back softly to the front of the house again, in order to take another survey of the kitchen. In passing the stable-door, she thought she heard a sound, as of a horse's foot, and after listening, she was sure of it. She tried to open the door and look in, but it was locked. However, she concluded they were the horses belonging to the soldiers, and she pursued her way.

Just as she turned the corner of the house, she heard the front door, which had been open when she arrived, banged to and locked; and when she reached the window, she saw that the three men had risen from their seats, and appeared to be preparing to go to bed. One of the soldiers opened a closet, and deposited in it the bottle she had seen on the table, whilst the other raked the ashes over the wood fire to keep it smouldering till the morning. The young stranger, in the meantime, lighted a candle, and making a salutation to the others, quitted the room; and in a moment or two more, she saw a light in the room above, which had been occupied by herself and the young ladies, and could distinguish his shadow, as he moved backwards and forwards, undressing himself.

It thus became perfectly clear that her young ladies were no longer there; and when, presently afterwards, the two soldiers having quitted the kitchen, she discerned them in the apartment that had been occupied by the Le Clercs, all doubts of the departure of the inn's former inmates were removed.

But next she had to consider how she was to dispose of herself for the night; for as she had not ventured to present herself to the men before, she gave up all idea of doing it now; and the only shelter that seemed at her disposal, was Rauque's den. It did not appear very probable that she would be disturbed there, for some hours at least; and besides, there was the accommodation of a rude bed, consisting of a mattress and coverlet on the ground, which, in her present state of fatigue, was not to be despised.

So back she crept, and having examined the place as well as she could by the pale moonlight, and seeing nothing to excite distrust, she drew the wooden bolt that formed the fastening of the door; and then, resolving to retrace her steps to Lisle with the early dawn, she stretched herself on the coarse bed, and soon fell into a sound sleep.

She had slept some time, but was yet so heavy from her previous fatigue that she could not rouse herself, when she became aware of a noise near her. She turned on the other side, and "addressed herself again to sleep;" but the sound became louder, and apparently nearer. Still slumber sat heavy upon her; and though she heard it, she was not awake enough to heed it, nor to reflect on what it might be. Presently, however, there came the sound as of a heavy blow; and its suddenness, as well as its loudness, caused her to open her eyes. But she could discern nothing particular; everything appeared, as far as she could see, to be as it was when she lay down; and she was about to close her eyes again, when the blow was so distinctly repeated, that she started up in her bed, and looked towards the door, expecting to see it open. Whilst she was yet looking, the sound was again repeated; and now, being more awake, she perceived that it did not proceed from the door, but, as it appeared to her, from under the ground. It was much too loud, and altogether unlike a noise produced by rats, or any subterraneous inhabitants of that description; and she sat aghast with terror as it continued, evidently at each concussion becoming more distinct.

Suddenly she fancied her bed moved under her; and, seized with horror, she sprung into the middle of the room. The faint moonlight, which only penetrated through a small window, was too feeble to permit her to distinguish any motion in the mattress, but she fancied she heard it stir; and being determined to satisfy herself whether it was her imagination that had got the better of her, or whether her apprehensions were really founded, she softly approached, and stooping down, laid her hand upon it. At that instant, a heave from beneath, that almost lifted it from the ground, left no further room for doubt, and springing to the door, she quickly undrew the bolt and rushed out.

There, for a moment or two, she stood breathless, listening to the still increasing noise within, and lost in wonder as to the cause of so strange a phenomenon. That the sounds were produced by human agency she felt assured; but how should any living being be buried there? And who could it be? Suddenly it occurred to her, "Can it be the inhabitants of the inn that have disappeared?" The thing certainly was to the last degree improbable; but the circumstance of anybody being there at all was so inexplicable, that it left room for all manner of conjecture. They might have concealed themselves to escape some danger, or to avoid the police, or they might have been confined by force.

In fine, Susan ended by making up her mind that it was certainly them; and, impelled by anxiety and curiosity, she ventured softly to approach the still open door, and peep in.

Precisely at that moment the mattress gave a great heave, and, turning over, disclosed underneath a part of the stone floor, that appeared to be lifted up by the agency of some one beneath. Slowly it moved, and great efforts seemed to be required to raise it; and Susan felt so strong a suspicion that it was her friends, and was so deeply interested in the result, that she felt disposed to advance and lend her assistance; but she forbore a moment, and as she stood, hesitating what to do, she distinctly heard a man's voice proceed from the vault, and an answer returned by another.

Neither, she felt certain, was the voice of Rauque, and both were much too vigorous to have proceeded from Monsieur Le Clerc; they could not, therefore, be those she expected. Still, anxious to see the explanation of so extraordinary an adventure, she did not quit the door; but, placing herself at the side, where she could not be seen by those who were about to emerge, she awaited the result.

She was not kept much longer in suspense—the stone was presently turned over, and a head protruded. Then there was a pause, and some conversation passed with a person lower down; next, the first stepped out, and, after looking about him a little, stooped down, and assisted the other to emerge. Susan could discern that both were men, but more than that, she could not distinguish. One thing, however, was clear; they were not those she had imagined. Almost overcome by fear and wonder, when the second was about to step out, she retired from the door, and, hiding herself behind a water-butt that was at hand, she watched what was to come next.

The two men soon appeared at the door, and she had now an opportunity of observing that they were both attired as sailors. They stood for some minutes in conversation, as if consulting what they should do next. They pointed to the stars, and seemed to be calculating how far the night was advanced; and they pointed to the house, apparently speaking of that or its inhabitants. Presently, they put their hands in their pockets, and Susan descried something glittering in their hands—they were armed. Could they be thieves—assassins—midnight murderers?

After some brief colloquy, they stepped from the door, and proceeded towards the front of the house. When they had turned the corner, Susan moved after them, and as she drew nearer could distinctly hear them trying the latch of the door. It was fast, and as she ventured to peep round, she saw them make an attempt to open the window. That was fast too; but it was in the lattice fashion, and composed of very small panes of glass.

One of these they easily extracted, and having put in a hand, the window was unlatched, and they both climbed in.

Susan often said afterwards that she could never explain what impelled her, but she had an idea that they were going to assassinate the young gentleman she had seen sitting with the soldiers, and she felt an uncontrollable desire to endeavour to save him. So overpowering was this sentiment, that she was utterly indifferent, or at least insensible, to the danger she might incur by her interference; and, without pausing a moment to reflect, they no sooner disappeared within the room, than she approached the window, still keeping, however, out of sight.

For a minute or two she could distinguish their footsteps and their whispering voices; and then she heard them softly open the door and leave the room. Upon this she advanced, and, following their example, climbed into the yet open window, and pursuing their steps (fortunately, in her haste she had not put on her shoes, which besides her bonnet, was the only article of her dress she had taken off when she lay down) she noiselessly proceeded along the passage, and just reached the bottom of the stairs as they reached the top.

Here were the two bed-rooms; the one that had formerly been hers, and to which she had seen the young gentleman retire, on the right, and the one occupied by the soldiers on the left. The men stopped on the landing-place, and seemed uncertain which to enter; they listened at both sides, and then, having whispered something, the foremost laid his hand on the latch of the right-hand room, and softly opening the door, they entered.

The instant they were within, with a light and fleet step Susan darted up the stairs, burst open the door of the opposite room, rushed to the bed, and seizing the arms of the men who were lying there, cried with all her force to them to awake.

"Rise! rise! awake!" she cried; "murder and thieves are in the house!"

Alarmed by her screams, though not knowing what she said, the soldiers sprang out of bed, and seized their sabres.

"This way," she cried, dragging them to the door, which they just reached as the men, scared by the uproar, were making the best of their way down stairs, whilst two figures in white emerged from the opposite room, crying out in good set English, to know "what in the name of God was the matter?"

"There were villains in the house going to murder you," replied Susan; "they have just escaped down stairs, and the soldiers are gone after them!"

"The Lord look down upon us!" cried a voice Susan thought she recognised.

"I'll dress myself and follow them," said the other person; "my pistols may be of use."

"You shall do no such thing," returned the first, seizing him by the arm; "I shall die of the fright if you leave me. Let the soldiers look after them; it's their business, not ours."

"Gracious me!" cried Susan, who at that moment got a glimpse of the last speaker's face, "sure it's master's voice! Mr. Cripps, sir, is it you?"

"To be sure it's me," returned Mr. Cripps; "why, Susan, how came you here?—where are the girls?"

"Lord knows, sir," said Susan; "I went away two days ago to put a letter in the post for you; and for some reason I can't make out, the seized me and put me in prison. To-day they set me free, and I made the best of my way back here; but seeing the soldiers through the window below, and none of the people of the inn, I was afraid to enter. Lucky it was, or we might all have been murdered in our beds!"

"Jemima's safe enough," said Mr. Cripps; "but I can hear nothing of the other two. We traced you all the way along the road from Paris, till we reached this house this evening, where we found the soldiers, who told us the people of the inn were seized and carried to Lisle yesterday, and a little English girl with them; and as our horses were tired, and the men said there were beds at our service, we resolved to remain here till to-morrow."

During this conversation, the other stranger had partly dressed himself, and now came forward with his pistols in his hand, prepared to follow the soldiers, and give what assistance he could in apprehending the villains.

"You shan't go," cried Mr. Cripps, resolutely seizing him.

"Hark!" cried Susan, "there's a scuffle below;" and the young man, disregarding Mr. Cripps's entreaties, burst from him and rushed down the stairs.

"Mr. Leeson! Mr. Leeson!" cried Mr. Cripps. "Lord, Lord! we shall all be murdered!"

"Mr. Leeson!" exclaimed Susan; "it's Master Harry, as I live;" and away she darted down the stairs after him.

When she reached the kitchen, the two men were already in the power of the soldiers, and Harry was standing with his pistols directed to their heads, ready to fire if they made further resistance.

"Strike a light, will you?" said he to her; "let us see the faces of these scoundrels."

Susan struck a light, but she was more anxious to see his face. She approached him, and held the candle to it. "Master Harry," she said, "don't you know me?"

"Good Heavens!" cried he, "Susan, is it you?"

"It is, indeed, Master Harry," said she. "Oh, how many a weary day I've sighed to know what was become of you!"

"Let us first secure these villains," he said, "and then we shall have plenty of time to talk of the past."

The men, whom it is unnecessary to say were the two Rodolphes, were then, by the mutual aid of the soldiers and Harry, bound, and shut up in a dark closet, which was just large enough to hold them; and from which, having no window, they could only escape by the door, and upon that the soldiers kept guard till morning.

B B

Their next business was to relieve Mr. Cripps's alarm, who being by this time dressed, was very glad to come down stairs and join the party at the fire, which Susan soon blew into a blaze.

"And so you never heard of me?" said Harry.

"One letter we heard Mrs. Gaveston had, soon after you went away," replied Susan, "but no more."

"I wrote one every year," replied Harry, "to say I was safe and doing well, and that she should soon see me again; and I have been only waiting till I was received as a partner into the house where I am now head-clerk—which I am to be shortly— because I wished to present myself to Gaveston as an independent man."

The remainder of the night was passed in relating their separate adventures, and in discussing the mystery of the young ladies' disappearance; and on the following morning they proceeded to Lisle to claim Jemima and prosecute further inquiries; whilst the soldiers, their object being gained by the arrest of the two smugglers, shut up the house, and took the same road.

CHAPTER LVIII.

THE CONCLUSION.

It was on a fine morning in the month of October, that a great number of people might be seen assembled round the doors of the Court House at Lisle, in the hope of getting a sight of the two Englishmen, Remorden and Dillon, as they were conducted from their place of confinement to the Hall of Justice.

Their indictment was for the murder of the Duc de Rochechouart and his servant, which was of itself a subject of much indigna- tion and excitement amongst the populace, to whose capricious favour the duke's magnificence, munificence, and personal beauty had strongly recommended him. It was moreover expected that, although the murder was the crime they were to be tried for, many curious particulars regarding their other misdemeanors would be elicited in the course of the examination, especially regarding their extensive contraband dealings, and their carrying off the young English ladies, about which latter circumstance very strange stories were afloat.

Added to these sources of unusual interest was another—the two Rodolphes of Nantes, the celebrated foster-brothers, were also to be brought up on the same day. Their extraordinary attachment, desperate characters, and bold enterprises, had long been the theme of curiosity, wonder, and fear, along the whole of the north coast and the frontier towns. Many dreaded them, a few admired them; and some, who happened to be themselves con- nected with the contraband trade, felt a deeper interest in the scene.

It was expected that the trial of the two Englishmen would take place first; and when the covered vehicle arrived which

contained the criminals, the mob were about to give utterance to
their feelings in a howl of indignation, but the door being opened,
instead of Remorden and Dillon, the two Rodolphes were handed
out. It needed none to say who they were; the curious similarity
of person, air, and dress that prevailed between them, was a
sufficient introduction to all who beheld them; besides that, there
was scarcely a hut for many a mile round the country that had
not a rude print of the foster-brothers pinned over the mantelpiece. It was then understood that a principal witness against
the Englishmen not having yet arrived, their trial was for the
present postponed.

As they stepped out, the howls which were just beginning to
assail their ears were hushed into silence; and when, manacled
and guarded as they were, they turned round after they had
ascended the steps, to take a survey of the crowd, a faint cheer
was heard to arise from a few scattered voices, which, had not the
officers hurried them out of sight, would probably have terminated in a general huzza!—so easily are the lower orders
dazzled by a reputation for daring deeds, and so prone to forget
the tendency of actions whose boldness they admire.

When the prisoners, officers, and those attached to the train
had passed in, amongst whom were several of the leading inhabitants, and strangers who had tickets entitling them to seats
in commodious situations, there was a general rush amongst the
crowd, which did not cease till the porter, announcing that the
hall was full, was about to shut the gates against the unsuccessful candidates, but he was stopt by the arrival of another cortége
—the carriages containing the witnesses.

Out of the first were handed Monsieur and Madame Le Clerc,
Rauque, the two soldiers that had guarded the inn, and other
persons whose testimony referred to some late smuggling tran-
sactions of importance, which had been the primary cause of the
efforts made to arrest the criminals. The second contained Mr.
Cripps, Harry Leeson, Susan, and Jemima; and when all these
had been introduced the gates were closed.

The indictment against the Rodolphes was on two counts—first,
as regarded their contraband dealings; and secondly, for having
burglariously entered the inn by night, armed with knives, and
with intent to rob and murder the inhabitants.

With the first we have little concern, it being sufficient to say,
that enterprises of the most desperate character were proved
against them by the testimony of many witnesses; in the course
of which such extraordinary traits of courage were related,
especially exercised in defence of each other, that it was several
times found necessary to call the audience to order, and threaten
a general expulsion, in order to repress the applause of the people,
and obtain silence. Nevertheless, in spite of all the evidence that
had been collected, owing to the great difficulty of distinguishing
between them, and appropriating to each their several deeds,
and the almost impossibility of inducing their confederates in

the contraband trade to come forward as witnesses, it was not found practicable to establish such proofs of criminality as could justify a capital conviction. A temporary imprisonment or confinement to the galleys appeared the severest sentence they had to expect; but when they came to the second clause of the indictment, the affair assumed a more unfavourable aspect.

The first witness called was Susan, and after her Mr. Cripps, Mr. Leeson, and the soldiers, all of whom narrated the circumstances as they were detailed to the reader in the last chapter; and the relation seemed to leave no doubt in the minds of the judges' that they had entered the house with the intent to commit murder; but whether they were in search of any particular victim did not appear so clear. Mr. Cripps and Harry both affirmed that when they opened their eyes, the men were standing one by each bed, with their weapons in their hands, apparently on the point of striking them; but that suddenly scared by Susan's screams, they had darted out of the room, and were down the stairs before they themselves could reach the door; but they could assign no motive, unless their object was plunder, as they knew nothing of the men, and had never seen them before.

"What could we hope to obtain in that house," said Rodolphe Bruneau, "that would make it worth our while to commit such a crime?"

"Have we ever been accused or in the slightest degree suspected of robbery?" said Grimaud; "or of shedding blood, except in self-defence?"

"And doubtless," said Bruneau, "you have caused the vault we emerged from to be searched, and must have discovered that if our design were plunder, there was no necessity for our entering the house to obtain a booty."

The advocate for the crown, however, suggested that their object in assassinating the inhabitants of the inn, was probably in order to make themselves masters of all the vault contained; and this appeared to be the general opinion of the court. They had found out, or been told, that such a receptacle for smuggled goods existed, and had concealed themselves there till a favourable opportunity offered for executing their purpose.

Madame Le Clerc and Rauque were then called, and asked whether they had shown or mentioned the vault to the Rodolphes. Rauque being questioned first, answered that he did not recollect; but Madame Le Clerc admitted that she had shown it to them, which confirmed the court in their previous opinion; and as nothing more could be elicited, the trial was about to be brought to a conclusion, when the prisoners, who saw clearly by the course things were taking that they would be found guilty, and probably be either condemned to death or to the galleys for life, begged to be heard.

"We are not guilty," said Rodolphe Bruneau, " of the intentions you impute to us; and we should consider it a heavy aggravation of the penalty we are to suffer, be it what it may, to leave the world with such a stigma attached to our names. We have ever been faithful to all who had dealings with us; there are many present in this court who know it. I cannot appeal to them by name, look, or gesture, but I appeal to their hearts if I do not speak the truth." There was here a murmur amongst the crowd, which testified that the appeal was not unfelt.

"We came to the house of the Le Clercs by invitation," continued Bruneau, having been informed that Madame Le Clerc had been long seeking an opportunity of confiding some speculations of importance to our management. We came without suspicion, relying on the same faith we practised to others—but you shall hear how our confidence was requited. We arrived in the evening, having obeyed her summons at considerable risk to ourselves, owing to the unusual alertness of the police and the preventive service, since the enterprise of the Englishmen. She received us hospitably, bade us welcome, and said she had long desired to see us, but deferred her intention of disclosing the particular business she wished to treat of till after supper, and the other persons present had retired.

"Accordingly, she conducted her husband and a little girl that she said belonged to the English prisoners, to bed; and when none remained up but herself and the boy called Rauque, she beckoned us to follow her, giving us to understand that she would now show us some valuable goods, of which she wished us to undertake the transportation. She then conducted us through a back door, into an outhouse, Rauque leading the way. When there, he lighted a candle from a dark lantern he had brought from the house, and pushing aside a mattress which lay on the floor, he asked our assistance in raising a square of the pavement, which to the eye was scarcely different to the others around it; a ladder, which was leaning against the wall in one corner of the outhouse was then let down, and we were invited to descend. Suspecting no evil, we did so, whilst Rauque held the light over the aperture to show us our way; but when we reached the bottom, and looked to see the others follow us, the ladder was suddenly drawn up, the stone returned to its place, the aperture closed, and we found ourselves in darkness and alone."

"Interred alive," said Grimaud; "left to die by starvation!"

The sensation this strange story created may be imagined. Some did not believe it; but those who best knew the Rodolphes, did, for more reasons than one.

"We finally escaped," continued Bruneau, "by piling what things we could find for the purpose to raise us, and then by standing on each other's shoulders alternately, till we succeeded in loosening and lifting the stone."

"Can it be matter of surprise," said Grimaud, "that on regaining our liberty we should have sought to avenge this unprovoked outrage—this glaring breach of faith—this cruel violation of hospitality? We had no means of knowing that the inmates of the inn had been changed during our confinement. The victims we sought were those who had injured us; and we believed the beds we stood by contained Madame Le Clerc and her husband."

Many were the eyes turned on Madame Le Clerc, as this extra-ordinary tale was unfolded; but though of a deadly paleness, she maintained an unmoved countenance and imperturbable composure; and as for Rauque, he preserved the same vacant stolid look as usual, which, however, from his answers in the course of the former examination, might be conjectured to be in a great degree assumed. Monsieur Le Clerc himself remained, as ever, absent and abstracted; and appeared to feel no interest in what was going on, further than that he was sensible of some little annoyance at being removed from his own accustomed hearth and easy chair.

"Is this account true?" said the advocate for the crown to Rauque; but Rauque did not appear to hear the question.

"Is it true, I ask you?—you Rauque? Is the account we have heard true?"

"I can't tell," said Rauque: "I know nothing of it."

"Do you admit that these persons have spoken the truth, Madame Le Clerc?" said the advocate.

"Ask them," said she to Rauque, "how they can credit such a story? What motive could I have for inviting these men to my house for such a purpose? or how could I hope to execute it? They are not persons to be so easily entrapped," she added, with a significant smile at the prisoners.

"Nevertheless," said Bruneau, "you know we have spoken the truth."

"The boy knows it too," said Grimaud.

But Madame Le Clerc shook her head with an air of contemptuous incredulity; and Rauque, who only spoke when he was obliged, said nothing.

"I confess," said the advocate, "the story does seem very improbable; and we must admit that it would be as difficult to find a motive for undertaking such an enterprise, as it would be to execute it. It seems much more likely that they went there for the purpose of plundering the vault, which they might have heard of from their confederates; and that when they pretended to quit the house they concealed themselves there."

"But," said Grimaud, "we might have emptied the vault of its contents by night, without any necessity for assassinating the people of the house."

"Tell them," said Madame Le Clerc to Rauque, "that they durst not, because our testimony against them, had we survived, would have been their ruin. They would have forfeited their characters, and been no more trusted—no more employed. They would have been betrayed to justice, and sufficient evidence offered to put them out of the way for ever."

As no testimony could be brought to reinforce either side, probability, and the credit to be attached to the assertions of the different parties, were all that remained to guide the decision; and it was considered that both these were against the Rodolphes.

In spite, therefore, of their reiterated asseverations that they had spoken the truth, they were condemned to the galleys for life; the authorities being extremely glad of this opportunity to get rid of two such obnoxious and troublesome individuals.

As they were led out they cast a vengeful look at Madame Le Clerc, who answered it by a smile of triumph.

The crowd, eager to see the last of the prisoners, rushed after them, and thus stopping up the way, prevented the immediate departure of the more orderly part of the audience, who waited for a clearer passage; and before these had time to retire, it was understood that the principal witness against the Englishmen having arrived, their trial would immediately take place.

On learning this, many persons resumed their seats; amongst whom were Mr. Cripps, Harry, and Susan, as also Madame Le Clerc, who had only been detained as a witness in the case of the Rodolphes, nothing having been proved against herself sufficient to justify her being placed at the bar. It is true, the contents of the vault were of an illegal description; but she affirmed that the whole was the property of the customers that came to the house, in which she had no interest. The goods were seized, and herself set free.

It was not long before a yell from the populace without announced the arrival of the prisoners; and presently afterwards the doors were thrown open, and they made their appearance, followed by the crowd. Whether from apprehension or confinement, their aspects were considerably changed since Susan had last seen them; their faces were pale, their cheeks sunk, their eyes hollow; and the looseness of their habiliments testified that their bodies had considerably shrunk from their former dimensions. They nevertheless aimed at bearing themselves as independently as possible; but the effort was unsuccessful—their depression involuntarily betrayed their consciousness of the desperate predicament in which they stood.

Many persons of distinction, friends and connexions of the late duke, were present, besides strangers; and altogether the court was crowded to suffocation, not an inch of room being left vacant in any part of it.

Amongst this great assemblage there was no one who felt a deeper interest in the scene than Susan. In Colonel Jones, for she yet knew him by no other name, she believed she saw the only person from whom there was the slightest hope of ever learning the truth respecting her brother's fate. As his character was unveiled, her first impressions had gained strength; till now she felt perfectly confirmed in her persuasion, and what had been but suspicion, amounted to conviction.

"What," said she to Harry Leeson, to whom she had related all the foregoing circumstances, and communicated all her suspicions—"what should bring such a person as that to Oakfield, to inquire when Mr. Wentworth was to return? Mr. Wentworth could have no acquaintance, nor no business with a man of his character. And I still believe, and shall to the day of my death, that I was not altogether asleep, but in a sort of trance, that night in your uncle's room, and that that man was there—and another too—Heaven forgive me if I'm wrong!"

"If anything had been missing," said Harry, "I should think so too. But nothing was."

"One thing was, Mr. Harry," replied Susan. "Your uncle's will."

"If it's certain one existed," answered Harry.

"I firmly believe it," replied Susan. "Mr. Franklyn, Mr. Rice, and Mr. Olliphant the lawyer, all declared there was a will; and Jeremy told me that he had been present when Mr. Wentworth signed it, and was one of the witnesses himself. And more than that, that there were two copies of it."

"I never heard this before," said Harry.

"No," answered Susan; "how should you? It would have been useless and cruel to tell it you at the time—you were but a child then. And since, you have seen no one who could tell it you. But in that will it is said that you were provided for handsomely, and that the greatest part of the fortune was settled on Miss Wentworth."

"If this man is condemned to die," said Harry, "we may possibly learn the truth yet. He will have no further interest in concealing it, and will probably feel little compunction at betraying his confederates."

When the indictment had been read, and the case stated by the advocate engaged for the prosecution, the first, and indeed only witness, (except the troop of cavalry that had arrested their flight,) was called by the name of "Madame Amabel Jean or Jons;" and to the surprise of Susan and of Harry, who perfectly remembered her, for even as a boy her extraordinary beauty had struck him, Mabel Lightfoot was introduced.

Though often interrupted by her tears, she gave her evidence clearly and succinctly. The purport of it the reader already knows; and it is sufficient to say, that, corroborated by the officers of the troop, and the balls found in the bodies of the victims, the crime was satisfactorily established.

The prisoners, however, had engaged an advocate of ability on their side; and it now became his turn to be heard.

"My lords and gentlemen," said he, "however satisfied I may be of the innocence of my clients—at least of their freedom from any criminal intention—and whatever confidence I may have in the grounds of their defence, I yet never rose to address your lordships with a more reluctant feeling on my own part, and a greater distrust in my own powers of producing that conviction in your minds which is firmly established in mine.

"This distrust, this apprehension, my lords, arises from the ungrateful course which in justice to my clients I am forced to adopt. I need not ask, for I cannot doubt, the impression that the evidence just elicited has made, not only on your lordships' minds, but on the mind of every individual in this numerous assembly. We are but men—but mortal—and alas! how difficult is it—how nearly impossible, to divest ourselves of prejudice, to be uninfluenced by appearance, to keep our judgment clear when our eyes are dazzled, our ears bewitched, our senses enthralled!—to elude, in short, the powerful spell flung over us by the most transcendent beauty, the most enchanting grace, reinforced by an intellect so clear, so subtle, so astute,—the apparent—alas! that it should be *but* apparent—the apparent innocence of youth, combined with the consummate art of age!—for there are lives in which experience is gathered so fast, that I will not say the wisdom, but the cunning of years is accumulated in a few short seasons.

"But, gentlemen, it is not in the lives of the innocent, the simple, the pure in thought, the virtuous in deed, that this premature consummation takes place; this unnatural maturity, where the core is ripe even to rottenness, whilst the outside, so smooth, so blooming, so brilliant, would deter the most sacrilegious hand, abash the boldest eye! Is it not rather where the seeds of vice have fallen in the rankest soil—where, to drop our metaphor, depravity has been nursed in the cradle,—where impurity has been imbibed with the first lessons of the horn-book,—where the earliest germ of the infant mind has been diseased,—where taint has grown upon taint by habit, encouragement, propinquity, association; till all that should be pure is defiled—all that should be innocent, depraved,—all that should be beautiful, deformed; in short, till all within is foul even to corruption, whilst all without still shines bright and unspotted as the snowy garments of the blest, misleading our judgments, betraying our passions, bewildering our senses, and perplexing our understandings?

"Your lordships will be disposed to ask me, 'to what purpose this exordium?' My lords, it is a feeble attempt to clear the path before me in some measure from the mass of prejudice I see accumulated against my unfortunate clients, and in favour of the witness for the prosecution. I say the witness, my lords, for in fact, there is but one witness. On the sole testimony of one person, the prisoners at the bar are to be judged; and it is therefore but equitable that that testimony should be nicely sifted, its value accurately weighed, its claims to confidence maturely considered.

"Now, my lords, how stands the case? In a certain family of high respectability and liberal fortune, who resided in one of the provinces of England, dwelt, in the capacity of dairy-maid, a young woman called Mabel Lightfoot, whose unparalleled beauty and extraordinary fascinations made her the envy of her own sex and the wonder and admiration of the other.

"It is to be supposed that a creature so gifted was not without innumerable suitors; and, in effect, there was not a servant in the family, nor a hind in the village, who did not lay his humble fortunes at her feet; but scorn was the meed of all—of all but one: to him only she stooped; and on him she lavished all those favours and all that devoted affection for which the sex are so remarkable, when given up to one devouring and exclusive passion.

"This fortunate individual, my lords, who bore the palm of victory from all competitors, held the situation of footman in the family that harboured the enchantress. He was one who, from peculiar circumstances, was regarded with especial kindness by his master; and whom, if obligations could bind mankind, ought

to have been ready to shed his blood in his defence. The peculiar esteem in which he was held, placed him much about the
person of the old gentleman, to whose private apartments he had
access at all hours. Well, my lords, will it be believed?—whether
tempted by the father of mischief himself, or seduced by the most
pernicious, the most beguiling of his emissaries—a lovely, crafty,
and abandoned woman,—this young man, this trusted servant, this
favoured dependant himself took the life he should have died to
save! stole upon the old man in his hours of repose, murdered
him in his sleep, broke open his portfolio, robbed him to a considerable amount, and then fled with his paramour; and so well
were their plans laid, so artfully was their escape contrived, that
all the researches instituted by private vengeance, or by public
justice, proved utterly ineffectual: pursuit was fruitless; their
track was never discovered.

"Though time inevitably relaxed perquisitions that promised
so little success, it may be easily conceived that the resentment
and the desire of vengeance on the part of the family, and of
those most immediately connected with them, lost nothing of its
force; and I leave it to your lordships' imaginations—to the imaginations of all present—to picture what must have been the sensa-
tions of an intimate and attached friend of the injured parties, on
suddenly and most unexpectedly meeting with one, and, as he first
supposed, both of these heinous criminals; for it happened that
the person of the unfortunate and lamented Duke de Rochechouart,
his height, and his complexion, bore a singular resemblance to the
young man whose history I have been detailing.

"Was it not natural, my lords, that the first impulse should
have been pursuit?—that a seizure should be attempted?—that
resistance should be opposed?—that prudence, forbearance, the
possibility of error, and the dangers of rashness, should have been
overlooked and forgotten in the excitement of the chase? The
trigger was drawn—the ball did its mission; and when it was too
late my unfortunate clients discovered their mistake—their mistake of one of the parties, not of the other; for the companion of
the Duke de Rochechouart, his mistress, his paramour, was the
lovely woman, the sorceress, that pernicious emanation of evil
clothed in the robes of glory, the beautiful and seducing dairy-
maid—in short, the Mabel Lightfoot, whose story you have just
heard, and whose powerful spells you can scarcely yet shake off.

"It was then that, aware of their danger, my ill-starred clients
turned to fly—that they became the fugitives; whilst she, who
had fled before, seeing her advantage, and mounted on a capital
horse, became the pursuer.

"The rest is known; and my simple and unvarnished tale is
told. But is this sufficient? Is my word all that is required to
support a statement so unexpected, and bring conviction to your
lordships' minds? Certainly not; and before I proceed further,
I will, if so permitted, summon a witness, whose testimony, of the
most unexceptionable nature, will, I believe, be found entirely
corroborative of my assertions."

Whatever effect this defence might have produced upon the judges, its influence on the minds of the audience in general was evident. The abhorrence with which the prisoners had been regarded was exceedingly mitigated; and the murmurs and exclamations which broke from the assembly at different points of the narrative, especially where the murder and subsequent elopement were detailed, evinced that the object of their displeasure was changed.

But there was one person in the court whose feelings, whilst she listened to the discourse, must rather be left to the imagination than be made the subject of analysis. The pain, the curiosity, the surprise, and, at the bottom of all, the hope, which she could not suppress, that the moment was perhaps arrived that was to vindicate her brother, and possibly even restore him to her, though of that she had less expectation, created a commotion in her breast, that without the kind support of her friend Harry, who sat beside her, would have scarcely permitted her to await the sequel; whilst he himself, most deeply interested, was prepared to observe with the closest attention the nature of the evidence to be adduced, holding himself ready for the moment when perhaps his own testimony, or that of Susan herself, might be offered with advantage. For whatever changes had been wrought in the minds of the other assistants, there was none in theirs. They still believed that Andrew was innocent; that Mabel, whatever had been her errors, was neither concerned in the murder nor the robbery; and that the prisoners at the bar were guilty of the crime imputed to them, with all its aggravations.

But how was the interest and excitement of the scene augmented when an usher of the court, who had disappeared for a few minutes, returned, leading in Mr. Gaveston! He, then, was the witness announced by the advocate for the defence, whose unimpeachable testimony was to establish the guilt of Andrew and of Mabel, invalidate her evidence, and vindicate the prisoners! It is needless to say that this avowed connexion with men of character so infamous, was to them the strongest confirmation of all their previous suspicions.

"Before this witness is sworn," continued Monsieur Périer, the advocate, "it is necessary that we should prove his identity; and not only that, but also his respectability, that your lordships may be enabled to judge of the degree of credibility to be attached to his evidence. Fortunately, by the testimony of Monsieur Rigaud, Monsieur Moreau, and other worthy and well-known inhabitants of Lisle, we shall have no difficulty in doing that to your entire satisfaction."

The gentlemen named, who were persons concerned in the wine trade, and had had various opportunities of seeing Mr. Gaveston, were then called; and unanimously testified to his being a gentleman of fortune, a partner in the house, and connexion of the late Mr. Wentworth, and the husband of his daughter. Monsieur Moreau also declared that he had happened to be in England at the time the events above detailed had taken place; that he had

always heard them related as by Monsieur Périer; and that he
had himself seen bills posted on the walls and advertisements in
the newspapers, offering a reward for the apprehension of the footman and the dairy-maid.

These points being satisfactorily established, Mr. Gaveston's
evidence was then taken, which, it is unnecessary to say, was in
all respects a repetition of Monsieur Périer's story; and the
powerful effect it produced in favour of the prisoners may be conceived, especially when he acknowledged the gallant colonel as an
intimate friend of the family.

Towards the close of his examination, however, a circumstance
occurred, which appeared in some degree to give a shock to the
self-possession with which he had hitherto presented his testimony, and to shake the confidence of the acute lawyers who were
listening to it. A little boy, dressed in a sort of page's livery, was
seen quietly to steal across the hall, and to slip a note into the
hand of Monsieur Dumont, the principal advocate for the prosecution. The child then withdrew as he had come, and disappeared
amongst the assembly at the back of the hall.

After receiving this billet, Monsieur Dumont arose, and commenced a very close and subtle cross-examination of the witness;
in the course of which he put many questions that were evidently
unexpected and unpleasant, and which caused Mr. Gaveston frequently to hesitate and change colour. Amongst others, he was
particularly pressed as to whether he had not seen Mabel after
her elopement from Oakfield—whether he had not seen her on the
night she went away—whether he had not been accessory to her
departure—whether he had not afterwards seen her in London—
and whether he had not sent her to France as Miss Jones, and
paid the expenses of her journey, &c. &c. To all of which interrogations, however, he answered in the negative; but their effect
upon his nerves was beyond his control; whilst Susan and Harry,
who could not conceive whence the intimation had come that had
set Monsieur Dumont upon this track, became more and more
entranced with expectation, and elated by hope.

Their curiosity, however, on one point, was very soon relieved;
for no sooner was the cross-examination concluded, than Monsieur
Dumont begged to be allowed to bring forward some witnesses on
his side—witnesses, he admitted, whose appearance was to him
wholly unexpected—whom he had never seen, and whose names
and claims to authenticity he had yet to learn; and then addressing
his looks towards the quarter of the hall whence the page had
emerged, he requested that the persons who had intimated their
desire to be interrogated would advance; and immediately Mr.
Simpson and Mr. Olliphant stepped forward, and presented themselves with a salutation to the court.

After a few words exchanged with Monsieur Dumont, the wine-
merchants, Rigaud, Moreau, &c., were recalled, and testified most
fully to the identity, station, and respectability of the two strangers.
This done, Mr. Olliphant's evidence was first taken.

He began with admitting the fact of the murder and robbery,

and the suspicions that had fixed on Andrew and Mabel, from
their disappearance; and added, that till very lately, the whole
affair had been so enveloped in mystery, that a very few weeks
ago it would have been wholly out of his power to have thrown
any light on it, or to have shaken in any degree the testimony of
the last witness. But a combination of circumstances, he said,
when least looked for or expected, and when all attempts to discover the truth had long ceased, had suddenly lifted the veil, and
disclosed a tissue of villany, so far surpassing whatever the advocate for the prisoners had attempted to establish, that the only
apprehension he had was, that the evidence he and his friend had
to adduce would scarcely be credited, from the enormity of the
wickedness it portrayed.

He then, after mentioning the unaccountable disappearance of
the will, of whose existence he and others were perfectly aware,
and the consequences that resulted from its loss, went on to relate
the singular accident by which it had been recovered; their proceedings thereupon, and the suspicions that Mr. Gaveston's deportment had excited; the unexpected arrival and disclosures of
Mabel, which had led to the identification of Julia Clark; her
sudden and mysterious departure, which, together with their
desire to obtain an interview with Jones and to watch Gaveston,
had brought them to France: and finally, how, by a train of accidents, as singular as any of the preceding, they had only a few
nights before rescued her from a watery grave, to which that
monster of wickedness, Gaveston, had consigned her, in order to
annihilate her evidence with her life. In fact, he added, it was
her subsequent illness and incapacity for travelling which had
detained them and Mabel on the road, and prevented their arriving
till the day appointed for the trial. "Fortunately, probably," he
said; "for had our presence been known, the line of defence you
have heard would never have been adopted; and so favourable an
opportunity of vindicating the innocent and exposing the guilty
might never have recurred."

After this, Julia Clark was brought forward; and her evidence,
confirmed by Mr. Simpson's, was heard. She asserted, in conclusion, that Mr. Gaveston, or Godfrey, as she had always believed
him to be, had induced her to take a walk with him on the night
she was found in the water; and under pretence of making her
stoop down to see something which he said he saw floating, had
taken the opportunity of pushing her in; and that, but for the
sagacity of the little beggar-boy, she must infallibly have perished
before any assistance could have arrived to extricate her.

In order to establish beyond a doubt the truth of this latter
part of the story Mr. Simpson begged to call Basil; where-
upon the little page, now beggar-boy no longer, related how
he had been returning from the country with his sticks, and
how, immediately after he had heard a scream proceeding
from the water, he had been nearly knocked down by a gentleman, who seemed to be hastening from the spot whence the sound
had emanated. He then related how, after he had obtained

assistance, and she was saved, he had gone home; and that then the idea first occurred to him, that the man he had seen running away had pushed her into the water. "I recalled his features and appearance," said Basil, "and I thought I should know him if I met him again."

"And did you meet him again?" said Monsieur Dumont.

"I did," replied Basil. "On the following morning, when I went out early to look for work, I met a worthy couple, hurrying with their luggage to the mail-coach office, in the Rue de Bouloy. They had a basket that incommoded them, and I offered to carry it thither for a few pence, which they agreed to give me. Whilst I was standing there, seeing them off, and helping them to take care of their baggage, who should I see but my man! I recognised him directly. He came into the court with a porter, who carried his portmanteau, and inquired for the mail to Lisle. A thought struck me; and whilst he was busy speaking to the head clerk about his place, I took out my knife, and cut off a little corner of his coat. He mounted the mail and departed; and I went soon afterwards to my good master, Monsieur Simpson, and told him what I had done. He has the same coat on now. Examine it, and compare this little corner with it, and you'll see that it matches exactly."

But this verification of a fact, which, however, nobody doubted, for the opinions of the audience were once more changed, was found impracticable, Mr. Gaveston having already left the court-house; and, as it was discovered on inquiry, departed in great haste for Brussels.

One more confirmation of his villany yet remained. Harry Leeson, in compliance with Susan's entreaty, made known to Monsieur Dumont that there were yet two more English persons in court who requested permission to say a few words connected with this case, which, though perhaps unnecessary, were yet very important to the persons concerned.

He then narrated the circumstance of Mr. Gaveston's having given him, when a boy, some weeks after the murder of Mr. Wentworth, a half-crown, which the housemaid recognised as one she had seen laid by in Mr. Wentworth's portfolio to be preserved; and that, for particular reasons, this half-crown had been kept ever since. "This woman, the housemaid I allude to," said he, "is now in court; and I learn from her, that for some reason or other, which she cannot explain, a few days since, on coming to Lisle on business, she was seized and thrown into confinement, and the box containing the half-crown in question was taken, with other things, from her pockets, and not restored. We now request that inquiry may be made, and that it may be produced."

This being done, and the box opened, Julia Clark begged permission to see the coin, which, being handed to her, she immediately recognised as having been in her possession for some time. Mr. Dyson, she said, had desired her to keep it, lest she should make a mistake and pass it, which he did not wish to do, for particular reasons. "Afterwards," added she, "he asked me for it, saying that he had a bet to pay Mr. Godfrey, and that it would do for him." We may here observe, although it was not shown her till another occasion, that she also recognised the shirt button that Susan had brought from Maningtree, as one of a pair that she had given to Mr. Gaveston—the initials J. C. and W. G. being intended for Julia Clark and Walter Godfrey.

The trial was now concluded; and the prisoners, by the evidence of these unexpected witnesses, being replaced exactly in the situation they had held after Mabel's testimony, were found guilty, and condemned to death.

The recognitions and congratulations that were exchanged amongst parties so unexpectedly met, we will not detain the reader with describing; but there was one reunion still more unlooked for, if possible, than the others, which we must mention.

It had been observed by those near her, that when Julia Clark was introduced into the court, and named, Madame Le Clerc had suddenly started from her seat, as if about to rush forward, but had sunk back again, apparently fainting. As, owing to the great pressure, it would have been impossible to get her out, her neighbours contented themselves with procuring a glass of water from one of the ushers, and giving her such aid as they could, by means of which she was enabled to sit out the trial. But the moment the proceedings closed, and the assembly began to move, she was seen, preceded by Rauque, who cleared a path for her with his elbows, making her way eagerly into the centre of the hall, where the witnesses yet stood. When she reached Julia, who, supported by Mr. Simpson's arm, was in conversation with Susan, she laid her hand on her shoulder, and opened her lips; as if she was about to speak; but as her daughter turned round, and cried, "Oh, heavens! it's my mother!" the mysterious dumb woman, the hostess of the lone inn, the unfortunate Julie Le Moine, sunk upon the ground in strong convulsions. From thence she was carried to her bed: where, after a few days' illness, produced by the violent passions and agitations she had been subject to, she expired, having been affectionately attended by her daughter to the last.

When Monsieur Le Clerc, the father, the Valentine Clerk of Nantes, was introduced to his daughter, he recognised her, exclaiming, "Ah, my child!" and seemed for a short time to be somewhat roused from his lethargy; but when the excitement of novelty ceased, he fell into his usual state of abstraction, in which he passed the rest of his days, attended by his daughter, who, through Mr. Simpson's kindness, was again established in a respectable shop, far from the scene of her former adventures and abasement.

Previous to the execution of the prisoners Remorden and Dillon, several efforts were made to induce the former to make known the real particulars of Mr. Wentworth's murder, and more especially to disclose the fate of Andrew Hopley; but all persuasions were ineffectual. He had promised Gaveston, provided he would corroborate the story Monsieur Périer was instructed to relate, that he would appoint him heir to the Remorden property; and that, whether the defence proved successful or not, he would never betray the secret—and he kept his word.

But what human lips refused to reveal, the labours of the roadmakers ere long disclosed.

Mr. Gaveston, when he left the court, seeing that all that remained for him was a life of infamy or a disgraceful death, fled with all speed to Brussels; where, after making a will, bequeathing whatever he had at his disposal to little Julia, his only child, he retired to his chamber in the hotel, and blew out his brains.

As soon as his death was known in England, Mr. Borthwick naturally allowed the road to follow the line proposed; and when they broke up the grounds of the old Manor House, in the deep dry well alluded to by the crones in the early part of our story, under a heap of withered branches and furze, were found the remains of Andrew Hopley, with his clothes and other articles, amongst which were the remnants of a shirt stained with blood, marked "W. G.," and bearing in one of its sleeves the fellow stud to that in Susan's possession.

We may here close our volume in the words of Monsieur Périer —"Our simple and unvarnished tale is told;"—but, we venture to hope, with somewhat better success.

Mabel Lightfoot, notwithstanding many kind offers of protection and countenance in England, and the entreaties of Don Querubin, who on learning the death of the Duc de Rochechouart hastened to lay his title and fortunes at her feet, (being on the point of obtaining a divorce from the fair Dorothée, who had abandoned him for "metal more attractive,") declared her resolution of spending the remainder of her days as boarder in a convent.

Our English friends returned to their own country, where Mrs. Gaveston, who was never permitted to learn the particulars of her husband's crimes, joined them. She was, however, made acquainted with the existence of little Julia, whose education and welfare she kindly superintended. Harry Leeson, who was shortly after the above events received as a partner in the house of Mr. Glassford, the captain's brother, married the daughter of the latter, by whose interest it will be easily understood he had been placed in so advantageous a situation; and the moment he had a roof of his own to shelter her, he realized the generous projects of his boyhood, and made it a home and a refuge of peace and happiness for poor Susan Hopley.

THE END.

Savill & Edwards, Printers, 4, Chandos-street, Covent-garden.

Printed in Great Britain
by Amazon

47692817R00225